ULYSSES

JAMES JOYCE was born in Dublin in 1882, the eldest surviving son of the sociable but irresponsible father, John Joyce, and a pious and reserved mother, Mary Jane Murray. His childhood and early manhood coincided with a fall in the family fortunes from well-to-do to impoverished. In 1903 he began to write *Stephen Hero*, an autobiographical novel left unfinished. In the following year he left Ireland accompanied by Nora Barnacle, a young Galway girl, and remained with her for the rest of his life through an unending series of migrations from flat to flat and hotel to hotel, centring on the cities of Trieste, Zurich and Paris. In the course of this long odyssey, and in the face of great adversity, he composed, in addition to shorter works, four of the acknowledged masterpieces of English literature: *Dubliners, A Portrait of the Artist as a Young Man, Ulysses,* and *Finnegans Wake*. He died in Zurich in 1941 of undiagnosed peritonitis and was survived by his wife Nora (died 1951), two children, Giorgio (died 1976) and Lucia (died 1982), and a grandson, Stephen.

DANIS ROSE is one of the world's leading experts on James Joyce. He has written and edited some of the more important books and articles in the field. These include: *The James Joyce Archive: Volumes 28–63* (1977–78, with David Hayman); *The Index Manuscript* (1978); *The Lost Notebook* (1989, with John O'Hanlon); 'Ireland and James Joyce' (*Joyce Studies Annual 1992*); *The Textual Diaries of James Joyce* (1995); *Ulysses in Genesis* (forthcoming); and the four-part critical edition of *Finnegans Wake* (forthcoming). He was born in Dublin, where he now lives.

James Joyce

ULYSSES

Edited by Danis Rose

PICADOR

Originally published 1922 by Shakespeare and Company, Paris
First published in Great Britain 1922 by the Egoist Press, London
First published in Great Britain in an unlimited edition 1937 by the Bodley Head, London

This completely revised edition first published 1997 by Picador

This edition published 1998 by Picador
an imprint of Macmillan Publishers Ltd
25 Eccleston Place, London SW1W 9NF
Basingstoke and Oxford
Associated companies throughout the world
www.macmillan.co.uk

ISBN 0 330 35230 X

Original copyright James Joyce 1922
This edition, Preface, Introduction, *Ulysses* chronology, and all editorial matter
copyright © Danis Rose 1997

The right of Danis Rose to be identified as the
editor of this work has been asserted by him in accordance
with the Copyright, Designs and Patents Act 1988.

All rights reserved. No part of this publication may be
reproduced, stored in or introduced into a retrieval system, or
transmitted, in any form, or by any means (electronic, mechanical,
photocopying, recording or otherwise) without the prior written
permission of the publisher. Any person who does any unauthorized
act in relation to this publication may be liable to criminal
prosecution and civil claims for damages.

5 7 9 8 6 4

A CIP catalogue record for this book is available from
the British Library.

Typeset in Poppl-Pontifex by SetSystems Ltd, Saffron Walden, Essex
Printed and bound in Great Britain by
Mackays of Chatham plc, Chatham, Kent

This book is sold subject to the condition that it shall not,
by way of trade or otherwise, be lent, re-sold, hired out,
or otherwise circulated without the publisher's prior consent
in any form of binding or cover other than that in which
it is published and without a similar condition including this
condition being imposed on the subsequent purchaser.

Preface

> This is the most beautiful thing we'll ever have. We'll print it if it's the last effort of our lives.
>
> – Margaret Anderson, editor of the *Little Review*, on receiving 'Proteus'*

Ulysses – unquestionably one of the most outstanding novels in the English language and the text most expressive of the psyche of modern man and woman – tells the sadly comic story of Leopold Bloom, a good man led by love, attempting to come to terms with loss: the deaths of his son and of his father, the departure of his daughter from home, the passing of his youth and the adultery of his wife Marion (called Molly). Prefaced to this tale is another story, that of a sombre and intense young man, Stephen Dedalus, an aspiring writer bogged down in the stasis of Dublin life, in mourning for his mother and with little hope for the future. The paths of these two men cross, briefly join, and then part. Stephen Dedalus walks into eternity along the lane at the rear of Eccles Street, and Leopold Bloom lays himself down to sleep beside his wife (his head by her feet, his feet by her head) on the recently desecrated marital bed.

Even today, seventy-five years after its first publication, the history of the genesis of James Joyce's *Ulysses* is known only to a small minority of specialist scholars and to few if any general readers. While the novel is rightly esteemed by readers and scholars alike as a masterpiece, it is often viewed as a single cohesive work and its composition as the unfolding of a master plan. Joyce himself is principally responsible for this latter view. Very late in the day, in September 1920, he prepared just such a master plan – the so-called *Linati Schema* – in which he listed against each episode its Homeric correspondence, its time, its colour, its persons, its technic, its sense, its organ and its symbol. All terribly complicated, of course, of limited use to the reader and misleading with regard to the manner in which *Ulysses* was really constructed. Only recently, after prodigious effort by Joyce scholars (A. Walton Litz, Philip Herring, Myron Schwartzman, Michael Groden, Rodney Wilson Owen, Hans Walter Gabler,

---

* Richard Ellmann, *James Joyce* (Oxford: Oxford University Press, 1982), 421.

John O'Hanlon and the present writer, among others), has the true story of the writing of the book become known. *Ulysses* comprises no fewer than three sequentially related works all called 'Ulysses': an unwritten but conceptualized short story for *Dubliners*, a partly written sequel to *A Portrait of the Artist as a Young Man* and, finally, the narrative whose central character is Leopold Bloom. In this sense, the genesis of *Ulysses* resembles those of both *A Portrait of the Artist as a Young Man* and *Finnegans Wake*, which are to similar degrees nonlinear and composite creations.

In the Introduction, following a short account of the rationale of the Reader's Edition, I tell – briefly but for the first time – the story of *Ulysses*, its place in Joyce's biography, its composition, and the changing texts in which the narrative is embodied. This will allow the new reader (and indeed many an old one) to form a clear understanding of the whole saga.

James Joyce's *Ulysses* is quintessentially a work of literary art. Accordingly, the overriding criterion applied in creating this edition has been to maximize the pleasure of the reader. To this, the scholarship informing the edition – the initial preparation of the isotext and the worksheet-tagged text, the detection and elimination of textual faults and errors, small and large, the copyreading and other acts – must perforce remain secondary and subservient. To the best of my ability I have endeavoured to use the tools of scholarship to the greater ends of clarifying the sense and the sound of the individual sentences and freeing up the flow and the pace of the text as a whole. The Reader's Edition is presented to the reader as an integrated edition of a work of literary art and it is on these terms, primarily aesthetic, that it steps forth to be judged.

Dublin,
21 April 1997

vi

Contents

Introduction

I. The Rationale of the Reader's Edition

Since the completion of *Ulysses* I feel more and more tired but I have to hold on till the proofs are revised. I am extremely irritated by all those printer's errors. Working as I do amid piles of notes at a table in an hotel I cannot possibly do this mechanical part with my wretched eye and a half. Are these to be perpetuated in future editions? I hope not.[1]

It would today be presumptuous and unwise to assert that there is, or could ever be, such a thing as a definitive or 'single most authoritative' edition of *Ulysses*. It may even be that the hysteria surrounding the dispute over the Gabler edition of *Ulysses* was no more than the death rattle of that once potent idea, the fully determinate text. For many years now, since around the time of the publication of *Ulysses* in fact, the physicists have been telling us that we are in the era of inbuilt indeterminacy. With the passing away of the materialistic belief in certainties in favour of statistical probabilities, the contemporary but still widespread fallacy that the extirpation of mere printers' errors, important as it is, is the sole or even the primary function of a textual editor ought also to have passed away.

Textual scholarship began life as the quasi-archaeological science or art of sorting through mediated classical and biblical texts in pursuit of the reconstitution of the lost 'original texts'. The skills acquired in this enterprise remain an indispensable part, but only a part, of a modern editor's repertoire. It made and makes good sense to seek to identify and eliminate errors in a text that has descended through a non-critical line of transmission, where one inaccurate copy begat another, and the most important tool in this endeavour is a 'stemma', a reliable road map of the genesis of the work in question, allowing an informed judgement to be made as to the relative levels of authority to ascribe to the variants that are thrown up by a detailed comparison of text against text in the line of descent of the various copies of the work that have survived.

Such skills are primarily of value in the establishment of accurate editions of authors' manuscripts. But in the establishment of critical editions of works of literary art – books made for readers to be read for pleasure – further skills are needed: those of publishers' copyreaders, commonly disparaged by textual scholars, and those acquired by critics over long years of immersion in the study of the lives of authors and in multiple close readings of their texts. Not alone are these three sets of skills necessary for the competent editing of literary works; in addition they enrich each other. The textual faults underlined by the copyreader challenge the textual scholar to search for their origin in surviving or in reconstructed lost manuscripts, and the cruxes that defy both these disciplines are as often as not solvable by the critic or the biographer.

I have sought to bring all these skills to bear in editing *Ulysses*. Initially, I prepared a straight manuscript text, what I term an 'isotext'. Inasmuch as it is possible to achieve it, an isotext is an error-free, 'naked' transcription of the author's words as written down by him or by a surrogate, positive faults and all, with their individual diachronic interrelationships defined. It is not a transcription, however edited, of any single text, but a blending together of the members of a series or complex of texts. In the case of *Ulysses*, the isotext is not greatly dissimilar to the left-hand pages of Gabler's Critical and Synoptic Edition of *Ulysses* of 1984 which present in a linear fashion the 'continuous manuscript text', but it includes *all* the extant manuscripts which are in the main line of transmission, excludes the six 'lost final working drafts' Gabler imaginatively reconstructed (or created) which I argue never existed (see Section III, 'The Rosenbach Manuscript'), and replaces the remaining two 'lost final working drafts' with their corresponding protodrafts (which are not lost). The isotext of *Ulysses* (more fully described in 'A Technical Appendix') is in the actual case:

(1) *Incomplete*   Some documents are lost: for example, the typescripts of the early episodes, the typist's copy for 'Nausicaa' and 'Oxen of the Sun', and the protoversions of most of the other episodes. This is not always an insurmountable problem, as the lacunae in the manuscript line can be supplied by the corresponding text from the document next in sequence in the transmission (duplicate fair copy, typescript, or proof). It will not invariably be accurate, but has to suffice.

(2) *Uncompleted*   The documents as a group contain multiple and mutually cross-contaminating instances of every possible type of error that a person could conceivably make whilst repeatedly copying out

long convolute stretches of text: misspellings, misplacements, repetitions, missing words, erroneously omitted or imported marks of punctuation, and so on.

(3) *Overdetermined*   Because the isotext does not derive from a single document, alternative authorial versions or variants – which cannot be shown with any assurance to be straightforward revisions – exist for some words and phrases. (These cases are in fact relatively rare.) Alternative formats or styles of presentation of the text are also present: for example, the placement of the speech prefix, the punctuation in 'Eumaeus', and the apostrophes in 'Penelope'.

The isotext is literally '*Ulysses* as James Joyce wrote it'. Importantly, it is not as it stands a suitable candidate for a reading text (principally because of its self-reflexivity, complexity and uncompletedness), but insofar as it is based on documents within the main line of transmission it is *exactly* the text in Joyce's handwriting (in the main) from which the edition of *Ulysses* published in 1922 and all subsequent editions ultimately derive.

To convert an isotext into a text suitable for general reading, one needs to strip away all the diacritics and other codes and then, most importantly, to copyread the thus-reduced text. This is a performative act wholly distinct from the original preparation of the isotext itself, which is basically determinate: the documents are either there or are not there, those that are not there can be reconstructed to a high degree of accuracy, and the status of all variants can be coolly defined without choosing between any. Two radically different approaches to editing *Ulysses* are in this way combined: that which insists on the primacy of the author's manuscript, and that which takes account of the preparation of the raw manuscript for the public. These different editorial orientations, insofar as *Ulysses* is concerned, inform Hans Walter Gabler's and Jerome McGann's positions, respectively.[2]

Gabler's purely manuscript-based approach, if taken to its logical conclusion, should proceed no further than the unemended isotext. But as this would not allow for the extraction of a usable reading text, he solved the problem by declaring his 'continuous manuscript text' a copy-text. He then proceeded to emend this according to the methods of the more traditional 'final authorial intention' approach (which I discuss below).

McGann's idea – the 'social contract' theory of editing – is based on a simple insight known to authors and publishers since the days of the

Gutenberg press but not taken sufficiently seriously by textual editors before him: *no published book qua book is entirely the work of the author.* Literary production, he argues, is not an autonomous and self-reflexive activity, it is a social and institutional event. There is always a 'production crew' involved whose contribution to the book consists of copy-editing in the broad sense (typing, regularizing, house styling, correcting, censoring, formatting, typesetting, and so on) and of book designing (choosing the quality of the paper, the size of the page, the jacket and cover designs, the price, and so on). The author is equally a member of the production crew when, for example, he corrects proofs or when he approves or accedes to the alteration or deletion of text, or when – as Gabler has pointed out – he functions as a scribe in copying out his own work.

This insight underlies McGann's preference for the first edition as copy-text. Firstly, he contends, no book is ever produced without this sort of cooperative effort and, secondly, the particular cooperative effort that resulted in the first edition is part of the history of the book and the text of the first edition is the text that saw it enter into cultural history. At this point his argument loses its force: as many commentators have pointed out, the logic of his theory suggests that only facsimile editions ought to be produced since only in this way can the full contribution of the original production crew and the text that entered into cultural history be retained. McGann, however, knows that first editions are always imperfect. Accordingly, to move forward at all, the 'social contract' theory needs a rationale of emendation and for that it has to coopt some or all of the methods of the more traditional author-centred approach.

This approach, historically, has been based on the concept of 'final authorial intention'. It arose during the middle decades of this century when textual scholarship sought to provide a set of rules whereby any text could be transformed into a definitive edition (or a close approximation). It did not matter who did the editing, the result should in principle always be the same. The underlying model was evidently the paradigmatic requirement in the sciences that an experiment should be repeatable and should always give the same results, but for this requirement to be satisfied the sought-after definitive edition *must already exist,* if not in one place then at least spread out over the documents. If it does not, then clearly it cannot be recovered by formal rules of procedure and so the whole 'scientific' enterprise collapses.

A second requirement of traditional textual scholarship is that the work is entirely the work of the author alone. No other persons must be allowed to contribute. This is embodied in the concept of final authorial intention. The editor exercises his critical judgement to ascertain exactly what the author *intended* to write down or have written down and thus to form the book. This general approach has worked well enough in practice and has resulted in critical editions that are manifestly superior to mere reprints or facsimile editions, though they are far from being 'definitive'. However, the conceit that underlies this praxis – that the editor has replaced the contribution of the production crew (defined as textual corruption) with the author's own words – has been shown, by McGann and others, to be a sham.

For *Ulysses: A Reader's Edition*, the rationale for the copyreading of the isotext takes as its starting point not 'final authorial intention' but McGann's analysis of how books are actually produced. It then takes this analysis to its logical conclusion (not the same as that arrived at by previous commentators, McGann himself included): that the editor should replace the original production crew when copyreading, and the edition's publisher's typographers and designers should replace their original counterparts. Only in this way can one produce an edition that is of its own time and that can, intellectually and aesthetically, stand on its own two feet.

Few, if any, scholarly editors would describe what they do in these terms, yet to a greater or lesser degree this is what all textual editors and their publishers do when they make emendations. Yet they do so as surreptitiously as possible. Indeed, the long reign of the 'final authorial intention' theory and its fetishization of the author has led to a climate of opinion in which editors are, to some extent, afraid of their own shadows. *Every* emendation has to be justified as a return to the author's intention. For this reason, and even before McGann, the first-edition text was usually chosen as the copy-text. In this way, readings resulting from the work of the original production crew could be, and frequently were, coopted. The editor by a sleight of hand thus reduced his workload and his responsibility to a fraction of what it would otherwise have been; for while such readings do in fact constitute emendations they do not need to be defended as such, being already present in the copy-text.

In the traditional approach, and following W. W. Greg,[3] textual elements were separated into 'substantives' and 'accidentals'. Substantives are defined as those elements in a text that affect the author's meaning or the essence of his expression (mainly the actual wording) and accidentals are those elements, or 'accidents', mainly affecting the text's formal presentation (spelling, word-division, punctuation and the like). Allowing this division, the classic rules to be adopted in emendation are: (1) in dealing with substantives, emend according to the author's final revision, where demonstrable, otherwise follow the copy-text; and, (2) with accidentals, follow the copy-text. My own prescription is: (1) with substantives, follow the isotext; and, (2) with accidentals, follow sound practice. (I say sound practice rather than best practice because sound practice changes over time and also varies depending on the author and the kind of book that one is editing.)

It is my belief that an edition based on these principles generates a text that not only more closely preserves and represents the author's words (in that it deviates least from the isotext) but, somewhat paradoxically, also better recaptures the 'flavour' of the first edition. Readers' expectations change with the passage of time. When *Ulysses* was first published, it was received by the public as being thoroughly modern, absolutely the dernier cri. Simply to reproduce the 1922 text seventy-five years on, whether as a straight facsimile edition or as a 'corrected' 1922, is to produce nothing more worthwhile than a historical curiosity on the one hand or a 'genuine replica' on the other. I think that Joyce and *Ulysses* deserve better.

The craft of copyreading, as I mean it (apart from decisions concerning design features of the text, such as the matter of hyphenation in compound words[4] or the use of italics in unemphasized words, e.g. 'élite' as compared with '*élite*'), involves the determination of what I term 'textual faults'. The concept of 'error', although fundamental to editing, is notoriously difficult to define. In the preparation of the isotext, non-authorial transmissional variants are routinely eliminated as being corruptions. This is one easily defined category. But in the preparation of a reading text a serious difficulty immediately arises. Often a typist's or a compositor's intervention (an error in one sense) will in fact correct a textual flaw, and this emendation (having been made by someone other than the author) prevents it being remade by the author, and thus it can never be 'authorized' in the full sense. Despite the arguments that inevitably ensue – Why this? Why not that? – most editors accept some unauthorized emendations on the grounds that they were probably 'passively authorized', that is, seen by the author and approved by him (though in most cases, and especially with Joyce, they evidently were not). Going beyond the first edition, most editors also accept those emendations made during the author's lifetime as, again, these were possibly passively authorized. But what about the many textual faults that, purely by an accident of history, never got corrected during the author's lifetime? Must these be treated as sacrosanct? Why is it necessary, even in the first place, to appeal to passive authorization?

A textual fault (the straight errors, it will be remembered, have already been eliminated in preparing the isotext) can be suspected when one realizes that there is 'something wrong' with a particular sentence in the isotext, not simply where a word is misspelled but more subtly where the sentence is saying something that it should not, where the logic of the narrative is inexplicably broken. Once such a fault is suspected, the file on the genetic history of that particular sentence must be re-examined to determine if indeed a fault has taken place. The determination and correction of textual faults should be acted upon only where the full manuscript record indicates that a fault may have arisen in a straight-forward, and usually quite simple, way. (I shall cite a number of examples of this shortly.)

In *Ulysses* such a fault mainly arises where Joyce imperfectly copied out some earlier-drafted version of the text (in which the constituent elements may well be scattered on the page). For those episodes for which the protodrafts are missing it is necessary to extrapolate the probable history of the textual fault from extradraft (notesheet) material and from the types of faults one finds in those cases where the protoversion does exist (and we can see for ourselves where and how faults occur).[5]

In the examples of textual faults that follow, the first-quoted version is that of the 1922 edition and the emended version is that of the Reader's Edition.[6]

(1) Textual faults involving accidentals

In these cases, the editor detects an impossible reading and infers it to have arisen from the omission of punctuation when Joyce copied out an earlier (now lost) antecedent text. (We can confirm from many manu-script-attested instances that he frequently made such errors.) Take for example Bloom's musing, while having lunch in Davy Byrne's, on the distinctions one finds among different social classes in what they choose to eat. He thinks of the aristocracy, of hock in green glasses, of swell blowouts, of the women moving about:

> Lady this. Powdered bosom pearls. The *élite*. *Crème de la crème*. They want special dishes to pretend they're.

The shorter Rosenbach manuscript version, the earliest draft form available, is the simpler:

> Lady this. Powdered bosom pearls.

We have no other manuscripts to appeal to. But 'Powdered bosom pearls' is manifestly wrong. What is a 'bosom pearl' and why should bosom pearls be powdered? The logical explanation is that Joyce mistakenly dropped a comma after 'bosom' in copying out the protodraft. In this case, accordingly, the copyread version of the sentence includes the comma.

(2) Textual faults involving misplacement of interlineated readings

We have many manuscript-attested instances where we can see how Joyce, in copying out his piecemeal-structured paragraphs, misplaces an insertion originally correctly positioned or mislocates an insertion in the haste of composition. What results is a textual fault. Accordingly, in critically considering fair-copy or protoversions of texts for which an antecedent document is missing, the editor must remain vigilant for the possibility of such an error having arisen, as attention to it cannot be drawn by collation of documents. In other instances, accumulated interlineations over the typescripts and proofs can cause a fragment of prose to drift from its proper setting. An interesting case of this arises in the following passage from 'Lestrygonians' where Bloom, at the bar, is eating a sandwich:

> Mr Bloom ate his strips of sandwich, fresh clean bread, with relish of disgust, pungent mustard, the feety savour of green cheese.

This 1922 fragment can be traced back to the shorter Rosenbach form:

> Mr Bloom ate his strips of sandwich, relishing fresh clean bread, pungent mustard, the feety savour of green cheese.

The first thing to note here is the lucidity of the manuscript version and the relative obscurity of the (second) typescript version in which the new element 'with relish of disgust' has been shifted *into the sandwich*, between the bread and the mustard. It can reasonably be inferred, bearing in mind the likely supralineal position of the replacement in the (first) typescript, that, Joyce having crossed out the word 'relishing' and replacing it with 'with relish of disgust', the typist in retyping the page placed the replacement not in conjunction (as it should be) with the act of eating (Bloom ate) but in the middle of the sandwich ingredients after the word 'bread', where it remains, lost, unconnected and spoiling the whole flavour of the sentence. Accordingly, to restore full sense, the copyread text reads:

> Mr Bloom ate his strips of sandwich with relish of disgust, fresh clean bread, pungent mustard, the feety savour of green cheese.

A double example of bits of text drifting about is in 'Eumaeus', where the ever-opportunistic Bloom ponders on possible plans to profit himself and Stephen.

> All kinds of Utopian plans were flashing through his (Bloom's) busy brain. Education (the genuine article), literature, journalism, prize titbits, up to date billing, hydros and concert tours in English watering resorts packed with theatres, turning money away, duets in Italian with the accent perfectly true to nature and a quantity of other things, no necessity of course to tell the world and his wife from the housetops about it and a slice of luck. An opening was all was wanted.

This is nonsense: in the course of its transition through the documents of composition the text has become chopped up. What is this business about 'hydros' that Bloom sees as a Utopian plan and, more bizarre yet, what can we make of his prudent disapproval of telling 'the housetops about it and a slice of luck'? To recreate the sense of the passage one has to reassemble it, in the process allowing for the actual and probable arrangement of elements in the protoversion and in the (lost) first draft version. With other textual errors corrected, what emerges is the meaningful:

> All kinds of Utopian plans were flashing through his (Bloom's) busy brain, education (the genuine article), literature, journalism, prize titbits, up-to-date billing, concert tours in English watering resorts packed with hydros and seaside theatres, turning money away, duets in Italian with the accent perfectly true to nature, and a quantity of other things, no necessity of course to tell the world and his wife from the housetops about it. An opening was all was wanted and a slice of luck.

(3) Textual faults arising from Joyce's imperfect transcription

This, which is common enough, arises wherever Joyce fails accurately to copy a particular word (e.g. in miscopying 'anklet' as 'ankle') and leaves the misreading in the fair copy uncorrected. A striking example involves one of the central issues informing the book, the question of love. In 'Oxen of the Sun' we are told in stark terms (or we should have been) what primarily motivated Bloom's visit to the maternity hospital. The 1922 text reads:

> Stark ruth of man his errand that him lone led till that house.

The grammatical subject here is 'lone': Bloom was driven to go by 'lone'. The sentence fails to make sense. So what is wrong?

The sentence appears unchanged in all draft forms right back to the fair copy, so the problem is not that a textual error has arisen; but if we push further back, to the protodrafts, we can see that 'lone' in the above, its incongruity masked by our preformed notions of Bloom's loneliness and aloneness, is an authorial miscopying of 'love'. The sentence properly reads: 'Stark ruth of man his errand that him love led to that house.' Thus through a textual fault was love lost. Found and restored, it now praises Bloom's compassionate feelings for his fellow woman. That Joyce did not creatively change love to lone is clear from an echo of the same statement that occurs later on in the same episode: 'Ruth rede him, love led on with will to wander, loth to leave.'

Or again, what is one to make of the description of the girl Gerty in 'Nausicaa', one which cannot be 'corrected' even by the most exhaustive searching out of errors?

> Mayhap it was this, the love that might have been, that lent to her softlyfeatured face at whiles a look, tense with suppressed meaning that imparted a strange yearning tendency to the beautiful eyes, a charm few could resist.

The reader will be forgiven for straining at a 'yearning tendency' and for finding the grammatical construction illogical. Only by returning to the pre-faircopy manuscript text can we reassemble the passage's intended and sensible meaning:

> Mayhap it was this, the love that might have been, that lent to her softly featured face at whiles a look tense with suppressed meaning and that

imparted a strange yearning tenderness to the beautiful eyes, a charm few could resist.

(4) Textual faults arising through Joyce's omissions in creatively copying out a protodraft

Consider the following sentence from 'Oxen', which cannot further be 'corrected' by reference to the manuscript fair copy or to the typescript and proofs, yet I challenge the reader to find the verb:

> All the world saying, for aught they knew, the big wind of last February a year that did havoc the land so pitifully a small thing beside this barrenness.

Only by recourse to the protoversion can the mystery be solved and the original sense restored:

> All the world saying, for aught they knew, the big wind of last February a year that did havoc the land so pitifully was a small thing beside this barrenness.

As a final example, consider the following extract from 'Eumaeus', which exhibits a complex of errors and faults of various types. The version as published in 1922 is cited first. Then, to demonstrate the very different results obtained from editing according to traditional principles, I cite the version as edited by Gabler as well as the version as it appears in the Reader's Edition. The 1922 edition reads:

> The queer suddenly things he popped out with attracted the elder man who was several years the other's senior or like his father. But something substantial he certainly ought to eat, were it only an eggflip made on unadulterated maternal nutriment or, failing that, the homely Humpty Dumpty boiled.
>
> – At what o'clock did you dine? he questioned of the slim form and tired though unwrinkled face.
>
> – Some time yesterday, Stephen said.
>
> – Yesterday, exclaimed Bloom till he remembered it was already tomorrow, Friday. Ah, you mean it's after twelve!
>
> – The day before yesterday, Stephen said, improving on himself.
>
> Literally astounded at this piece of intelligence Bloom, reflected. Though they didn't see eye to eye in everything, a certain analogy there

somehow was, as if both their minds were travelling, so to speak, in the one train of thought.

Gabler's most notable contribution was to dispense with the punctuation that appeared at typescript stage (see below, page xxiv). His 1984 edition reads:

The queer suddenly things he popped out with attracted the elder man who was several years the other's senior or like his father but something substantial he certainly ought to eat even were it only an eggflip made on unadulterated maternal nutriment or, failing that, the homely Humpty Dumpty boiled.

   – At what o'clock did you dine? he questioned of the slim form and tired though unwrinkled face.

   – Some time yesterday, Stephen said.

   – Yesterday! exclaimed Bloom till he remembered it was already tomorrow Friday. Ah, you mean it's after twelve!

   – The day before yesterday, Stephen said, improving on himself.

   Literally astounded at this piece of intelligence Bloom reflected. Though they didn't see eye to eye in everything a certain analogy there somehow was as if both their minds were travelling, so to speak, in the one train of thought.

Finally, the reconstituted Reader's Edition text reads:

The queer things he suddenly popped out with, rather like his father, attracted the elder man. But something substantial he certainly ought to eat, even were it only an eggflip made on unadulterated maternal nutriment or, failing that, the homely Humpty Dumpty boiled.

   – At what o'clock did you dine? he questioned of the slim form and tired though unwrinkled face.

   – Some time yesterday, Stephen said.

   – Yesterday! exclaimed Bloom, till he remembered it was already tomorrow, Friday. Ah, you mean it's after twelve!

   – The day before yesterday, Stephen said, improving on himself.

   Literally astounded at this piece of intelligence, Bloom reflected. Though they didn't see eye to eye in everything, a certain analogy there somehow was, as if both their minds (though one was several years the other's senior) were travelling, so to speak, in the one train of thought.

I hope the above examples (and many others could be adduced)[7] will emphasize the necessity – if one really wants to make sense of *Ulysses*, if one wants *Ulysses* to make sense – to detect and emend these textual faults. This is a dimension of text-editing that has been largely ignored hitherto (possibly because previous editors did not have access to the prototextual documents and/or were unaware of how Joyce constructed his text), yet it is indisputably an indispensable ingredient in properly restoring the text.

As is illustrated in all of the above, there is a sharp distinction to be drawn between an error and a fault. An error is what a textual scholar would call an error – a mistake made as the text is transmitted from one copy to another by someone other than the author – whereas a fault is what an author would commonly call an error: a mistake *per se* in the sense of a sentence or, on a smaller scale, in the spelling of a word. No matter that they are manuscript-attested, misspellings should not remain uncorrected. Joyce himself asked that his spellings be checked and, if wrong, corrected:

> I cannot find information in the dictionaries here about two words you have corrected. Of course my notes are all locked up.
> *iris*: which plural is used? English or Latin?
> *feintruled*: my impression is that the correct term is with an 'e'.
> Will you please look them up and correct accordingly.[8]

On another occasion he accepted the unsolicited advice of an American reader and agreed to the correction in a later edition of the spelling of the names of two boxers, Corbett and Fitzsimmons.[9] Of course, there are a few instances in the text where the misspellings were deliberate, but these are always stressed so that the reader can tell the difference between them and typos. They would otherwise have no significance.

When Joyce referred to his hope that the errors in *Ulysses* would not be perpetuated throughout future editions, he did not imply that he hoped someone would check everything against the manuscripts, see that it matched, and, if it did, leave it at that. That was not what he meant at all. He meant that textual faults, as well as errors attributable to typists and compositors, would be corrected in the future. This is clear from his comments on 'Ithaca':

> Also I am afraid I must have the proofs of *Ithaca* (the ugly duckling of the book and therefore, I suppose, my favourite) read by a competent person – which will be another expense.[10]

As regards Ithaca the question of printer's errors is not the chief point. The episode should be read by some person who is a physicist, mathematician and astronomer and a number of other things.[11]

There are heaps of misprints in the last two episodes.[12]

In a second edition the mistakes must be corrected. Some of the blunders and omissions which disfigure *Ithaca* especially are lamentable.[13]

There are some loose sheets of Ulysses lying about. If I sent them to you could you, when you have time, put in the corrections you speak of. That would leave me free for the correction of the text only. But the printer says that the changes are to be as few as possible.[14]

Throughout the Reader's Edition textual errors, textual faults, misspellings of words and names of persons and places are corrected, but more extensive and invasive surgery is needed in the case of 'Ithaca' where the text has been emended in line with Joyce's own request that the mathematical, astronomical and other scientific facts be checked for mistakes. For the most part this has required emendations to some of Joyce's numerical computations and the occasional completion of his calculations.

'Eumaeus' and 'Penelope', fronting and backing 'Ithaca' respectively, present problems of a quite different nature. It has long been noted that in the matter of punctuation the typescript of 'Eumaeus' differs extensively from the fair copy: it contains a large number of commas and ellipses not present in the fair copy, and, contrary to Joyce's usual practice, all of the speeches have been enclosed within inverted commas. The currently accepted explanation for this is that the typist independently and without authorization made the changes while typing, but this explanation is not borne out unambiguously by Joyce's response. Before sending the typescript to the printer, he replaced the inverted commas with dashes (as in the fair copy) but he left stand nearly all the new punctuation. One may well ask why. My own view is that it is not really credible that the typist could have made so many intelligent changes on his or her own authority without marking up the fair copy in the process. The revised punctuation is too complex to have been introduced automatically while typing: in many cases it reproduces the punctuation as it was in the protodraft and there are no marks on the fair copy to indicate where the punctuation should go. As with the disputed episodes discussed in Section III, I suggest that it is likely that the extant typescript is a *second* typescript, and that the first typescript was heavily revised with regard to the punctuation either by Joyce or by the typist on Joyce's instructions. The presence of the very un-Joycean inverted commas is, paradoxically, not an argument against this interpretation if we recall that 'Eumaeus' is intended to be Bloom's episode, written by him for possible submission to *Tit-Bits*. Bloom undoubtedly would have used inverted commas and would have punctuated heavily. Only when he came to submitting the typescript to the printer did Joyce decide that he had perhaps gone a little too far and so struck out the inverted commas. But he left the heavy punctuation stand.

Something very similar occurred with 'Penelope', Molly's episode, which in deliberate gender contrast contains no punctuation at all. Due to its late completion, the draft that otherwise would have been the basis for a fair copy was the source of the typescript, which in turn (and without a second intervening typescript) was almost immediately sent to the printer. This left no opportunity for Joyce to reverse his decisions on the format. Of these the most controversial – and the most irritating to the reader – was the removal of all the apostrophes. This process began on the typescript and continued onto the proofs. (It was possibly first suggested to Joyce by his friend Robert McAlmon, who typed 'Penelope'.) The problem is that apostrophes are integral parts of their words, which in many cases ('wed', 'well', 'Ill', 'Id' etc.) cannot be understood without them. In practice, readers of *Ulysses* are compelled mentally to resupply the apostrophes, so that nothing really has been gained by their removal and a great deal – the undisturbed flow of the text – has been lost. For this reason the Reader's Edition includes two versions of 'Penelope', the first in the original format of the manuscript with the apostrophes included and with many of the numbers spelled out, and the second, following immediately in an Appendix, in the later, more experimental format of the first edition.

II. The History of the Composition of *Ulysses*

i. Early Days up to 'Proteus'

Although he was not aware of it at the time, James Joyce begin to make preparations for *Ulysses* as early as 1902, when only twenty years old. He began to compose what he called 'epiphanies', brief prose pieces in which the ordinary events of a day shine forth with an inner illumination and are thereby transcended. They are referred to in the 'Proteus' section of *Ulysses* when Stephen Dedalus, walking along Sandymount strand, reminisces:

> Remember your epiphanies, written on green oval leaves, so deeply deep, copies to be sent if you died to all the great libraries of the world, including Alexandria? Someone was to read them there after a few thousand years, a *mahamanvantara*.

Joyce continued to compose his epiphanies for about two years, gathering together some seventy-odd, of which only twenty-two survive. But they did not have to wait for thousands of years before being read. Some of them, by circuitous routes, ended up in *Ulysses*.[1]

> Two mourners push on through the crowd. The girl, one hand catching the woman's skirt, runs in advance. The girl's face is the face of a fish, discoloured and oblique-eyed; the woman's face is small and square, the face of a bargainer. The girl, her mouth distorted, looks up at the woman to see if it is time to cry; the woman, settling a flat bonnet, hurries on towards the mortuary chapel.

The above example, one of the young Joyce's observations, becomes converted in 'Hades' into part of Bloom's interior monologue:

> Mourners came out through the gates: woman and a girl. Lean-jawed harpy, hard woman at a bargain, her bonnet awry. Girl's face stained

with dirt and tears, holding the woman's arm, looking up at her for a sign to cry. Fish's face, bloodless and livid.

In the second example, a rather sad and sentimental evocation of the image of his mother becomes transformed, in 'Circe', into something more sinister.

She comes at night when the city is still; invisible, inaudible, all unsummoned. She comes from her ancient seat to visit the least of her children, mother most venerable, as though he had never been alien to her. She knows the inmost heart; therefore she is gentle, nothing exacting; saying, I am susceptible of change, an imaginative influence in the hearts of my children. Who has pity for you when you are sad among the strangers? Years and years I loved you when you lay in my womb.

This is the version in *Ulysses*:

Stephen's mother, emaciated, rises stark through the floor, in leper grey, with a wreath of faded orange blossoms and a torn bridal veil, her face worn and noseless, green with gravemould. Her hair is scant and lank. She fixes her blue-circled hollow eyesockets on Stephen and opens her toothless mouth, uttering a silent word. A choir of virgins and confessors sing voicelessly.

(…)
The Mother (*with the subtle smile of death's madness*) – I was once the beautiful May Goulding. I am dead.
Stephen (*horror-struck*) – Lemur, who are you? No. What bogeyman's trick is this?
(…)
The Mother (*comes nearer Stephen, breathing upon him softly her breath of wetted ashes*) – All must go through it, Stephen. More women than men in the world. You too. Time will come.
Stephen (*choking with fright, remorse and horror*) – They say I killed you, mother. He offended your memory. Cancer did it, not I. Destiny.
The Mother (*a green rill of bile trickling from a side of her mouth*) – You sang that song to me. *Love's bitter mystery*.
Stephen (*eagerly*) – Tell me the word, mother, if you know now. The word known to all men.
The Mother – Who saved you the night you jumped into the train at Dalkey with Paddy Lee? Who had pity for you when you were sad

among the strangers? Prayer is all powerful. Prayer for the suffering souls in the Ursuline manual and forty days indulgence. Repent, Stephen.

Stephen – The ghoul! Hyena!

The Mother – I pray for you in my other world. Get Dilly to make you that boiled rice every night after your brainwork. Years and years I loved you, O my son, my firstborn, when you lay in my womb.

The earliest concept for a work to be entitled 'Ulysses' dates from 25 September 1906, to a time when Joyce was trying to finish the writing of the *Dubliners* stories. In a letter to his brother Stanislaus dispatched from a sultry and inhospitable Rome he remarked:

> Sometimes thinking of Ireland it seems to me that I have been unnecessarily harsh. I have reproduced (in *Dubliners* at least) none of the attraction of the city for I have never felt at my ease in any city since I left it except in Paris. I have not reproduced its ingenuous insularity and its hospitality.[2]

Joyce (who is clearly intimating that he should remedy the oversight) is not here referring (as some commentators have supposed) to that altogether more sardonic tale 'The Dead', which he was not to conceive of, let alone to write, for another year, but to a plan for a story about an incident on a less sultry Irish evening when a putative Dublin Jew named Alfred H. Hunter, rumoured to be a cuckold, pulled up out of a gutter somewhere in Dublin (possibly the kips, i.e. 'nighttown') a drunken young man (James Joyce) and took him home with him and generally bucked him up with a restorative cup of cocoa or whatever. Four days later, again writing to Stanislaus, Joyce made this explicit:

> I have a new story for Dubliners in my head. It deals with Mr Hunter.[3]

For unspecified and still unclear reasons this story was to be called 'Ulysses'. In the event, the story 'never got any forrader than the title'.[4] Joyce laid aside his new plan and busied himself once more in the seemingly never-ending struggle to get *Dubliners* published.

The issue of 'Ulysses' did not arise again until around 1913 or 1914 when he came to add the finishing touches to *A Portrait of the Artist as a Young Man*. As the story of the genesis of *Ulysses* is so coupled with that of *A Portrait*, to explain it makes it necessary to consider briefly the rather convolute history of the earlier work.

Joyce returned to Trieste from Rome in March 1907. His first few months back in the city were spent trying to make ends meet. Then, shortly before the birth on 26 July 1907 of his daughter Lucia, he was struck down with rheumatic fever. In the few months of ill-health that followed he wrote 'The Dead' and with it ended the composition of *Dubliners*.

That book now out of the way (though still some seven years from being published), he moved on to a completely new work. He had finally and firmly decided to abandon *Stephen Hero*, but he retained the general idea of an autobiographical novel and he recycled much of what he had already written into a new five-chapter work.[5] Progress was swift at first and by 7 April 1908 he had completed three chapters. Then he began to freeze up. In February 1909 he sent what he had managed to write to his friend Ettore Schmitz (the writer Italo Svevo): the first three chapters (which were distinct from those as later published) and a draft opening for a proposed fourth chapter. Schmitz's enthusiastic response to the new novel encouraged Joyce – at the time still poor, struggling to establish himself as an author and responsible for the upkeep of a young family – to find the energy to complete the fourth chapter and begin a fifth. Then in 1911, 'in a fit of rage on account of the trouble over *Dubliners*', he committed the entire manuscript as it then stood (some 313 manuscript leaves) to the stove.[6] Fortunately, the pages were rescued by a 'family fire brigade' and apparently suffered no harm from their near combustion.[7] He tied up the 'charred remains' of the manuscript in an old sheet and only came back to it months later when he sorted and pieced it together as best he could. He revised and then wrote out afresh the first three chapters, incorporated Chapter IV and the beginning of Chapter V from the earlier manuscript, and completed the latter (though possibly not in that order). Lastly, he inserted the final version of the villanelle and freshly wrote out the end of Chapter III.[8] Though now near completion, it lacked the diary entries which conclude it in its published form.

When in early 1914 Joyce came to complete *A Portrait*, the quality it had inherited from *Stephen Hero* of being autobiographical posed a serious problem for him, as the time-frame envisaged for the earlier novel extended to 8 October 1904 and included the date (13 August 1903) of the death of Joyce's mother, an event that he could neither omit nor include in *A Portrait* as it then stood. It would disrupt his treatment of the development of Stephen's spirituality and falsify the impulses occasioning his flight to Paris, the event with which he now intended to end the novel.

His initial solution to the problem, I suggest, was not simply to end *A Portrait* on the eve of his real (and Stephen's fictional) first departure for Paris in 1902 (and thus before the death of his mother with its concomitant crisis of emotion), but to backdate all of the events from 1903 and 1904 that he had intended to include in *Stephen Hero* to the period before 13 August 1903 and thereby project the death of the mother into some as yet unactualized future. This stratagem accounts for the collapsing (in *A Portrait*) of the events of Stephen's university experience into a single year. It also throws some light on an abandoned fragment of *A Portrait* written contemporaneously with its final fair copy and now in the British Library.[9] It is evident from the text of this document that Joyce had at one point actually written into the narrative of *A Portrait* events falling beyond the point of closure as it now stands. In the piece, Stephen is invited by Doherty (later renamed Buck Mulligan) to cohabit with him in the tower:

> Dedalus, we must retire to the tower, you and I. Our lives are precious. I'll try to touch the aunt. We are the super-artists. *Dedalus and Doherty have left Ireland for the Omphalos.*

This is followed by a scene set in the kitchen of Stephen's parents' house in which Stephen argues about religious faith with his pious mother, evidently still very much alive. It follows that Joyce had originally redated the Martello Tower episode to a period before her death.

By virtue of its non-incorporation into the text of *A Portrait*, the piece bears witness to the birth of the idea of 'Ulysses' as a sequel to *A Portrait*. Splitting his personal history into two, Joyce cut off *A Portrait* early, terminating it on the eve of Stephen's first departure for Paris, and, by reusing and postdating the extension as a seminal basis for the opening of a 'sequel', he was able to bury the painful period of the mother's death in the graveyard of the interregnum between the time-frames of the two books.

It was therefore during the period when Joyce was on the verge of completing *A Portrait of the Artist as a Young Man* that the second 'Ulysses' (the 'sequel') came into being. The join between the two books is perhaps best immortalized by the datelines on their closing pages: 1904–1914 and 1914–1922 respectively. Yet there still persisted a serious problem with the issue of the meshing of the time-frames of the book he had all but completed and its planned but unwritten sequel: in what month of what year to end *A Portrait*, 8 October 1904 (*Stephen Hero*'s terminal date) being now excluded.

According to the 'Proteus' protodraft and the Rosenbach Manuscript of the same episode, Stephen is in Paris in irrational fear of being arrested on a charge of murder in February 1902. This would necessarily place the ending of *A Portrait* in 1901. Hans Walter Gabler, who first noted this early date, concluded: 'the events of the final chapter of *A Portrait* occur in the spring in term-time of what could be conceived of as Stephen's first and only year [at University College. Thus, it would have been spring 1901] according to *A Portrait*'s overall implicit chronological framework … permitting Stephen to be thought of as living in Paris in February 1902.' The date, he continues, may well be a 'vestige of an abandoned time-scheme linking *A Portrait* in progress with the opening of a proto-*Ulysses* for which the date 16 June 1904 was not fixed.'[10]

Once more, some time was to pass between the idea and the execution. On 16 June 1915 (the date is a coincidence) Joyce wrote (in German) to his brother Stanislaus:

> I have written something. The first episode of my new novel *Ulysses* is written. The first part, the Telemachiad, consists of four episodes: the second of fifteen, that is Ulysses' wanderings: and the third, Ulysses' return home, of three more episodes.[11]

A few weeks later, writing to H. L. Mencken, Joyce explained that the novel he was working on was 'a continuation of *A Portrait of the Artist* and also of *Dubliners*.'[12] This theme, that *Ulysses* was to be a sequel, was to remain a constant refrain in Joyce's letters through 1915 and 1916.

Returning to 1914 and Gabler's account of the close of *A Portrait*, it should be evident that the 'proto-*Ulysses*' to which he refers is in fact the projected but abandoned extension of the earlier book in which were to be included, before the mother's death, events that in real life followed it. The 1901/1902 chronology derives from that earlier time when the two books were not as yet separate and the diary entries that now close *A Portrait* had not as yet been conceived of. After Joyce had decided upon a sequel, which by hindsight we know he intended to take place in 1904, he felt compelled to alter the 1901 terminal date of *A Portrait* by pushing it forward; a gap in the life of 1901 to 1904 was simply unworkable. He shifted dates by sleight by hand: by the inclusion of the diary entries with which the novel concludes. A close examination of the events described

– the meeting with Davin on his way to a GAA hurley match on 3 April, the visit to the library on 24 March – shows that in only one available year, 1904, do these two dates fall, as they must to remain realistic, on a Sunday and on a weekday respectively.[13]

We can now establish Joyce's 1914 chronology for his linked books:

> April 1904: *A Portrait* ends
> 28 April – summer 1904: Stephen is in Paris
> Midsummer 1904: Death of May Dedalus
> Autumn 1904: The action of 'Ulysses as sequel'

This chronology accords with many of the impressions one receives on reading the opening episodes of *Ulysses* (inherited from the 'Ulysses' as sequel): that Stephen has been to Paris only once; that he is not long returned, having come home on receiving news of the death of his mother; and that, when one encounters him in his mourning garb, she is not long dead. Other, finer impressions (e.g. that it is the day on which the milkwoman is paid) suggest moreover that the earlier 'Ulysses' was set on a Saturday, not a Thursday. Further, bearing in mind that the *Hamlet* episode most probably followed directly upon 'Proteus' in the first version of 'Ulysses as sequel', the timing is credible: Stephen would leave the school around noon, take the train to Lansdowne Road, walk to Sandymount for his stroll (or, alternatively, the might-have-been liquid lunch at The Ship) and from there move on to the National Library.

As to which Saturday in the autumn of 1904, the most reasonable inference is 8 October 1904, the same day he had planned as the terminus for *Stephen Hero*: precisely the day when, in real life, James Joyce and Nora Barnacle left Dublin for Europe and their destiny while, in the parallel world of *Ulysses*, Stephen Dedalus, unloved and unloving, walked along the strand at Sandymount.

To summarize, one notes that by its internal chronological consistency *A Portrait* closes in 1901; by the historical validity of the diary entries it closes in 1904. *Ulysses*, in its initial manifestation as a Stephen-centred sequel, falls not on Bloomsday, but on Stephensday, 8 October 1904.

On 10 October 1916, writing to Harriet Shaw Weaver, the woman who was later to become his patron, Joyce reported progress:

> I thank you also for your kind enquiry about the book I am writing. I am working at it as well as I can. It is called *Ulysses* and the action takes place in Dublin in 1904. I have almost finished the first part and have written out part of the middle and end.[14]

In all probability, the parts of the book written at this time were versions of 'Telemachus', 'Nestor', 'Proteus', the *Hamlet* chapter ('Scylla and Charybdis'), and some part of what became 'Circe' and 'Eumaeus': the Martello Tower scene, Stephen teaching, Stephen en route to the city, Stephen in the library, and an affray involving a scene of conflict (probably in Westland Row Station) between Stephen and his companions, his fall and his rescue by the fictional counterpart of Alfred H. Hunter.

From this point on, talk of *Ulysses* as sequel ended. Joyce had used up all the incidents intended for *Stephen Hero* that he had left out of *A Portrait*. He had also incorporated all his ideas for the planned short story from *Dubliners*. He was now adrift. He had now to turn his attention to the development of the character of that Good Samaritan, Alfred H. Hunter: how to flesh him out, how to give him a life independent of Stephen Dedalus and how to encompass him more fully in the Homeric paradigm implicit in the title of his new book. Given his long-standing preoccupation with the preoccupied Stephen, this was no easy matter. He had in consequence (as betimes before and more often afterwards) a nervous breakdown.[15]

With no port to steer towards and drifting in his barque on the waters of directionlessness, he began to gather notes on modern Greek. On loose sheets and in small notebooks he listed words and short sentences; he jotted down bits from newspaper reports; he wrote several sample business letters; and he studied the grammar.[16] Presumably (unless he had in mind emigrating to Greece) and logically (given his literary concerns), his main purpose in this research was to facilitate a detailed investigation into Homer's *Odyssey*. In order to find a way forward, he would immerse himself in his model.

In the midst of this work, in February 1917, fate (in the form of Harriet Weaver, acting anonymously) showed herself kind to the burdened author and he received a letter, literally out of the blue, from the firm of Slack, Monro, Saw & Company, London solicitors. It read:

> We are instructed to write to you on behalf of an admirer of your writing, who desires to be anonymous, to say that we are to forward you a cheque for £50 on the 1st May, August, November and February next, making a total of £200, which we hope you will accept without any enquiry as to the source of the gift.[17]

This windfall changed winter to spring. Joyce was in pocket for the first time. He had real cash and a lot of it, with great expectations of more to come. (In 1917 the exchange rate between the pound and the dollar was one to five, about two and a half times what it is today. For a very rough 1997 equivalent, multiply the pounds by thirty and the dollars by ten; thus, Joyce's early 1917 income – which was soon to increase substantially – of £17 or $85 would be worth today about £500 or $850.) In response, he ended for ever his narrow obsession with Stephen Dedalus and began his wider obsession with Leopold Bloom. Introspection gave way to extroversion, neurosis to humour.[18] The mourning and introverted single young man with his soul-smothering poverty made way for the married, affable and extroverted man-about-town. It was in these new circumstances, then, that Joyce returned to *Ulysses*. He saw it now not as a mere sequel to *A Portrait*, but as divorced from it, a book revolving round a new sun: a well-heeled, mature Dubliner walking about the metropolis on a real day, Thursday 16 June 1904.

It should be recalled that since early adolescence Joyce had been living on or below the poverty line. As he himself often said, he had little imagination. It was not an easy thing for him realistically to delineate the character of a man who, while not by any means rich, was nevertheless what in Dublin parlance was termed 'comfortable', not having nonstop to wonder where the next shilling was coming from. To write about Bloom, Joyce had to become Bloom, and this is what he did do over the next few years. And, with the memories of his own youth added, Zurich became Dublin. Harriet Weaver, then, may in a way be said to be the real creator of Leopold Bloom, and world literature owes her an inestimable debt of gratitude.

At first the work on the new *Ulysses* went slowly. In March he suffered another bout of illness: rheumatic iritis. On 22 April he wrote to Harriet Weaver: 'I can read and write however and am continuing my book at the usual snail's pace.'[19] On 13 June he continued: 'I am better but still in cure. I can also read and write more easily ... In these circumstances I have not been able to do very much with my book *Ulysses*: but I have done what I could.'[20] By 24 July he explained to Pound: 'As regards *Ulysses* I write and think and write and think all day and part of the night. It goes on as it has been going these five or six years. But the ingredients will not fuse until they have reached a certain temperature.'[21]

Apropos of these 'ingredients', it was around this time that he began to compile in a small notebook (now lost, but surviving in part as a partial transcription in one of the *Finnegans Wake* notebooks) words and themes from the newspapers of June 1904, slang and colloquial expressions from the turn of the century, and notes on Homer's *Odyssey* from Victor Bérard's 1902 geographical exploration *Les Phéniciens et l'Odyssée*. This notebook represents the earliest known document in the line of the textual genesis of *Ulysses* as it has come down to us. It includes the earliest traceable reference to the day finally settled on for the date of the action, 16 June 1904, and the first sketching out of Bloom's personal chronology.[22]

At the end of July Nora took the family to Locarno to enable Joyce to get on with his work. On 1 August she wrote to him: 'I suppose now that you are alone you ought to be able to write as you havent me always to bother you.'[23] By 10 August 1917 he evidently felt that he had at last broken through, for he wrote to the *Little Review*: 'I (...) hope very soon to be able to arrange through Mr Pound the transportation of some chapters of *Ulysses* for your consideration.'[24] On 5 November he himself went to Locarno, where he remained for two months. There he quickly finished the fair copies of the first two episodes, 'Telemachus' and 'Nestor', and, on his return to Zurich in January, 'Proteus'. These were then typed in three copies, one for the *Little Review*, one for Harriet Weaver (for the *Egoist*) and one for Joyce to retain. The fair copies he kept himself. Their story, which was to have many repercussions, is related in Section III, 'The Rosenbach Manuscript'.

ii. 'Calypso' to 'Sirens'

I am doing it, as Aristotle would say, by different means in different parts.

– James Joyce[25]

From the point of Leopold Bloom's smooth emergence into daylight in February/March 1918, the story of *Ulysses* simplifies itself (for a while at least) and all its loose strands entwine. Joyce's stout ship was on an even keel at last as it weighed anchor before long wandering.

And plain sailing it was to be, for a year and a half, for what we might call the second or middle period: the writing of the episodes from 'Calypso' to 'Sirens'.[26] It must have been the happiest time in Joyce's life: he was relatively untroubled; was assured of an income; received £50 ($250) from the *Egoist* for the British serial rights and £10 ($50) per episode from the *Little Review* for the American rights; was in communication through Harriet Weaver (to whom he ceded the British rights) with Ben Huebsch with regard to the American book rights; and had mapped out for himself the literary route he wished to take. While the Homeric correspondences and even the hours, not to mention the other details, of the 'Linati Schema' are a little forced in the first three episodes – having had to be imposed, so to speak, on material already drafted – the case is different for the Bloom episodes. Joyce had settled on a general plan: each episode was to reflect *sub specie tempora nostra* one of the 'adventures' in Homer's *Odyssey*, and the hour of the day for each was also settled. Less certain is the applicability of the other details of the 'Schema': the colour, the organ, the science, the sense, and so on. Some are evidently pertinent to some episodes, but not all equally to each.[27]

But to the extent that they did apply, the constrictions and variations acted as a kind of spur to Joyce's creative abilities and imparted to the whole project a sense of uniformity that it might otherwise have lacked. He was keenly sensitive to this as the cohesiveness of his novel was by no means guaranteed, given its choppy origins. For this reason, in correspondence he insisted upon the almost self-defining quality of each of his episodes.

With Stephen out of the way the sky was clear. Armed with a sort of rough guide to the narrative (a copy of the *Odyssey*), a double map of the land/sea lanes (Thom's *Dublin Directory* and his notes from Victor Bérard delineating the Mediterranean routes taken by the wily Phoenician mariner),[28] the furniture of the day (notes culled from the newspapers of June 1904), the characters (friends of his father's, mostly, and others, sketched out in the so-called 'Alphabetical Notebook' compiled in Trieste after his return from Dublin in December 1909) and their language (notes on period slang and colloquial speech taken from dictionaries), he set to work on his most ambitious undertaking to date: the transformation of a day in the life of Leopold Bloom not into a short story or a series of epiphanies, but into an epic.

The self-contained episodes of this middle period, despite the restrictions imposed in corralling the narrative within the schematic limitations he set out for himself (limitations which thereby freed him from the tyranny and the terror of the void), are borne aloft by a pitch-perfectness and delicacy of touch unique in literature. From the first word the touch is sure:

> Mr Leopold Bloom ate with relish the inner organs of beasts and fowls. He liked thick giblet soup, nutty gizzards, a stuffed roast heart, liver slices fried with crustcrumbs, fried hen-cod's roe. Most of all he liked grilled mutton kidneys which gave to his palate a fine tang of faintly scented urine.

Unusually, given Joyce's long-standing working practices, these central episodes were, for the most part, drafted as individual literary compositions in the traditional sense and were not compiled from earlier fragments intermeshed and expanded. They came freshly minted. Of the exceptions, Bloom's journey to the *zophos* or underworld, 'Hades', and the *Hamlet* chapter, 'Scylla and Charybdis', are restructurings of material already written or printed.[29]

The middle episodes, unlike the later ones, are not at all 'encyclopaedic' in nature and, if less challenging, are much more transparent and more pleasant to read. The commonly held notion of how Joyce wrote *Ulysses* – as a sustained and brilliant original composition – is indeed mostly true of these eight episodes. And as Joyce progressed through them his mastery of his medium improved; by the time he had reached 'Sirens' his performance was that of a virtuoso. This episode is surely the apotheosis of purely literary writing, writerly writing, as clean as the voice of larks in clear air, and is a maximal approximation to a state of pure music without sacrificing the movement of the narrative sense. The inner ear and the inner eye are equally delighted:

> Pat served, uncovered dishes. Leopold cut liver slices. As said before he ate with relish the inner organs, nutty gizzards, fried cod's roe, while Richie Goulding, Collis, Ward ate steak and kidney, steak then kidney, bite by bite of pie he ate Bloom ate they ate.

Joyce was justly proud of the performance that was 'Sirens'. But, paradoxically, it was not well received. It was perhaps too outré for his contemporaries. Ezra Pound, no literary traditionalist himself, was the first to lay his cards on the table:

> In face of *mss* just arrived, I think however I may adjoin personal op. that you have once again gone 'down where the asparagus grows' and gone down as far as the lector most bloody benevolens can be expected to respire. I dont arsk you to erase – But express opinion that a few sign posts. perhaps twenty words coherent in bunches of 3 to 5 *wd*. not only clarify but even improve 1st. page (...) I am sending *mss* today to Egoist

and L.R. and if you have any relentings, please communic. direct to said offices … Also even the assing girouette of a postfuturo Gertrudo Steino protopublic dont demand a new style per chapter.[30]

Even Harriet Weaver complained and, thereby adding to them, tactlessly suggested that Joyce's writing had been affected to some extent by his recent worries.[31] Exasperated, Joyce explained and justified his technique to his friend George Borach, who has left us this account of the conversation:

> I finished the Sirens chapter during the last few days. A big job. I wrote this chapter with the technical resources of music. It is a fugue with all musical notations: *piano, forte, rallentando,* and so on. A quintet occurs in it, too, as in the *Meistersinger,* my favourite Wagner opera. The barmaids have the upper parts of women and the lower of fish. From in front you see bosom and head. But if you stand behind the bar, you see filth, the empty bottles on the floor, the ugly shoes of the women, and so on. Only disgusting things.[32]

iii. 'Cyclops' to End

> He had eaten all the whilepaper, swallowed the lustres, devoured forty flights of styearcases, chewed up all the mensas and seccles, ronged the records, made mundballs of the ephemerids and vorasioused most glutinously with the very timeplace in the ternitary – not too dusty a cicada of neuteriment for a chittinous chip so mity.
>
> – From *Finnegans Wake*

After the experimental 'Sirens', things had to change. James Joyce had become the writer who could do anything with language, who could twist it into any shape, but there was a downside to his new-realized genius. He had lost his own voice, his own style, his own words. Though he had up to that time written in a variety of styles – the exiguous prose of the *Epiphanies,* the fragile rhythms of *Chamber Music,* the rough-hewn honesty of *Stephen Hero,* the 'scrupulous meanness' of *Dubliners,* the spirituality of *A Portrait of the Artist as a Young Man* and its extension into the early chapters of *Ulysses,* the light yet inimitable so-called initial style of the early Bloom episodes and even the music of 'Sirens' itself – these had all been *his* styles and all had registered no more than milestones along the path of his artistic development as a master wordsmith. But with 'Sirens' he had overreached himself. There was nowhere left to go except perhaps to the region of pure sound, but it was too soon, much too soon, for him to begin to explore that forbidding territory. He had *Ulysses* to finish.

He had also used up the cream of the assembled fragments from his early life. This led to a further loss, the loss of copy. How he was to overcome this latter difficulty was to determine the mechanics of his literary practice for most of the remainder of his life.

To progress with 'Cyclops', he first sorted out what he could use of the residual notes at his disposal. He then began to collect new notes, slowly at first but soon compendiously, listing them on large loose pages which we now term 'notesheets'.[33] Gathering together this as yet undigested raw material, rearranging the words and phrases into new patterns in draft passages, and putting these together to form longer textual units was to become the norm for the rest of the *Ulysses* years and beyond. These notesheets are a sight to behold: column upon column of words and phrases, some destined to become the basic building blocks of his work in progress. Indeed, as certain sheets now lost can be identified as members of the original set by the logic of Joyce's own internal system of recycling of elements, their saturation of the text must be even greater than what is presently demonstrable.

Accordingly, while each episode from 'Cyclops' to 'Penelope' is written in its own unique style, each is also largely a compilation arising out of the imaginative reordering of notesheet elements. These elements, so far as we have been able to establish, are derived from external printed sources (magazines, books, newspapers etc.) and possess no substantial internal ordering apart from their initial sequentiality in the source texts. In this innovative enterprise of 'borrowing' on a massive and unprecedented scale, Joyce solicited help from companions in finding suitable, thematically apt sources, for example from Frank Budgen:

> If you or Sargent can pick up any handbook *cheap* on Freemasonry or any ragged, dirty, smudged, torn, defiled, effaced, dogeared, coverless, undated, anonymous misprinted book on mathematics, or algebra or trig. or Eucl. from a cart for 1d or at most 2¼d tant mieux.[34]

This attributes a binary level of significance to a great many, if not most, of the words in the second half of *Ulysses* – to how they cohere in their new context and how they cohered in the *undisclosed* original context from which they were taken. This is not quite the same as embedding quotations in a new text, when the meaning of the text transmitted is common to both contexts. In *Ulysses*, both 'meanings' can sometimes combine to enrich the reading experience (usually in a second or later reading); at other times the 'meanings' of the words in their original context are completely irrelevant.

A direct effect of this noncontinuous approach to shaping a text, this jigsaw-puzzle writing, writing not linearly but rather by way of conjoining preformed elements and adjusting the boundaries – so that they fit smoothly, where the elements are handled, as it were, with a tweezers, looked at and surgically inserted into the growing culture of the context – is that the 'genetic profile' of any paragraph from these later episodes (the full history of its coming into being) is perforce of an intricacy and intertextuality several orders higher than in the early episodes. (This 'isotextual' aspect of the text is described in more detail in 'A Technical Appendix', p. lxxv.) Composition by accretion also permits increased compression and compactness and an unlimited heterogeneity of reference, as the author can easily introduce any manner and variety of material. What emerges is a text of ever-increasing complexity and mounting extradimensionality (and, concurrently, an exaggerated potential for textual fault at the seams). At points the text, although self-evidently *written*, seems somehow 'unwritable', yet it always retains Joyce's characteristic signature, his precision in expression, while as readers we are presented with wholly new depths and densities.

To show the reader just how deceptive and innocuous-looking the text thus produced can be, yet how it came to be written, here are some sample passages from the later episodes deconstructed into their preformed source elements. In these, the elements (all drawn from notesheets) are demarcated by raised diacritics ⌜ ... ⌝. Elements placed within other elements are enclosed by diacritics ⌐ ... ⌐. The reader is invited to consider how a seemingly continuous linear passage is in fact a *text mosaic*. The new order of the elements is Joyce's: the old order is invisible.

Ba. Again. ⌜Wonder why they come out at night like mice.⌝ They're a mixed breed. Birds are like ⌜hopping mice⌝. ⌜What frightens them, light or noise?⌝ Better sit still. All instinct. ⌜Like the bird in drouth got water out of the end of a jar by throwing in pebbles.⌝ Like a ⌜little man in a

cloak he is with tiny hands⌐. Are they birds or what? ⌐Weeny bones.
Almost see them glimmering, kind of a bluey white.⌐ Colours depend
on the light you see. ⌐Stare at the sun for example⌐ like the eagle then
look at a shoe see a blotch blob yellowish. Wants to stamp his trademark
on everything. Instance, that ⌐cat this morning on the staircase⌐ colour
of ⌐brown turf⌐. Say you never see them with three colours. Not true.
That half-tabby white ⌐tortoiseshell in the City Arms with the letter em
on her forehead.⌐ Body fifty different colours. Howth a while ago
amethyst. Glass flashing. That's how that wise man what's his name
with the ⌐burning glass⌐. ⌐Then the heather goes on fire.⌐ It can't be
tourists' matches. What? Perhaps the ⌐sticks dry rub together in the
wind and light⌐. Or broken bottles in the furze act as a ⌐burning glass⌐
in the sun. ⌐Archimedes.⌐ I have it! My memory's not so bad.

(From 'Nausicaa')

After which effusion the redoubtable specimen ⌐duly arrived on the
scene⌐ and, ⌐regaining his seat⌐, he ⌐sank rather than sat⌐ heavily on the
form provided.

Skin-the-Goat, assuming he was he, evidently with an ⌐axe to grind⌐,
was ⌐airing his grievances⌐ in a ⌐forcible-feeble philippic⌐ anent the
natural resources of Ireland, or ⌐something of that sort⌐, which he
⌐described ⌐in his ⌐lengthy⌐ dissertation⌐ as the richest country bar
none⌐ on the face of God's earth, far and away superior to England, with
⌐coal in large quantities⌐, ⌐six million pounds worth of pork exported⌐
every year, ⌐ten millions between butter and eggs⌐, and all the riches
drained out of it by England levying taxes on the poor people that ⌐paid
through the nose⌐ always, and ⌐gobbling up the best meat⌐ in the
market, and a lot more ⌐surplus steam⌐ ⌐in the same vein⌐. The
⌐conversation accordingly became general⌐ and all agreed that that was
⌐a fact⌐. You could grow any mortal thing in Irish soil, he stated, and
there was ⌐Colonel Everard down there in Navan growing tobacco⌐.

(From 'Eumaeus')

Meditations of ⌐evolution⌐ increasingly vaster: of the moon invisible in
incipient lunation, approaching perigee: of the infinite lactiginous scintillating ⌐uncondensed⌐ ⌐Milky Way⌐, ⌐discernible by daylight by an
observer placed at the lower end of a ⌐cylindrical   vertical⌐ shaft⌐ 5000
ft deep sunk from the surface towards the centre of the earth: of ⌐Sirius
(Alpha in Canis Major) 9 light-years (51,000,000,000,000 miles) distant
and in volume 3,000,000 times the dimension of our planet⌐: of
⌐Arcturus⌐: of the precession of equinoxes: of ⌐Orion with belt and

sextuple sun Theta and Nebula in which myriads of our solar systems could be contained⌝: of ⌜moribund and of nascent new stars⌝ such as ⌜Nova in 1901⌝: of our system plunging towards the constellation of Hercules: of the ⌜parallax ⌞or parallactic drift⌟ of so-called fixed stars⌝, in reality evermoving wanderers from immeasurably remote eons to infinitely remote futures, in comparison with which the years, ⌜threescore and ten⌝, of allotted human life formed a parenthesis of infinitesimal brevity.   *(From 'Ithaca')*

I ⌜remember that day with the waves⌝ and the ⌜boats with their high heads rocking⌝ and the ⌜smell of ship⌝ those ⌜Officers' uniforms ⌞on shore leave⌟ made me seasick⌝ he didn't say anything he was very serious I had the ⌜high-buttoned boots⌝ on and my skirt was blowing she kissed me six or seven times ⌜didn't I cry yes⌝ I believe I did or near it my lips were taittering when I said goodbye ⌜she had a Gorgeous wrap of some special kind⌝ of blue colour ⌜on her for the voyage⌝ made very peculiarly to one side like and it was ⌜extremely pretty⌝ it got as dull as the devil after they went I was almost planning to ⌜run away mad⌝ out of it somewhere ⌜we're never easy where we are father or aunt or marriage⌝   *(From 'Penelope')*

To revert to the question of style, we note how each episode from 'Cyclops' onwards is written in a unique and essentially imported style. No longer possessed of a natural style of his own, Joyce was obliged to seek them from outside. This he did consummately and he made each his own for the duration of the writing of the episode in question. The first, and possibly the least successful and least integrated, is 'Cyclops', which consists of a bar-counter recitation (male gossip) by a nameless, deadbeat Dubliner, the whole interrupted by a series of disjointed parodies. As Joyce explained to his friend Budgen:

The chapter of the *Cyclops* is being lovingly moulded in the way you know. The Fenian is accompanied by a wolfhound who speaks (or curses) in Irish. He unburdens his soul about the Saxo-Angles in the best Fenian style and with colossal vituperativeness alluding to their standard industry. The epic proceeds explanatorily 'He spoke of the English, a noble race, rulers of the waves, who sit on thrones of alabaster, silent as the deathless gods'.[35]

It was tough going. As he explained to Harriet Weaver: 'it is impossible for me to write these episodes quickly. The elements needed will fuse only after a prolonged existence together (...) I understand that you may begin to regard the various styles of the episodes with dismay and prefer the initial style much as the wanderer did who longed for the rock of Ithaca. But in the compass of one day to compress all these wanderings and clothe them in the form of this day is for me only possible by such variation which, I beg you to believe, is not capricious.'[36] Ezra Pound was impressed. He thought that 'Cyclops' was perhaps the best thing that Joyce had yet done and he attributed its motley of styles to a trick borrowed from Rabelais, 'but never done better'.[37]

The next episode, 'Nausicaa', was written as a variant of a cheap novelette for young ladies in, as Joyce put it in a letter to Budgen, 'a namby-pamby jammy marmalady drawersy (alto là!) style with effects of incense, mariolatry, masturbation, stewed cockles, painter's palette, chit chat, circumlocution, etc., etc.'[38] The execution is superb and 'Nausicaa' is a joy to read.

'Oxen of the Sun', which followed, in which Mrs Mina Purefoy gives birth in the maternity hospital, is perhaps the most complex episode in *Ulysses* and the hardest to get to grips with. The first-time reader should perhaps skip it rather than become bogged down, stop reading and thereby miss out on the more accessible pleasures of the final four episodes. On 25 February 1920 Joyce wrote to Harriet Weaver: 'I am working now on the *Oxen of the Sun* the most difficult episode in an odyssey, I think, both to interpret and to execute.'[39] He expatiated at length on his ideas to Budgen:

Am working hard at *Oxen of the Sun*, the idea being the crime committed against fecundity by sterilizing the act of coition. Scene, lying-in hospital. Technique: a nineparted episode without divisions introduced by a Sallustian-Tacitean prelude (the unfertilized ovum), then by way of earliest English alliterative and monosyllabic and Anglo-Saxon ('Before born the babe had bliss. Within the womb he won worship.' 'Bloom dull dreamy heard: in held hat stony staring') then by way of Mandeville ('there came forth a scholar of medicine that men clepen etc') then Malory's *Morte d'Arthur* ('but that franklin Lenehan was prompt ever to pour them so that at the least way mirth should not lack'), then the Elizabethan chronicle style ('about that present time young Stephen filled all cups'), then a passage solemn, as of Milton, Taylor, Hooker, followed by a choppy Latin-gossipy bit, style of Burton-Browne, then a passage Bunyanesque ('the reason was that in the way he fell in with a certain whore whose name she said is Bird in the Hand') after a diarystyle bit Pepys-Evelyn ('Bloom sitting snug with a party of wags, among then Dixon jun., Ja. Lynch, Doc. Madden and Stephen D. for a languor he had before and was now better, he having dreamed tonight a strange fancy and Mistress Purefoy there to be delivered, poor body, two days past her time and the midwives hard put to it, God send her quick issue') and so on through Defoe-Swift and Steele-Addison-Sterne and Landor-Pater-Newman until it ends in a frightful jumble of Pidgin English, nigger English, Cockney, Irish, Bowery slang and broken doggerel. This progression is also linked back at each part subtly with some foregoing episode of the day and, besides this, with the natural stages of development in the embryo and the periods of faunal evolution in general. The double-thudding Anglo-Saxon motive recurs from time to time ('Loth to move from Horne's house') to give the sense of the hoofs of oxen. Bloom is the spermatozoon, the hospital the womb, the nurse the ovum, Stephen the embryo. How's that for high?[40]

In 'Circe', the longest episode in the book and the last of the adventures or wanderings, the action takes place in a brothel. Literally pornographic, it is an oneiric phantasmagoria written out in the style of a costume drama (Bloom, for instance, appears in five or six different suits). The innermost fears and desires of Bloom and Stephen are acted out as if in the real life of the novel, objects become animated and speak, ghosts from the past enter bearing their burdens, the text is enantiomorphized, and the events of the day are replayed in nightmarish caricature. It is at once the funniest and the most sordid of the episodes of *Ulysses*.

'Eumaeus', the first episode of the close or end (Nostos: the homecoming), is a tour de force of composition: magical writing written in the style of bad prose. The ostensible author of the piece is Leopold Bloom himself. During the day he had been contemplating writing a short piece for *Tit-Bits*, a lowbrow magazine. He even grants the episode (within it, of course) its title: *My Experiences in a Cabman's Shelter*.

'Ithaca', which follows, is again dramatically different, cold, dry, and catechetical, but nonetheless the most intensely moving episode in the book. Joyce described the technique to Budgen:

I am writing *Ithaca* in the form of a mathematical catechism. All events are resolved into their cosmic, physical, psychical etc. equivalents, e.g. Bloom jumping down the area, drawing water from the tap, the micturation in the garden, the cone of incense, lighted candle and statue, so that not only will the reader know everything and know it in the baldest coldest way, but Bloom and Stephen thereby become heavenly bodies, wanderers like the stars at which they gaze. The last word (human, all too human) is left to Penelope. This is the indispensable countersign to Bloom's passport to eternity.[41]

As may be inferred, Joyce interrupted the composition of 'Ithaca' to write 'Penelope', the finale of his book and perhaps the most famous single chapter in literary history: a long unpunctuated sustained amplitudinous curvilinear uninhibited wildly self-contradictory female monologue:

> *Penelope* is the clou of the book. The first sentence contains 2500 words. There are eight sentences in the episode. It begins and ends with the female word *yes*. It turns like the huge earth ball slowly surely and evenly round spinning, its four cardinal points being the female breasts, arse, womb and cunt expressed by the words *because*, *bottom* (in all senses bottom button, bottom of the class, bottom of the sea, bottom of his heart), *woman*, *yes*. Though probably more obscene than any preceding episode it seems to me to be perfectly sane full amoral fertilisable untrustworthy engaging shrewd limited prudent indifferent *Weib. Ich bin der* [sic] *Fleisch der stets bejaht.*[42]

The writing of *Ulysses* thus divides into three periods: the first and least Ulyssean ('Telemachus', 'Nestor', 'Proteus', 'Scylla and Charybdis', and some elements of the close that were later utterly transformed) was the earliest drafted, and engrosses material from texts and notebooks from the years up to the completion of *A Portrait*. In their original forms, these characterized Stephen Dedalus, the young artist in conflict. The style is more or less uniform: straight narration typically interrupted by dialogue and 'interior(ized) monologue' (thinking aloud to oneself on the text page): pellucid, sharp, and clean-cut writing. The style of the middle period ('Calypso' to 'Sirens') is lighter, while remaining tightly controlled, and is in part a return to the 'scrupulously mean' writing of *Dubliners*. 'Aeolus' and 'Wandering Rocks', innovative as they are, do not depart a great deal from the initial style. The headlines, captions or interrupting voices that disfigure 'Aeolus' were a late addition to what was originally continuous narrative, and the archipelago of prose that is 'Wandering Rocks' is disjunctive in focus but not in style. In 'Sirens', the style is simply taken to extremes. The episodes from the third period ('Cyclops' to 'Penelope') are individually *sui generis*, contrived, expansive, superdense, encyclopaedic.

The first period permits a form of critical scholarship in which autobiographical elements can be isolated and pinned to their original context. (This has already been largely done and published by scholars.) The group from the middle period is only tangentially indebted to notes and suchlike material and is more open to traditional criticism. That from the final period is by contrast massively indebted to other texts but, with the exception of the Nora Barnacle centred and *Exiles* derived aspect of 'Penelope', purely non-autobiographical. The concatenation of Joyce's text with root elements in these cases and, by extension, with the original non-Joyce contexts has been accomplished to date only partly and it promises by far the richest lode for future fine-point exegesis.

III. The Rosenbach Manuscript

I cannot dictate to a stenographer or type. I write all with my hand. When the fair copy is ready I send it to a typist.

— James Joyce[1]

I did not buy the Ulysses MS for commercial reasons. I daresay if I tried to sell it tomorrow I could not get $500 for it. But I bought it because I am interested in the book and the author and for my own personal library.

— A. S. W. Rosenbach[2]

The central document in the manuscript record of *Ulysses* (here taken to include the notes, early drafts, typescripts, and proofs) is the 'Rosenbach manuscript'. This document consists of a handwritten copy of each of the eighteen episodes of Joyce's novel at an intermediate stage of development. It is the only handwritten copy of the *entire* book at any stage of its development and, as such, it has been termed 'the manuscript of *Ulysses*'. It is accordingly of critical importance. Surprisingly, it is to date the most consistently misconstrued and denigrated document in the entire Joyce corpus, and it has been at the epicentre of at least two scholarly controversies occasioning, if not yet bodily harm, bloodied reputations. Insofar as the germ and germane cause of these controversies ultimately arose from James Joyce's financial vicissitudes, the issues are best understood and the problems best resolved by keeping one's eye on the trail of 'the money'.

In spring 1917, before Joyce physically wrote down any part of what was to become the Rosenbach manuscript, Harriet Weaver unexpectedly and anonymously arranged for him to receive a quarterly allowance of £50, approximately £17/$85 per month. In October, although early drafts of some parts of *Ulysses* existed, he undertook the systematic composition of each episode in the order in which it appears in the published volume. It was his practice, when he was satisfied that the structure and content of each episode had attained a state of at least temporary finality and respectability, to prepare a fair copy. This he then revised, chiefly by adding new material in the margins or between the lines, before passing it over to be typed. When made, the typescript was corrected (not always thoroughly) and further revised before Joyce turned to composing the next episode in the sequence.

In late February 1918, while finishing the fourth episode, 'Calypso', he was informed to his undoubted delight that a wealthy American heiress, Mrs Edith Rockefeller McCormick, had arranged for him to be subsidized to the tune of a further 1,000 Swiss francs per month. The subvention was to begin immediately. Joyce's net income was thereby raised to the very respectable sum of £57/$285 per month. Not only was this more than adequate to live on, it enabled him to become an impresario of sorts. With his friend Claud Sykes he set up the 'English Players', a travelling road show which sought to bring the best of English and Irish drama to the (supposedly) culturally deprived residents of the cantons. Fifteen months later, in May 1919, Harriet Weaver, once again acting anonymously and unaware of the McCormick subvention, generously settled on Joyce £5,000 in War Bonds, giving him, in lieu of the £50 per quarter, a *guaranteed* permanent income of £250 per year and in the process augmenting his monthly income by nearly £4/$20.

On 26 June 1919, by which time he had started on the twelfth episode, 'Cyclops', John Quinn, an Irish-American lawyer and patron of the arts, wrote to him:

> Would you care to dispose of the manuscript of 'Ulysses'? How many pages will it run? Is it finished? If it is not finished and you wish to dispose of it, to me, I should be glad to send you a draft on account.[3]

Quinn had first learned about Joyce from Ezra Pound and had two years earlier purchased the manuscript of *Exiles* for £25 ($125). In his reply, written on 3 August 1919, Joyce showed little or no interest in taking up Quinn's offer as he was, as shown, not at the time in particular need of money. Paring his fingernails, he would only observe:

> *Ulysses* will not be finished probably till the end of next year – if even then. A chapter takes me about four or five months to write.[4]

In the midst of this exchange of letters, Joyce was badly embarrassed. On 9 July he wrote to Slack, Monro, Saw and Co. informing them that he had guessed the name of his anonymous benefactor: it was Lady Cunard. Possibly he thought it appropriate that *Ulysses* should be subsidized by the wife of a shipping magnate. This letter was hardly posted when another arrived, dated 6 July, from Harriet Weaver, confessing that it was she who had been 'communicating' with him through the solicitors. She begged his forgiveness.[5] The consternation in the Joyce household can only be imagined. Red-faced, after a long pause he replied to her on 20 July asking *her* forgiveness.[6]

Some months later his horizons unexpectedly contracted. On the morning of 1 October 1919, dressed in a black suit (de rigueur in visiting a Swiss bank), scrubbed and brushed, he marched into the Eidgenössiche Bank in Zurich to collect his regular stipend of 1,000 Swiss francs, only to be told: *Der Kredit ist erschöpft.* Mrs McCormick, inexplicably, had cancelled her bequest. Deeply concerned, he wrote informing her that he was about to quit Zurich and return to Trieste (which he had left in 1915) and asked if they could perhaps meet before he left. She replied stonily on 10 October to state that she was not in a position to meet him and would therefore say goodbye in her letter. Genuinely worried at this point, he gathered together the manuscript of his book (at the time comprising the fair manuscripts of all of the episodes up to and including 'Cyclops') and dispatched these forthwith to her. Alas, even this last-ditch effort failed to have the desired effect. She responded on 13 October:

> Thank you for the fine manuscript, – which I am glad to keep for you with the understanding that, when for any reason, you want it, you have only to write for it. As the Bank told you, I am not able to help you any longer financially, but now that the difficult years of the war are past, you will find publishers and will come forward yourself, I know.[7]

Two days later, John Quinn received a rather cryptic cable from Joyce:

> Starting cable maximum advance manuscript Ulysses via Sanita two Trieste.[8]

The very next day, with his income now deflated to a relatively paltry £21/$105 a month, a mere third of what he had enjoyed during the happier days in Zurich, the troubled author left for Trieste. For him, the difficult years of the post-war period had begun.

By the time Quinn's reply reached him (by cable of 22 November 1919 sent in error to Zurich and offering £25/$125 advance on the manuscript of *Ulysses*)[9], the urgency of his desire to sell it had abated somewhat. The family were now living with Stanislaus (an uncomfortable situation but at least cheap) and he had made arrangements for a part-time teaching job at the Scuola Superiore di Commercio Revoltella. Writing on 3 January 1920 to Frank Budgen, he confided his new strategy:

Quinn replied after a month offering 700 frs down on account of *Ulysses* MS. I did not answer. He now offers 1500 frs down, without naming the ultimate sum. I shall write to Mrs M [McCormick] to know if she wants it.[10]

In point of fact Quinn had not increased his offer from £25 (625 francs) to £60 (1500 francs) and one can only quiz how Joyce got it into his head that he had. At the beginning of February he updated Budgen: 'Wrote to Mrs M to know whether she wants MS of *Ulysses*. No reply! How the hell am I to get it back?'[11] There was no immediate reply from Budgen either for, as Joyce explained to Harriet Weaver, several of the letters posted by him at this time had gone astray. Eventually, the Post Office sorting itself out, he heard from Budgen and presumably also from Mrs McCormick. At this point he sought in vain to persuade Budgen to visit him in Trieste: 'I thought if you came you could bring the MS of *Ulysses*.'[12] It is uncertain how exactly Joyce repossessed himself of his manuscript, adrift since October, but he had it safely back in his hands by at the latest June 1920. He had in the interval finally opted to sell it to Quinn. On 4 February (while still manuscriptless) he sent him a telegram: 'Cable immediately advance manuscript Ulysses.'[13] Quinn telegraphed at once, generously rounding up the figures to 3,000 lire (£31 or $155). Having made it explicit that he did not want a fragment or a series of fragments but only the complete manuscript, he stipulated the arrangement: Joyce could have the advance payment, but only when he had received *all* of the manuscript could he estimate its value, basing this on the number of pages, the general appearance of the document, and suchlike considerations, and only then would he send the outstanding balance. There was thus no question *at this time* of Joyce dispatching to Quinn that part of the manuscript already written. Effectively, Joyce had mortgaged it without handing over a page.

By the middle of May 1920 he had finished the technically very complex fourteenth episode, 'Oxen of the Sun', and was understandably exhausted. He was also bored with Trieste. He had not relished the return to relative impecuniosity and he felt, quite correctly, that he was travelling backwards. A change, though, necessitated a fresh influx of money. But from where or from whose pocket?

In early June, he wended his way to Lago di Garda, where he met Ezra Pound for the first time. Inevitably, the two men – adepts at surmounting life's little exigencies – teased out the Irishman's problems. Pound suggested that the most sensible thing was for Joyce to move to Paris, rather than somewhere in Ireland or England where he had intimated he might go. Pound was himself going to Paris and, like another John the Baptist, would prepare the way. Having no better alternative Joyce agreed to try it, even if only temporarily, and he returned to Trieste to make final preparations for the move.

On 24 June 1920 he wrote to Quinn:

I shall send you tomorrow five chapters or episodes, *Wandering Rocks*, *Sirens*, *Cyclops*, *Nausikaa* and *Oxen of the Sun* [Episodes 10 to 14] and a few days later nine more [Episodes 1 to 9], making the entire MS so far. The final adventure [Episode 15] and close of the book [Episodes 16 to 18] I shall remit you as written during the next few months.[14]

By way of explanation for this, he asked Quinn to cable him in Paris an additional advance 'or, if you prefer, the balance of the total price'. He dutifully sent off the first parcel on the following day. Then, on 4 July, he quit Trieste for Paris and from there on 12 July posted the second parcel, containing the first nine episodes.

That day he dropped in to see Sylvia Beach in her little bookshop on the rue Dupuytren. They had met for the first time at a party given by the poet André Spire the previous evening. Beach's account of the first real conversation between the Irish writer and the young American woman who was to become the first publisher of *Ulysses* is as follows:

Joyce (…) had spent his entire savings on the removal to Paris. He must look for pupils (…) I wondered when Joyce found time to write. At night, he said, after the lessons were over (…) Did he sometimes dictate? 'Never!' he exclaimed. He always wrote by hand. He liked to be held back, would otherwise go too fast. He had to see his work as he shaped it word by word (…) It appeared that Mr. John Quinn, the brilliant Irish-American lawyer in New York, was buying the manuscript of *Ulysses* bit by bit. As soon as Joyce completed an instalment, he made a fair copy and sent it off to Quinn, who, in return, sent Joyce the sum agreed on – small sums, but they helped.[15]

It should be clear from this that Beach has confused Joyce's plans with respect to sending Quinn the later episodes with the facts of the case regarding the earlier ones.

The second parcel of fair manuscripts arrived in New York in advance of the first, confusing Quinn and worrying Joyce. He thought the latter lost and lamented to Stanislaus: 'I suppose I have to write it out all over again! Curse them again!'[16] On 16 August 1920 Quinn sent Joyce £50/$250; on 27 September – the first parcel having belatedly turned up – £20/$100; on 24 January 1921 – in response to a cable of desperation – £40/$200; during August 1921, while on a visit to Paris, £52/$260; and, finally, on 20 November 1922, the balance outstanding of £47/$235, thereby bringing the total – his considered estimate of the value of the manuscript of *Ulysses* – to £240/$1,200 (in 1997 terms, approximately £7,200 or $12,000). For his part, Joyce sent Quinn episodes fifteen and sixteen, 'Circe' and 'Eumaeus', on 8 April 1921 and the penultimate and ultimate episodes, 'Ithaca' and 'Penelope', on or about 1 May 1922.

While all this was going on Joyce's circumstances had slowly improved. In August 1920 Harriet Weaver paid an additional £2,000 into his trust fund, lifting his monthly income to about £30/$150. On 2 February 1922 *Ulysses* was published. In March the incorrigible Miss Weaver added a yet further £1,500 to the fund, increasing his income to £35/$165 a month. Thus, taking into account the royalties from *Ulysses* and the cheaper cost of living in Paris, he was now no less well off than he had been in Zurich. Finally, in July 1923, as a *coup de grâce*, his truly extraordinary benefactress added £12,000 to his account, rendering it well-nigh unnecessary for him (or for me) to have to stoop to calculate the monthly yield. James Joyce was now as rich as he ever was or would be ever again. Totting up her total bequest, Harriet Weaver had signed over to Joyce the equivalent in today's money of approximately £600,000 or $1,000,000.

Quinn, meanwhile, had elected to sell his extensive library by public auction. This amounted to some 18,000 items, including the recently acquired manuscript of *Ulysses*. In November 1923, lest he feel in any degree poorly treated by him, Quinn generously offered to share with Joyce any profit made on its resale, adding that in his opinion, given that Joyce was relatively unknown in the United States, the manuscript was unlikely to fetch as much as $1,000. There was always the slim possibility on the other hand that one or two 'nuts' would be willing to bid for it and drive the price perhaps as high as $2,500.

The auction took place on 14 January 1924. The bidding was slow but the price eventually inched up to $1,975. As this was so close to Quinn's reserve price of $2,000 the auctioneer prudently decided to let it go, and Dr A. S. W. Rosenbach, an American rare-book dealer, became the new owner of the manuscript. (He later boasted that he had been prepared to spend as much as $3,500 on the manuscript.)

With auctioneers' fees and the $1,200 already paid deducted and with the resultant figure halved, the sale realized for Joyce the sum of $239.37 – a sum to be paid only on receipt by Quinn of the purchase price (the auction house having allowed the purchaser six months in which to pay). Quinn wrote to Joyce on 21 January 1924 informing him of the results of the sale and asking him to forward the manuscript of the last six pages of the book, which, he noted, had not been included in the parcel sent on 1 May 1922. On learning of the figure, and in his new *persona* of man of substance, Joyce was overcome with 'stupor and indignation'.[17] He assured Quinn that the final pages had been added on proof (in fact they had not been: he had retained the manuscript of these pages) and he ungratefully, if politely, disdained the $239.37. He even toyed with the idea of buying back the manuscript. For what figure, he asked, would 'Mr (or Dr) Rosenbach relinquish his grip on his (my) MS?'[18] Quinn advised him in a letter of 29 February 1924 to tread carefully: if Rosenbach smelled a rat and thought that Joyce's interest was commercial and not (as of course it *now* was) sentimental, he would ask for a figure substantially higher than $1,975. Indeed, Quinn urged, Joyce would be foolhardy to pay anything like $2,000 for the manuscript and would be well advised to keep his money intact for his old age.[19] In the event, absolutely nothing came of Joyce's outrage. In April 1924 H. Bacon Collamore, the underbidder at the Quinn sale, sought to buy the manuscript. Rosenbach was willing to let it go for $3,000, but Collamore felt that the price was too high.

And so it all ended. The manuscript, which one presumes would today fetch as much as a million dollars, was destined to remain in Rosenbach's possession until his death in 1952 and thereafter to become part of a memorial collection in Philadelphia named in his and his brother's honour: the Philip H. and A. S. W. Rosenbach Foundation. There, today, the interested scholar can freely fingerponder it: the erstwhile seriously undervalued, much disputed, surprisingly small and fragile, calligraphically scripted manuscript of *Ulysses*.

The Controversies

When John Quinn purchased the manuscript of *Ulysses* he quite naturally assumed that he was getting the actual manuscript of *Ulysses*, in other words the fair copies which the typist had used in preparing the typescripts. That the manuscript he did buy was indeed the real McCoy was equally the view held by most Joyce scholars prior to 1975. In that year the Rosenbach Foundation, in association with Faber and Faber, published a truly splendid facsimile edition of the manuscript, edited by Clive Driver and with an introduction by Harry Levin. The facsimiles are so near-perfect that, with care, one can not only distinguish between pencilled and inked inscriptions but also read overwritten and partly erased words. In his introduction Levin entertains no doubt that, as he writes, 'the printers [of *Ulysses*] worked from typescripts based on the text before us'. Clive Driver was equally convinced of the manuscript's authenticity and ascribed what he felt was scholarly neglect of it to a groundless, if not malicious, rumour.

> At least part of the reason for this neglect is a long-standing myth, originating with Sylvia Beach, that the Quinn manuscript is merely a fair copy, that Joyce, after completing each episode, sat down and wrote out by hand a duplicate of the final text to sell to Quinn.[20]

While it is true that Sylvia Beach had made a claim in her 1959 autobiography *Shakespeare and Company* (see p. liii) that might be construed as positing the fresh inscription of a duplicate manuscript, this had not resulted in neglect: Joyce scholars had not even followed it up. Had they done so, the manuscript would have become the focus of intense scrutiny – which, ironically, is precisely what did happen on the publication of the facsimile and of Driver's overzealous counterclaim.

The current generally accepted evaluation of the true status of the Rosenbach manuscript was thrashed out between 1975 and 1977 in a series of reviews, letters to each other, and letters to the editor by four experts on Joyce's text: A. Walton Litz, Philip Gaskell, Hans Walter Gabler, and Michael Groden. If, as they pointed out, one carefully compares the text in the manuscript against that in the extant typescripts certain anomalies come to light. For eight of the episodes – 'Lotus Eaters' (5), 'Hades' (6), 'Aeolus' (7), 'Lestrygonians' (8), 'Scylla and Charybdis' (9), 'Sirens' (11), 'Nausicaa' (13), and 'Oxen of the Sun' (14) – the texts do not match point for point: the typescripts not only incorporate material *not* in the manuscript but also some phrases in the manuscript appear in altered form in the typescript. It seemed to Litz, Groden, and Gaskell that these differences could be explained: either Joyce sent the typist instructions for additional revisions to be made, or the typescript was returned to Joyce, revised, and a second typescript (the extant typescript) prepared.

Gabler argued that the number and nature of the changes involved flatly ruled out the first proposal, and the two-typescript theory could be discounted on the grounds that Joyce could not have afforded such a luxury. Furthermore, in the case of three episodes for which early drafts survive, some of the variant readings in the typescript match those in the early drafts, while the Rosenbach manuscript incorporates some readings that are undoubtedly later revisions of those in the early-draft text. This textual situation could only have arisen, he concluded, if the typescript had been made from a different draft or fair copy of which the Rosenbach manuscript is a duplicate copy. He termed the original draft or fair copy (which, for each of the episodes in question, is 'lost') the 'final working draft' or FWD. As Gabler saw it, noting that the Rosenbach manuscript of the episodes in question appears to have been copied out in haste, Joyce made fresh revisions while writing them out. Some of these revisions he failed to copy back into the FWD, and, finally, after he had finished writing out the duplicate (Rosenbach) fair copy, he went back to the original draft (the FWD) and further revised this before submitting it to the typist. This hypothesis was eventually agreed by all concerned,[21] and the first controversy ended in unison. The main losers were Clive Driver, whose reputation as a bibliographer took a dent or two, and the Rosenbach Foundation, whose crown jewel had (apparently) been shown to be forty per cent paste.

The second controversy, which centred on the Critical and Synoptic Edition of *Ulysses* edited by Gabler with Wolfhard Steppe and Claus Melchior and published in 1984, was much more far-reaching and embittered, and involved not only virtually the entire man- and woman-power of the Joycean community but also a turbulence of journalists, reviewers, trustees, editors, grandsons, persons-of-letters, scandalmongers, men in macintoshes and literary hangers-on: everyone had their own point of view, although not everybody knew what they were meant to be looking at.

The apple of discord was Gabler's treatment of the Rosenbach manuscript in the case of the eight episodes for which, according to received opinion (originating in Gabler himself), that particular manuscript lay outside the line of direct descent of the text. According to Gabler, some of Joyce's revisions of these episodes were overlooked, and since these new readings (a minority of a minority) remained as it were 'marooned' in the backwater of the Rosenbach manuscript, he had to decide whether to incorporate them into his critical edition. In the event he opted for their inclusion, except where subsequent changes (on the typescript or the proofs) made it impossible or inappropriate to incorporate them, reasoning that if Joyce had not intended to include the revisions, then, taken as a group, they would have been unique and essentially meaningless, particularly so as he was ever parsimonious of his own composition.

Gabler's stance seemed sensible to me at the time, and would today if I though it still relevant. But it failed to satisfy Clive Hart and Philip Gaskell, two of the edition's three-member Advisory Committee. Hart and Gaskell argued that only material *inside* the line of direct descent of the text – Joyce's draft, the typist's copy (in these cases the lost 'final working draft'), the typescripts, and the proofs – should in principle be included. Their view was picked up by John Kidd, the young American Joycean who soon emerged as the most vociferous of Gabler's opponents. In addition to many other *improperia* which he listed against the edition ('errors of execution' which turn out on closer inspection to be mainly procedural, theoretical, and typographical, and only in a small number of cases actual errors as one would normally understand the term), he vehemently objected to the incorporation of readings from the Rosenbach manuscript in the case of the eight so-called collateral (duplicate) fair copies.

The hypothesis that eight of the eighteen episodes of the *Ulysses* manuscript sold to John Quinn are 'authorial fakes' constitutes a very serious charge and posits bizarre – consistently bizarre – behaviour on James Joyce's part. One would therefore expect the evidence to be, if not compelling, at least substantial. In fact it virtually evaporates in the case of the first six of the eight episodes, and it suggests a somewhat different scenario for the remaining two.

A New Hypothesis

The currently accepted theory requires that on eight separate occasions one of the fair copies at issue was written out shortly *before* the corresponding typescript was made and – more significantly – at a time when Joyce was still engaged in composing the relevant episode.[22] Certain aspects of this scenario have long disquieted me; namely, (i) on eight separate occasions Joyce chose to prepare the 'for sale' fair copy not *after* he had finished preparing the 'true' typist's copy (the lost 'final working draft'), but shortly *before* he did so; and (ii) on eight separate occasions, although he went to the trouble of preparing a new fair copy, which he thus had to hand, he chose to pass on to the typist the *earlier* and less legible copy.

These aspects of the theory are best illustrated by considering the actual circumstances in which the typescripts were prepared. The pattern of Joyce's state of mind as he approached the point of completion of an episode is clear from his correspondence. He grew increasingly excited, impatient and exhausted, as evidenced, for example, in two of his letters to Budgen: 'Gloria in excelsis Deo! Nausikaa episode finished. Typing: and will send you a copy at once';[23] and, 'The oxen of the bloody bleeding sun are finished. Typing nearly so.'[24] It is hardly credible that he interrupted his composition to prepare a duplicate fair copy, one for which he had no immediate use. The only conceivable immediate use of such a distracting labour would have been to provide a clean fair manuscript to hand to the typist.

According to the theory, Joyce initiated his strange practice of preparing a duplicate (to be sold in the indeterminate future) *whilst in the midst of composition* in April 1918, a mere month after Mrs McCormick's subsidy had increased his income to a level at which he was no longer in need of the relatively small sum that he knew his manuscript would bring. Furthermore, because of the very large number of revisions that postdate the Rosenbach, the typescripts for these episodes would necessarily have been made from very complex manuscripts indeed (the lost 'final working drafts') and we would naturally expect them to be less accurate than the typescripts made directly from the Rosenbach manuscript.

It was precisely in the period March 1918 to October 1919 (during which time he prepared the first six of the eight disputed episodes) that Joyce had the means and the motive to have his typescripts (average length eighteen single-spaced pages) retyped. Writing to Harriet Weaver on 20 March 1918, he indicated that he planned something of the sort:

I have sent [Episode 4] to Mr Pound but I must apologise for the very bad typescript. I shall try to have the following episodes done better. I hope it is legible in spite of the typist's mistakes.[25]

The typescripts that followed (with two exceptions) bear out Joyce's declared intention. They are clean, legible, and contain relatively few mistakes. This seems odd if we accept the theory that they were made directly from the 'final working drafts' which, given the large number of additions and revisions they must have contained, would have been difficult for a typist to work from. The exceptions are episodes 10 and 12

('Wandering Rocks' and 'Cyclops') which were indisputably made from the Rosenbach manuscript. According to the theory, the only discernible differences between these two typescripts and the typescripts made from the 'final working drafts' should be that the latter should be worse than the former. The reverse is the case. Joyce was aware of this. On 28 October 1919 he wrote to Harriet Weaver:

> A few days before I left [Zurich] I forwarded to Mr Pound the episode of the *Cyclops* but I suppose there are many mistakes as I had not time to revise the typescript carefully.[26]

The first part of my own proposal for a solution to the problem of the Rosenbach manuscript is as follows: in the case of episodes 5–9 and 11, all written in Zurich, Joyce wrote out the extant Rosenbach fair copies specifically for the purpose of providing clean copy for the typist. The typescript, when returned, was then carefully revised by Joyce and sent out for retyping. The purpose of the retyping was to provide clean copy for the serial publication in the *Little Review* and *Egoist*.

In addition to assessing the biographical evidence for this interpretation of the facts (summarized above), I have carefully examined the textual situation. There are no readings in the typescript which cannot be accounted for on the basis of the two-typescript theory. There are, on the other hand, many mistakes in the typescript which can be directly linked to the particularities of the handwriting and to the disposition of revisions in the Rosenbach manuscript. In one case only (Episode 11, 'Sirens') is there an early draft extant. This draft is the immediate antecedent of the Rosenbach manuscript and shares with the typescript only two or three readings differing in the Rosenbach. These agreements can easily be accounted for as corrections made by Joyce on the first typescript. If the Rosenbach was collateral for this episode then we would expect a much larger number of agreements between the draft and the typescript.

For episodes 5–9 and 11, all the available evidence supports the two-typescript theory and therefore for these episodes the Rosenbach manuscript is not collateral (is not a duplicate) but rather lies within the line of direct descent of the text. For episodes 13 and 14, there is evidence to corroborate the view that the Rosenbach manuscript is collateral. But here also, and for the same reasons as recounted above, I do not agree that they were written out while Joyce was still engaged in composition. The second part of my proposed solution is: in the case of episodes 13 and 14, both composed after Joyce had returned to Trieste, the typist's copy was written down in small notebooks. In June 1920, when he came to gather together the episodes for posting to John Quinn, Joyce realized that the notebooks were not uniform with the rest of the manuscript (which consisted entirely of single leaves). Aware that Quinn had advised him that the appearance of the manuscript would be a factor in the estimation of its value, Joyce decided to copy them out on single leaves. The copying took place not *before* but *after* the typescripts had been returned and revised and when Joyce was no longer composing. This implies that the Rosenbach fair copies for these two episodes do not incorporate any new revisions and that they contain no new readings other than copying errors. There is no text 'marooned', so to speak, in the Rosenbach manuscript.

The most likely date when the copying took place was sometime during the period mid-May to late June 1920. This was the sole occasion when he had the means, the motive, and the opportunity to prepare for Quinn a duplicate manuscript. It was only at this time, we should recall, that the question arose of his actually forwarding it. In pressing need of money, he clearly bore in mind Quinn's intention of estimating its monetary value on the basis of its appearance and quality. This, after all, is the only sane reason why Joyce should have made any duplicate copies in the first place: there must have been something wrong with the 'true' manuscripts; otherwise, why not simply and sensibly send these to Quinn?

For both of these duplicated episodes, 'Nausicaa' and 'Oxen of the Sun', early-draft versions have survived, and when these are compared with the extant typescripts and with the Rosenbach it is found that the early draft and typescript agree against the Rosenbach in about two hundred instances, far more than could reasonably be accounted for as Joyce's corrections on a first typescript. In addition, the Rosenbach manuscripts for the two episodes share a peculiar feature: a small number of pencil-strokes coincide (hardly coincidentally) with page-breaks in the extant typescripts. These pencil-strokes, unless they are the result of outrageous and oddly coincidental behaviour on the part of an unusually knowl-edgeable Joyce scholar (and we must remember that the manuscript and the typescript were not directly compared, as far as I am aware, until after the facsimile had been published), can only have been added after mid-May 1920, when the typescript of 'Oxen' had been prepared, and before 25 June 1920, when Joyce sent off the first parcel to Quinn. The most likely reason for the pencil-marks is that Joyce was spot-checking the manuscript against the typescript to ensure that it was complete, not word by word but at least section by section. This would have been necessary only if he had in the first place copied from sundry notebooks. The bibliographical evidence suggests that this is indeed the case for 'Oxen' at least.

Despite the fact that the Rosenbach manuscript was not the copy for the typist for these two episodes, it is probable that a second typescript was prepared. According to the first part of my thesis this had become standard procedure for Joyce, and although his income in Trieste was much less than it had been in Zurich he still was a long way from being penniless and he still needed to provide clean copy for the *Little Review*.

Conclusion

In the case of six of the disputed episodes, Litz, Groden, and Gaskell's original hypothesis of a double typing is overwhelmingly the most likely correct interpretation of the evidence. For the remaining two episodes, Gabler's idea of a duplicate fair copy is almost certainly correct, except that these copies were made after, and not before, the typescripts had been prepared.

In establishing the text of *Ulysses* on critical and historical principles of text-editing, the position of the Rosenbach manuscript within the overall stemma of *Ulysses* is of pivotal importance. While the story, recounted above, of that manuscript's creation, sale, history, and critical reception is of great interest in itself, I trust that the reader will appreciate that its greater significance lies in the fact that a truer grasp of its status yields a truer text of *Ulysses*.

Notes

I. The Rationale of the Reader's Edition

1. Letter to Harriet Weaver dated 6 November 1921. *Letters* I, 176.

2. Hans Walter Gabler, 'The Synchrony and Diachrony of Texts: Practice and Theory of the Critical Edition of James Joyce's *Ulysses*', *Text*, vol. 1 (1984), 305–26; Jerome McGann, *A Critique of Modern Textual Criticism* (Chicago: University of Chicago Press, 1983); and D. F. McKenzie, *Bibliography and the Sociology of Texts* (London: British Library, 1985). For an overview of the field, see Michael Groden, 'Contemporary Textual and Literary Theory', in George Bornstein, ed., *Representing Modernist Texts: Editing as Interpretation* (Ann Arbor: University of Michigan Press, 1991), 259–86.

3. W. W. Greg, 'The Rationale of Copy-Text', *Studies in Bibliography*, vol. 3 (1950–1951), 19–36.

4. Hyphenation in early twentieth-century standard British English was excessive and ill thought-out. Hence, in *Ulysses*, Joyce's general aversion to, incomprehension of and thoroughly inconsistent use of hyphenation/nonhyphenation in compound words. Modern usage, particularly in America, is much more sparing and intelligent: the hyphen is used ordinarily to prevent ambiguity and/or as an aid to the eye in reading. In the Reader's Edition, compound words formed for the sole purpose of eliminating a necessary, or hypothetically necessary, hyphen (as in 'illusing', 'wellknown' or snotgreen') are converted into hyphenated or, where more appropriate in context, two-word forms (e.g. 'ill-using', 'well-known'/ 'well known' and 'snot-green'/'snot green'). Common compound words (e.g. 'kneebreeches', 'hairdresser', 'searchlight') or true Joycean neologisms (mostly verbal forms, e.g. 'blueglancing') are of course left stand. Finally, Joyce's hyphenated 'no-one' (he evidently balking at 'noone') is replaced by the two-word form 'no one'.

5. Regarding textual faults, it may be instructive to consider the apparently trivial case of the lost and found postcard. The now notorious

Kidd–Gabler dispute opened at the April 1985 conference of the Society for Textual Scholarship in New York when Kidd read a paper entitled 'Errors of Execution in the 1984 *Ulysses*'. One of Kidd's complaints was that Gabler had not done all his homework:

> By not examining the *unpublished* correspondence, a postcard from Joyce to Claud Sykes, his first typist, was overlooked. This document at SUNY-Buffalo, dated 19.xii.1917, requested a revision in the Nestor episode which was never carried out. (John Kidd, 'Errors of Execution in the 1984 *Ulysses*', paper delivered to the Society for Textual Scholarship, New York City, 26 April 1985. Reprinted in *Studies in the Novel*, vol. 22, no. 2 (Summer 1990), 245.)

Gabler replied:

> The Poetry Collection at Buffalo have by most recent communication affirmed my own record of the case: they assert that they have no such unpublished postcard, under such or other date, as cited – but, you will note, not quoted – by Dr Kidd. Does the postcard exist at all? If so, where? And what are its instructions? Until Dr Kidd gets his facts straight, we cannot deal with consequent facts potentially relevant to the edition. (Hans Walter Gabler, 'A Response to John Kidd', delivered to the Society for Textual Scholarship, New York City, 26 April 1985. Ibid., 250.)

As it happens, the disputed postcard was indeed in Buffalo, mislaid amongst some uncatalogued material. It has since resurfaced. Before the STS meeting, neither Kidd nor Gabler had seen it or a copy of it. What they both had seen was an index card describing the postcard prepared in the 1970s by the late Jack Dalton, who had seen it. On the card, Joyce instructed Sykes to insert in 'Nestor' the phrase 'History is to blame' after the words 'His seacold eyes looked over the empty bay'. The curiosity is that the fair copy (which Sykes had and was typing) reads: 'His seacold eyes looked on the empty bay'. Dalton sensibly decided that the postcard could not be construed as a request to Sykes also to change 'on' to 'over', and he made a notation to this effect. Later, copies of Dalton's index cards found their way to Gabler's office in Munich. He agreed with Dalton in this instance, but, the decision being a negative one (not to change), by 1985 had forgotten all about it. While on a visit to Munich some months prior to the STS meeting, Kidd was permitted to read through Gabler's assorted files. Coming across the index card, he evidently misunderstood it, made his own private note, but did not alert Gabler to its source. Hence the unnecessary exchange in New York.

My view of the matter is that Dalton was correct: the postcard by itself does not constitute a request to change 'on' to 'over', and Gabler acted correctly in not making the change *on that basis*; but, looked at from a broader perspective, it does provide sufficient *indirect* evidence on which to base an argument for the change to be made.

With regard to the word 'over' in the postcard, Dalton and Gabler assumed that Joyce was simply misremembering the fair copy, while Kidd assumed that it was a request for a revision. I believe that Joyce was simply *quoting* the protodraft (now lost), which he had retained and from which the fair copy was prepared. The latter was completed in mid-December 1917 and sent to Sykes on the 16th.

The phrase quoted in the postcard of 19 December 1917 is a conscious echo of a passage in 'Telemachus' which, in the fair copy, reads:

> He gazed southward over the bay. Eyes, pale as the sea the wind had freshened, paler, firm and prudent. The seas' ruler he gazed over the bay, empty save for a sail tacking by the Muglins.

If I am correct, then the 'Nestor' protodraft read 'over the empty bay' in close correlation with the phrasing in 'Telemachus'. The question then becomes: is the 'on' of the 'Nestor' fair copy an authorized revision of the 'over' of the protodraft, or is it no more than a copying slip? I believe that the latter explanation is the more probable: Joyce had written out the fair copy only a few days before sending the postcard and he would surely have remembered such an odd revision, which spoils a carefully constructed 'echo'.

While the difference in context between 'on' and 'over' is not of itself likely to be of much concern to the general reader, the argument regarding it underlines a fact that is important: the fair copies are all *copies* of earlier drafts and they will inevitably contain some quantum of errors made by Joyce in copying them out.

6. In these examples, attention is drawn only to the textual fault at issue and not to other errors in the 1922 versions.

7. In an unpublished article, 'Miles of porches of ears' (presently under review at the *James Joyce Quarterly*), John Turner identifies and discusses six additional textual faults. Of these, the most interesting is from 'Aeolus'. In a segment dealing with Daniel O'Connell, the phrase 'Miles of ears of

porches' occurs. Noting that the words 'of porches' first appear in the extant typescript (the fair copy reads 'miles of ears' and the intermediate document is lost), Turner argues sensibly that Joyce's probable instruction regarding the insertion (to position it after 'miles') was either faulty or was misunderstood by the typist.

8. Letter to Harriet Weaver dated 29 September 1922. BL Add. MS 57346, fol. 161.

9. John Kidd, 'A Catechism for the *Ulysses* Repair Kit', *James Joyce Literary Supplement*, vol. 5, No 2 (Fall 1991), 13. The reader was David Klarfeld of Holyoke, Massachussetts.

10. Letter to Harriet Weaver dated 25 November 1921. BL Add. MS 57346, fol. 71.

11. Letter to Harriet Weaver dated 6 December 1921. *Letters* I, 178.

12. Letter to Robert McAlmon dated 1 March 1922. Ibid., 181.

13. Letter to Harriet Weaver dated 11 March 1922. Ibid., 183.

14. Letter to Harriet Weaver dated 16 May 1922. Ibid., 184.

II. *The History of the Composition of* Ulysses

1. *James Joyce Archive*, vol. 7, 27–33.

2. *Letters* II, 166.

3. Ibid., 168.

4. Ibid., 209.

5. *Letters* I, 136. From the outset Joyce seems not to have wanted to reuse the (frankly wanting) title 'Stephen Hero' suggested to him by his brother Stanislaus. Before settling on the present title he contemplated both 'A Portrait of the Artist' (again) and 'Chapters in the Life of a Young Man' (*Letters* II, 83). Also, as a reverse match for Doherty (see p. xxxi), he considered changing the surname of his protagonist, Dedalus, to Daly.

6. Trouble indeed and it was to continue seemingly interminably. In 1917 Joyce complained with only slight exaggeration: 'Ten years of my life have been consumed in correspondence and litigation about my book

Dubliners. It was rejected by 40 publishers; three times set up, and once burnt. It cost me about 3,000 francs in postage, fees, train and boat fare, for I was in correspondence with 110 newspapers, 7 solicitors, 3 societies, 40 publishers and several men of letters about it. In the end it was published, in 1914, word for word as I wrote it in 1905' (*Letters* I, 105). Until Joyce was well over thirty years of age his sole published volume was the suite of thirty-six poems written between 1901 and 1904 (*Chamber Music*).

7. *Letters* I, 136.

8. *A Portrait* was not completed until 1914. Published serially and intermittently in somewhat censored form in instalments in the *Egoist* from 2 February 1914 to 1 September 1915, it first appeared in book form on 29 December 1916 when it was published in New York by Ben W. Huebsch. The Egoist Press of London, using the same sheets, brought out the first English publication on 12 February 1917.

9. BL Add. MS. 49975; reproduced in the *James Joyce Archive*, vol. 10, pp. 1219–22. This 'Doherty piece' is essentially an assemblage of phrases drawn from the 'Gogarty', 'Mother', and 'Ireland' sections of Joyce's 1909 Trieste (or 'Alphabetical') notebook (item 25 in the Cornell Joyce papers) and from *Stephen Hero*. Of these, a number descended in modified form into the final text of 'Telemachus' (e.g. [of Gogarty/Doherty/Mulligan], 'He has a horse-like face and hair grained and hued like pale oak' and 'Dubliners who slighted me esteemed him as peasants esteem a bonesetter or the redskins their medicine-man'). The line of development of 'Telemachus', accordingly, is: root: Trieste notebook → *Portrait* extension (1913–1914) <revision of plan> → *Ulysses* as sequel (1914) <revision of plan> → *Ulysses* as finally realized (1917).

10. 'Stephen in Paris', *James Joyce Quarterly*, vol. 17, 3 (Spring 1980), 306–11. One finds towards the end of *Giacomo Joyce* (probably written in August 1914 though drafted earlier and perhaps added to for some time thereafter) an early explicit reference to this new 'Ulysses' included in a description of a dream: 'Gogarty came yesterday to be introduced. *Ulysses* is the reason' (*James Joyce Archive*, vol. 2, 306).

11. *Selected Letters*, 209. In this early 'Ulysses' the correspondence with the Homeric model was very tentative. Stephen starred as Telemachus, of course, but in search more of a future than a father. The windswept

Martello Tower by the seashore stood in nicely for narrow, rocky Ithaca. An emaciated May Dedalus inappropriately played the voluptuous Penelope, while plump Buck Mulligan excelled in the villain's role of usurper. By the time Joyce had reconceptualized the book, by the time Bloom (growing as he did out of Alfred H. Hunter) came into the picture, Ithaca had switched to Eccles Street, Penelope was recast as the generously endowed Molly, and the handsome blackguard type Blazes Boylan more than consummately portrayed the despoiling interloper.

12. Letter dated 7 July 1915. *Letters* I, 83.

13. The dates of the diary, in this reckoning, span a canonical period of 40 days, in 1904 beginning on Passion Sunday (March 20), the 40th day in Lent, and coincident (as is highly appropriate) with a period set aside by the Church for the 'Contemplation of the Man of Sorrows'.

14. *Letters* II, 387. As regards the 'middle', a document of great significance which was once available (but, alas, no copies were taken) has been lost. John Slocum and Herbert Cahoon, *A Bibliography of James Joyce* (London: Hart-Davis, p. 140), describe a manuscript of the *Hamlet* episode ('Scylla and Charybdis') consisting of 'fragmentary conversations, which appear altered in the final version'.

15. *Letters* I, 97.

16. The latest such listing can be dated April 1917. See in this context *James Joyce Archive*, vol. 4, 288–352, and Rodney Wilson Owen, *James Joyce and the Beginnings of 'Ulysses'* (Ann Arbor: UMI Research Press, 1983), 96–102.

17. Richard Ellmann (1982), 413.

18. That Stephen's excessive egocentrism is purely fictional is absurd: Joyce drew him out of his own pocket. One has only to think of the outrageous dedication in his prose play, *A Brilliant Career*, that he sent to William Archer on 30 August 1900: 'To – My own Soul I dedicate the first true work of my life' (*Letters* II, 7).

19. *Letters* I, 102.

20. *Letters* II, 397.

21. Unpublished letter, Yale.

22. For further information in this connection see the introduction to *The Lost Notebook*, eds. Danis Rose and John O'Hanlon (Edinburgh: Split Pea Press, 1989).

23. *Letters* II, 400.

24. See Philip R. Yanella, 'James Joyce to the *Little Review*: ten letters', *Journal of Modern Literature* vol. 1, no. 3 (March 1971), 394.

25. Letter dated 9 April 1917 to Ezra Pound. *Letters* I, 101.

26. This nomenclature may be confusing. The division of the writing of *Ulysses* into phases was initiated by A. Walton Litz, who in *The Art of James Joyce* (Oxford: Oxford University Press, 1961) defined two distinct periods. Michael Groden refined this in *Ulysses in Progress* (Princeton: Princeton University Press, 1977) into three periods. My division is a further refinement of Groden's scheme.

27. Joyce provided a complete description of this conditioning skeleton in the somewhat perplexing 'Linati Schema'. Encouraged by Joyce, this kind of systematization has led the credulous to assume that each episode is written in a unique style. This is not the case. Only the episodes from 'Sirens' to the end can accurately be said to be each *sui generis*.

28. See in this connection Clive Hart and Leo Knuth, *A Topographical Guide to James Joyce's Ulysses* (Colchester: A Wake Newsletter Press, 1975); Danis Rose and John O'Hanlon, eds., *The Lost Notebook* (Edinburgh: Split Pea Press, 1989); Philip Herring, ed., *Joyce's Notes and Early Drafts for Ulysses* (Charlottesville: University Press of Virginia, 1977); and Michael Seidel, *Epic Geography* (Princeton: Princeton University Press, 1976).

29. 'Hades' was in part pieced together from material already written or gathered (in this case, the account in *Stephen Hero* XXII of the death of Joyce's sister and her subsequent funeral attended by him, his father, and his father's friends, and an account from the *Evening Telegraph* of 13 July 1904 of the funeral of Dubliner Mat Kane who perished while bathing off a boat in Kingstown Harbour). 'Scylla and Charybdis', the *Hamlet* chapter, was composed by restructuring the earlier-written fragment from 'Ulysses as sequel' and adding to it information gleaned from an exchange of correspondence in November 1918 with the German Shakespeare scholar

Carl Bleibtreu (who appears as a 'character' in the episode). See in this context Charles Skinner, 'Two Joyce Letters Concerning *Ulysses* and a Reply', *James Joyce Quarterly* vol. 15 (Summer 1978), 376–9.

30. Forrest Read, ed., *Pound/Joyce: The Letters of Ezra Pound to James Joyce* (New York: New Directions, 1970), 157.

31. John Firth, ed., 'Harriet Weaver's Letters to James Joyce 1915–1920', *Studies in Bibliography*, vol. XX (1967), 182.

32. Willard Potts, ed., *Portraits of the Artist in Exile* (Dublin: Wolfhound Press, 1970), 72.

33. These papers have been edited and (to a degree) annotated by Philip F. Herring in *Joyce's Ulysses Notesheets in the British Museum* (Charlottes-ville: University Press of Virginia, 1972). Significantly, it is at this point in his career that Joyce began more comprehensively to conserve for poster-ity his working notes and draft materials. Commenting on this, Hans Walter Gabler writes:

> In the course of his writing career, Joyce's artistic self-awareness and attitude to his art underwent a significant paradigm shift. It is hardly by the accident of external circumstances alone that little or no note and draft materials have survived for the earlier part of the *oeuvre*. He purposely destroyed his juvenile poems, left no traces at all (apart from versional variants) of *Chamber Music*, and discarded, as of apparently no further significance, most workshop materials for *Dubliners* and *A Portrait of the Artist as a Young Man* (and, with the materials for the latter, two-thirds of *Stephen Hero*). The aspect of these works with which Joyce identified was clearly that of their finished state, to which he signed his name. In allegiance to traditional notions of authorship, he seems to have mentally divorced the published accomplishment from its material states of origin. Overtly, this attitude persists, indeed, through *Exiles* and *Ulysses*. An undercurrent indicating the paradigm shift manifests itself in the survival of copious notes for *Exiles* and the increasingly systematic preservation of notesheets and drafts for *Ulysses* from 'Cyclops' onwards. To our critical and retrospective view, these prefigure the gradual and segmental emergence of the work that in conclusion acquires the title *Finnegans Wake*. Its title under evolution is also the name for the new paradigm: *Work in Progress* (*James Joyce Quarterly*, vol. 33 [Summer 1996], 621–5).

34. Letter of [?28] February 1921, *Selected Letters*, 279. On different occasions he asked Budgen to send him books on fortune-telling, British Freemasonry, stamp collecting, palmistry, any old bookseller's catalogue, *My Three Husbands* by Anon., and so on and on. He even asked him to read some of the books and send him lists of words and phrases.

35. Letter dated 19 June 1919. *Letters* I, 126.

36. Letters dated 20 July and 6 August 1919. Ibid., 128–9.

37. Letter from Ezra Pound to John Quinn dated 25 October 1919. *Pound/Joyce*, 161.

38. Letter dated 3 January 1920. *Letters* I, 135.

39. Ibid., 137.

40. Letter dated 20 March 1920. *Selected Letters*, 251–2.

41. Letter of [?28] February 1921. Ibid., 278.

42. Letter to Frank Budgen dated 16 August 1921. Ibid., 285.

III. The Rosenbach Manuscript

1. Letter to John Quinn dated 13 May 1917. *Letters* II, 396.

2. Myron Schwartzman, 'Quinnigans Quake! John Quinn's Letters to James Joyce, 1921–1924', *Bulletin of Research in the Humanities* vol. 83 (1980), vol. 64.

3. Myron Schwartzman, 'Quinnigans Quake! John Quinn's Letters to James Joyce, 1916–1920', *Bulletin of Research in the Humanities* vol. 81 (1978), 237.

4. *Letters* II, 448.

5. Ellmann (1982), 480–81.

6. *Selected Letters*, 240–41.

7. *Letters* II, 454.

8. Schwartzman (1978), 239–40.

9. Ibid., 240.

10. *Selected Letters*, 245.

11. *Letters* II, 458.

12. *Selected Letters*, 251.

13. Schwartzman (1978), 241–2.

14. Ibid., 244.

15. Sylvia Beach, *Shakespeare and Company*, reprint of 1959 edition (London: Plantin Publishers, 1987), 38–9.

16. Letter dated 14 September 1920. *Letters* III, 21.

17. Schwartzman (1980), 62.

18. Letter dated 5 February 1924. Ibid.

19. Ibid., 66.

20. James Joyce, *Ulysses*, a facsimile of the manuscript, edited by Clive Driver (London and Philadelphia: Faber and Faber in association with the Philip H. and A. S. W. Rosenbach Foundation, 1975), 32.

21. Although the scholars prefaced the word 'probably' to their accounts to indicate that the matter had not been unequivocally proven, for all practical purposes it was treated as if it had been and the Joyce establishment accepted the hypothesis as constituting a given. To explain the need for duplicate copies in the first place, it was contended that the eight copies were made by Joyce with a view to their possible future sale, though not necessarily to John Quinn. I shall return to this point later. A. Walton Litz, *James Joyce Quarterly* vol. 14 (1976), 101–11; Philip Gaskell, *Times Literary Supplement* (25 June 1976), 803; Michael Groden, *Ulysses in Progress* (Princeton: Princeton University Press, 1977), 205–19; Hans Walter Gabler, *The Library* vol. 32 (1977), 177–82.

22. The approximate dates are April 1918 ('Lotus Eaters'), May 1918 ('Hades'), August 1918 ('Aeolus'), October 1918 ('Lestrygonians'), December 1918 ('Scylla and Charybdis'), May 1919 ('Sirens'), February 1920 ('Nausicaa'), and May 1920 ('Oxen of the Sun').

23. Letter, undated but *c.* February 1920. *Letters* II, 458.

24. Letter dated 18 May 1920. Ibid., 464.

25. *Letters* I, 112.

26. *Letters* II, 455.

A Technical Appendix:
an isotext and a reader's edition

I should like briefly to draw the reader's closer attention to what exactly constitutes an 'isotext edition' and a 'reader's edition' and what distinguishes these from the text of the first edition or that of Gabler's Critical and Synoptic Edition and why, of these four forms, versions or instantiations of what passes for the same text, the Reader's Edition is the most suitable for general reading.

Consider the following sample passage from 'Oxen of the Sun', detailing Bloom's initial interaction with Stephen and his companions on his arrival at the maternity hospital. In its 1922 first-publication form this reads:

> And the learning knight let pour for childe Leopold a draught and halp thereto the while all they that were there drank every each. And childe Leopold did up his beaver for to pleasure him and took apertly somewhat in amity for he never drank no manner of mead which he then put by and anon full privily he voided the more part in his neighbour glass and his neighbour nist not of his wile. And he sat down in that castle with them for to rest him there awhile. Thanked be Almighty God.
>
> This meanwhile this good sister stood by the door and begged them at the reverence of Jesu our alther liege lord to leave their wassailing for there was above one quick with child a gentle dame, whose time hied fast. Sir Leopold heard on the upfloor cry on high and he wondered what cry that it was whether of child or woman and I marvel, said he, that it be not come or now. Meseems it dureth overlong. And he was ware and saw a franklin that hight Lenehan on that side the table that was older than any of the tother and for that they both were knights virtuous in the one emprise and eke by cause that he was elder he spoke to him full gently. But, said he, or it be long too she will bring forth by God His bounty and have joy of her childing for she hath waited marvellous long. And the franklin that had drunken said, Expecting each moment to be her next. Also he took the cup that stood tofore him for him needed never none asking nor

desiring of him to drink, and Now drink, said he, fully delectably, and he quaffed as far as he might to their both's health for he was a passing good man of his lustiness. And sir Leopold that was the goodliest guest that ever sat in scholars' hall and that was the meekest man and the kindest that ever laid husbandly hand under hen and that was the very truest knight of the world one that ever did minion service to lady gentle pledged him courtly in the cup. Woman's woe with wonder pondering.

Now let us speak of that fellowship that was there to the intent to be drunken an they might. There was a sort of scholars along either side the board, that is to wit, Dixon yclept junior of saint Mary Merciable's with other his fellows Lynch and Madden, scholars of medicine, and the franklin that hight Lenehan and one from Alba Longa, one Crotthers, and young Stephen that had mien of a frere that was at head of the board and Costello that men clepen Punch Costello all long of a mastery of him erewhile gested (and of all them, reserved young Stephen, he was the most drunken that demanded still of more mead) and beside the meek sir Leopold. But on young Malachi they waited for that he promised to have come and such as intended to no goodness said how he had broke his avow. And sir Leopold sat with them for he bore fast friendship to sir Simon and to this his son young Stephen and for that his langour becalmed him there after longest wanderings insomuch as they feasted him for that time in the honourablest manner. Ruth red him, love led on with will to wander, loth to leave.

This, then, is Joyce's text as it appeared in the first edition and as proofread by him. Insofar as it could be argued that he approved it as truly representing his own work by not further altering or emending it (and this applies by extension to the rest of the 1922 *Ulysses*), the version could accurately be described as de facto 'error' free (depending on how you want to define an error). The covert facts of the matter are that the passage as presented above conceals a total of nineteen variants and five omissions of words from the text one would establish by the most informed condensation of the complete isotext and a further eleven variants from what one would wish for in a Reader's Edition. The passage as it stands, moreover, misinforms in that it isolates Bloom and Dixon from the attention of the others present ('the while they … drank every each') and records that Bloom's stratagem of discreetly emptying part of the contents of his unwanted glass of ale into a neighbour's *was* noticed by Dixon (as 'nist not' means 'was not unaware', while 'wist not', meaning 'was not aware', is meant).

The text of the Reader's Edition, by contrast, is as follows:

And the learning knight let pour for Childe Leopold a draught of fellowship and a halp thereto the which all they that were there drank every each. And Childe Leopold did up his beaver for to pleasure him and took apertly somewhat in amity for he never drank no manner of mead which he then put by and anon privily he voided it the more part in his neighbour glass and his neighbour wist not of this wile. And he sat down in that castle with them for to rest him there awhile. Thanked be Almighty God.

This meanwhile the good sister stood by the door and begged them at the reverence of Jesu our alther liege Lord to leave their wassailing for there was above one quick with child, a gentle dame, whose time hied fast. Sir Leopold heard in the upfloor cry on high and he wondered what cry that it was, whether of child or woman. I marvel, said he, it be not come or now. Meseems it dureth overlong. And he was ware of and saw a franklin that hight Lenehan on that side the table that was older than any of the tother and for that they both were knights venturous in the one emprise and eke by cause that he was elder he spoke to him fully gently. But, said he, or it be long too she will bring forth by God His bounty and have joy of her childing for she hath waited marvellous long. And the franklin that had drunken said, Expecting each moment to be her next. Also he took the cup that stood tofore him for him needed never none asking nor desiring of him to drink and, Now drink, said he full delectably, and he quaffed as far as he might to their both's health for he was a passing good man of his lustiness. And Sir Leopold that was the goodliest guest that ever sat in scholars' hall and that was the meekest man and the kindest that ever laid husbandly hand under hen and that was the very gentlest knight of the world, one that ever did minion service to lady gentle, pledged him courtly in the cup. Woman's woe with wonder pondering.

Now let us speak of that fellowship that was there to the intent to be drunken an they might. There was a sort of scholars along either side the board, that is to wit, Dixon yclept junior of Saint Mary Merciable's with other his fellows Lynch and Madden, scholars of medicine, and the franklin that hight Lenehan and one from Alba Longa, one Crotthers, and young Stephen that had mien of a frere that was at head of the board and Costello that men clepen Punch Costello all long of a mastery of him erewhile gested (and of all them, reserved young Stephen, he was the most drunken that demanded still of more mead) and beside the meek Sir Leopold. But on young Malachi they waited for that he promised to have come and such as intended to no goodness said how he had broke his avow. And Sir Leopold sat with them for he bore fast friendship to Sir Simon and to this his son young Stephen and for that his languor becalmed him there after longest wanderings insomuch as they feasted him for that time in the honourablest manner. Ruth rede him, love led on with will to wander, loth to leave.

As the above text is difficult to follow, even for *Ulysses*, the reader may appreciate the following annotations:

learning knight let pour = apprentice knight (in context = medical
    student [Dixon]) poured
Childe = Sir
did up his beaver = (in context) pushed back or took off his hat
apertly = openly
amity = friendship
anon privily = shortly and secretly
voided = emptied
wist not = was unaware
wile = trick
This meanwhile the good sister = While this was going on, the nurse
alther liege Lord = Lord of all
wassailing = carousing
quick with child = pregnant
in the upfloor = upstairs
it be not come or now = it (the birth) had not ended before now
it dureth = it has gone on
ware = aware
that hight = that was named
on that side = on the far side
the tother = the others
venturous = adventurous
emprise = chivalrous enterprise
eke by cause = also because
or it be long too = before long
tofore him = before him
as far as he might = as much as he could manage

to the intent to be drunken an they might = with the intention of
  getting drunk if they could
a sort of = some
that is to wit = namely
yclept = called
other his fellows = his companions
mien of a frere = the look of a priest
clepen = named
all long of = owing to
reserved = except
for that = because
had broke his avow = had broken his promise
Ruth rede him = Compassion directed him
loth = reluctant

Two phrases in the passage – 'a halp thereto the which all they that
were there drank every each' and 'all long of a mastery of him erewhile
gested' – remain ambiguous, and are possibly incoherent: the former, in
which 'halp' simply means 'help', seems to wish to convey that all of the
students acknowledged Bloom's presence by drinking to his health; the
latter, in which 'erewhile' means 'previously' and 'gest' means 'exploit',
seems somehow to refer to the origin of Costello's nickname 'Punch',
which we know to hinge on the bigness of his head. A further irony in
the passage is in the use of the phrase 'her time hieth fast', meaning that
she was shortly to give birth. In the context from which Joyce took the
phrase, 'my tyme hyeth fast' was used to mean 'I am not long for this
world'.

This Reader's Edition text is itself derived from a more complex and
richer isotext in which are arrayed all textual operations that in any way
altered the passage in the course of its protracted formation. This differs
from Gabler's somewhat similar synoptic version (apart from differences
of editorial judgement in the evaluation of some variants) in that it is
more extensive, engrossing as it does the two prototextual versions of the
text that lie behind the (missing) typist's copy. In preparing this, moreover,
a further version of the same text was also considered: one in which it is
deconstructed not diachronically as in the former (by displaying the
hidden strata of its development), but synchronically and contextually
(by showing the boundaries of the discrete elements of which it is a
composite). That is to say, the text was spliced both ways. This latter

editorial undertaking is necessary to show up any textual faults that may have arisen in the process of Joyce's transference of elements from source to notesheet to draft (in the present case, the textual faults 'full privily', 'nist', 'virtuous', 'full gently' and 'fully delectably').

Both of these versions of the text are cited below.

In the first case, the isotext, the diacritics indicate the level of development at which a particular textual operation took place. Thus, '⌐³⁺[the traveller] Childe⌐³⁺' indicates that Joyce replaced the reading 'the traveller' with the reading 'Childe' at genetic level 3+, the 1921 revision of the typescript. Levels 0 and 1 are prototextual, 1 having been copied from 0 and further revised; (missing) level 2 is the fair manuscript copied from 1; levels 3 and 3+ are the twice-revised extant typescript; and levels 4 and 5 are proof stages. Virtual levels of operation are designated not by the superscript ⌐ but by its fellow ˂. These are 'interdraft' textual transformations which occur not as a change on any page but mentally in the act of the author creatively copying one version into another: they are not 'intradraft', on-the-page operations. These latter, which are visibly marked on the manuscript, typescript or proof page, are designated by raised carets rotating ^ ˃ ˅ ˂ in order of ascent. Thus, a ˃ class addition is necessarily a second-order addition made to a first-order addition. Angle brackets enclose *currente calamo* deletions. In the notes on variants, 'R' denotes the Rosenbach manuscript version of the passage, a lateral level-2 copy lying outside the line of transmission of the text, and 'matrix' denotes the base-text at any level inherited from a preceding level. The abbreviations *cc* and *r* denote 'contrived correction' and 'revision', respectively, while the symbols □ and △ mean 'illegible word' and 'indicated but unmade insertion at this point', respectively. The reader need not necessarily be concerned with the fine-point details of this deconstruction, only to note its extent and nature.

« »

And { And] *mx* [matrix] 3; and 0–1 } ^[that scholar] ⁽²[this scholar] the learning knight { learning knight] *mx* 3; learningknight *mx* R } ²⁾^ let pour for { for] 0, *mx* 1, 3, and R; to *r*1; } ⁽²[him] ⌐³⁺[the traveller] Childe Leopold⌐³²⁾ a draught of fellowship { of fellowship] 0, 1; *absent* 3 and R } ^˃and ˅a { a] 0; *absent* 1 }˅ halp thereto˂ the which { which] 0–1; while *mx* 3 and R } ˃all˂ they { all they] *r* 0; they all 0 } ⁽²that were there²⁾ drank { drank] 0–3; drank drank *mx* R } every each^ ⁽²[whereof]. And²⁾ ^[he] ⁽²[sir]

⌐⊤[the traveller] Childe⁺³²⁾ Leopold ¶⁽²[having put up his vizard] did up his
⌐⊤[vizor] beaver⁺³²⁾¶ ᐳᐸ[for to pleasure him ᐸᐸ ⁽²and²⁾ took ^[but little] ᐳ[only
little] ᵛapertlyᵛ somewhat in ᵛ[friendship] ᐊ[fellowship] amityᐳ ᶜfor he
ᐊ[drank never no ale] never drank no manner of meadᐳᐳᵛᐸ ¶which he
then put byᵈ ⁽²[but] and²⁾ anon [ᐊ full part] privily { privily] e; full part
privily 0; full privily mx 1 } ^he^ voided it { it] 0; absent mx 3 } ^[clean] the
more part^ ⁽²[into] in²⁾ his neighbour glass ^[ᐳfor he drank never no ale]^
⁽²[, he nothing of that wile perceiving] and his neighbour nist not of this {
this mx R; his mx 3 } wile²⁾. ^[So sat he] ᐊ[Thus] ⁽²[So] And he²⁾ᐳ sat ⁽²down²⁾
ᐳ[Master Bloom] [⁽²sir Leopold]ᐸᐸ ⁽²in that { that] mx 3; the R } castle with
^[those merry scholars] ⁽²[those drunken scholars] them²⁾^ ⁽²[to rest] for to
rest him there awhile²⁾. ^[Loth to move in Horne's house.] [⁽²Loth to move
from Horne's house.] ¶Thanked be Almighty God.¶

This meanwhile the { the] 0, 1; this R, mx 3 } good ⁽²[nun] sister²⁾ stood
by the door and ^[bade] begged^ them ᐸof their gentlenessᐳ ^ᐳ[by Jesu
□] at { at] mx 1; At 0 } the reverence of Jesu our alther liege Lord { Lord] r
1; lord 0–1 }ᐸ^ to leave their wassailing for there was above one { above
one] r 1; one above 0 } ¶quick with child¶, { child,] 1, mx R; ~ mx 3 } a
gentle dame, whose time hied fast. ¶⁽²[And sir] Sir²⁾ Leopold heard in { in]
1, mx R; on mx 3 } the ^[upper chamber] upfloor^ cry on high and he
⁽²[marvelled] wondered²⁾ what cry ⁽²that²⁾ it was ^[for he nist not whether
of — -] whether of child or woman^¶ and I marvel, said ᐊ[sir Leopold] heᐳ,
it be not come or now ^ᐳ[for that]. Meseems^ { now. Meseems] r 1; ~
meseems 0–1 } it dureth overlong ᐸin the comingᐳ^. And ^[a franklin]
he was ware of { of] 0; deleted 0; not restored 1 } ^and { and] mx 1; & 0 }
saw^ ^ ᐊ[scholar] franklinᐳ that^ hight Lenehan ᐸthat heard himᐳ on that
side the ⁽²[board] table²⁾^[, one elder] that was older^ than any of the tother
and ᐸto him sir Leopoldᐳ ᐸfor that heᐳ ^[known to sir Leopold] [ᐊknown
of him] ᐳᐊ[by cause] for thatᐳ they ⁽²both²⁾ were ᵛ[fellowknights] ᐊ[fellows]
knights venturous { venturous] 1; virtuous mx 3 and R }ᐳᵛ in the one
emprise ᐊand eke by cause that he was elder he spoke to him fully { fully]
1, mx R; full mx 3 } gentlyᐳᐸ^. But, said ᐊ[sir Leopold to him] heᐳ ^[ᐊeke
by cause he was elder]^, or it be long too she will bring forth by God His {
His] mx 3; his 0–1 } ᐊ[grace] bountyᐳ and have joy ⁵of her childing⁵ for
she ^[is in marvellous pain] hath waited marvellous long^. And the
^[squire] franklin that had drunken^ said ^△^, Expecting each moment
to be her next. Also he took the cup that stood ᐊ[afore] toforeᐳ him for
him needed ^never^ none asking ^nor desiring ᐊofᐳ him to drink^ and {
and] 0–1; ~, mx 3 } ^Now drink, said he ¶full { full] 1, mx R; fully mx 3 }

delectably[n], and^ he ^[drank] quaffed^ as far as he might to their both's
health for he was a passing good man of his lustiness. ^And^ sir ⊲Leopold⊳
that was the ‖[meekest knight] goodliest guest[n] that ever sat in ⊲scholars'⊳
hall { hall] *mx* 1; hall, 0 } ⊲and that was the meekest man ‖and the
kindest[n] that ever laid ‖husbandly[n] hand under hen and that was the
‖very[n] gentlest { gentlest] *mx* 3; *absent* 4; truest *cc* 4 } knight ⑫of the world
one⑫ { of ... one] *mx* 3; *absent* R } that ever did minion service to lady
gentle⊳ pledged him courtly in the cup. Woman's woe with wonder
⊲[feeling] ⑫[weening] pondering⑫⊳.

  Now let us speak of that fellowship that was there to the intent to be
drunken { drunken] *mx* 1; ~, 0 } an they might. There ^[were] was a sort
of scholars ‖along either side the board[n], that is to wit, Dixon { Dixon] *mx*
1; ~, 0 } yclept junior { junior] *mx* 1; ~, 0 } ⑫of saint Mary Merciable's {
of ... Merciable's] *mx* 3; *absent* R }⑫ with other his fellows^ [⊲Dixon,]
[^yclept junior, and] Lynch and Madden, scholars of medicine, { medicine,]
0, *mx* 3; ~ *mx* 1 and R } and the franklin ^that^ hight Lenehan and one
from Alba ^Longa^, one { one] *deleted and restored* 0 } Crotthers, and
[⊲the] young [^knight] Stephen { Stephen] *mx* 3; ~, *mx* 1 and R } ^that
had mien of a ⊳[friar] frere^⊲ that was at head of the board { board] 0, *mx*
3; ~, 1 } and <a jester> Costello { Costello] *mx* 1; ~, 0 } that men clepen
Punch { Punch] 0–1, *mx* R; Bighead *r* 1 } Costello ^⊳[for things] all long
⊲[upon] of⊳ a mastery< of him ⊲erewhile⊳ gested^ (and of all them,
reserved young Stephen { reserved young Stephen] *r* 0; young Stephen
reserved 0 }, { them, ... Stephen,] 0, *mx* 3; ~...~ *mx* R } he was the most
drunken<) and> that demanded ^[ever] still^ of more ⊲[ale] mead⊳) and
beside the meek sir Leopold. But { Leopold. But] *mx* 1; ~, but 0 } on ^[sir]
young^ Malachi they waited for that he promised to have come and such
as intended to no goodness said how he had broke his avow. And sir
Leopold sat with them for he ^[had] bore ⊳fast^⊲ friendship to sir Simon
and to this his son young Stephen { Stephen] 0, *mx* 3; ~, *mx* 1 } ^and for
that his languor { languor] 0–1, *mx* R, 1932; langour *mx* 3 } ⊳[calmed]
becalmed< him there ⊳after longest wanderings< ⊳[where] insomuch as<
they feasted him for that time in the honourablest manner^. Ruth ⊲[led]
rede { rede] *mx* 1; red *mx* 3 and R }⊳ him, [^knight,] ^love^ led on { on] *mx*
1; ~, 0 } with ⊲[lust] will⊳ to wander, { wander,] 0, *mx* 3; ~ *mx* 1 and R }
[^ yet] loth to ⊲[go] leave⊳. ‖[⑫Loth to move from Horne's house]‖

The above text has been copyread and further editorially emended (*e*) in
the following instances:

wist] *e*; nist (= wist + ne) 0
was, whether] *e*; was whether 1
woman. And] *e*; woman and 0
world, … gentle,] *e*; world … gentle *mx* 3
Sir Leopold] *e*; sir Leopold 0
Saint Mary] *e*; saint Mary *mx* 3
Sir Simon] *e*; sir Simon 0

Thus, bypassing the 1922 text, the text of the Reader's Edition is arrived at by (a) constructing an isotext in which all manuscript-attested textual operations are described and critically evaluated and prioritized, (b) condensing this into a text free of apparatus, and (c) subjecting the latter to a final copyreading process. In evaluating variants in the isotext (and thereby necessarily making editorial decisions regarding the authorial status of the variants), a further level of information about the history of the text has been considered: (d) the deconstructed, worksheet-tagged analysis of its component parts. For the passage at issue this is as follows. (For the sake of simplicity I do not specify from what particular notesheet a particular element derives.)

{Structure: ⌜And … And … And.⌝}

And the learning knight ⌜let pour⌝ for Childe Leopold a draught of fellowship and a ⌜halp⌝ thereto ⌜the which⌝ all they that were there drank ⌜every each⌝. And Childe Leopold did up his ⌜beaver⌝ for ⌜to pleasure him⌝ and took ⌜apertly⌝ somewhat in amity for ⌜he never drank no⌝ manner of mead which he then put by and ⌜anon⌝ privily he ⌜voided⌝ it the more part in his neighbour glass and his neighbour ⌜wist not⌝ of this wile. And he sat down in that castle with them for to rest him there awhile. ⌜Thanked be Almighty God.⌝

⌜This meanwhile⌝ the good sister stood by the door and begged them at the reverence of ⌜Jesu⌝ ⌜our alther liege Lord⌝ ⌜to leave their wassailing⌝ for there was above one ⌜quick with child⌝, a gentle dame, ⌜whose time hied fast⌝. ⌜Sir Leopold heard ⌞in the upfloor⌟ cry on high⌝ and he wondered what cry that it was, whether of child or woman. ⌜I marvel⌝, said he, it be not come ⌜or now⌝. Meseems it ⌜dureth⌝ overlong. And ⌜he was ware⌝ of and saw ⌜a franklin that hight⌝ Lenehan ⌜on that side the table⌝ that was older ⌜than any of the tother⌝ and for that they both were knights ⌜venturous⌝ in the one emprise and ⌜eke by cause⌝ that he was elder he spoke to him ⌜fully gently⌝. ⌜But, said he, or it be long too she⌝ will bring forth by God His bounty and have joy of her childing for she hath waited ⌜marvellous⌝ long. And the franklin that had drunken said, Expecting ⌜each moment to be her next⌝. ⌜Also⌝ he took the cup ⌜that stood tofore him⌝ for ⌜him needed never none asking⌝ nor ⌜desiring of him to drink⌝ and, Now drink, said he ⌜full delectably⌝, and he quaffed ⌜as far as he might⌝ ⌜to their both's health⌝ for he was ⌜a passing good man of his lustiness⌝. And Sir Leopold that was the goodliest guest that ever sat in scholars' hall and that was ⌜the meekest man and the kindest⌝ that ever laid husbandly hand under hen and that was the ⌜very gentlest knight of the world⌝, one that ever did minion service to lady gentle, pledged him courtly in the cup. Woman's woe with wonder pondering.

⌜Now let us speak of⌝ that fellowship that was there ⌜to the intent to be⌝ drunken ⌜an they might⌝. There was ⌜a sort of⌝ scholars along either side the board, ⌜that is to wit⌝, Dixon yclept junior of Saint Mary Merciable's with ⌜other his fellows⌝ Lynch and Madden, scholars of medicine, and the franklin that ⌜hight⌝ Lenehan and one from Alba Longa, one Crotthers, and young Stephen that had mien of a frere that was at head of the board and Costello that men ⌜clepen⌝ Punch Costello ⌜all long of⌝ a mastery of him erewhile gested (and of all them, ⌜reserved⌝ young Stephen, he was the most drunken that ⌜demanded still⌝ of more mead) and beside the meek Sir Leopold. But on young Malachi they waited ⌜for that⌝ he promised to have come and ⌜such as intended to no goodness said how he had broke his avow⌝. And Sir Leopold sat with them for he bore fast friendship to Sir Simon and to ⌜this his son⌝ young Stephen and for that his ⌜languor⌝ becalmed him there after ⌜longest wanderings⌝ ⌜insomuch as⌝ ⌜they feasted him for that time in the honourablest manner⌝. Ruth rede him, love led on with will to wander, loth to leave.

Each of the textual elements demarcated above can (e) further be referred via the notesheets to its appearance in an external context, insofar as this has been traced, and its sense thereby clarified. Thus, for example, Joyce's explanation for Bloom's waiting in the maternity hospital – 'insomuch as they feasted him for that time in the honourablest manner' – derives from a sentence in Sir Thomas North's account of the banishment of Caius Martius Coriolanus from the city of Rome and of his subsequent defection to Rome's enemy Tullus Aufidius, king of the Volsceans, 'Tullus hearing what he [Coriolanus] said, was a marvellous glad man, and … he feasted him for that time, and entertained him in the honourablest manner he could, talking with him of no other matter at that present'.

Regarding all of the above, several things will be clear to the reader. Firstly, the 'evidence' by which the text of the present edition has been established (acts (a) to (e) above) cannot properly be presented reductively and linearly in the form of a historical collation. Such a lemmatization of differences – between it and the 1922 edition, say – shrouds the all-important matter of the strictly nonlinear frames of reference involved. Only a complete edition of the isotext would adequately define the scholarly basis of the Reader's Edition in this respect. On the other hand, there are serious practical, legal, and financial difficulties in preparing for publication and publishing such an enterprise, not the least being that the number of actual users of such a manuscript edition would be too few commercially to justify the expense involved in bringing it out. A more practical project would be to produce an updating of Gabler's synoptic text, along with a companion set of volumes on the genesis of *Ulysses* containing an annotated edition of the worksheets (a revision of Philip Herring's edition), an edition of all of the protodrafts, and an edition of the early and late copybooks pertinent to the novel. Hopefully such an archive can be prepared at some time in the future, perhaps as an integral part of a comprehensive hypertext of *Ulysses*.

ULYSSES

PART I

STATELY, plump Buck Mulligan came from the stairhead bearing a bowl of lather on which a mirror and a razor lay crossed. A yellow dressing gown, ungirdled, was sustained gently behind him on the mild morning air. He held the bowl aloft and intoned:

— *Introibo ad altare Dei.*

Halted, he peered down the dark winding stairs and called out coarsely:

— Come up, Kinch! Come up, you fearful Jesuit!

Solemnly he came forward and mounted the round gunrest. He faced about and blessed gravely thrice the tower, the surrounding country and the awaking mountains. Then, catching sight of Stephen Dedalus, he bent towards him and made rapid crosses in the air, gurgling in his throat and shaking his head. Stephen Dedalus, displeased and sleepy, leaned his arms on the top of the staircase and looked coldly at the shaking gurgling face that blessed him, equine in its length, and at the light untonsured hair, grained and hued like pale oak.

Buck Mulligan peeped an instant under the mirror and then covered the bowl smartly.

— Back to barracks! he said sternly.

He added in a preacher's tone:

— For this, O dearly beloved, is the genuine Christine: body and soul and blood and ouns. Slow music, please. Shut your eyes, gents. One moment. A little trouble about those white corpuscles. Silence, all.

He peered sideways up and gave a long low whistle of call, then paused awhile in rapt attention, his even white teeth glistening here and there with gold points. Chrysostomos. Two strong shrill whistles answered through the calm.

— Thanks, old chap, he cried briskly. That will do nicely. Switch off the current, will you?

He skipped off the gunrest and looked gravely at his watcher, gathering about his legs the loose folds of his gown. The plump shadowed face and sullen oval jowl recalled a prelate, patron of arts in the middle ages. A pleasant smile broke quietly over his lips.

—The mockery of it! he said gaily. Your absurd name, an ancient Greek!

He pointed his finger in friendly jest and went over to the parapet, laughing to himself. Stephen Dedalus stepped up, followed him wearily halfway and sat down on the edge of the gunrest, watching him still as he propped his mirror on the parapet, dipped the brush in the bowl and lathered cheeks and neck.

Buck Mulligan's gay voice went on:

—My name is absurd too: Malachi Mulligan, two dactyls. But it has a Hellenic ring, hasn't it? Tripping and sunny like the buck himself. We must go to Athens. Will you come if I can get the aunt to fork out twenty quid?

He laid the brush aside and, laughing with delight, cried:

—Will he come? The jejune Jesuit!

Ceasing, he began to shave with care.

—Tell me, Mulligan, Stephen said quietly.

—Yes, my love?

—How long is Haines going to stay in this tower?

Buck Mulligan showed a shaven cheek over his right shoulder.

—God, isn't he dreadful? he said frankly. A ponderous Saxon. He thinks you're not a gentleman. God, these bloody English! Bursting with money and indigestion. Because he comes from Oxford. You know, Dedalus, you have the real Oxford manner. He can't make you out. O, my name for you is the best: Kinch, the knifeblade.

He shaved warily over his chin.

—He was raving all night about a black panther, Stephen said. Where is his guncase?

—A woeful lunatic! Mulligan said. Were you in a funk?

—I was, Stephen said with energy and growing fear. Out here in the dark with a man I don't know raving and moaning to himself about shooting a black panther. You saved men from drowning. I'm not a hero, however. If he stays on here I am off.

Buck Mulligan frowned at the lather on his razor blade. He hopped down from his perch and began to search his trouser pockets hastily.

—Scutter! he cried thickly.

He came over to the gunrest and, thrusting a hand into Stephen's upper pocket, said:

—Lend us a loan of your noserag to wipe my razor.

Stephen suffered him to pull out and hold up on show by its corner a dirty crumpled handkerchief. Buck Mulligan wiped the razor blade neatly. Then, gazing over the handkerchief, he said:

— The bard's noserag! A new art colour for our Irish poets: snot green. You can almost taste it, can't you?

He mounted to the parapet again and gazed out over Dublin Bay, his fair oak-pale hair stirring slightly.

— God! he said quietly. Isn't the sea what Algy calls it: a great sweet mother? The snot-green sea. The scrotumtightening sea. *Epi oinopa ponton.* Ah, Dedalus, the Greeks! I must teach you. You must read them in the original. *Thalatta! Thalatta!* She is our great sweet mother. Come and look.

Stephen stood up and went over to the parapet. Leaning on it, he looked down on the water and on the mailboat clearing the harbour-mouth of Kingstown.

— Our mighty mother! Buck Mulligan said.

He turned abruptly his grey searching eyes from the sea to Stephen's face.

— The aunt thinks you killed your mother, he said. That's why she won't let me have anything to do with you.

— Someone killed her, Stephen said gloomily.

— You could have knelt down, damn it, Kinch, when your dying mother asked you, Buck Mulligan said. I'm hyperborean as much as you. But to think of your mother begging you with her last breath to kneel down and pray for her. And you refused. There is something sinister in you . . .

He broke off and lathered again lightly his farther cheek. A tolerant smile curled his lips.

— But a lovely mummer! he murmured to himself. Kinch, the loveliest mummer of them all!

He shaved evenly and with care, in silence, seriously.

Stephen, an elbow rested on the jagged granite, leaned his palm against his brow and gazed at the fraying edge of his shiny black coatsleeve. Pain, that was not yet the pain of love, fretted his heart. Silently, in a dream, she had come to him after her death, her wasted body within its loose brown graveclothes giving off an odour of wax and rosewood, her breath, that had bent upon him, mute, reproachful, a faint odour of wetted ashes. Across the threadbare cuff-edge he saw the sea hailed as a great sweet mother by the well-fed voice beside him. The ring of bay and skyline held a dull green mass of liquid. A bowl of white china had stood beside her deathbed holding the green sluggish bile which she had torn up from her rotting liver by fits of loud groaning vomiting.

Buck Mulligan wiped again his razor blade.

— Ah, poor dogsbody! he said in a kind voice. I must give you a shirt and a few noserags. How are the secondhand breeks?

— They fit well enough, Stephen answered.

Buck Mulligan attacked the hollow beneath his underlip.

— The mockery of it, he said contentedly. Secondleg they should be. God knows what poxy bowsy left them off. I have a lovely pair with a hair stripe, grey. You'll look spiffing in them. I'm not joking, Kinch. You look damn well when you're dressed.

— Thanks, Stephen said. I can't wear them if they are grey.

— He can't wear them, Buck Mulligan told his face in the mirror. Etiquette is etiquette. He kills his mother but he can't wear grey trousers.

He folded his razor neatly and with stroking palps of fingers felt the smooth skin.

Stephen turned his gaze from the sea and to the plump face with its smoke-blue mobile eyes.

— That fellow I was with in the Ship last night, said Buck Mulligan, says you have g.p.i. He's up in Dottyville with Conolly Norman. General paralysis of the insane!

He swept the mirror a half circle in the air to flash the tidings abroad in sunlight now radiant on the sea. His curling shaven lips laughed and the edges of his white glittering teeth. Laughter seized all his strong well-knit trunk.

— Look at yourself, he said, you dreadful bard!

Stephen bent forward and peered at the mirror held out to him, cleft by a crooked crack. Hair on end. As he and others see me. Who chose this face for me? This dogsbody to rid of vermin. It asks me too.

— I pinched it out of the skivvy's room, Buck Mulligan said. It does her all right. The aunt always keeps plain-looking servants for Malachi. Lead him not into temptation. And her name is Ursula.

Laughing again, he brought the mirror away from Stephen's peering eyes.

— The rage of Caliban at not seeing his face in a mirror, he said. If Wilde were only alive to see you!

Drawing back and pointing, Stephen said with bitterness:

— It is a symbol of Irish art. The cracked looking glass of a servant.

Buck Mulligan suddenly linked his arm in Stephen's and walked with him round the tower, his razor and mirror clacking in the pocket where he had thrust them.

—It's not fair to tease you like that, Kinch, is it? he said kindly. God knows you have more spirit than any of them.

Parried again. He fears the lancet of my art as I fear that of his. The cold steel pen.

—Cracked looking glass of a servant! Tell that to the oxy chap downstairs and touch him for a guinea. He's stinking with money and thinks you're not a gentleman. His old fellow made his tin by selling jalap to Zulus or some bloody swindle or other. God, Kinch, if you and I could only work together we might do something for the island. Hellenise it.

Cranly's arm. His arm.

—And to think of your having to beg from these swine. I'm the only one that knows what you are. Why don't you trust me more? What have you up your nose against me? Is it Haines? If he makes any noise here I'll bring down Seymour and we'll give him a ragging worse than they gave Clive Kempthorpe.

Young shouts of moneyed voices in Clive Kempthorpe's rooms. Pale-faces: they hold their ribs with laughter, one clasping another. O, I shall expire! Break the news to her gently, Aubrey! I shall die! With slit ribbons of his shirt whipping the air he hops and hobbles round the table, with trousers down at heels, chased by Ades of Magdalen with the tailor's shears. A scared calf's face gilded with marmalade. I don't want to be debagged! Don't you play the giddy ox with me!

Shouts from the open window startling evening in the quadrangle. A deaf gardener, aproned, masked with Matthew Arnold's face, pushes his mower on the sombre lawn, watching narrowly the dancing motes of grasshalms.

—To ourselves ... new paganism ... omphalos.

—Let him stay, Stephen said. There's nothing wrong with him except at night.

—Then what is it? Buck Mulligan asked impatiently. Cough it up. I'm quite frank with you. What have you against me now?

They halted, looking towards the blunt cape of Bray Head that lay on the water like the snout of a sleeping whale. Stephen freed his arm quietly.

—Do you wish me to tell you? he asked.

—Yes, what is it? Buck Mulligan answered. I don't remember anything.

He looked in Stephen's face as he spoke. A light wind passed his brow, fanning softly his fair uncombed hair and stirring silver points of anxiety in his eyes.

Stephen, depressed by his own voice, said:

— Do you remember the first day I went to your house after my mother's death?

Buck Mulligan frowned quickly and said:

— What? Where? I can't remember anything. I remember only ideas and sensations. Why? What happened in the name of God?

— You were making tea, Stephen said, and went across the landing to get more hot water. Your mother and some visitor came out of the drawing room. She asked you who was in your room.

— Yes? Buck Mulligan said. What did I say? I forget.

— You said, Stephen answered, *O, it's only Dedalus whose mother is beastly dead.*

A flush which made him seem younger and more engaging rose to Buck Mulligan's cheek.

— Did I say that? he asked. Well? What harm is that?

He shook his constraint from him nervously.

— And what is death, he asked, your mother's or yours or my own? You saw only your mother die. I see them pop off every day in the Mater and Richmond and cut up into tripes in the dissecting room. It is a beastly thing and nothing else. It simply doesn't matter. You wouldn't kneel down to pray for your mother on her deathbed when she asked you. Why? Because you have the cursed Jesuit strain in you, only it's injected the wrong way. To me it's all a mockery and beastly. Her cerebral lobes are not functioning. She calls the doctor Sir Peter Teazle and picks buttercups off the quilt. Humour her till it's over. You crossed her last wish in death and yet you sulk with me because I don't whinge like some hired mute from Lalouette's. Absurd! I suppose I did say it. I didn't mean to offend the memory of your mother.

He had spoken himself into boldness. Stephen, shielding the gaping wounds which the words had left in his heart, said very coldly:

— I am not thinking of the offence to my mother.

— Of what then? Buck Mulligan asked.

— Of the offence to me, Stephen answered.

Buck Mulligan swung round on his heel.

— O, an impossible person! he exclaimed.

He walked off quickly round the parapet. Stephen stood at his post, gazing over the calm sea towards the headland. Sea and headland now grew dim. Pulses were beating in his eyes, veiling their sight, and he felt the fever of his cheeks.

A voice within the tower called loudly:

— Are you up there, Mulligan?

— I'm coming, Buck Mulligan answered.

He turned towards Stephen and said:

— Look at the sea. What does it care about offences? Chuck Loyola, Kinch, and come on down. The Sassenach wants his morning rashers.

His head halted again for a moment at the top of the staircase, level with the roof:

— Don't mope over it all day, he said. I'm inconsequent. Give up the moody brooding.

His head vanished but the drone of his descending voice boomed out of the stairhead:

— *And no more turn aside and brood*
Upon love's bitter mystery
For Fergus rules the brazen cars.

Woodshadows floated silently by through the morning peace from the stairhead seaward where he gazed. Inshore and farther out the mirror of water whitened, spurned by light-shod hurrying feet. White breast of the dim sea. The twining stresses, two by two. A hand plucking the harpstrings, merging their twining chords. Wave-white wedded words shimmering on the dim tide.

A cloud began to cover the sun slowly, wholly, shadowing the bay in deeper green. It lay beneath him, a bowl of bitter waters. Fergus's song: I sang it alone in the house, holding down the long dark chords. Her door was open: she wanted to hear my music. Silent with awe and pity I went to her bedside. She was crying in her wretched bed. For those words, Stephen: love's bitter mystery.

Where now?

Her secrets: old feather fans, tasselled dancecards powdered with musk, a gaud of amber beads in her locked drawer. A birdcage hung in the sunny window of her house when she was a girl. She heard old Royce sing in the pantomime of *Turko the Terrible* and laughed with others when he sang:

— *I am the boy*
That can enjoy
Invisibility.

Phantasmal mirth, folded away: musk-perfumed.

And no more turn aside and brood.

Folded away in the memory of nature with her toys. Memories beset his brooding brain. Her glass of water from the kitchen tap when she had approached the sacrament. A cored apple, filled with brown sugar, roasting for her at the hob on a dark autumn evening. Her shapely fingernails reddened by the blood of squashed lice from the children's shirts.

In a dream, silently, she had come to him, her wasted body within its loose graveclothes giving off an odour of wax and rosewood, her breath, bent over him with mute secret words, a faint odour of wetted ashes.

Her glazing eyes, staring out of death to shake and bend my soul. On me alone. The ghostcandle to light her agony. Ghostly light on her tortured face. Her hoarse loud breath rattling in horror while all prayed on their knees. Her eyes on me to strike me down. *Liliata rutilantium te confessorum turma circumdet: jubilantium te virginum chorus excipiat.*

Ghoul! Chewer of corpses!

No, mother! Let me be and let me live.

— Kinch ahoy!

Buck Mulligan's voice sang from within the tower. It came nearer up the staircase, calling again. Stephen, still trembling at his soul's cry, heard warm running sunlight and in the air behind him friendly words.

— Dedalus, come down, like a good mosey. Breakfast is ready. Haines is apologising for waking us last night. It's all right.

— I'm coming, Stephen said, turning.

— Do, for Jesus' sake, Buck Mulligan said. For my sake and for all our sakes.

His head disappeared and reappeared.

— I told him your symbol of Irish art. He says it's very clever. Touch him for a quid, will you? A guinea, I mean.

— I get paid this morning, Stephen said.

— The school kip? Buck Mulligan said. How much? Four quid? Lend us one.

— If you want it, Stephen said.

— Four shining sovereigns, Buck Mulligan cried with delight. We'll have a glorious drunk to astonish the druidy druids. Four omnipotent sovereigns.

He flung up his hands and tramped down the stone stairs, singing out of tune with a Cockney accent:

— *O, won't we have a merry time,*

Drinking whisky, beer and wine!
On Coronation,
Coronation Day!
O, won't we have a merry time
On Coronation Day!

Warm sunshine merrying over the sea. The nickel shaving bowl shone, forgotten, on the parapet. Why should I bring it down? Or leave it there all day, forgotten friendship?

He went over to it, held it in his hands awhile, feeling its coolness, smelling the clammy slaver of the lather in which the brush was stuck. So I carried the boat of incense then at Clongowes. I am another now and yet the same. A servant too. A server of a servant.

In the gloomy domed living room of the tower Buck Mulligan's gowned form moved briskly to and fro about the hearth, hiding and revealing its yellow glow. Two shafts of soft daylight fell across the flagged floor from the high barbicans: and at the meeting of their rays a cloud of coalsmoke and fumes of fried grease floated, turning.

— We'll be choked, Buck Mulligan said. Haines, open that door, will you?

Stephen laid the shaving bowl on the locker. A tall figure rose from the hammock where it had been sitting, went to the doorway and pulled open the inner doors.

— Have you the key? a voice asked.

— Dedalus has it, Buck Mulligan said. Janey Mack, I'm choked!

He howled, without looking up from the fire:

— Kinch!

— It's in the lock, Stephen said, coming forward.

The key scraped round harshly twice and, when the heavy door had been set ajar, welcome light and bright air entered. Haines stood at the doorway, looking out. Stephen hauled his upended valise to the table and sat down to wait. Buck Mulligan tossed the fry on to the dish beside him. Then he carried the dish and a large teapot over to the table, set them down heavily and sighed with relief.

— I'm melting, he said, as the candle remarked when … But, hush! Not a word more on that subject! Kinch, wake up! Bread, butter, honey. Haines, come in. The grub is ready. Bless us, O Lord, and these Thy gifts. Where's the sugar? O jay, there's no milk.

Stephen fetched the loaf and the pot of honey and the buttercooler from the locker. Buck Mulligan sat down in a sudden pet.

— What sort of a kip is this? he said. I told her to come after eight.

— We can drink it black, Stephen said thirstily. There's a lemon in the locker.

— O, damn you and your Paris fads! Buck Mulligan said. I want Sandycove milk.

Haines came in from the doorway and said quietly:

— That woman is coming up with the milk.

— The blessings of God on you! Buck Mulligan cried, jumping up from his chair. Sit down. Pour out the tea there. The sugar is in the bag. Here, I can't go fumbling at the damned eggs.

He hacked through the fry on the dish and slapped it out on three plates, saying:

— *In nomine Patris et Filii et Spiritus Sancti.*

Haines sat down to pour out the tea.

— I'm giving you two lumps each, he said. But, I say, Mulligan, you do make strong tea, don't you?

Buck Mulligan, hewing thick slices from the loaf, said in an old woman's wheedling voice:

— *When I makes tea I makes tea,* as old Mother Grogan said. *And when I makes water I makes water.*

— By Jove, it is tea, Haines said.

Buck Mulligan went on hewing and wheedling:

— *So I do, Mrs Cahill,* says she. *Begob, ma'am,* says Mrs Cahill, *God send you don't make them in the one pot.*

He lunged towards his messmates in turn a thick slice of bread impaled on his knife.

— That's folk, he said very earnestly, for your book, Haines. Five lines of text and ten pages of notes about the folk and the fishgods of Dundrum. Printed by the weird sisters in the year of the big wind.

He turned to Stephen and asked in a fine puzzled voice, lifting his brows:

— Can you recall, brother, is Mother Grogan's tea-and-water pot spoken of in the *Mabinogion* or is it in the Upanishads?

— I doubt it, said Stephen gravely.

— Do you now? Buck Mulligan said in the same tone. Your reasons, pray?

— I fancy, Stephen said as he ate, it did not exist in or out of the *Mabinogion*. Mother Grogan was, one imagines, a kinswoman of Mary Anne.

Buck Mulligan's face smiled with delight.

— Charming! he said in a finical sweet voice, showing his white teeth and blinking his eyes pleasantly. Do you think she was? Quite charming!

Then, suddenly overclouding all his features, he growled in a hoarsened rasping voice as he hewed again vigorously at the loaf:

— *For old Mary Anne*
  She doesn't care a damn
  But, hising up her petticoats …

He crammed his mouth with fry and munched and droned.

The doorway was darkened by an entering form.

— The milk, sir.

— Come in, ma'am, Mulligan said. Kinch, get the jug.

An old woman came forward and stood by Stephen's elbow.

— That's a lovely morning, sir, she said. Glory be to God.

— To whom? Mulligan said, glancing at her. Ah, to be sure!

Stephen reached back and took the milkjug from the locker.

— The islanders, Mulligan said to Haines casually, speak frequently of the collector of prepuces.

— How much, sir? asked the old woman.

— A quart, Stephen said.

He watched her pour into the measure and thence into the jug rich white milk, not hers. Old shrunken paps. She poured again a measureful and a tilly. Old and secret she had entered from a morning world, maybe a messenger. She praised the goodness of the milk, pouring it out. Crouching by a patient cow at daybreak in the lush field, a witch on her toadstool, her wrinkled fingers quick at the squirting dugs. They lowed about her whom they knew, dewsilky cattle. Silk of the kine and poor old woman, names given her in old times. A wandering crone, lowly form of an immortal, serving her conqueror and her gay betrayer, their common cuckquean, a messenger from the secret morning. To serve or to upbraid, whether he could not tell: but scorned to beg her favour.

— It is indeed, ma'am, Buck Mulligan said, pouring milk into their cups.

— Taste it, sir, she said.

He drank at her bidding.

— If we could only live on good food like that, he said to her somewhat loudly, we wouldn't have the country full of rotten teeth and rotten guts. Living in a bogswamp, eating cheap food and the streets paved with dust, horsedung and consumptives' spits.

15

— Are you a medical student, sir? the old woman asked.

— I am, ma'am, Buck Mulligan answered.

— Look at that now, she said.

Stephen listened in scornful silence. She bows her old head to the voice that speaks to her loudly, her bonesetter, her medicine man: me she slights. To the voice that will shrive and oil for the grave all there is of her but her woman's unclean loins, of man's flesh made not in God's likeness, the serpent's prey. And to the loud voice that now bids her be silent with wondering unsteady eyes.

— Do you understand what he says? Stephen asked her.

— Is it French you are talking, sir? the old woman said to Haines.

Haines spoke to her again a longer speech, confidently.

— Irish, Buck Mulligan said. Is there Gaelic on you?

— I thought it was Irish, she said, by the sound of it. Are you from the west, sir?

— I am an Englishman, Haines answered.

— He's English, Buck Mulligan said, and he thinks we ought to speak Irish in Ireland.

— Sure we ought to, the old woman said, and I'm ashamed I don't speak the language myself. I'm told it's a grand language by them that knows.

— Grand is no name for it, said Buck Mulligan. Wonderful entirely. Fill us out some more tea, Kinch. Would you like a cup, ma'am?

— No, thank you, sir, the old woman said, slipping the ring of the milkcan on her forearm and about to go.

Haines said to her:

— Have you your bill? We had better pay her, Mulligan, hadn't we?

Stephen filled again the three cups.

— Bill, sir? she said, halting. Well, it's seven mornings a pint at twopence is seven twos is a shilling and twopence over and these three mornings a quart at fourpence is three quarts is a shilling. That's a shilling and one and two is two and two, sir.

Buck Mulligan sighed and, having filled his mouth with a crust thickly buttered on both sides, stretched forth his legs and began to search his trouser pockets.

— Pay up and look pleasant, Haines said to him, smiling.

Stephen filled a third cup, a spoonful of tea colouring faintly the thick rich milk. Buck Mulligan brought up a florin, twisted it round in his fingers and cried:

— A miracle!

He passed it along the table towards the old woman, saying:

— *Ask nothing more of me, sweet.*
All I can give you I give.

Stephen laid the coin in her uneager hand.

— We'll owe twopence, he said.

— Time enough, sir, she said, taking the coin. Time enough. Good morning, sir.

She curtseyed and went out, followed by Buck Mulligan's tender chant:

— *Heart of my heart, were it more,*
More would be laid at your feet.

He turned to Stephen and said:

— Seriously, Dedalus. I'm stony. Hurry out to your school kip and bring us back some money. Today the bards must drink and junket. Ireland expects that every man this day will do his duty.

— That reminds me, Haines said, rising, that I have to visit your national library today.

— Our swim first, Buck Mulligan said.

He turned to Stephen and asked blandly:

— Is this the day for your monthly wash, Kinch?

Then he said to Haines:

— The unclean bard makes a point of washing once a month.

— All Ireland is washed by the Gulf Stream, Stephen said as he let honey trickle over a slice of the loaf.

Haines from the corner where he was knotting easily a scarf about the loose collar of his tennis shirt spoke:

— I intend to make a collection of your sayings if you will let me.

Speaking to me. They wash and tub and scrub. Agenbite of inwit. Conscience. Yet here's a spot.

— That one about the cracked looking glass of a servant being the symbol of Irish art is deuced good.

Buck Mulligan kicked Stephen's foot under the table and said with warmth of tone:

— Wait till you hear him on *Hamlet*, Haines.

— Well, I mean it, Haines said, still speaking to Stephen. I was just thinking of it when that poor old creature came in.

— Would I make any money by it? Stephen asked.

Haines laughed and, as he took his soft grey hat from the holdfast of the hammock, said:

— I don't know, I'm sure.

He strolled out to the doorway. Buck Mulligan bent across to Stephen and said with coarse vigour:

— You put your hoof in it now. What did you say that for?

— Well? Stephen said. The problem is to get money. From whom? From the milkwoman or from him. It's a toss-up, I think.

— I blow him out about you, Buck Mulligan said, and then you come along with your lousy leer and your gloomy Jesuit jibes.

— I see little hope, Stephen said, from her or from him.

Buck Mulligan sighed tragically and laid his hand on Stephen's arm.

— From me, Kinch, he said.

In a suddenly changed tone he added:

— To tell you the God's truth I think you're right. Damn all else they are good for. Why don't you play them as I do? To hell with them all. Let us get out of the kip.

He stood up, gravely ungirdled and disrobed himself of his gown, saying resignedly:

— Mulligan is stripped of his garments.

He emptied his pockets on to the table.

— There's your snotrag, he said.

And putting on his stiff collar and rebellious tie he spoke to them, chiding them, and to his dangling watchchain. His hands plunged and rummaged in his trunk while he called for a clean handkerchief. God, we'll simply have to dress the character. I want puce gloves and green boots. Contradiction. Do I contradict myself? Very well then, I contradict myself. Mercurial Malachi. A limp black missile flew out of his talking hands.

— And there's your Latin Quarter hat, he said.

Stephen picked it up and put it on. Haines called to them from the doorway:

— Are you coming, you fellows?

— I'm ready, Buck Mulligan answered, going towards the door. Come out, Kinch. You have eaten all we left, I suppose.

Resigned, he passed out with grave words and gait, saying well-nigh with sorrow:

— And going forth he met Butterly.

Stephen, taking his ashplant from its leaning place, followed them out and, as they went down the ladder, pulled to the slow iron door and locked it. He put the huge key in his inner pocket.

At the foot of the ladder Buck Mulligan asked:

— Did you bring the key?

— I have it, Stephen said, preceding them.

He walked on. Behind him he heard Buck Mulligan club with his heavy bathtowel the leader shoots of ferns or grasses.

— Down, sir! How dare you, sir!

Haines asked:

— Do you pay rent for this tower?

— Twelve quid, Buck Mulligan said.

— To the secretary of state for war, Stephen added over his shoulder.

They halted while Haines surveyed the tower and said at last:

— Rather bleak in wintertime, I should say. Martello you call it?

— Billy Pitt had them built, Buck Mulligan said, when the French were on the sea. But ours is the omphalos.

— What is your idea of *Hamlet*? Haines asked Stephen.

— No, no, Buck Mulligan shouted in pain. I'm not equal to Thomas Aquinas and the fifty-five reasons he has made out to prop it up. Wait till I have a few pints in me first.

He turned to Stephen, saying, as he pulled down neatly the peaks of his primrose waistcoat:

— You couldn't manage it under three pints, Kinch, could you?

— It has waited so long, Stephen said listlessly, it can wait longer.

— You pique my curiosity, Haines said amiably. Is it some paradox?

— Pooh! Buck Mulligan said. We have grown out of Wilde and paradoxes. It's quite simple. He proves by algebra that Hamlet's grandson is Shakespeare's grandfather and that he himself is the ghost of his own father.

— What? Haines said, beginning to point at Stephen. He himself?

Buck Mulligan slung his towel stolewise round his neck and, bending in loose laughter, said to Stephen's ear:

— O shade of Kinch the elder! Japhet in search of a father!

— I'm always tired in the morning, Stephen said to Haines. And it is rather long to tell.

Buck Mulligan, walking forward again, raised his hands.

— The sacred pint alone can unbind the tongue of Dedalus, he said.

— I mean to say, Haines explained to Stephen as they followed, this tower and these cliffs here remind me somehow of Elsinore. *That beetles o'er his base into the sea*, isn't it?

Buck Mulligan turned suddenly for an instant towards Stephen but did not speak. In the bright silent instant Stephen saw his own image in cheap dusty mourning between their gay attires.

— It's a wonderful tale, Haines said, bringing them to halt again.

He gazed southward over the bay. Eyes pale as the sea the wind had freshened: paler, firm and prudent. The seas' ruler, he gazed over the bay, empty save for the smokeplume of the mailboat, vague on the bright skyline, and a sail tacking by the Muglins.

— I read a theological interpretation of it somewhere, he said bemused. The Father and the Son idea. The Son striving to be atoned with the Father.

Buck Mulligan at once put on a blithe, broadly smiling face. He looked at them, his well-shaped mouth open happily, his eyes, from which he had suddenly withdrawn all shrewd sense, blinking with mad gaiety. He moved a doll's head to and fro, the brims of his Panama hat quivering, and began to chant in a quiet happy foolish voice:

— *I'm the queerest young fellow that ever you heard.*
  My mother's a Jew, my father's a bird.
  With Joseph the Joiner I cannot agree,
  So here's to disciples and Calvary.

He held up a forefinger of warning.

— *If anyone thinks that I amn't divine*
  He'll get no free drinks when I'm making the wine
  But have to drink water and wish it were plain
  That I make when the wine becomes water again.

He tugged swiftly at Stephen's ashplant in farewell and, running forward to a brow of the cliff, fluttered his hands at his sides like fins or wings of one about to rise in the air and chanted:

— *Goodbye, now, goodbye! Write down all I said*
  And tell Tom, Dick and Harry I rose from the dead.
  What's bred in the bone cannot fail me to fly
  And Olivet's breezy – Goodbye, now, goodbye!

He capered before them down towards the Forty Foot hole, fluttering his winglike hands, leaping nimbly, Mercury's hat quivering in the fresh wind that bore back to them his brief birdlike cries.

Haines, who had been laughing guardedly, walked on beside Stephen and said:

— We oughtn't to laugh, I suppose. He is rather blasphemous. I'm not a believer myself, that is to say. Still, his gaiety takes the harm out of it somehow, doesn't it? What did he call it? *Joseph the Joiner*?

— *The Ballad of Joking Jesus*, Stephen answered.

— O, Haines said, you have heard it before?

— Three times a day, after meals, Stephen said drily.

— You're not a believer, are you? Haines asked. I mean, a believer in the narrow sense of the word. Creation from nothing and miracles and a personal God.

— There is only one sense of the word, it seems to me, Stephen said.

Haines stopped to take out a smooth silver case in which twinkled a green stone. He sprang it open with his thumb and offered it.

— Thank you, Stephen said, taking a cigarette.

Haines helped himself and snapped the case to. He put it back in his side pocket and took from his waistcoat pocket a nickel tinderbox, sprang it open too and, having lit his cigarette, held the flaming spunk towards Stephen in the shell of his hands.

— Yes, of course, he said, as they went on again. Either you believe or you don't, isn't it? Personally I couldn't stomach that idea of a personal God. You don't stand for that, I suppose?

— You behold in me, Stephen said with grim displeasure, a horrible example of free thought.

He walked on, waiting to be spoken to, trailing his ashplant by his side. Its ferrule followed lightly on the path, squealing at his heels. My familiar, after me, calling, Steeeeeeeeeeeephen! A wavering line along the path. They will walk on it tonight, coming here in the dark. He wants that key. It is mine. I paid the rent. Now I eat his salt bread. Give him the key too. All. He will ask for it. That was in his eyes.

— After all, Haines began . . .

Stephen turned and saw that the cold gaze which had measured him was not all unkind.

— After all, I should think you are able to free yourself. You are your own master, it seems to me.

— I am the servant of two masters, Stephen said, an English and an Italian.

— Italian? Haines said.

A crazy queen, old and jealous. Kneel down before me.

— And a third, Stephen said, there is who wants me for odd jobs.

— Italian? Haines said again. What do you mean?

– The Imperial British State, Stephen answered, his colour rising, and the Holy Roman Catholic and Apostolic Church.

Haines detached from his underlip some fibres of tobacco before he spoke.

– I can quite understand that, he said calmly. An Irishman must think like that, I daresay. We feel in England that we have treated you rather unfairly. It seems history is to blame.

The proud potent titles clanged over Stephen's memory the triumph of their brazen bells: *et in unam sanctam catholicam et apostolicam ecclesiam*: the slow growth and change of rite and dogma, like his own rare thoughts a chemistry of stars. Symbol of the apostles in the mass for Pope Marcellus, the voices blended, singing alone, loud in affirmation: and behind their chant the vigilant angel of the Church militant disarmed and menaced her heresiarchs. A horde of heresies fleeing with mitres awry: Photius and the brood of mockers, of whom Mulligan was one, and Arius, warring his life long upon the consubstantiality of the Son with the Father, and Valentine, spurning Christ's terrene body, and the subtle African here-siarch Sabellius who held that the Father was Himself His own Son. Words Mulligan had spoken a moment since in mockery to the stranger. Idle mockery. The void awaits surely all them that weave the wind: a menace, a disarming and a worsting from those embattled angels of the Church, Michael's host, who defend her ever in the hour of conflict with their lances and their shields.

Hear, hear! Prolonged applause. *Zut! Nom de Dieu!*

– Of course I'm a Britisher, Haines's voice said, and I feel as one. I don't want to see my country fall into the hands of German Jews either. That's our national problem, I'm afraid, just now.

Two men stood at the verge of the cliff, watching: businessman, boatman.

– She's making for Bullock Harbour.

The boatman nodded towards the north of the bay with some disdain.

– There's five fathoms out there, he said. It'll be swept up that way when the tide comes in about one. It's nine days today.

The man that was drowned. A sail veering about the blank bay waiting for a swollen bundle to bob up, roll over to the sun a puffy face, salt white. Here I am.

They followed the winding path down to the creek. Buck Mulligan stood on a stone, in shirtsleeves, his unclipped tie rippling over his shoulder. A young man clinging to a spur of rock near him moved slowly frogwise his green legs in the deep jelly of the water.

— Is the brother with you, Malachi?

— Down in Westmeath. With the Bannons.

— Still there? I got a card from Bannon. Says he found a sweet young thing down there. Photo girl he calls her.

— Snapshot, eh? Brief exposure.

Buck Mulligan sat down to unlace his boots. An elderly man shot up near the spur of rock a blowing red face. He scrambled up by the stones, water glistening on his pate and on its garland of grey hair, water rilling over his chest and paunch and spilling jets out of his black sagging loincloth.

Buck Mulligan made way for him to scramble past and, glancing at Haines and Stephen, crossed himself piously with his thumbnail at brow and lips and breastbone.

— Seymour's back in town, the young man said, grasping again his spur of rock. Chucked medicine and going in for the army.

— Ah, go to God! Buck Mulligan said.

— Going over next week to stew. You know that red Carlisle girl, Lily?

— Yes.

— Spooning with him last night on the pier. The father is rotto with money.

— Is she up the pole?

— Better ask Seymour that.

— Seymour a bleeding officer! Buck Mulligan said.

He nodded to himself as he drew off his trousers and stood up, saying tritely:

— *Redheaded women buck like goats* . . .

He broke off in alarm, feeling his side under his flapping shirt.

— My twelfth rib is gone, he cried. I'm the Übermensch. Toothless Kinch and I, the supermen.

He struggled out of his shirt and flung it behind him to where his clothes lay.

— Are you going in here, Malachi?

— Yes. Make room in the bed.

The young man shoved himself backward through the water and reached the middle of the creek in two long clean strokes. Haines sat down on a stone, smoking.

— Are you not coming in? Buck Mulligan asked.

— Later on, Haines said. Not on my breakfast.

Stephen turned away.

— I'm going, Mulligan, he said.

— Give us that key, Kinch, Buck Mulligan said, to keep my chemise flat.

Stephen handed him the key. Buck Mulligan laid it across his heaped clothes.

— And twopence, he said, for a pint. Throw it there.

Stephen threw two pennies on the soft heap. Dressing, undressing. Buck Mulligan erect, with joined hands before him, said solemnly:

— He who stealeth from the poor lendeth to the Lord. Thus spake Zarathustra.

His plump body plunged.

— We'll see you again, Haines said, turning as Stephen walked up the path and smiling at wild Irish.

Horn of a bull, hoof of a horse, smile of a Saxon.

— The Ship, Buck Mulligan cried. Half twelve.

— Good, Stephen said.

He walked along the upward-curving path.

> *Liliata rutilantium.*
> *Turma circumdet.*
> *Jubilantium te virginum.*

The priest's grey nimbus in a niche where he dressed discreetly. I will not sleep here tonight. Home also I cannot go.

A voice, sweet-toned and sustained, called to him from the sea. Turning the curve he waved his hand. It called again. A sleek brown head, a seal's, far out on the water, round.

Usurper.

— You, Cochrane, what city sent for him?

— Tarentum, sir.

— Very good. Well?

— There was a battle, sir.

— Very good. Where?

The boy's blank face asked the blank window.

Fabled by the daughters of memory. And yet it was in some way if not as memory fabled it. A phrase, then, of impatience, thud of Blake's wings of excess. I hear the ruin of all space, shattered glass and toppling masonry, and time one livid final flame. What's left us then?

— I forget the place, sir. 279 B.C.

— Asculum, Stephen said, glancing at the name and year in the gore-scarred book.

— Yes, sir. And he said: *Another victory like that and we are done for.*

That phrase the world had remembered. A dull ease of the mind. From a hill above a corpse-strewn plain a general speaking to his officers, leaning upon his spear. Any general to any officers. They lend ear.

— You, Armstrong, Stephen said. What was the end of Pyrrhus?

— End of Pyrrhus, sir?

— I know, sir. Ask me, sir, Comyn said.

— Wait. You, Armstrong. Do you know anything about Pyrrhus?

A bag of figrolls lay snugly in Armstrong's satchel. He curled them between his palms at whiles and swallowed them softly. Crumbs adhered to the tissue of his lips. A sweetened boy's breath. Well-off people, proud that their eldest son was in the navy. Vico Road, Dalkey.

— Pyrrhus, sir? Pyrrhus, a pier.

All laughed. Mirthless high malicious laughter. Armstrong looked round at his classmates, silly glee in profile. In a moment they will laugh more loudly, aware of my lack of rule and of the fees their papas pay.

— Tell me now, Stephen said, poking the boy's shoulder with the book, what is a pier.

— A pier, sir, Armstrong said. A thing out in the water. A kind of bridge. Kingstown Pier, sir.

Some laughed again: mirthless but with meaning. Two in the back bench whispered. Yes. They knew: had never learned nor ever been innocent. All. With envy he watched their faces. Edith, Ethel, Gerty, Lily. Their likes, their breaths too, sweetened with tea and jam, their bracelets tittering in the struggle.

— Kingstown Pier, Stephen said. Yes, a disappointed bridge.

The words troubled their gaze.

— How, sir? Comyn asked. A bridge is across a river.

For Haines's chapbook. No one here to hear. Tonight, deftly amid wild drink and talk, to pierce the polished mail of his mind. What then? A jester at the court of his master, indulged and disesteemed, winning a clement master's praise. Why had they chosen all that part? Not wholly for the smooth caress. For them too history was a tale like any other too often heard, their land a pawnshop.

Had Pyrrhus not fallen by a beldam's hand in Argos or Julius Caesar not been knifed to death. They are not to be thought away. Time has branded them and, fettered, they are lodged in the room of the infinite possibilities they have ousted. But can those have been possible seeing that they never were? Or was that only possible which came to pass? Weave, weaver of the wind.

— Tell us a story, sir.

— O, do, sir. A ghost story.

— Where do you begin in this? Stephen asked, opening another book.

— *Weep no more*, Comyn said.

— Go on then, Talbot.

— And the story, sir?

— After, Stephen said. Go on, Talbot.

A swarthy boy opened a book and propped it nimbly under the breastwork of his satchel. He recited jerks of verse with odd glances at the text:

— *Weep no more, woeful shepherds, weep no more,*
  For Lycidas, your sorrow, is not dead,
  Sunk though he be beneath the watery floor . . .

It must be a movement then, an actuality of the possible as possible. Aristotle's phrase formed itself within the gabbled verses and floated out into the studious silence of the library of Sainte Geneviève where he had read, sheltered from the sin of Paris, night by night. By his elbow a delicate Siamese conned a handbook of strategy. Fed and feeding brains

26

about me: under glowlamps, impaled, with faintly beating feelers: and in my mind's darkness a sloth of the underworld, reluctant, shy of brightness, shifting her dragon-scaly folds. Thought is the thought of thought. Tranquil brightness. The soul is in a manner all that is: the soul is the form of forms. Tranquillity sudden, vast, candescent: form of forms.

Talbot repeated:

— *Through the dear might of Him that walked the waves,*
   Through the dear might…

— Turn over, Stephen said quietly. I don't see anything.

— What, sir? Talbot asked simply, bending forward.

His hand turned the page over. He leaned back and went on again, having just remembered.

Of Him that walked the waves. Here also over these craven hearts His shadow lies and on the scoffer's heart and lips and on mine. It lies upon their eager faces who offered Him a coin of the tribute. To Caesar what is Caesar's, to God what is God's. A long look from dark eyes, a riddling sentence to be woven and woven on the church's looms. Ay.

> *Riddle me, riddle me, randy ro.*
> *My father gave me seeds to sow.*

Talbot slid his closed book into his satchel.

— Have I heard all? Stephen asked.

— Yes, sir. Hockey at ten, sir.

— Half-day, sir. Thursday.

— Who can answer a riddle? Stephen asked.

They bundled their books away, pencils clacking, pages rustling. Crowding together they strapped and buckled their satchels, all gabbling gaily:

— A riddle, sir? Ask me, sir.

— O, ask me, sir.

— A hard one, sir.

— This is the riddle, Stephen said:

> *The cock crew,*
> *The sky was blue,*
> *The bells in heaven*
> *Were striking eleven.*
> *'Tis time for this poor soul*
> *To go to heaven.*

— What is that?

— What, sir?

— Again, sir. We didn't hear.

Their eyes grew bigger as the lines were repeated. After a silence Cochrane said:

— What is it, sir? We give it up.

Stephen, his throat itching, answered:

— The fox burying his grandmother under a holly bush.

He stood up and gave a shout of nervous laughter to which their cries echoed dismay.

A stick struck the door and a voice in the corridor called:

— Hockey!

They broke asunder, sidling out of their benches, leaping them. Quickly they were gone, and from the lumber room came the rattle of sticks and clamour of their boots and tongues.

Sargent, who alone had lingered, came forward slowly, showing an open copybook. His tangled hair and scraggy neck gave witness of unreadiness and through his misty glasses weak eyes looked up pleading. On his cheek, dull and bloodless, a soft stain of ink lay, date-shaped, recent and damp as a snail's bed.

He held out his copybook. The word *Sums* was written on the headline. Beneath were sloping figures and at the foot a crooked signature with blind loops and a blot. Cyril Sargent: his name and seal.

— Mr Deasy told me to write them out all again, he said, and show them to you, sir.

Stephen touched the edges of the book. Futility.

— Do you understand how to do them now? he asked.

— Numbers eleven to fifteen, Sargent answered. Mr Deasy said I was to copy them off the board, sir.

— Can you do them now yourself? Stephen asked.

— No, sir.

Ugly and futile: lean neck and thick hair and a stain of ink, a snail's bed. Yet someone had loved him, borne him in her arms and in her heart. But for her the race of the world would have trampled him underfoot, a squashed boneless snail. She had loved his weak watery blood drained from her own. Was that then real? The only true thing in life? His mother's prostrate body the fiery Columbanus in holy zeal bestrode. She was no more: the trembling skeleton of a twig burned in the fire, an odour of rosewood and wetted ashes. She had saved him from being trampled underfoot and had gone, scarcely having been. A poor soul gone to heaven: and on a heath beneath winking stars a fox, red reek of rapine in his fur, with merciless bright eyes scraped in the earth, listened, scraped up the earth, listened, scraped and scraped.

Sitting at his side Stephen solved out the problem. He proves by algebra that Shakespeare's ghost is Hamlet's grandfather. Sargent peered askance through his slanted glasses. Hockeysticks rattled in the lumber room: the hollow knock of a ball and calls from the hockey field.

Across the page the symbols moved in grave morrice, in the mummery of their letters, wearing quaint caps of squares and cubes. Give hands, traverse, bow to partner, so: imps of fancy of the Moors. Gone too from the world, Averroës and Moses Maimonides, dark men in mien and movement, flashing in their mocking mirrors the obscure soul of the world, a darkness shining in brightness which brightness could not comprehend.

— Do you understand now? Can you work the second for yourself?

— Yes, sir.

In long shaky strokes Sargent copied the data. Waiting always for a word of help, his hand moved faithfully the unsteady symbols, a faint hue of shame flickering behind his dull skin. *Amor matris*: subjective and objective genitive. With her weak blood and whey-sour milk she had fed him and hid from sight of others his swaddling bands.

Like him was I, these sloping shoulders, this gracelessness. My childhood bends beside me. Too far for me to lay a hand of comfort there, once or lightly. Mine is far, and his secret as our eyes. Secrets, silent, stony, sit in the dark palaces of both our hearts: secrets weary of their tyranny: tyrants willing to be dethroned.

The sum was done.

— It is very simple, Stephen said as he stood up.

— Yes, sir. Thanks, Sargent answered.

He dried the page with a sheet of thin blotting paper and carried his copybook back to his desk.

— You had better get your stick and go out to the others, Stephen said as he followed towards the door the boy's graceless form.

— Yes, sir.

In the corridor his name was heard, called from the playfield.

— Sargent!

— Run on, Stephen said. Mr Deasy is calling you.

He stood in the porch and watched the laggard hurry towards the scrappy field where sharp voices were in strife. They were sorted in teams and Mr Deasy came away, stepping over wisps of grass with gaitered feet. When he had reached the schoolhouse voices again contending called to him. He turned his angry white moustache.

— What is it now? he cried continually without listening.

— Cochrane and Halliday are on the same side, sir, Stephen said.

— Will you wait in my study for a moment, Mr Deasy said, till I restore order here.

And as he stepped fussily back across the field his old man's voice cried sternly:

— What is the matter? What is it now?

Their sharp voices cried about him on all sides: their many forms closed round him, garish sunshine bleaching the honey of his illdyed head.

Stale smoky air hung in the study with the smell of drab abraded leather of its chairs. As on the first day he bargained with me here. As it was in the beginning, is now. On the sideboard the tray of Stuart coins, base treasure of a bog: and ever shall be. And snug in their spooncase of purple plush, faded, the twelve apostles, having preached to all the gentiles: world without end.

A hasty step over the stone porch and in the corridor. Blowing out his rare moustache Mr Deasy halted at the table.

— First, our little financial settlement, he said.

He brought out of his coat a pocketbook bound by a leather thong. It slapped open and he took from it two notes, one of joined halves, and laid them carefully on the table.

— Two, he said, strapping and stowing his pocketbook away.

And now his strongroom for the gold. Stephen's embarrassed hand moved over the shells heaped in the cold stone mortar: whelks and money cowries and leopard shells: and this, whorled as an emir's turban, and this, the scallop of Saint James. An old pilgrim's hoard, dead treasure, hollow shells.

A sovereign fell, bright and new, on the soft pile of the tablecloth.

— Three, Mr Deasy said, turning his little savings box about in his hand. These are handy things to have. See. This is for sovereigns. This is for shillings. Sixpences, half crowns. And here crowns. See.

He shot from it two crowns and two shillings.

— Three twelve, he said. I think you'll find that's right.

— Thank you, sir, Stephen said, gathering the money together with shy haste and putting it all in a pocket of his trousers.

— No thanks at all, Mr Deasy said. You have earned it.

Stephen's hand, free again, went back to the hollow shells. Symbols too of beauty and of power. A lump in my pocket. Symbols soiled by greed and misery.

— Don't carry it like that, Mr Deasy said. You'll pull it out somewhere and lose it. You just buy one of these machines. You'll find them very handy.

Answer something.

— Mine would be often empty, Stephen said.

The same room and hour, the same wisdom: and I the same. Three times now. Three nooses round me here. Well? I can break them in this instant if I will.

— Because you don't save, Mr Deasy said, pointing his finger. You don't know yet what money is. Money is power. When you have lived as long as I have. I know, I know. *If youth but knew.* But what does Shakespeare say? *Put but money in thy purse.*

— Iago, Stephen murmured.

He lifted his gaze from the idle shells to the old man's stare.

— He knew what money was, Mr Deasy said. He made money. A poet, yes, but an Englishman too. Do you know what is the pride of the English? Do you know what is the proudest word you will ever hear from an Englishman's mouth?

The seas' ruler. His sea-cold eyes looked over the empty bay: it seems history is to blame: on me and on my words, unhating.

— That on his empire, Stephen said, the sun never sets.

— Ba! Mr Deasy cried. That's not English. A French Celt said that.

He tapped his savings box against his thumbnail.

— I will tell you, he said solemnly, what is his proudest boast. *I paid my way.*

Good man, good man.

— *I paid my way. I never borrowed a shilling in my life.* Can you feel that? *I owe nothing.* Can you?

Mulligan, nine pounds, three pairs of socks, one pair brogues, ties. Curran, ten guineas. McCann, one guinea. Fred Ryan, two shillings. Temple, two lunches. Russell, one guinea. Cousins, ten shillings. Bob Reynolds, half a guinea. Keohler, three guineas. Mrs McKernan, five weeks' board. The lump I have is useless.

— For the moment, no, Stephen answered.

Mr Deasy laughed with rich delight, putting back his savings box.

—I knew you couldn't, he said joyously. But one day you must feel it. We are a generous people but we must also be just.

—I fear those big words, Stephen said, which make us so unhappy.

Mr Deasy stared sternly for some moments over the mantelpiece at the shapely bulk of a man in tartan filibegs: Albert Edward, Prince of Wales.

—You think me an old fogey and an old Tory, his thoughtful voice said. I saw three generations since O'Connell's time. I remember the famine in '46. Do you know that the Orange lodges agitated for repeal of the Union twenty years before O'Connell did or before the prelates of your communion denounced him as a demagogue? You Fenians forget some things.

Glorious, pious and immortal memory. The lodge of Diamond in Armagh the Splendid behung with corpses of papishes. Hoarse, masked and armed, the planters' covenant. The black north and true blue bible. Croppies, lie down.

Stephen sketched a brief gesture.

—I have rebel blood in me too, Mr Deasy said. On the spindle side. But I am descended from Sir John Blackwood who voted for the Union. We are all Irish, all kings' sons.

—Alas, Stephen said.

—*Per vias rectas*, Mr Deasy said firmly, was his motto. He voted for it and put on his topboots to ride to Dublin from the Ards of Down to do so.

> Lal the ral the ra
> The rocky road to Dublin.

A gruff squire on horseback with shiny topboots. Soft day, Sir John! Soft day, your honour! ... Day! ... Day! ... Two topboots jog dangling on to Dublin. Lal the ral the ra. Lal the ral the raddy.

—That reminds me, Mr Deasy said. You can do me a favour, Mr Dedalus, with some of your literary friends. I have a letter here for the press. Sit down a moment. I have just to copy the end.

He went to the desk near the window, pulled in his chair twice and read off some words from the sheet on the drum of his typewriter.

—Sit down. Excuse me, he said over his shoulder, *the dictates of common sense.* Just a moment.

He peered from under his shaggy brows at the manuscript by his elbow and, muttering, began to prod the stiff buttons of the keyboard slowly, sometimes blowing as he screwed up the drum to erase an error.

Stephen seated himself noiselessly before the princely presence. Framed around the walls images of vanished horses stood in homage, their meek heads poised in air: Lord Hastings' *Repulse*, the duke of Westminster's *Shotover*, the duke of Beaufort's *Ceylon*, Prix de Paris, 1866. Elfin riders sat them, watchful of a sign. He saw their speeds, backing king's colours, and shouted with the shouts of vanished crowds.

— Full stop, Mr Deasy bade his keys. *But prompt ventilation of this all-important question...*

Where Cranly led me to get rich quick, hunting his winners among the mud-splashed brakes, amid the bawls of bookies on their pitches and reek of the canteen, over the motley slush. *Fair Rebel! Fair Rebel!* Even money the favourite. Ten to one the field. Dicers and thimbleriggers we hurried by after the hoofs, the vying caps and jackets, and past the meat-faced woman, a butcher's dame, nuzzling thirstily her clove of orange.

Shouts rang shrill from the boys' playfield and a whirring whistle. Again: a goal. I am among them, among their battling bodies in a medley, the joust of life. You mean that knock-kneed mother's darling who seems to be slightly crawsick? Jousts. Time shocked rebounds, shock by shock. Jousts, slush and uproar of battles, the frozen deathspew of the slain, a shout of spearspikes baited with men's bloodied guts.

— Now then, Mr Deasy said, rising.

He came to the table, pinning together his sheets. Stephen stood up.

— I have put the matter into a nutshell, Mr Deasy said. It's about the foot-and-mouth disease. Just look through it. There can be no two opinions on the matter.

May I trespass on your valuable space. That doctrine of laissez faire which so often in our history. Our cattle trade. The way of all our old industries. Liverpool ring which jockeyed the Galway Harbour scheme. European conflagration. Grain supplies through the narrow waters of the Channel. The pluterperfect imperturbability of the Department of Agriculture. Pardoned a classical allusion. Cassandra. By a woman who was no better than she should be. To come to the point at issue.

— I don't mince words, do I? Mr Deasy asked as Stephen read on.

Foot-and-mouth disease. Known as Koch's preparation. Serum and virus. Percentage of salted horses. Rinderpest. Emperor's horses at Mürzsteg, lower Austria. Veterinary surgeons. Mr Henry Blackwood Price. Courteous offer a fair trial. Dictates of common sense. All-important question. In every sense of the word take the bull by the horns. Thanking you for the hospitality of your columns.

—I want that to be printed and read, Mr Deasy said. You will see at the next outbreak they will put an embargo on Irish cattle. And it can be cured. It is cured. My cousin, Blackwood Price, writes to me it is regularly treated and cured in Austria by cattle doctors there. They offer to come over here. I am trying to work up influence with the Department. Now I'm going to try publicity. I am surrounded by difficulties, by ... intrigues, by ... backstairs influence, by ...

He raised his forefinger and beat the air oldly before his voice spoke.

—Mark my words, Mr Dedalus, he said. England is in the hands of the Jews. In all the highest places: her finance, her press. And they are the signs of a nation's decay. Wherever they gather they eat up the nation's vital strength. I have seen it coming these years. As sure as we are standing here the Jew merchants are already at their work of destruction. Old England is dying.

He stepped swiftly off, his eyes coming to blue life as they passed a broad sunbeam. He faced about and back again.

—Dying, he said, if not dead by now.

> *The harlot's cry from street to street*
> *Shall weave old England's winding sheet.*

His eyes open wide in vision stared sternly across the sunbeam in which he halted.

—A merchant, Stephen said, is one who buys cheap and sells dear, Jew or gentile, is he not?

—They sinned against the Light, Mr Deasy said gravely. And you can see the darkness in their eyes. And that is why they are wanderers on the earth to this day.

On the steps of the Paris Stock Exchange the gold-skinned men quoting prices on their gemmed fingers. Gabble of geese. They swarmed loud, uncouth, about the temple, their heads thickplotting under maladroit silk hats. Not theirs: these clothes, this speech, these gestures. Their full slow eyes belied the words, the gestures eager and unoffending, but knew the rancours massed about them and knew their zeal was vain. Vain patience to heap and hoard. Time surely would scatter all. A hoard heaped by the roadside: plundered and passing on. Their eyes knew their years of wandering and, patient, knew the dishonours of their flesh.

—Who has not? Stephen said.

—What do you mean? Mr Deasy asked.

He came forward a pace and stood by the table. His underjaw fell sideways open uncertainly. Is this old wisdom? He waits to hear from me.

— History, Stephen said, is a nightmare from which I am trying to awake.

From the playfield the boys raised a shout. A whirring whistle: goal. What if that nightmare gave you a back kick?

— The ways of the Creator are not our ways, Mr Deasy said. All human history moves towards one great goal, the manifestation of God.

Stephen jerked his thumb towards the window, saying:

— That is God.

Hooray! Ay! Whrrwhee!

— What? Mr Deasy asked.

— A shout in the street, Stephen answered, shrugging his shoulders.

Mr Deasy looked down and held for awhile the wings of his nose tweaked between his fingers. Looking up again he set them free.

— I am happier than you are, he said. We have committed many errors and many sins. A woman brought sin into the world. For a woman who was no better than she should be, Helen, the runaway wife of Menelaus, ten years the Greeks made war on Troy. A faithless wife first brought the strangers to our shore here, MacMurrough's wife and her leman, O'Rourke, prince of Breffni. A woman too brought Parnell low. Many errors, many failures, but not the one sin. I am a struggler now at the end of my days. But I will fight for the right till the end.

> *For Ulster will fight*
> *And Ulster will be right.*

Stephen raised the sheets in his hand.

— Well, sir, he began . . .

— I foresee, Mr Deasy said, that you will not remain here very long at this work. You were not born to be a teacher, I think. Perhaps I am wrong.

— A learner rather, Stephen said.

And here what will you learn more?

Mr Deasy shook his head.

— Who knows? he said. To learn one must be humble. But life is the great teacher.

Stephen rustled the sheets again.

— As regards these, he began . . .

— Yes, Mr Deasy said. You have two copies there. If you can have them published at once.

Telegraph. Irish Homestead.

— I will try, Stephen said, and let you know tomorrow. I know two editors slightly.

— That will do, Mr Deasy said briskly. I wrote last night to Mr Field M.P. There is a meeting of the Cattle Traders Association today at the City Arms Hotel. I asked him to lay my letter before the meeting. You see if you can get it into your two papers. What are they?

— The *Evening Telegraph* ...

— That will do, Mr Deasy said. There is no time to lose. Now I have to answer that letter from my cousin.

— Good morning, sir, Stephen said, putting the sheets in his pocket. Thank you.

— Not at all, Mr Deasy said as he searched the papers on his desk. I like to break a lance with you, old as I am.

— Good morning, sir, Stephen said again, bowing to his bent back.

He went out by the open porch and down the gravel path under the trees, hearing the cries of voices and crack of sticks from the playfield. The lions couchant on the pillars as he passed out through the gate: toothless terrors. Still, I will help him in his fight. Mulligan will dub me a new name: the bullock-befriending bard.

— Mr Dedalus!

Running after me. No more letters, I hope.

— Just one moment.

— Yes, sir, Stephen said, turning back at the gate.

Mr Deasy halted, breathing hard and swallowing his breath.

— I just wanted to say, he said. Ireland, they say, has the honour of being the only country which never persecuted the Jews. Do you know that? No. And do you know why?

He frowned sternly on the bright air.

— Why, sir? Stephen asked, beginning to smile.

— Because she never let them in, Mr Deasy said solemnly.

A coughball of laughter leaped from his throat dragging after it a rattling chain of phlegm. He turned back quickly, coughing, laughing, his lifted arms waving to the air.

— She never let them in, he cried again through his laughter as he stamped on gaitered feet over the gravel of the path. That's why.

On his wise shoulders through the checkerwork of leaves the sun flung spangles, dancing coins.

Ineluctable modality of the visible: at least that if no more, thought through my eyes. Signatures of all things I am here to read: seaspawn and seawrack, the nearing tide, that rusty boot. Snot green, blue silver, rust: coloured signs. Limits of the diaphane. But he adds: in bodies. Then he was aware of them bodies before of them coloured. How? By knocking his sconce against them, sure. Go easy. Bald he was and a millionaire, *maestro di color che sanno*. Limit of the diaphane in. Why in? Diaphane, adiaphane. If you can put your five fingers through it, it is a gate; if not, a door. Shut your eyes and see.

Stephen closed his eyes to hear his boots crush crackling wrack and shells. You are walking through it howsomever. I am, a stride at a time. A very short space of time through very short times of space. Five, six: the *nacheinander*. Exactly: and that is the ineluctable modality of the audible. Open your eyes. No. Jesus! If I fell over a cliff that beetles o'er his base, fell through the *nebeneinander* ineluctably. I am getting on nicely in the dark. My ash sword hangs at my side. Tap with it: they do. My two feet in his boots are at the ends of his legs, *nebeneinander*. Sounds solid: made by the mallet of Los. *Demiourgos*. Am I walking into eternity along Sandymount Strand? Crush, crack, crick, crick. Wild sea money. Dominie Deasy kens them a'.

> *Won't you come to Sandymount,*
> *Madeleine the mare?*

Rhythm begins, you see. I hear. A catalectic tetrameter of iambs marching. No, agallop: *deleine the mare*.

Open your eyes now. I will. One moment. Has all vanished since? If I open and am for ever in the black adiaphane? *Basta!* I will see if I can see.

See now. There all the time without you: and ever shall be, world without end.

They came down the steps from Leahy's Terrace prudently, *Frauenzimmer*, and down the shelving shore flabbily, their splayed feet sinking in the silted sand. Like me, like Algy, coming down to our mighty mother. Number one swung lourdily her midwife's bag, the other's gamp poked in the beach. From the Liberties, out for the day. Mrs Florence MacCabe, relict of the late Patk MacCabe, deeply lamented, of Bride Street. One of her sisterhood lugged me squealing into life. Creation from nothing. What has she in the bag? A misbirth with a trailing navelcord, hushed in ruddy wool. The cords of all link back, strand-entwining cable of all flesh. That is why mystic monks. Will you be wise as gods? Gaze in your omphalos. Hello! Kinch here. Put me on to Edenville. Aleph, alpha; nought, nought, one.

Spouse and helpmate of Adam Kadmon: Heva, naked Eve. She had no navel. Gaze. Belly without blemish, bulging big, a buckler of taut vellum, no, white-heaped corn, orient and immortal, standing from everlasting to everlasting. Womb of sin.

Wombed in sin darkness I was too, made not begotten. By them, the man with my voice and my eyes and a ghostwoman with ashes on her breath. They clasped and sundered, did the coupler's will. From before the ages He willed me and now may not will me away or ever. A *lex aeterna* stays about Him. Is that then the divine substance wherein Father and Son are consubstantial? Where is poor dear Arius to try conclusions? Warring his life long on the contransmagnificandjewbangtantiality. Ill-starred heresiarch! In a Greek watercloset he breathed his last: euthanasia. With beaded mitre and with crozier, stalled upon his throne, widower of a widowed see, with upstiffed omophorion, with clotted hinder parts.

Airs romped round him, nipping and eager airs. They are coming: waves. The white-maned seahorses, champing, brightwindbridled, the steeds of Mananaan.

I mustn't forget his letter for the press. And after? The Ship, half twelve. By the way, go easy with that money like a good young imbecile. Yes, I must.

His pace slackened. Here. Am I going to aunt Sara's or not? My consubstantial father's voice. Did you see anything of your artist brother Stephen lately? No? Sure he's not down in Strasburg Terrace with his aunt Sally? Couldn't he fly a bit higher than that, eh? And and and and tell us, Stephen, and how is uncle Si? O weeping God, the things I married into! De boys up in de hayloft. The drunken little costdrawer and his brother the cornet player. Highly respectable gondoliers! And skew-eyed Walter sirring his father, no less! Sir. Yes, sir. No, sir. Jesus wept: and no wonder, by Christ!

I pull the wheezy bell of their shuttered cottage: and wait. Twice. They take me for a dun, peer out from a coign of vantage.

— It's Stephen, sir.

— Let him in. Let Stephen in.

A bolt drawn back and Walter welcomes me.

— We thought you were someone else.

In his broad bed nuncle Richie, pillowed and blanketed, extends over the hillock of his knees a sturdy forearm. Clean-chested. He has washed the upper moiety.

— Morrow, nephew. Sit down and take a walk.

He lays aside the lapboard whereon he drafts his bills of costs for the eyes of Master Goff and Master Shapland Tandy, filing consents and common searches and a writ of *duces tecum*. A bogoak frame over his bald head: Wilde's *Requiescat*. The drone of his misleading whistle brings Walter back.

— Yes, sir?

— Malt for Richie and Stephen, tell mother. Where is she?

— Bathing Crissie, sir.

Papa's little bedpal. Lump of love.

— No, uncle Richie...

— Call me Richie. Damn your lithia water. It lowers. Whusky!

— Uncle Richie, really...

— Sit down or by the law Harry I'll knock you down.

Walter squints vainly for a chair.

— He has nothing to sit down on, sir.

— He has nowhere to put it, you mug. Bring in our Chippendale chair. Would you like a bite of something? None of your damned lawdeedaw airs here. The rich of a rasher fried with a herring? Sure? So much the better. We have nothing in the house but backache pills.

All'erta!

He drones bars of Ferrando's *aria di sortita*. The grandest number, Stephen, in the whole opera. Listen.

His tuneful whistle sounds again, finely shaded, with rushes of the air, his fists bigdrumming on his padded knees.

This wind is sweeter.

Houses of decay, mine, his and all. You told the Clongowes gentry you had an uncle a judge and an uncle a general in the army. Come out of them, Stephen. Beauty is not there. Nor in the stagnant bay of Marsh's Library where you read the fading prophecies of Joachim Abbas. For whom? The hundred-headed rabble of the cathedral close. A hater of his kind, he ran from them to the wood of madness, his mane foaming in the moon, his eyeballs stars. Houyhnhnm: horse-nostrilled. The oval equine faces: Temple, Buck Mulligan, Foxy Campbell. Lanternjaws. Abbas father, furious dean, what offence laid fire to their brains? Paff! *Descende, calve, ut ne amplius decalveris.* A garland of grey hair on his comminated head: see him me clambering down to the footpace (*descende!*) clutching a monstrance, basilisk-eyed. Get down, baldpoll! A choir gives back menace and echo, assisting about the altar's horns, the snorted Latin of jackpriests moving burly in their albs, tonsured and oiled and gelded, fat with the fat of kidneys of wheat.

And at the same instant perhaps a priest round the corner is elevating it. Dringdring! And two streets off another locking it into a pyx. Dringadring! And in a Lady chapel another taking housel all to his own cheek. Dringdring! Down, up, forward, back. Dan Occam thought of that, invincible doctor. A misty English morning the imp hypostasis tickled his brain. Bringing his host down and kneeling he heard twine with his second bell the first bell in the transept (he is lifting his) and, rising, heard (now I am lifting) their two bells (he is kneeling) twang in diphthong.

Cousin Stephen, you will never be a saint. Isle of saints. You were awfully holy, weren't you? You prayed to the Blessed Virgin that you might not have a red nose. You prayed to the devil in Serpentine Avenue that the fubsy widow in front might lift her clothes still more from the wet street. *O si, certo!* Sell your soul for that, do, dyed rags pinned round a squaw. More tell me, more still! On the top of the Howth tram alone, crying to the rain: *Naked women! Naked women!* What about that, eh?

What about what? What else were they invented for?

You are a highly intellectual fellow, with your Oxford manner. Reading two pages apiece of seven books every night, eh? I was young. You bowed to yourself in the mirror, stepping forward to applause earnestly, striking face. Hurray for the goddamned idiot! Hray! No one saw: tell no one. Books you were going to write with letters for titles. Have you read his F? O yes, but I prefer Q. Yes, but W is wonderful. O yes, W. Remember your epiphanies, written on green oval leaves, so deeply deep, copies to be sent if you died to all the great libraries of the world, including Alexandria? Someone was to read them there after a few thousand years, a *mahamanvantara*. Pico della Mirandola like. Ay, very like a whale. When one reads these strange pages of one long gone one feels that one is at one with one who once . . .

The grainy sand had gone from under his feet. His boots trod again a damp crackling mast, razorshells, squeaking pebbles, that on the unnumbered pebbles beats, wood sieved by the shipworm, lost Armada. Unwholesome sandflats waited to suck his treading soles, breathing upward sewage breath. A pocket of seaweed smouldered in sea fire under a midden of man's ashes. He coasted them, walking warily. A porter bottle stood up, stogged to its waist, in the cakey sand dough. A sentinel: isle of dreadful thirst. Broken hoops on the shore; at the land's end a maze of dark cunning nets; farther away chalk-scrawled back doors; and on the higher beach a drying line with two crucified shirts. Ringsend: wigwams of brown steersmen and master mariners. Human shells.

He halted. I have passed the way to aunt Sara's. Am I not going there? Seems not. No one about. He turned northeast and crossed the firmer sand towards the Pigeon House.

— *Qui vous a mise dans cette fichue position?*
— *C'est le pigeon, Joseph!*

Patrice, home on furlough, lapped warm milk with me in the bar MacMahon. Son of the wild goose, Kevin Egan of Paris. My father's a bird. He lapped the sweet *lait chaud* with pink young tongue, a plump bunny's face. Lap, *lapin*. He hopes to win in the *gros lots*. About the nature of women he read in Michelet. But he must send me *La vie de Jésus* by M. Léo Taxil. Lent it to his friend.

— *C'est tordant, vous savez. Moi, je suis socialiste. Je ne crois pas en l'existence de Dieu. Faut pas le dire à mon père.*
— *Il croit?*
— *Mon père, oui.*
Schluss. He laps.

My Latin Quarter hat. God, we simply must dress the character. I want puce gloves. You were a student, weren't you? Of what, in the other devil's name? Paysayenn. P.C.N., you know: *physiques, chimiques et naturelles.* Aha! Eating your groatsworth of *mou en civet*, fleshpots of Egypt, elbowed by belching cabmen. Just say in the most natural tone: when I was in Paris, boul'Mich', I used to. Yes, you used to carry punched tramtickets for weeks in your pocket to prove an alibi if they arrested you for murder somewhere. Justice. On the night of the seventeenth of February 1904 the prisoner was seen by two witnesses. Other fellow did it: other me. Hat, tie, overcoat, nose. *Lui, c'est moi.* Allee samee. You seem to have enjoyed yourself.

Proudly walking. Whom were you trying to walk like? Forget: a dispossessed. With mother's money order, eight shillings, the banging door of the post office slammed in your face by the usher. Hunger

41

toothache. *Encore deux minutes*. Look clock. Must get. *Fermé*. Hired dog! Shoot him to bloody bits with a bang shotgun, bits man spattered walls all brass buttons. Bits all khrrrrklak in place clack back. Not hurt? O, that's all right. Shake hands. See what I meant, see? O, that's all right. Shake a shake. O, that's all only all right.

You were going to do wonders, what? Missionary to Europe after fiery Columbanus. Fiacre and Scotus on their creepystools in heaven spilt from their pintpots, loudlatinlaughing: *Euge! Euge!* Pretending to speak broken English as you dragged your valise, porter threepence, across the slimy pier at Newhaven. *Comment?* Rich booty you brought back. *Le Tutu*, five tattered numbers of *Pantalon Blanc et Culotte Rouge*, a blue French telegram, curiosity to show:

> Mother dying come home father.

The aunt thinks you killed your mother. That's why she won't ...

> Then here's a health to Mulligan's aunt
> And I'll tell you the reason why.
> She always kept things decent in
> The Hannigan famileye.

His feet marched in sudden proud rhythm over the sand furrows along by the boulders of the South Wall. He stared at them proudly, piled stone mammoth skulls. Gold light on sea, on sand, on boulders. The sun is there, the slender trees, the lemon houses.

Paris rawly waking, crude sunlight on her lemon streets. Moist pith of farls of bread, the frog-green wormwood, her matin incense, court the air. Belluomo rises from the bed of his wife's lover's wife. The kerchiefed housewife is astir, a saucer of acetic acid in her hand. In Rodot's Yvonne and Madeleine, belated, new-make their tumbled beauties, shattering with gold teeth *chaussons* of pastry, their mouths yellowed with the *pus* of *flan breton*. Faces of Paris men go by, their well-pleased pleasers, curled *conquistadores*.

Noon slumbers. Kevin Egan rolls gunpowder cigarettes through fingers smeared with printers' ink, sipping his green fairy as Patrice his white. About us gobblers fork spiced beans down their gullets. *Un demi-setier!* A jet of coffee steam from the burnished cauldron. She serves me at his beck. *Il est irlandais. Hollandais? Non fromage. Deux irlandais, nous, Irlande, vous savez? Ah, oui!* She thought you wanted a cheese *hollandais*. Your postprandial. Do you know that word? Postprandial. There was a fellow I knew once in Barcelona, queer fellow, used to call it his postprandial. Well, *sláinte!* Around the slabbed tables the tangle of wined breaths and grumbling gorges. His breath hangs over our sauce-stained plates, the green fairy's fang thrusting between his lips. Of Ireland, the Dalcassians, of hopes, conspiracies. Of Arthur Griffith now, AE, pimander, good shepherd of men. To yoke me as his yokefellow, our crimes our common cause. You're your father's son. I know the voice. His fustian shirt, sanguine-flowered, trembles its Spanish tassels at his secrets. M. Drumont, famous journalist, Drumont, know what he called Queen Victoria? Old hag with the yellow teeth. *Vieille ogresse* with the *dents jaunes.* Maud Gonne, beautiful woman, *La Patrie,* M. Millevoye. Félix Faure, know how he died? Licentious men. The *froeken, bonne à tout faire,* who rubs male nakedness in the bath at Uppsala. *Moi faire,* she said, *tous les messieurs.* Not this *monsieur,* I said. Most licentious custom. Bath a most private thing. I wouldn't let my brother, not even my own brother, most lascivious thing. Green eyes, I see you! Fang, I feel. Lascivious people.

The blue fuse burns deadly between his hands and burns clear. Loose tobacco shreds catch fire: a flame and acrid smoke light our corner. Raw facebones under his peep-of-day-boy's hat. How the head centre got away, authentic version. Got up as a young bride, man, veil, orange blossoms, drove out the road to Malahide. Did, faith. Of lost leaders, the betrayed, wild escapes. Disguises, clutched at, gone, not here.

Spurned lover. I was a strapping young gossoon at that time, I tell you. I'll show you my likeness one day. I was, faith. Lover, for her love he prowled with Colonel Richard Burke, tanist of his sept, under the walls of Clerkenwell and, crouching, saw a flame of vengeance hurl them upward in the fog. Shattered glass and toppling masonry. In gay Paree he hides, Egan of Paris, unsought by any save by me. Making his day's stations, the dingy printing case, his three taverns, the Montmartre lair he sleeps short night in, rue de la Goutte-d'Or, damascened with flyblown faces of the gone. Loveless, landless, wifeless. She is quite nicey comfy without her outcast man, madame in rue Gît-le-Cœur, canary and two buck lodgers. Peachy cheeks, a zebra skirt, frisky as a young thing's. Spurned and undespairing. Tell Pat you saw me, won't you? I wanted to get poor Pat a job one time. *Mon fils,* soldier of France. I taught him to sing *The boys of Kilkenny are stout roaring blades.* Know that old lay? I taught Patrice that. Old Kilkenny: Saint Canice, Strongbow's castle on the Nore. Goes like this. *O, O.* He takes me, Napper Tandy, by the hand.

Weak wasting hand on mine. They have forgotten Kevin Egan, not he
them. Remembering thee, O Sion.

He had come nearer the edge of the sea and wet sand slapped his
boots. The new air greeted him, harping in wild nerves, wind of wild air
of seeds of brightness. Here, I am not walking out to the Kish Lightship,
am I? He stood suddenly, his feet beginning to sink slowly in the quaking
soil. Turn back.

Turning, he scanned the shore south, his feet sinking again slowly in
new sockets. The cold domed room of the tower waits. Through the
barbicans the shafts of light are moving ever, slowly ever, as my feet
are sinking, creeping duskward over the dial floor. Blue dusk, night-
fall, deep blue night. In the darkness of the dome they wait, their pushed
back chairs, my obelisk valise, around a board of abandoned platters.
Who to clear it? He has the key. I will not sleep there when this night
comes. A shut door of a silent tower entombing their blind bodies, the
panthersahib and his pointer. Call: no answer. He lifted his feet up from
the suck and turned back by the mole of boulders. Take all, keep all. My
soul walks with me, form of forms. So in the moon's midwatches I pace
the path above the rocks, in sable silvered, hearing Elsinore's tempting
flood.

The flood is following me. I can watch it flow past from here. Get back
then by the Poolbeg road to the strand there. He climbed over the sedge
and eely oarweeds and sat on a stool of rock, resting his ashplant in a
grike.

A bloated carcass of a dog lay lolled on bladderwrack. Before him the
gunwale of a boat, sunk in sand. *Un coche ensablé*, Louis Veuillot called
Gautier's prose. These heavy sands are language tide and wind have silted
here. And these the stoneheaps of dead builders, a warren of weasel rats.
Hide gold there. Try it. You have some. Sands and stones. Heavy of the
past. Sir Lout's toys. Mind you don't get one bang on the ear. I'm the
bloody well gigant rolls all them bloody well boulders, bones for my
steppingstones. Feefawfum. I zmellz de bloodz odz an Iridzman.

A point, live dog, grew into sight running across the sweep of sand.
Lord, is he going to attack me? Respect his liberty. You will not be master
of others or their slave. I have my stick. Sit tight. From farther away,
walking shoreward across from the crested tide, figures: two. The two

Marys. They have tucked it safe among the bulrushes. Peekaboo, I see you. No, the dog. He is running back to them. Who?

Galleys of the Lochlanns ran here to beach in quest of prey, their blood-beaked prows riding low on a molten pewter surf. Dane vikings, torcs of tomahawks aglitter on their breasts. When Malachi wore the collar of gold. A school of turlehide whales stranded in hot noon, spouting, hobbling in the shallows. Then from the starving cagework city a horde of jerkined dwarfs, my people, with flayers' knives, running, scaling, hacking in green blubbery whalemeat. Famine, plague and slaughter. Their blood is in me, their lusts my waves. I moved among them on the frozen Liffey, that I, a changeling, among the spluttering resin fires. I spoke to no one: none to me.

The dog's bark ran towards him, stopped, ran back. Dog of my enemy. I just simply stood pale, silent, bayed about. *Terribilia meditans.* A primrose doublet, fortune's knave, smiled on my fear. For that are you pining, the bark of their applause? Pretenders: live their lives. The Bruce's brother; Thomas Fitzgerald, silken knight; Perkin Warbeck, York's false scion, in breeches of silk of white-rose ivory, wonder of a day; and Lambert Simnel, with a tail of nans and sutlers, a scullion crowned. All kings' sons. Paradise of pretenders then and now. He saved men from drowning and you shake at a cur's yelping? But the courtiers who mocked Guido in Or San Michele were in their own house. House of ... We don't want any more of your medieval abstrusiosities. Would you do what he did? A boat would be near, a lifebuoy. *Natürlich*, put there for you. Would you or would you not? The man that was drowned nine days ago off Maiden's Rock. They are waiting for him now. The truth, spit it out! I would want to. I would try. I am not a strong swimmer. Water cold soft. When I put my face into it in the basin at Clongowes. Can't see! Who's behind me? Out quickly, quickly! Do you see the tide flowing quickly in on all sides, sheeting the lows of sand quickly, shellcocoa-coloured? If I had land under my feet. I want his life still to be his, mine still to be mine. A drowning man. His human eyes scream to me out of horror of his death. I ... With him together down ... I could not save her. Waters: bitter death: lost.

A woman and a man. I see her skirties. Pinned up, I bet.

Their dog ambled about a bank of dwindling sand, trotting, sniffing on all sides. Looking for something lost in a past life. Suddenly he made off like a bounding hare, ears flung back, chasing the shadow of a low-skimming gull. The man's shrieked whistle struck his limp ears. He turned, bounded back, came nearer, trotted on twinkling shanks. On a field tenny a buck trippant, proper, unattired. At the lacefringe of the tide he halted with stiff forehoofs, seaward-pointed ears. His snout lifted barked at the wavenoise, herds of sea morse. They serpented towards his feet, curling, unfurling many crests, every ninth breaking, plashing, from far, from farther out, waves and waves.

Cocklepickers. They waded a little way into the water and, stooping, soused their bags and, lifting them again, waded out. The dog yelped running to them, reared up and pawed them, dropping on all fours, again reared up at them with mute bearish fawning. Unheeded he kept by them as they came towards the drier sand, a rag of wolf's tongue redpanting from his jaws. His speckled body ambled ahead of them and then loped off at a calf's gallop. The carcass lay on his path. He stopped, sniffed, stalked round it, brother, nosing closer, went round it sniffing rapidly like a dog all over the dead dog's bedraggled fell. Dogskull, dogsniff, eyes on the ground, moves to one great goal. Ah, poor dogsbody! Here lies poor dogsbody's body.

– Tatters! Outofthat, you mongrel!

The cry brought him skulking back to his master and a blunt bootless kick sent him unscathed across a spit of sand, crouched in flight. He slunk back in a curve. Doesn't see me. Along by the edge of the mole he lolloped, dawdled, smelt a rock and from under a cocked hind leg pissed against it. He trotted forward and, lifting again his hind leg, pissed quick short at an unsmelt rock. The simple pleasures of the poor. His hind paws then scattered the sand: then his forepaws dabbled and delved. Something he buried there: his grandmother. He rooted in the sand, dabbling, delving, and stopped to listen to the air, scraped up the sand again with a fury of his claws, soon ceasing. A pard, a panther got in spousebreach, vulturing the dead.

After he woke me up last night same dream. Or was it? Wait. Open hallway. Street of harlots. Remember. Haroun al-Raschid. I am almosting it. That man led me, spoke. I was not afraid. The melon he had he held against my face. Smiled: creamfruit smell. That was the rule, said. In. Come. Red carpet spread. You will see who.

Shouldering their bags they trudged, the red Egyptians. His blued feet out of turned-up trousers slapped the clammy sand, a dull brick muffler strangling his unshaven neck. With woman steps she followed: the ruffian and his strolling mort. Spoils slung at her back. Loose sand and shellgrit crusted her bare feet. About her wind-raw face her hair trailed. Behind her lord, his helpmate, bing awast to Romeville. When night hides her body's flaws, calling under her brown shawl from an archway where dogs have mired. Her fancy man is treating two Royal Dublins in O'Loughlin's of Blackpitts. Buss her, wap in rogues' rum lingo, O, my dimber wapping dell! A she-fiend's whiteness under her rancid rags. Fumbally's Lane that night: the tanyard smells.

> *White thy fambles, red thy gan*
> *And thy quarrons dainty is.*
> *Couch a hogshead with me then.*
> *In the darkmans clip and kiss.*

Morose delectation Aquinas tunbelly calls this, *frate porcospino*. Unfallen Adam rode and not rutted. Call away, let him and welcome: for thy quarrons dainty is. Language no whit worse than his. Monkwords, marybeads jabber on their girdles: roguewords, tough nuggets patter in their pockets.

Passing now.

A side-eye at my Hamlet hat. If I were suddenly naked here as I sit? I am not. Across the sands of all the world, followed by the sun's flaming sword, to the west, trekking to evening lands, she trudges, schlepps, trains, drags, trascines her load. A tide westering, moondrawn, in her wake. Tides, myriad-islanded, within her, blood not mine, *oinopa ponton*, a wine-dark sea. Behold the handmaid of the moon. In sleep the wet sign calls her hour, bids her rise. Bridebed, childbed, bed of death, ghostcandled. *Omnis caro ad te veniet*. He comes, pale vampire, through storm his eyes, his batsails bloodying the sea, mouth to her mouth's kiss.

Here. Put a pin in that chap, will you? My tablets. Mouth to her kiss. No. Must be two of 'em. Glue 'em well. Mouth to her mouth's kiss.

His lips lipped and mouthed fleshless lips of air: mouth to her moomb. Oomb, all-wombing tomb. His mouth moulded issuing breath, unspeeched: ooeeehah: roar of cataractic planets, globed, blazing, roaring wayawayawayawayaway. Paper. The banknotes, blast them. Old Deasy's letter. Here. Thanking you for the hospitality, tear the blank end off. Turning his back to the sun he bent over far to a table of rock and scribbled words. That's twice I forgot to take slips from the library counter.

His shadow lay dark over the rocks as he bent, ending. Why not endless till the farthest star? Darkly they are there behind this light, darkness shining in the brightness, Delta of Cassiopeia, worlds. Me sits there, with his augur's rod of ash, in borrowed sandals, by day beside a livid sea, unbeheld, in violet night walking beneath a reign of uncouth stars. I throw this ended shadow from me, manshape ineluctable, call it back. Endless, would it be mine, form of my form? Who watches me here? Who ever anywhere will read these written words? Signs on a white field. Somewhere to someone in your flutiest voice. The good bishop of Cloyne took the veil of the temple out of his shovel hat: veil of space with coloured emblems hatched on its field. Hold hard. Coloured on a flat: yes, that's right. Flat I see, then think distance, near, far: flat I see, east, back. Ah, see now! Falls back suddenly, frozen in stereoscope. Click does the trick. You find my words dark. Darkness is in our souls, do you not think? Flutier. Our souls, shamewounded by our sins, cling to us yet more, a woman to her lover clinging, the more the more.

She trusts me, her hand gentle, the long-lashed eyes. Now where the blue hell am I bringing her beyond the veil? Into the ineluctable modality of the ineluctable visuality. She, she, she. What she? The virgin at Hodges Figgis' window on Monday looking in for one of the alphabet books you were going to write. Keen glance you gave her. Wrist through the braided jesses of her sunshade. She lives in Leeson Park with a grief and kickshaws, a lady of letters. Talk that to someone else, Stevie: a pick-me-up. Bet she wears those curse of God stays suspenders and yellow stockings darned with lumpy wool. Talk about apple dumplings, *piuttosto*. Where are your wits?

Touch me. Soft eyes. Soft soft soft hand. I am lonely here. O, touch me soon, now. What is that word known to all men? I am quiet here alone. Sad too. Touch, touch me.

He lay back at full stretch over the sharp rocks, cramming the scribbled note and pencil into a pocket, his hat tilted down on his eyes. That is Kevin Egan's movement I made, nodding for his nap. Sabbath sleep. *Et vidit Deus. Et erant valde bona.* H'lo! *Bonjour.* Welcome as the flowers in May. Under its leaf he watched through peacock-twittering lashes the southing sun. I am caught in this burning scene. Pan's hour, the faunal noon. Among gum-heavy serpentplants, milk-oozing fruits, where on the tawny waters leaves lie wide. Pain is far.

And no more turn aside and brood.

His gaze brooded on his broad-toed boots, a buck's castoffs, *nebeneinander.* He counted the creases of rucked leather wherein another's foot had nested warm. The foot that beat the ground in tripudium: foot I dislove. But you were delighted when Esther Osvalt's shoe went on you:

48

girl I knew in Paris. *Tiens, quel petit pied!* Staunch friend: a brother soul. Wilde's love that dare not speak its name. His arm: Cranly's arm. He now will leave me. And the blame? As I am. As I am. All or not at all.

In long lassoes from the Cock Lake the water flowed full, covering greengoldenly lagoons of sand, rising, flowing. My ashplant will float away. I shall wait. No, they will pass on, passing, chafing against the low rocks, swirling, passing.

Better get this job over quick. Listen: a four-worded wavespeech: seesoo, hrss, rsseeiss, ooos. Vehement breath of water amid sea snakes, rearing horses, rocks. In cups of rocks it slops: flop, slop, slap: bounded in barrels. And, spent, its speech ceases. It flows purling, widely flowing, floating foampool, flower unfurling.

Under the upswelling tide he saw the writhing weeds lift languidly and sway reluctant arms, in whispering water swaying, hising up their petti-coats, upturning coy silver fronds. Day by day, night by night: lifted, flooded and let fall. Lord, they are weary; and, whispered to, they sigh. Saint Ambrose heard it, sigh of leaves and waves, waiting, awaiting the fullness of their times, *diebus ac noctibus injurias patiens ingemiscit.* To no end gathered: vainly then released, forth flowing, wending back, loom of the moon. Weary too in sight of lovers, lascivious men, a naked woman shining in her courts, she draws a toil of waters.

Five fathoms out there. Full fathom five thy father lies. At one, he said. Found drowned. High water at Dublin Bar. Driving before it a loose drift of rubble, fanshoals of fishes, silly shells. A corpse rising salt-white from the undertow, bobbing landward, a pace a pace a porpoise. There he is. Hook it quick. Sunk though he be beneath the watery floor. Pull. We have him. Easy now.

Bag of corpsegas sopping in foul brine. A quiver of minnows, fat of a spongy titbit, flash through the slits of his buttoned trouserfly. God becomes man becomes fish becomes barnacle goose becomes featherbed mountain. Dead breaths I living breathe, tread dead dust, devour a urinous offal from all dead. Hauled stark over the gunwale he breathes upward the stench of his green grave, his leprous nosehole snoring to the sun.

A sea change this, brown eyes salt-blue. Sea death, mildest of all deaths known to man. Old Father Ocean. Prix de Paris, 1866: beware of imita-tions. Just you give it a fair trial. We enjoyed ourselves immensely.

Come. I thirst. Clouding over. No black clouds anywhere, are there? Thunderstorm. All-bright he falls, proud lightning of the intellect, *Lucifer, dico, qui nescit occasum.* No. My cockle hat and staff and his my sandal shoon. Where? To evening lands. Evening will find itself.

He took the hilt of his ashplant, lunging with it softly, dallying still. Yes, evening will find itself: in me, without me. All days make their end. By the way, next when is it Tuesday will be the longest day. Of all the glad new year, mother, the rum tum tiddledy tum. Lawn Tennyson, gentleman poet. *Già.* For the old hag with the yellow teeth. And Monsieur Drumont, gentleman journalist. *Già.* My teeth are very bad. Why, I wonder? Feel. That one is going too. Shells. Ought I go to a dentist, I wonder, with that money? That one. This. Toothless Kinch, the superman. Why is that, I wonder, or does it mean something perhaps?

My handkerchief. He threw it. I remember. Did I not take it up?

His hand groped vainly in his pockets. No, I didn't. Better buy one.

He laid the dry snot picked from his nostril on a ledge of rock, carefully. For the rest let look who will.

Behind. Perhaps there is someone.

He turned his face over a shoulder, rear regardant. Moving through the air high spars of a three-master, her sails brailed up on the crosstrees, homing, upstream, silently moving, a silent ship.

PART II

MR LEOPOLD BLOOM ate with relish the inner organs of beasts and fowls. He liked thick giblet soup, nutty gizzards, a stuffed roast heart, liver slices fried with crustcrumbs, fried hen-cod's roe. Most of all he liked grilled mutton kidneys which gave to his palate a fine tang of faintly scented urine.

Kidneys were in his mind as he moved about the kitchen softly, righting her breakfast things on the humpy tray. Gelid light and air were in the kitchen but out of doors gentle summer morning everywhere. Made him feel a bit peckish.

The coals were reddening.

Another slice of bread and butter: three, four: right. She didn't like her plate full. Right. He turned from the tray, lifted the kettle off the hob and set it sideways on the fire. It sat there, dull and squat, its spout stuck out. Cup of tea soon. Good. Mouth dry.

The cat walked stiffly round a leg of the table with tail on high.

— Mkgnao!

— O, there you are, Mr Bloom said, turning from the fire.

The cat mewed in answer and stalked again stiffly round a leg of the table, mewing. Just how she stalks over my writing table. Prr. Scratch my head. Prr.

Mr Bloom watched curiously, kindly, the lithe black form. Clean to see: the gloss of her sleek hide, the white button under the butt of her tail, the green flashing eyes. He bent down to her, his hands on his knees.

— Milk for the pussens, he said.

— Mrkgnao! the cat cried.

They call them stupid. They understand what we say better than we understand them. She understands all she wants to. Vindictive too. Cruel. Her nature. Curious mice never squeal. Seem to like it. Wonder what I look like to her. Height of a tower? No, she can jump me.

— Afraid of the chickens she is, he said mockingly. Afraid of the chookchooks. I never saw such a stupid pussens as the pussens.

— Mrkrgnao! the cat said loudly.

She blinked up out of her avid shameclosing eyes, mewing plaintively and long, showing him her milk-white teeth. He watched the dark eyeslits narrowing with greed till her eyes were green stones. Then he went to the dresser, took the jug Hanlon's milkman had just filled for him, poured warmbubbled milk on a saucer and set it slowly on the floor.

— Gurrhr! she cried, running to lap.

He watched the bristles shining wirily in the weak light as she tipped three times and licked lightly. Wonder is it true if you clip them they can't mouse after. Why? They shine in the dark, perhaps, the tips. Or kind of feelers in the dark, perhaps.

He listened to her licking lap. Ham and eggs, no. No good eggs with this drouth. Want pure fresh water. Thursday: not a good day either for a mutton kidney at Buckley's. Fried with butter, a shake of pepper. Better a pork kidney at Dlugacz's. While the kettle is boiling. She lapped slower, then licked the saucer clean. Why are their tongues so rough? To lap better, all porous holes. Nothing she can eat? He glanced round him. No.

On quietly creaky boots he went up the staircase to the hall, paused by the bedroom door. She might like something tasty. Thin bread and butter she likes in the morning. Still perhaps: once in a way.

He said softly in the bare hall:

— I'm going round the corner. Be back in a minute.

And when he had heard his voice say it he added:

— You don't want anything for breakfast?

A sleepy soft grunt answered:

— Mn.

No. She didn't want anything. He heard then a warm heavy sigh, softer, as she turned over and the loose brass quoits of the bedstead jingled. Must get those settled really. Pity. All the way from Gibraltar. Forgotten any little Spanish she knew. Wonder what her father gave for it. Old style. Ah yes! Of course. Bought it at the governor's auction. Got a short knock. Hard as nails at a bargain, old Tweedy. Yes, sir. At Plevna that was. I rose from the ranks, sir, and I'm proud of it. Still, he had brains enough to make that corner in stamps. Now that was farseeing.

His hand took his hat from the peg over his initialled heavy overcoat and his lost property office secondhand waterproof. Stamps: stickyback pictures. Daresay lots of officers are in the swim too. Course they do. The sweated legend in the crown of his hat told him mutely: Plasto's high-grade ha. He peeped quickly inside the leather headband. White slip of paper. Quite safe.

On the doorstep he felt in his hip pocket for the latchkey. Not there. In the trousers I left off. Must get it. Potato I have. Creaky wardrobe. No use disturbing her. She turned over sleepily that time. He pulled the hall door to after him very quietly, more, till the footleaf dropped gently over the threshold, a limp lid. Looked shut. All right till I come back anyhow.

He crossed to the bright side, avoiding the loose cellarflap of number seventy-five. The sun was nearing the steeple of George's Church. Be a warm day I fancy. Specially in these black clothes feel it more. Black conducts, reflects (refracts is it?) the heat. But I couldn't go in that light suit. Make a picnic of it. His eyelids sank quietly often as he walked in happy warmth. Boland's breadvan delivering with trays our daily, but she prefers yesterday's, loaves turnovers crisp crowns hot. Makes you feel young. Somewhere in the east, early morning: set off at dawn. Travel round in front of the sun, steal a day's march on him. Keep it up for ever never grow a day older technically. Walk along a strand, strange land, come to a city gate, sentry there, old ranker too, old Tweedy's big moustaches, leaning on a long kind of a spear. Wander through awned streets. Turbaned faces going by. Dark caves of carpet shops, big man, Turko the Terrible, seated cross-legged smoking a coiled pipe. Cries of sellers in the streets. Drink water scented with fennel, sherbet. Dander along all day. Might meet a robber or two. Well, meet him. Getting on to sundown. The shadows of the mosques among the pillars: priest with a scroll rolled up. A shiver of the trees, signal, the evening wind. I pass on. Fading gold sky. A mother watches me from her doorway. She calls her children home in their dark language. High wall: beyond, strings twanged. Night sky, moon, violet, colour of Molly's new garters. Strings. Listen. A girl playing one of those instruments what do you call them: dulcimers. I pass.

Probably not a bit like it really. Kind of stuff you read: in the track of the sun. Sunburst on the title page. He smiled, pleasing himself. What Arthur Griffith said about the headpiece over the *Freeman* leader: a Home Rule sun rising up in the northwest from the laneway behind the Bank of Ireland. He prolonged his pleased smile. Ikey touch that: Home Rule sun rising up in the northwest.

He approached Larry O'Rourke's. From the cellar grating floated up the flabby gush of porter. Through the open doorway the bar squirted out whiffs of ginger, tea dust, biscuit mush. Good house, however: just the end of the city traffic. For instance M'Auley's down there: n.g. as position. Of course if they ran a tramline along the North Circular from the cattle market to the quays value would go up like a shot.

Bald head over the blind. Cute old codger. No use canvassing him for an order. Still, he knows his own business best. There he is, sure enough, my bold Larry, leaning against the sugarbin in his shirtsleeves, watching the aproned curate swab up with mop and bucket. Simon Dedalus takes him off to a tee with his eyes screwed up. Do you know what I'm going to tell you? What's that, Mr O'Rourke? Do you know what? The Russians, they'd only be an eight o'clock breakfast for the Japanese.

Stop and say a word: about the funeral perhaps. Sad thing about poor Dignam, Mr O'Rourke.

Turning into Dorset Street he said freshly in greeting through the doorway:

— Good day, Mr O'Rourke.

— Good day to you.

— Lovely weather, sir.

— 'Tis all that.

Where do they get the money? Coming up redheaded curates from the county Leitrim, rinsing empties and old man in the cellar. Then, lo and behold, they blossom out as Adam Findlaters or Dan Tallons. Then think of the competition. General thirst. Good puzzle would be cross Dublin without passing a pub. Save it they can't. Off the drunks perhaps. Put down three and carry five. What is that? A bob here and there, dribs and drabs. On the wholesale orders perhaps. Doing a double shuffle with the town travellers. Square it with the boss and we'll split the job, see?

How much would that tot to off the porter in the month? Say ten barrels of stuff. Say he got ten per cent off. Or more. Fifteen. He passed Saint Joseph's National School. Brats' clamour. Windows open. Fresh air helps memory. Or a lilt. Ahbeesee defeegee kelomen opeecue rustyouvee doubleyou. Boys are they? Yes. Inishturk, Inishark, Inishboffin. At their joggerfry. Mine. Slieve Bloom.

He halted before Dlugacz's window, staring at the hanks of sausages, polonies, black and white. Fifteen multiplied by. The figures whitened in his mind, unsolved: displeased, he let them fade. The shiny links packed with forcemeat fed his gaze and he breathed in tranquilly the lukewarm breath of cooked spicy pig's blood.

A kidney oozed bloodgouts on the willow-patterned dish: the last. He stood by the next-door girl at the counter. Would she buy it too, calling the items from a slip in her hand? Chapped: washing soda. And a pound and a half of Denny's sausages. His eyes rested on her vigorous hips. Woods his name is. Wonder what he does. Wife is oldish. New blood. No followers allowed. Strong pair of arms. Whacking a carpet on the clothes-line. She does whack it, by George. The way her crooked skirt swings at each whack.

The ferret-eyed pork butcher folded the sausages he had snipped off with blotchy fingers, sausage-pink. Sound meat there: like a stall-fed heifer.

He took up a page from the pile of cut sheets: the model farm at Kinnereth on the lakeshore of Tiberias. Can become ideal winter sanatorium. Moses Montefiore. I thought he was. Farmhouse, wall round it, blurred cattle cropping. He held the page from him: interesting: read it nearer, the title, the blurred cropping cattle, the page rustling. A young white heifer. Those mornings in the cattle market, the beasts lowing in their pens, branded sheep, flop and fall of dung, the breeders in hobnailed boots trudging through the litter, slapping a palm on a ripe-meated hindquarter, there's a prime one, unpeeled switches in their hands. He held the page aslant, patiently, bending his senses and his will, his soft subject gaze at rest. The crooked skirt swinging, whack by whack by whack.

The pork butcher snapped two sheets from the pile, wrapped up her prime sausages and made a red grimace.

– Now, my miss, he said.

She tendered a coin, smiling boldly, holding her thick wrist out.

– Thank you, my miss. And one shilling threepence change. For you, please?

Mr Bloom pointed quickly. To catch up and walk behind her if she went slowly, behind her moving hams. Pleasant to see first thing in the morning. Hurry up, damn it. Make hay while the sun shines. She stood outside the shop in sunlight and sauntered lazily to the right. He sighed down his nose: they never understand. Soda-chapped hands. Crusted toenails too. Brown scapulars in tatters, defending her both ways. The sting of disregard glowed to weak pleasure within his breast. For another: a constable off duty cuddling her in Eccles Lane. They like them sizeable. Prime sausage. O please, Mr Policeman, I'm lost in the wood.

– Threepence, please.

His hand accepted the moist tender gland and slid it into a side pocket. Then it fetched up three coins from his trousers pocket and laid them on the rubber prickles. They lay, were read quickly and quickly slid, disk by disk, into the till.

– Thank you, sir. Another time.

A speck of eager fire from foxeyes thanked him. He withdrew his gaze after an instant. No: better not: another time.

— Good morning, he said, moving away.

— Good morning, sir.

No sign. Gone. What matter?

He walked back along Dorset Street, reading gravely. Agudath Netaim: planters' company. To purchase waste sandy tracts from Turkish government and plant with eucalyptus trees. Excellent for shade, fuel and construction. Orange groves and immense melon fields north of Jaffa. You pay eighty marks and they plant a dunam of land for you with olives, oranges, almonds or citrons. Olives cheaper: oranges need artificial irrigation. Every year you get a sending of the crop. Your name entered for life as owner in the book of the union. Can pay ten down and the balance in yearly instalments. Bleibtreustrasse 34, Berlin W. 15.

Nothing doing. Still, an idea behind it.

He looked at the cattle, blurred in silver heat. Silver-powdered olive trees. Quiet long days: pruning, ripening. Olives are packed in jars, eh? I have a few left from Andrews. Molly spitting them out. Knows the taste of them now. Oranges in tissue paper packed in crates. Citrons too. Wonder is poor Citron still in Saint Kevin's Parade. And Masliansky with the old cither. Pleasant evenings we had then. Molly in Citron's basket chair. Nice to hold, cool waxen fruit, hold in the hand, lift it to the nostrils and smell the perfume. Like that, heavy, sweet, wild perfume. Always the same, year after year. They fetched high prices too, Moisel told me. Arbutus Place: Pleasants Street: pleasant old times. Must be without a flaw, he said. Coming all that way: Spain, Gibraltar, Mediterranean, the Levant. Crates lined up on the quayside at Jaffa, chap ticking them off in a book, navvies handling them barefoot in soiled dungarees. There's whatdoyoucallhim out of. How do you? Doesn't see. Chap you know just to salute bit of a bore. His back is like that Norwegian captain's. Wonder if I'll meet him today. Watering cart. To provoke the rain. On earth as it is in heaven.

A cloud began to cover the sun slowly, wholly. Grey. Far.

No, not like that. A barren land, bare waste. Volcanic lake, the dead sea: no fish, weedless, sunk deep in the earth. No wind could lift those waves, grey metal, poisonous foggy waters. Brimstone they called it raining down: the cities of the plain: Sodom, Gomorrah, Edom. All dead names. A dead sea in a dead land, grey and old. Old now. It bore the oldest, the first race. A bent hag crossed from Cassidy's clutching a noggin bottle by the neck. The oldest people. Wandered far away over all the earth, captivity to captivity, multiplying, dying, being born everywhere. It lay there now. Now it could bear no more. Dead: an old woman's: the grey sunken cunt of the world.

Desolation.

Grey horror seared his flesh. Folding the page into his pocket he turned into Eccles Street, hurrying homeward. Cold oils slid along his veins, chilling his blood: age crusting him with a salt cloak. Well, I am here now. Yes, I am here now. Morning mouth, bad images. Got up wrong side of the bed. Must begin again those Sandow's exercises. On the hands down. Blotchy brown brick houses. Number eighty still unlet. Why is that? Valuation is only seventeen. Towers, Battersby, North, MacArthur: parlour windows plastered with bills. Plasters on a sore eye. To smell the gentle smoke of tea, fume of the pan, sizzling butter. Be near her ample bed-warmed flesh. Yes, yes.

Quick warm sunlight came running from Berkeley Road, swiftly, in slim sandals, along the brightening footpath. Runs, she runs to meet me, a girl with gold hair on the wind.

Two letters and a card lay on the hall floor. He stooped and gathered them. Mrs Marion Bloom. His quickened heart slowed at once. Bold hand. Mrs Marion...

— Poldy!

Entering the bedroom he half closed his eyes and walked through warm yellow twilight towards her tousled head.

— Who are the letters for?

He looked at them. Mullingar. Milly.

— A letter for me from Milly, he said carefully, and a card to you. And a letter for you.

He laid her card and letter on the twill bedspread near the curve of her knees.

— Do you want the blind up?

Letting the blind up by gentle tugs halfway his backward eye saw her glance at the letter and tuck it under her pillow.

— That do? he asked, turning.

She was reading the card, propped on her elbow.

— She got the things, she said.

He waited till she had laid the card aside and curled herself back slowly with a snug sigh.

— Hurry up with that tea, she said. I'm parched.

– The kettle is boiling, he said.

But he delayed to clear the chair: her striped petticoat, tossed soiled linen: and lifted all in an armful on to the foot of the bed.

As he went down the kitchen stairs she called:

– Poldy!

– What?

– Scald the teapot.

On the boil sure enough: a plume of steam from the spout. He scalded and rinsed out the teapot and put in four full spoons of tea, tilting the kettle then to let the water flow in. Having set it to draw he took off the kettle, crushed the pan flat on the live coals and watched the lump of butter slide and melt. While he unwrapped the kidney the cat mewed hungrily against him. Give her too much meat she won't mouse. Say they won't eat pork. Kosher. Here. He let the blood-smeared paper fall to her and dropped the kidney amid the sizzling butter sauce. Pepper. He sprinkled it through his fingers, ringwise, from the chipped eggcup.

Then he slit open his letter, glancing down the page and over. Thanks: new tam: Mr Coghlan: Lough Owel picnic: young student: Blazes Boylan's seaside girls.

The tea was drawn. He filled his own moustache cup, sham Crown Derby, smiling. Silly Milly's birthday gift. Only five she was then. No, wait: four. I gave her the amberoid necklace she broke. Putting pieces of folded brown paper in the letterbox for her. He smiled, pouring.

> *O, Milly Bloom, you are my darling.*
> *You are my looking glass from night to morning.*
> *I'd rather have you without a farthing*
> *Than Katey Keogh with her ass and garden.*

Poor old Professor Goodwin. Dreadful old case. Still, he was a courteous old chap. Old-fashioned way he used to bow Molly off the platform. And the little mirror in his silk hat. The night Milly brought it into the parlour. O, look what I found in Professor Goodwin's hat! All we laughed. Sex breaking out even then. Pert little piece she was.

He prodded a fork into the kidney and slapped it over: then fitted the teapot on the tray. Its hump bumped as he took it up. Everything on it? Bread and butter, four, sugar, spoon, her cream. Yes. He carried it upstairs, his thumb hooked in the teapot handle.

Nudging the door open with his knee he carried the tray in and set it on the chair by the bedhead.

— What a time you were! she said.

She set the brasses jingling as she raised herself briskly, an elbow on the pillow. He looked calmly down on her bulk and between her large soft bubs, sloping within her nightdress like a she-goat's udder. The warmth of her couched body rose on the air, mingling with the fragrance of the tea she poured.

A strip of torn envelope peeped from under the dimpled pillow. In the act of going he stayed to straighten the bedspread.

— Who was the letter from? he asked.

Bold hand. Marion.

— O, Boylan, she said. He's bringing the programme.

— What are you singing?

— *Là ci darem* with J.C. Doyle, she said, and *Love's Old Sweet Song.*

Her full lips, drinking, smiled. Rather stale smell that incense leaves next day. Like foul flowerwater.

— Would you like the window open a little?

She doubled a slice of bread into her mouth, asking:

— What time is the funeral?

— Eleven, I think, he answered. I didn't see the paper.

Following the pointing of her finger he took up a leg of her soiled drawers from the bed. No? Then a twisted grey garter looped round a stocking: rumpled, shiny sole.

— No: that book.

Other stocking. Her petticoat.

— It must have fell down, she said.

He felt here and there. *Voglio e non vorrei.* Wonder if she pronounces that right: *voglio.* Not in the bed. Must have slid down. He stooped and lifted the valance. The book, fallen, sprawled against the bulge of the orange-keyed chamberpot.

— Show here, she said. I put a mark in it. There's a word I wanted to ask you.

She swallowed a draught of tea from her cup held by not handle and, having wiped her fingertips smartly on the blanket, began to search the text with the hairpin till she reached the word.

— Met him what? he asked.

— Here, she said. What does that mean?

He leaned downward and read near her polished thumbnail.

— Metempsychosis?

— Yes. Who's he when he's at home?

— Metempsychosis, he said, frowning. It's Greek; from the Greek. That means the transmigration of souls.

— O rocks! she said. Tell us in plain words.

He smiled, glancing askance at her mocking eyes. Young still. The same young eyes. The first night after the charades. Dolphin's Barn. He turned over the smudged pages. *Ruby: the Pride of the Ring.* Hello. Illustration. Fierce Italian with carriagewhip. Must be Ruby pride of the on the floor naked. Sheet kindly lent. *The monster Maffei desisted and flung his victim from him with an oath.* Cruelty behind it all. Doped animals. Trapeze at Hengler's. Had to look the other way. Mob gaping. Break your neck and we'll break our sides. Families of them. Bone them young so they metempsychosis. That we live after death. Our souls. That a man's soul after he dies. Dignam's soul . . .

— Did you finish it? he asked.

— Yes, she said. There's nothing smutty in it. Is she in love with the first fellow all the time?

— Never read it. Do you want another?

— Yes. Get another of Paul de Kock's. Nice name he has.

She poured more tea into her cup, watching it flow sideways.

Must get that Capel Street Library book renewed or they'll write to Kearney, my guarantor. Reincarnation: that's the word.

— Some people believe, he said, that we go on living in another body after death, that we lived before. They call it reincarnation. That we all lived before on the earth thousands of years ago or some other planet. They say we have forgotten it. Some say they remember their past lives.

The sluggish cream wound curdling spirals through her tea. Better remind her of the word: metempsychosis. An example would be better. An example?

The Bath of the Nymph over the bed. Given away with the Easter number of *Photo Bits*: splendid masterpiece in art colours. Tea before you put milk in. Not unlike her with her hair down: slimmer. Three and six I gave for the frame. She said it would look nice over the bed. Naked nymphs: Greece: and for instance all the people that lived then.

He turned the pages back.

— Metempsychosis, he said, is what the ancient Greeks called it. They used to believe you could be changed into an animal or a tree, for instance. What they called nymphs, for example.

Her spoon ceased to stir up the sugar. She gazed straight before her, inhaling through her arched nostrils.

– There's a smell of burn, she said. Did you leave anything on the fire?

– The kidney! he cried suddenly.

He fitted the book roughly into his inner pocket and, stubbing his toes against the broken commode, hurried out towards the smell, stepping hastily down the stairs with a flurried stork's legs. Pungent smoke shot up in an angry jet from a side of the pan. By prodding a prong of the fork under the kidney he detached it and turned it turtle on its back. Only a little burned. He tossed it off the pan on to a plate and let the scanty brown gravy trickle over it.

Cup of tea now. He sat down, cut and buttered a slice of the loaf. He shore away the burnt flesh and flung it to the cat. Then he put a forkful into his mouth, chewing with discernment the toothsome pliant meat. Done to a turn. A mouthful of tea. Then he cut away dies of bread, sopped one in the gravy and put it in his mouth. What was that about some young student and a picnic? He creased out the letter at his side, reading it slowly as he chewed, sopping another die of bread in the gravy and raising it to his mouth.

Dearest Papli

Thanks ever so much for the lovely birthday present. It suits me splendid. Everyone says I'm quite the belle in my new tam. I got mummy's lovely box of creams and am writing. They are lovely. I am getting on swimming in the photo business now. Mr Coghlan took one of me and Mrs, will send when developed. We did great biz yesterday. Fair Day and all the beef to the heels were in. We are going to Lough Owel on Monday with a few friends to make a scrap picnic. Give my love to mummy and to yourself a big kiss and thanks. I hear them at the piano downstairs. There is to be a concert in the Greville Arms on Saturday. There is a young student comes here some evenings named Bannon his cousins or something are big swells he sings Boylan's (I was on the pop of writing Blazes Boylan's) song about those seaside girls. Tell him Silly Milly sends my best respects. I must now close with fondest love

Your fond daughter

Milly

P.S. Excuse bad writing, am in hurry. Byby.

M.

Fifteen yesterday. Curious, fifteenth of the month too. Her first birthday away from home. Separation. Remember the summer morning she was born, running to knock up Mrs Thornton in Denzille Street. Jolly old woman. Lots of babies she must have helped into the world. She knew from the first poor little Rudy wouldn't live. Well, God is good, sir. She knew at once. He would be eleven now if he had lived.

His vacant face stared pitying at the postscript. Excuse bad writing. Hurry. Piano downstairs. Coming out of her shell. Row with her in the XL Café about the bracelet. Wouldn't eat her cakes or speak or look. Saucebox. He sopped other dies of bread in the gravy and ate piece after piece of kidney. Twelve and six a week. Not much. Still, she might do worse. Music-hall stage. Young student. He drank a draught of cooler tea to wash down his meal. Then he read the letter again: twice.

O well: she knows how to mind herself. But if not? No, nothing has happened. Of course it might. Wait in any case till it does. A wild piece of goods. Her slim legs running up the staircase. Destiny. Ripening now. Vain: very.

He smiled with troubled affection at the kitchen window. Day I caught her in the street pinching her cheeks to make them red. Anemic a little. Was given milk too long. On the *Erin's King* that day round the Kish. Damned old tub pitching about. Not a bit funky. Her pale blue scarf loose in the wind with her hair.

> *All dimpled cheeks and curls,*
> *Your head it simply swirls.*

Seaside girls. Torn envelope. Hands stuck in his trousers pockets, jarvey off for the day, singing. Friend of the family. *Swurls*, he says. Pier with lamps, summer evening, band.

> *Those girls, those girls,*
> *Those lovely seaside girls.*

Milly too. Young kisses: the first. Far away now, past. Mrs Marion. Reading lying back now, counting the strands of her hair, smiling, braiding.

A soft qualm, regret, flowed down his backbone, increasing. Will happen, yes. Prevent. Useless: can't move. Girl's sweet light lips. Will happen too. He felt the flowing qualm spread over him. Useless to move now. Lips kissed, kissing, kissed. Full gluey woman's lips.

Better where she is down there: away. Occupy her. Wanted a dog to pass the time. Might take a trip down there. August bank holiday, only two and six return. Six weeks off, however. Might work a press pass. Or through M'Coy.

The cat, having cleaned all her fur, returned to the meat-stained paper, nosed at it and stalked to the door. She looked back at him, mewing. Wants to go out. Wait before a door sometime it will open. Let her wait. Has the fidgets. Electric. Thunder in the air. Was washing at her ear with her back to the fire too.

He felt full, heavy: then a gentle loosening of his bowels. He stood up, undoing the waistband of his trousers. The cat mewed to him.

— Miaow! he said in answer. Wait till I'm ready.

Heaviness: hot day coming. Too much trouble to fag up the stairs to the landing.

A paper. He liked to read at stool. Hope no ape comes knocking just as I'm.

In the table drawer he found an old number of *Tit-Bits*. He folded it under his armpit, went to the door and opened it. The cat went up in soft bounds. Ah, wanted to go upstairs, curl up in a ball on the bed.

Listening, he heard her voice:

— Come, come, pussy. Come.

He went out through the back door into the garden: stood to listen towards the next garden. No sound. Perhaps hanging clothes out to dry. The maid was in the garden. Fine morning.

He bent down to regard a lean file of spearmint growing by the wall. Make a summerhouse here. Scarlet runners. Virginia creepers. Want to manure the whole place over, scabby soil. A coat of liver of sulphur. All soil like that without dung. Household slops. Loam, what is this that is? The hens in the next garden: their droppings are very good top dressing. Best of all though are the cattle, especially when they are fed on those oilcakes. Mulch of dung. Best thing to clean ladies' kid gloves. Dirty cleans. Ashes too. Reclaim the whole place. Grow peas in that corner there. Lettuce. Always have fresh greens then. Still, gardens have their drawbacks. That bee or bluebottle here Whit Monday.

He walked on. Where is my hat, by the way? Must have put it back on the peg. Or hanging up on the floor. Funny I don't remember that. Hallstand too full. Four umbrellas, her raincloak. Picking up the letters. Drago's shopbell ringing. Queer I was just thinking that moment. Brown brilliantined hair over his collar. Just had a wash and brushup. Wonder have I time for a bath this morning. Tara Street. Chap in the paybox there got away James Stephens, they say. O'Brien.

Deep voice that fellow Dlugacz has. Agudath what is it? Now, my miss. Enthusiast.

He kicked open the crazy door of the jakes. Better be careful not to get these trousers dirty for the funeral. He went in, bowing his head under the low lintel. Leaving the door ajar, amid the stench of mouldy limewash and stale cobwebs he undid his braces. Before sitting down he peered through a chink up at the next-door windows. The king was in his counting house. Nobody.

Asquat on the cuckstool he folded out his paper, turning its pages over on his bared knees. Something new and easy. No great hurry. Keep it a bit. Our prize titbit. *Matcham's Masterstroke*. Written by Mr Philip Beaufoy, Playgoers' Club, London. Payment at the rate of one guinea a column has been made to the writer. Three and a half. Three pounds three. Three pounds thirteen and six.

Quietly he read, restraining himself, the first column and, yielding but resisting, began the second. Midway, his last resistance yielding, he allowed his bowels to ease themselves quietly as he read, reading still patiently, that slight constipation of yesterday quite gone. Hope it's not too big, bring on piles again. No, just right. So. Ah! Costive. One tabloid of cascara sagrada. Life might be so. It did not move or touch him but it was something quick and neat. Print anything now. Silly season. He read on, seated calm above his own rising smell. Neat certainly. *Matcham often thinks of the masterstroke by which he won the laughing witch who now*. Begins and ends morally. *Hand in hand*. Smart. He glanced back through what he had read and, while feeling his water flow quietly, he envied kindly Mr Beaufoy who had written it and received payment of three pounds thirteen and six.

Might manage a sketch. By Mr and Mrs L.M. Bloom. Invent a story for some proverb. Which? Time I used to try jotting down on my cuff what she said dressing. Dislike dressing together. Nicked myself shaving. Biting her nether lip hooking the placket of her skirt. Timing her. 9.15. Did Roberts pay you yet? 9.20. What had Gretta Conroy on? 9.23. What possessed me to buy this comb? 9.24. I'm swelled after that cabbage. A speck of dust on the patent leather of her boot. Rubbing smartly in turn each welt against her stockinged calf. Morning after the bazaar dance when May's band played Ponchielli's dance of the hours. Explain that: morning hours, noon, then evening coming on, then night hours. Washing her teeth. That was the first night. Her head dancing. Her fansticks clicking. Is that Boylan well off? He has money. Why? I noticed he had a good rich smell off his breath dancing. No use humming then. Allude to it. Strange kind of music that last night. The mirror was in shadow.

She rubbed her handglass briskly on her woollen vest against her full wagging bub. Peering into it. Lines in her eyes. It wouldn't pan out somehow.

Evening hours, girls in grey gauze. Night hours then: black with daggers and eyemasks. Poetical idea: pink, then golden, then grey, then black. Still, true to life also. Day: then the night.

He tore away half the prize story sharply and wiped himself with it. Then he girded up his trousers, braced and buttoned himself. He pulled back the jerky shaky door of the jakes and came forth from the gloom into the air.

In the bright light, lightened and cooled in limb, he eyed carefully his black trousers: the ends, the knees, the houghs of the knees. What time is the funeral? Better find out in the paper.

A creak and a dark whirr in the air high up. The bells of George's Church. They tolled the hour, loud dark iron:

— *Heigho! Heigho!*
  Heigho! Heigho!
  Heigho! Heigho!

Quarter to. There again: the overtone following through the air. A third.

Poor Dignam!

By lorries along Sir John Rogerson's Quay Mr Bloom walked soberly, past Windmill Lane, Leask's the linseed crusher's, the postal telegraph office. Could have given that address too. And past the Sailors' Home. He turned from the morning noises of the quayside and walked through Lime Street. By Brady's Cottages a boy for the skins lolled, his bucket of offal linked, smoking a chewed fagbutt. A smaller girl with scars of eczema on her forehead eyed him, listlessly holding her battered caskhoop. Tell him if he smokes he won't grow. O, let him! His life isn't such a bed of roses. Waiting outside pubs to bring da home. Come home to ma, da. Slack hour: won't be many there. He crossed Townsend Street, passing the frowning face of Bethel. El, yes: house of: Aleph, Beth. And past Nichols' the undertaker's. At eleven it is. Time enough. Daresay Corny Kelleher bagged the job for O'Neill's. Singing with his eyes shut. Corny. *Met her once in the park. In the dark. What a lark.* Police tout. *Her name and address she then told with my tooraloom tooraloom tay.* O, surely he bagged it. Bury him cheap in a what-you-may-call-it. *With my tooraloom, tooraloom, tooraloom, tooraloom.*

In Westland Row he halted before the window of the Belfast and Oriental Tea Company and read the legends of lead-papered packets: choice blend, finest quality, family tea. Rather warm. Tea. Must get some from Tom Kernan. Couldn't ask him at a funeral, though. While his eyes still read blandly he took off his hat, quietly inhaling his hairoil, and sent his right hand with slow grace over his brow and hair. Very warm morning. Under their dropped lids his eyes found the tiny bow of the leather headband inside his high-grade ha. Just there. His right hand came down into the bowl of his hat. His fingers found quickly a card behind the headband and transferred it to his waistcoat pocket.

So warm. His right hand once more more slowly went over his brow and hair. Then he put on his hat again, relieved: and read again: choice blend, made of the finest Ceylon brands. The Far East. Lovely spot it must be: the garden of the world, big lazy leaves to float about on, cactuses, flowery meads, snaky lianas they call them. Wonder is it like that. Those Cingalese lolling about in the sun in *dolce far niente*, not doing a hand's turn all day. Sleep six months out of twelve. Too hot to quarrel. Influence of the climate. Lethargy. Flowers of idleness. The air feeds most. Azote. Hothouse in Botanic Gardens. Sensitive plants. Water lilies. Petals too tired to. Sleeping sickness in the air. Walk on roseleaves. Imagine trying to eat tripe and cowheel. Where was the chap I saw in that picture somewhere? Ah, yes, in the Dead Sea, floating on his back, reading a book with a parasol open. Couldn't sink if you tried: so thick with salt. Because the weight of the water, no, the weight of the body in the water is equal to the weight of the what? Or is it the volume is equal to the weight? It's a law something like that. Vance in High School cracking his fingerjoints, teaching. The college curriculum. Cracking curriculum. What is weight really when you say the weight? Thirty-two feet per second per second. Law of falling bodies: per second per second. They all fall to the ground. The earth. It's the force of gravity of the earth is the weight.

He turned away and sauntered across the road. How did she walk with her sausages? Like that, something. As he walked he took the folded *Freeman* from his side pocket, unfolded it, rolled it lengthwise in a baton and tapped it at each sauntering step against his trouserleg. Careless air: just drop in to see. Per second per second. Per second for every second it means. From the curbstone he darted a keen glance through the door of the post office. Too late box. Post here. No one. In.

He handed the card through the brass grill.

— Are there any letters for me? he asked.

While the postmistress searched a pigeonhole he gazed at the recruiting poster with soldiers of all arms on parade: and held the tip of his baton against his nostrils, smelling fresh printed ragpaper. No answer probably. Went too far last time.

The postmistress handed him back through the grill his card with a letter. He thanked her and glanced rapidly at the typed envelope.

Henry Flower Esq,
c/o P.O. Westland Row,
City.

Answered anyhow. He slipped card and letter into his side pocket, reviewing again the soldiers on parade. Where's old Tweedy's regiment? Castoff soldier. There: bearskin cap and hackle plume. No, he's a grenadier. Pointed cuffs. There he is: Royal Dublin Fusiliers. Redcoats. Too showy. That must be why the women go after them. Uniform. Easier to enlist and drill. Maud Gonne's letter about taking them off O'Connell

Street at night: disgrace to our Irish capital. Griffith's paper is on the same tack now: an army rotten with venereal disease: overseas or half-seas over empire. Half baked they look: hypnotised like. Eyes front! Mark time! Table: able. Bed: ed. The King's Own. Never see him dressed up as a fireman or a bobby. A mason, yes.

He strolled out of the post office and turned to the right. Talk: as if that would mend matters. His hand went into his pocket and a forefinger felt its way under the flap of the envelope, ripping it open in jerks. Women will pay a lot of heed, I don't think. His fingers drew forth the letter and crumpled the envelope in his pocket. Something pinned on: photo perhaps. Hair? No.

M'Coy. Get rid of him quickly. Take me out of my way. Hate company when you.

— Hello, Bloom. Where are you off to?

— Hello, M'Coy. Nowhere in particular.

— How's the body?

— Fine. How are you?

— Just keeping alive, M'Coy said.

His eyes on the black tie and clothes, he asked with low respect:

— Is there any . . . no trouble I hope? I see you're . . .

— O no, Mr Bloom said. Poor Dignam, you know. The funeral is today.

— To be sure, poor fellow. So it is. What time?

A photo it isn't. A badge maybe.

— E . . . eleven, Mr Bloom answered.

— I must try to get out there, M'Coy said. Eleven, is it? I only heard it last night. Who was telling me? Holohan. You know Hoppy?

— I know.

Mr Bloom gazed across the road at the outsider drawn up before the door of the Grosvenor. The porter hoisted the valise up on the well. She stood still, waiting, while the man, husband, brother, like her, searched his pockets for change. Stylish kind of coat with that roll collar, warm for a day like this, looks like blanket cloth. Careless stand of her with her hands in those patch pockets. Like that haughty creature at the polo match. Women all for caste till you touch the spot. Handsome is and handsome does. Reserved about to yield. The Honourable Mrs, and Brutus is an honourable man. Possess her once take the starch out of her.

— I was with Bob Doran, he's on one of his periodical bends, and what do you call him Bantam Lyons. Just down there in Conway's we were.

Doran, Lyons, in Conway's. She raised a gloved hand to her hair.

— In came Hoppy. Having a wet.

Drawing back his head and gazing far from beneath his vailed eyelids he saw the bright fawn skin shine in the glare, the braided drums. Clearly I can see today. Moisture about gives long sight perhaps. Talking of one thing or another. Lady's hand. Which side will she get up?

— And he said: *Sad thing about our poor friend Paddy! What Paddy?* I said. *Poor little Paddy Dignam,* he said.

Off to the country: Broadstone probably. High brown boots with laces dangling. Well-turned foot. What is he foostering over that change for? Sees me looking. Eye out for other fellow always. Good fallback. Two strings to her bow.

— *Why?* I said. *What's wrong with him?* I said.

Proud: rich: silk stockings.

— Yes, Mr Bloom said.

He moved a little to the side of M'Coy's talking head. Getting up in a minute.

— *What's wrong with him?* he said. *He's dead,* he said. And, faith, he filled up. *Is it Paddy Dignam?* I said. I couldn't believe it when I heard it. I was with him no later than Friday last or Thursday was it in the Arch. *Yes,* he said. *He's gone. He died on Monday, poor fellow.*

Watch! Watch! Silk flash rich stockings white. Watch!

A heavy tramcar honking its gong slewed between.

Lost it. Curse your noisy pugnose. Feels locked out of it. Paradise and the peri. Always happening like that. The very moment. Girl in Eustace Street hallway Monday was it settling her garter. Her friend covering the display of. *Esprit de corps.* Well, what are you gaping at?

— Yes, yes, Mr Bloom said after a dull sigh. Another gone.

— One of the best, M'Coy said.

The tram passed. They drove off towards the Loop Line bridge, her rich gloved hand on the steel grip. Flicker, flicker: the laceflare of her hat in the sun: flicker, flick.

— Wife well, I suppose? M'Coy's changed voice said.

— O yes, Mr Bloom said. Tiptop, thanks.

He unrolled the newspaper baton and read idly:

> *What is home without*
> *Plumtree's Potted Meat?*
> *Incomplete.*
> *With it an abode of bliss.*

71

— My missus has just got an engagement. At least it's not settled yet.

Valise tack again. By the way no harm. I'm off that, thanks.

Mr Bloom turned his large-lidded eyes with unhasty friendliness.

— My wife too, he said. She's going to sing at a swagger affair in the Ulster Hall, Belfast, on the twenty-fifth.

— That so? M'Coy said. Glad to hear that, old man. Who's getting it up?

Mrs Marion Bloom. Not up yet. Queen was in her bedroom eating bread and. No book. Blackened court cards laid along her thigh by sevens. Dark lady and fair man. Letter. Cat furry black ball. Torn strip of envelope.

> *Love's*
> *Old*
> *Sweet*
> *Song.*
> *Comes lo-ove's old . . .*

— It's a kind of a tour, don't you see? Mr Bloom said thoughtfully. *Sweeeet song.* There's a committee formed. Part shares and part profits.

M'Coy nodded, picking at his moustache stubble.

— O well, he said. That's good news.

He moved to go.

— Well, glad to see you looking fit, he said. Meet you knocking around.

— Yes, Mr Bloom said.

— Tell you what, M'Coy said. You might put down my name at the funeral, will you? I'd like to go but I mightn't be able, you see. There's a drowning case at Sandycove may turn up and then the coroner and myself would have to go down if the body is found. You just shove in my name if I'm not there, will you?

— I'll do that, Mr Bloom said, moving to get off. That'll be all right.

— Right, M'Coy said brightly. Thanks, old man. I'd go if I possibly could. Well, tolloll. Just C. P. M'Coy will do.

— That will be done, Mr Bloom answered firmly.

Didn't catch me napping, that wheeze. The quick touch. Soft mark. I'd like my job. Valise I have a particular fancy for. Leather. Capped corners, rivetted edges, double action lever lock. Bob Cowley lent him his for the Wicklow Regatta concert last year and never heard tidings of it from that good day to this.

Mr Bloom, strolling towards Brunswick Street, smiled. My missus has just got an. Reedy freckled soprano. Cheeseparing nose. Nice enough in its way: for a little ballad. No guts in it. You and me, don't you know? In the same boat. Softsoaping. Give you the needle that would. Can't he hear the difference? Think he's that way inclined a bit. Against my grain somehow. Thought that Belfast would fetch him. I hope that smallpox up there doesn't get worse. Suppose she wouldn't let herself be vaccinated again. Your wife and my wife.

Wonder is he pimping after me.

Mr Bloom stood at the corner, his eyes wandering over the multi-coloured hoardings. Cantrell and Cochrane's Ginger Ale (Aromatic). Clery's Summer Sale. No, he's going on straight. Hello. *Leah* tonight: Mrs Bandmann-Palmer. Like to see her in that again. Hamlet she played last night. Male impersonator. Perhaps he was a woman. Why Ophelia committed suicide. Poor papa! How he used to talk about Kate Bateman in that! Outside the Adelphi in London waiting all the afternoon to get in. Year before I was born that was: sixty-five. And Ristori in Vienna. What is this the right name is? By Mosenthal it is. *Rachel*, is it? No. The scene he was always talking about where the old blind Abraham recognises the voice and puts his fingers on his face.

Nathan's voice! His son's voice! I hear the voice of Nathan who left his father to die of grief and misery in my arms, who left the house of his father and left the God of his father.

Every word is so deep, Leopold.

Poor papa! Poor man! I'm glad I didn't go into the room to look at his face. That day! O, dear! O, dear! Ffoo! Well, perhaps it was the best for him.

Mr Bloom went round the corner and passed the drooping nags of the hazard. No use thinking of it any more. Nosebag time. Wish I hadn't met that M'Coy fellow.

He came nearer and heard a crunching of gilded oats, the gently champing teeth. Their full buck eyes regarded him as he went by, amid the sweet oaten reek of horsepiss. Their El Dorado. Poor jugginses! Damn all they know or care about anything with their long noses stuck in nosebags. Too full for words. Still, they get their feed all right and their doss. Gelded too: a stump of black gutta-percha wagging limp between their haunches. Might be happy all the same that way. Good poor brutes they look. Still, their neigh can be very irritating.

He drew the letter from his pocket and folded it into the newspaper he carried. Might just walk into her here. The lane is safer.

He passed the cabman's shelter. Curious the life of drifting cabbies: all

weathers, all places, time or setdown, no will of their own. *Voglio e non.*
Like to give them an odd cigarette. Sociable. Shout a few flying syllables
as they pass. He hummed:

— *Là ci darem la mano*
  La la lala la la.

He turned into Cumberland Street and, going on some paces, halted in
the lee of the station wall. No one. Meade's timberyard. Piled balks. Ruins
and tenements. With careful tread he passed over a hopscotch court with
its forgotten pickeystone. Not a sinner. Near the timberyard a squatted
child at marbles, alone, shooting the taw with a cunnythumb. A wise
tabby, a blinking sphinx, watched from her warm sill. Pity to disturb
them. Mohammed cut a piece out of his mantle not to wake her. Open it.
And once I played marbles when I went to that old dame's school. She
liked mignonette. Mrs Ellis's. And Mr? He opened the letter within the
newspaper.

A flower. I think it's a. A yellow flower with flattened petals. Not
annoyed then? What does she say?

Dear Henry

   I got your last letter to me and thank you very much for it. I am sorry
you did not like my last letter. Why did you enclose the stamps? I am
awfully angry with you. I do wish I could punish you for that. I called
you naughty boy because I do not like that other world. Please tell me
what is the real meaning of that word. Are you not happy in your home,
you poor little naughty boy? I do wish I could do something for you.
Please tell me what you think of poor me. I often think of the beautiful
name you have. Dear Henry, when will we meet? I think of you so often
you have no idea. I have never felt myself so much drawn to a man as
you. I feel so bad about. Please write me a long letter and tell me more.
Remember if you do not I will punish you. So now you know what I will
do to you, you naughty boy, if you do not wrote. O how I long to meet
you. Henry dear, do not deny my request before my patience are
exhausted. Then I will tell you all. Goodbye now, naughty darling. I
have such a bad headache today. and write *by return* to your longing

   Martha

P.S. Do tell me what kind of perfume does your wife use. I want to
know.

   X X X X

He tore the flower gravely from its pinhold, smelt its almost no smell
and placed it in his heart pocket. Language of flowers. They like it because

no one can hear. Or a poison bouquet to strike him down. Then, walking slowly forward, he read the letter again, murmuring here and there a word. Angry tulips with you darling manflower punish your cactus if you don't please poor forget-me-not how I long violets to dear roses when we soon anemone meet all naughty nightstalk wife Martha's perfume. Having read it all he took it from the newspaper and put it back in his side pocket.

Weak joy opened his lips. Changed since the first letter. Wonder did she wrote it herself. Doing the indignant: a girl of good family like me, respectable character. Could meet one Sunday after the rosary. Thank you: not having any. Usual love scrimmage. Then running round corners. Bad as a row with Molly. Cigar has a cooling effect. Narcotic. Go further next time. Naughty boy: punish: afraid of words, of course. Brutal, why not? Try it anyhow. A bit at a time.

Fingering still the letter in his pocket he drew the pin out of it. Common pin, eh? He threw it on the road. Out of her clothes somewhere: pinned together. Queer the number of pins they always have. No roses without thorns.

Flat Dublin voices bawled in his head. Those two sluts that night in the Coombe, linked together in the rain.

> O, Mairy lost the pin of her drawers.
> She didn't know what to do
> To keep it up,
> To keep it up.

It? Them. Such a bad headache. Has her roses probably. Or sitting all day typing. Eyefocus bad for stomach nerves. What perfume does your wife use? Now could you make out a thing like that?

> To keep it up.

Martha, Mary. I saw that picture somewhere I forget now. Old master or faked for money. He is sitting in their house, talking. Mysterious. Also, the two sluts in the Coombe would listen.

> To keep it up.

Nice kind of evening feeling. No more wandering about. Just loll there: quiet dusk: let everything rip. Forget. Tell about places you have been, strange customs. The other one, jar on her head, was getting the supper: fruit, olives, lovely cool water out of the well, stone cold like the hole in the wall at Ashtown. Must carry a paper goblet next time I go to the trotting matches. She listens with big dark soft eyes. Tell her: more and more: all. Then a sigh: silence. Long long long rest.

Going under the railway arch he took out the envelope, tore it swiftly in shreds and scattered them towards the road. The shreds fluttered away, sank in the dank air: a white flutter, then all sank.

Henry Flower. You could tear up a cheque for a hundred pounds in the same way. Simple bit of paper. Lord Iveagh once cashed a seven-figure cheque for a million in the Bank of Ireland. Shows you the money to be made out of porter. Still, the other brother Lord Ardilaun has to change his shirt four times a day, they say. Skin breeds lice or vermin. A million pounds, wait a moment. Twopence a pint, fourpence a quart, eightpence a gallon of porter, no, one and fourpence a gallon of porter. One and four into twenty: fifteen about. Yes, exactly. Fifteen millions of barrels of porter.

What am I saying, barrels? Gallons. About a million barrels all the same.

An incoming train clanked heavily above his head, coach after coach. Barrels bumped in his head: dull porter slopped and churned inside. The bungholes sprang open and a huge dull flood leaked out, flowing together, winding through mudflats all over the level land, a lazy pooling swirl of liquor bearing along wide-leaved flowers of its froth.

He had reached the open back door of All Hallows. Stepping into the porch he doffed his hat, took the card from his pocket and tucked it again behind the leather headband. Damn it. I might have tried to work M'Coy for a pass to Mullingar.

Same notice on the door. Sermon by the Very Reverend John Conmee S.J. on Saint Peter Claver S.J. and the African Mission. Prayers for the conversion of Gladstone they had too when he was almost unconscious. The Protestants are the same. Convert Dr William J. Walsh D.D. to the true religion. Save China's millions. Wonder how they explain it to the heathen Chinee. Prefer an ounce of opium. Celestials. Rank heresy for them. Buddha their god lying on his side in the museum. Taking it easy with hand under his cheek. Joss sticks burning. Not like Ecce Homo. Crown of thorns and cross. Clever idea Saint Patrick the shamrock. Chopsticks? Conmee: Martin Cunningham knows him: distinguished looking. Sorry I didn't work him about getting Molly into the choir instead of that Father Farley who looked a fool but wasn't. They're taught that. He's not going out in bluey specs with the sweat rolling off him to baptise blacks, is he? The glasses would take their fancy, flashing. Like to see them sitting round in a ring with blub lips, entranced, listening. Still life. Lap it up like milk, I suppose.

The cold smell of sacred stone called him. He trod the worn steps, pushed the swingdoor and entered softly by the rear.

Something going on: some sodality. Pity so empty. Nice discreet place to be next some girl. Who is my neighbour? Jammed by the hour to slow music. That woman at midnight mass. Seventh heaven. Women knelt in the benches with crimson halters round their necks, heads bowed. A batch knelt at the altar rails. The priest went along by them, murmuring, holding the thing in his hands. He stopped at each, took out a communion, shook a drop or two (are they in water?) off it and put it neatly into her mouth. Her hat and head sank. Then the next one. Her hat sank at once. Then the next one: a small old woman. The priest bent down to put it into her mouth, murmuring all the time. Latin. The next one. Shut your eyes and open your mouth. What? *Corpus.* Body. Corpse. Good idea the Latin. Stupefies them first. Hospice for the dying. They don't seem to chew it: only swallow it down. Rum idea: eating bits of a corpse. Why the cannibals cotton to it.

He stood aside watching their blind masks pass down the aisle, one by one, and seek their places. He approached a bench and seated himself in its corner, nursing his hat and newspaper. These pots we have to wear. We ought to have hats modelled on our heads. They were about him here and there with heads still bowed in their crimson halters, waiting for it to melt in their stomachs. Something like those matzoth: it's that sort of bread: unleavened shewbread. Look at them. Now I bet it makes them feel happy. Lollipop. It does. Yes, bread of angels it's called. There's a big idea behind it, kind of kingdom of God is within you feel. First communicants. Hokypoky penny a lump. Then feel all like one family party, same in the theatre, all in the same swim. They do. I'm sure of that. Not so lonely. In our confraternity. Then come out a bit spreeish. Let off steam. Thing is if you really believe in it. Lourdes cure, waters of oblivion, and the Knock apparition, statues bleeding. Old fellow asleep near that confession box. Hence those snores. Blind faith. Safe in the arms of kingdom come. Lulls all pain. Wake this time next year.

He saw the priest stow the communion cup away, well in, and kneel an instant before it, showing a large grey bootsole from under the lace affair he had on. Suppose he lost the pin of his. He wouldn't know what to do to. Bald spot behind. Letters on his back: I.N.R.I? No: I.H.S. Molly told me one time I asked her. I have sinned: or no: I have suffered, it is. And the other one? Iron nails ran in.

Meet one Sunday after the rosary. Do not deny my request. Turn up with a veil and black bag. Dusk and the light behind her. She might be here with a ribbon round her neck and do the other thing all the same on the sly. Their character. That fellow that turned Queen's evidence on the Invincibles he used to receive the, Carey was his name, the communion every morning. This very church. Peter Carey. No, Peter Claver I am thinking of. Denis Carey. And just imagine that. Wife and six children at home. And plotting that murder all the time. Those crawthumpers, now that's a good name for them, there's always something shifty-looking about them. They're not straight men of business either. O no, she's not here: the flower: no, no. By the way, did I tear up that envelope? Yes: under the bridge.

The priest was rinsing out the chalice: then he tossed off the dregs smartly. Wine. Makes it more aristocratic than for example if he drank what they are used to, Guinness's porter or some temperance beverage, Wheatley's Dublin hop bitters or Cantrell and Cochrane's ginger ale (aromatic). Doesn't give them any of it: shew wine: only the other. Cold comfort. Pious fraud but quite right: otherwise they'd have one old boozer worse than another coming along cadging for a drink. Queer the whole atmosphere of the. Quite right. Perfectly right that is.

Mr Bloom looked back towards the choir. Not going to be any music. Pity. Who has the organ here I wonder. Old Glynn, he knew how to make that instrument talk, the *vibrato*: fifty pounds a year they say he had in Gardiner Street. Molly was in fine voice that day, the *Stabat Mater* of Rossini. Father Bernard Vaughan's sermon first. Christ or Pilate? Christ, but don't keep us all night over it. Music they wanted. Footdrill stopped. Could hear a pin drop. I told her to pitch her voice against that corner. I could feel the thrill in the air, the full, the people looking up:

Quis est homo.

Some of that old sacred music is splendid. Mercadante: *Seven Last Words*. Mozart's *Twelfth Mass*: the Gloria in that. Those old popes were keen on music, on art and statues and pictures of all kinds. Palestrina for example too. They had a gay old time while it lasted. Healthy too, chanting, regular hours, then brew liqueurs. Benedictine. Green Chartreuse. Still, having eunuchs in their choir that was coming it a bit thick. What kind of voice is it? Must be curious to hear after their own strong basses. Connoisseurs. Suppose they wouldn't feel anything after. Kind of a placid. No worry. Fall into flesh, don't they? Gluttons, tall, long legs. Who knows? Eunuch. One way out of it.

He saw the priest bend down and kiss the altar and then face about and bless all the people. All crossed themselves and stood up. Mr Bloom glanced about him and then stood up, looking over the risen hats. Stand up at the gospel of course. Then all settled down on their knees again and he sat back quietly in his bench. The priest came down from the altar, holding the thing out from him, and he and the massboy answered each other in Latin. Then the priest knelt down and began to read off a card:

— O God, our refuge and our strength . . .

Mr Bloom put his face forward to catch the words. English. Throw them the bone. I remember slightly. How long since your last mass? Glorious and immaculate Virgin. Joseph her spouse. Peter and Paul. More interesting if you understood what it was all about. Wonderful organisation certainly, goes like clockwork. Confession. Everyone wants to. Then I will tell you all. Penance. Punish me, please. Great weapon in their hands. More than doctor or solicitor. Woman dying to. And I schschschschschsch. And did you chachachachacha? And why did you? Look down at her ring to find an excuse. Whispering gallery. Walls have ears. Husband learn to his surprise. God's little joke. Then out she comes. Repentance skin-deep. Lovely shame. Pray at an altar. Hail Mary and Holy Mary. Flowers, incense, candles melting. Hide her blushes. Salvation Army blatant imitation. Reformed prostitute will address the meeting. How I found the Lord. Squareheaded chaps those must be in Rome: they work the whole show. And don't they rake in the money too! Bequests also: to the P.P. for the time being in his absolute discretion. Masses for the repose of my soul to be said publicly with open doors. Monasteries and convents. The priest in that Fermanagh will case in the witness-box. No browbeating him. He had his answer pat for everything. Liberty and exaltation of our holy mother the Church. The doctors of the Church: they mapped out the whole theology of it.

The priest prayed:

— Blessed Michael, archangel, defend us in the hour of conflict. Be our safeguard against the wickedness and snares of the devil (may God restrain him, we humbly pray): and do thou, O prince of the heavenly host, by the power of God thrust Satan down to hell and with him those other wicked spirits who wander through the world for the ruin of souls.

The priest and the massboy stood up and walked off. All over. The women remained behind: thanksgiving.

Better be shoving along. Brother Buzz. Come around with the plate perhaps. Pay your Easter duty.

He stood up. Hello. Were those two buttons of my waistcoat open all the time? Women enjoy it. Never tell you. But we. Excuse, miss, there's a (whh!) just a (whh!) fluff. Annoyed if you don't. Why didn't you tell me before? Or their skirt behind, placket unhooked. Glimpses of the moon. Still, like you better untidy. Good job it wasn't farther south. He passed, discreetly buttoning, down the aisle and out through the main door into the light. He stood a moment unseeing by the cold black marble bowl while before him and behind two worshippers dipped furtive hands in the low tide of holy water. Trams: a car of Prescott's dyeworks: a widow in her weeds. Notice because I'm in mourning myself. He covered himself. How goes the time? Quarter past. Time enough yet. Better get that lotion made up. Where is this? Ah yes, the last time, Sweny's in Lincoln Place. Chemists rarely move. Their green and gold beaconjars too heavy to stir. Hamilton Long's, founded in the year of the flood. Huguenot churchyard near there. Visit some day.

He walked southward along Westland Row. But the recipe is in the other trousers. O, and I forgot that latchkey too. Bore this funeral affair. O well, poor fellow, it's not his fault. When was it I got it made up last? Wait. I changed a sovereign I remember. First of the month it must have been or the second. O, he can look it up in the prescriptions book.

The chemist turned back page after page. Sandy shrivelled smell he seems to have. Shrunken skull. And old. Quest for the philosophers' stone. The alchemists. Drugs age you after mental excitement. Lethargy then. Why? Reaction. A lifetime in a night. Gradually changes your character. Living all the day among herbs, ointments, disinfectants. All his alabaster lilypots. Mortar and pestle. *Aq. dest. Fol. laur. The. virid.* Smell almost cure you like the dentist's doorbell. Doctor Whack. He ought to physic himself a bit. Electuary or emulsion. The first fellow that picked an herb to cure himself had a bit of pluck. Simples. Want to be careful. Enough stuff here to chloroform you. Test: turns blue litmus paper red. Chloroform. Overdose of laudanum. Sleeping draughts. Love philtres. Paragoric poppy syrup bad for cough. Clogs the pores or the phlegm. Poisons the only cures. Remedy where you least expect it. Clever of nature.

— About a fortnight ago, sir?

— Yes, Mr Bloom said.

He waited by the counter, inhaling the keen reek of drugs, the dusty dry smell of sponges and loofahs. Lot of time taken up telling your aches and pains.

— Sweet almond oil and tincture of benzoin, Mr Bloom said, and then orangeflower water...

It certainly did make her skin so delicate white like wax.

— And white wax also, he said.

Brings out the darkness of her eyes. Looking at me, the sheet up to her eyes, Spanish, smelling herself, when I was fixing the links in my cuffs. Those homely recipes are often the best: strawberries for the teeth: nettles and rainwater: oatmeal they say steeped in buttermilk. Skin food. One of the old queen's sons, duke of Albany was it, had only one skin. Leopold, yes. Three we have. Warts, bunions and pimples to make it worse. But you want a perfume too. What perfume does your? *Peau d'Espagne.* That orangeflower water is so fresh. Pure curd soap. Nice smell these soaps have. Time to get a bath round the corner. Hammam. Turkish. Massage. Dirt gets rolled up in your navel. Nicer if a nice girl did it. Also I think I. Yes I. Do it in the bath. Curious longing I. Water to water. Combine business with pleasure. Pity no time for massage. Feel fresh then all day. Funeral be rather glum.

— Yes, sir, the chemist said. That was two and nine. Have you brought a bottle?

— No, Mr Bloom said. Make it up, please. I'll call later in the day and I'll take one of those soaps. How much are they?

— Fourpence, sir.

Mr Bloom raised a cake to his nostrils. Sweet lemony wax.

— I'll take this one, he said. That makes three and a penny.

— Yes, sir, the chemist said. You can pay all together, sir, when you come back.

— Good, Mr Bloom said.

He strolled out of the shop, the newspaper baton under his armpit, the coolwrappered soap in his left hand.

At his armpit Bantam Lyons's voice and hand said:

— Hello, Bloom, what's the best news? Is that today's? Show us a minute.

Shaved off his moustache again, by Jove! Long cold upper lip. To look younger. He does look balmy. Younger than I am.

Bantam Lyons's yellow black-nailed fingers unrolled the baton. Wants a wash too. Take off the rough dirt. Good morning, have you used Pears' soap? Dandruff on his shoulders. Scalp wants oiling.

— I want to see about that French horse that's running today, Bantam Lyons said. Where the bugger is it?

He rustled the pleated pages, jerking his chin on his high collar. Barber's itch. Tight collar he'll lose his hair. Better leave him the paper and get shut of him.

— You can keep it, Mr Bloom said.

— Ascot. Gold Cup. Wait, Bantam Lyons muttered. Half a mo. *Maximum the Second.*

— I was just going to throw it away, Mr Bloom said.

Bantam Lyons raised his eyes suddenly and leered weakly.

— What's that? his sharp voice said.

— I say you can keep it, Mr Bloom answered. I was going to throw it away that moment.

Bantam Lyons doubted an instant, leering: then thrust the outspread sheets back on Mr Bloom's arms.

— I'll risk it, he said. Here, thanks.

He sped off towards Conway's corner. God speed, scut.

Mr Bloom folded the sheets again to a neat square and lodged the soap in it, smiling. Silly lips of that chap. Betting. Regular hotbed of it lately. Messenger boys stealing to put on sixpence. Raffle for large tender turkey. Your Christmas dinner for threepence. Jack Fleming embezzling to gamble then smuggled off to America. Keeps a hotel now. They never come back. Fleshpots of Egypt.

He walked cheerfully towards the mosque of the baths. Remind you of a mosque, red-baked bricks, the minarets. College sports today I see. He eyed the horseshoe poster over the gate of College Park: cyclist doubled up like a cod in a pot. Damn bad ad. Now if they had made it round like a wheel. Then the spokes: sports, sports, sports: and the hub big: College. Something to catch the eye.

There's Hornblower standing at the porter's lodge. Keep him on hand: might take a turn in there on the nod. How do you do, Mr Hornblower? How do you do, sir?

Heavenly weather really. If life was always like that. Cricket weather. Sit around under sunshades. Over after over. Out. They can't play it here. Duck for six wickets. Still, Captain Buller broke a window in the Kildare Street Club with a slog to square leg. Donnybrook Fair more in their line. And the skulls we were a-cracking when M'Carthy took the floor. Heat wave. Won't last. Always passing, the stream of life, which in the stream of life we trace is dearer thaaan them all.

Enjoy a bath now: clean trough of water, cool enamel, the gentle tepid stream. This is my body.

He foresaw his pale body reclined in it at full, naked, in a womb of warmth, oiled by scented melting soap, softly laved. He saw his trunk and limbs riprippled over and sustained, buoyed lightly upward, lemon yellow: his navel, bud of flesh: and saw the dark tangled curls of his bush floating, floating hair of the stream around the limp father of thousands, a languid floating flower.

Martin Cunningham, first, poked his silk-hatted head into the creaking carriage and, entering deftly, seated himself. Mr Power stepped in after him, curving his height with care.

— Come on, Simon.

— After you, Mr Bloom said.

Mr Dedalus covered himself quickly and got in, saying:

— Yes, yes.

— Are we all here now? Martin Cunningham asked. Come along, Bloom.

Mr Bloom entered and sat in the vacant place. He pulled the door to after him and slammed it twice till it shut tight. He passed an arm through the armstrap and looked seriously from the open carriage window at the lowered blinds of the avenue. One dragged aside: an old woman peeping. Nose whiteflattened against the pane. Thanking her stars she was passed over. Extraordinary the interest they take in a corpse. Glad to see us go we give them such trouble coming. Job seems to suit them. Huggermugger in corners. Slop about in slipperslappers for fear he'd wake. Then getting it ready. Laying it out. Molly and Mrs Fleming making the bed. Pull it more to your side. Our winding sheet. Never know who will touch you dead. Wash and shampoo. I believe they clip the nails and the hair. Keep a bit in an envelope. Grows all the same after. Unclean job.

All waited. Nothing was said. Stowing in the wreaths probably. I am sitting on something hard. Ah, that soap in my hip pocket. Better shift it out of that. Wait for an opportunity.

All waited. Then wheels were heard from in front, turning: then nearer: then horses' hoofs. A jolt. Their carriage began to move, creaking and swaying. Other hoofs and creaking wheels started behind. The lowered blinds of the avenue passed and number nine with its craped knocker, door ajar. At walking pace.

They waited still, their knees jogging, till they had turned and were passing along the tramtracks. Tritonville Road. Quicker. The wheels rattled rolling over the cobbled causeway and the crazy glasses shook rattling in the doorframes.

— What way is he taking us? Mr Power asked through both windows.

— Irishtown, Martin Cunningham said. Ringsend. Brunswick Street.

Mr Dedalus nodded, looking out.

— That's a fine old custom, he said. I'm glad to see it has not died out.

All watched awhile through their windows caps and hats lifted by passers. Respect. The carriage swerved from the tramtrack to the smoother road past Watery Lane. Mr Bloom at gaze saw a lithe young man, clad in mourning, a wide hat.

— There's a friend of yours gone by, Dedalus, he said.

— Who is that?

— Your son and heir.

— Where is he? Mr Dedalus said, stretching over.

The carriage, passing the open drains and mounds of ripped-up roadway before the tenement houses, lurched round the corner and, swerving back to the tramtrack, rolled on noisily with chattering wheels. Mr Dedalus fell back, saying:

— Was that Mulligan cad with him? His *fidus Achates*!

— No, Mr Bloom said. He was alone.

— Down with his aunt Sally, I suppose, Mr Dedalus said, and the Goulding faction, the drunken little costdrawer and Crissie, papa's little lump of dung, the wise child that knows her own father.

Mr Bloom smiled joylessly on Ringsend Road. Wallace Bros. The bottleworks. Dodder Bridge.

Richie Goulding and the legal bag. Goulding, Collis and Ward he calls the firm. His jokes are getting a bit damp. Great card he was. Waltzing in Stamer Street with Ignatius Gallaher on a Sunday morning, the landlady's two hats pinned on his head. Out on the rampage all night. Beginning to tell on him now: that backache of his, I fear. Wife ironing his back. Thinks he'll cure it with pills. All breadcrumbs they are. About six hundred per cent profit.

— He's in with a lowdown crowd, Mr Dedalus snarled. That Mulligan is a contaminated bloody double-dyed ruffian by all accounts. His name stinks all over Dublin. But with the help of God and His blessed mother I'll make it my business to write a letter one of those days to his mother or his aunt or whatever she is that will open her eye as wide as a gate. I'll tickle his catastrophe, believe you me.

He cried above the clatter of the wheels:

— I won't have her bastard of a nephew ruin my son. A counterjumper's son. Selling tapes in my cousin's, Peter Paul M'Swiney's. Not likely.

He ceased. Mr Bloom glanced from his angry moustache to Mr Power's mild face and Martin Cunningham's eyes and beard, gravely shaking. Noisy self-willed man. Full of his son. He is right. Something to hand on. If little Rudy had lived. See him grow up. Hear his voice in the house. Walking beside Molly in an Eton suit. My son. Me in his eyes. Strange feeling it would be. From me. Just a chance. Must have been that morning in Raymond Terrace she was at the window watching the two dogs at it by the wall of the cease-to-do-evil. And the sergeant grinning up. She had that cream gown on with the rip she never stitched. Give us a touch, Poldy. God, I'm dying for it. How life begins.

Got big then. Had to refuse the Greystones concert. My son inside her. I could have helped him on in life. I could. Make him independent. Learn German too.

— Are we late? Mr Power asked.

— Ten minutes, Martin Cunningham said, looking at his watch.

Molly. Milly. Same thing watered down. Her tomboy oaths. O jumping Jupiter! Ye gods and little fishes! Still, she's a dear girl. Soon be a woman. Mullingar. Dearest Papli. Young student. Yes, yes: a woman too. Life, life.

The carriage heeled over and back, their four trunks swaying.

— Corny might have given us a more commodious yoke, Mr Power said.

— He might, Mr Dedalus said, if he hadn't that squint troubling him. Do you follow me?

He closed his left eye. Martin Cunningham began to brush away crustcrumbs from under his thighs.

— What is this, he said, in the name of God? Crumbs?

— Someone seems to have been making a picnic party here lately, Mr Power said.

All raised their thighs and eyed with disfavour the mildewed buttonless leather of the seats. Mr Dedalus, twisting his nose, frowned downward and said:

— Unless I'm greatly mistaken ... What do you think, Martin?

— It struck me too, Martin Cunningham said.

Mr Bloom set his thigh down. Glad I took that bath. Feel my feet quite clean. But I wish Mrs Fleming had darned these socks better.

Mr Dedalus sighed resignedly.

— After all, he said, it's the most natural thing in the world.

— Did Tom Kernan turn up? Martin Cunningham asked, twirling the peak of his beard gently.

— Yes, Mr Bloom answered. He's behind with Ned Lambert and Hynes.

— And Corny Kelleher himself? Mr Power asked.

— At the cemetery, Martin Cunningham said.

— I met M'Coy this morning, Mr Bloom said. He said he'd try to come.

The carriage halted short.

— What's wrong?

— We're stopped.

— Where are we?

Mr Bloom put his head out of the window.

— The Grand Canal, he said.

Gasworks. Whooping cough they say it cures. Good job Milly never got it. Poor children! Doubles them up black and blue in convulsions. Shame really. Got off lightly with illnesses compared. Only measles. Flaxseed tea. Scarlatina, influenza epidemics. Canvassing for death. Don't miss this chance. Dogs' Home over there. Poor old Athos! Be good to Athos, Leopold, is my last wish. Thy will be done. We obey them in the grave. A dying scrawl. He took it to heart, pined away. Quiet brute. Old men's dogs usually are.

A raindrop spat on his hat. He drew back and saw an instant of shower spray dots over the grey flags. Apart. Curious. Like through a colander. I thought it would. My boots were creaking, I remember now.

— The weather is changing, he said quietly.

— A pity it did not keep up fine, Martin Cunningham said.

— Wanted for the country, Mr Power said. There's the sun again coming out.

Mr Dedalus, peering through his glasses towards the veiled sun, hurled a mute curse at the sky.

— It's as uncertain as a child's bottom, he said.

— We're off again.

The carriage turned again its stiff wheels and their trunks swayed gently. Martin Cunningham twirled more quickly the peak of his beard.

— Tom Kernan was immense last night, he said. And Paddy Leonard taking him off to his face.

— O, draw him out, Martin, Mr Power said eagerly. Wait till you hear him, Simon, on Ben Dollard's singing of *The Croppy Boy*.

— Immense, Martin Cunningham said pompously. *His singing of that simple ballad, Martin, is the most trenchant rendering I ever heard in the whole course of my experience.*

— *Trenchant*, Mr Power said laughing. He's dead nuts on that. And the *retrospective arrangement.*

— Did you read Dan Dawson's speech? Martin Cunningham asked.

— I did not then, Mr Dedalus said. Where is it?

— In the paper this morning.

Mr Bloom took the paper from his inside pocket. That book I must change for her.

— No, no, Mr Dedalus said quickly. Later on, please.

Mr Bloom's glance travelled down the edge of the paper, scanning the deaths. Callan, Coleman, Dignam, Fawcett, Lowry, Naumann, Peake. What Peake is that? Is it the chap was in Crosbie and Alleyne's? No. Sexton, Urbright. Inked characters fast fading on the frayed breaking paper. Thanks to the Little Flower. Sadly missed. To the inexpressible grief of his. Aged 88 after a long and tedious illness. Month's mind: Quinlan. On whose soul Sweet Jesus have mercy.

> It is now a month since dear Henry fled
> To his home up above in the sky
> While his family weeps and mourns his loss
> Hoping some day to meet him on high.

I tore up the envelope? Yes. Where did I put her letter after I read it in the bath? He patted his waistcoat pocket. There all right. Dear Henry fled. Before my patience are exhausted.

National School. Meade's yard. The hazard. Only two there now. Nodding. Full as a tick. Too much bone in their skulls. The other trotting round with a fare. An hour ago I was passing there. The jarvies raised their hats.

A pointsman's back straightened itself upright suddenly against a tramway standard by Mr Bloom's window. Couldn't they invent something automatic so that the wheel itself, much handier? Well, but that fellow would lose his job then? Well, but then another fellow would get a job making the new invention.

Antient Concert Rooms. Nothing on there. A man in a buff suit with a crape armlet. Not much grief there. Quarter mourning. People-in-law perhaps.

They went past the bleak pulpit of Saint Mark's, under the railway bridge, past the Queen's Theatre: in silence. Hoardings. Eugene Stratton. Mrs Bandmann-Palmer. Could I go to see *Leah* tonight, I wonder. I said I. Or the *Lily of Killarney*? Elster-Grime Opera Company. Big powerful change. Wet bright bills for next week. *Fun on the Bristol*. Martin Cunningham could work a pass for the Gaiety. Have to stand a drink or two. As broad as it's long.

He's coming in the afternoon. Her songs.

Plasto's. Sir Philip Crampton's memorial fountain bust. Who was he?

— How do you do? Martin Cunningham said, raising his palm to his brow in salute.

— He doesn't see us, Mr Power said. Yes, he does. How do you do?

— Who? Mr Dedalus asked.

— Blazes Boylan, Mr Power said. There he is, airing his quiff.

Just that moment I was thinking.

Mr Dedalus bent across to salute. From the door of the Red Bank the white disk of a straw hat flashed reply: passed.

Mr Bloom reviewed the nails of his left hand, then those of his right hand. The nails, yes. Is there anything more in him that they she sees? Fascination. Worst man in Dublin. That keeps him alive. They sometimes feel what a person is. Instinct. But a type like that. My nails. I am just looking at them: well pared. And after: thinking alone. Body getting a bit softy. I would notice that: from remembering. What causes that? I suppose the skin can't contract quickly enough when the flesh falls off. But the shape is there. The shape is there still. Shoulders. Hips. Plump. Night of the dance, dressing. Shift stuck between the cheeks behind.

He clasped his hands between his knees and, satisfied, sent his vacant glance over their faces.

Mr Power asked:

— How is the concert tour getting on, Bloom?

— O, very well, Mr Bloom said. I hear great accounts of it. It's a good idea, you see ...

— Are you going yourself?

— Well, no, Mr Bloom said. In point of fact I have to go down to the county Clare on some private business. You see, the idea is to tour the chief towns. What you lose on one you can make up on the other.

— Quite so, Martin Cunningham said. Mary Anderson is up there now. Have you good artists?

— Louis Werner is touring her, Mr Bloom said. O yes. We'll have all topnobbers. J.C. Doyle and John MacCormack I hope and. The best, in fact.

— And *Madame*, Mr Power said, smiling. Last but not least.

Mr Bloom unclasped his hands in a gesture of soft politeness and clasped them. Smith O'Brien. Someone has laid a bunch of flowers there. Woman. Must be his deathday. For many happy returns. The carriage wheeling by Farrell's statue united noiselessly their unresisting knees.

– Four bootlaces for a penny!

Oot: a dull-garbed old man from the curbstone tendered his wares, his mouth opening: oot.

– Four bootlaces for a penny!

Wonder why he was struck off the rolls. Had his office in Hume Street. Same house as Molly's namesake, Tweedy, crown solicitor for Waterford. Has that silk hat ever since. Relics of old decency. Mourning too. Terrible comedown, poor old wretch! Kicked about like snuff at a wake. O'Callaghan on his last legs.

And *Madame.* Twenty past eleven. Up. Mrs Fleming is in to clean. Doing her hair, humming: *voglio e non vorrei.* No: *vorrei e non.* Looking at the tips of her hairs to see if they are split. *Mi trema un poco il.* Beautiful on that *tre* her voice is: weeping tone. A thrush. A throstle. There is a word throstle that expresses that.

His eyes passed lightly over Mr Power's good-looking face. Greyish over the ears. *Madame*: smiling. I smiled back. A smile goes a long way. Only politeness perhaps. Nice fellow. Who knows is that true about the woman he keeps? Not pleasant for the wife. Yet they say, who was it told me, there is no carnal. You would imagine that would get played out pretty quick. Yes, it was Crofton met him one evening bringing her a pound of rump steak. What is this she was? Barmaid in Jury's. Or the Moira, was it?

They passed under the huge-cloaked Liberator's form.

Martin Cunningham nudged Mr Power.

– Of the tribe of Reuben, he said.

A tall black-bearded figure, bent on a stick, stumping round the corner of Elvery's Elephant House, showed them a curved hand rested open on his spine.

– In all his pristine beauty, Mr Power said.

Mr Dedalus looked after the stumping figure and said mildly:

– The devil break the hasp of your back!

Mr Power, collapsing in laughter, shaded his face from the window as the carriage passed Gray's statue.

– We have all been there, Martin Cunningham said broadly.

His eyes met Mr Bloom's eyes. He caressed his beard, adding:

– Well, nearly all of us.

90

Mr Bloom began to speak with sudden eagerness to his companions' faces:

— That's an awfully good one that's going the rounds about Reuben J. and the son.

— About the boatman? Mr Power asked.

— Yes. Isn't it awfully good?

— What is that? Mr Dedalus asked. I didn't hear it.

— There was a girl in the case, Mr Bloom began, and he determined to send him to the Isle of Man out of harm's way but when they were both...

— What? Mr Dedalus asked. That confirmed bloody hobbledehoy is it?

— Yes, Mr Bloom said. They were both on the way to the boat and he tried to drown...

— Drown Barabbas! Mr Dedalus cried. I wish to Christ he did!

Mr Power sent a long laugh down his shaded nostrils.

— No, Mr Bloom said, the son himself...

Martin Cunningham thwarted his speech rudely:

— Reuben J. and the son were piking it down the quay next the river on their way to the Isle of Man boat and the young chiseller suddenly got loose and over the wall with him into the Liffey.

— For God's sake! Mr Dedalus exclaimed in fright. Is he dead?

— Dead! Martin Cunningham cried. Not he! A boatman got a pole and fished him out by the slack of the breeches and he was landed up to the father on the quay more dead than alive. Half the town was there.

— Yes, Mr Bloom said. But the funny part is...

— And Reuben J., Martin Cunningham said, gave the boatman a florin for saving his son's life.

A stifled sigh came from under Mr Power's hand.

— O, he did, Martin Cunningham affirmed. Like a hero. A silver florin.

— Isn't it awfully good? Mr Bloom said eagerly.

— One and eightpence too much, Mr Dedalus said drily.

Mr Power's choked laugh burst quietly in the carriage.

Nelson's Pillar.

— Eight plums a penny! Eight for a penny!

— We had better look a little serious, Martin Cunningham said.

Mr Dedalus sighed.

— Ah then indeed, he said, poor little Paddy wouldn't grudge us a laugh. Many a good one he told himself.

— The Lord forgive me! Mr Power said, wiping his wet eyes with his fingers. Poor Paddy! I little thought a week ago when I saw him last and he was in his usual health that I'd be driving after him like this. He's gone from us.

— As decent a little man as ever wore a hat, Mr Dedalus said. He went very suddenly.

— Breakdown, Martin Cunningham said. Heart.

He tapped his chest sadly.

Blazing face: red-hot. Too much John Barleycorn. Cure for a red nose. Drink like the devil till it turns adelite. A lot of money he spent colouring it.

Mr Power gazed at the passing houses with rueful apprehension.

— He had a sudden death, poor fellow, he said.

— The best death, Mr Bloom said.

Their wide-open eyes looked at him.

— No suffering, he said. A moment and all is over. Like dying in sleep.

No one spoke.

Dead side of the street this. Dull business by day: land agents, temperance hotel, Falconer's *Railway Guide*, Civil Service College, Gill's, Catholic Club, the Industrious Blind. Why? Some reason. Sun or wind. At night too. Chummies and slaveys. Under the patronage of the late Father Mathew. Foundation stone for Parnell. Breakdown. Heart.

White horses with white frontlet plumes came round the Rotunda corner, galloping. A tiny coffin flashed by. In a hurry to bury. A mourning coach. Unmarried. Black for the married. Piebald for bachelors. Dun for a nun.

— Sad, Martin Cunningham said. A child.

A dwarf's face, mauve and wrinkled like little Rudy's was. Dwarf's body, weak as putty, in a white-lined deal box. Burial Friendly Society pays. Penny a week for a sod of turf. Our. Little. Beggar. Baby. Meant nothing. Mistake of nature. If it's healthy it's from the mother. If not, from the man. Better luck next time.

— Poor little thing, Mr Dedalus said. It's well out of it.

The carriage climbed more slowly the hill of Rutland Square. Rattle his bones. Over the stones. Only a pauper. Nobody owns.

— In the midst of life, Martin Cunningham said.

— But the worst of all, Mr Power said, is the man who takes his own life.

Martin Cunningham drew out his watch briskly, coughed, and put it back.

— The greatest disgrace to have in the family, Mr Power added.

— Temporary insanity, of course, Martin Cunningham said decisively. We must take a charitable view of it.

— They say a man who does it is a coward, Mr Dedalus said.

— It is not for us to judge, Martin Cunningham said.

Mr Bloom, about to speak, closed his lips again. Martin Cunningham's large eyes. Looking away now. Sympathetic human man he is. Intelligent. Like Shakespeare's face. Always a good word to say. They have no mercy on that here, or infanticide. Refuse Christian burial. They used to drive a stake of wood through his heart in the grave. As if it wasn't broken already. Yet sometimes they repent too late. Found in the riverbed clutching rushes. He looked at me. And that awful drunkard of a wife of his. Setting up house for her time after time and then pawning the furniture on him every Saturday almost. Leading him the life of the damned. Wear the heart out of a stone, that. Monday morning. Start afresh. Shoulder to the wheel. Lord, she must have looked a sight that night Dedalus told me he was in there. Drunk about the place and capering with Martin's umbrella.

> *And they call me the jewel of Asia,*
> *Of Asia,*
> *The geisha.*

He looked away from me. He knows. Rattle his bones.

That afternoon of the inquest. The red-labelled bottle on the table. The room in the hotel with hunting pictures. Stuffy it was. Sunlight through the slats of the Venetian blinds. The coroner's sunlit ears, big and hairy. Boots giving evidence. Thought he was asleep first. Then saw like yellow streaks on his face. Had slipped down to the foot of the bed. Verdict: overdose. Death by misadventure. The letter. For my son Leopold.

No more pain. Wake no more. Nobody owns.

The carriage rattled swiftly along Blessington Street. Over the stones.

— We are going the pace, I think, Martin Cunningham said.

— God grant he doesn't upset us on the road, Mr Power said.

— I hope not, Martin Cunningham said. That will be a great race tomorrow in Germany. The Gordon Bennett.

— Yes, by Jove, Mr Dedalus said. That will be worth seeing, faith.

As they turned into Berkeley Street a street organ near the Basin sent over and after them a rollicking rattling song of the halls. Has anybody here seen Kelly? Kay ee double ell wy. Dead March from *Saul.* He's as bad as old Antonio. He left me on my ownio. Pirouette! The Mater

Misericordiae. Eccles Street. My house down there. Big place. Ward for incurables there. Very encouraging. Our Lady's Hospice for the Dying. Deadhouse handy underneath. Where old Mrs Riordan died. They look terrible, the women. Her feeding cup and rubbing her mouth with the spoon. Then the screen round her bed for her to die. Nice young student that was dressed that bite the bee gave me. He's gone over to the lying-in hospital they told me. From one extreme to the other.

The carriage galloped round a corner: stopped.

– What's wrong now?

A divided drove of branded cattle passed the windows, lowing, slouching by on padded hoofs, whisking their tails slowly on their clotted bony croups. Outside them and through them ran raddled sheep bleating their fear.

– Emigrants, Mr Power said.

– Huuuh! the drover's voice cried, his switch sounding on their flanks. Huuuh out of that!

Thursday, of course. Tomorrow is killing day. Springers. Cuffe sold them about twenty-seven quid each. For Liverpool probably. Roast beef for old England. They buy up all the juicy ones. And then the fifth quarter is lost: all that raw stuff, hide, hair, horns. Comes to a big thing in a year. Dead meat trade. By-products of the slaughterhouses for tanneries, soap, margarine. Wonder if that dodge works now getting dicky meat off the train at Clonsilla.

The carriage moved on through the drove.

– I can't make out why the Corporation doesn't run a tramline from the park gate to the quays, Mr Bloom said. All those animals could be taken in trucks down to the boats.

– Instead of blocking up the thoroughfare, Martin Cunningham said. Quite right. They ought to.

– Yes, Mr Bloom said, and another thing I often thought is to have municipal funeral trams like they have in Milan, you know. Run the line out to the cemetery gates and have special trams, hearse and carriage and all. Don't you see what I mean?

– O, that be damned for a story, Mr Dedalus said. Pullman car and saloon dining room.

– A poor lookout for Corny, Mr Power added.

– Why? Mr Bloom asked, turning to Mr Dedalus. Wouldn't it be more decent than galloping two abreast?

— Well, there's something in that, Mr Dedalus granted.

— And, Martin Cunningham said, we wouldn't have scenes like that when the hearse capsized round Dunphy's and upset the coffin on to the road.

— That was terrible, Mr Power's shocked face said, and the corpse fell about the road. Terrible!

— First round Dunphy's, Mr Dedalus said, nodding. Gordon Bennett Cup.

— Praises be to God! Martin Cunningham said piously.

Bom! Upset. A coffin bumped out on to the road. Burst open. Paddy Dignam shot out and rolling over stiff in the dust in a brown habit too large for him. Red face: grey now. Mouth fallen open. Asking what's up now. Quite right to close it. Looks horrid open. Then the insides decompose quickly. Much better to close up all the orifices. Yes. Also. With wax. The sphincter loose. Seal up all.

— Dunphy's, Mr Power announced as the carriage turned right.

Dunphy's Corner. Mourning coaches drawn up, drowning their grief. A pause by the wayside. Tiptop position for a pub. Expect we'll pull up here on the way back to drink his health. Pass round the consolation. Elixir of life.

But suppose now it did happen. Would he bleed if a nail say cut him in the knocking about? He would and he wouldn't, I suppose. Depends on where. The circulation stops. Still, some might ooze out of an artery. It would be better to bury them in red: a dark red.

In silence they drove along Phibsborough Road. An empty hearse trotted by, coming from the cemetery: looks relieved.

Crossguns Bridge: the Royal Canal.

Water rushed roaring through the sluices. A man stood on his dropping barge between clamps of turf. On the towpath by the lock a slack-tethered horse. Aboard of the *Bugabu*.

Their eyes watched him. On the slow weedy waterway he had floated on his raft coastward over Ireland, drawn by a haulage rope past beds of reeds, over slime, mud-choked bottles, carrion dogs. Athlone, Mullingar, Moyvalley. I could make a walking tour to see Milly by the canal. Or cycle down. Hire some old crock, safety. Wren had one the other day at the auction but a lady's. Developing waterways. James M'Cann's hobby to row me o'er the ferry. Cheaper transit. By easy stages. Houseboats. Camping out. Also hearses. To heaven by water. Perhaps I will without writing. Come as a surprise. Leixlip, Clonsilla. Dropping down lock by lock to Dublin. With turf from the midland bogs. Salute. He lifted his brown straw hat, saluting Paddy Dignam.

They drove on past Brian Boroimh House. Near it now.

— I wonder how is our friend Fogarty getting on, Mr Power said.

— Better ask Tom Kernan, Mr Dedalus said.

— How is that? Martin Cunningham said. Left him weeping, I suppose.

— Though lost to sight, Mr Dedalus said, to memory dear.

The carriage steered left for Finglas Road.

The stonecutter's yard on the right. Last lap. Crowded on the spit of land silent shapes appeared: white, sorrowful, holding out calm hands, knelt in grief, pointing. Fragments of shapes, hewn. In white silence: appealing. The best obtainable. Thos. H. Dennany, monumental builder and sculptor.

Passed.

On the curbstone before Jimmy Geary's, the sexton's, an old tramp sat, grumbling, emptying the dirt and stones out of his huge dust-brown yawning boot. After life's journey.

Gloomy gardens then went by, one by one: gloomy houses.

Mr Power pointed.

— That is where Childs was murdered, he said. The last house.

— So it is, Mr Dedalus said. A gruesome case. Seymour Bushe got him off. Murdered his brother. Or so they said.

— The Crown had no evidence, Mr Power said.

— Only circumstantial, Martin Cunningham said. That's the maxim of the law. Better for ninety-nine guilty to escape than for one innocent person to be wrongfully condemned.

They looked. Murderer's ground. It passed darkly. Shuttered, tenantless, unweeded garden. Whole place gone to hell. Wrongfully condemned. Murder. The murderer's image in the eye of the murdered. They love reading about it. Man's head found in a garden. Her clothing consisted of. How she met her death. Recent outrage. The weapon used. Murderer is still at large. Clues. A shoelace. The body to be exhumed. Murder will out.

Cramped in this carriage. She mightn't like me to come that way without letting her know. Must be careful about women. Catch them once with their pants down. Never forgive you after. Fifteen.

The high railings of Prospect rippled past their gaze. Dark poplars, rare white forms. Forms more frequent, white shapes thronged amid the trees, white forms and fragments streaming by mutely, sustaining vain gestures on the air.

The felly harshed against the curbstone: stopped. Martin Cunningham put out his arm and, wrenching back the handle, shoved the door open with his knee. He stepped out. Mr Power and Mr Dedalus followed.

Change that soap now. Mr Bloom's hand unbuttoned his hip pocket swiftly and transferred the paper-stuck soap to his inner handkerchief pocket. Give it a nice smell. He stepped out of the carriage, replacing the newspaper his other hand still held.

Paltry funeral: coach and three carriages. It's all the same. Pallbearers, gold reins, requiem mass, firing a volley. Pomp of death. Beyond the hind carriage a hawker stood by his barrow of cakes and fruit. Simnel cakes those are, stuck together: cakes for the dead. Dog biscuits. Who ate them? Mourners coming out.

He followed his companions. Mr Kernan and Ned Lambert followed, Hynes walking after them. Corny Kelleher stood by the opened hearse and took out the two wreaths. He handed one to the boy.

Where is that child's funeral disappeared to?

A team of horses passed from Finglas with toiling plodding tread, dragging through the funereal silence a creaking waggon on which lay a granite block. The waggoner marching at their head saluted.

Coffin now. Got here before us, dead as he is. Horse looking round at it with his plume skewways. Dull eye: collar tight on his neck, pressing on a blood vessel or something. Do they know what they cart out here every day? Must be twenty or thirty funerals every day. Then Mount Jerome for the Protestants. Funerals all over the world everywhere every minute. Shovelling them under by the cartload doublequick. Thousands every hour. Too many in the world.

Mourners came out through the gates: woman and a girl. Lean-jawed harpy, hard woman at a bargain, her bonnet awry. Girl's face stained with dirt and tears, holding the woman's arm, looking up at her for a sign to cry. Fish's face, bloodless and livid.

The mutes shouldered the coffin and bore it in through the gates. So much dead weight. Felt heavier myself stepping out of that bath. First the stiff: then the friends of the stiff. Corny Kelleher and the boy followed with their wreaths. Who is that beside them? Ah, the brother-in-law.

All walked after.

Martin Cunningham whispered:

— I was in mortal agony with you talking of suicide before Bloom.

— What? Mr Power whispered. How so?

— His father poisoned himself, Martin Cunningham whispered. Had the Queen's Hotel in Ennis. You heard him say he was going to Clare. Anniversary.

— O God! Mr Power whispered. First I heard of it. Poisoned himself!

He glanced behind him to where a face with dark thinking eyes followed towards the cardinal's mausoleum. Speaking.

— Was he insured? Mr Bloom asked.

— I believe so, Mr Kernan answered, but the policy was heavily mortgaged. Martin is trying to get the youngster into Artane.

— How many children did he leave?

— Five. Ned Lambert says he'll try to get one of the girls into Todd's.

— A sad case, Mr Bloom said gently. Five young children.

— A great blow to the poor wife, Mr Kernan added.

— Indeed yes, Mr Bloom agreed.

Has the laugh at him now.

He looked down at the boots he had blacked and polished. She had outlived him. Lost her husband. More dead for her than for me. One must outlive the other. Wise men say. There are more women than men in the world. Condole with her. Your terrible loss. I hope you'll soon follow him. For Hindu widows only. She would marry another. Him? No. Yet who knows after? Widowhood not the thing since the old queen died. Drawn on a gun carriage. Victoria and Albert. Frogmore memorial mourning. But in the end she put a few violets in her bonnet. Vain in her heart of hearts. All for a shadow. Consort not even a king. Her son was the substance. Something new to hope for, not like the past she wanted back, waiting. It never comes. One must go first: alone, under the ground: and lie no more in her warm bed.

— How are you, Simon? Ned Lambert said softly, clasping hands. Haven't seen you for a month of Sundays.

— Never better. How are all in Cork's own town?

— I was down there for the Cork Park races on Easter Monday, Ned Lambert said. Same old six and eightpence. Stopped with Dick Tivy.

— And how is Dick, the solid man?

— Nothing between himself and heaven, Ned Lambert answered.

— By the holy Paul! Mr Dedalus said in subdued wonder. Dick Tivy bald?

— Martin is going to get up a whip for the youngsters, Ned Lambert said, pointing ahead. A few bob a skull. Just to keep them going till the insurance muddle is cleared up.

— Yes, yes, Mr Dedalus said dubiously. Is that the eldest boy in front?

— Yes, Ned Lambert said, with the wife's brother. John Henry Menton is behind. He put down his name for a quid.

— I'll engage he did, Mr Dedalus said. I often told poor Paddy he ought to mind that job. John Henry is not the worst in the world.

— How did he lose it? Ned Lambert asked. Liquor, what?

— Many a good man's fault, Mr Dedalus said with a sigh.

They halted about the door of the mortuary chapel. Mr Bloom stood behind the boy with the wreath, looking down at his sleek-combed hair and at the slender furrowed neck inside his brand-new collar. Poor boy! Was he there when the father? Both unconscious. Lighten up at the last moment and recognise for the last time. All he might have done. I owe three shillings to O'Grady. Would he understand? The mutes bore the coffin into the chapel. Which end is his head?

After a moment he followed the others in, blinking in the screened light. The coffin lay on its bier before the chancel, four tall yellow candles at its corners. Always in front of us. Corny Kelleher, laying a wreath at each fore corner, beckoned to the boy to kneel. The mourners knelt here and there in praying desks. Mr Bloom stood behind near the font and, when all had knelt, dropped carefully his unfolded newspaper from his pocket and knelt his right knee upon it. He fitted his black hat gently on his left knee and, holding its brim, bent over piously.

A server, bearing a brass bucket with something in it, came out through a door. The white-smocked priest came after him, tidying his stole with one hand, balancing with the other a little book against his toad's belly. Who'll read the book? I, said the rook.

They halted by the bier and the priest began to read out of his book with a fluent croak.

Father Coffey. I knew his name was like a coffin. *Dominenamine.* Bully about the muzzle he looks. Bosses the show. Muscular Christian. Woe betide anyone that looks crooked at him: priest. Thou art Peter. Burst sideways like a sheep in clover, Dedalus says he will. With a belly on him like a poisoned pup. Most amusing expressions that man finds. Hhhn: burst sideways.

— *Non intres in judicium cum servo tuo, Domine.*

Makes them feel more important to be prayed over in Latin. Requiem mass. Crape weepers. Black-edged notepaper. Your name on the altar list.

Chilly place this. Want to feed well, sitting in there all the morning in the gloom kicking his heels waiting for the next please. Eyes of a toad too. What swells him up that way? Molly gets swelled after cabbage. Air of the place maybe. Looks full up of bad gas. Must be an infernal lot of bad gas round the place. Butchers, for instance: they get like raw beefsteaks. Who was telling me? Mervyn Browne. Down in the vaults of Saint Werburgh's, lovely old organ hundred and fifty, they have to bore a hole in the coffins sometimes to let out the bad gas and burn it. Out it rushes: blue. One whiff of that and you're a goner.

My kneecap is hurting me. Ow. That's better.

The priest took a stick with a knob at the end of it out of the boy's bucket and shook it over the coffin. Then he walked to the other end and shook it again. Then he came back and put it back in the bucket. As you were before you rested. It's all written down: he has to do it.

— *Et ne nos inducas in tentationem.*

The server piped the answers in the treble. I often thought it would be better to have boy servants. Up to fifteen or so. After that of course . . .

Holy water that was, I expect. Shaking sleep out of it. He must be fed up with that job, shaking that thing over all the corpses they trot up. What harm if he could see what he was shaking it over. Every mortal day a fresh batch: middle-aged men, old women, children, women dead in childbirth, men with beards, baldheaded businessmen, consumptive girls with little sparrows' breasts. All the year round he prayed the same thing over them all and shook water on top of them: sleep. On Dignam now.

— *In paradisum.*

Said he was going to paradise or is in paradise. Says that over everybody. Tiresome kind of a job. But he has to say something.

The priest closed his book and went off, followed by the server. Corny Kelleher opened the side doors and the gravediggers came in, hoisted the coffin again, carried it out and shoved it on their cart. Corny Kelleher gave one wreath to the boy and the other to the brother-in-law. All followed them out of the side doors into the mild grey air. Mr Bloom came last, folding his paper again into his pocket. He gazed gravely at the ground till the coffincart wheeled off to the left. The metal wheels ground the gravel with a sharp grating cry and the pack of blunt boots followed the trundled barrow along a lane of sepulchres.

The ree the ra the ree the ra the roo. Lord, I mustn't lilt here.

— The O'Connell circle, Mr Dedalus said about him.

Mr Power's soft eyes went up to the apex of the lofty cone.

— He's at rest, he said, in the middle of his people, old Dan O'. But his heart is buried in Rome. How many broken hearts are buried here, Simon!

— Her grave is over there, Jack, Mr Dedalus said. I'll soon be stretched beside her. Let Him take me whenever He likes.

Breaking down, he began to weep to himself quietly, stumbling a little in his walk. Mr Power took his arm.

— She's better where she is, he said kindly.

— I suppose so, Mr Dedalus said with a weak gasp. I suppose she is in heaven if there is a heaven.

Corny Kelleher stepped aside from his rank and allowed the mourners to plod by.

— Sad occasions, Mr Kernan began politely.

Mr Bloom closed his eyes and sadly twice bowed his head.

— The others are putting on their hats, Mr Kernan said. I suppose we can do so too. We are the last. This cemetery is a treacherous place.

They covered their heads.

— The reverend gentleman read the service too quickly, don't you think? Mr Kernan said with reproof.

Mr Bloom nodded gravely, looking in the quick bloodshot eyes. Secret eyes, secretsearching eyes. Mason, I think: not sure. Beside him again. We are the last. In the same boat. Hope he'll say something else.

Mr Kernan added:

— The service of the Irish Church, used in Mount Jerome, is simpler, more impressive, I must say.

Mr Bloom gave prudent assent. The language of course was another thing.

Mr Kernan said with solemnity:

— *I am the resurrection and the life.* That touches a man's inmost heart.

— It does, Mr Bloom said.

Your heart perhaps but what price the fellow in the six feet by two with his toes to the daisies? No touching that. Seat of the affections. Broken heart. A pump after all, pumping thousands of gallons of blood every day. One fine day it gets bunged up and there you are. Lots of them lying around here: lungs, hearts, livers. Old rusty pumps: damn the thing else. The resurrection and the life. Once you are dead you are dead. That last day idea. Knocking them all up out of their graves. Come forth, Lazarus! And he came fifth and lost the job. Get up! Last day! Then every fellow mousing around for his liver and his lights and the rest of his traps. Find damn all of himself that morning. Pennyweight of powder in a skull. Twelve grammes one pennyweight. Troy measure.

Corny Kelleher fell into step at their side.

— Everything went off A1, he said. What?

He looked on them from his drawling eye. Policeman's shoulders. With your tooraloom tooraloom.

— As it should be, Mr Kernan said.

— What? Eh? Corny Kelleher said.

Mr Kernan assured him.

— Who is that chap behind with Tom Kernan? John Henry Menton asked. I know his face.

Ned Lambert glanced back.

— Bloom, he said. Madam Marion Tweedy that was, is, I mean, the soprano. She's his wife.

— O, to be sure, John Henry Menton said. I haven't seen her for some time. She was a fine-looking woman. I danced with her, wait, fifteen, seventeen golden years ago, at Mat Dillon's in Roundtown. And a good armful she was.

He looked behind through the others.

— What is he? he asked. What does he do? Wasn't he in the stationery line? I fell foul of him one evening, I remember, at bowls.

Ned Lambert smiled.

— Yes, he was, he said, in Wisdom Hely's. A traveller for blotting paper.

— In God's name, John Henry Menton said, what did she marry a coon like that for? She had plenty of game in her then.

— Has still, Ned Lambert said. He does some canvassing for ads.

John Henry Menton's large eyes stared ahead.

The barrow turned into a side lane. A portly man, ambushed among the grasses, raised his hat in homage. The gravediggers touched their caps.

— John O'Connell, Mr Power said, pleased. He never forgets a friend.

Mr O'Connell shook all their hands in silence. Mr Dedalus said:

— I am come to pay you another visit.

— My dear Simon, the caretaker answered in a low voice. I don't want your custom at all.

Saluting Ned Lambert and John Henry Menton he walked on at Martin Cunningham's side, puzzling two long keys at his back.

— Did you hear that one, he asked them, about Mulcahy from the Coombe?

— I did not, Martin Cunningham said.

They bent their silk hats in concert and Hynes inclined his ear. The caretaker hung his thumbs in the loops of his gold watchchain and spoke in a discreet tone to their vacant smiles.

— They tell the story, he said, that two drunks came out here one foggy evening to look for the grave of a friend of theirs. They asked for Mulcahy from the Coombe and were told where he was buried. After traipsing about in the fog they found the grave, sure enough. One of the drunks spelt out the name: Terence Mulcahy. The other drunk was blinking up at a statue of our Saviour the widow had got put up.

The caretaker blinked up at one of the sepulchres they passed. He resumed:

— And, after blinking up at the sacred figure, *Not a bloody bit like the man*, says he. *That's not Mulcahy*, says he, *whoever done it*.

Rewarded by smiles he fell back and spoke with Corny Kelleher, accepting the dockets given him, turning them over and scanning them as he walked.

— That's all done with a purpose, Martin Cunningham explained to Hynes.

— I know, Hynes said, I know that.

— To cheer a fellow up, Martin Cunningham said. It's pure goodheartedness: damn the thing else.

Mr Bloom admired the caretaker's prosperous bulk. All want to be on good terms with him. Decent fellow, John O'Connell, real good sort. Keys: like Keyes's ad: no fear of anyone getting out. No pass-out checks. Habeas corpus. I must see about that ad after the funeral. Did I write Ballsbridge on the envelope I took to cover when she disturbed me writing to Martha? Hope it's not chucked in the dead-letter office. Be the better of a shave. Grey sprouting beard. That's the first sign when the hairs come out grey. And temper getting cross. Silver threads among the grey. Fancy being his wife. Wonder how he had the gumption to propose to any girl. Come out and live in the graveyard. Dangle that before her. It might thrill her first. Courting death. Shades of night hovering here with all the dead stretched about: the shadows of the tombs when churchyards yawn. Daniel O'Connell must be a descendant I suppose. Who is this used to say he was? A queer breedy man, great Catholic all the same, like a big giant in the dark.

Will-o'-the-wisp. Gas of graves. Want to keep her mind off it to conceive at all. Women especially are so touchy. Tell her a ghost story in bed to make her sleep. Have you ever seen a ghost? Well, I have. It was a pitch-dark night. The clock was on the stroke of twelve. Still, they'd kiss all right if properly keyed up. Whores in Turkish graveyards. Learn anything if taken young. You might pick up a young widow here. Men like that. Love among the tombstones. Romeo. Spice of pleasure. In the midst of death we are in life. Both ends meet. Tantalising for the poor dead. Smell of grilled beefsteaks to the starving. Gnawing their vitals. Desire to grig people. Molly wanting to do it at the window. Eight children he has anyway.

He has seen a fair share go under in his time, lying around him field after field. Holy fields. More room if they buried them standing. Sitting or kneeling you couldn't. Standing? His head might come up some day above ground in a landslip with his hand pointing. All honeycombed the ground must be: oblong cells. And very neat he keeps it too, trim grass and edgings. His garden, Major Gamble calls Mount Jerome. Well, so it is. Ought to be flowers of sleep. Chinese cemeteries with giant poppies growing produce the best opium Masliansky told me. The Botanic Gardens are just over there. It's the blood sinking in the earth gives new life. Same idea those Jews they said killed the Christian boy. Every man his price. Well-preserved fat corpse, gentleman, epicure, invaluable for fruit garden. A bargain. By carcass of William Wilkinson, auditor and accountant, lately deceased, three pounds thirteen and six. With thanks.

I daresay the soil would be quite fat with corpse manure, bones, flesh, nails. Charnelhouses. Dreadful. Turning green and pink, decomposing. Rot quick in damp earth. The lean old ones tougher. Then a kind of a tallowy kind of a cheesy. Then begin to get black, black treacle oozing out of them. Then dried up. Deathmoths. Of course the cells or whatever they are go on living. Changing about. Live for ever practically. Nothing to feed on feed on themselves.

But they must breed a devil of a lot of maggots. Soil must be simply swirling with them. *Your head it simply swurls. Those pretty little seaside gurls.* He looks cheerful enough over it. Gives him a sense of power seeing all the others go under first. Wonder how he looks at life. Cracking his jokes too: warms the cockles of his heart. The one about the bulletin. Spurgeon went to heaven 4 a.m. this morning. 11 p.m. (closing time). Not arrived yet. Peter. The dead themselves the men anyhow would like to hear an odd joke or the women to know what's in fashion. A juicy pear or ladies' punch, hot, strong and sweet. Keep out the damp. You must laugh sometimes so better do it that way. Gravediggers in *Hamlet*. Shows the profound knowledge of the human heart. Daren't joke about the dead for two years at least. *De mortuis nil nisi prius.* Go out of mourning first. Hard to imagine his funeral. Seems a sort of a joke. Read your own obituary notice they say you live longer. Gives you second wind. New lease of life.

– How many have you for tomorrow? the caretaker asked.

– Two, Corny Kelleher said. Half ten and eleven.

The caretaker put the papers in his pocket. The barrow had ceased to trundle. The mourners split and moved to each side of the hole, stepping with care round the graves. The gravediggers bore the coffin and set its nose on the brink, looping the bands round it.

Burying him. We come to bury Caesar. His ides of March or June. He doesn't know who is here nor care.

Now who is that lanky-looking galoot over there in the macintosh? Now who is he I'd like to know. Now I'd give a trifle to know who he is. Always someone turns up you never dreamt of. A fellow could live on his lonesome all his life. Yes, he could. Still, he'd have to get someone to sod him after he died though he could dig his own grave. We all do. Only man buries. No, ants too. First thing strikes anybody. Bury the dead. Say Robinson Crusoe was true to life. Well, then Friday buried him. Every Friday buries a Thursday if you come to look at it.

> *O, poor Robinson Crusoe,*
> *How could you possibly do so?*

Poor Dignam! His last lie on the earth in his box. When you think of them all it does seem a waste of wood. All gnawed through. They could invent a handsome bier with a kind of panel sliding, let it down that way. Ay, but they might object to be buried out of another fellow's. They're so particular. Lay me in my native earth. Bit of clay from the Holy Land. Only a mother and deadborn child ever buried in the one coffin. I see what it means. I see. To protect him as long as possible even in the earth. The Irishman's house is his coffin. Embalming in catacombs, mummies, the same idea.

Mr Bloom stood far back, his hat in his hand, counting the bared heads. Twelve. I'm thirteen. No. The chap in the macintosh is thirteen. Death's number. Where the deuce did he pop out of? He wasn't in the chapel, that I'll swear. Silly superstition that about thirteen.

Nice soft tweed Ned Lambert has in that suit. Tinge of purple. I had

105

one like that when we lived in Lombard Street West. Dressy fellow he was once. Used to change three suits in the day. Must get that grey suit of mine turned by Mesias. Hello. It's dyed. His wife, I forgot he's not married, or his landlady ought to have picked out those threads for him.

The coffin dived out of sight, eased down by the men straddled on the grave trestles. They struggled up and out: and all uncovered. Twenty.

Pause.

If we were all suddenly somebody else.

Far away a donkey brayed. Rain. No such ass. Never see a dead one, they say. Shame of death. They hide. Also poor papa went away.

Gentle sweet air blew round the bared heads in a whisper. Whisper. The boy by the gravehead held his wreath with both hands, staring quietly in the black open space. Mr Bloom moved behind the portly kindly caretaker. Well-cut frockcoat. Weighing them up perhaps to see which will go next. Well, it is a long rest. Feel no more. It's the moment you feel. Must be damned unpleasant. Can't believe it at first. Mistake must be: someone else. Try the house opposite. Wait, I wanted to. I haven't yet. Then darkened death chamber. Light they want. Whispering around you. Would you like to see a priest? Then rambling and wandering. Delirium. All you hid all your life. The death struggle. His sleep is not natural. Press his lower eyelid. Watching is his nose pointed, is his jaw sinking, are the soles of his feet yellow. Pull the pillow away and finish it off on the floor since he's doomed. Devil in that picture of sinner's death showing him a woman. Dying to embrace her in his shirt. Last act of *Lucia. Shall I nevermore behold thee?* Bam! He expires. Gone at last. People talk about you a bit: forget you. Don't forget to pray for him. Remember him in your prayers. Even Parnell. Ivy Day dying out. Then they follow: dropping into a hole one after the other.

We are praying now for the repose of his soul. Hoping you're well and not in hell. Nice change of air. Out of the frying pan of life into the fire of purgatory.

Does he ever think of the hole waiting for himself? They say you do when you shiver in the sun. Someone walking over it. Callboy's warning. Near you. Mine over there towards Finglas, the plot I bought. Mamma, poor mamma, and little Rudy.

The gravediggers took up their spades and flung heavy clods of clay in on the coffin. Mr Bloom turned his face. And if he was alive all the time! Whew! By Jingo, that would be awful! No, no: he is dead, of course. Of course he is dead. Monday he died. They ought to have some law to pierce the heart and make sure or an electric clock or a telephone in the coffin and some kind of a canvas airhole. Flag of distress. Three days. Rather long to keep them in summer. Just as well to get shut of them as soon as you are sure there's no ...

The clay fell softer. Begin to be forgotten. Out of sight, out of mind.

The caretaker moved away a few paces and put on his hat. Had enough of it. The mourners took heart of grace, one by one, covering themselves without show. Mr Bloom put on his hat and saw the portly figure make its way deftly through the maze of graves. Quietly, sure of his ground, he traversed the dismal fields.

Hynes jotting down something in his notebook. Ah, the names. But he knows them all. No: coming to me.

— I am just taking the names, Hynes said below his breath. What is your Christian name? I'm not sure.

— L., Mr Bloom said. Leopold. And you might put down M'Coy's name too. He asked me to.

— Charley, Hynes said, writing. I know. He was on the *Freeman* once.

So he was, before he got the job in the morgue under Louis Byrne. Good idea a postmortem for doctors. Find out what they imagine they know. He died of a Tuesday. Got the run. Levanted with the cash of a few ads. Charley, you're my darling. That was why he asked me to. O well, does no harm. I saw to that, M'Coy. Thanks, old chap: much obliged. Leave him under an obligation: costs nothing.

— And tell us, Hynes said, do you know that fellow in the, fellow was over there in the ...

He looked around.

— Macintosh. Yes, I saw him, Mr Bloom said. Where is he now?

— M'Intosh, Hynes said, scribbling. I don't know who he is. Is that his name?

He moved away, looking about him.

— No, Mr Bloom began, turning and stopping. I say, Hynes!

Didn't hear.

What? Where has he disappeared to? Not a sign. Well, of all the. Has anybody here seen? Kay ee double ell. Become invisible. Good Lord, what became of him?

A seventh gravedigger came beside Mr Bloom to take up an idle spade.

— O, excuse me!

He stepped aside nimbly.

Clay, brown, damp, began to be seen in the hole. It rose. Nearly over. A mound of damp clods rose more, rose, and the gravediggers rested their spades. All uncovered again for a few instants. The boy propped his wreath against a corner: the brother-in-law his on a lump. The grave-diggers put on their caps and carried their earthy spades towards the barrow. Then knocked the blades lightly on the turf: clean. One bent to pluck from the haft a long tuft of grass. One, leaving his mates, walked slowly on with shouldered weapon, its blade blueglancing. Silently at the gravehead another coiled the coffinband. His navelcord. The brother-in-law, turning away, placed something in his free hand. Thanks in silence. Sorry, sir: trouble. Headshake. I know that. For yourselves just.

The mourners moved away slowly, without aim, by devious paths, staying at whiles to read a name on a tomb.

— Let us go round by the chief's grave, Hynes said. We have time.

— Let us, Mr Power said.

They turned to the right, following their slow thoughts. With awe Mr Power's blank voice spoke:

— Some say he is not in that grave at all. That the coffin was filled with stones. That one day he will come again.

Hynes shook his head.

— Parnell will never come again, he said. He's there, all that was mortal of him. Peace to his ashes.

Mr Bloom walked unheeded along his grove by saddened angels, crosses, broken pillars, family vaults, stone hopes praying with upcast eyes, old Ireland's hearts and hands. More sensible to spend the money on some charity for the living. Pray for the repose of the soul of. Does anybody really? Plant him and have done with him. Like down a coalshoot. Then lump them together to save time. All Souls' Day. Twenty-seventh I'll be at his grave. Ten shillings for the gardener. He keeps it free of weeds. Old man himself. Bent down double with his shears, clipping. Near death's door. Who passed away. Who departed this life. As if they did it of their own accord. Got the shove, all of them. Who kicked the bucket. More interesting if they told you what they were. So-and-so, wheelwright. I travelled for cork lino. I paid five shillings in the pound. Or a woman's with her saucepan. I cooked good Irish stew. Eulogy in a country church-yard it ought to be, that poem of whose is it Wordsworth or Thomas Campbell. Entered into rest, the Protestants put it. Old Dr Murren's. The great physician called him home. Well, it's God's acre for them. Nice country residence. Newly plastered and painted. Ideal spot to have a quiet smoke and read the *Church Times*. Marriage ads they never try to beautify.

Rusty wreaths hung on knobs, garlands of bronzefoil. Better value that for the money. Still, the flowers are more poetical. The other gets rather tiresome, never withering. Expresses nothing. Immortelles.

A bird sat tamely perched on a poplar branch. Like stuffed. Like the wedding present Alderman Hooper gave us. Hu! Not a budge out of him. Knows there are no catapults to let fly at him. Dead animal even sadder. Silly Milly burying the little dead bird in the kitchen matchbox, a daisychain and bits of broken chainies on the grave.

The Sacred Heart that is: showing it. Heart on his sleeve. Ought to be sideways and red it should be painted, like a real heart. Ireland was dedicated to it or whatever that. Seems anything but pleased. Why this infliction? Would birds come then and peck like the boy with the basket of fruit? But he said no because they ought to have been afraid of the boy. Apollo that was.

How many! All these here once walked round Dublin. Faithful departed. As you are now so once were we.

Besides how could you remember everybody? Eyes, walk, voice. Well, the voice, yes: gramophone. Have a gramophone in every grave or keep it in the house. After dinner on a Sunday. Put on poor old great-grandfather. Kraahraark! Hellohellohello amawfullyglad kraark awfullygladaseeagain hellohello amawf krpthsth. Remind you of the voice like the photograph reminds you of the face. Otherwise you couldn't remember the face after fifteen years, say. For instance who? For instance some fellow that died when I was in Wisdom Hely's.

Rtststr! A rattle of pebbles. Wait. Stop.

He looked down intently into a stone crypt. Some animal. Wait. There he goes.

An obese grey rat toddled along the side of the crypt, moving the pebbles. An old stager: great-grandfather: he knows the ropes. The grey alive crushed itself in under the plinth, wriggled itself in under it. Good hiding place for treasure.

Who lives there? Are laid the remains of Robert Emery. Robert Emmet was buried here by torchlight, wasn't he? Making his rounds.

Tail gone now.

One of those chaps would make short work of a fellow. Pick the bones clean no matter who it was. Ordinary meat for them. A corpse is meat gone bad. Well, and what's cheese? Corpse of milk. I read in that *Voyages in China* that the Chinese say a white man smells like a corpse. Cremation better. Priests dead against it. Devilling for the other firm. Wholesale burners and Dutch oven dealers. Time of the plague. Quicklime feverpits to eat them. Lethal chamber. Ashes to ashes. Or bury at sea. Where is that Parsee tower of silence? Eaten by birds. Earth, fire, water. Drowning they say is the pleasantest. See your whole life in a flash. But being brought back to life, no. Can't bury in the air however. Out of a flying machine. Wonder does the news go about whenever a fresh one is let down. Underground communication. We learned that from them. Wouldn't be surprised. Regular square feed for them. Flies come before he's well dead. Got wind of Dignam. They wouldn't care about the smell of it. Salt-white crumbling mush of corpse: smell, taste like raw white turnips.

The gates glimmered in front: still open. Back to the world again. Enough of this place. Brings you a bit nearer every time. Last time I was here was Mrs Sinico's funeral. Poor papa too. The love that kills. And even scraping up the earth at night with a lantern like that case I read of to get at fresh buried females or even putrefied with running gravesores. Give you the creeps after a bit. I will appear to you after death. You will see my ghost after death. My ghost will haunt you after death. There is another world after death named hell. I do not like that other world, she wrote. No more do I. Plenty to see and hear and feel yet. Feel live warm beings near you. Let them sleep in their maggoty beds. They are not going to get me this innings. Warm beds: warm full-blooded life.

Martin Cunningham emerged from a side path, talking gravely.

Solicitor, I think. I know his face. Menton, John Henry, solicitor, commissioner for oaths and affidavits. Dignam used to be in his office. Mat Dillon's long ago. Jolly Mat. Convivial evenings. Cold fowl, cigars, the Tantalus glasses. Heart of gold really. Yes, Menton. Got his rag out that evening on the bowling green because I sailed inside him. Pure fluke of mine: the bias. Why he took such a rooted dislike to me. Hate at first sight. Molly and Floey Dillon linked under the lilac tree, laughing. Fellow always like that, mortified if women are by.

Got a dinge in the side of his hat. Carriage probably.

— Excuse me, sir, Mr Bloom said beside them.

They stopped.

— Your hat is a little crushed, Mr Bloom said, pointing.

John Henry Menton stared at him for an instant without moving.

— There, Martin Cunningham helped, pointing also.

John Henry Menton took off his hat, bulged out the dinge and smoothed the nap with care on his coatsleeve. He clapped the hat on his head again.

— It's all right now, Martin Cunningham said.

John Henry Menton jerked his head down in acknowledgment.

— Thank you, he said shortly.

They walked on towards the gates. Mr Bloom, chapfallen, drew behind a few paces so as not to overhear. Martin laying down the law. Martin could wind a sappyhead like that round his little finger without his seeing it.

Oyster eyes. Never mind. Be sorry after perhaps when it dawns on him. Get the pull over him that way.

Thank you. How grand we are this morning!

IN THE HEART OF THE HIBERNIAN METROPOLIS

Before Nelson's Pillar trams slowed, shunted, changed trolley, started for Blackrock, Kingstown and Dalkey, Clonskeagh, Rathgar and Terenure, Palmerston Park and Upper Rathmines, Sandymount Green, Rathmines, Ringsend and Sandymount Tower, Harold's Cross. The hoarse Dublin United Tramway Company's timekeeper bawled them off:

– Rathgar and Terenure!

– Come on, Sandymount Green!

Right and left parallel clanging ringing a double-decker and a single-deck moved from their railheads, swerved to the down line, glided parallel.

– Start, Palmerston Park!

THE WEARER OF THE CROWN

Under the porch of the General Post Office shoeblacks called and polished. Parked in North Prince's Street His Majesty's vermilion mailcars, bearing on their sides the royal initials E.R., received loudly flung sacks of letters, postcards, lettercards, parcels, insured and paid, for local, provincial, British and overseas delivery.

GENTLEMEN OF THE PRESS

Grossbooted draymen rolled barrels dullthudding out of Prince's Stores and bumped them up on the brewery float. On the brewery float bumped dullthudding barrels rolled by grossbooted draymen out of Prince's Stores.

– There it is, Red Murray said. Alexander Keyes.

– Just cut it out, will you? Mr Bloom said, and I'll take it round to the *Telegraph* office.

The door of Ruttledge's office creaked again. Davy Stephens, minute in a large capecoat, a small felt hat crowning his ringlets, passed out with a roll of papers under his cape, a king's courier.

Red Murray's long shears sliced out the advertisement from the newspaper in four clean strokes. Scissors and paste.

—I'll go through the printing works, Mr Bloom said, taking the cut square.

—Of course, if he wants a par, Red Murray said earnestly, a pen behind his ear, we can do him one.

—Right, Mr Bloom said with a nod. I'll rub that in.

We.

WILLIAM BRAYDEN, ESQUIRE, OF OAKLANDS, SANDYMOUNT

Red Murray touched Mr Bloom's arm with the shears and whispered:

—Brayden.

Mr Bloom turned and saw the liveried porter raise his lettered cap as a stately figure entered between the newsboards of the *Weekly Freeman and National Press* and the *Freeman's Journal and National Press*. Dull-thudding Guinness's barrels. It passed stately up the staircase, steered by an umbrella, a solemn beard-framed face. The broadcloth back ascended each step: back. All his brains are in the nape of his neck, Simon Dedalus says. Welts of flesh behind on him. Fat folds of neck, fat, neck, fat, neck.

—Don't you think his face is like our Saviour? Red Murray whispered.

The door of Ruttledge's office whispered: ee: cree. They always build one door opposite another for the wind to. Way in. Way out.

Our Saviour: beard-framed oval face: talking in the dusk. Mary, Martha. Steered by an umbrella sword to the footlights: Mario the tenor.

—Or like Mario, Mr Bloom said.

—Yes, Red Murray agreed. But Mario was said to be the picture of our Saviour.

Jesus Mario with rougy cheeks, doublet and spindlelegs. Hand on his heart. In *Martha*.

> *Co-ome thou lost one,*
> *Co-ome thou dear one!*

THE CROZIER AND THE PEN

—His Grace phoned down twice this morning, Red Murray said gravely.

They watched the knees, legs, boots vanish. Neck.

A telegram boy stepped in nimbly, threw an envelope on the counter and stepped off posthaste, with a word:

— *Freeman*!

Mr Bloom said slowly:

— Well, he is one of our saviours also.

A meek smile accompanied him as he lifted the counterflap, as he passed in through a side door and along the warm dark stairs and passage, along the now reverberating boards. But will he save the circulation? Thumping, thumping.

He pushed in the glass swingdoor and entered, stepping over strewn packing paper. Through a lane of clanking drums he made his way towards Nannetti's reading closet.

Hynes here too: account of the funeral probably. Thumping, thump.

WITH UNFEIGNED REGRET IT IS WE ANNOUNCE
THE DISSOLUTION OF A MOST RESPECTED DUBLIN BURGESS

This morning the remains of the late Mr Patrick Dignam. Machines. Smash a man to atoms if they got him caught. Rule the world today. His machineries are pegging away too. Like these, got out of hand: fermenting. Working away, tearing away. And that old grey rat tearing to get in.

HOW A GREAT DAILY ORGAN IS TURNED OUT

Mr Bloom halted behind the foreman's spare body, admiring the glossy crown.

Strange he never saw his real country. Ireland my country. Member for College Green. He boomed that workaday worker tack for all it was worth. It's the ads and side features sell a weekly, not the stale news in the official gazette. Queen Anne is dead. Published by authority in the year one thousand and. Demesne situate in the townland of Rosenallis, barony of Tinnehinch. To all whom it may concern schedule pursuant to statute showing return of number of mules and jennets exported from Ballina. Nature notes. Cartoons. Phil Blake's weekly Pat and Bull story. Uncle Toby's page for tiny tots. Country bumpkins' queries. Dear Mr Editor, what is a good cure for flatulence? I'd like that part. Learn a lot teaching others. The personal note. M.A.P. Mainly all pictures. Shapely bathers on golden strand. World's biggest balloon. Double marriage of sisters celebrated. Two bridegrooms laughing heartily at each other. Caprani too, printer. More Irish than the Irish.

The machines clanked in threefour time. Thump, thump, thump. Now if he got paralysed there and no one knew how to stop them they'd clank on and on the same, print it over and over and up and back. Monkeydoodle the whole thing. Want a cool head.

— Well, get it into the evening edition, councillor, Hynes said.

Soon be calling him my lord mayor. Long John is backing him, they say.

The foreman, without answering, scribbled press on a corner of the sheet and made a sign to a typesetter. He handed the sheet silently over the dirty glass screen.

— Right, thanks, Hynes said, moving off.

Mr Bloom stood in his way.

— If you want to draw, the cashier is just going to lunch, he said, pointing backward with his thumb.

— Did you? Hynes asked.

— Mm, Mr Bloom said. Look sharp and you'll catch him.

— Thanks, old man, Hynes said. I'll tap him too.

He hurried on eagerly towards the *Freeman's Journal* office.

Three bob I lent him in Meagher's. Three weeks. Third hint.

WE SEE THE CANVASSER AT WORK

Mr Bloom laid his cutting on Mr Nannetti's desk.

— Excuse me, councillor, he said. This ad, you see. Keyes, you remember?

Mr Nannetti considered the cutting awhile and nodded.

— He wants it in for July, Mr Bloom said.

The foreman moved his pencil towards it.

— But wait, Mr Bloom said. He wants it changed. Keyes, you see. He wants two keys at the top.

Hell of a racket they make. He doesn't hear it. Nannan. Iron nerves. Maybe he understands what I . . .

The foreman turned round to hear patiently and, lifting an elbow, began to scratch slowly in the armpit of his alpaca jacket.

— Like that, Mr Bloom said, crossing his forefingers at the top.

Let him take that in first.

Mr Bloom, glancing sideways up from the cross he had made, saw the foreman's sallow face, think he has a touch of jaundice, and, beyond, the obedient reels feeding in huge webs of paper. Clank it. Clank it. Miles of it unreeled. What becomes of it after? O, wrap up meat, parcels: various uses, thousand and one things.

Slipping his words deftly into the pauses of the clanking he drew swiftly on the scarred woodwork.

HOUSE OF KEY(E)S

— Like that, see. Two crossed keys here. A circle. Then here the name. Alexander Keyes, tea, wine and spirit merchant. So on.

Better not teach him his own business.

— You know yourself, councillor, just what he wants. Then round the top in leaded: the House of Keys. You see? Do you think that's a good idea?

The foreman moved his scratching hand to his lower ribs and scratched there quietly.

— The idea, Mr Bloom said, is the House of Keys, you know, councillor, the Manx Parliament. Innuendo of Home Rule. Tourists, you know, from the Isle of Man. Catches the eye, you see. Can you do that?

I could ask him perhaps about how to pronounce that *voglio*. But then if he didn't know only make it awkward for him. Better not.

— We can do that, the foreman said. Have you the design?

— I can get it, Mr Bloom said. It was in a Kilkenny paper. He has a house there too. I'll just run out and ask him. Well, you can do that and just a little par calling attention. You know, the usual. High-class licensed premises. Long-felt want. So on.

The foreman thought for an instant.

— We can do that, he said. Let him give us a three months' renewal.

A typesetter brought him a limp galley page. He began to check it silently. Mr Bloom stood by, hearing the loud throbs of cranks, watching the silent typesetters at their cases.

ORTHOGRAPHICAL

Want to be sure of his spelling. Proof fever. Martin Cunningham forgot to give us his spelling-bee conundrum this morning. It is amusing to view the unpar one ar alleled embarra two ars is it double ess ment of a harassed pedlar while gauging au the symmetry with a y of a peeled pear under a cemetery wall. Silly, isn't it? Cemetery put in of course on account of the symmetry.

I could have said when he clapped on his topper. Thank you. I ought to have said something about an old hat or something. No. I could have said. Looks as good as new now. See his phiz then.

Sllt. The nethermost deck of the first machine jogged forward its flyboard with sllt the first batch of quire-folded papers. Sllt. Almost human the way it sllt to call attention. Doing its level best to speak. That door too sllt creaking, asking to be shut. Everything speaks in its own way. Sllt.

NOTED CHURCHMAN AN OCCASIONAL CONTRIBUTOR

The foreman handed back the galley page suddenly, saying:

— Wait. Where's the archbishop's letter? It's to be repeated in the *Telegraph*. Where's what's his name?

He looked about him round his loud unanswering machines.

— Monks, sir? a voice asked from the casting box.

— Ay. Where's Monks?

— Monks!

Mr Bloom took up his cutting. Time to get out.

— Then I'll get the design, Mr Nannetti, he said, and you'll give it a good place, I know.

— Monks!

— Yes, sir.

Three months' renewal. Want to get some wind off my chest first. Try it anyhow. Rub in August: good idea: Horse Show month. Ballsbridge. Tourists over for the show.

A DAYFATHER

He walked on through the caseroom, passing an old man, bowed, spectacled, aproned. Old Monks, the dayfather. Queer lot of stuff he must have put through his hands in his time: obituary notices, pubs' ads, speeches, divorce suits, found drowned. Nearing the end of his tether now. Sober serious man with a bit in the savings bank I'd say. Wife a good cook and washer. Daughter working the machine in the parlour. Plain Jane, no damn nonsense.

AND IT WAS THE FEAST OF THE PASSOVER

He stayed in his walk to watch a typesetter neatly distributing type. Reads it backwards first. Quickly he does it. Must require some practice that. mangiD kcirtaP. Poor papa with his haggadah book, reading backwards with his finger to me. Pessach. Next year in Jerusalem. Dear, O, dear! All that long business about that brought us out of the land of Egypt and into the house of bondage. Alleluia. *Shema Israel Adonai Elohenu.* No, that's the other. Then the twelve brothers, Jacob's sons. And then the lamb and the cat and the dog and the stick and the water and the butcher and then the angel of death kills the butcher and he kills the ox and the dog kills the cat. Sounds a bit silly till you come to look into it well. Justice it means but it's everybody eating everyone else. That's what life is after all. How quickly he does that job. Practice makes perfect. Seems to see with his fingers.

Mr Bloom passed on out of the clanking noises through the gallery on to the landing. Now am I going to tram it out all the way and then catch him out perhaps? Better phone him up first. Number? Yes. Same as Citron's house. Twenty-eight. Twenty-eight double four.

ONLY ONCE MORE THAT SOAP

He went down the house staircase. Who the deuce scrawled all over these walls with matches? Looks as if they did it for a bet. Heavy greasy smell there always is in those works. Lukewarm glue in Thom's next door when I was there.

He took out his handkerchief to dab his nose. Citronlemon? Ah, the soap I put there. Lose it out of that pocket. Putting back his handkerchief he took out the soap and stowed it away, buttoned, in the hip pocket of his trousers.

What perfume does your wife use? I could go home still: tram: something I forgot. Just to see: before: dressing. No. Here. No.

A sudden screech of laughter came from the *Evening Telegraph* office. Know who that is. What's up? Pop in a minute to phone. Ned Lambert it is.

He entered softly.

ERIN, GREEN GEM OF THE SILVER SEA

— The ghost walks, Professor MacHugh murmured softly, biscuitfully, to the dusty windowpane.

Mr Dedalus, staring from the empty fireplace at Ned Lambert's quizzing face, asked of it sourly:

— Agonising Christ, wouldn't it give you a heartburn on your arse?

Ned Lambert, seated on the table, read on:

— *Or again, note the meanderings of some purling rill as it babbles on its way, tho' quarrelling with the stony obstacles, to the tumbling waters of Neptune's blue domain, 'mid mossy banks fanned by gentlest zephyrs, played on by the glorious sunlight or 'neath the shadows cast o'er its pensive bosom by the overarching leafage of the giants of the forest.* What about that, Simon? he asked over the fringe of his newspaper. How's that for high?

— Changing his drink, Mr Dedalus said.

Ned Lambert, laughing, struck the newspaper on his knees, repeating:

— *The pensive bosom and the overarsing leafage.* O boys! O boys!

— And Xenophon looked upon Marathon, Mr Dedalus said, looking again on the fireplace and to the window, and Marathon looked on the sea.

— That will do, Professor MacHugh cried from the window. I don't want to hear any more of the stuff.

He ate off the crescent of water biscuit he had been nibbling and, hungered, made ready to nibble the biscuit in his other hand.

Highfalutin stuff. Bladderbags. Ned Lambert is taking a day off I see. Rather upsets a man's day, a funeral does. He has influence, they say. Old Chatterton, the vice-chancellor, is his granduncle or his great-granduncle. Close on ninety they say. Subleader for his death written this long time perhaps. Living to spite them. Might go first himself. Johnny, make room for your uncle. The Right Honourable Hedges Eyre Chatterton. Daresay he writes him an odd shaky cheque or two on gale days. Windfall when he kicks out. Alleluia.

— Just another spasm, Ned Lambert said.

— What is it? Mr Bloom asked.

— A recently discovered fragment of Cicero, Professor MacHugh answered with pomp of tone. *Our lovely land.*

SHORT BUT TO THE POINT

— Whose land? Mr Bloom said simply.

— Most pertinent question, the professor said between his chews, with an accent on the whose.

— Dan Dawson's land, Mr Dedalus said.

— Is it his speech last night? Mr Bloom asked.

Ned Lambert nodded.

— But listen to this, he said.

The doorknob hit Mr Bloom in the small of the back as the door was pushed in.

— Excuse me, J. J. O'Molloy said, entering.

Mr Bloom moved nimbly aside.

— I beg yours, he said.

— Good day, Jack.

— Come in. Come in.

— Good day.

— How are you, Dedalus?

— Well. And yourself?

J. J. O'Molloy shook his head.

SAD

Cleverest fellow at the junior bar he used to be. Decline, poor chap. That hectic flush spells finis for a man. Touch and go with him. What's in the wind, I wonder. Money worry.

— *Or again if we but climb the serried mountain peaks.*

— You're looking extra.

— Is the editor to be seen? J. J. O'Molloy asked, looking towards the inner door.

— Very much so, Professor MacHugh said. To be seen and heard. He's in his sanctum with Lenehan.

J. J. O'Molloy strolled to the sloping desk and began to turn back the pink pages of the file.

Practice dwindling. A might-have-been. Losing heart. Gambling. Debts of honour. Reaping the whirlwind. Used to get good retainers from D. and T. Fitzgerald. Their wigs to show the grey matter. Brains on their sleeve like the statue in Glasnevin. Believe he does some literary work for the *Express* with Gabriel Conroy. Well-read fellow. Myles Crawford began on the *Independent.* Funny the way those newspapermen veer about when they get wind of a new opening. Weathercocks. Hot and cold in the same breath. Wouldn't know which to believe. One story good till you hear the next. Go for one another baldheaded in the papers and then all blows over. Hail-fellow well met the next moment.

— Ah, listen to this for God's sake, Ned Lambert pleaded. *Or again if we but climb the serried mountain peaks...*

—Bombast! the professor broke in testily. Enough of the inflated windbag!

—*Peaks*, Ned Lambert went on, *towering high on high, to bathe our souls, as it were...*

—Bathe his lips, Mr Dedalus said. Blessed and eternal God! Yes? Is he taking anything for it?

—*As 'twere, in the peerless panorama of Ireland's portfolio, unmatched, despite their well-praised prototypes in other vaunted prize regions, for very beauty, of bosky grove and undulating plain and luscious pastureland of vernal green, steeped in the transcendent translucent glow of our mild mysterious Irish twilight...*

—The moon, Professor MacHugh said. He forgot *Hamlet.*

HIS NATIVE DORIC

—*That mantles the vista far and wide and waits till the glowing orb of the moon shines forth to irradiate her silver effulgence...*

—O! Mr Dedalus cried, giving vent to a hopeless groan. Shite and onions! That'll do, Ned. Life is too short.

He took off his silk hat and, blowing out impatiently his bushy moustache, welshcombed his hair with raking fingers.

Ned Lambert tossed the newspaper aside, chuckling with delight. An instant after, a hoarse bark of laughter burst over Professor MacHugh's unshaven black-spectacled face.

—Doughy Daw! he cried.

WHAT WETHERUP SAID

All very fine to jeer at it now in cold print but it goes down like hot cake that stuff. He was in the bakery line too, wasn't he? Why they call him Doughy Daw. Feathered his nest well anyhow. Daughter engaged to that chap in the Inland Revenue office with the motor. Hooked that nicely. Entertainments. Open house. Big blowout. Wetherup always said that. Get a grip of them by the stomach.

The inner door was opened violently and a scarlet beaked face, crested by a comb of feathery hair, thrust itself in. The bold blue eyes stared about them and the harsh voice asked:

—What is it?

— And here comes the sham squire himself, Professor MacHugh said grandly.

— Getonouthat, you bloody old pedagogue! the editor said in recognition.

— Come, Ned, Mr Dedalus said, putting on his hat. I must get a drink after that.

— Drink! the editor cried. No drinks served before mass.

— Quite right too, Mr Dedalus said, going out. Come on, Ned.

Ned Lambert sidled down from the table. The editor's blue eyes roved towards Mr Bloom's face, shadowed by a smile.

— Will you join us, Myles? Ned Lambert asked.

MEMORABLE BATTLES RECALLED

— North Cork Militia! the editor cried, striding to the mantelpiece. We won every time! North Cork and Spanish officers!

— Where was that, Myles? Ned Lambert asked with a reflective glance at his toecaps.

— In Ohio! the editor shouted.

— So it was, begad, Ned Lambert agreed.

Passing out, he whispered to J. J. O'Molloy:

— Incipient jigs. Sad case.

— Ohio! the editor crowed in high treble from his uplifted scarlet face. My Ohio!

— A perfect cretic! the professor said. Long, short and long.

O, HARP EOLIAN!

He took a reel of dental floss from his waistcoat pocket and, breaking off a piece, twanged it smartly between two and two of his resonant unwashed teeth.

— Bingbang, bangbang.

Mr Bloom, seeing the coast clear, made for the inner door.

— Just a moment, Mr Crawford, he said. I just want to phone about an ad.

He went in.

— What about that leader this evening? Professor MacHugh asked, coming to the editor and laying a firm hand on his shoulder.

— That'll be all right, Myles Crawford said more calmly. Never you fret. Hello, Jack. That's all right.

— Good day, Myles, J.J. O'Molloy said, letting the pages he held slip limply back on the file. Is that Canada Swindle case on today?

The telephone whirred inside.

— Twenty-eight ... No, twenty ... Double four ... Yes.

SPOT THE WINNER

Lenehan came out of the inner office with *Sport*'s tissues.

— Who wants a dead cert for the Gold Cup? he asked. *Sceptre* with O. Madden up.

He tossed the tissues on to the table.

Screams of newsboys barefoot in the hall rushed near and the door was flung open.

— Hush, Lenehan said. I hear feetstoops.

Professor MacHugh strode across the room and seized the cringing urchin by the collar as the others scampered out of the hall and down the steps. The tissues rustled up in the draught, floated softly in the air blue scrawls and under the table came to earth.

— It wasn't me, sir. It was the big fellow shoved me, sir.

— Throw him out and shut the door, the editor said. There's a hurricane blowing.

Lenehan began to paw the tissues up from the floor, grunting as he stooped twice.

— Waiting for the racing special, sir, the newsboy said. It was Pat Farrell shoved me, sir.

He pointed to two faces peering in round the doorframe.

— Him, sir.

— Out of this with you, Professor MacHugh said gruffly.

He hustled the boy out and banged the door to.

J.J. O'Molloy turned the files cracklingly over, murmuring, seeking:

— Continued on page six, column four.

— Yes ... *Evening Telegraph* here, Mr Bloom phoned from the inner office. Is the boss ...? Yes, *Telegraph* ... To where? ... Aha! Which auction rooms? ... Aha! I see ... Right. I'll catch him.

A COLLISION ENSUES

The bell whirred again as he rang off. He came in quickly and bumped against Lenehan who was struggling up with the second tissue.

— *Pardon, monsieur*, Lenehan said, clutching him for an instant and making a grimace.

— My fault, Mr Bloom said, suffering his grip. Are you hurt? I'm in a hurry.

— Knee, Lenehan said.

He made a comic face and whined, rubbing his knee:

— The accumulation of the *anno Domini*.

— Sorry, Mr Bloom said.

He went to the door and, holding it ajar, paused. J.J. O'Molloy slapped the heavy pages over. The noise of two shrill voices, a mouth organ, echoed in the bare hallway from the newsboys squatted on the doorsteps:

— *We are the boys of Wexford*
  Who fought with heart and hand.

EXIT BLOOM

— I'm just running round to Bachelor's Walk, Mr Bloom said, about this ad of Keyes's. Want to fix it up. They tell me he's round there in Dillon's.

He looked indecisively for a moment at their faces. The editor who, leaning against the mantelshelf, had propped his head on his hand suddenly stretched forth an arm amply.

— Begone! he said. The world is before you.

— Back in no time, Mr Bloom said, hurrying out.

J.J. O'Molloy took the tissues from Lenehan's hand and read them, blowing them apart gently, without comment.

— He'll get that advertisement, the professor said, staring through his black-rimmed spectacles over the crossblind. Look at the young scamps after him.

— Show! Where? Lenehan cried, running to the window.

A STREET CORTÈGE

Both smiled over the crossblind at the file of capering newsboys in Mr Bloom's wake, the last zigzagging white on the breeze a mocking kite, a tail of white bowknots.

— Look at the young guttersnipe behind him hue and cry, Lenehan said, and you'll kick. O, my rib risible! Taking off his flat spaugs and the walk. Small nines. Steal upon larks.

He began to mazurka in swift caricature across the floor on sliding feet past the fireplace to J.J. O'Molloy who placed the tissues in his receiving hands.

— What's that? Myles Crawford said with a start. Where are the other two gone?

— Who? the professor said, turning. They're gone round to the Oval for a drink. Paddy Hooper is there with Jack Hall. Came over last night.

— Come on then, Myles Crawford said. Where's my hat?

He walked jerkily into the office behind, parting the vent of his jacket and jingling his keys in his back pocket. They jingled then in the air and against the wood as he locked his desk drawer.

— He's pretty well on, Professor MacHugh said in a low voice.

— Seems to be, J.J. O'Molloy said, taking out a cigarette case in murmuring meditation, but it is not always as it seems. Who has the most matches?

THE CALUMET OF PEACE

He offered a cigarette to the professor and took one himself. Lenehan promptly struck a match for them and lit their cigarettes in turn. J.J. O'Molloy opened his case again and offered it.

— *Thanky vous*, Lenehan said, helping himself.

The editor came from the inner office, a straw hat awry on his brow. He declaimed in song, pointing sternly at Professor MacHugh:

— *'Twas rank and fame that tempted thee,*
  'Twas empire charmed thy heart.

The professor grinned, locking his long lips.

— Eh? Your bloody old Roman empire? Myles Crawford said.

He took a cigarette from the open case. Lenehan, lighting it for him with quick grace, said:

— Silence for my brand-new riddle!

— *Imperium Romanum*, J.J. O'Molloy said gently. It sounds nobler than British or Brixton. The word reminds one somehow of fat in the fire.

Myles Crawford blew his first puff violently towards the ceiling.

— That's it, he said. We are the fat. You and I are the fat in the fire. We haven't got the chance of a snowball in hell.

— Wait a moment, Professor MacHugh said, raising two quiet claws. We mustn't be led away by words, by sounds of words. We think of Rome, imperial, imperious, imperative.

He extended elocutionary arms from frayed stained shirtcuffs, pausing:

— What was their civilisation? Vast, I allow: but vile. Cloacae: sewers. The Jews in the wilderness and on the mountaintop said: *It is meet to be here. Let us build an altar to Jehovah.* The Roman, like the Englishman who follows in his footsteps, brought to every new shore on which he set his foot (on our shore he never set it) only his cloacal obsession. He gazed about him in his toga and he said: *It is meet to be here. Let us construct a watercloset.*

— Which they accordingly did do, Lenehan said. Our old ancient ancestors, as we read in the first chapter of Guinness's, were partial to the running stream.

— They were nature's gentlemen, J.J. O'Molloy murmured. But we have also Roman law.

— And Pontius Pilate is its prophet, Professor MacHugh responded.

— Do you know that story about Chief Baron Palles? J.J. O'Molloy asked. It was at the Royal University dinner. Everything was going swimmingly . . .

— First my riddle, Lenehan said. Are you ready?

Mr O'Madden Burke, tall in copious grey of Donegal tweed, came in from the hallway. Stephen Dedalus, behind him, uncovered as he entered.

— *Entrez, mes enfants!* Lenehan cried.

— I escort a suppliant, Mr O'Madden Burke said melodiously. Youth led by Experience visits Notoriety.

— How do you do? the editor said, holding out a hand. Come in. Your governor is just gone.

? ? ?

Lenehan said to all:

— Silence! What opera resembles a railway line? Reflect, ponder, excogitate, reply.

Stephen handed over the typed sheets, pointing to the title and signature.

– Who? the editor asked.

Bit torn off.

– Mr Garrett Deasy, Stephen said.

– That old pelters, the editor said. Who tore it? Was he short taken?

> *On swift sail flaming*
> *From storm and south*
> *He comes, pale vampire,*
> *Mouth to my mouth.*

– Good day, Stephen, the professor said, coming to peer over their shoulders. Foot-and-mouth...? Are you turned...?

Bullock-befriending bard.

SHINDY IN WELL-KNOWN RESTAURANT

– Good day, sir, Stephen answered, blushing. The letter is not mine. Mr Garrett Deasy asked me to ...

– O, I know him, Myles Crawford said, and knew his wife too. The bloodiest old tartar God ever made. By Jesus, she had the foot-and-mouth disease and no mistake! The night she threw the soup in the waiter's face in the Star and Garter. Oho!

A woman brought sin into the world. For Helen, the runaway wife of Menelaus, ten years the Greeks. O'Rourke, prince of Breffni.

– Is he a widower? Stephen asked.

– Ay, a grass one, Myles Crawford said, his eye running down the typescript. Emperor's horses. Habsburg. An Irishman saved his life on the ramparts of Vienna. Don't you forget! Maximilian Karl O'Donnell, graf von Tirconnell in Ireland. Sent his heir over to make the king an Austrian field marshal now. Going to be trouble there one day. Wild geese. O yes, every time. Don't you forget that!

– The moot point is did he forget it, J.J. O'Molloy said quietly, turning a horseshoe paperweight. Saving princes is a thank-you job.

Professor MacHugh turned on him.

– And if not? he said.

– I'll tell you how it was, Myles Crawford began. A Hungarian it was one day ...

— We were always loyal to lost causes, the professor said. Success for us is the death of the intellect and of the imagination. We were never loyal to the successful. We serve them. I teach the blatant Latin language. I speak the tongue of a race the acme of whose mentality is the maxim: time is money. Material domination. *Dominus*! Lord! Where is the spirituality? Lord Jesus! Lord Salisbury! A sofa in a West End club. But the Greek!

KYRIE ELEISON!

A smile of light brightened his dark-rimmed eyes, lengthened his long lips.

— The Greek! he said again. *Kyrios!* Shining word! The vowels the Semite and the Saxon know not. *Kyrie!* The radiance of the intellect. I ought to profess Greek, the language of the mind. *Kyrie eleison!* The closetmaker and the cloacamaker will never be lords of our spirit. We are liege subjects of the Catholic chivalry of Europe that foundered at Trafalgar and of the empire of the spirit, not an *imperium*, that went under with the Athenian fleets at Aegospotami. Yes, yes. They went under. Pyrrhus, misled by an oracle, made a last attempt to retrieve the fortunes of Greece. Loyal to a lost cause.

He strode away from them towards the window.

— They went forth to battle, Mr O'Madden Burke said greyly, but they always fell.

— Boohoo! Lenehan wept with a little noise. Owing to a brick received in the latter half of the matinée. Poor, poor, poor Pyrrhus!

He whispered then near Stephen's ear:

LENEHAN'S LIMERICK

— *There's a ponderous pundit MacHugh*
  Who wears goggles of ebony hue.
  As he mostly sees double,
  To wear them why trouble?
  I can't see the Joe Miller. Can you?

In mourning for Sallust, Mulligan says. Whose mother is beastly dead.

Myles Crawford crammed the sheets into a side pocket.

— That'll be all right, he said. I'll read the rest after. That'll be all right.

Lenehan extended his hands in protest.

— But my riddle! he said. What opera is like a railway line?

— Opera? Mr O'Madden Burke's sphinx face reriddled.

Lenehan announced gladly:

— *The Rose of Castile.* See the wheeze? Rows of cast steel. Gee!

He poked Mr O'Madden Burke mildly in the spleen. Mr O'Madden Burke fell back with grace on his umbrella, feigning a gasp.

— Help! he sighed. I feel a strong weakness.

Lenehan, rising to tiptoe, fanned his face rapidly with the rustling tissues.

The professor, returning by way of the files, swept his hand across Stephen's and Mr O'Madden Burke's loose ties.

— Paris, past and present, he said. You look like communards.

— Like fellows who had blown up the Bastille, J.J. O'Molloy said in quiet mockery. Or was it you shot the lord lieutenant of Finland between you? You look as though you had done the deed. General Bobrikoff.

— We were only thinking about it, Stephen said.

OMNIUM GATHERUM

— All the talents, Myles Crawford said. Law, the classics ...

— The turf, Lenehan put in.

— Literature, the press.

— If Bloom were here, the professor said. The gentle art of advertisement.

— And Madam Bloom, Mr O'Madden Burke added. The vocal muse. Dublin's prime favourite.

Lenehan gave a loud cough.

— Ahem! he said very softly. O, for a fresh of breath air! I caught a cold in the park. The gate was open.

"YOU CAN DO IT!"

The editor laid a nervous hand on Stephen's shoulder.

— I want you to write something for me, he said. Something with a bite in it. You can do it. I see it in your face. *In the lexicon of youth* ...

See it in your face. See it in your eye. Lazy idle little schemer.

— Foot-and-mouth disease! the editor cried in scornful invective. Great nationalist meeting in Borris-in-Ossory. All balls! Bulldozing the public! Give them something with a bite in it. Put us all into it, damn its soul. Father, Son and Holy Ghost and Jakes M'Carthy.

— We can all supply mental pabulum, Mr O'Madden Burke said.

Stephen raised his eyes to the bold unheeding stare.

— He wants you for the press gang, J.J. O'Molloy said.

THE GREAT GALLAHER

— You can do it, Myles Crawford repeated, clenching his hand in emphasis. Wait a minute. We'll paralyse Europe, as Ignatius Gallaher used to say when he was on the shaughraun, doing billiard-marking in the Clarence. Gallaher, that was a pressman for you. That was a pen. You know how he made his mark? I'll tell you. That was the smartest piece of journalism ever known. That was in eighty-two, sixth of May, time of the Invincibles, murder in the Phoenix Park, before you were born, I suppose. I'll show you.

He pushed past them to the files.

— Look at here, he said, turning. The *New York World* cabled for a special. Remember that time?

Professor MacHugh nodded.

— The *New York World*, the editor said excitedly, pushing back his straw hat. Where it took place. Tim Kelly, or Kavanagh I mean, Joe Brady and the rest of them. Where Skin-the-Goat drove the car. Whole route, see?

— Skin-the-Goat, Mr O'Madden Burke said. Fitzharris. He has that cabman's shelter, they say, down there at Butt Bridge. Holohan told me. You know Holohan?

— Hop and carry one, is it? Myles Crawford said.

— And poor Gumley is down there too, so he told me, minding stones for the Corporation. A night watchman.

Stephen turned in surprise.

— Gumley? he said. You don't say so? A friend of my father's, is it?

— Never mind Gumley, Myles Crawford cried angrily. Let Gumley mind the stones, see they don't run away. Look at here. What did Ignatius Gallaher do? I'll tell you. Inspiration of genius. Cabled right away. Have you *Weekly Freeman* of 17 March? Right. Have you got that?

He flung back pages of the files and stuck his finger on a point.

— Take page four, advertisement for Bransome's coffee, let us say. Have you got that? Right.

The telephone whirred.

A DISTANT VOICE

— I'll answer it, the professor said, going.

— B is Parkgate. Good.

His finger leaped and struck point after point, vibrating.

— T is viceregal lodge. C is where murder took place. K is Knockmaroon gate.

The loose flesh of his neck shook like a cock's wattles. An ill-starched dicky jutted up and with a rude gesture he thrust it back into his waistcoat.

— Hello? *Evening Telegraph* here ... Hello? ... Who's there? ... Yes ... Yes ... Yes.

— F to P is the route Skin-the-Goat drove the car for an alibi: Inchicore, Roundtown, Windy Arbour, Palmerston Park, Ranelagh. F.A.B.P. Got that? X is Davy's public house in Upper Leeson Street.

The professor came to the inner door.

— Bloom is at the telephone, he said.

— Tell him go to hell, the editor said promptly. X is Davy's public house, see?

CLEVER, VERY

— Clever, Lenehan said. Very.

— Gave it to them on a hot plate, Myles Crawford said, the whole bloody history.

Nightmare from which you will never awake.

— I saw it, the editor said proudly. I was present. Dick Adams, the best-hearted bloody Corkman the Lord ever put the breath of life in, and myself.

Lenehan bowed to a shape of air, announcing:

— Madam, I'm Adam. And Able was I ere I saw Elba.

— History! Myles Crawford cried. The Old Woman of Prince's Street was there first. There was weeping and gnashing of teeth over that. Out of an advertisement. Gregor Grey made the design for it. That gave him

131

the leg up. Then Paddy Hooper worked Tay Pay who took him on to the *Star*. Now he's got in with Blumenfeld. That's press. That's talent. Pyat! He was all their daddies!

— The father of scare journalism, Lenehan confirmed, and the brother-in-law of Chris Callanan.

— Hello? ... Are you there? ... Yes, he's here still. Come across yourself.

— Where do you find a pressman like that now, eh? the editor cried.

He flung the pages down.

— Clamn dever, Lenehan said to Mr O'Madden Burke.

— Very smart, Mr O'Madden Burke said.

Professor MacHugh came from the inner office.

— Talking about the Invincibles, he said, did you see that some hawkers were up before the recorder...

— O yes, J.J. O'Molloy said eagerly. Lady Dudley was walking home through the park to see all the trees that were blown down by that cyclone last year and thought she'd buy a view of Dublin. And it turned out to be a commemoration postcard of Joe Brady or Number One or Skin-the-Goat. Right outside the viceregal lodge, imagine!

— They're only in the hook and eye department, Myles Crawford said. Psha! Press and the bar! Where have you a man now at the bar like those fellows, like Whiteside, like Isaac Butt, like silver-tongued O'Hagan? Eh? Ah, bloody nonsense! Only in the halfpenny place!

His mouth continued to twitch unspeaking in nervous curls of disdain.

Would anyone wish that mouth for her kiss? How do you know? Why did you write it then?

RHYMES AND REASONS

Mouth, south. Is the mouth south someway? Or the south a mouth? Must be some. South, pout, out, shout, drouth. Rhymes: two men dressed the same, looking the same, two by two.

> .... *la tua pace*
> .... *che parlar ti piace*
> *Mentre che il vento, come fa, si tace.*

He saw them three by three, approaching girls, in green, in rose, in russet, entwining, *per l'aere perso*, in mauve, in purple, *quella pacifica oriflamma*, in gold of oriflamme, *di rimirar fè più ardenti*. But I old men,

132

penitent, leaden-footed, underdarkneath the night: mouth, south: tomb, womb.

— Speak up for yourself, Mr O'Madden Burke said.

SUFFICIENT FOR THE DAY ...

J.J. O'Molloy, smiling palely, took up the gage.

— My dear Myles, he said, flinging his cigarette aside, you put a false construction on my words. I hold no brief, as at present advised, for the third profession *qua* profession but your Cork legs are running away with you. Why not bring in Henry Grattan and Flood and Demosthenes and Edmund Burke? Ignatius Gallaher we all know and his Chapelizod boss, Harmsworth of the farthing press, and his American cousin of the Bowery gutter sheet, not to mention *Paddy Kelly's Budget*, *Pue's Occurrences* and our watchful friend *The Skibbereen Eagle*. Why bring in a master of forensic eloquence like Whiteside? Sufficient for the day is the newspaper thereof.

LINKS WITH BYGONE DAYS OF YORE

— Grattan and Flood wrote for this very paper, the editor cried in his face. Irish Volunteers. Where are you now? Established 1763. Dr Lucas. Who have you now like John Philpot Curran? Psha!

— Well, J.J. O'Molloy said, Bushe K.C. for example.

— Bushe? the editor said. Well, yes: Bushe, yes. He has a strain of it in his blood. Kendal Bushe or I mean Seymour Bushe.

— He would have been on the bench long ago, the professor said, only for ... But no matter.

J.J. O'Molloy turned to Stephen and said quietly and slowly:

— One of the most polished periods I think I ever listened to in my life fell from the lips of Seymour Bushe. It was in that case of fratricide, the Childs murder case. Bushe defended him.

And in the porches of mine ear did pour.

By the way how did he find that out? He died in his sleep. Or the other story, beast with two backs?

— What was that? the professor asked.

133

– He spoke on the law of evidence, J.J. O'Molloy said, of Roman justice as contrasted with the earlier Mosaic code, the *lex talionis*. And he cited the *Moses* of Michelangelo in the Vatican.

– Ha.

– A few well-chosen words, Lenehan prefaced. Silence!

Pause. J.J. O'Molloy took out his cigarette case.

False lull. Something quite ordinary.

Messenger took out his matchbox thoughtfully and lit his cigar.

I have often thought since on looking back over that strange time that it was that small act, trivial in itself, that striking of that match, that determined the whole aftercourse of both our lives.

A POLISHED PERIOD

J.J. O'Molloy resumed, moulding his words:

– He said of it: *that stony effigy in frozen music, horned and terrible, of the human form divine, that eternal symbol of wisdom and of prophecy which, if aught that the imagination or the hand of sculptor has wrought in marble of soul-transfigured and of soul-transfiguring deserves to live, deserves to live.*

His slim hand with a wave graced echo and fall.

– Fine! Myles Crawford said at once.

– The divine afflatus, Mr O'Madden Burke said.

– You like it? J.J. O'Molloy asked Stephen.

Stephen, his blood wooed by grace of language and gesture, blushed. He took a cigarette from the case. J.J. O'Molloy offered his case to Myles Crawford. Lenehan lit their cigarettes as before and took his trophy, saying:

– *Muchibus thankibus.*

A MAN OF HIGH MORALE

– Professor Magennis was speaking to me about you, J.J. O'Molloy said to Stephen. What do you think really of that hermetic crowd, the Opal Hush poets: AE the master mystic? That Blavatsky woman started it. She was a nice old bag of tricks. AE has been telling some Yankee interviewer that you came to him in the small hours of the morning to ask him about planes of consciousness. Magennis thinks you must have been pulling AE's leg. He is a man of the very highest morale, Magennis.

Speaking about me. What did he say? What did he say? What did he say about me? Don't ask.

— No, thanks, Professor MacHugh said, waving the cigarette case aside. Wait a moment. Let me say one thing. The finest display of oratory I ever heard was a speech made by John F. Taylor at the College Historical Society. Mr Justice Fitzgibbon, the present lord justice of appeal, had spoken and the paper under debate was an essay (new for those days) advocating the revival of the Irish tongue.

He turned towards Myles Crawford and said:

— You know Gerald Fitzgibbon. Then you can imagine the style of his discourse.

— He is sitting with Tim Healy, J.J. O'Molloy said, rumour has it, on the Trinity College Estates Commission.

— He is sitting with a sweet thing in a child's frock, Myles Crawford said. Go on. Well?

— It was the speech, mark you, the professor said, of a finished orator, full of courteous haughtiness and pouring in chastened diction I will not say the vials of his wrath but pouring the proud man's contumely upon the new movement. It was then a new movement. We were weak, therefore worthless.

He closed his long thin lips an instant but, eager to be on, raised an outspanned hand to his spectacles and, with trembling thumb and ring finger touching lightly the black rims, steadied them to a new focus.

IMPROMPTU

In ferial tone he addressed J.J. O'Molloy:

— Taylor had come there, you must know, from a sickbed. That he had prepared his speech I do not believe, for there was not even one shorthand writer in the hall. His dark lean face had a growth of shaggy beard round it. He wore a loose white silk neckcloth and altogether he looked (though he was not) a dying man.

His gaze turned at once but slowly from J.J. O'Molloy's towards Stephen's face and then bent at once to the ground, seeking. His unglazed linen collar appeared behind his bent head, soiled by his withering hair. Still seeking, he said:

– When Fitzgibbon's speech had ended John F. Taylor rose to reply. Briefly, as well as I can bring them to mind, his words were these.

He raised his head firmly. His eyes bethought themselves once more. Witless shellfish swam in the gross lenses to and fro, seeking outlet.

He began:

– *Mr Chairman, ladies and gentlemen: Great was my admiration in listening to the remarks addressed to the youth of Ireland a moment since by my learned friend. It seemed to me that I had been transported into a country far away from this country, into an age remote from this age, that I stood in ancient Egypt and that I was listening to the speech of some high priest of that land addressed to the youthful Moses.*

His listeners held their cigarettes poised to hear, their smokes ascending in frail stalks that flowered with his speech. *And let our crooked smokes.* Noble words coming. Look out. Could you try your hand at it yourself?

– *And it seemed to me that I heard the voice of that Egyptian high priest raised in a tone of like haughtiness and like pride. I heard his words and their meaning was revealed to me.*

FROM THE FATHERS

It was revealed to me that those things are good which yet are corrupted, which neither if they were supremely good nor unless they were good could be corrupted. Ah, curse you! That's Saint Augustine.

– *Why will you Jews not accept our culture, our religion and our language? You are a tribe of nomad herdsmen: we are a mighty people. You have no cities nor no wealth: our cities are hives of humanity and our galleys, trireme and quadrireme, laden with all manner merchandise furrow the waters of the known globe. You have but emerged from primitive conditions: we have a literature, a priesthood, an agelong history and a polity.*

Nile.

Child, man, effigy.

By the Nilebank the babemaries kneel, a cradle of bulrushes: a man supple in combat: stone horned, stone bearded, heart of stone.

– *You pray to a local and obscure idol: our temples, majestic and mysterious, are the abodes of Isis and Osiris, of Horus and Ammon Ra. Yours serfdom, awe and humbleness: ours thunder and the seas. Israel is weak and few are her children: Egypt is an host and terrible are her arms. Vagrants and daylabourers are you called: the world trembles at our name.*

A dumb belch of hunger cleft his speech. He lifted his voice above it boldly:

— *But, ladies and gentlemen, had the youthful Moses listened to and accepted that view of life, had he bowed his head and bowed his will and bowed his spirit before that arrogant admonition, he would never have brought the chosen people out of their house of bondage nor followed the pillar of the cloud by day. He would never have spoken with the Eternal amid lightnings on Sinai's mountaintop nor ever have come down with the light of inspiration shining in his countenance and bearing in his arms the tables of the law, graven in the language of the outlaw.*

He ceased and looked at them, enjoying silence.

OMINOUS – FOR HIM!

J.J. O'Molloy said not without regret:

— And yet he died without having entered the land of promise.

— A - sudden - at - the - moment - though - from - lingering - illness - often - previously - expectorated - demise, Lenehan said. And with a great future behind him.

The troop of bare feet was heard rushing along the hallway and pattering up the staircase.

— That is oratory, the professor said, uncontradicted.

Gone with the wind. Hosts at Mullaghmast and Tara of the kings. Miles of porches of ears. The tribune's words, howled and scattered to the four winds. A people sheltered within his voice. Dead noise. Akasic records of all that ever anywhere wherever was. Love and laud him: me no more.

I have money.

— Gentlemen, Stephen said. As the next motion on the agenda paper may I suggest that the house do now adjourn?

— You take my breath away. It is not perchance a French compliment? Mr O'Madden Burke asked. 'Tis the hour, methinks, when the winejug, metaphorically speaking, is most grateful in Ye Ancient Hostelry.

— That it be and hereby is resolutely resolved. All who are in favour say ay, Lenehan announced. The contrary no. I declare it carried. To which particular boozing shed...? My casting vote is: Mooney's!

He led the way, admonishing:

— We will sternly refuse to partake of strong waters, will we not? Yes, we will not. By no manner of means.

137

Mr O'Madden Burke, following close, said with an ally's lunge of his umbrella:

— Lay on, Macduff!

— Chip of the old block! the editor cried, slapping Stephen on the shoulder. Let us go. Where are those blasted keys?

He fumbled in his pocket, pulling out the crushed typesheets.

— Foot-and-mouth. I know. That'll be all right. That'll go in. Where are they? That's all right.

He thrust the sheets back and went into the inner office.

LET US HOPE

J.J. O'Molloy, about to follow him in, said quietly to Stephen:

— I hope you will live to see it published. Myles, one moment.

He went into the inner office, closing the door behind him.

— Come along, Stephen, the professor said. That is fine, isn't it? It has the prophetic vision. *Fuit Ilium!* The sack of windy Troy. Kingdoms of this world. The masters of the Mediterranean are fellaheen today.

The first newsboy came pattering down the stairs at their heels and rushed out into the street, yelling:

— Racing special!

Dublin. I have much, much to learn.

They turned to the left along Abbey Street.

— I have a vision too, Stephen said.

— Yes? the professor said, skipping to get into step. Crawford will follow.

Another newsboy shot past them, yelling as he ran:

— Racing special!

DEAR DIRTY DUBLIN

Dubliners.

— Two Dublin vestals, Stephen said, elderly and pious, have lived fifty and fifty-three years in Fumbally's Lane.

— Where is that? the professor asked.

— Off Blackpitts, Stephen said.

Damp night reeking of hungry dough. Against the wall. Face glistening tallow under her fustian shawl. Frantic hearts. Akasic records. Quicker, darlint!

On now. Dare it. Let there be life.

138

— They want to see the views of Dublin from the top of Nelson's Pillar. They save up three and tenpence in a red tin letterbox moneybox. They shake out the threepenny bits and a sixpence and coax out the pennies with the blade of a knife. Two and three in silver and one and seven in coppers. They put on their bonnets and best clothes and take their umbrellas for fear it may come on to rain.

— Wise virgins, Professor MacHugh said.

LIFE ON THE RAW

— They buy one-and-fourpenceworth of brawn and four slices of pan loaf at the North City Dining Rooms in Marlborough Street from Miss Kate Collins, proprietress. They purchase four and twenty ripe plums from a girl at the foot of Nelson's Pillar to take off the thirst of the brawn. They give two threepenny bits to the gentleman at the turnstile and begin to waddle slowly up the winding staircase, grunting, encouraging each other, afraid of the dark, panting, one asking the other have you the brawn, praising God and the Blessed Virgin, threatening to come down, peeping at the airslits. Glory be to God. They had no idea it was that high.

Their names are Anne Kearns and Florence MacCabe. Anne Kearns has the lumbago for which she rubs on Lourdes water given her by a lady who got a bottleful from a Passionist father. Florence MacCabe takes a crubeen and a bottle of double X for supper every Saturday.

— Antithesis, the professor said, nodding twice. Vestal virgins. I can see them. What's keeping our friend?

He turned.

A bevy of scampering newsboys rushed down the steps, scattering in all directions, yelling, their white papers fluttering. Hard after them Myles Crawford appeared on the steps, his hat aureoling his scarlet face, talking with J. J. O'Molloy.

— Come along, the professor cried, waving his arm.

He set off again to walk by Stephen's side.

— Yes, he said. I see them.

RETURN OF BLOOM

Mr Bloom, breathless, caught in a whirl of wild newsboys near the offices of the *Irish Catholic* and *Dublin Penny Journal*, called:

— Mr Crawford! A moment!

— *Telegraph*! Racing special!

— What is it? Myles Crawford said, falling back a pace.

A newsboy cried in Mr Bloom's face:

— Terrible tragedy in Rathmines! A child bit by a bellows!

INTERVIEW WITH THE EDITOR

—Just this ad, Mr Bloom said, pushing through towards the steps, puffing, and taking the cutting from his pocket. I spoke with Mr Keyes just now. He'll give a renewal for two months, he says. After he'll see. But he wants a par to call attention in the *Telegraph* too, the Saturday pink. And he wants it copied if it's not too late, I told councillor Nannetti, from the *Kilkenny People*. I can have access to it in the National Library. House of Keys, don't you see? His name is Keyes. It's a play on the name. But he practically promised he'd give the renewal. But he wants just a little puff. What will I tell him, Mr Crawford?

K.M.A.

— Will you tell him he can kiss my arse? Myles Crawford said, throwing out his arm for emphasis. Tell him that straight from the stable.

A bit nervy. Look out for squalls. All off for a drink. Arm in arm. Lenehan's yachting cap on the cadge beyond. Usual blarney. Wonder is that young Dedalus the moving spirit. Has a good pair of boots on him today. Last time I saw him he had his heels on view. Been walking in muck somewhere. Careless chap. What was he doing in Irishtown?

— Well, Mr Bloom said, his eyes returning, if I can get the design I suppose it's worth a short par. He'd give the ad, I think. I'll tell him …

K.M.R.I.A.

— He can kiss my royal Irish arse, Myles Crawford cried loudly over his shoulder. Any time he likes, tell him.

While Mr Bloom stood weighing the point and about to smile he strode on jerkily.

— *Nulla bona*, Jack, he said, raising his hand to his chin. I'm up to here. I've been through the hoop myself. I was looking for a fellow to back a bill for me no later than last week. Sorry, Jack. You must take the will for the deed. With a heart and a half if I could raise the wind anyhow.

J.J. O'Molloy pulled a long face and walked on silently. They caught up on the others and walked abreast.

— When they have eaten the brawn and the bread and wiped their twenty fingers in the paper the bread was wrapped in they go nearer to the railings.

— Something for you, the professor explained to Myles Crawford. Two old Dublin women on the top of Nelson's Pillar.

SOME COLUMN!
THAT'S WHAT WADDLER ONE SAID

— That's new, Myles Crawford said. That's copy. Out for the waxies' Dargle. Two old trickies, what?

— But they are afraid the pillar will fall, Stephen went on. They see the roofs and argue about where the different churches are: Rathmines' blue dome, Adam and Eve's, Saint Laurence O'Toole's. But it makes them giddy to look so they pull up their skirts . . .

THOSE SLIGHTLY RAMBUNCTIOUS FEMALES

— Easy all, Myles Crawford said. No poetic licence. We're in the archdiocese here.

— And settle down on their striped petticoats, peering up at the statue of the one-handled adulterer.

— One-handled adulterer! the professor cried. I like that. I see the idea. I see what you mean.

DAMES DONATE DUBLIN'S CITS.
SPEEDPILLS VELOCITOUS AEROLITHS, BELIEF.

— It gives them a crick in their necks, Stephen said, and they are too tired to look up or down or to speak. They put the bag of plums between them and eat the plums out of it, one after another, wiping off with their handkerchiefs the plum juice that dribbles out of their mouths and spitting the plumstones slowly out between the railings.

He gave a sudden loud young laugh as a close. Lenehan and Mr O'Madden Burke, hearing, turned, beckoned and led on across towards Mooney's.

— Finished? Myles Crawford said. So long as they do no worse.

SOPHIST WALLOPS HAUGHTY HELEN SQUARE ON PROBOSCIS.
SPARTANS GNASH MOLARS.
ITHACANS VOW PEN IS CHAMP.

— You remind me of Antisthenes, the professor said, a disciple of Gorgias, the sophist. It is said of him that none could tell if he were bitterer against others or against himself. He was the son of a noble and a bondwoman. And he wrote a book in which he took away the palm of beauty from Argive Helen and handed it to poor Penelope.

Poor Penelope. Penelope Rich.

They made ready to cross O'Connell Street.

HELLO THERE, CENTRAL!

At various points along the eight lines tramcars with motionless trolleys stood in their tracks, bound for or from Rathmines, Rathfarnham, Blackrock, Kingstown and Dalkey, Sandymount Green, Ringsend and Sandymount Tower, Donnybrook, Palmerston Park and Upper Rathmines, all still, becalmed in short circuit. Hackney cars, cabs, delivery waggons, mailvans, private broughams, aerated mineral water floats with rattling crates of bottles, rattled, rolled, horsedrawn, rapidly.

WHAT? – AND LIKEWISE – WHERE?

— But what do you call it? Myles Crawford asked. Where did they get the plums?

VIRGILIAN, SAYS PEDAGOGUE.
SOPHOMORE PLUMPS FOR OLD MAN MOSES.

— Call it, wait, the professor said, opening his long lips wide to reflect. Call it, let me see. Call it: *Deus nobis haec otia fecit.*

— No, Stephen said, I call it *A Pisgah Sight of Palestine* or *The Parable of the Plums*.

— I see, the professor said.

He laughed richly.

— I see, he said again with new pleasure. Moses and the promised land. We gave him that idea, he added to J.J. O'Molloy.

HORATIO IS CYNOSURE THIS FAIR JUNE DAY

J.J. O'Molloy sent a weary sidelong glance towards the statue and held his peace.

— I see, the professor said.

He halted on Sir John Gray's pavement island and peered aloft at Nelson through the meshes of his wry smile.

DIMINISHED DIGITS PROVE
TOO TITILLATING FOR FRISKY FRUMPS.
ANNE WIMBLES, FLO WANGLES.
YET, CAN YOU BLAME THEM?

— One-handled adulterer, he said, smiling grimly. That tickles me, I must say.

— Tickled the old ones too, Myles Crawford said, if the God Almighty's truth was known.

Pineapple rock, lemon platt, butterscotch. A sugarsticky girl shovelling scoopfuls of creams for a Christian Brother. Some school treat. Bad for their tummies. Lozenge and comfit manufacturer to His Majesty the King. God. Save. Our. Sitting on his throne, sucking red jujubes white.

A sombre Y.M.C.A. young man, watchful among the warm sweet fumes of Graham Lemon's, placed a throwaway in the hand of Mr Bloom.

Heart-to-heart talks.

Bloo ... Me? No.

Blood of the Lamb.

His slow feet walked him riverward, reading. Are you saved? All are washed in the blood of the Lamb. God wants blood victim. Birth, hymen, martyr, war, foundation of a building, sacrifice, kidney burnt offering, druids' altars. Elijah is coming. Dr John Alexander Dowie, restorer of the church in Zion, is coming.

Is coming! Is coming!! Is coming!!!

All heartily welcome.

Paying game. Torrey and Alexander last year. Polygamy. His wife will put the stopper on that. Where was that ad some Birmingham firm the luminous crucifix? Our Saviour. Wake up in the dead of night and see Him on the wall, hanging. Pepper's Ghost idea. Iron Nails Ran In.

Phosphorus it must be done with. If you leave a bit of codfish for instance. I could see the bluey silver over it. Night I went down to the pantry in the kitchen. Don't like all the smells in it waiting to rush out. What was it she wanted? The Malaga raisins. Thinking of Spain. Before Rudy was born. The phosphorescence, that bluey greeny. Very good for the brain.

From Butler's Monument House corner he glanced along Bachelor's Walk. Dedalus' daughter there still outside Dillon's auction rooms. Must be selling off some old furniture. Knew her eyes at once from the father. Lolling about waiting for him. Home always breaks up when the mother goes. Fifteen children he had. Birth every year almost. That's in their theology or the priest won't give the poor woman the confession, the absolution. Increase and multiply. Did you ever hear such an idea? Eat you out of house and home. No families themselves to feed. Living on the fat of the land. Their butteries and larders. I'd like to see them do the black fast Yom Kippur. Crossbuns. One meal and a collation for fear he'd collapse on the altar. A housekeeper of one of those fellows if you could pick it out of her. Never pick it out of her. Like getting £ s.d. out of him. Does himself well. No guests. All for number one. Watching his water. Bring your own bread and butter. His reverence. Mum's the word.

Good Lord, that poor child's dress is in flitters. Underfed she looks too. Potatoes and marge, marge and potatoes. It's after they feel it. Proof of the pudding. Undermines the constitution.

As he set foot on O'Connell Bridge a puffball of smoke plumed up from the parapet. Brewery barge with export stout. England. Sea air sours it, I heard. Be interesting some day get a pass through Hancock to see the brewery. Regular world in itself. Vats of porter, wonderful. Rats get in too. Drink themselves bloated as big as a collie floating. Dead drunk on the porter. Drink till they puke again like Christians. Imagine drinking that! Rats: vats. Well of course if we knew all the things.

Looking down he saw flapping strongly, wheeling between the gaunt quay walls, gulls. Rough weather outside. If I threw myself down? Reuben J.'s son must have swallowed a good bellyful of that sewage. One and eightpence too much. Hhhhm. It's the droll way he comes out with the things. Knows how to tell a story too.

They wheeled lower. Looking for grub. Wait.

He threw down among them a crumpled paper ball. Elijah thirty-two feet per sec is com. Not a bit. The ball bobbed unheeded on the wake of swells, floated under by the bridge piers. Not such damn fools. Also the day I threw that stale cake out of the *Erin's King* picked it up in the wake fifty yards astern. Live by their wits. They wheeled, flapping.

The hungry famished gull
Flaps o'er the waters dull.

That is how poets write, the similar sounds. But then Shakespeare has no rhymes: blank verse. The flow of the language it is. The thoughts. Solemn.

Hamlet, I am thy father's spirit
Doomed for a certain time to walk the earth.

— Two apples a penny! Two for a penny!

His gaze passed over the glazed apples serried on her stand. Australians

145

they must be this time of year. Shiny peels: polishes them up with a rag or a handkerchief.

Wait. Those poor birds.

He halted again and bought from the old applewoman two Banbury cakes for a penny and broke the brittle paste and threw its fragments down into the Liffey. See that? The gulls swooped silently, two, then all, from their heights, pouncing on prey. Gone. Every morsel.

Aware of their greed and cunning he shook the powdery crumb from his hands. They never expected that. Manna. Live on fish, fishy flesh they have, all seabirds, gulls, sea goose. Swans from Anna Liffey swim down here sometimes to preen themselves. No accounting for tastes. Wonder what kind is swan meat. Robinson Crusoe had to live on them.

They wheeled, flapping weakly. I'm not going to throw any more. Penny quite enough. Lot of thanks I get. Not even a caw. They spread foot-and-mouth disease too. If you cram a turkey, say, on chestnut meal it tastes like that. Eat pig, like pig. But then why is it that saltwater fish are not salty? How is that?

His eyes sought answer from the river and saw a rowboat rock at anchor on the treacly swells lazily its plastered board.

Kino's
11/-
Trousers

Good idea that. Wonder if he pays rent to the Corporation. How can you own water really? It's always flowing in a stream, never the same, which in the stream of life we trace. Because life is a stream. All kinds of places are good for ads. That quack doctor for the clap used to be stuck up in all the greenhouses. Never see it now. Strictly confidential. Dr Hy Franks. Didn't cost him a red cent. Like Maginni the dancing master self-advertisement. Got fellows to stick them up or stick them up himself for that matter on the q.t. running in to loosen a button. Fly-by-night. Just the place too. POST NO BILLS. POST IIO PILLS. Some chap with a dose burning him.

If he ... ?

O!

Eh?

No ... No.

No, no. I don't believe it. He wouldn't surely?

No, no.

146

Mr Bloom moved forward, raising his troubled eyes. Think no more about that. After one. Timeball on the Ballast Office is down. Dunsink time. Fascinating little book that is of Sir Robert Ball's. Parallax. I never exactly understood. There's a priest. Could ask him. Par, it's Greek: parallel, parallax. Met him pike hoses she called it till I told her about the transmigration idea. O rocks!

Mr Bloom smiled O rocks at two windows of the Ballast Office. She's right after all. Only big words for ordinary things on account of the sound. She's not exactly witty. Can be rude too. Blurt out what I was thinking. Still, I don't know. She used to say Ben Dollard had a base barreltone voice. He has legs like barrels and you'd think he was singing into a barrel. Now, isn't that wit? They used to call him Big Ben. Not half as witty as calling him base barreltone. Appetite like an albatross. Get outside of a baron of beef. Powerful man he was at stowing away number one Bass. Barrel of Bass. See? It all works out.

A procession of white-smocked sandwich men marched slowly towards him along the gutter, scarlet sashes across their boards. Bargains. Like that priest they are this morning: we have sinned: we have suffered. He read the scarlet letters on their five tall white hats: H.E.L.Y.'S. Wisdom Hely's. Y lagging behind drew a chunk of bread from under his foreboard, crammed it into his mouth and munched as he walked. Our staple food. Three bob a day, walking along the gutters, street after street. Just keep skin and bone together, bread and skilly. They are not Boyl: no: M'Glade's men. Doesn't bring in any business either. I suggested to him about a transparent showcart with two smart girls sitting inside writing letters: copybooks, envelopes, blotting paper. I bet that would have caught on. Smart girl writing something catch the eye at once. Everyone dying to know what she's writing. Get twenty of them round you if you stare at nothing. Have a finger in the pie. Women too. Curiosity. Pillar of salt. Wouldn't have it of course because he didn't think of it himself first. Or the inkbottle I suggested with a false stain of black celluloid. His ideas for ads like Plumtree's Potted under the obituaries, cold meat department. You can't lick 'em. What? Our envelopes. Hello, Jones, where are you going? Can't stop, Robinson, I am hastening to purchase the only reliable ink eraser, *Kansell*, sold by Hely's Ltd., 27–30 Dame Street. Well out of that ruck I am. Devil of a job it was collecting accounts of those convents. Tranquilla Convent. That was a nice nun there, really sweet face. Wimple suited her small head. Sister? Sister? I am sure she was crossed in love by her eyes. Very hard to bargain with that sort of woman. I disturbed her at her devotions that morning. But glad to communicate with the outside world. Our great day, she said. Feast of Our Lady of Mount Carmel. Sweet name too: caramel. She knew, I think she knew by the way she. If she had married she would have changed. I suppose they really were short of money. Fried everything in the best butter all the same. No lard for them. My heart's broke eating dripping. They like buttering themselves in and out. Molly tasting it, her veil up. Sister? Pat Claffey, the pawnbroker's daughter. It was a nun they say invented barbed wire.

He crossed Westmoreland Street when apostrophe S had plodded by. Rover cycle shop. Those races are on today. How long ago is that? Year Phil Gilligan died. We were in Lombard Street West. Wait. Was in Thom's. Got the job in Wisdom Hely's year we married. Six years. Ten years ago: ninety-four he died, yes that's right, the big fire at Arnott's. Val Dillon was lord mayor. The Glencree dinner. Alderman Robert O'Reilly emptying the port into his soup before the flag fell. Bobbob lapping it for the inner alderman. Couldn't hear what the band played. For what we have already received may the Lord make us. Milly was a kiddy then. Molly had that elephant-grey dress with the braided frogs. Man-tailored with self-covered buttons. She didn't like it because I sprained my ankle first day she wore it, choir picnic at the Sugarloaf. As if that. Old Goodwin's tall hat done up with some sticky stuff. Flies' picnic too. Never put a dress on her back like it. Fitted her like a glove, shoulders and hips. Just beginning to plump it out well. Rabbit pie we had that day. People looking after her.

Happy. Happier then. Snug little room that was with the red wallpaper. Dockrell's, one and ninepence a dozen. Milly's tubbing night. American soap I bought: elderflower. Cosy smell of her bathwater. Funny she looked soaped all over. Shapely too. Now photography. Poor papa's daguerreotype atelier he told me of. Hereditary taste.

He walked along the curbstone.

Stream of life. What was the name of that priesty-looking chap was always squinting in when he passed? Weak eyes, woman. Stopped in Citron's, Saint Kevin's Parade. Pen something. Pendennis? My memory is getting. Pen...? Of course it's years ago. Noise of the trams probably. Well, if he couldn't remember the dayfather's name that he sees every day.

Bartell d'Arcy was the tenor, just coming out then. Seeing her home after practice. Conceited fellow with his waxed-up moustache. Gave her that song *Winds that blow from the south*.

Windy night that was I went to fetch her, there was that lodge meeting on about those lottery tickets, after Goodwin's concert in the Supper Room or Oak Room of the Mansion House. He and I behind. Sheet of her music blew out of my hand against the High School railings. Lucky it didn't. Thing like that spoils the effect of a night for her. Professor Goodwin linking her in front. Shaky on his pins, poor old sot. His farewell concerts. Positively last appearance on any stage. May be for months and may be for never. Remember her laughing at the wind, her blizzard collar up. Corner of Harcourt Road remember that gust. Brrfoo! Blew up all her skirts and her boa nearly smothered old Goodwin. She did get flushed in the wind. Remember when we got home raking up the fire and frying up those pieces of lap of mutton for her supper with the chutney sauce she liked. And the mulled rum. Could see her in the bedroom from the hearth unclamping the busk of her stays. White.

Swish and soft flop her stays made on the bed. Always warm from her. Always liked to let herself out. Sitting there after till near two, taking out her hairpins. Milly tucked up in beddyhouse. Happy. Happy. That was the night . . .

— O, Mr Bloom, how do you do?

— O, how do you do, Mrs Breen?

— No use complaining. How is Molly those times? Haven't seen her for ages.

— In the pink, Mr Bloom said gaily. Milly has a position down in Mullingar, you know.

— Go away! Isn't that grand for her?

— Yes, in a photographer's there. Getting on like a house on fire. How are all your charges?

— All on the baker's list, Mrs Breen said.

How many has she? No other in sight.

— You're in black I see. You have no . . .?

— No, Mr Bloom said. I have just come from a funeral.

Going to crop up all day, I foresee. Who's dead, when and what did he die of? Turn up like a bad penny.

— O, dear me, Mrs Breen said, I hope it wasn't any near relation.

May as well get her sympathy.

— Dignam, Mr Bloom said. An old friend of mine. He died quite suddenly, poor fellow. Heart trouble, I believe. Funeral was this morning.

Your funeral's tomorrow
While you're coming through the rye.

149

Diddlediddle dumdum
Diddlediddle...

– Sad to lose the old friends, Mrs Breen's womaneyes said melancholily.

Now that's quite enough about that. Just: quietly: husband.

– And your lord and master?

Mrs Breen turned up her two large eyes. Hasn't lost them anyhow.

– O, don't be talking! she said. He's a caution to rattlesnakes. He's in there now with his lawbooks finding out the law of libel. He has me heartscalded. Wait till I show you.

Hot mock turtle vapour and steam of new-baked jampuffs rolypoly poured out from Harrison's. The heavy noonreek tickled the top of Mr Bloom's gullet. Want to make good pastry, butter, best flour, demerara sugar, or they'd taste it with the hot tea. Or is it from her? A barefoot arab stood over the grating, breathing in the fumes. Deaden the gnaw of hunger that way. Pleasure or pain is it? Penny dinner. Knife and fork chained to the table.

Opening her handbag, chipped leather. Hatpin: ought to have a guard on those things. Stick it in a chap's eye in the tram. Rummaging. Open. Money. Please take one. Devils if they lose sixpence. Raise Cain. Husband barging. Where's the ten shillings I gave you on Monday? Are you feeding your little brother's family? Soiled handkerchief: medicine bottle. Pastille that was fell. What is she...?

– There must be a new moon out, she said. He's always bad then. Do you know what he did last night?

Her hand ceased to rummage. Her eyes fixed themselves on him, wide in alarm, yet smiling.

– What? Mr Bloom asked.

Let her speak. Look straight in her eyes. I believe you. Trust me.

– Woke me up in the night, she said. Dream he had, a nightmare.

Indiges.

– Said the ace of spades was walking up the stairs.

– The ace of spades! Mr Bloom said.

She took a folded postcard from her handbag.

– Read that, she said. He got it this morning.

– What is it? Mr Bloom asked, taking the card. U.P?

– U.P: up, she said. Someone taking a rise out of him. It's a great shame for them, whoever he is.

– Indeed it is, Mr Bloom said.

She took back the card, sighing.

— And now he's going round to Mr Menton's office. He's going to take an action for ten thousand pounds, he says.

She folded the card into her untidy bag and snapped the catch.

Same blue serge dress she had two years ago, the nap bleaching. Seen its best days. Wispish hair over her ears. And that dowdy toque, three old grapes to take the harm out of it. Shabby genteel. She used to be a tasty dresser. Lines round her mouth. Only a year or so older than Molly.

See the eye that woman gave her, passing. Cruel. The unfair sex.

He looked still at her, holding back behind his look his discontent. Pungent mock turtle, oxtail, mulligatawny. I'm hungry too. Flakes of pastry on the gusset of her dress: daub of sugary flour stuck to her cheek. Rhubarb tart with liberal fillings, rich fruit interior. Josie Powell that was. In Luke Doyle's long ago. Dolphin's Barn, the charades. U.P: up.

Change the subject.

— Do you ever see anything of Mrs Beaufoy? Mr Bloom asked.

— Mina Purefoy? she said.

Philip Beaufoy I was thinking. Playgoers' Club. Matcham often thinks of the masterstroke. Did I pull the chain? Yes. The last act.

— Yes.

— I just called to ask on the way in is she over it. She's in the lying-in hospital in Holles Street. Dr Horne got her in. She's three days bad now.

— O, Mr Bloom said. I'm sorry to hear that.

— Yes, Mrs Breen said. And a houseful of kids at home. It's a very stiff birth, the nurse told me.

— O, Mr Bloom said.

His heavy pitying gaze absorbed her news. His tongue clacked in compassion. Dth! Dth!

— I'm sorry to hear that, he said. Poor thing! Three days! That's terrible for her.

Mrs Breen nodded.

— She was taken bad on the Tuesday . . .

Mr Bloom touched her funny bone gently, warning her:

— Mind! Let this man pass.

A bony form strode along the curbstone from the river, staring with a rapt gaze into the sunlight through a heavy-stringed glass. Tight as a skullpiece a tiny hat gripped his head. From his arm a folded dustcoat, a stick and an umbrella dangled to his stride.

— Watch him, Mr Bloom said. He always walks outside the lampposts. Watch!

— Who is he if it's a fair question? Mrs Breen asked. Is he dotty?

— His name is Cashel Boyle O'Connor Fitzmaurice Tisdall Farrell, Mr Bloom said, smiling. Watch!

— He has enough of them, she said. Denis will be like that one of these days.

She broke off suddenly.

— There he is, she said. I must go after him. Goodbye. Remember me to Molly, won't you?

— I will, Mr Bloom said.

He watched her dodge through passers towards the shopfronts. Denis Breen in skimpy frockcoat and blue canvas shoes shuffled out of Harrison's, hugging two heavy tomes to his ribs. Blown in from the bay. Like old times. He suffered her to overtake him without surprise and thrust his dull grey beard towards her, his loose jaw wagging as he spoke earnestly.

Meshuggah. Off his chump.

Mr Bloom walked on again easily, seeing ahead of him in sunlight the tight skullpiece, the dangling stick, umbrella, dustcoat. Going the two days. Watch him! Out he goes again. One way of getting on in the world. And that other old mosey lunatic in those duds. Hard time she must have with him.

U.P: up. I'll take my oath that's Alf Bergan or Richie Goulding. Wrote it for a lark in the Scotch House I bet anything. Round to Menton's office. His oyster eyes staring at the postcard. Be a feast for the gods.

He passed the *Irish Times*. There might be other answers lying there. Like to answer them all. Good system for criminals. Code. At their lunch now. Clerk with the glasses there doesn't know me. O, leave them there to simmer. Enough bother wading through forty-four of them. Wanted, smart lady typist to aid gentleman in literary work. I called you naughty darling because I do not like that other world. Please tell me what is the meaning. Please tell me what perfume does your wife. Tell me who made the world. The way they spring those questions on you. And the other one, Lizzie Twigg. My literary efforts have had the good fortune to meet with the approval of the eminent poet AE (Mr Geo. Russell). No time to do her hair drinking sloppy tea with a book of poetry.

Best paper by long chalks for a small ad. Got the provinces now. Cook and general, exc. cuisine, housemaid kept. Wanted, live man for spirit counter. Resp. girl (R.C.) wishes to hear of post in fruit or pork shop. James Carlyle made that. Six and a half per cent dividend. Made a big deal on Coats's shares. Ca'canny. Cunning old Scotch hunks. All the toady news. Our gracious and popular vicereine. Bought the *Irish Field* now. Lady Mount-Cashell has quite recovered after her confinement and rode out with the Ward Union staghounds at the enlargement yesterday at Rathoath. Uneatable fox. Pothunters too. Fear injects juices make it tender enough for them. Riding astride. Sits her horse like a man. Weightcarrying huntress. No sidesaddle or pillion for her, not for Joe. First to the meet and in at the death. Strong as a brood mare some of those horsey women. Swagger around livery stables. Toss off a glass of brandy neat while you'd say knife. That one at the Grosvenor this morning. Up with her on the car: wishswish. Stone wall or five-barred gate put her mount to it. Think that pugnosed driver did it out of spite. Who is this she was like? O yes! Mrs Miriam Dandrade that sold me her old wraps and black underclothes in the Shelbourne Hotel. Divorced Spanish-American. Didn't take a feather out of her my handling them. As if I was her clotheshorse. Saw her in the viceregal party when Stubbs the park ranger got me in with Whelan of the *Express*. Scavenging what the quality left. High tea. Mayonnaise I poured on the plums thinking it was custard. Her ears ought to have tingled for a few weeks after. Want to be a bull for her. Born courtesan. No nursery work for her, thanks.

Poor Mrs Purefoy! Methodist husband. Method in his madness. Saffron bun and milk and soda lunch in the Educational Dairy. Y.M.C.A. Eating with a stopwatch, thirty-two chews to the minute. And still his mutton-chop whiskers grew. Supposed to be well connected. Theodore's cousin in Dublin Castle. One tony relative in every family. Hardy annuals he presents her with. Saw him out at the Three Jolly Topers marching along bareheaded and his eldest boy carrying one in a market net. The squallers. Poor thing! Then having to give the breast year after year all hours of the night. Selfish those t.t.'s are. Dog in the manger. Only one lump of sugar in my tea, if you please.

He stood at Fleet Street crossing. Luncheon interval. A sixpenny at Rowe's? Must look up that ad in the National Library. An eightpenny in the Burton. Better. On my way.

He walked on past Bolton's Westmoreland House. Tea. Tea. Tea. I forgot to tap Tom Kernan.

Sss. Dth, dth, dth! Three days imagine groaning on a bed with a vinegared handkerchief round her forehead, her belly swollen out. Phew!

Dreadful simply! Child's head too big: forceps. Doubled up inside her trying to butt its way out blindly, groping for the way out. Kill me that would. Lucky Molly got over hers lightly. They ought to invent something to stop that. Life with hard labour. Twilight sleep idea: Queen Victoria was given that. Nine she had. A good layer. Old woman that lived in a shoe she had so many children. Suppose he was consumptive. Time someone thought about it instead of gassing about the what was it the pensive bosom of the silver effulgence. Flapdoodle to feed fools on. They could easily have big establishments. Whole thing quite painless. Out of all the taxes give every child born five quid at compound interest up to twenty-one, five per cent is a hundred shillings and five, tiresome pounds multiply by twenty decimal system, encourage people to put by money save, hundred and ten and a bit twenty-one years, want to work it out on paper come to a tidy sum. More than you think.

Not stillborn of course. They are not even registered. Trouble for nothing.

Funny sight two of them together, their bellies out. Molly and Mrs Moisel. Mothers' meeting. Phthisis retires for the time being, then returns. How flat they look after all of a sudden! Peaceful eyes. Weight off their minds. Old Mrs Thornton was a jolly old soul. All my babies, she said. The spoon of pap in her mouth before she fed them. O, that's nyumnyum. Got her hand crushed by old Tom Wall's son. His first bow to the public. Head like a prize pumpkin. Snuffy Dr Murren. People knocking them up at all hours. For God's sake, doctor. Wife in her throes. Then keep them waiting months for their fee. To attendance on your wife. No gratitude in people. Humane doctors, most of them.

Before the huge high door of the Irish House of Parliament a flock of pigeons flew. Their little frolic after meals. Who will we do it on? I pick the fellow in black. Here goes. Here's good luck. Must be thrilling from the air. Apjohn, myself and Owen Goldberg up in the trees near Goose-green playing the monkeys. Mackerel they called me.

A squad of constables debouched from College Street, marching in Indian file. Goose step. Food-heated faces, sweating helmets, patting their truncheons. After their feed with a good load of fat soup under their belts. Policeman's lot is oft a happy one. They split up into groups and scattered, saluting, towards their beats. Let out to graze. Best moment to attack one, in pudding time. A punch in his dinner. A squad of others, marching irregularly, rounded Trinity railings making for the station.

Bound for their troughs. Prepare to receive cavalry. Prepare to receive soup.

He crossed under Tommy Moore's roguish finger. They did right to put him up over a urinal: meeting of the waters. Ought to be places for women. Running into cake shops. Settle my hat straight. *There is not in this wide world a vallee.* Great song of Julia Morkan's. Kept her voice up to the very last. Pupil of Michael Balfe's, wasn't she?

He gazed after the last broad tunic. Nasty customers to tackle. Jack Power could a tale unfold: father a G-man. If a fellow gives them trouble being lagged they let him have it hot and heavy in the bridewell. Can't blame them after all with the job they have, especially the young hornies. That horse policeman the day Joe Chamberlain was given his degree in Trinity: he got a run for his money. My word he did! His horse's hoofs clattering after us down Abbey Street. Lucky I had the presence of mind to dive into Manning's or I was souped. He did come a wallop, by George. Must have cracked his skull on the cobblestones. I oughtn't to have got myself swept along with those medicals. And the Trinity jibs in their mortarboards. Looking for trouble. Still, I got to know that young Dixon who dressed that sting for me in the Mater and now he's in Holles Street where Mrs Purefoy. Wheels within wheels. Police whistle in my ears still. All skedaddled. Why he fixed on me. Give me in charge. Right here it began.

– Up the Boers!

– Three cheers for DeWet!

– We'll hang Joe Chamberlain on a sour-apple tree.

Silly billies: mob of young cubs yelling their guts out. Vinegar Hill. The Butter Exchange band. Few years' time half of them magistrates and civil servants. War comes on: into the army helterskelter: same fellows used to: *whether on the scaffold high.*

Never know who you're talking to. Corny Kelleher he has Harvey Duff in his eye. Like that Peter or Denis or James Carey that blew the gaff on the Invincibles. Member of the Corporation too. Egging raw youths on to get in the know. All the time drawing Secret Service pay from the Castle. Drop him like a hot potato. Why those plainclothesmen are always courting slaveys. Easily twig a man used to uniform. Squarepushing up against a back door. Maul her a bit. Then the next thing on the menu. And who is the gentleman does be visiting then? Was the young master saying anything? Peeping Tom through the keyhole. Decoy duck. Hot-blooded young student fooling round her fat arms ironing.

— Are those yours, Mary?

— I don't wear such things ... Stop or I'll tell the missus on you. Out half the night.

— There are great times coming, Mary. Wait till you see.

— Ah, ge'long with your great times coming.

Barmaids too. Tobacco-shop girls.

James Stephens' idea was the best. He knew them. Circles of ten so that a fellow couldn't round on more than his own ring. Sinn Féin. Back out you get the knife. Hidden hand. Stay in. The firing squad. Turnkey's daughter got him out of Richmond, off from Lusk. Putting up in the Buckingham Palace Hotel under their very noses. Irish Garibaldi.

You must have a certain fascination: Parnell. Arthur Griffith is a squareheaded fellow but he has no go in him for the mob or gas about our lovely land. Gammon and spinach. Dublin Bakery Company's tearoom. Debating societies. That republicanism is the best form of government. That the language question should take precedence of the economic question. Have your daughters inveigling them to your house. Stuff them up with meat and drink. Michaelmas goose. Here's a good lump of thyme seasoning under the apron for you. Have another quart of goose grease before it gets too cold. Half-fed enthusiasts. Penny roll and a walk with the band. No grace for the carver. The thought that the other chap pays best sauce in the world. Make themselves thoroughly at home. Show us over those apricots, meaning peaches. The not far distant day. Home Rule sun rising up in the northwest.

His smile faded as he walked, a heavy cloud hiding the sun slowly, shadowing Trinity's surly front. Trams passed one another, ingoing, outgoing, clanging. Useless words. Things go on same day after day: squads of police marching out, back: trams in, out. Those two loonies mooching about. Dignam carted off. Mina Purefoy swollen belly on a bed groaning to have a child tugged out of her. One born every second somewhere. Other dying every second. Since I fed the birds five minutes. Three hundred kicked the bucket. Other three hundred born, washing the blood off, all are washed in the blood of the Lamb, bawling maaaaaa.

Cityful passing away, other cityful coming, passing away too: other coming on, passing on. Houses, lines of houses, streets, miles of pavements, piled-up bricks, stones. Changing hands. This owner, that. Landlord never dies they say. Other steps into his shoes when he gets his notice to quit. They buy the place up with gold and still they have all the gold. Swindle in it somewhere. Piled up in cities, worn away age after age. Pyramids in sand. Built on bread and onions. Slaves. Chinese wall. Babylon. Big stones left. Round towers. Rest rubble, sprawling suburbs, jerry-built. Kirwan's mushroom houses, built of breeze. Shelter for the night.

No one is anything.

This is the very worst hour of the day. Vitality. Dull, gloomy: hate this hour. Feel as if I had been eaten and spewed.

Provost's house. The Reverend Dr Salmon: tinned salmon. Well tinned in there. Like a mortuary chapel. Wouldn't live in it if they paid me. Hope they have liver and bacon today. Nature abhors a vacuum.

The sun freed itself slowly and lit glints of light among the silverware opposite in Walter Sexton's window by which John Howard Parnell passed, unseeing.

There he is: the brother. Image of him. Haunting face. Now that's a coincidence. Course hundreds of times you think of a person and don't meet him. Like a man walking in his sleep. No one knows him. Must be a Corporation meeting today. They say he never put on the city marshal's uniform since he got the job. Charley Kavanagh used to come out on his high horse, cocked hat, puffed, powdered and shaved. Look at the woebegone walk of him. Eaten a bad egg. Poached eyes on ghost. I have a pain. Great man's brother: his brother's brother. He'd look nice on the city charger. Drop into the D.B.C. probably for his coffee, play chess there. His brother used men as pawns. Let them all go to pot. Afraid to pass a remark on him. Freeze them up with that eye of his. That's the fascination: the name. All a bit touched. Mad Fanny and his other sister Mrs Dickinson driving about with scarlet harness. Bolt upright like surgeon M'Ardle. Still, David Sheehy beat him for South Meath. Apply for the Chiltern Hundreds and retire into public life. The patriot's banquet. Eating orange peels in the park. Simon Dedalus said when they put him in Parliament that Parnell would come back from the grave and lead him out of the House of Commons by the arm.

– Of the two-headed octopus, one of whose heads is the head upon which the ends of the world have forgotten to come while the other speaks with a Scotch accent. The tentacles ...

They passed from behind Mr Bloom along the curbstone. Beard and bicycle. Young woman.

And there he is too. Now that's really a coincidence: second time. Coming events cast their shadows before. With the approval of the

157

eminent poet Mr Geo. Russell. That might be Lizzie Twigg with him. AE: what does that mean? Initials perhaps. Albert Edward, Arthur Edmund, Alphonsus Eb Ed El Esquire. What was he saying? The ends of the world with a Scotch accent. Tentacles: octopus. Something occult: symbolism. Holding forth. She's taking it all in. Not saying a word. To aid gentleman in literary work.

His eyes followed the high figure in homespun, beard and bicycle, a listening woman at his side. Coming from the vegetarian. Only weggebobbles and fruit. Don't eat a beefsteak. If you do, the eyes of that cow will pursue you through all eternity. They say it's healthier. Wind and watery though. Tried it. Keep you on the run all day. Bad as a bloater. Dreams all night. Why do they call that thing they gave me nut steak? Nutarians. Fruitarians. To give you the idea you are eating rump steak. Absurd. Salty too. They cook in soda. Keep you sitting by the tap all night.

Her stockings are loose over her ankles. I detest that: so tasteless. Those literary ethereal people they are all. Dreamy, cloudy, symbolistic. Esthetes they are. I wouldn't be surprised if it was that kind of food you see produces the like waves of the brain the poetical. For example one of those policemen sweating Irish stew into their shirts you couldn't squeeze a line of poetry out of him. Don't know what poetry is even. Must be in a certain mood.

> *The dreamy cloudy gull*
> *Waves o'er the waters dull.*

He crossed at Nassau Street corner and stood before the window of Yeates and Son, pricing the field glasses. Or will I drop into old Harris's and have a chat with young Sinclair? Well-mannered fellow. Probably at his lunch. Must get those old glasses of mine set right. Goerz lenses six guineas. Germans making their way everywhere. Sell on easy terms to capture trade. Undercutting. Might chance on a pair in the railway lost property office. Astonishing the things people leave behind them in trains and cloakrooms. What do they be thinking about? Women too. Incredible. Last year travelling to Ennis had to pick up that farmer's daughter's bag and hand it to her at Limerick Junction. Unclaimed money too. There's a little watch up there on the roof of the bank to test those glasses by.

His lids came down on the lower rims of his irides. Can't see it. If you imagine it's there you can almost see it. Can't see it.

He faced about and, standing between the awnings, held out his right hand at arm's length towards the sun. Wanted to try that often. Yes:

completely. The tip of his little finger blotted out the sun's disk. Must be the focus where the rays cross. If I had black glasses. Interesting. There was a lot of talk about those sunspots when we were in Lombard Street West. Terrific explosions they are. There will be a total eclipse this year: autumn some time.

Now that I come to think of it, that ball falls at Greenwich time. It's the clock is worked by an electric wire from Dunsink. Must go out there some first Saturday of the month. If I could get an introduction to Professor Joly or learn up something about his family. That would do to: man always feels complimented. Flattery where least expected. Nobleman proud to be descended from some king's mistress. His foremother. Lay it on with a trowel. Cap in hand goes through the land. Not go in and blurt out what you know you're not to: what's parallax? Show this gentleman the door.

Ah.

His hand fell to his side again.

Never know anything about it. Waste of time. Gasballs spinning about, crossing each other, passing. Same old dingdong always. Gas, then solid, then world, then cold, then dead shell drifting around, frozen rock like that pineapple rock. The moon. Must be a new moon out, she said. I believe there is.

He went on by La Maison Claire.

Wait. The full moon was the night we were Sunday fortnight exactly there is a new moon. Walking down by the Tolka. Not bad for a Fairview moon. She was humming. *The young May moon she's beaming, love.* He other side of her. Elbow, arm. He. *Glowworm's la-amp is gleaming, love.* Touch. Fingers. Asking. Answer. Yes.

Stop. Stop. If it was it was. Must.

Mr Bloom, quickbreathing, slowlier walking, passed Adam Court.

With ah quiet keep quiet relief his eyes took note: this is street here middle of the day Bob Doran's bottle shoulders. On his annual bend, M'Coy said. They drink in order to say or do something or *cherchez la femme.* Up in the Coombe with chummies and streetwalkers and then the rest of the year as sober as a judge.

Yes. Thought so. Sloping into the Empire. Gone. Plain soda would do him good. Where Pat Kinsella had his Harp Theatre before Whitbread ran the Queen's. Broth of a boy. Dion Boucicault business with his harvest-moon face in a poky bonnet. *Three Purty Maids from School.* How time flies, eh? Showing long red pantaloons under his skirts. Drinkers, drinking, laughed spluttering, their drink against their breath. More power, Pat!

Coarse red: fun for drunkards: guffaw and smoke. Take off that white hat! His parboiled eyes. Where is he now? Beggar somewhere. The harp that once did starve us all.

I was happier then. Or was that I? Or am I now I? Twenty-eight I was. She twenty-three. When we left Lombard Street West something changed. Could never like it again after Rudy. Can't bring back time. Like holding water in your hand. Would you go back to then? Just beginning then. Would you? Are you not happy in your home, you poor little naughty boy? Wants to sew on buttons for me. I must answer. Write it in the library.

Grafton Street gay with housed awnings lured his senses. Muslin prints, silk, dames and dowagers, jingle of harnesses, hoofthuds lowringing on the baking causeway. Thick feet that woman has in the white stockings. Hope the rain mucks them up on her. Country-bred chawbacon. All the beef to the heels were in. Always gives a woman clumsy feet. Molly looks out of plumb.

He passed, dallying, the windows of Brown Thomas, silk mercers. Cascades of ribbons. Flimsy China silks. A tilted urn poured from its mouth a flood of blood-hued poplin: lustrous blood. The Huguenots brought that here. *Lacaus esant tara tara*. Great chorus that. *Taree tara*. Must be washed in rainwater. Meyerbeer. *Tara: bom bom bom*.

Pincushions. I'm a long time threatening to buy one. Sticks them all over the place. Needles in window curtains.

He bared slightly his left forearm. Scrape: nearly gone. Not today anyhow. Must go back for that lotion. For her birthday perhaps. Junejulyaugseptember eighth. Nearly three months off. Then she mightn't like it. Women won't pick up pins. Say it cuts lo.

Gleaming silks, petticoats on slim brass rails, rays of flat silk stockings.

Useless to go back. Had to be. Tell me all.

High voices. Sun-warm silk. Jingling harnesses. All for a woman, home and houses, silk webs, silver, rich fruits spicy from Jaffa. Agudath Netaim. Wealth of the world.

A warm human plumpness settled down on his brain. His brain yielded. Perfume of embraces all him assailed. With hungered flesh obscurely, he mutely craved to adore.

Duke Street. Here we are. Must eat. The Burton. Feel better then.

He turned Combridge's corner, still pursued. Jingling, hoofthuds. Perfumed bodies, warm, full. All kissed, yielded: in deep summer fields, tangled pressed grass, in trickling hallways of tenements, along sofas, creaking beds.

— Jack, love!

— Darling!

— Kiss me, Reggy!

— My boy!

— Love!

His heart astir he pushed in the door of the Burton restaurant. Stink gripped his trembling breath: pungent meatjuice, slush of greens. See the animals feed.

Men, men, men.

Perched on high stools by the bar, hats shoved back, at the tables calling for more bread, no charge, swilling, wolfing gobfuls of sloppy food, their eyes bulging, wiping wetted moustaches. A pallid suet-faced young man polished his tumbler knife fork and spoon with his napkin. New set of microbes. A man with an infant's sauce-stained napkin tucked round him shovelled gurgling soup down his gullet. A man spitting back on his plate: half-masticated gristle: gums: no teeth to chewchewchew it. Chump chop from the grill. Bolting to get it over. Sad boozer's eyes. Bitten off more than he can chew. Am I like that? See ourselves as others see us. Hungry man is an angry man. Working tooth and jaw. Don't! O! A bone! That last pagan king of Ireland Cormac in the school poem choked himself at Sletty southward of the Boyne. Wonder what he was eating. Something goloptious. Saint Patrick converted him to Christianity. Couldn't swallow it all however.

— Roast beef and cabbage.

— One stew.

Smells of men. Spat-on sawdust, sweetish warmish cigarette smoke, reek of plug, spilt beer, men's beery piss, the stale of ferment.

His gorge rose.

Couldn't eat a morsel here. Fellow sharpening knife and fork to eat all before him, old chap picking his tootles. Slight spasm, full, chewing the cud. Before and after. Grace after meals. Look on this picture then on that. Scoffing up stew gravy with sopping sippets of bread. Lick it off the plate, man! Get out of this.

He gazed round the stooled and tabled eaters, tightening the wings of his nose.

— Two stouts here.

— One corned and cabbage.

That fellow ramming a knifeful of cabbage down as if his life depended on it. Good stroke. Give me the fidgets to look. Safer to eat from his three hands. Tear it limb from limb. Second nature to him. Born with a silver knife in his mouth. That's witty, I think. Or no. Silver means born rich. Born with a knife. But then the allusion is lost.

An ill-girt server gathered sticky clattering plates. Rock, the bailiff, standing at the bar blew the foamy crown from his tankard. Well up: it splashed yellow near his boot. A diner, knife and fork upright, elbows on table, ready for a second helping stared towards the foodlift across his stained square of newspaper. Other chap telling him something with his mouth full. Sympathetic listener. Table talk. I munched hum un thu Unchster Bunk un Munchday. Ha? Did you, faith?

Mr Bloom raised two fingers doubtfully to his lips. His eyes said:

— Not here. Don't see him.

Out. I hate dirty eaters.

He backed towards the door. Get a light snack in Davy Byrne's. Stopgap. Keep me going. Had a good breakfast.

— Roast and mashed here.

— Pint of stout.

Every fellow for his own, tooth and nail. Gulp. Grub. Gulp. Gobstuff.

He came out into clearer air and turned back towards Grafton Street. Eat or be eaten. Kill! Kill!

Suppose that communal kitchen years to come perhaps. All trotting down with porringers and tommycans to be filled. Devour contents in the street. John Howard Parnell, example, the provost of Trinity, every mother's son. *Don't talk of your provosts and provost of Trinity.* Women and children, cabmen, priests, parsons, field marshals, archbishops. From Ailesbury Road, Clyde Road, artisans' dwellings, North Dublin Union, lord mayor in his gingerbread coach, old queen in a Bath chair. My plate's empty. After you with the incorporated drinking cup. Like Sir Philip Crampton's fountain. Rub off the microbes with your handkerchief. Next chap rubs on a new batch with his. *Father O'Flynn would make hares of them all.* Have rows all the same. All for number one. Children fighting for the scrapings of the pot. Want a soup pot as big as the Phoenix Park. Harpooning flitches and hindquarters out of it. Hate people all round you. City Arms Hotel *table d'hôte* she called it. Soup, joint and sweet. Never know whose thoughts you're chewing. Then who'd wash up all the plates and forks? Might be all feeding on tabloids that time. Teeth getting worse and worse.

After all there's a lot in that vegetarian, the fine flavours of things from the earth: garlic, of course it stinks after, Italian organ grinders, crisp of onions, mushrooms, truffles. Pain to the animal too. Pluck and draw fowl. Wretched brutes there at the cattle market waiting for the poleaxe to split their skulls open. Moo. Poor trembling calves. Meh. Staggering bob. Bubble and squeak. Butchers' buckets, wobbly lights. Give us that brisket off the hook. Plup. Raw head and bloody bones. Flayed glass-eyed sheep hung from their haunches, sheepsnouts bloody-papered snivelling nose-jam on sawdust. Top and lashers going out. Don't maul them pieces, young one.

Hot fresh blood they prescribe for decline. Blood always needed. Insidious. Lick it up smoking hot, thick sugary. Famished ghosts.

Ah, I'm hungry.

He entered Davy Byrne's. Moral pub. He doesn't chat. Stands a drink now and then. But in leap year once in four. Cashed a cheque for me once.

What will I take now? He drew his watch. Let me see now. Shandygaff?

— Hello, Bloom, Nosey Flynn said from his nook.

— Hello, Flynn.

— How's things?

— Tiptop ... Let me see. I'll take a glass of burgundy and ... let me see.

Sardines on the shelves. Almost taste them by looking. Sandwich? Ham and his descendants mustered and bred there. Potted meats. What is home without Plumtree's potted meat? Incomplete. What a stupid ad! Under the obituary notices they stuck it. All up a plum tree. Dignam's potted meat. Cannibals would with lemon and rice. White missionary too salty. Like pickled pork. Expect the chief consumes the parts of honour. Ought to be tough from exercise. His wives in a row to watch the effect. *There was a right royal old nigger. Who ate or something the somethings of the Reverend Mr MacTrigger.* With it an abode of bliss. Lord knows what concoction. Cauls mouldy tripes windpipes faked and minced up. Puzzle find the meat. Kosher. No meat and milk together. Hygiene that was what they call now. Yom Kippur fast, spring-cleaning of inside. Peace and war depend on some fellow's digestion. Religions. Christmas turkeys and geese. Slaughter of innocents. Eat, drink and be merry. Then casual wards full after. Heads bandaged. Cheese digests all but itself. Mity cheese.

— Have you a cheese sandwich?

— Yes, sir.

Like a few olives too if they had them. Italian I prefer. Good glass of burgundy, take away that feeling. Lubricate. A nice salad, cool as a cucumber. Tom Kernan can dress. Puts gusto into it. Pure olive oil. Milly served me that cutlet with a sprig of parsley. Take one Spanish onion. God made food, the devil the cooks. Devilled crab.

— Wife well?

— Quite well, thanks … A cheese sandwich, then. Gorgonzola, have you?

— Yes, sir.

Nosey Flynn sipped his grog.

— Doing any singing those times?

Look at his mouth. Could whistle in his own ear. Flap ears to match. Music. Knows as much about it as my coachman. Still, better tell him. Does no harm. Free ad.

— She's engaged for a big tour end of this month. You may have heard perhaps.

— No. O, that's the style. Who's getting it up?

The curate served.

— How much is that?

— Seven *d*, sir … Thank you, sir.

Mr Bloom cut his sandwich into slender strips. *Mr MacTrigger.* Easier than the dreamy creamy stuff. *His five hundred wives. Had the time of their lives.*

— Mustard, sir?

— Thank you.

He studded under each lifted strip yellow blobs. *Their lives.* I have it. *It grew bigger and bigger and bigger.*

— Getting it up? he said. Well, it's like a company idea, you see. Part shares and part profits.

— Ay, now I remember, Nosey Flynn said, putting his hand in his pocket to scratch his groin. Who is this was telling me? Isn't Blazes Boylan mixed up in it?

A warm shock of air, heat of mustard, hanched on Mr Bloom's heart. He raised his eyes and met the stare of a bilious clock. Two. Pub clock five minutes fast. Time going on. Hands moving. Two. Not yet.

His midriff yearned then upward, sank within him, yearned more longly, longingly.

Wine.

He smellsipped the cordial juice and, bidding his throat strongly to speed it, set his wineglass delicately down.

— Yes, he said. He's the organiser in point of fact.

No fear. No brains.

Nosey Flynn snuffled and scratched. Flea having a good square meal.

— He had a good slice of luck, Jack Mooney was telling me, over that boxing match Myler Keogh won again' that soldier in the Portobello barracks. By God, he had the little kipper down in the county Carlow, he was telling me...

Hope that dewdrop doesn't come down into his glass. No, snuffled it up.

— For near a month, man, before it came off. Sucking duck eggs, by God, till further orders. Keep him off the booze, see? O, by God, Blazes is a hairy chap.

Davy Byrne came forward from the hind bar in tuck-stitched shirt-sleeves, cleaning his lips with two wipes of his napkin. Herring's blush. Whose smile upon each feature plays with such and such replete. Too much fat on the parsnips.

— And here's himself and pepper on him, Nosey Flynn said. Can you give us a good one for the Gold Cup?

— I'm off that, Mr Flynn, Davy Byrne answered. I never put anything on a horse.

— You're right there, Nosey Flynn said.

Mr Bloom ate his strips of sandwich with relish of disgust, fresh clean bread, pungent mustard, the feety savour of green cheese. Sips of his wine soothed his palate. Not logwood that. Tastes fuller this weather with the chill off.

Nice quiet bar. Nice piece of wood in that counter. Nicely planed. Like the way it curves there.

— I wouldn't do anything at all in that line, Davy Byrne said. It ruined many a man the same horses.

Vintners' sweepstake. Licensed for the sale of beer, wine and spirits for consumption on the premises. Heads I win, tails you lose.

— True for you, Nosey Flynn said. Unless you're in the know. There's no straight sport going now. Lenehan gets some good ones. He's giving *Sceptre* today. *Zinfandel*'s the favourite, Lord Howard de Walden's, won at Epsom. Morny Cannon is riding him. I could have got seven to one against *Saint Amant* a fortnight before.

— That so? Davy Byrne said.

He went towards the window and, taking up the petty-cash book, scanned its pages.

— I could, faith, Nosey Flynn said, snuffling. That was a rare bit of horseflesh. *Saint Frusquin* was her sire. She won in a thunderstorm, Rothschild's filly, with wadding in her ears. Blue jacket and yellow cap. Bad luck to Big Ben Dollard and his *John o'Gaunt.* He put me off it. Ay.

He drank resignedly from his tumbler, running his fingers down the flutes.

— Ay, he said, sighing.

Mr Bloom, champing, standing, looked upon his sigh. Nosey numbskull. Will I tell him that horse Lenehan? He knows already. Better let him forget. Go and lose more. Fool and his money. Dewdrop coming down again. Cold nose he'd have kissing a woman. Still, they might like. Prickly beards they like. Dogs' cold noses. Old Mrs Riordan with the rumbling stomach's Skye terrier in the City Arms Hotel. Molly fondling him in her lap. O, the big doggybowwowsywowsy!

Wine soaked and softened rolled pith of bread mustard a moment mawkish cheese. Nice wine it is. Taste it better because I'm not thirsty. Bath of course does that. Just a bite or two. Then about six o'clock I can. Six, six. Time will be gone then. She . . .

Mild fire of wine kindled his veins. I wanted that badly. Felt so off colour. His eyes unhungrily saw shelves of tins: sardines, gaudy lobsters' claws. All the odd things people pick up for food. Out of shells, periwinkles with a pin, off trees, snails out of the ground the French eat, out of the sea with bait on a hook. Silly fish learn nothing in a thousand years. If you didn't know risky putting anything into your mouth. Poisonous berries. Johnny Magories. Roundness you think good. Gaudy colour warns you off. One fellow told another and so on. Try it on the dog first. Led on by the smell or the look. Tempting fruit. Ice cones. Cream. Instinct. Orange groves for instance. Need artificial irrigation. Bleibtreustrasse. Yes, but what about oysters? Unsightly like a clot of phlegm. Filthy shells. Devil to open them too. Who found them out? Garbage, sewage they feed on. Fizz and Red Bank oysters. Effect on the sexual. Aphrodis. He was in the Red Bank this morning. Was he oysters old fish at table? Perhaps he young flesh in bed. No. June has no ar no oysters. But there are people like things high. Tainted game. Jugged hare. First catch your hare. Chinese eating eggs fifty years old, blue and green again. Dinner of thirty courses. Each dish harmless might mix inside. Idea for a poison mystery. Or who was it used to eat the scruff off his own head? Cheapest lunch in town. That Archduke Leopold was it, no, yes, or was it Otto one of those Habsburgs?

Of course, aristocrats. Then the others copy to be in the fashion. Milly too, rock oil and flour. Raw pastry I like myself. Half the catch of oysters they throw back in the sea to keep up the price. Cheap, no one would buy. Caviare. Do the grand. Especially with fish. Hock in green glasses. Swell blowout. Lady this. Powdered bosom, pearls. The élite. Crème de la crème. They want special dishes to pretend they're. Hermit with a platter of pulse keep down the stings of the flesh. Know me come eat with me. Royal sturgeon high sheriff. Coffey, the butcher, right to venisons of the forest from His Ex. Send him back the half of a cow. Spread I saw down in the Master of the Rolls' kitchen area. White-hatted chef like a rabbi. Combustible duck. Curly cabbage *à la duchesse de Parme*. Just as well to write it on the bill of fare so you can know what you've eaten. Too many drugs spoil the broth. I know it myself. Dosing it with Edwards' desiccated soup. Geese stuffed silly for them. Lobsters boiled alive. Do ptake some ptarmigan. Wouldn't mind being a waiter in a swell hotel. Tips, evening dress, half-naked ladies. May I tempt you to a little more filleted lemon sole, Miss DuBedat? Yes, do bedad. And she did bedad. Huguenot name I expect that. A Miss DuBedat lived in Killiney I remember. *Du, de la*, French. Still, it's the same fish perhaps old Mickey Hanlon of Moore Street ripped the guts out of, making money hand over fist, finger in fishes' gills. Can't write his name on a cheque, think he was painting the landscape with his mouth twisted. Moooikill A Aitcha Ha. Ignorant as a kish of brogues, worth fifty thousand pounds.

Stuck on the pane two flies buzzed, stuck.

Glowing wine on his palate lingered, swallowed. Crushing in the winepress grapes of Burgundy. Sun's heat it is. Seems a secret touch telling me, memory. Touched, his sense moistened remembered. Hidden under wild ferns on Howth: below us bay sleeping: sky. No sound. The sky. The bay purple by the Lion's Head. Green by Drumleck. Yellow-green towards Sutton. Fields of undersea, the lines faint brown in grass, buried cities. Pillowed on my coat she had her hair, earwigs in the heather scrub, my hand under her nape, you'll toss me all. O wonder! Coolsoft with ointments her hand touched me, caressed: her eyes upon me did not turn away. Ravished over her I lay, full lips full open, kissed her mouth. Yum. Softly she gave me in my mouth the seedcake warm and chewed. Mawkish pulp her mouth had mumbled sweet and sour with spittle. Joy: I ate it: joy. Young life, her lips that gave me pouting. Soft warm sticky gumjelly lips. Flowers her eyes were, take me, willing eyes. Pebbles fell. She lay still. A goat. No one. High on Ben Howth rhododendrons a nannygoat walking surefooted, dropping currants. Screened under ferns she laughed, warmfolded. Wildly I lay on her, kissed her: eyes, her lips, her stretched neck beating, woman's breasts full in her blouse of nun's veiling, fat nipples upright. Hot I tongued her. She kissed me. I was kissed. All yielding she tossed my hair. Kissed, she kissed me.

Me. And me now.

Stuck, the flies buzzed.

His downcast eyes followed the silent veining of the oaken slab. Beauty: it curves: curves are beauty. Shapely goddesses: Juno, Venus: curves the world admires. Can see them library museum standing in the round hall, naked goddesses. Aids to digestion. They don't care what man looks. All to see. Never speaking. I mean to say to fellows like Flynn. Suppose she did Pygmalion and Galatea what would she say first? Mortal! Put you in your proper place. Quaffing nectar at mess with gods, golden dishes, all ambrosial. Not like a tanner lunch we have, boiled mutton, carrots and turnips, bottle of Allsopp. Nectar, imagine it like drinking electricity: gods' food. Lovely forms of woman sculped. Junonian. Immortal, lovely. And we stuffing food in one hole and out behind: food, chyle, blood, dung, earth, food: have to feed it like stoking an engine. They have no. Never looked. I'll look today. Keeper won't see. Bend down, let something drop. See if she.

Dribbling, a quiet message from his bladder came to go to do not to do there to do. A man and ready he drained his glass to the lees and walked, to men too they gave themselves, manly conscious, lay with men lovers, a youth enjoyed her, to the yard.

When the sound of his boots had ceased Davy Byrne said from his book:

— What is this he is? Isn't he in the insurance line?

— He's out of that long ago, Nosey Flynn said. He does canvassing for the *Freeman.*

— I know him well to see, Davy Byrne said. Is he in trouble?

— Trouble? Nosey Flynn said. Not that I heard of. Why?

— I noticed he was in mourning.

— Was he? Nosey Flynn said. So he was, faith. I asked him how was all at home. You're right, by God. So he was.

— I never broach the subject, Davy Byrne said humanely, if I see a gentleman is in trouble that way. It only brings it up fresh in their minds.

— It's not the wife anyhow, Nosey Flynn said. I met him the day before yesterday and he coming out of that Irish Farm Dairy John Wyse Nolan's wife has in Henry Street with a jar of cream in his hand taking it home to his better half. She's well nourished, I tell you. Plovers on toast.

— And is he doing much for the *Freeman*? Davy Byrne said.

Nosey Flynn pursed his lips.

— He doesn't buy cream on the ads he picks up. You can make bacon of that.

— How so? Davy Byrne asked, coming from his book.

Nosey Flynn made swift passes in the air with juggling fingers. He winked.

— He's in the craft, he said.

— Do you tell me so? Davy Byrne said.

— Very much so, Nosey Flynn said. Ancient, free and accepted order. Light, life and love, by God. They give him a leg up. I was told that by a … well, I won't say who.

— Is that a fact?

— O, it's a fine order, Nosey Flynn said. They stick to you when you're down. I know a fellow was trying to get into it, but they're as close as damn it. By God, they did right to keep the women out of it.

Davy Byrne smiledyawnednodded all in one:

— Iiiiiichaaaaaaach!

— There was one woman, Nosey Flynn said, hid herself in a clock to find out what they do be doing. But be damned but they smelt her out and swore her in on the spot a master mason. That was one of the Saint Legers of Doneraile.

Davy Byrne, sated after his yawn, said with tear-washed eyes:

— And is that a fact? Decent quiet man he is. I often saw him in here and I never once saw him … you know, over the line.

— God Almighty couldn't make him drunk, Nosey Flynn said firmly. Slips off when the fun gets too hot. Didn't you see him look at his watch? Ah, you weren't there. If you ask him to have a drink first thing he does he outs with the watch to see what he ought to imbibe. Declare to God he does.

— There are some like that, Davy Byrne said. He's a safe man, I'd say.

— He's not too bad, Nosey Flynn said, snuffling it up. He has been known to put his hand down too to help a fellow. Give the devil his due. O, Bloom has his good points. But there's one thing he'll never do.

His hand scrawled a dry pen signature beside his grog.

— I know, Davy Byrne said.

— Nothing in black and white, Nosey Flynn said.

Paddy Leonard and Bantam Lyons came in. Tom Rochford followed, frowning, a plaining hand on his claret waistcoat.

— Day, Mr Byrne.

— Day, gentlemen.

They paused at the counter.

— Who's standing? Paddy Leonard asked.

— I'm sitting anyhow, Nosey Flynn answered.

— Well, what'll it be? Paddy Leonard asked.

— I'll take a stone ginger, Bantam Lyons said.

— How much? Paddy Leonard cried. Since when, for God's sake? What's yours, Tom?

— How is the main drainage? Nosey Flynn asked, sipping.

For answer Tom Rochford pressed his hand to his breastbone and hiccuped.

— Would I trouble you for a glass of fresh water, Mr Byrne? he said.

— Certainly, sir.

Paddy Leonard eyed his alemates.

— Lord love a duck, he said, look at what I'm standing drinks to! Cold water and ginger pop! Two fellows that would suck whiskey off a sore leg.

Tom Rochford spilt powder from a twisted paper into the water set before him.

— That cursed dyspepsia, he said before drinking.

— Bread soda is very good, Davy Byrne said.

Tom Rochford nodded and drank.

— He has some bloody horse up his sleeve, Paddy Leonard said of Lyons. For the Gold Cup. A dead snip.

— *Zinfandel* is it? Nosey Flynn asked. Is it *Zinfandel*?

— Say nothing, Bantam Lyons winked. I'm going to plunge five bob on my own.

— Tell us if you're worth your salt and be damned to you, Paddy Leonard said. Who gave it to you?

Mr Bloom on his way out raised three fingers in greeting.

— So long! Nosey Flynn said.

The others turned.

— That's the man now that gave it to me, Bantam Lyons whispered.

— Prrwht! Paddy Leonard said with scorn. Mr Byrne, sir, we'll take two of your small Jamesons after that and a . . .

— Stone ginger, Davy Byrne added civilly.

— Ay, Paddy Leonard said. A sucking bottle for the baby.

Mr Bloom walked towards Dawson Street, his tongue brushing his teeth smooth. Something green it would have to be: spinach, say. Then with those Röntgen rays searchlight you could.

At Duke Lane a ravenous terrier choked up a sick knuckly cud on the cobblestones and lapped it with new zest. Surfeit. Returned with thanks having fully digested the contents. First sweet then savoury. Mr Bloom coasted warily. Ruminants. His second course. Their upper jaw they move. Wonder if Tom Rochford will do anything with that invention of his. Wasting time explaining it to Flynn's mouth. Lean people long mouths. Ought to be a hall or a place where inventors could go in and invent free. Course then you'd have all the cranks pestering.

He hummed, prolonging in solemn echo, the closes of the bars:

— *Don Giovanni, a cenar teco*
  M'invitasti.

Feel better. Burgundy. Good pick-me-up. Who distilled first? Some chap in the blues. Dutch courage. That *Kilkenny People* in the National Library now I must.

Bare clean close-stools, waiting, in the window of William Miller, plumber, turned back his thoughts. They could: and watch it all the way down changing biliary duct spleen squirting liver gastric juice coils of intestines like pipes. But the poor buffer would have to stand all the time with his entrails on show. Science. Swallow a pin, sometimes comes out of the ribs years after, tour round the body.

— *A cenar teco.*

What does that *teco* mean? Tonight perhaps.

— *Don Giovanni, thou hast me invited*
  To come to supper tonight,
  The rum the rumdum.

Doesn't go properly.

Keyes: two months if I get Nannetti to. That'll be two pounds ten, about two pounds eight. Three Hynes owes me. Two eleven. Prescott's dyeworks van over there. If I get Billy Prescott's ad. Two fifteen. Five guineas about. On the pig's back.

Could buy one of those silk petticoats for Molly, colour of her new garters.

Today. Today. Not think.

Tour the south then. What about English watering places? Brighton,

Margate. Piers by moonlight. Her voice floating out. Those lovely seaside girls. Against John Long's a drowsing loafer lounged in heavy thought, gnawing a crusted knuckle. Handyman wants job. Small wages. Will eat anything.

Mr Bloom turned at Gray's confectioner's window of unbought tarts and passed the Reverend Thomas Connellan's bookstore. *Why I Left the Church of Rome.* Bird's Nest women run him. They say they used to give pauper children soup to change to Protestants in the time of the potato blight. Society over the way papa went to for the conversion of poor Jews. Same bait. Why we left the Church of Rome.

A blind stripling stood tapping the curbstone with his slender cane. No tram in sight. Wants to cross.

— Do you want to cross? Mr Bloom asked.

The blind stripling did not answer. His wallface frowned weakly. He moved his head uncertainly.

— You're in Dawson Street, Mr Bloom said. Molesworth Street is opposite. Do you want to cross? There's nothing in the way.

The cane moved out trembling to the left. Mr Bloom's eye followed its line and saw again the dyeworks van drawn up before Drago's. Where I saw his brilliantined hair just when I was. Horse drooping. Driver in John Long's. Slaking his drouth.

— There's a van there, Mr Bloom said, but it's not moving. I'll see you across. Do you want to go to Molesworth Street?

— Yes, the stripling answered. South Frederick Street.

— Come, Mr Bloom said.

He touched the thin elbow gently: then took the limp seeing hand to guide it forward.

Say something to him. Better not do the condescending. They mistrust what you tell them. Pass a common remark:

— The rain kept off.

No answer.

Stains on his coat. Slobbers his food, I suppose. Tastes all different for him. Have to be spoonfed first. Like a child's hand his hand. Like Milly's was. Sensitive. Sizing me up I daresay from my hand. Wonder if he has a name. Van. Keep his cane clear of the horse's legs: tired drudge get his doze. That's right. Clear. Behind a bull: in front of a horse.

— Thanks, sir.

Knows I'm a man. Voice.

— Right now? First turn to the left.

The blind stripling tapped the curbstone and went on his way, drawing his cane back, feeling again.

Mr Bloom walked behind the eyeless feet, a flat-cut suit of herringbone tweed. Poor young fellow! How on earth did he know that van was there? Must have felt it. See things in their foreheads perhaps. Kind of sense of volume. Weight or size of it, something blacker than the dark. Wonder would he feel it if something was removed. Feel a gap. Queer idea of Dublin he must have, tapping his way round by the stones. Could he walk in a beeline if he hadn't that cane? Bloodless pious face like a fellow going in to be a priest.

Penrose! That was that chap's name.

Look at all the things they can learn to do. Read with their fingers. Tune pianos. Or we are surprised they have any brains. Why we think a deformed person or a hunchback clever if he says something we might say. Of course the other senses are more. Embroider. Plait baskets. People ought to help. Workbasket I could buy for Molly's birthday. Hates sewing. Might take an objection. Dark men they call them.

Sense of smell must be stronger too. Smells on all sides, bunched together. Each street different smell. Each person too. Then the spring, the summer: smells. Tastes? They say you can't taste wines with your eyes shut or a cold in the head. Also smoke in the dark they say get no pleasure.

And with a woman, for instance. More shameless not seeing. That girl passing the Stewart Institution, head in the air. Look at me. I have them all on. Must be strange not to see her. Kind of a form in his mind's eye. The voice, temperature. When he touches her with his fingers must almost see the lines, the curves. His hands on her hair, for instance. Say it was black, for instance. Good. We call it black. Then passing over her white skin. Different feel perhaps. Feeling of white.

Post office. Must answer. Fag today. Send her a postal order two shillings, half a crown. Accept my little present. Stationer's just here too. Wait. Think over it.

With a gentle finger he felt ever so slowly the hair combed back above his ears. Again. Fibres of fine fine straw. Then gently his finger felt the skin of his right cheek. Downy hair there too. Not smooth enough. The belly is the smoothest. No one about. There he goes into Frederick Street. Perhaps to Levenston's dancing academy piano. Might be settling my braces.

Walking by Doran's public house he slid his hand between his waistcoat and trousers and, pulling aside his shirt gently, felt a slack fold of his belly. But I know it's whitey yellow. Want to try in the dark to see.

He withdrew his hand and pulled his dress to.

Poor fellow! Quite a boy. Terrible. Really terrible. What dreams would he have, not seeing? Life a dream for him. Where is the justice being born that way? All those women and children excursion beanfeast burned and drowned in New York. Holocaust. Karma they call that, transmigration for sins you did in a past life, the reincarnation, met him pike hoses. Dear, dear, dear. Pity of course: but somehow you can't cotton on to them someway.

Sir Frederick Falkiner going into the Freemasons' Hall. Solemn as Troy. After his good lunch in Earlsfort Terrace. Old legal cronies cracking a magnum. Tales of the bench and assizes and annals of the Blue Coat School. I sentenced him to ten years. I suppose he'd turn up his nose at that stuff I drank. Vintage wine for them, the year marked on a dusty bottle. Has his own ideas of justice in the recorder's court. Well-meaning old man. Police chargesheets crammed with cases, get their percentage manufacturing crime. Sends them to the rightabout. The devil on money-lenders. Gave Reuben J. a great strawcalling. Now, he's really what they call a dirty Jew. Power those judges have. Crusty old topers in wigs. Bear with a sore paw. And may the Lord have mercy on your soul.

Hello, placard. Mirus Bazaar. His Excellency the lord lieutenant. Sixteenth. Today it is. In aid of funds for Mercer's Hospital. The *Messiah* was first given for that. Yes. Handel. What about going out there? Ballsbridge. Drop in on Keyes. No use sticking to him like a leech. Wear out my welcome. Sure to know someone on the gate.

Mr Bloom came to Kildare Street. First I must. Library.

Straw hat in sunlight. Tan shoes. Turned-up trousers. It is. It is.

His heart quopped softly. To the right. Museum. Goddesses. He swerved to the right.

Is it? Almost certain. Don't look. Wine in my face. Why did I? Too heady. Yes, it is. The walk. Not see. Not see. Get on.

Making for the museum gate with long windy steps he lifted his eyes. Handsome building. Sir Thomas Deane designed. Not following me?

Didn't see me perhaps. Light in his eyes.

The flutter of his breath came forth in short sighs. Quick. Cold statues: quiet there. Safe in a minute.

No, didn't see me. After two. Just at the gate.

My heart!

His eyes beating looked steadfastly at cream curves of stone. Sir Thomas Deane was the. Greek architecture.

Look for something I.

His hasty hand went quick into a pocket, took out, read unfolded Agudath Netaim. Where did I?

Busy looking for.

He thrust back quickly Agudath.

Afternoon she said.

I am looking for that. Yes, that. Try all pockets. Handker. *Freeman*. Where did I? Ah, yes. Trousers. Purse. Potato. Where did I?

Hurry. Walk quietly. Moment more. My heart.

His hand looking for the where did I put found in his hip pocket soap lotion have to call tepid paper stuck. Ah, soap there I yes. Gate.

Safe!

Urbane to comfort them, the Quaker librarian purred:

— And we have, have we not, those priceless pages of *Wilhelm Meister*? A great poet on a great brother poet. A hesitating soul taking arms against a sea of troubles, torn by conflicting doubts, as one sees in real life.

He came a step a sink-a-pace forward on neat's-leather creaking and a step backward creaking a sink-a-pace on the solemn floor.

A noiseless attendant, setting open the door but slightly, made him a noiseless beck.

— Directly, said he, creaking to go, albeit lingering. The beautiful ineffectual dreamer who comes to grief against hard facts. One always feels that Goethe's judgments are so true. True in the larger analysis.

Twicreakingly analysis he corantoed off. Bald, most zealous, by the door he gave his large ear all to the attendant's words: heard them: and was gone.

Two left.

— Monsieur de la Palice, Stephen sneered, was alive fifteen minutes before his death.

— Have you found those six brave medicals, John Eglinton asked with elder's gall, to write *Paradise Lost* at your dictation? *The Sorrows of Satan* he calls it.

Smile. Smile Cranly's smile.

> *First he tickled her*
> *Then he patted her*
> *Then he passed the female catheter*
> *For he was a medical*
> *Jolly old medi...*

— I feel you would need one more for *Hamlet*. Seven is dear to the mystic mind. The Shining Seven W. B. calls them.

Glitter-eyed, his rufous skull close to his green-capped desklamp sought the face, bearded amid darkgreener shadow, an ollav, holy-eyed. He laughed low: a sizar's laugh of Trinity: unanswered.

Orchestral Satan, weeping many a rood
Tears such as angels weep.
Ed egli avea del cul fatto trombetta.

He holds my follies hostage.

Cranly's eleven true Wicklowmen to free their sireland. Gaptoothed Kathleen, her four beautiful green fields, the stranger in her house. And one more to hail him: *Ave, Rabbi.* The Tinahely twelve. In the shadow of the glen he cooees for them. My soul's youth I gave him, night by night. God speed. Good hunting.

Mulligan has my telegram.

Folly. Persist.

— Our young Irish bards, John Eglinton censured, have yet to create a figure which the world will set beside Saxon Shakespeare's Hamlet though I admire him, as old Ben did, on this side idolatry.

— All these questions are purely academic, Russell oracled out of his shadow. I mean, whether Hamlet is Shakespeare or James I or Essex. Clergymen's discussions of the historicity of Jesus. Art has to reveal to us ideas, formless spiritual essences. The supreme question about a work of art is out of how deep a life does it spring. The painting of Gustave Moreau is the painting of ideas. The deepest poetry of Shelley, the words of Hamlet, bring our minds into contact with the eternal wisdom, Plato's world of ideas. All the rest is the speculation of schoolboys for schoolboys.

AE has been telling some Yankee interviewer. Wall, tarnation strike me!

— The schoolmen were schoolboys first, Stephen said superpolitely. Aristotle was once Plato's schoolboy.

— And has remained so, one should hope, John Eglinton sedately said. One can see him, a model schoolboy with his diploma under his arm.

He laughed again at the now smiling bearded face.

Formless spiritual. Father, Word and Holy Breath. Allfather, the heavenly man. Hiesos Kristos, magician of the beautiful, the Logos who suffers in us at every moment. This verily is that. I am the fire upon the altar. I am the sacrificial butter.

Dunlop, Judge, the noblest Roman of them all, AE, Arval, the Name Ineffable, in heaven hight, K.H., their master, whose identity is no secret to adepts. Brothers of the Great White Lodge always watching to see if they can help. The Christ with the bride-sister, moisture of light, born of an ensouled virgin, repentant sophia, departed to the plane of buddhi. The life esoteric is not for ordinary person. O.P. must work off bad karma first. Mrs Cooper-Oakley once glimpsed our very illustrious sister H.P.B.'s elemental.

O, fie! Out on't! *Pfuiteufel!* You naughtn't to look, missus, so you naughtn't, when a lady's ashowing of her elemental.

Mr Best entered, tall, young, mild, light. He bore in his hand with grace a notebook, new, large, clean, bright.

— That model schoolboy, Stephen said, would find Hamlet's musings about the afterlife of his princely soul, the improbable, insignificant and undramatic monologue, as shallow as Plato's.

John Eglinton, frowning, said, waxing wroth:

— Upon my word, it makes my blood boil to hear anyone compare Aristotle with Plato.

— Which of the two, Stephen asked, would have banished me from his commonwealth?

Unsheathe your dagger definitions. Horseness is the whatness of allhorse. Streams of tendency and eons they worship. God: noise in the street: very peripatetic. Space: what you damn well have to see. Through spaces smaller than red globules of man's blood they creepycrawl after Blake's buttocks into eternity of which this vegetable world is but a shadow. Hold to the now, the here, through which all future plunges to the past.

Mr Best came forward, amiable, towards his colleague.

— Haines is gone, he said.

— Is he?

— I was showing him Jubainville's book. He's quite enthusiastic, don't you know, about Hyde's *Love Songs of Connacht.* I couldn't bring him in to hear the discussion. He's gone to Gill's to buy it.

> *Bound thee forth, my booklet, quick*
> *To greet the callous public.*
> *Writ, I ween, 'twas not my wish,*
> *In lean unlovely English.*

— The peatsmoke is going to his head, John Eglinton opined.

We feel in England. Penitent thief. Gone. I smoked his baccy. Green twinkling stone. An emerald set in the ring of the sea.

— People do not know how dangerous love songs can be, the auric egg of Russell warned occultly. The movements which work revolutions in

178

the world are born out of the dreams and visions in a peasant's heart on the hillside. For them the earth is not an exploitable ground but the living mother. The rarefied air of the academy and the arena produce the six-shilling novel, the music-hall song. France produces the finest flower of corruption in Mallarmé but the desirable life is revealed only to the poor of heart, the life of Homer's Phaeacians.

From these words Mr Best turned an unoffending face to Stephen.

— Mallarmé, don't you know, he said, has written those wonderful prose poems Stephen MacKenna used to read to me in Paris. The one about *Hamlet*. He says: *il se promène, lisant au livre de lui-même*, don't you know, *reading the book of himself*. He describes *Hamlet* given in a French town, don't you know, a provincial town. They advertised it.

His free hand graciously wrote tiny signs in air.

Hamlet
ou
Le Distrait
Pièce de Shakespeare

He repeated to John Eglinton's new-gathered frown:

— *Pièce de Shakespeare*, don't you know. It's so French, the French point of view. *Hamlet ou*...

— The absentminded beggar, Stephen ended.

John Eglinton laughed.

— Yes, I suppose it would be, he said. Excellent people, no doubt, but distressingly shortsighted in some matters.

Sumptuous and stagnant exaggeration of murder.

— A deathsman of the soul Robert Greene called him, Stephen said. Not for nothing was he a butcher's son, wielding the sledded poleaxe and spitting in his palms. Nine lives are taken off for his father's one. Our Father who art in purgatory. Khaki Hamlets don't hesitate to shoot. The blood-boltered shambles in Act Five is a forecast of the concentration camp sung by Mr Swinburne.

Cranly, I his mute orderly, following battles from afar.

> *Whelps and dams of murderous foes whom none*
> *But we had spared*...

Between the Saxon smile and Yankee yawp. The devil and the deep sea.

— He will have it that *Hamlet* is a ghost story, John Eglinton said for Mr

Best's behoof. Like the fat boy in Pickwick he wants to make our flesh creep.

List! List! O, list!

My flesh hears him: creeping, hears.

If thou didst ever...

— What is a ghost? Stephen said with tingling energy. One who has faded into impalpability through death, through absence, through change of manners. Elizabethan London lay as far from Stratford as corrupt Paris lies from virgin Dublin. Who is the ghost from *limbo patrum*, returning to the world that has forgotten him? Who is King Hamlet?

John Eglinton shifted his spare body, leaning back to judge.

Lifted.

— It is this hour of a day in mid-June, Stephen said, begging with a swift glance their hearing. The flag is up on the playhouse by the bankside. The bear Sackerson growls in the pit near it, Paris Garden. Canvas climbers who sailed with Drake chew their sausages among the groundlings.

Local colour. Work in all you know. Make them accomplices.

— Shakespeare has left the Huguenot's house in Silver Street and walks by the swan mews along the riverbank. But he does not stay to feed the pen chevying her game of cygnets towards the rushes. The Swan of Avon has other thoughts.

Composition of place. Ignatius Loyola, make haste to help me!

— The play begins. A player comes on under the shadow, made up in the castoff mail of a court buck, a well-set man with a bass voice. It is the ghost, the king, a king and no king, and the player is Shakespeare who has studied *Hamlet* all the years of his life which were not vanity in order to play the part of the spectre. He speaks the words to Burbage, the young player who stands before him beyond the rack of cerecloth, calling him by a name, *Hamlet, I am thy father's spirit*, bidding him list. To a son he speaks, the son of his soul, the prince, young Hamlet, and to the son of his body, Hamnet Shakespeare, who has died in Stratford that his namesake may live for ever.

— Is it possible that that player Shakespeare, a ghost by absence, and in the vesture of buried Denmark, a ghost by death, speaking his own words to his own son's name (had Hamnet Shakespeare lived he would have been Prince Hamlet's twin), is it possible, I want to know, or probable that he did not draw or foresee the logical conclusion of those premises: you are the dispossessed son: I am the murdered father: your mother is the guilty queen, Anne Shakespeare, born Hathaway?

—But this prying into the family life of a great man, Russell began impatiently.

Art thou there, truepenny?

—Interesting only to the parish clerk. I mean, we have the plays. I mean, when we read the poetry of *King Lear* what is it to us how the poet lived? As for living, our servants can do that for us, Villiers de l'Isle has said. Peeping and prying into the greenroom gossip of the day, the poet's drinking, the poet's debts. We have *King Lear*: and it is immortal.

Mr Best's face, appealed to, agreed.

> *Flow over them with your waves and with your waters, Mananaan,*
> *Mananaan MacLir . . .*

How now, sirrah, that pound he lent you when you were hungry?

Marry, I wanted it.

Take thou this noble.

Go to! You spent most of it in Georgina Johnson's bed, clergyman's daughter. Agenbite of inwit.

Do you intend to pay it back?

O, yes.

When? Now?

Well . . . no.

When, then?

I paid my way. I paid my way.

Steady on. He's from beyant Boyne water. The northeast corner. You owe it.

Wait. Five months. Molecules all change. I am other I now. Other I got pound.

Buzz. Buzz.

But I, entelechy, form of forms, am I by memory because under everchanging forms.

I that sinned and prayed and fasted.

A child Conmee saved from pandies.

I, I and I. I.

A.E.I.O.U.

—Do you mean to fly in the face of the tradition of three centuries? John Eglinton's carping voice asked. Her ghost at least has been laid for ever. She died, for literature at least, before she was born.

181

— She died, Stephen retorted, sixty-seven years after she was born. She saw him into and out of the world. She took his first embraces. She bore his children and she laid pennies on his eyes to keep his eyelids closed when he lay on his deathbed.

Mother's deathbed. Candle. The sheeted mirror. Who brought me into this world lies there, bronze-lidded, under a few cheap flowers. *Liliata rutilantium.*

I wept alone.

John Eglinton looked in the tangled glowworm of his lamp.

— The world believes that Shakespeare made a mistake, he said, and got out of it as quickly and as best he could.

— Bosh! Stephen said rudely. A man of genius makes no mistakes. His errors are volitional and are the portals of discovery.

Portal of discovery opened to let in the Quaker librarian, softcreak-footed, bald, eared and assiduous.

— A shrew, John Eglinton said shrewdly, is not a useful portal of discovery, one should imagine. What useful discovery did Socrates learn from Xanthippe?

— Dialectic, Stephen answered: and from his mother how to bring thoughts into the world. What he learnt from his other wife Myrto (*absit nomen!*), Socratididion's Epipsychidion, no man, not a woman, will ever know. But neither the midwife's lore nor the Caudle lectures saved him from the archons of Sinn Féin and their noggin of hemlock.

— But Anne Hathaway? Mr Best's quiet voice said forgetfully. Yes, we seem to be forgetting her as Shakespeare himself forgot her.

His look went from brooder's beard to carper's skull, to remind, to chide them not unkindly, then to the baldpink lollard costard, guiltless though maligned.

— He had a good groatsworth of wit, Stephen said, and no truant memory. He carried a memory in his wallet as he trudged to Romeville whistling *The girl I left behind me*. If the earthquake did not time it we should know where to place poor Wat, sitting in his form, the cry of hounds, the studded bridle and her blue windows. That memory, *Venus and Adonis*, lay in the bedchamber of every light-o'-love in London. Is Katharine the shrew ill-favoured? Hortensio calls her young and beautiful. Do you think the writer of *Antony and Cleopatra*, a passionate pilgrim, had his eyes in the back of his head that he chose the ugliest doxy in all Warwickshire to lie withal? Good: he left her and gained the world of men. But his boy-women are the women of a boy. Their life, thought, speech are lent them by males. He chose badly? He was chosen, it seems to me. If others have their will Anne hath a way. By cock, she was to blame. She put the comether on him, sweet and twenty-six. The grey-eyed goddess who bends over the boy Adonis, stooping to conquer, as prologue to the swelling act, is a bold-faced Stratford wench who tumbles in a cornfield a lover younger than herself.

And my turn? When?

Come!

— Ryefield, Mr Best said brightly, gladly, raising his new book, gladly, brightly.

He murmured then with blond delight for all:

— *Between the acres of the rye*
   These pretty countryfolk would lie.

Paris: the well-pleased pleaser.

A tall figure in bearded homespun rose from shadow and unveiled its cooperative watch.

— I am afraid I am due at the *Homestead*.

Whither away? Exploitable ground.

— Are you going? John Eglinton's active eyebrows asked. Shall we see you at Moore's tonight? Pyper is coming.

— Pyper! Mr Best piped. Is Pyper back?

Peter Piper pecked a peck of pick of peck of pickled pepper.

— I don't know if I can. Thursday. We have our meeting. If I can get away in time.

Yogibogeybox in Dawson Chambers. *Isis Unveiled*. Their Pali book we tried to pawn. Cross-legged under an umbrel umbershoot he thrones, an Aztec logos, functioning on astral levels, their oversoul, mahamahatma. The faithful hermetists await the Light, ripe for chelaship, ringroundabout him. Louis H. Victory. T. Caulfield Irwin. Lotus ladies tend them i'the eyes, their pineal glands aglow. Filled with his god he thrones, Buddh under plantain. Gulfer of souls, engulfer. He-souls, she-souls, shoals of souls. Engulfed with wailing creecries, whirled, whirling, they bewail.

> *In quintessential triviality*
> *For years in this fleshcase a she-soul dwelt.*

— They say we are to have a literary surprise, the Quaker librarian said, friendly and earnest. Mr Russell, rumour has it, is gathering together a sheaf of our younger poets' verses. We are all looking forward anxiously.

Anxiously he glanced in the cone of lamplight where three faces, lighted, shone.

See this. Remember.

Stephen looked down on a wide headless caubeen hung on his ashplant handle over his knee. My casque and sword. Touch lightly with two index fingers. Aristotle's experiment. One or two? Necessity is that in virtue of which it is impossible that one can be otherwise. Argal, one hat is one hat.

Listen.

Young Colum and Starkey. George Roberts is doing the commercial part. Longworth will give it a good puff in the *Express*. O, will he? I liked Colum's *Drover*. Yes, I think he has that queer thing, genius. Do you think he has genius really? Yeats admired his line: *As in wild earth a Grecian vase*. Did he? I hope you'll be able to come tonight. Malachi Mulligan is coming too. Moore asked him to bring Haines. Did you hear Miss Mitchell's joke about Moore and Martyn? That Moore is Martyn's wild oats? Awfully clever, isn't it? They remind one of Don Quixote and Sancho Panza. Our national epic has yet to be written, Dr Sigerson says. Moore is the man for it. A knight of the rueful countenance here in Dublin. With a saffron kilt? O'Neill Russell? O yes, he must speak the grand old tongue. And his Dulcinea? James Stephens is doing some clever sketches. We are becoming important, it seems.

Cordelia. *Cordoglio*. Lir's loneliest daughter.

Nookshotten. Now your best French polish.

— Thank you very much, Mr Russell, Stephen said, rising. If you will be so kind as to give the letter to Mr Norman . . .

— O yes. If he considers it important it will go in. We have so much correspondence.

— I understand, Stephen said. Thanks.

God ild you. The pigs' paper. Bullock-befriending.

— Synge has promised me an article for *Dana* too. Are we going to be read? I feel we are. The Gaelic League wants something in Irish. I hope you will come round tonight. Bring Starkey.

Stephen sat down.

The Quaker librarian came from the leavetakers. Blushing, his mask said:

— Mr Dedalus, your views are most illuminating.

He creaked to and fro, tiptoeing up nearer heaven by the altitude of a chopine, and, covered by the noise of outgoing, said low:

— Is it your view, then, that she was not faithful to the poet?

Alarmed face asks me. Why did he come? Courtesy or an inward light?

— Where there is a reconciliation, Stephen said, there must have been first a sundering.

— Yes.

Christfox in leather trews, hiding, a runaway in blighted treeforks from hue and cry. Knowing no vixen, walking lonely in the chase. Women he won to him, tender people, a whore of Babylon, ladies of justices, bully tapsters' wives. Fox and geese. And in New Place a slack dishonoured body that once was comely, once as sweet, as fresh as cinnamon, now her leaves falling, all, bare, frighted of the narrow grave and unforgiven.

— Yes. So you think . . .

The door closed behind the outgoer.

Rest, suddenly, possessed the discreet vaulted cell, rest of warm and brooding air.

A vestal's lamp.

Here he ponders things that were not: what Caesar would have lived to do had he believed the soothsayer: what might have been: possibilities of the possible as possible: on things not known: what name Achilles bore when he lived among women.

Coffined thoughts around me, in mummy cases, embalmed in spice of words. Thoth, god of libraries, a birdgod, moony-crowned. And I heard the voice of that Egyptian high priest. In *painted chambers loaded with tilebooks*.

They are still. Once quick in the brains of men. Still: but an itch of death is in them, to tell me in my ear a maudlin tale, urge me to wreak their will.

— Certainly, John Eglinton mused, of all great men he is the most enigmatic. We know nothing but that he lived and suffered. Not even so much. Others abide our question. A shadow hangs over all the rest.

— But *Hamlet* is so personal, isn't it? Mr Best pleaded. I mean, a kind of private paper, don't you know, of his private life. I mean, I don't care a button, don't you know, who is killed or who is guilty . . .

He rested an innocent book on the edge of the desk, smiling his defiance. His private papers in the original. *Tá an bád ar an tír. Táim i mo shagart.* Put Béarla on it, littlejohn.

Quoth littlejohn Eglinton:

— I was prepared for paradoxes from what Malachi Mulligan told us but I may as well warn you that if you want to shake my belief that Shakespeare is Hamlet you have a stern task before you.

Bear with me.

Stephen withstood the bane of miscreant eyes glinting stern under wrinkled brows. A basilisk. *E quando vede l'uomo l'attosca*. Messer Brunetto, I thank thee for the word.

— As we, or Mother Dana, weave and unweave our bodies, Stephen said, from day to day, their molecules shuttled to and fro, so does the artist weave and unweave his image. And as the mole on my right breast is where it was when I was born, though all my body has been woven of new stuff time after time, so through the ghost of the unquiet father the image of the unliving son looks forth. In the intense instant of imagination, when the mind, Shelley says, is a fading coal, that which I was is that which I am and that which in possibility I may come to be. So in the future, the sister of the past, I may see myself as I sit here now but by reflection from that which then I shall be.

Drummond of Hawthornden helped you at that stile.

— Yes, Mr Best said youngly. I feel Hamlet quite young. The bitterness might be from the father but the passages with Ophelia are surely from the son.

Has the wrong sow by the lug. He is in my father. I am in his son.

— That mole is the last to go, Stephen said, laughing.

John Eglinton made a nothing pleasing mow.

— If that were the birthmark of genius, he said, genius would be a drug in the market. The plays of Shakespeare's later years, which Renan admired so much, breathe another spirit.

— The spirit of reconciliation, the Quaker librarian breathed.

— There can be no reconciliation, Stephen said, if there has not been a sundering.

Said that.

— If you want to know what are the events which cast their shadow over the hell of time of *King Lear, Othello, Hamlet, Troilus and Cressida*, look to see when and how the shadow lifts. What softens the heart of a man, shipwrecked in storms dire, Tried, like another Ulysses, Pericles, prince of Tyre?

Head, redcone-capped, buffeted, brine-blinded.

— A child, a girl placed in his arms, Marina.

– The leaning of sophists towards the bypaths of apocrypha is a constant quantity, John Eglinton detected. The highroads are dreary but they lead to the town.

Good Bacon: gone musty. Shakespeare Bacon's wild oats. Cypher-jugglers going the highroads. Seekers on the great quest. What town, good masters? Mummed in names: AE, eon: Magee, John Eglinton. East of the sun, west of the moon: *Tir na nÓg.* Booted the twain and staved.

> *How many miles to Dublin?*
> *Three score and ten, sir.*
> *Will we be there by candlelight?*

– Mr Brandes accepts it, Stephen said, as the first play of the closing period.

– Does he? What does Mr Sidney Lee, or Mr Simon Lazarus, as some aver his name is, say of it?

– Marina, Stephen said, a child of storm, Miranda, a wonder, Perdita, that which was lost. What was lost is given back to him: his daughter's child. *My dearest wife*, Pericles says, *was like this maid.* Will any man love the daughter if he has not loved the mother?

– The art of being a grandfather, Mr Best gan murmur. *L'art d'être grandp...*

– Will he not see reborn in her, with the memory of his own youth added, another image? His own image to a man with that queer thing genius is the standard of all experience, material and moral. Such an appeal will touch him. The images of other males of his blood will repel him. He will see in them grotesque attempts of nature to foretell or repeat himself.

The benign forehead of the Quaker librarian enkindled rosily with hope.

– I hope Mr Dedalus will work out his theory for the enlightenment of the public. And we ought to mention another Irish commentator, Mr George Bernard Shaw. Nor should we forget Mr Frank Harris. His articles on Shakespeare in the *Saturday Review* were surely brilliant. Oddly enough, he too draws for us an unhappy relation with the dark lady of the sonnets. The favoured rival is William Herbert, earl of Pembroke. I own that if the poet must be rejected such a rejection would seem more in harmony with – what shall I say? – our notions of what ought not to have been.

187

Felicitously he ceased and held out a meek head among them, auk's egg, prize of their fray.

He thous and thees her with grave husbandwords. Dost love, Miriam? Dost love thy man?

— That may be too, Stephen said. There is a saying of Goethe's which Mr Magee likes to quote. Beware of what you wish for in youth because you will get it in middle life. Why does he send to one who is a *buonaroba*, a bay where all men ride, a maid of honour with a scandalous girlhood, a lordling to woo for him? He was himself a lord of language and had made himself a coistrel gentleman and had written *Romeo and Juliet*. Why? Belief in himself has been untimely killed. He was overborne in a cornfield first (a ryefield, I should say) and he will never be a victor in his own eyes after nor play victoriously the game of laugh and lie down. Assumed dongiovannism will not save him. No later undoing will undo the first undoing. The tusk of the boar has wounded him there where love lies ableeding. If the shrew is worsted there yet remains to her woman's invisible weapon. There is, I feel in the words, some goad of the flesh driving him into a new passion, a darker shadow of the first, darkening even his own understanding of himself. A like fate awaits him and the two rages commingle in a whirlpool.

They list. And in the porches of their ears I pour.

— The soul has been before stricken mortally, a poison poured in the porch of a sleeping ear. But those who are done to death in sleep cannot know the manner of their quell unless their Creator endow their souls with that knowledge in the life to come. The poisoning, and the beast with two backs that urged it, King Hamlet's ghost could not know of were he not endowed with knowledge by his Creator. That is why the speech (his lean unlovely English) is always turned elsewhere, backward. Ravisher and ravished, what he would but would not, go with him from Lucrece's blue-circled ivory globes to Imogen's breast, bare, with its mole cinque-spotted. He goes back, weary of the creation he has piled up, to hide him from himself, an old dog licking an old sore. But, because loss is his gain, he passes on towards eternity in undiminished personality, untaught by the wisdom he has written or by the laws he has revealed. His beaver is up. He is a ghost, a shadow now, the wind by Elsinore's rocks or what you will, the sea's voice, a voice heard only in the heart of him who is the substance of his shadow, the son consubstantial with the father.

— Amen! Buck Mulligan responded from the doorway.

Hast thou found me, O mine enemy?

Entr'acte.

A ribald face, sullen as a dean's, came forward, then blithe in motley, towards the greeting of their smiles. My telegram.

— You were speaking of the gaseous vertebrate, if I mistake not? he asked of Stephen.

Primrose-vested, he greeted gaily with his doffed Panama as with a bauble.

They make him welcome. *Was Du verlachst wirst Du noch dienen.*

Brood of mockers: Photius, pseudo-Malachi, Johann Most.

He who himself begot, middler the Holy Ghost, and Himself sent himself, Agenbuyer, between Himself and others, who, put upon by His fiends, stripped and whipped, was nailed like bat to barn door, starved on crosstree, who let Him bury, stood up, harrowed hell, fared into heaven and there these nineteen hundred years sitteth on the right hand of His own self but yet shall come in the latter day to doom the quick and dead when all the quick shall be dead already.

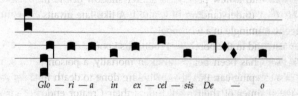

Glo — ri — a   in   ex — cel — sis   De — o

He lifts his hands. Veils fall. O, flowers! Bells with bells with bells aquiring.

— Yes, indeed, the Quaker librarian said. A most instructive discussion. Mr Mulligan, I'll be bound, has his theory too of the play and of Shakespeare. All sides of life should be represented.

He smiled on all sides equally.

Buck Mulligan thought, puzzled.

— Shakespeare? he said. I seem to know the name.

A flying sunny smile rayed in his loose features.

— To be sure, he said, remembering brightly. The chap that writes like Synge.

Mr Best turned to him.

— Haines missed you, he said. Did you meet him? He'll see you after at the D.B.C. He's gone to Gill's to buy Hyde's *Love Songs of Connacht.*

189

— I came through the museum, Buck Mulligan said. Was he here?

— The bard's fellow countrymen, John Eglinton answered, are rather tired perhaps of our brilliancies of theorising. I hear that an actress played Hamlet for the four-hundred-and-eighth time last night in Dublin. Vining held that the prince was a woman. Has no one made him out to be an Irishman? Judge Barton, I believe, is searching for some clues. He swears (His Highness not His Lordship) by Saint Patrick.

— The most brilliant of all is that story of Wilde's, Mr Best said, lifting his brilliant notebook. That *Portrait of Mr W.H.* where he proves that the sonnets were written by a Willie Hughes, a man all hues.

— For Willie Hughes, is it not? the Quaker librarian asked.

Or Hughie Wills. Mr William Himself. W.H: who am I?

— I mean, for Willie Hughes, Mr Best said, amending his gloss easily. Of course it's all paradox, don't you know, Hughes and hews and hues the colour, but it's so typical the way he works it out. It's the very essence of Wilde, don't you know. The light touch.

His glance touched their faces lightly as he smiled, a blond ephebe. Tame essence of Wilde.

You're darned witty. Three drams of usquebaugh you drank with Dan Deasy's ducats.

How much did I spend? O, a few shillings.

For a plump of pressmen. Humour wet and dry.

Wit. You would give your five wits for youth's proud livery he pranks in. Lineaments of gratified desire.

There be many mo. Take her for me. In pairing time. Jove, a cool ruttime send them. Yea, turtledove her.

Eve. Naked wheatbellied sin. A snake coils her, fang in's kiss.

— Do you think it is only a paradox? the Quaker librarian was asking. The mocker is never taken seriously when he is most serious.

They talked seriously of mocker's seriousness.

Buck Mulligan's again heavy face eyed Stephen awhile. Then, his head wagging, he came near, drew a folded telegram from his pocket. His mobile lips read, smiling with new delight.

— Telegram! he said. Wonderful inspiration! Telegram! A papal bull!

He sat on a corner of the unlit desk, reading aloud joyfully:

— *The sentimentalist is he who would enjoy without incurring the immense debtorship for a thing done.* Signed: Dedalus. Where did you launch it from? The kips? No. College Green. Have you drunk the four quid? The aunt is going to call on your unsubstantial father. Telegram! Malachi

Mulligan, The Ship, Lower Abbey Street. O, you peerless mummer! O, you priestified kinchite!

Joyfully he thrust message and envelope into a pocket but keened in querulous brogue:

— It's what I'm telling you, mister honey, it's queer and sick we were, Haines and myself, the time himself brought it in. 'Twas murmur we did for a gallus potion would rouse a friar, I'm thinking, and he limp with leching. And we one hour and two hours and three hours in Connery's sitting civil waiting for pints apiece.

He wailed softly:

— And we to be there, mavrone, and you to be unbeknownst sending us your conglomerations the way we to have our tongues out a yard long like the drouthy clerics do be fainting for a pussful.

Stephen laughed.

Quickly, warningfully, Buck Mulligan bent down.

— The tramper Synge is looking for you, he said, to murder you. He heard you pissed on his hall door in Glasthule. He's out in pampooties to murder you.

— Me! Stephen exclaimed. That was your contribution to literature.

Buck Mulligan gleefully bent back, laughing to the dark eavesdropping ceiling.

— Murder you! he laughed.

Harsh gargoyle face that warred against me over our mess of hash of lights in rue Saint-André-des-Arts. In words of words for words, *palabras*. Oisín with Patrick. Faunman he met in Clamart woods, brandishing a winebottle. *C'est vendredi saint!* Murthering Irish. His image, wandering, he met. I mine. I met a fool i'the forest.

— Mr Lyster, an attendant said from the door ajar.

— ... in which everyone can find his own. So Mr Justice Madden in his *Diary of Master William Silence* has found the hunting terms ... Yes? What is it?

— There's a gentleman here, sir, the attendant said, coming forward and offering a card. From the *Freeman*. He wants to see the files of the *Kilkenny People* for last year.

— Certainly, certainly, certainly. Is the gentleman ...?

He took the eager card, glanced, not saw, laid down, unglanced, looked, asked, creaked, asked:

— Is he ...? O, there!

Brisk in a galliard he was off and out. In the daylit corridor he talked with voluble pains of zeal, in duty bound, most fair, most kind, most honest broadbrim.

— This gentleman? *Freeman's Journal*? *Kilkenny People*? To be sure. Good day, sir. *Kilkenny* ... We have certainly ...

A patient silhouette waited, listening.

— All the leading provincial ... *Northern Whig, Cork Examiner, Enniscorthy Guardian* ... 1903 ... Will you please ...? Evans, conduct this gentleman ... If you just follow the atten ... Or please allow me ... This way ... Please, sir ...

Voluble, dutiful, he led the way to all the provincial papers, a bowing dark figure following his hasty heels.

The door closed.

— The sheeny! Buck Mulligan cried.

He jumped up and snatched the card.

— What's his name? Ikey Moses? Bloom.

He rattled on:

— Jehovah, collector of prepuces, is no more. I found him over in the museum where I went to hail the foamborn Aphrodite. The Greek mouth that has never been twisted in prayer. Every day we must do homage to her. *Life of life, thy lips enkindle.*

Suddenly he turned to Stephen:

— He knows you. He knows your old fellow. O, I fear me, he is Greeker than the Greeks. His pale Galilean eyes were upon her mesial groove. Venus Kallipyge. O, the thunder of those loins! *The god pursuing, the maiden hid.*

— We want to hear more, John Eglinton decided with Mr Best's approval. We begin to be interested in Mrs S. Till now we had thought of her, if at all, as a patient Griselda, a Penelope stay-at-home.

— Antisthenes, pupil of Gorgias, Stephen said, took the palm of beauty from Kyrios Menelaus' brood dam, Argive Helen, the wooden mare of Troy in whom a score of heroes slept, and handed it to poor Penelope. Twenty years he lived in London and, during part of that time, he drew a salary equal to that of the lord chancellor of Ireland. His life was rich. His art, more than the art of feudalism, as Walt Whitman called it, is the art of surfeit. Hot herring pies, green mugs of sack, honey sauces, sugar of roses, marchpane, gooseberried pigeons, ringocandies. Sir Walter Raleigh, when they arrested him, had half a million francs on his back including a pair of fancy stays. The gombeen woman Eliza Tudor had underlinen enough to vie with her of Sheba. Twenty years he dallied there between conjugal love and its chaste delights and scortatory love and its foul pleasures. You know Manningham's story of the burgher's wife who bade Dick Burbage to her bed after she had seen him in *Richard III* and how Shakespeare, overhearing, without more ado about nothing, took the cow by the horns and, when Burbage came knocking at the gate, answered from the capon's blankets: *William the Conqueror came before Richard III.* And the gay lakin, Mistress Fitton, mount and cry *O*, and his dainty birdsnies, Lady Penelope Rich, a clean quality woman is suited for a player, and the punks of the bankside, a penny a time.

Cours-la-Reine. *Encore vingt sous. Nous ferons de petites cochonneries. Minette? Tu veux?*

— The height of fine society. And Sir William Davenant of Oxford's mother with her cup of canary for every cock canary.

Buck Mulligan, his pious eyes upturned, prayed:

— Blessed Margaret Mary Anycock!

— And Harry of six wives' daughter. And other lady friends from neighbour seats, as Lawn Tennyson, gentleman poet, sings. But all those twenty years what do you suppose poor Penelope in Stratford was doing behind the diamond panes?

Do and do. Thing done. Thing done. In a rosery of Fetter Lane of Gerard, herbalist, he walks, greyed auburn. An azured harebell, like her veins. Lids of Juno's eyes: violets. He walks. One life is all. One body. Do. But do. Afar, in a reek of lust and squalor, hands are laid on whiteness.

Buck Mulligan rapped John Eglinton's desk sharply.

— Whom do you suspect? he challenged.

— Say that he is the spurned lover in the sonnets. Once spurned, twice spurned. But the court wanton spurned him for a lord, his dear-my-love.

Love that dare not speak its name.

— As an Englishman, you mean, John sturdy Eglinton put in, he loved a lord.

Old wall where sudden lizards flash. At Charenton I watched them.

— It seems so, Stephen said, when he wants to do for him, and for all other and singular uneared wombs, the holy office an ostler does for the stallion. Maybe, like Socrates, he had a midwife to mother as he had a shrew to wife. But she, the giglot wanton, did not break a bedvow. Two deeds are rank in that ghost's mind: a broken vow and the dull-brained yokel on whom her favour has declined, deceased husband's brother. Sweet Anne, I take it, was hot in the blood. Once a wooer, twice a wooer.

Stephen turned boldly in his chair.

— The burden of proof is with you, not with me, he said, frowning. If you deny that in the fifth scene of *Hamlet* he has branded her with infamy, tell me why there is no mention of her during the thirty-four years between the day she married him and the day she buried him. All those women saw their men down and under: Mary, her goodman John, Anne, her poor dear Willun, when he went and died on her, raging that he was the first to go, Joan, her four brothers, Judith, her husband and all her sons, Susan, her husband too, while Susan's daughter, Elizabeth, to use grandaddy's words, wed her second, having killed her first.

O yes, mention there is. In the years when he was living richly in royal London, to pay a debt she had to borrow forty shillings from her father's shepherd. Explain you then. Explain the swan song too wherein he has commended her to posterity.

He faced their silence.

To whom thus Eglinton:

You mean the will.

That has been explained, I believe, by jurists.

She was entitled to her widow's dower

At common law. His legal knowledge was great

Our judges tell us.

Him Satan fleers,

Mocker:

And therefore he left out her name

From the first draft but he did not leave out

The presents for his granddaughter, for his daughters,

For his sister, for his old cronies in Stratford

And in London. And therefore when he was urged,

As I believe, to name her

He left her his

Second-best

Bed.

Punkt.

Leftherhis

Secondbest

Leftherhis

Bestabed

Secabest

Leftabed.

Woa!

—Pretty countryfolk had few chattels then, John Eglinton observed, as they have still if our peasant plays are true to type.

—He was a rich country gentleman, Stephen said, with a coat of arms and landed estate at Stratford and a house in Ireland Yard, a capitalist shareholder, a bill promoter, a tithe farmer. Why did he not leave her his best bed if he wished her to snore away the rest of her nights in peace?

—It is clear that there were two beds, a best and a second-best, Mr Secondbest Best said finely.

—*Separatio a mensa et a thalamo*, bettered Buck Mulligan and was smiled on.

—Antiquity mentions famous beds, Second Eglinton puckered, bedsmiling. Let me think.

—Antiquity mentions that Stagyrite school urchin and bald heathen sage, Stephen said, who when dying in exile frees and endows his slaves, pays tribute to his elders, wills to be laid in earth near the bones of his dead wife and bids his friends be kind to an old mistress (don't forget Nell Gwyn Herpyllis) and let her live in his villa.

—Do you mean he died so? Mr Best asked with slight concern. I mean...

—He died dead drunk, Buck Mulligan capped. *A quart of ale is a dish for a king.* O, I must tell you what Dowden said!

—What? asked Besteglinton.

William Shakespeare and Company, Limited. The people's William. For terms apply: E. Dowden, Highfield House...

—Lovely! Buck Mulligan suspired amorously. I asked him what he thought of the charge of pederasty brought against the bard. He lifted his hands and said: *All we can say is that life ran very high in those days.* Lovely!

Catamite.

—The sense of beauty leads us astray, said beautifulinsadness Best to ugling Eglinton.

Steadfast John replied severe:

—The doctor can tell us what those words mean. You cannot eat your cake and have it.

Sayest thou so? Will they wrest from us, from me, the palm of beauty?

—And the sense of property, Stephen said. He drew Shylock out of his own long pocket. The son of a maltjobber and moneylender, he was himself a cornjobber and moneylender with ten tods of corn hoarded in the famine riots. His borrowers are no doubt those divers of worship mentioned by Chettle Falstaff who reported his uprightness of dealing. He sued a fellow player for the price of a few bags of malt and exacted his pound of flesh in interest for every money lent. How else could Aubrey's ostler and callboy get rich quick? All events brought grist to his mill. Shylock chimes with the Jew-baiting that followed the hanging and quartering of the queen's leech Lopez, his Jew's heart being plucked forth while the sheeny was yet alive: *Hamlet* and *Macbeth* with the coming to the throne of a Scotch philosophaster with a turn for witch-roasting. The lost Armada is his jeer in *Love's Labour's Lost.* His pageants, the histories, sail full-bellied on a tide of Mafeking enthusiasm. Warwickshire Jesuits are tried and we have a porter's theory of equivocation. The *Sea Venture* comes home from the Bermudas and the play Renan admired is written with Patsy Caliban, our American cousin. The sugared sonnets follow Sidney's. As for fay Elizabeth, otherwise carroty Bess, the gross virgin who inspired *The Merry Wives of Windsor,* let some Meinherr from Almany grope his life long for deep-hid meanings in the depths of the buckbasket.

I think you're getting on very nicely. Just mix up a mixture of mixed theolologicophilolological. *Mingo, minxi, mictum, mingere.*

—Prove that he was a Jew, John Eglinton dared, expectantly. Your dean of studies holds he was a Holy Roman.

Sufflaminandus sum.

—He was made in Germany, Stephen replied, as the champion French polisher of Italian scandals.

—A myriad-minded man, Mr Best reminded. Coleridge called him myriad-minded.

Amplius. In societate humana hoc est maxime necessarium ut sit amicitia inter multos.

—Saint Thomas, Stephen began...

—*Ora pro nobis,* Monk Mulligan groaned, sinking to a chair.

There he keened a wailing rune:

—*Pogue mahone! Acushla machree!* It's destroyed we are from this day! It's destroyed we are surely!

All smiled their smiles.

—Saint Thomas, Stephen, smiling, said, whose gorbellied works I enjoy reading in the original, writing of incest from a standpoint different from that of the new Viennese school Mr Magee spoke of, likens it in his wise and curious way to an avarice of the emotions. He means that the love so given to one near in blood is covetously withheld from some stranger who, it may be, hungers for it. Jews, whom Christians tax with avarice, are of all races the most given to intermarriage. Accusations are made in anger. The Christian laws which built up the hoards of the Jews (for whom, as for the lollards, storm was shelter) bound their affections too with hoops of steel. Whether these be sins or virtues old Nobodaddy will tell us at doomsday leet. But a man who holds so tightly to what he calls his rights over what he calls his debts will hold tightly also to what he calls his rights over her whom he calls his wife. No Sir Smile neighbour shall covet his ox or his wife or his manservant or his maidservant or his jackass.

— Or his jennyass, Buck Mulligan antiphoned.

— Gentle Will is being roughly handled, gentle Mr Best said gently.

— Which will? gagged sweetly Buck Mulligan. We are getting mixed.

— The will to live, John Eglinton philosophised, for poor Anne, Will's widow, is the will to die.

— *Requiescat*! Stephen prayed.

> *What of all the will to do?*
> *It has vanished long ago…*

— She lies laid out in stark stiffness in that second-best bed, the mobled queen, even though you prove that a bed in those days was as rare as a motorcar is now and that its carvings were the wonder of seven parishes. In old age she takes up with gospellers (one stayed at New Place and drank a quart of sack the town paid for but in which bed he slept it skills not to ask) and heard she had a soul. She read or had read to her his chapbooks, preferring them to the *Merry Wives* and, loosing her nightly waters on the jordan, she thought over *Hooks and Eyes for Believers' Breeches* and *The Most Spiritual Snuffbox, to Make the Most Devout Souls Sneeze*. Venus has twisted her lips in prayer. Agenbite of inwit: remorse of conscience. It is an age of exhausted whoredom groping for its god.

— History shows that to be true, *inquit Eglintonus Chronolologos*. The ages succeed one another. But we have it on high authority that a man's worst enemies shall be those of his own house and family. I feel that Russell is right. What do we care for his wife or father? I should say that only family poets have family lives. Falstaff was not a family man. I feel that the fat knight is his supreme creation.

Lean, he lay back. Shy, deny thy kindred, the unco guid. Shy, supping with the godless, he sneaks the cup. A sire in Ultonian Antrim bade it him. Visits him here on quarter days. Mr Magee, sir, there's a gentleman to see you. Me? Says he's your father, sir. Give me my Wordsworth. Enter Magee Mór Matthew, a rugged rough rug-headed kern, in strossers with a buttoned codpiece, his nether stocks bemired with clauber of ten forests, a wand of wilding in his hand.

Your own? He knows your old fellow. The widower.

Hurrying to her squalid deathlair from gay Paris, on the quayside I touched his hand. The voice, new warmth, speaking. Dr Bob Kenny is attending her. The eyes that wish me well. But do not know me.

— A father, Stephen said, battling against hopelessness, is a necessary evil. He wrote the play in the months that followed his father's death. If you hold that he, a greying man with two marriageable daughters, with thirty-five years of life, *nel mezzo del cammin di nostra vita*, with fifty of experience, is the beardless undergraduate from Wittenberg then you must hold that his seventy-year-old mother is the lustful queen. No. The corpse of John Shakespeare does not walk the night. From hour to hour it rots and rots. He rests, disarmed of fatherhood, having devised that mystical estate upon his son. Boccaccio's Calandrino was the first and last man who felt himself with child. Fatherhood, in the sense of conscious begetting, is unknown to man. It is a mystical estate, an apostolic succession, from only begetter to only begotten. On that mystery and not on the Madonna which the cunning Italian intellect flung to the mob of Europe the church is founded, and founded irremovably because founded, like the world, macro and microcosm, upon the void. Upon incertitude, upon unlikelihood. *Amor matris*, subjective and objective genitive, may be the only true thing in life. Paternity may be a legal fiction. Who is the father of any son that any son should love him or he any son?

What the hell are you driving at?

I know. Shut up. Blast you! I have reasons.

Amplius. Adhuc. Iterum. Postea.

Are you condemned to do this?

— They are sundered by a bodily shame so steadfast that the criminal annals of the world, stained with all other incests and bestialities, hardly record its breach. Sons with mothers, sires with daughters, lesbic sisters, loves that dare not speak their name, nephews with grandmothers, jailbirds with keyholes, queens with prize bulls. The son unborn mars beauty: born, he brings pain, divides affection, increases care. He is a male: his growth is his father's decline, his youth his father's envy, his friend his father's enemy.

In rue Monsieur-le-Prince I thought it.

— What links them in nature? An instant of blind rut.

Am I a father? If I were?

Shrunken uncertain hand.

— Sabellius, the African, subtlest heresiarch of all the beasts of the field, held that the Father was himself His own Son. The bulldog of Aquin, with whom no word shall be impossible, refutes him. Well: if the father who has not a son be not a father, can the son who has not a father be a son? When Rutlandbaconsouthamptonshakespeare or another poet of the same name in the comedy of errors wrote *Hamlet* he was not the father of his own son merely but, being no more a son, he was and felt himself the father of all his race, the father of his own grandfather, the father of his unborn grandson, who, by the same token, never was born, for nature, as Mr Magee understands her, abhors perfection.

Eglintoneyes, quick with pleasure, looked up shybrightly. Gladly glancing, a merry puritan, through the twisted eglantine.

Flatter. Rarely. But flatter.

— Himself his own father, Sonmulligan told himself. Wait. I am big with child. I have an unborn child in my brain. Pallas Athena! A play! The play's the thing! Let me parturiate!

He clasped his paunchbrow with both birth-aiding hands.

— As for his family, Stephen said, his mother's name lives in the forest of Arden. Her death brought from him the scene with Volumnia in *Coriolanus*. His boy-son's death is the death scene of young Arthur in *King John*. Hamlet, the black prince, is Hamnet Shakespeare. Who the girls in *The Tempest*, in *Pericles*, in *Winter's Tale* are we know. Who Cleopatra, fleshpot of Egypt, and Cressida and Venus are we may guess. But there is another member of his family who is recorded.

— The plot thickens, John Eglinton said.

The Quaker librarian, quaking, tiptoed in, quake, his mask, quake, with haste, quake, quack.

Door closed. Cell. Day.

They list. Three. They.

I you he they.

Come, mess.

Stephen – He had three brothers, Gilbert, Edmund, Richard. Gilbert in his old age told some cavaliers he got a pass for nowt from Maister Gatherer one time, mass he did, and he seen his brud Maister Wull the playwriter up in Lunnon in a wrastling play wud a man on's back. The playhouse sausage filled Gilbert's soul. He is nowhere: but an Edmund and a Richard are recorded in the works of Sweet William.

Mageeglinjohn – Names! What's in a name?

Best – That is my name, Richard, don't you know. I hope you are going to say a good word for Richard, don't you know, for my sake.

(*Laughter.*)

Buckmulligan (*piano, diminuendo*)

– Then outspoke medical Dick
  To his comrade medical Davy ...

Stephen – In his trinity of Black Wills, the villain Shakebags, Iago, Richard Crookback, Edmund in *King Lear*, two bear the wicked uncles' names. Nay, that last play was written or being written while his brother Edmund lay dying in Southwark.

Best – I hope Edmund is going to catch it. I don't want Richard, my name ...

(*Laughter.*)

Quakerlyster (*a tempo*) – But he that filches from me my good name ...

Stephen (*stringendo*) – He has hidden his own name, a fair name, William, in the plays, a super here, a clown there, as a painter of old Italy set his face in a dark corner of his canvas. He has revealed it in the sonnets where there is Will in overplus. Like John o'Gaunt his name is dear to him, as dear as the coat of arms he toadied for, *or* on a bend *sable* a spear *or* steeled *argent*, honorificabilitudinitatibus, dearer than his glory of the greatest shakescene in the country. What's in a name? That is what we ask ourselves in childhood when we write the name that we are told is ours. A star, a daystar, a firedrake, rose at his birth. It shone by day in the heavens alone, brighter than Venus in the night, and by night it shone over Delta in Cassiopeia, the recumbent constellation which is the signature of his initial among the stars. His eyes watched it, low-lying on the horizon, eastward of the Bear, as he walked by the slumberous summer fields at midnight, returning from Shottery and from her arms.

Both satisfied. I too.

Don't tell them he was nine years old when it was quenched.

And from her arms.

Wait to be wooed and won. Ay, meacock. Who will woo you?

Read the skies. *Autontimorumenos. Bous Stephanoumenos.* Where's your configuration? Stephen, Stephen, cut the bread even. S.D: *sua donna. Già: di lui. Gelindo risolve di non amare S.D.*

— What is that, Mr Dedalus? the Quaker librarian asked. Was it a celestial phenomenon?

— A star by night, Stephen said, a pillar of the cloud by day.

What more's to speak?

Stephen looked on his hat, his stick, his boots.

Stephanos: my crown. My sword. His boots are spoiling the shape of my feet. Buy a pair. Holes in my socks. Handkerchief too.

— You make good use of the name, John Eglinton allowed. Your own is strange enough. I suppose it explains your fantastical humour.

Me, Magee and Mulligan.

Fabulous artificer, the hawklike man. You flew. Whereto? Newhaven-Dieppe, steerage passenger. Paris and back. Lapwing. Icarus. *Pater, ait.* Sea-bedabbled, fallen, weltering. Lapwing you are. Lapwing be.

Mr Best eagerquietly lifted his book to say:

— That's very interesting because that brother motive, don't you know, we find also in the old Irish myths. Just what you say. The three brothers Shakespeare. In Grimm too, don't you know, the fairy tales. The third brother that always marries the sleeping beauty and wins the best prize.

Best of Best brothers. Good, better, best.

The Quaker librarian springhalted near.

— I should like to know, he said, which brother you ... I understand you to suggest there was misconduct with one of the brothers ... But perhaps I am anticipating?

He caught himself in the act: looked at all: refrained.

An attendant from the doorway called:

— Mr Lyster! Father Dinneen wants ...

— O! Father Dinneen! Directly.

Swiftly rectly creaking rectly rectly he was rectly gone.

John Eglinton touched the foil.

— Come, he said. Let us hear what you have to say of Richard and Edmund. You kept them for the last, didn't you?

— In asking you to remember those two noble kinsmen nuncle Richie and nuncle Edmund, Stephen answered, I feel I am asking too much perhaps. A brother is as easily forgotten as an umbrella.

Lapwing.

Where is your brother? Apothecaries' Hall. My whetstone. Him, then Cranly, Mulligan: now these. Speech, speech. But act. Act speech. They mock to try you. Act. Be acted on.

Lapwing.

I am tired of my voice, the voice of Esau. My kingdom for a drink.

On.

— You will say those names were already in the chronicles from which he took the stuff of his plays. Why did he take them rather than others? Richard, a whoreson crookback, misbegotten, makes love to a widowed Anne (what's in a name?), woos and wins her, a whoreson merry widow. Richard the conqueror, third brother, came after William the conquered. The other four acts of that play hang limply from that first. Of all his kings Richard is the only king unshielded by Shakespeare's reverence, the angel of the world. Why is the underplot of *King Lear* in which Edmund figures lifted out of Sidney's *Arcadia* and spatchcocked on to a Celtic legend older than history?

— That was Will's way, John Eglinton defended. We should not now combine a Norse saga with an excerpt from a novel by George Meredith. *Que voulez-vous?* Moore would say. He puts Bohemia on the seacoast and makes Ulysses quote Aristotle.

— Why? Stephen answered himself. Because the theme of the false or the usurping or the adulterous brother or all three in one is to Shakespeare, what the poor are not, always with him. The note of banishment, banishment from the heart, banishment from the home, sounds uninterruptedly from *The Two Gentlemen of Verona* onward till Prospero breaks his staff, buries it certain fathoms in the earth and drowns his book. It doubles itself in the middle of his life, reflects itself in another, repeats itself. Protasis, epitasis, catastasis, catastrophe. It repeats itself again when he is near the grave, when his married daughter Susan, chip of the old block, is accused of adultery. But it was the original sin that darkened his understanding, weakened his will and left in him a strong inclination to evil (the words are those of my lords bishops of Maynooth), an original sin and, like original sin, committed by another in whose sin he too has sinned. It is between the lines of his last written words, it is petrified on his tombstone under which her four bones are not to be laid. Age has not withered it. Beauty and peace have not done it away. It is in infinite variety everywhere in the world he has created, in *Much Ado about Nothing*, twice in *As You Like It*, in *The Tempest*, in *Hamlet*, in *Measure for Measure* and in all the other plays which I have not read.

He laughed to free his mind from his mind's bondage.

Judge Eglinton summed up.

— The truth is midway, he affirmed. He is the ghost and the prince. He is all in all.

— He is, Stephen said. The boy of Act One is the mature man of Act Five. All in all. In *Cymbeline*, in *Othello*, he is bawd and cuckold. He acts and is acted on. Lover of an ideal or a perversion, like José he kills the real Carmen. His unremitting intellect is the horn-mad Iago ceaselessly willing that the Moor in him shall suffer.

— Cuckoo! Cuckoo! Cuck Mulligan clucked lewdly. O word of fear!

Dark dome received, reverbed.

— And what a character is Iago! undaunted John Eglinton exclaimed. When all is said, Dumas *fils* (or is it Dumas *père*?) is right. After God Shakespeare has created most.

— Man delights him not nor woman neither, Stephen said. He returns after a life of absence to that spot of earth where he was born, where he has always been, man and boy, a silent witness, and there, his journey of life ended, he plants his mulberry tree in the earth. Then dies. The motion is ended. Gravediggers bury Hamlet *père* and Hamlet *fils*. A king and a prince at last in death, with incidental music. And, what though murdered and betrayed, bewept by all frail tender hearts for, Dane or Dubliner, sorrow for the dead is the only husband from whom they refuse to be divorced. If you like the epilogue look long on it: prosperous Prospero, the good man rewarded, Lizzie, grandpa's lump of love, and nuncle Richie, the bad man taken off by poetic justice to the place where the bad niggers go. Strong curtain. He found in the world without as actual what was in his world within as possible. Maeterlinck says: *If Socrates leave his house today he will find the sage seated on his doorstep. If Judas go forth tonight it is to Judas his steps will tend.* Every life is many days, day after day. We walk through ourselves, meeting robbers, ghosts, giants, old men, young men, wives, widows, brothers-in-love, but always meeting ourselves. The playwright who wrote the folio of this world and wrote it badly (He gave us light first and the sun two days later), the lord of things as they are whom the most Roman of Catholics call *dio boia*, hangman god, is doubtless all in all in all of us, ostler and butcher, and would be bawd and cuckold too but that in the economy of heaven, foretold by Hamlet, there are no more marriages, glorified man, an androgynous angel, being a wife unto himself.

— Eureka! Buck Mulligan cried. Eureka!

Suddenly happied, he jumped up and reached in a stride John Eglinton's desk.

— May I? he said. The Lord has spoken to Malachi.

He began to scribble on a slip of paper.

Take some slips from the counter going out.

— Those who are married, Mr Best, douce herald, quoted, all save one, shall live. The rest shall keep as they are.

He laughed, unmarried, at Eglinton Johannes, of arts a bachelor.

Unwed, unfancied, ware of wiles, they fingerponder nightly each his variorum edition of *The Taming of the Shrew*.

— You are a delusion, said roundly John Eglinton to Stephen. You have brought us all this way to show us a French triangle. Do you believe your own theory?

— No, Stephen said promptly.

— Are you going to write it? Mr Best asked. You ought to make it a dialogue, don't you know, like the Platonic dialogues Wilde wrote.

John Eclecticon doubly smiled.

— Well, in that case, he said, I don't see why you should expect payment for it since you don't believe it yourself. Dowden believes there is some mystery in *Hamlet* but will say no more. Herr Bleibtreu, the man Pyper met in Berlin, who is working up that Rutland theory, believes that the secret is hidden in the Stratford monument. He is going to visit the present duke, Pyper says, and prove to him that his ancestor wrote the plays. It will come as a surprise to His Grace. But he believes his theory.

I believe. O Lord, help my unbelief. That is, help me to believe or help me to unbelieve? Who helps to believe? *Egomen*. Who to unbelieve? Other chap.

— You are the only contributor to *Dana* who asks for pieces of silver. Then I don't know about the next number. Fred Ryan wants space for an article on economics.

Fraidrine. Two pieces of silver he lent me. Tide you over. Economics.

— For a guinea, Stephen said, you can publish this interview.

Buck Mulligan stood up from his laughing scribbling, laughing: and then gravely said, honeying malice:

— I called upon the bard Kinch at his summer residence in Upper Mecklenburgh Street and found him deep in the study of the *Summa contra Gentiles* in the company of two gonorrheal ladies, Fresh Nelly and Rosalie, the coalquay whore.

He broke away.

— Come, Kinch. Come, wandering Aengus of the birds.

Come, Kinch, you have eaten all we left. Ay. I will serve you your orts and offals.

Stephen rose.

Life is many days. This will end.

— We shall see you tonight, John Eglinton said. *Notre ami Moore* says Malachi Mulligan must be there.

Buck Mulligan flaunted his slip and Panama.

— Monsieur Moore, he said, lecturer on French letters to the youth of Ireland. I'll be there. Come, Kinch, the bards must drink. Can you walk straight?

Laughing, he ...

Swill till eleven. Irish nights' entertainment.

Lubber ...

Stephen followed a lubber ...

One day in the National Library we had a discussion. Shakes. After. His lub back. I followed. I gall his kibe.

Stephen, greeting, then all amort, followed a lubber jester, a wellkempt head, new-barbered, out of the vaulted cell into a shattering daylight of no thoughts.

What have I learned? Of them? Of me?

Walk like Haines now.

The constant readers' room. In the readers' book Cashel Boyle O'Connor Fitzmaurice Tisdall Farrell paraphs his polysyllables. Item: was Hamlet mad? The Quaker's pate godlily with a priesteen in booktalk.

— O please do, sir ... I shall be most pleased ...

Amused, Buck Mulligan mused in pleasant murmur with himself, self-nodding:

— A pleased bottom.

The turnstile.

Is that ...? Blue-ribboned hat ... Idly writing ... What? Looked ...?

The curving balustrade: smoothsliding Mincius.

Puck Mulligan, Panama-helmeted, went step by step, iambing, trolling:

— *John Eglinton, my jo, John,*
   Why won't you wed a wife?

He spluttered to the air:

— O, the chinless Chinaman! Chin Chon Eg Lin Ton. We went over to their playbox, Haines and I, the Plumbers' Hall. Our players are creating a new art for Europe, like the Greeks or M. Maeterlinck. Abbey Theatre! I smell the pubic sweat of monks.

He spat blank.

Forgot: any more than he forgot the whipping lousy Lucy gave him. And left the *femme de trente ans*. And why no other children born? And his first child a girl?

Afterwit. Go back.

The dour recluse still there (he has his cake) and the douce youngling, minion of pleasure, Phaedo's toyable fair hair.

Eh ... I just eh ... wanted ... I forgot ... eh ...

— Longworth and McCurdy Atkinson were there ...

Puck Mulligan footed featly, trilling:

> — *I hardly hear the purlieu cry*
> *Or a Tommy talk as I pass one by*
> *Before my thoughts begin to run*
> *On F. McCurdy Atkinson,*
> *The same that had the wooden leg,*
> *And that filibustering filibeg*
> *That never dared to slake his drouth,*
> *Magee that had the chinless mouth.*
> *Being afraid to marry on earth*
> *They masturbated for all they were worth.*

Jest on. Know thyself.

Halted, below me, a quizzer looks at me. I halt.

— Mournful mummer, Buck Mulligan moaned. Synge has left off wearing black to be like nature. Only crows, priests and English coal are black.

A laugh tripped over his lips.

— Longworth is awfully sick, he said, after what you wrote about that old hake Gregory. O, you inquisitional drunken Jew Jesuit! She gets you a job on the paper and then you go and slate her drivel to Jaysus. Couldn't you do the Yeats touch?

He went on and down, mopping, chanting with waving graceful arms:

— The most beautiful book that has come out of our country in my time. One thinks of Homer.

He stopped at the stairfoot.

— I have conceived a play for the mummers, he said solemnly.

The pillared Moorish hall, shadows entwined. Gone the nine men's morrice with caps of indices.

In sweetly varying voices Buck Mulligan read his tablet:

Everyman His Own Wife

or

A Honeymoon in the Hand
(a national immorality in three orgasms)

by

Ballocky Mulligan

He turned a happy patch's smirk to Stephen, saying:

— The disguise, I fear, is thin. But listen.

He read, *marcato*:

CHARACTERS:
Toby Tostoff (*a ruined Pole*)
Crab (*a bushranger*)
Medical Dick
and   } (*two birds with one stone*)
Medical Davy
Mother Grogan (*a watercarrier*)
Fresh Nelly
and
Rosalie (*the coalquay whore*).

He laughed, lolling a to-and-fro head, walking on, followed by Stephen: and mirthfully he told the shadows, souls of Moors:

— O, the night in the Camden Hall when the daughters of Erin had to lift their skirts to step over you as you lay in your mulberry-coloured, multicoloured, multitudinous vomit!

— The most innocent son of Erin, Stephen said, for whom they ever lifted them.

About to pass through the doorway, feeling one behind, he stood aside.

Part. The moment is now. Where then? If Socrates leave his house today, if Judas go forth tonight. Why? That lies in space which I in time must come to, ineluctably.

My will: his will that fronts me. Seas between.

A man passed out between them, bowing, greeting.

— Good day again, Buck Mulligan said.

The portico.

207

Here I watched the birds for augury. Aengus of the birds. They go, they come. Last night I flew. Easily flew. Men wondered. Street of harlots after. A creamfruit melon he held to me. In. You will see.

— The wandering Jew, Buck Mulligan whispered with clown's awe. Did you see his eye? He looked upon you to lust after you. I fear thee, ancient mariner. O, Kinch, thou art in peril. Get thee a breechpad.

Manner of Oxenford.

Day. Wheelbarrow sun over arch of bridge.

A dark back went before them, step of a pard, down, out by the gateway, under portcullis barbs.

They followed.

Offend me still. Speak on.

Kind air defined the coigns of houses in Kildare Street. No birds. Frail from the housetops two plumes of smoke ascended, pluming, and in a flow of softness softly were blown.

Cease to strive. Peace of the druid priests of *Cymbeline*, hierophantic: from wide earth an altar.

> *Laud we the gods*
> *And let our crooked smokes climb to their nostrils*
> *From our bless'd altars.*

The superior, the Very Reverend John Conmee S.J., reset his smooth watch in his interior pocket as he came down the presbytery steps. Five to three. Just nice time to walk to Artane. What was that boy's name again? Dignam. Yes. *Vere dignum et justum est.* Brother Swan was the person to see. Mr Cunningham's letter. Yes. Oblige him, if possible. Good practical Catholic: useful at mission time.

A one-legged sailor, swinging himself onward by lazy jerks of his crutches, growled some notes. He jerked short before the convent of the Sisters of Charity and held out a peaked cap for alms towards the Very Reverend John Conmee S.J. Father Conmee blessed him in the sun for his purse held, he knew, one silver crown.

Father Conmee crossed to Mountjoy Square. He thought, but not for long, of soldiers and sailors whose legs had been shot off by cannon-balls ending their days in some pauper ward, and of Cardinal Wolsey's words: *If I had served my God as I have served my king, He would not have abandoned me in my old days.* He walked by the treeshade of sunnywinking leaves: and towards him came the wife of Mr David Sheehy M.P.

— Very well, indeed, father. And you, father?

Father Conmee was wonderfully well indeed. He would go to Buxton probably for the waters. And her boys, were they getting on well at Belvedere? Was that so? Father Conmee was very glad indeed to hear that. And Mr Sheehy himself? Still in London. The House was still sitting, to be sure it was. Beautiful weather it was, delightful indeed. Yes, it was very probable that Father Bernard Vaughan would come again to preach. O yes: a very great success. A wonderful man really.

Father Conmee was very glad to see the wife of Mr David Sheehy M.P. looking so well and he begged to be remembered to Mr David Sheehy M.P. Yes, he would certainly call.

— Good afternoon, Mrs Sheehy.

Father Conmee doffed his silk hat and smiled, as he took leave, at the jet beads of her mantilla inkshining in the sun. And smiled yet again, in going. He had cleaned his teeth, he knew, with areca-nut paste.

Father Conmee walked and, walking, smiled for he thought on Father Bernard Vaughan's droll eyes and cockney voice.

Pilate! W'y don't you 'old back that 'owlin mob?

A zealous man, however. Really he was. And really did great good in his way. Beyond a doubt. He loved Ireland, he said, and he loved the Irish. Of good family too, would one think it? Welsh, were they not?

O, lest he forget. That letter to father provincial.

Father Conmee stopped three little schoolboys at the corner of Mountjoy Square. Yes: they were from Belvedere. The little house. Aha. And were they good boys at school? O. That was very good now. And what was his name? Jack Sohan. And his name? Ger Gallaher. And the other little man? His name was Brunny Lynam. O, that was a very nice name to have.

Father Conmee gave a letter from his breast to Master Brunny Lynam and pointed to the red pillarbox at the corner of Fitzgibbon Street.

— But mind you don't post yourself into the box, little man, he said.

The boys sixeyed Father Conmee and laughed:

— O, sir.

— Well, let me see if you can post a letter, Father Conmee said.

Master Brunny Lynam ran across the road and put Father Conmee's letter to father provincial into the mouth of the bright red letterbox. Father Conmee smiled and nodded and smiled and walked along Mountjoy Square East.

Mr Denis J. Maginni, professor of dancing &c., in silk hat, slate frockcoat with silk facings, white kerchief tie, tight lavender trousers, canary gloves and pointed patent boots, walking with grave deportment most respectfully took the curbstone as he passed Lady Maxwell at the corner of Dignam's Court.

Was that not Mrs M'Guinness?

Mrs M'Guinness, stately, silver-haired, bowed to Father Conmee from the farther footpath along which she sailed. And Father Conmee smiled and saluted. How did she do?

A fine carriage she had. Like Mary, queen of Scots, something. And to think that she was a pawnbroker! Well, now! Such a ... what should he say? ... such a queenly mien.

Father Conmee walked down Great Charles Street and glanced at the shut-up Free Church on his left. The Reverend T. R. Greene B.A. will (D.V.) speak. The incumbent they called him. He felt it incumbent on him to say a few words. But one should be charitable. Invincible ignorance. They acted according to their lights.

Father Conmee turned the corner and walked along the North Circular Road. It was a wonder that there was no tramline in such an important thoroughfare. Surely, there ought to be.

A band of satchelled schoolboys crossed from Richmond Street. All raised untidy caps. Father Conmee greeted them more than once benignly. Christian Brother boys.

Father Conmee smelt incense on his right hand as he walked. Saint Joseph's Church, Portland Row. For aged and virtuous females. Father Conmee raised his hat to the Blessed Sacrament. Virtuous: but occasionally they were also bad-tempered.

Near Aldborough House Father Conmee thought of that spendthrift nobleman. And now it was an office or something.

Father Conmee began to walk along the North Strand Road and was saluted by Mr William Gallagher who stood in the doorway of his shop. Father Conmee saluted Mr William Gallagher and perceived the odours that came from bacon flitches and ample cools of butter. He passed Grogan's the tobacconist's against which newsboards leaned and told of a dreadful catastrophe in New York. In America those things were continually happening. Unfortunate people to die like that, unprepared. Still, an act of perfect contrition.

Father Conmee went by Daniel Bergin's public house against the window of which two unlabouring men lounged. They saluted him and were saluted.

Father Conmee passed H. J. O'Neill's funeral establishment where Corny Kelleher totted figures in the daybook while he chewed a blade of hay. A constable on his beat saluted Father Conmee and Father Conmee saluted the constable. In Youkstetter's the pork butcher's Father Conmee observed pig's puddings, white and black and red, lying neatly curled in tubes.

Moored under the trees of Charleville Mall Father Conmee saw a turfbarge, a tow horse with pendent head, a bargeman with a hat of dirty straw seated amidships smoking and staring at a branch of poplar above him. It was idyllic: and Father Conmee reflected on the providence of the Creator who had made turf to be in bogs whence men might dig it out and bring it to town and hamlet to make fires in the houses of poor people.

On Newcomen Bridge the Very Reverend John Conmee S.J. of Saint

Francis Xavier's Church, Upper Gardiner Street, stepped on to an outward-bound tram.

Off an inward-bound tram stepped the Reverend John Dudley C.C. of Saint Agatha's Church, North William Street, on to Newcomen Bridge.

At Newcomen Bridge Father Conmee stepped into an outward-bound tram for he disliked to traverse on foot the dingy way past Mud Island.

Father Conmee sat in a corner of the tramcar, a blue ticket tucked with care in the eye of one plump kid glove, while four shillings, a sixpence and five pennies chuted from his other plump glovepalm into his purse. Passing the Ivy Church he reflected that the ticket inspector usually made his visit when one had carelessly thrown away the ticket. The solemnity of the occupants of the car seemed to Father Conmee excessive for a journey so short and cheap. Father Conmee liked cheerful decorum.

It was a peaceful day. The gentleman with the glasses opposite Father Conmee had finished explaining and looked down. His wife, Father Conmee supposed. A tiny yawn opened the mouth of the wife of the gentleman with the glasses. She raised her small gloved fist, yawned ever so gently, tiptapping her small gloved fist on her opening mouth and smiled tinily, sweetly.

Father Conmee perceived her perfume in the car. He perceived also that the awkward man at the other side of her was sitting on the edge of the seat.

Father Conmee at the altar rails placed the host with difficulty in the mouth of the awkward old man who had the shaky head.

At Annesley Bridge the tram halted and, when it was about to go, an old woman rose suddenly from her place to alight. The conductor pulled the bellstrap to stay the car for her. She passed out with her basket and a market net: and Father Conmee saw the conductor help her and net and basket down: and Father Conmee thought that, as she had nearly passed the end of the penny fare, she was one of those good souls who had always to be told twice *bless you, my child,* that they have been absolved, *pray for me.* But they had so many worries in life, so many cares, poor creatures.

From the hoardings Mr Eugene Stratton grinned with thick nigger lips at Father Conmee.

Father Conmee thought of the souls of black and brown and yellow men and of his sermon on Saint Peter Claver S.J. and the African Mission and of the propagation of the faith and of the millions of black and brown and yellow souls that had not received the baptism of water when their last hour came like a thief in the night. That book by the Belgian Jesuit, *Le Nombre des élus*, seemed to Father Conmee a reasonable plea. Those were millions of human souls created by God in His own likeness to whom the faith had not (D.V.) been brought. But they were God's souls, created by God. It seemed to Father Conmee a pity that they should all be lost, a waste, if one might say.

At the Howth road stop Father Conmee alighted, was saluted by the conductor and saluted in his turn.

The Malahide road was quiet. It pleased Father Conmee, road and name. The joybells were ringing in gay Malahide. Lord Talbot de Malahide, immediate hereditary lord admiral of Malahide and the seas adjoining. Then came the call to arms and she was maid, wife and widow in one day. Those were old-worldish days, loyal times in joyous townlands, old times in the barony.

Father Conmee, walking, thought of his little book *Old Times in the Barony* and of the book that might be written about Jesuit houses and of Mary Rochfort, daughter of Lord Molesworth, first countess of Belvedere.

A listless lady, no more young, walked alone the shore of Lough Ennel, Mary, first countess of Belvedere, listlessly walking in the evening, not startled when an otter plunged. Who could know the truth? Not the jealous Lord Belvedere, and not her confessor if she had not committed adultery fully, *ejaculatio seminis inter vas naturale mulieris*, with her husband's brother. She would half confess if she had not all sinned as women did. Only God knew and she and he, her husband's brother.

Father Conmee thought of that tyrannous incontinence, needed however for man's race on earth, and of the ways of God which were not our ways.

Don John Conmee walked and moved in times of yore. He was humane and honoured there. He bore in mind secrets confessed and he smiled at smiling noble faces in a beeswaxed drawing room ceiled with full fruit clusters. And the hands of a bride and of a bridegroom, noble to noble, were impalmed by Don John Conmee.

It was a charming day.

The lychgate of a field showed Father Conmee breadths of cabbages curtseying to him with ample underleaves. The sky showed him a flock of small white clouds going slowly down the wind. *Moutonné*, the French said. A just and homely word.

Father Conmee, reading his office, watched a flock of muttoning clouds over Rathcoffey. His thin-socked ankles were tickled by the stubble of

Clongowes field. He walked there, reading in the evening, and heard the cries of the boys' lines at their play, young cries in the quiet evening. He was their rector: his reign was mild.

Father Conmee drew off his gloves and took his red-edged breviary out. An ivory bookmark told him the page.

Nones. He should have read that before lunch. But Lady Maxwell had come.

Father Conmee read in secret *Pater* and *Ave* and crossed his breast. *Deus in adjutorium.*

He walked calmly and read mutely the nones, walking and reading till he came to *Res* in *Beati immaculati: Principium verborum tuorum veritas: in aeternum omnia judicia justitiae tuae.*

A flushed young man came from a gap of a hedge and after him came a young woman with wild nodding daisies in her hand. The young man raised his cap abruptly: the young woman abruptly bent and with slow care detached from her light skirt a clinging twig.

Father Conmee blessed both gravely and turned a thin page of his breviary. *Sin: Principes persecuti sunt me gratis: et a verbis tuis formidavit cor meum.*

« »

Corny Kelleher closed his long daybook and glanced with his drooping eye at a pine coffinlid sentried in a corner. He pulled himself erect, went to it and, spinning it on its axle, viewed its shape and brass furnishings. Chewing his blade of hay, he laid the coffinlid by and came to the doorway. There he tilted his hatbrim to give shade to his eyes and leaned against the doorcase, looking idly out.

Father John Conmee stepped into the Dollymount tram on Newcomen Bridge.

Corny Kelleher locked his large-footed boots and gazed, his hat downtilted, chewing his blade of hay.

Constable 57C, on his beat, stood to pass the time of day.

— That's a fine day, Mr Kelleher.

— Ay, Corny Kelleher said.

— It's very close, the constable said.

Corny Kelleher sped a silent jet of hayjuice arching from his mouth while a generous white arm from a window in Eccles Street flung forth a coin.

– What's the best news? he asked.

– I seen that particular party last evening, the constable said with bated breath.

« »

A one-legged sailor crutched himself round MacConnell's corner, skirting Rabaiotti's ice-cream car, and jerked himself up Eccles Street. Towards Larry O'Rourke, in shirtsleeves in his doorway, he growled unamiably:

– *For England* ...

He swung himself violently forward past Katey and Boody Dedalus, halted and growled:

– *home and beauty.*

J.J. O'Molloy's white careworn face was told that Mr Lambert was in the warehouse with a visitor.

A stout lady stopped, took a copper coin from her purse and dropped it into the cap held out to her. The sailor grumbled thanks, glanced sourly at the unheeding windows, sank his head and swung himself forward four strides.

He halted and growled angrily:

– *For England* ...

Two barefoot urchins, sucking long liquorice laces, halted near him, gaping at his stump with their yellow-slobbered mouths.

He swung himself forward in vigorous jerks, halted, lifted his head towards a window and bayed deeply:

– *home and beauty.*

The gay sweet chirping whistling within went on a bar or two, ceased. The blind of the window was drawn aside. A card *Unfurnished Apartments* slipped from the sash and fell. A plump bare generous arm shone, was seen, held forth from a white petticoat bodice and taut shiftstraps. A woman's hand flung forth a coin over the area railings. It fell on the path.

One of the urchins ran to it, picked it up and dropped it into the minstrel's cap, saying:

– There, sir.

« »

215

Katey and Boody Dedalus shoved in the door of the close steaming kitchen.

– Did you put in the books? Boody asked.

Maggy at the range rammed down a greyish mass beneath bubbling suds twice with her potstick and wiped her brow.

– They wouldn't give anything on them, she said.

Father Conmee walked through Clongowes fields, his thin-socked ankles tickled by stubble.

– Where did you try? Boody asked.

– M'Guinness's.

Boody stamped her foot and threw her satchel on the table.

– Bad cess to her big face! she cried.

Katey went to the range and peered with squinting eyes.

– What's in the pot? she asked.

– Shirts, Maggy said.

Boody cried angrily:

– Crikey, is there nothing for us to eat?

Katey, lifting the kettle lid in a pad of her stained skirt, asked:

– And what's in this?

A heavy fume gushed in answer.

– Pea soup, Maggy said.

– Where did you get it? Katey asked.

– Sister Mary Patrick, Maggy said.

The lacquey rang his bell.

– Barang!

Boody sat down at the table and said hungrily:

– Give us it here!

Maggy poured yellow thick soup from the kettle into a bowl. Katey, sitting opposite Boody, said quietly as her fingertip lifted to her mouth random crumbs:

– A good job we have that much. Where's Dilly?

– Gone to meet father, Maggy said.

Boody, breaking big chunks of bread into the yellow soup, added:

– Our father who art not in heaven.

Maggy, pouring yellow soup in Katey's bowl, exclaimed:

– Boody! For shame!

A skiff, a crumpled throwaway, Elijah is coming, rode lightly down the Liffey, under Loopline Bridge, shooting the rapids where water chafed around the bridge piers, sailing eastward past hulls and anchorchains, between the Customhouse Old Dock and George's Quay.

« »

The blond girl in Thornton's bedded the wicker basket with rustling fibre. Blazes Boylan handed her the bottle swathed in pink tissue paper and a small jar.

— Put these in first, will you? he said.

— Yes, sir, the blond girl said, and the fruit on top.

— That'll do, game ball, Blazes Boylan said.

She bestowed fat pears neatly, head by tail, and among them ripe shame-faced peaches.

Blazes Boylan walked here and there in new tan shoes about the fruit-smelling shop, lifting fruits, eyeing juicy crinkled and plump red tomatoes, sniffing smells.

H.E.L.Y.'S filed before him, tallwhitehatted, past Tangier Lane, plodding towards their goal.

He turned suddenly from a chip of strawberries, drew a gold watch from his fob and held it at its chain's length.

— Can you send them by tram? Now?

A dark-backed figure under Merchants' Arch scanned books on the hawker's cart.

— Certainly, sir. Is it in the city?

— O, yes, Blazes Boylan said. Ten minutes.

The blond girl handed him a docket and pencil.

— Will you write the address, sir?

Blazes Boylan at the counter wrote and pushed the docket to her.

— Send it at once, will you? he said. It's for an invalid.

— Yes, sir. I will, sir.

Blazes Boylan rattled merry money in his trousers pocket.

— What's the damage? he asked.

The blond girl's slim fingers reckoned the fruits.

Blazes Boylan looked into the cut of her blouse. A young pullet. He took a red carnation from the tall stem-glass.

— This for me? he asked gallantly.

The blond girl glanced sideways at him, got up regardless, with his tie a bit crooked, blushing.

217

— Yes, sir, she said.

Bending archly she reckoned again fat pears and blushing peaches.

Blazes Boylan looked in her blouse with more favour, the stalk of the red flower between his smiling teeth.

— May I say a word to your telephone, missy? he asked roguishly.

« »

— *Ma!* Almidano Artifoni said.

He gazed over Stephen's shoulder at Goldsmith's knobby poll.

Two carfuls of tourists passed slowly, their women sitting fore, gripping the handrests. Palefaces. Men's arms frankly round their stunted forms. They looked from Trinity to the blind columned porch of the Bank of Ireland where pigeons roocoocooed.

— *Anch'io ho avuto di queste idee*, Almidano Artifoni said, *quand' ero giovine come Lei. Eppoi mi sono convinto che il mondo è una bestia. È peccato. Perchè la sua voce ... sarebbe un cespite di rendita, via. Invece, Lei si sacrifica.*

— *Sacrifizio incruento*, Stephen said smiling, swaying his ashplant in slow swingswang from its midpoint, lightly.

— *Speriamo*, the round mustachioed face said pleasantly. *Ma, dia retta a me. Ci rifletta.*

By the stern stone hand of Grattan, bidding halt, an Inchicore tram unloaded straggling Highland soldiers of a band.

— *Ci rifletterò*, Stephen said, glancing down the solid trouserleg.

— *Ma, sul serio, eh?* Almidano Artifoni said.

His heavy hand took Stephen's firmly. Human eyes. They gazed curiously an instant and turned quickly towards a Dalkey tram.

— *Eccolo*, Almidano Artifoni said in friendly haste. *Venga a trovarmi e ci pensi. Addio, caro.*

— *Arrivederla, maestro*, Stephen said, raising his hat when his hand was freed. *E grazie.*

— *Di che?* Almidano Artifoni said. *Scusi, eh? Tante belle cose!*

Almidano Artifoni, holding up a baton of rolled music as a signal, trotted on stout trousers after the Dalkey tram. In vain he trotted, signalling in vain among the rout of barekneed gillies smuggling implements of music through Trinity gates.

« »

Miss Dunne hid the Capel Street Library copy of *The Woman in White* far back in her drawer and rolled a sheet of gaudy notepaper into her typewriter.

Too much mystery business in it. Is he in love with that one, Marion? Change it and get another by Mary Cecil Haye.

The disk shot down the groove, wobbled a while, ceased and ogled them: six.

Miss Dunne clicked on the keyboard:

— 16 June 1904.

Five tallwhitehatted sandwich men, between Monypeny's corner and the slab where Wolfe Tone's statue was not, eeled themselves, turning H.E.L.Y.'S, and plodded back as they had come.

Then she stared at the large poster of Marie Kendall, charming soubrette, and, listlessly lolling, scribbled on the jotter sixteens and capital esses. Mustard hair and dauby cheeks. She's not nice-looking, is she? The way she's holding up her bit of a skirt. Wonder will that fellow be at the band tonight. If I could get that dressmaker to make a concertina skirt like Susy Nagle's. They kick out grand. Shannon and all the boat-club swells never took their eyes off her. Hope to goodness he won't keep me here till seven.

The telephone rang rudely by her ear.

— Hello. Yes, sir. No, sir. Yes, sir. I'll ring them up after five. Only those two, sir, for Belfast and Liverpool. All right, sir. Then I can go after six if you're not back? A quarter after. Yes, sir. Twenty-seven and six. I'll tell him. Yes: one, seven, six.

She scribbled three figures on an envelope.

— Mr Boylan! Hello! That gentleman from *Sport* was in looking for you. Mr Lenehan, yes. He said he'll be in the Ormond at four. No, sir. Yes, sir. I'll ring them up after five.

« »

Two pink faces turned in the flare of the tiny torch.

— Who's that? Ned Lambert asked. Is that Crotty?

— Ringabella and Crosshaven, a voice replied, groping for foothold.

— Hello, Jack, is that yourself? Ned Lambert said, raising in salute his pliant lath among the flickering arches. Come on. Mind your steps there.

The vesta in the clergyman's uplifted hand consumed itself in a long soft flame and was let fall. At their feet its red speck died: and mouldy air closed round them.

— How interesting! a refined accent said in the gloom.

— Yes, sir, Ned Lambert said heartily. We are standing in the historic council chamber of Saint Mary's Abbey where Silken Thomas proclaimed himself a rebel in 1534. This is the most historic spot in all Dublin. O'Madden Burke is going to write something about it one of these days. The old Bank of Ireland was over the way till the time of the Union and the original Jews' Temple was here too before they built their synagogue over in Adelaide Road. You were never here before, Jack, were you?

— No, Ned.

— He rode down through Dame Walk, the refined accent said, if my memory serves me. The mansion of the Kildares was in Thomas Court.

— That's right, Ned Lambert said. That's quite right, sir.

— If you will be so kind then, the clergyman said, the next time to allow me perhaps . . .

— Certainly, Ned Lambert said. Bring the camera whenever you like. I'll get those bags cleared away from the windows. You can take it from here or from here.

In the still faint light he moved about, tapping with his lath the piled seedbags and points of vantage on the floor.

From a long face a beard and gaze hung on a chessboard.

— I'm deeply obliged, Mr Lambert, the clergyman said. I won't trespass on your valuable time . . .

— You're welcome, sir, Ned Lambert said. Drop in whenever you like. Next week, say. Can you see?

— Yes, yes. Good afternoon, Mr Lambert. Very pleased to have met you.

— Pleasure is mine, sir, Ned Lambert answered.

He followed his guest to the outlet and then whirled his lath away among the pillars. With J.J. O'Molloy he came forth slowly into Mary's Abbey where draymen were loading floats with sacks of carob and palm-nut meal: O'Connor, Wexford.

He stood to read the card in his hand:

— The Reverend Hugh C. Love, Rathcoffey. Present address: Saint Michael's, Sallins. Nice young chap he is. He's writing a book about the Fitzgeralds, he told me. He's well up in history, faith.

The young woman with slow care detached from her light skirt a clinging twig.

—I thought you were at a new gunpowder plot, J.J. O'Molloy said.

Ned Lambert cracked his fingers in the air.

—God! he cried. I forgot to tell him that one about the earl of Kildare after he set fire to Cashel Cathedral. You know that one? *I'm bloody sorry I did it*, says he, *but I declare to God I thought the archbishop was inside*. He mightn't like it, though. What? God, I'll tell him anyhow. That was the great earl, the Fitzgerald Mór. Hot members they were all of them, the Geraldines.

The horses he passed started nervously under their slack harness. He slapped a piebald haunch quivering near him and cried:

—Woa, sonny!

He turned to J.J. O'Molloy and asked:

—Well, Jack. What is it? What's the trouble? Wait a while. Hold hard.

With gaping mouth and head far back he stood still and, after an instant, sneezed loudly.

—Chow! he said. Blast you!

—The dust from those sacks, J.J. O'Molloy said politely.

—No, Ned Lambert gasped, I caught a ... cold night before ... blast your soul ... night before last ... and there was a hell of a lot of draught ...

He held his handkerchief ready for the coming ...

—I was ... Glasnevin this morning ... poor little ... what do you call him ... Chow! ... Mother of Moses!

« »

Tom Rochford took the top disk from the pile he clasped against his claret waistcoat.

—See? he said. Say it's turn six. In here, see. Turn Now On.

He slid it into the left slot for them. It shot down the groove, wobbled a while, ceased, ogling them: six.

Lawyers of the past, haughty, pleading, beheld pass from the Consolidated Taxing Office to Nisi Prius Court Richie Goulding carrying the costbag of Goulding, Collis and Ward and heard rustling from the Admiralty Division of King's Bench to the Court of Appeal an elderly female with false teeth smiling incredulously and a black silk skirt of great amplitude.

—See? he said. See now the last one I put in is over here: Turns Over. The impact. Leverage, see?

He showed them the rising column of disks on the right.

— Smart idea, Nosey Flynn said, snuffling. So a fellow coming in late can see what turn is on and what turns are over.

— See? Tom Rochford said.

He slid in a disk for himself: and watched it shoot, wobble, ogle, stop: four. Turn Now On.

— I'll see him now in the Ormond, Lenehan said, and sound him. One good turn deserves another.

— Do, Tom Rochford said. Tell him I'm Boylan with impatience.

— Good night, M'Coy said abruptly. When you two begin...

Nosey Flynn stooped towards the lever, snuffling at it.

— But how does it work here, Tommy? he asked.

— Tooraloo, Lenehan said. See you later.

He followed M'Coy out across the tiny square of Crampton Court.

— He's a hero, he said simply.

— I know, M'Coy said. The drain, you mean.

— Drain? Lenehan said. It was down a manhole.

They passed Dan Lowrey's music hall where Marie Kendall, charming soubrette, smiled on them from a poster a dauby smile.

Going down the path of Sycamore Street beside the Empire music hall Lenehan showed M'Coy how the whole thing was. One of those manholes like a bloody gaspipe and there was the poor devil stuck down in it, half choked with sewer gas. Down went Tom Rochford anyhow, bookie's vest and all, with the rope round him. And be damned but he got the rope round the poor devil and the two were hauled up.

— The act of a hero, he said.

At the Dolphin they halted to allow the ambulance car to gallop past them for Jervis Street.

— This way, he said, walking to the right. I want to pop into Lynam's to see *Sceptre*'s starting price. What's the time by your gold watch and chain?

M'Coy peered into Marcus Tertius Moses' sombre office, then at O'Neill's clock.

— After three, he said. Who's riding her?

— O. Madden, Lenehan said. And a game filly she is.

While he waited in Temple Bar M'Coy dodged a banana peel with gentle pushes of his toe from the path to the gutter. Fellow might damn easy get a nasty fall there coming along tight in the dark.

The gates of the drive opened wide to give egress to the viceregal cavalcade.

— Even money, Lenehan said returning. I knocked against Bantam Lyons in there going to back a bloody horse someone gave him that hasn't an earthly. Through here.

They went up the steps and under Merchants' Arch. A dark-backed figure scanned books on the hawker's cart.

— There he is, Lenehan said.

— Wonder what he's buying, M'Coy said, glancing behind.

— *Leopoldo* or *The Bloom is on the Rye*, Lenehan said.

— He's dead nuts on sales, M'Coy said. I was with him one day and he bought a book from an old one in Liffey Street for two bob. There were fine plates in it worth double the money, the stars and the moon and comets with long tails. Astronomy it was about.

Lenehan laughed.

— I'll tell you a damn good one about comets' tails, he said. Come over in the sun.

They crossed to the metal bridge and went along Wellington Quay by the river wall.

Master Patrick Aloysius Dignam came out of Mangan's, late Fehrenbach's, carrying a pound and a half of pork steaks.

— There was a big spread out at Glencree Reformatory, Lenehan said eagerly. The annual dinner, you know. Boiled shirt affair. The lord mayor was there, Val Dillon it was, and Sir Charles Cameron and Dan Dawson spoke and there was music. Bartell d'Arcy sang and Benjamin Dollard . . .

— I know, M'Coy broke in. My missus sang there once.

— Did she? Lenehan said.

A card *Unfurnished Apartments* reappeared on the window sash of number 7 Eccles Street.

He checked his tale a moment but broke out in a wheezy laugh.

— But wait till I tell you, he said. Delahunt of Camden Street had the catering and yours truly was chief bottlewasher. Bloom and the wife were there. Lashings of stuff we put up: port wine and sherry and curaçoa to which we did ample justice. Fast and furious it was. After liquids came solids. Cold joints galore and mince pies . . .

— I know, M'Coy said. The year the missus was there . . .

Lenehan linked his arm warmly.

— But wait till I tell you, he said. We had a midnight lunch too after all the jollification and when we sallied forth it was blue o'clock the morning after the night before. Coming home it was a gorgeous winter's night on the Featherbed mountain. Bloom and Chris Callanan were on one side of the car and I was with the wife on the other. We started singing glees and duets: *Lo, the early beam of morning.* She was well primed with a good load of Delahunt's port under her bellyband. Every jolt the bloody car gave I had her bumping up against me. Hell's delights! She has a fine pair, God bless her. Like that.

He held his caved hands a cubit from him, frowning:

– I was tucking the rug under her and settling her boa all the time. Know what I mean?

His hands moulded ample curves of air. He shut his eyes tight in delight, his body shrinking, and blew a sweet chirp from his lips.

– The lad stood to attention anyhow, he said with a sigh. She's a gamey mare and no mistake. Bloom was pointing out all the stars and the comets in the heavens to Chris Callanan and the jarvey: the Great Bear and Hercules and the Dragon and the whole jingbang lot. But, by God, I was lost, so to speak, in the Milky Way. He knew them all, faith. At last she spotted a weeny weeshy one miles away. *And what star is that, Poldy?* says she. By God, she had Bloom cornered. *That one, is it?* says Chris Callanan. *Sure that's only what you might call a pinprick.* By God, he wasn't far wide of the mark.

Lenehan stopped and leaned on the river wall, panting with soft laughter.

– I'm weak, he gasped.

M'Coy's white face smiled about it at instants and grew grave. Lenehan walked on again. He lifted his yachting cap and scratched his hind head rapidly. He glanced sideways in the sunlight at M'Coy.

– He's a cultured all-round man, Bloom is, he said seriously. He's not one of your common or garden … you know … There's a touch of the artist about old Bloom.

« »

Mr Bloom turned over idly pages of *The Awful Disclosures of Maria Monk*, then of Aristotle's *Masterpiece*. Crooked botched print. Plates: infants cuddled in a ball in blood-red wombs like livers of slaughtered cows. Lots of them like that at this moment all over the world. All butting with their skulls to get out of it. Child born every minute somewhere. Mrs Purefoy.

He laid both books aside and glanced at the third: *Tales of the Ghetto* by Leopold von Sacher-Masoch.

– That I had, he said, pushing it by.

The shopman let two volumes fall on the counter.

– Them are two good ones, he said.

Onions of his breath came across the counter out of his ruined mouth. He bent to make a bundle of the other books, hugged them against his unbuttoned waistcoat and bore them off behind the dingy curtain.

On O'Connell Bridge many persons observed the grave deportment and gay apparel of Mr Denis J. Maginni, professor of dancing &c.

Mr Bloom, alone, looked at the titles. *Fair Tyrants* by James Lovebirch. Know the kind that is. Had it? Yes.

He opened it. Thought so.

A woman's voice behind the dingy curtain. Listen: the man.

No: she wouldn't like that much. Got her it once.

He read the other title: *Sweets of Sin.* More in her line. Let us see.

He read where his finger opened:

All the dollar bills her husband gave her were spent in the stores on wondrous gowns and costliest frillies. For him! For Raoul!

Yes. This. Here. Try.

Her mouth glued on his in a luscious voluptuous kiss while his hands felt for the opulent curves inside her deshabille.

Yes. Take this. The end.

You are late, he spoke hoarsely, eyeing her with a suspicious glare.

The beautiful woman threw off her sable-trimmed wrap, displaying her queenly shoulders and heaving embonpoint. An imperceptible smile played round her perfect lips as she turned to him calmly.

Mr Bloom read again: *The beautiful woman* ...

Warmth showered gently over him, cowing his flesh. Flesh yielded amply amid rumpled clothes: whites of eyes swooning up. His nostrils arched themselves for prey. Melting breast ointments (*for him! for Raoul!*). Armpits' oniony sweat. Fish-gluey slime (*her heaving embonpoint!*). Feel! Press! Chrished! Sulphur dung of lions!

Young! Young!

An elderly female, no more young, left the building of the Courts of Chancery, King's Bench, Exchequer and Common Pleas, having heard in the Lord Chancellor's Court the case in lunacy of Potterton, in the Admiralty Division the summons, ex parte motion, of the owners of the *Lady Cairns* versus the owners of the barque *Mona,* in the Court of Appeal reservation of judgment in the case of Harvey versus the Ocean Accident and Guarantee Corporation.

Phlegmy coughs shook the air of the bookshop, bulging out the dingy curtains. The shopman's uncombed grey head came out and his unshaven reddened face, coughing. He raked his throat rudely, puked phlegm on the floor. He put his boot on what he had spat, wiping his sole along it, and bent, showing a raw-skinned crown, scantily haired.

Mr Bloom beheld it.

Mastering his troubled breath, he said:

— I'll take this one.

The shopman lifted eyes bleared with old rheum.

— *Sweets of Sin*, he said, tapping on it. That's a good one.

« »

The lacquey by the door of Dillon's auction rooms shook his handbell twice again and viewed himself in the chalked mirror of the cabinet.

Dilly Dedalus, loitering by the curbstone, heard the beats of the bell, the cries of the auctioneer within. Four and nine. Those lovely curtains. Five shillings. Cosy curtains. Selling new at two guineas. Any advance on five shillings? Going for five shillings.

The lacquey lifted his handbell and shook it:

— Barang!

Bang of the last-lap bell spurred the half-mile wheelmen to their sprint. J.A. Jackson, W.E. Wylie, A. Munro and W.H.T. Gahan, their stretched necks wagging, negotiated the curve by the College library.

Mr Dedalus, tugging a long moustache, came round from Williams's Row. He halted near his daughter.

— It's time for you, she said.

— Stand up straight for the love of the Lord Jesus, Mr Dedalus said. Are you trying to imitate your uncle John the cornet player, head upon shoulders? Melancholy God!

Dilly shrugged her shoulders. Mr Dedalus placed his hands on them and held them back.

— Stand up straight, girl, he said. You'll get curvature of the spine. Do you know what you look like?

He let his head sink suddenly down and forward, hunching his shoulders and dropping his underjaw.

— Give it up, father, Dilly said. All the people are looking at you.

Mr Dedalus drew himself upright and tugged again at his moustache.

— Did you get any money? Dilly asked.

226

— Where would I get money? Mr Dedalus said. There is no one in Dublin would lend me fourpence.

— You got some, Dilly said, looking in his eyes.

— How do you know that? Mr Dedalus asked, his tongue in his cheek.

Mr Kernan, pleased with the order he had booked, walked boldly along James's Street.

— I know you did, Dilly answered. Were you in the Scotch House now?

— I was not, then, Mr Dedalus said, smiling. Was it the little nuns taught you to be so saucy? Here.

He handed her a shilling.

— See if you can do anything with that, he said.

— I suppose you got five, Dilly said. Give me more than that.

— Wait awhile, Mr Dedalus said threateningly. You're like the rest of them, are you? An insolent pack of little bitches since your poor mother died. But wait awhile. You'll all get a short shrift and a long day from me. Low blackguardism! I'm going to get rid of you. Wouldn't care if I was stretched out stiff. He's dead. The man upstairs is dead.

He left her and walked on. Dilly followed quickly and pulled his coat.

— Well, what is it? he said, stopping.

The lacquey rang his bell behind their backs:

— Barang!

— Curse your bloody blatant soul, Mr Dedalus cried, turning on him.

The lacquey, aware of comment, shook the lolling clapper of his bell: but feebly:

— Bang!

Mr Dedalus stared at him.

— Watch him, he said. It's instructive. I wonder will he allow us to talk.

— You got more than that, father, Dilly said.

— I'm going to show you a little trick, Mr Dedalus said. I'll leave you all where Jesus left the Jews. Look, there's all I have. I got two shillings from Jack Power and I spent twopence for a shave for the funeral.

He drew forth a handful of copper coins nervously.

— Can't you look for some money somewhere? Dilly said.

Mr Dedalus thought and nodded.

— I will, he said gravely. I looked all along the gutter in O'Connell Street. I'll try this one now.

— You're very funny, Dilly said, grinning.

— Here, Mr Dedalus said, handing her two pennies. Get a glass of milk for yourself and a bun or a something. I'll be home shortly.

He put the other coins in his pocket and started to walk on.

The viceregal cavalcade passed, greeted by obsequious policemen, out of Parkgate.

— I'm sure you have another shilling, Dilly said.

The lacquey banged loudly.

Mr Dedalus amid the din walked off, murmuring to himself with a pursing mincing mouth:

— The little nuns! Nice little things! O, sure they wouldn't do anything! O, sure they wouldn't really! Is it little Sister Monica?

« »

From the sundial towards James's Gate walked Mr Kernan, pleased with the order he had booked for Pulbrook Robertson, boldly along James's Street, past Shackleton's offices. Got round him all right. How do you do, Mr Crimmins? First rate, sir. I was afraid you might be up in your other establishment in Pimlico. How are things going? Just keeping alive. Lovely weather we're having. Yes, indeed. Good for the country. Those farmers are always grumbling. I'll just take a thimbleful of your best gin, Mr Crimmins. A small gin, sir. Yes, sir. Terrible affair that *General Slocum* explosion. Terrible, terrible! A thousand casualties. And heartrending scenes. Men trampling down women and children. Most brutal thing. What do they say was the cause? Spontaneous combustion. Most scandalous revelation. Not a single lifeboat would float and the firehose all burst. What I can't understand is how the inspectors ever allowed a boat like that ... Now you're talking straight, Mr Crimmins. You know why? Palm oil. Is that a fact? Without a doubt. Well now, look at that. And America they say is the land of the free. I thought we were bad here.

I smiled at him. *America*, I said quietly, just like that. *What is it? The sweepings of every country including our own. Isn't that true?* That's a fact.

Graft, my dear sir. Well, of course, where there's money going there's always someone to pick it up.

Saw him looking at my frockcoat. Dress does it. Nothing like a dressy appearance. Bowls them over.

— Hello, Simon, Father Cowley said. How are things?

— Hello, Bob, old man, Mr Dedalus answered, stopping.

Mr Kernan halted and preened himself before the sloping mirror of Peter Kennedy, hairdresser. Stylish coat, beyond a doubt. Scott of Dawson Street. Well worth the half sovereign I gave Neary for it. Never built under three guineas. Fits me down to the ground. Some Kildare Street Club toff had it probably. John Mulligan, the manager of the Hibernian Bank, gave me a very sharp eye yesterday on Carlisle Bridge as if he remembered me.

Aham! Must dress the character for those fellows. Knight of the road. Gentleman. And now, Mr Crimmins, may we have the honour of your custom again, sir. The cup that cheers but not inebriates, as the old saying has it.

North Wall and Sir John Rogerson's Quay, with hulls and anchorchains, sailing westward, sailed by a skiff, a crumpled throwaway, rocked on the ferrywash, Elijah is coming.

Mr Kernan glanced in farewell at his image. High colour, of course. Grizzled moustache. Returned Indian officer. Bravely he bore his stumpy body forward on spatted feet, squaring his shoulders. Is that Ned Lambert's brother over the way: Sam? What? Yes. He's as like it as damn it. No. The windscreen of that motorcar in the sun there. Just a flash like that. Damn like him.

Aham! Hot spirit of juniper juice warmed his vitals and his breath. Good drop of gin, that was. His frocktails winked in bright sunshine to his fat strut.

Down there Emmet was hanged, drawn and quartered. Greasy black rope. Dogs licking the blood off the street when the lord lieutenant's wife drove by in her noddy.

Bad times those were. Well, well. Over and done with. Great topers too. Four-bottle men.

Let me see. Is he buried in Saint Michan's? No, there was a midnight burial in Glasnevin. Corpse brought in through a secret door in the wall. Dignam is there now. Went out in a puff. Well, well. Better turn down here. Make a detour.

Mr Kernan turned and walked down the slope of Watling Street by the corner of Guinness's visitors' waiting room. Outside the Dublin Distillers Company's stores an outside car without fare or jarvey stood, the reins knotted to the wheel. Damn dangerous thing. Some Tipperary bosthoon endangering the lives of the citizens. Runaway horse.

Denis Breen with his tomes, weary of having waited an hour in John Henry Menton's office, led his wife over O'Connell Bridge, bound for the office of Messrs Collis and Ward.

Mr Kernan approached Island Street.

Times of the troubles. Must ask Ned Lambert to lend me those reminiscences of Sir Jonah Barrington. When you look back on it all now in a kind of retrospective arrangement. Gaming at Daly's. No cardsharping then. One of those fellows got his hand nailed to the table by a dagger. Somewhere here Lord Edward Fitzgerald escaped from Major Sirr. Stables behind Moira House.

Damn good gin that was.

Fine dashing young nobleman. Good stock, of course. That ruffian, that sham squire with his violet gloves, gave him away. Course they were on the wrong side. They rose in dark and evil days. Fine poem that is: Ingram. They were gentlemen. Ben Dollard does sing that ballad touchingly. Masterly rendition.

At the siege of Ross did my father fall.

A cavalcade in easy trot along Pembroke Quay passed, outriders leaping, leaping in their, in their saddles. Frockcoats. Cream sunshades.

Mr Kernan hurried forward, blowing pursily.

His Excellency! Too bad! Just missed that by a hair. Damn it! What a pity!

« »

Stephen Dedalus watched through the webbed window the lapidary's fingers prove a time-dulled chain. Dust webbed the window and the showtrays. Dust darkened the toiling fingers with their vulture nails. Dust slept on dull coils of bronze and silver, lozenges of cinnabar, on rubies, leprous and wine-dark stones.

Born all in the dark wormy earth, cold specks of fire, evil, lights shining in the darkness. Where fallen archangels flung the stars of their brows. Muddy swine snouts, hands, root and root, gripe and wrest them.

She dances in a foul gloom where gum burns with garlic. A sailorman, rust-bearded, sips from a beaker rum and eyes her. A long and sea-fed silent rut. She dances, capers, wagging her sowish haunches and her hips, on her gross belly flapping a ruby egg.

Old Russell with a smeared shammy rag burnished again his gem, turned it and held it at the point of his Moses beard. Grandfather ape gloating on a stolen hoard.

And you who wrest old images from the burial earth? The brainsick words of sophists: Antisthenes. A lore of drugs. Orient and immortal wheat standing from everlasting to everlasting.

Two old women fresh from their whiff of the briny trudged through

Irishtown along Londonbridge Road, one with a sanded umbrella, one with a midwife's bag in which eleven cockles rolled.

The whirr of flapping leathern bands and hum of dynamos from the powerhouse urged Stephen to be on. Beingless beings. Stop! Throb always without you and the throb always within. Your heart you sing of. I between them. Where? Between two roaring worlds where they swirl, I. Shatter them, one and both. But stun myself too in the blow. Shatter me you who can. Bawd and butcher were the words. I say! Not yet awhile. A look around.

Yes, quite true. Very large and wonderful and keeps famous time. You say right, sir. A Monday morning. 'Twas so, indeed.

Stephen went down Bedford Row, the handle of the ash clacking against his shoulderblade. In Clohisey's window a faded 1860 print of Heenan boxing Sayers held his eye. Staring backers with square hats stood round the roped prize ring. The heavyweights in tight loincloths proposed gently each to other his bulbous fists. And they are throbbing: heroes' hearts.

He turned and halted by the slanted bookcart.

— Twopence each, the huckster said. Four for sixpence.

Tattered pages. *The Irish Beekeeper. Life and Miracles of the Curé of Ars. Pocket Guide to Killarney.*

I might find here one of my pawned school prizes. *Stephano Dedalo, alumno optimo, palmam ferenti.*

Father Conmee, having read his little hours, walked through the hamlet of Donnycarney, murmuring vespers.

Binding too good probably. What is this? Eighth and ninth book of Moses. Secret of all secrets. Seal of King David. Thumbed pages: read and read. Who has passed here before me? How to soften chapped hands. Recipe for white-wine vinegar. How to win a woman's love. For me this. Say the following talisman three times with hands folded:

— *Se el yilo nebrakada femininum! Amor me solo! Sanktus! Amen.*

Who wrote this? Charms and invocations of the most blessed abbot Pater Salanka to all true believers divulged. As good as any other abbot's charms, as mumbling Joachim's. Down, baldynoddle, or we'll wool your wool.

— What are you doing here, Stephen?

Dilly's high shoulders and shabby dress.

Shut the book quick. Don't let see.

— What are you doing? Stephen said.

231

A Stuart face of nonesuch Charles, lank locks falling at its sides. It glowed as she crouched feeding the fire with broken boots. I told her of Paris. Late lie-abed under a quilt of old overcoats, fingering a pinchbeck bracelet, Dan Kelly's token. *Nebrakada femininum.*

— What have you there? Stephen asked.

— I bought it from the other cart for a penny, Dilly said, laughing nervously. Is it any good?

My eyes they say she has. Do others see me so? Quick, far and daring. Shadow of my mind.

He took the coverless book from her hand. Chardenal's French primer.

— What did you buy that for? he asked. To learn French?

She nodded, reddening and closing tight her lips.

Show no surprise. Quite natural.

— Here, Stephen said. It's all right. Mind Maggy doesn't pawn it on you. I suppose all my books are gone.

— Some, Dilly said. We had to.

She is drowning. Agenbite. Save her. Agenbite. All against us. She will drown me with her, eyes and hair. Lank coils of seaweed hair around me, my heart, my soul. Salt-green death.

We.

Agenbite of inwit. Inwit's agenbite.

Misery! Misery!

« »

— Hello, Simon, Father Cowley said. How are things?

— Hello, Bob, old man, Mr Dedalus answered, stopping.

They clasped hands loudly outside Reddy and Daughter's. Father Cowley brushed his moustache often downward with a scooping hand.

— What's the best news? Mr Dedalus said.

— Why then not much, Father Cowley said. I'm barricaded up, Simon, with two men prowling around the house trying to effect an entrance.

— Jolly, Mr Dedalus said. Who is it?

— O, Father Cowley said. A certain gombeen man of our acquaintance.

— With a broken back, is it? Mr Dedalus asked.

— The same, Simon, Father Cowley answered. Reuben of that ilk. I'm just waiting for Ben Dollard. He's going to say a word to Long John to get him to take those two men off. All I want is a little time.

He looked with vague hope up and down the quay, a big apple bulging in his neck.

— I know, Mr Dedalus said, nodding. Poor old bockedy Ben! He's always doing a good turn for someone. Hold hard!

He put on his glasses and gazed towards the metal bridge an instant.

— Here he is, by God, he said, arse and pockets.

Ben Dollard's loose blue cutaway and square hat above large slops crossed the quay in full gait from the metal bridge. He came towards them at an amble, scratching actively behind his coattails.

As he came near Mr Dedalus greeted:

— Hold that fellow with the bad trousers.

— Hold him now, Ben Dollard said.

Mr Dedalus eyed with cold wandering scorn various points of Ben Dollard's figure. Then, turning to Father Cowley with a nod, he muttered sneeringly:

— That's a pretty garment, isn't it, for a summer's day?

— Why, God eternally curse your soul, Ben Dollard growled furiously, I threw out more clothes in my time than you ever saw.

He stood beside them beaming, on them first and on his roomy clothes from points of which Mr Dedalus flicked fluff, saying:

— They were made for a man in his health, Ben, anyhow.

— Bad luck to the Jewman that made them, Ben Dollard said. Thanks be to God he's not paid yet.

— And how is that *basso profondo*, Benjamin? Father Cowley asked.

Cashel Boyle O'Connor Fitzmaurice Tisdall Farrell, murmuring, glassy-eyed, strode past the Kildare Street Club.

Ben Dollard frowned and, making suddenly a chanter's mouth, gave forth a deep note.

— Aw! he said.

— That's the style, Mr Dedalus said, nodding to its drone.

— What about that? Ben Dollard said. Not too dusty? What?

He turned to both.

— That'll do, Father Cowley said, nodding also.

The Reverend Hugh C. Love walked from the old chapter house of Saint Mary's Abbey past James and Charles Kennedy's, rectifiers, attended by Geraldines tall and personable, towards the Tholsel beyond the Ford of Hurdles.

Ben Dollard with a heavy list towards the shopfronts led them forward, his joyful fingers in the air.

233

— Come along with me to the subsheriff's office, he said. I want to show you the new beauty Rock has for a bailiff. He's a cross between Lobengula and Lynchehaun. He's well worth seeing, mind you. Come along. I saw John Henry Menton casually in the Bodega just now and it will cost me a fall if I don't … Wait awhile … We're on the right lay, Bob, believe you me.

— For a few days tell him, Father Cowley said anxiously.

Ben Dollard halted and stared, his loud orifice open, a dangling button of his coat wagging bright-backed from its thread, as he wiped away the heavy shraums that clogged his eyes to hear aright.

— What few days? he boomed. Hasn't your landlord distrained for rent?

— He has, Father Cowley said.

— Then our friend's writ is not worth the paper it's printed on, Ben Dollard said. The landlord has the prior claim. I gave him all the particulars. 29 Windsor Avenue. Love is the name?

— That's right, Father Cowley said. The Reverend Mr Love. He's a minister in the country somewhere. But are you sure of that?

— You can tell Barabbas from me, Ben Dollard said, that he can put that writ where Jacko put the nuts.

He led Father Cowley boldly forward, linked to his bulk.

— Filberts I believe they were, Mr Dedalus said, as he dropped his glasses on his coatfront, following them.

« »

— The youngster will be all right, Martin Cunningham said, as they passed out of the Castleyard gate.

The policeman touched his forehead.

— God bless you, Martin Cunningham said cheerily.

He signed to the waiting jarvey who chucked at the reins and set on towards Lord Edward Street.

Bronze by gold, Miss Kennedy's head by Miss Douce's head, appeared above the crossblind of the Ormond Hotel.

— Yes, Martin Cunningham said, fingering his beard. I wrote to Father Conmee and laid the whole case before him.

— You could try our friend, Mr Power suggested backward.

— Boyd? Martin Cunningham said shortly. Touch me not.

John Wyse Nolan, lagging behind, reading the list, came after them quickly down Cork Hill.

On the steps of the City Hall Councillor Nannetti, descending, hailed Alderman Cowley and Councillor Abraham Lyon, ascending.

The Castle car wheeled empty into Upper Exchange Street.

— Look here, Martin, John Wyse Nolan said, overtaking them at the *Mail* office. I see Bloom put his name down for five shillings.

— Quite right, Martin Cunningham said, taking the list. And put down the five shillings too.

— Without a second word either, Mr Power said.

— Strange but true, Martin Cunningham added.

John Wyse Nolan opened wide eyes.

— I'll say there is much kindness in the Jew, he quoted elegantly.

They went down Parliament Street.

— There's Jimmy Henry, Mr Power said, just heading for Kavanagh's.

— Righto, Martin Cunningham said. Here goes.

Outside La Maison Claire Blazes Boylan waylaid Jack Mooney's brother-in-law, humpy, tight, making for the Liberties.

John Wyse Nolan fell back with Mr Power, while Martin Cunningham took the elbow of a dapper little man in a shower-of-hail suit who walked uncertainly with hasty steps past Micky Anderson's watches.

— The assistant town clerk's corns are giving him some trouble, John Wyse Nolan told Mr Power.

They followed round the corner towards James Kavanagh's winerooms. The empty Castle car fronted them at rest in Essex Gate. Martin Cunningham, speaking always, showed often the list at which Jimmy Henry did not glance.

— And Long John Fanning is here too, John Wyse Nolan said, as large as life.

The tall form of Long John Fanning filled the doorway where he stood.

— Good day, Mr Subsheriff, Martin Cunningham said, as all halted and greeted.

Long John Fanning made no way for them. He removed his large Henry Clay decisively and his large fierce eyes scowled intelligently over all their faces.

— Are the conscript fathers pursuing their peaceful deliberations? he said with rich acrid utterance to the assistant town clerk.

— Hell open to Christians they were having, Jimmy Henry said pettishly, about their damned Irish language.

Where was the marshal, he wanted to know, to keep order in the council chamber. And old Barlow the macebearer laid up with asthma, no mace on the table, nothing in order, no quorum even, and Hutchinson, the lord mayor, in Llandudno and little Lorcan Sherlock doing *locum tenens* for him. Damned Irish language, language of our forefathers.

Long John Fanning blew a plume of smoke from his lips.

Martin Cunningham spoke by turns, twirling the peak of his beard, to the assistant town clerk and the subsheriff, while John Wyse Nolan held his peace.

— What Dignam was that? Long John Fanning asked.

Jimmy Henry made a grimace and lifted his left foot.

— O, my corns! he said plaintively. Come upstairs for goodness' sake till I sit down somewhere. Uff! Ooo! Mind!

Testily he made room for himself beside Long John Fanning's flank and passed in and up the stairs.

— Come on up, Martin Cunningham said to the subsheriff. I don't think you knew him or perhaps you did, though.

With John Wyse Nolan, Mr Power followed them in.

— Decent little soul he was, Mr Power said to the stalwart back of Long John Fanning ascending towards Long John Fanning in the mirror.

— Rather low-sized. Dignam of Menton's office that was, Martin Cunningham said.

Long John Fanning could not remember him.

Clatter of horsehoofs sounded from the air.

— What's that? Martin Cunningham said.

All turned where they stood. John Wyse Nolan came down again. From the cool shadow of the doorway he saw the horses pass Parliament Street, harness and glossy pasterns in sunlight shimmering. Gaily they went past before his cool unfriendly eyes, not quickly. In saddles of the leaders, leaping leaders, rode outriders.

— What was it? Martin Cunningham asked, as they went on up the staircase.

— The lord lieutenant general and general governor of Ireland, John Wyse Nolan answered from the stairfoot.

« »

As they trod across the thick carpet Buck Mulligan whispered behind his Panama to Haines:

— Parnell's brother. There in the corner.

They chose a small table near the window, opposite a long-faced man whose beard and gaze hung intently down on a chessboard.

– Is that he? Haines asked, twisting round in his seat.

– Yes, Mulligan said. That's John Howard, his brother, our city marshal.

John Howard Parnell translated a white bishop quietly and his grey claw went up again to his forehead whereat it rested. An instant after, under its screen, his eyes looked quickly, ghost bright, at his foe and fell once more upon a working corner.

– I'll take a mélange, Haines said to the waitress.

– Two mélanges, Buck Mulligan said. And bring us some scones and butter and some cakes as well.

When she had gone he said, laughing:

– We call it D.B.C. because they have damn bad cakes. O, but you missed Dedalus on *Hamlet*.

Haines opened his new-bought book.

– I'm sorry, he said. Shakespeare is the happy hunting ground of all minds that have lost their balance.

The one-legged sailor growled at the area of 14 Nelson Street:

– *England expects* . . .

Buck Mulligan's primrose waistcoat shook gaily to his laughter.

– You should see him, he said, when his body loses its balance. Wandering Aengus I call him.

– I am sure he has an *idée fixe*, Haines said, pinching his chin thoughtfully with thumb and forefinger. Now I am speculating what it would be likely to be. Such persons always have.

Buck Mulligan bent across the table gravely.

– They drove his wits astray, he said, by visions of hell. He will never capture the Attic note, the note of Swinburne, of all poets, the white death and the ruddy birth. That is his tragedy. He can never be a poet. The joy of creation . . .

– Eternal punishment, Haines said, nodding curtly. I see. I tackled him this morning on belief. There was something on his mind, I saw. It's rather interesting because Professor Pokorny of Vienna makes an interesting point out of that.

Buck Mulligan's watchful eyes saw the waitress come. He helped her to unload her tray.

– He can find no trace of hell in ancient Irish myth, Haines said amid the cheerful cups. The moral idea seems lacking, the sense of destiny, of retribution. Rather strange he should have just that fixed idea. Does he write anything for your movement?

He sank two lumps of sugar deftly longwise through the whipped cream. Buck Mulligan slit a steaming scone in two and plastered butter over its smoking pith. He bit off a soft piece hungrily.

– Ten years, he said, chewing and laughing. He is going to write something in ten years.

– Seems a long way off, Haines said, thoughtfully lifting his spoon. Still, I shouldn't wonder if he did after all.

He tasted a spoonful from the creamy cone of his cup.

– This is real Irish cream I take it, he said with forbearance. I don't want to be imposed on.

Elijah, skiff, light crumpled throwaway, sailed eastward by flanks of ships and trawlers, amid an archipelago of corks, beyond New Wapping Street, past Benson's ferry and by the three-masted schooner *Rosevean* from Bridgwater with bricks.

« »

Almidano Artifoni walked past Holles Street, past Sewell's yard. Behind him Cashel Boyle O'Connor Fitzmaurice Tisdall Farrell with stickumbrelladustcoat dangling shunned the lamp before Mr Law Smith's house and, crossing, walked along Merrion Square. Distantly behind him a blind stripling tapped his way by the wall of College Park.

Cashel Boyle O'Connor Fitzmaurice Tisdall Farrell walked as far as Mr Louis Werner's cheerful windows, then turned and strode back along Merrion Square, his stickumbrelladustcoat dangling.

At the corner of Wilde's house he halted, frowned at Elijah's name announced on the Metropolitan Hall, frowned at the distant pleasance of Duke's Lawn. His eyeglass flashed frowning in the sun. With rat's teeth bared he muttered:

– *Coactus volui.*

He strode on for Clare Street, grinding his fierce word.

As he strode past Mr Bloom's dental windows the sway of his dustcoat brushed rudely from its angle a slender tapping cane and swept onwards, having buffeted a thewless body. The blind stripling turned his sickly face after the striding form.

— God's curse on you, he said sourly, whoever you are! You're blinder nor I am, you bitch's bastard!

« »

Opposite Ruggy O'Donohoe's Master Patrick Aloysius Dignam, pawing the pound and a half of Mangan's, late Fehrenbach's, pork steaks he had been sent for, went along warm Wicklow Street, dawdling. It was too blooming dull sitting in the parlour with Mrs Stoer and Mrs Quigley and Mrs MacDowell and the blind down and they all at their sniffles and sipping sups of the superior tawny sherry uncle Barney brought from Tunney's. And they eating crumbs of the cottage fruitcake, jawing the whole blooming time and sighing.

After Wicklow Lane the window of Madame Doyle, court dress milliner, stopped him. He stood looking in at the two puckers stripped to their pelts and putting up their props. From the side mirrors two mourning Masters Dignam gaped silently. Myler Keogh, Dublin's pet lamb, will meet Sergeant Major Bennett, the Portobello bruiser, for a purse of fifty sovereigns. Gob, that'd be a good pucking match to see. Myler Keogh, that's the chap sparring out to him with the green sash. Two bar entrance, soldiers half price. I could easy do a bunk on ma. Master Dignam on his left turned as he turned. That's me in mourning. When is it? May the twenty-second. Sure, the blooming thing is all over. He turned to the right and on his right Master Dignam turned, his cap awry, his collar sticking up. Buttoning it down, his chin lifted, he saw the image of Marie Kendall, charming soubrette, beside the two puckers. One of them mots that do be in the packets of fags Stoer smokes that his old fellow welted hell out of him for one time he found out.

Master Dignam got his collar down and dawdled on. The best pucker going for strength was Fitzsimmons. One puck in the wind from that fellow would knock you into the middle of next week, man. But the best pucker for science was Jem Corbett before Fitzsimmons knocked the stuffings out of him, dodging and all.

In Grafton Street Master Dignam saw a red flower in a toff's mouth and a swell pair of kicks on him and he listening to what the drunk was telling him and grinning all the time.

No Sandymount tram.

Master Dignam walking along Nassau Street shifted the pork steaks to his other hand. His collar sprang up again and he tugged it down. The blooming stud was too small for the buttonhole of the shirt, blooming end to it. He met schoolboys with satchels. I'm not going tomorrow either, stay away till Monday. He met other schoolboys. Do they notice I'm in mourning? Uncle Barney said he'd get it into the paper tonight. Then they'll all see it in the paper and read my name printed and pa's name.

His face got all grey instead of being red like it was and there was a fly walking over it up to his eye. The scrunch that was when they were screwing the screws into the coffin: and the bumps when they were bringing it downstairs.

Pa was inside it and ma crying in the parlour and uncle Barney telling the men how to get it round the bend. A big coffin it was, and high and heavy-looking. How was that? The last night pa was boozed he was standing on the landing there bawling out for his boots to go out to Tunney's for to booze more and he looked butty and short in his shirt. Never see him again. Death, that is. Pa is dead. My father is dead. He told me to be a good son to ma. I couldn't hear the other things he said but I saw his tongue and his teeth trying to say it better. Poor pa. That was Mr Dignam, my father. I hope he is in purgatory now because he went to confession to Father Conroy on Saturday night.

« »

William Humble, earl of Dudley, and Lady Dudley, accompanied by Lieutenant Colonel Heseltine, drove out after luncheon from the Viceregal Lodge. In the following carriage were the Honourable Mrs Paget, Miss de Courcy and the Honourable Gerald Ward A.D.C. in attendance.

The cavalcade passed out by the lower gate of Phoenix Park saluted by obsequious policemen and proceeded past Kingsbridge along the northern quays. The viceroy was most cordially greeted on his way through the metropolis. At Bloody Bridge Mr Thomas Kernan beyond the river greeted him vainly from afar. Between Queen's and Whitworth Bridges Lord Dudley's viceregal carriages passed and were unsaluted by Mr Dudley White B.L., M.A., who stood on Arran Quay outside Mrs M.E. White's, the pawnbroker's, at the corner of Arran Street West stroking his nose with his forefinger, undecided whether he should arrive at Phibsborough more quickly by a triple change of tram or by hailing a car or on foot through Smithfield, Constitution Hill and Broadstone terminus. In the porch of the Four Courts Richie Goulding with the costbag of

Goulding, Collis and Ward saw him with surprise. Past Richmond Bridge at the doorstep of the office of Reuben J. Dodd, solicitor, agent for the Patriotic Insurance Company, an elderly female about to enter changed her plan and, retracing her steps by King's windows, smiled credulously on the representative of His Majesty. From its sluice in Wood Quay wall under Tom Devin's office Poddle River hung out in fealty a tongue of liquid sewage. Above the crossblind of the Ormond Hotel, gold by bronze, Miss Kennedy's head by Miss Douce's head watched and admired. On Ormond Quay Mr Simon Dedalus, steering his way from the greenhouse for the subsheriff's office, stood still in midstreet and brought his hat low. His Excellency graciously returned Mr Dedalus' greeting. From Cahill's corner the Reverend Hugh C. Love M.A. made obeisance unperceived, mindful of lords deputy whose hands benignant had held of yore rich advowsons. On Grattan Bridge Lenehan and M'Coy, taking leave of each other, watched the carriages go by. Passing by Roger Greene's office and Dollard's big red printing house Gerty MacDowell, carrying the Catesby's cork lino letters for her father who was laid up, knew by the style it was the lord and lady lieutenant but she couldn't see what Her Excellency had on because the tram and Spring's big yellow furniture van had to stop in front of her on account of its being the lord lieutenant. Beyond Lundy Foot's from the shaded door of Kavanagh's winerooms John Wyse Nolan smiled with unseen coldness towards the lord lieutenant general and general governor of Ireland. The Right Honourable William Humble, earl of Dudley, G.C.V.O., passed Micky Anderson's all times ticking watches and Henry and James's wax smart-suited, fresh-cheeked models, the gentleman Henry, *le dernier cri* James. Over against Dame Gate Tom Rochford and Nosey Flynn watched the approach of the cavalcade. Tom Rochford, seeing the eyes of Lady Dudley fixed on him, took his thumbs quickly out of the pockets of his claret waistcoat and doffed his cap to her. A charming soubrette, great Marie Kendall, with dauby cheeks and lifted skirt smiled daubily from her poster upon William Humble, earl of Dudley, and upon Lieutenant Colonel C. Heseltine and also upon the Honourable Gerald Ward A.D.C. From the window of the D.B.C. Buck Mulligan gaily, and Haines gravely, gazed down on the viceregal equipage over the shoulders of eager guests, whose mass of forms darkened the chessboard whereon John Howard Parnell looked intently. In Fownes's Street Dilly Dedalus, straining her sight upward from Chardenal's first French primer, saw sunshades spanned and wheelspokes spinning in the glare. John Henry Menton, filling the doorway of Commercial Buildings, stared from wine-big oyster eyes, holding a fat gold hunter watch not looked at in his fat left hand not feeling it. Where the foreleg of King Billy's horse pawed the air Mrs Breen plucked her hastening husband back from under the hoofs of the outriders. She shouted in his ear the tidings. Understanding, he shifted his tomes to his left breast and saluted the second carriage. The Honourable Gerald Ward A.D.C., agreeably surprised, made haste to reply. At Ponsonby's corner a jaded white flagon H. halted and four tall-hatted white flagons halted behind him, E.L.Y.'S, while outriders pranced past and carriages. Opposite Pigott's music warerooms Mr Denis J. Maginni, professor of dancing &c., gaily apparelled, gravely walked, outpassed by a viceroy and unobserved. By the provost's wall came jauntily Blazes Boylan, stepping in tan shoes and socks with sky-blue clocks to the refrain of *My girl's a Yorkshire girl.* Blazes Boylan presented to the leaders' sky-blue frontlets and high action a sky-blue tie, a wide-brimmed straw hat at a rakish angle and a suit of indigo serge. His hands in his jacket pockets forgot to salute but he offered to the three ladies the bold admiration of his eyes and the red flower between his lips. As they drove along Nassau Street His Excellency drew the attention of his bowing consort to the programme of music which was being discoursed in College Park. Unseen brazen Highland laddies blared and drumthumped after the cortège:

> But though she's a factory lass
> And wears no fancy clothes.
> Baraabum.
> Yet I've a sort of a
> Yorkshire relish for
> My little Yorkshire rose.
> Baraabum.

Thither of the wall the quarter-mile flat handicappers, M.C. Greene, H. Thrift, T.M. Patey, C. Scaife, J.B. Jones, G.N. Morphy, F. Stevenson, C. Adderley and W.C. Huggard, started in pursuit. Striding past Finn's Hotel Cashel Boyle O'Connor Fitzmaurice Tisdall Farrell stared through a fierce eyeglass across the carriages at the head of Mr M.E. Solomons in the window of the Austro-Hungarian Vice-consulate. Deep in Leinster Street, by Trinity's postern a loyal king's man, Hornblower, touched his tallyho cap. As the glossy horses pranced by Merrion Square Master Patrick Aloysius Dignam, waiting, saw salutes being given to the gent with the topper and raised also his new black cap with fingers greased by pork-steak paper. His collar too sprang up. The viceroy, on his way to inaugurate the Mirus Bazaar in aid of funds for Mercer's Hospital, drove with his following towards Lower Mount Street. He passed a blind stripling opposite Broadbent's. In Lower Mount Street a pedestrian in a brown macintosh, eating dry bread, passed swiftly and unscathed across the viceroy's path. At the Grand Canal Bridge, from his hoarding Mr Eugene Stratton, his blub lips agrin, bade all comers welcome to Pembroke township. At Haddington Road corner two sanded women halted themselves, an umbrella and a bag in which eleven cockles rolled to view with wonder the lord mayor and lady mayoress without his golden chain. On Northumberland and Lansdowne Roads His Excellency acknowledged punctually salutes from rare male walkers, the salute of two small schoolboys at the garden gate of the house said to have been admired by the late queen when visiting the Irish capital with her husband, the prince consort, in 1849, and the salute of Almidano Artifoni's sturdy trousers swallowed by a closing door.

Bronze by gold heard the hoofirons, steelyringing.

   Imperthnthn thnthnthn.

   Chips, picking chips off rocky thumbnail, chips.

   Horrid! And gold flushed more.

   A husky fifenote blew.

   Blew. Blue bloom is on the.

   Gold pinnacled hair.

   A jumping rose on satiny breasts of satin, rose of Castile.

   Trilling, trilling: Idolores.

   Peep! Who's in the ... peepofgold?

   Tink cried to bronze in pity.

   And a call, pure, long and throbbing. Long in dying call.

   Decoy. Soft word. But look! The bright stars fade. Notes chirruping answer.

   O rose! Castile. The morn is breaking.

   Jingle jingle jaunted jingling.

   Coin rang. Clock clacked.

   Avowal. *Sonnez*. I could. Rebound of garter. Not leave thee. Smack. *La cloche!* Thigh smack. Avowal. Warm. Sweetheart, goodbye!

   Jingle. Bloo.

   Boomed crashing chords. When love absorbs. War! War! The tympanum.

   A sail! A veil awave upon the waves.

   Lost. Throstle fluted. All is lost now.

   Horn. Hawhorn.

   When first he saw. Alas!

   Full tup. Full throb.

   Warbling. Ah, lure! Alluring.

   Martha! Come!

   Clapclop. Clipclap. Clappyclap.

   Goodgod henev erheard inall.

   Deaf bald Pat brought pad knife took up.

   A moonlight nightcall: far, far.

244

I feel so sad. P.S. So lonely blooming.

Listen!

The spiked and winding cold seahorn.

Have you the? Each, and for other, plash and silent roar.

Pearls: when she. Liszt's rhapsodies. Hissss.

You don't?

Did not: no, no: believe: Lidlyd. With a cock with a carra.

Black. Deepsounding. Do, Ben, do.

Wait while you wait. Hee hee. Wait while you hee.

But wait!

Low in dark middle earth. Embedded ore.

Naminedamine.

All gone. All fallen.

Tiny, her tremulous fernfoils of maidenhair.

Amen! He gnashed in fury.

Fro. To, fro. A baton cool protruding.

Bronzelydia by Minagold.

By bronze, by gold, in ocean-green of shadow. Bloom. Old Bloom.

One rapped, one tapped, with a carra, with a cock.

Pray for him! Pray, good people!

His gouty fingers nakkering.

Big Benaben. Big Benben.

Last rose Castile of summer left bloom I feel so sad alone.

Pwee! Little wind piped wee.

True men. Lid Ker Cow De and Doll. Ay, ay. Like you men. Will lift your tschink with tschunk.

Fff! Oo!

Where bronze from anear? Where gold from afar? Where hoofs?

Rrrpr. Kraa. Kraandl.

Then, not till then. My eppripfftaph. Be pfrwritt.

Done.

Begin!

Bronze by gold, Miss Douce's head by Miss Kennedy's head, over the crossblind of the Ormond bar heard the viceregal hoofs go by, ringing steel.

— Is that her? asked Miss Kennedy.

Miss Douce said yes, sitting with His Ex, pearl grey and *eau de Nil*.

— Exquisite contrast, Miss Kennedy said.

When all agog Miss Douce said eagerly:

— Look at the fellow in the tall silk.

— Who? Where? gold asked more eagerly.

— In the second carriage, Miss Douce's wet lips said, laughing in the sun. He's looking. Mind till I see.

She darted, bronze, to the backmost corner, flattening her face against the pane in a halo of hurried breath.

Her wet lips tittered:

— He's killed looking back.

She laughed:

— O wept! Aren't men frightful idiots?

With sadness.

Miss Kennedy sauntered sadly from bright light, twining a loose hair behind an ear. Sauntering sadly, gold no more, she twisted twined a hair. Sadly she twined in sauntering gold hair behind a curving ear.

— It's them has the fine times, sadly then she said.

A man.

Bloowho went by by Moulang's pipes bearing in his breast the sweets of sin, by Wine's antiques in memory bearing sweet sinful words, by Carroll's dusky battered plate, for Raoul.

The boots to them, them in the bar, them barmaids came. For them unheeding him he banged on the counter his tray of chattering china. And

— There's your teas, he said.

Miss Kennedy with manners transposed the tea tray down to an upturned lithia crate, safe from eyes, low.

— What is it? loud boots unmannerly asked.

— Find out, Miss Douce retorted, leaving her spying point.

— Your beau, is it?

A haughty bronze replied:

— I'll complain to Mrs de Massey on you if I hear any more of your impertinent insolence.

— Imperthnthn thnthnthn, boots' snout sniffed rudely, as he retreated as she threatened as he had come.

Bloom.

On her flower frowning Miss Douce said:

— Most aggravating that young brat is. If he doesn't conduct himself I'll wring his ear for him a yard long.

Ladylike in exquisite contrast

— Take no notice, Miss Kennedy rejoined.

She poured in a teacup tea, then back in the teapot tea. They cowered under their reef of counter, waiting on footstools, crates upturned, waiting for their teas to draw. They pawed their blouses, both of black satin, two and nine a yard, waiting for their teas to draw, and two and seven.

Yes, bronze from anear, by gold from afar, heard steel from anear, hoofs ring from afar, and heard steelhoofs ringhoof ringsteel.

— Am I awfully sunburnt?

Miss bronze unbloused her neck.

— No, said Miss Kennedy. It gets brown after. Did you try the borax with the cherry-laurel water?

Miss Douce half stood to see her skin askance in the bar mirror gilded-lettered where hock and claret glasses shimmered and in their midst a shell.

— And leave it to my hands, she said.

— Try it with the glycerine, Miss Kennedy advised.

Bidding her neck and hands adieu

— Those things only bring out a rash, Miss Douce replied, reseated. I asked that old fogey in Boyd's for something for my skin.

Miss Kennedy, pouring now a full-drawn tea, grimaced and prayed:

— O, don't remind me of him for mercy' sake!

— But wait till I tell you, Miss Douce entreated.

Sweet tea Miss Kennedy having poured with milk plugged both two ears with little fingers.

— No, don't, she cried.

— I won't listen, she cried.

But Bloom?

Miss Douce grunted in snuffy fogey's tone:

— *For your what?* says he.

Miss Kennedy unplugged her ears to hear, to speak: but said, but prayed again:

— Don't let me think of him or I'll expire. The hideous old wretch! That night in the Antient Concert Rooms.

She sipped distastefully her brew, hot tea, a sip, sipped sweet tea.

— Here he was, Miss Douce said, cocking her bronze head three quarters, ruffling her nosewings. *Hufa! Hufa!*

Shrill shriek of laughter sprang from Miss Kennedy's throat. Miss Douce huffed and snorted down her nostrils that quivered imperthnthn like a snout in quest.

— O! shrieking, Miss Kennedy cried. Will you ever forget his goggle eye?

Miss Douce chimed in in deep bronze laughter, shouting:

— And your other eye!

Bloowhose dark eye read Aaron Figatner's name. Why do I always think Figather? Gathering figs, I think. And Prosper Loré's Huguenot name. By Bassi's blessed virgins Bloom's dark eyes went by. Blue-robed, white under, come to me. God they believe she is: or goddess. Those today. I could not see. That fellow spoke. A student. After with Dedalus' son. He might be Mulligan. All comely virgins. That brings those rakes of fellows in: her white.

By went his eyes. The sweets of sin. Sweet are the sweets.

Of sin.

In a giggling peal young goldbronze voices blended, Douce with Kennedy your other eye. They threw young heads back, bronze gigglegold, to let freefly their laughter, screaming, your other, signals to each other, high piercing notes.

Ah, panting, sighing, sighing, ah, fordone, their mirth died down.

Miss Kennedy lipped her cup again, raised, drank a sip and gigglegiggled. Miss Douce, bending again over the tea tray, ruffled again her nose and rolled droll fattened eyes. Again Kennygiggles, stooping, her fair pinnacles of hair, stooping, her tortoise napecomb showed, spluttered out of her mouth her tea, choking in tea and laughter, coughing with choking, crying:

— O greasy eyes! Imagine being married to a man like that, she cried. With his bit of beard!

Douce gave full vent to a splendid yell, a full yell of full woman, delight, joy, indignation.

— Married to the greasy nose! she yelled.

Shrill, with deep laughter, bronze after gold, they urged each each to peal after peal, ringing in changes, bronzegold, goldbronze, shrilldeep, to laughter after laughter. And then laughed more. Greasy I knows. Exhausted, breathless, their shaken heads they laid, braided and pinnacled by glossy-combed, against the counter ledge. All flushed (O!), panting, sweating (O!), all breathless.

Married to Bloom, to greaseabloom.

— O saints above! Miss Douce said, sighed above her jumping rose. I wished I hadn't laughed so much. I feel all wet.

— O, Miss Douce! Miss Kennedy protested. You horrid thing!

And flushed yet more (you horrid!), more goldenly.

By Cantwell's offices roved Greaseabloom, by Ceppi's virgins, bright of their oils. Nannetti's father hawked those things about, wheedling at doors as I. Religion pays. Must see him about Keyes's par. Eat first. I want. Not yet. At four, she said. Time ever passing. Clock hands turning. On. Where eat? The Clarence, Dolphin. On. For Raoul. Eat. If I net five guineas with those ads. The violet silk petticoats. Not yet. The sweets of sin.

Flushed less, still less, goldenly paled.

Into their bar strolled Mr Dedalus. Chips, picking chips off one of his rocky thumbnails. Chips. He strolled.

— O, welcome back, Miss Douce.

He held her hand. Enjoyed her holidays?

— Tiptop.

He hoped she had nice weather in Rostrevor.

— Gorgeous, she said. Look at the holy show I am. Lying out on the strand all day.

Bronze whiteness.

— That was exceedingly naughty of you, Mr Dedalus told her and pressed her hand indulgently. Tempting poor simple males.

Miss Douce of satin douced her arm away.

— O, go away! she said. You're very simple, I don't think.

He was.

— Well now, I am, he mused. I looked so simple in the cradle they christened me simple Simon.

— You must have been a doaty, Miss Douce made answer. And what did the doctor order today?

— Well now, he mused, whatever you say yourself. I think I'll trouble you for some fresh water and a half glass of whiskey.

Jingle.

— With the greatest alacrity, Miss Douce agreed.

With grace of alacrity towards the mirror gilt Cantrell and Cochrane's she turned herself. With grace she tapped a measure of gold whiskey from her crystal keg. Forth from the skirt of his coat Mr Dedalus brought pouch and pipe. Alacrity she served. He blew through the flue two husky fifenotes.

— By Jove, he mused, I often wanted to see the Mourne Mountains. Must be a great tonic in the air down there. But a long threatening comes at last, they say. Yes, yes.

Yes. He fingered shreds of hair, her maidenhair, her mermaid's, into the bowl. Chips. Shreds. Musing. Mute.

None not said nothing. Yes.

Gaily Miss Douce polished a tumbler, trilling:

— *O, Idolores, queen of the eastern seas!*

— Was Mr Lidwell in today?

In came Lenehan. Round him peered Lenehan. Mr Bloom reached Essex Bridge. Yes, Mr Bloom crossed bridge of Yessex. To Martha I must write. Buy paper. Daly's. Girl there civil. Bloom. Old Bloom. Blue bloom is on the rye.

— He was in at lunchtime, Miss Douce said.

Lenehan came forward.

— Was Mr Boylan looking for me?

He asked. She answered:

— Miss Kennedy, was Mr Boylan in while I was upstairs?

She asked. Miss voice of Kennedy answered, a second teacup poised, her gaze upon a page:

— No. He was not.

Miss gaze of Kennedy, heard, not seen, read on. Lenehan round the sandwich bell wound his round body round.

— Peep! Who's in the corner?

No glance of Kennedy rewarding him he yet made overtures. To mind her stops. To read only the black ones: round o and crooked ess.

Jingle jaunty jingle.

Girlgold she read and did not glance. Take no notice. She took no notice while he read by rote a solfa fable for her, plappering flatly:

— Ah fox met ah stork. Said thee fox too thee stork: Will you put your bill down inn my troath and pull upp ah bone?

He droned in vain. Miss Douce turned to her tea aside.

He sighed aside:

– Ah me! O my!

He greeted Mr Dedalus and got a nod.

– Greetings from the famous son of a famous father.

– Who may he be? Mr Dedalus asked.

Lenehan opened most genial arms. Who?

– *Who may he be?* he asked. Can you ask? Stephen, the youthful bard. Dry.

Mr Dedalus, famous father, laid by his dry filled pipe.

– I see, he said. I didn't recognise him for the moment. I hear he is keeping very select company. Have you seen him lately?

He had.

– I quaffed the nectar bowl with him this very day, said Lenehan. In Mooney's *en ville* and in Mooney's *sur mer*. He had received the rhino for the labour of his muse.

He smiled at bronze's tea-bathed lips, at listening lips and eyes.

– The élite of Erin hung upon his lips. The ponderous pundit Hugh MacHugh, Dublin's most brilliant scribe and editor and that minstrel boy of the wild wet west who is known by the euphonious appellation of the O'Madden Burke.

After an interval Mr Dedalus raised his grog and

– That must have been highly diverting, said he. I see.

He see. He drank. With faraway mourning mountain eye. Set down his glass.

He looked towards the saloon door.

– I see you have moved the piano.

– The tuner was in today, Miss Douce replied, tuning it for the smoking concert and I never heard such an exquisite player.

– Is that a fact?

– Didn't he, Miss Kennedy? The real classical, you know. And blind too, poor fellow. Not twenty I'm sure he was.

– Is that a fact? Mr Dedalus said.

He drank and strayed away.

– So sad to look at his face, Miss Douce condoled.

God's curse on bitch's bastard.

Tink to her pity cried a diner's bell. To the door of the dining room came bald Pat, came bothered Pat, came Pat, waiter of Ormond. Lager for diner. Lager without alacrity she served.

With patience Lenehan waited for Boylan with impatience, for jingle jaunty blazes boy.

Upholding the lid he (who?) gazed in the coffin (coffin?) at the oblique triple (piano!) wires. He pressed (the same who pressed indulgently her hand), soft-pedalling, a triple of keys to see the thicknesses of felt advancing, to hear the muffled hammerfall in action.

Two sheets cream vellum paper one reserve two envelopes when I was in Wisdom Hely's wise Bloom in Daly's Henry Flower bought. Are you not happy in your home? Flower to console me and a pin cuts lo. Means something, language of flow. Was it a daisy? Innocence that is. Respectable girl meet after mass. Thanks awfully muchly. Wise Bloom eyed on the door a poster, a swaying mermaid smoking 'mid the waves. Smoke mermaids, coolest whiff of all. Hair streaming: lovelorn. For some man. For Raoul. He eyed and saw afar on Essex Bridge a gay hat riding on a jaunting car. It is. Third time. Coincidence.

Jingling on supple rubbers it jaunted from the bridge to Ormond Quay. Follow. Risk it. Go quick. At four. Near now. Out.

– Twopence, sir, the shopgirl dared to say.

– Aha . . . I was forgetting . . . Excuse . . .

– And four.

At four she. Winsomely she on Bloohimwhom smiled. Bloo smi qui go. Ternoon. Think you're the only pebble on the beach? Does that to all. For men.

In drowsy silence gold bent on her page.

From the saloon a call came, long in dying. That was a tuning fork the tuner had that he forgot that he now struck. A call again. That he now poised that it now throbbed. You hear? It throbbed, pure, purer, softly and softlier, its buzzing prongs. Longer in dying call.

Pat paid for diner's pop-corked bottle: and over tumbler, tray and pop-corked bottle ere he went he whispered, bald and bothered, with Miss Douce.

– *The bright stars fade,*

A voiceless song sang from within, singing:

– *The morn is breaking,*

A duodene of birdnotes chirruped bright treble answer under sensitive hands. Brightly the keys, all twinkling, linked, all harpsichording, called to a voice to sing the strain of dewy morn, of youth, of love's leavetaking, life's, love's, morn.

– *The dewdrops pearl* . . .

Lenehan's lips over the counter lisped a low whistle of decoy.

– But look this way, he said, rose of Castile.

Jingle jaunted by the curb and stopped.

She rose and closed her reading, rose of Castile: fretted, forlorn, dreamily rose.

— Did she fall or was she pushed? he asked her.

She answered, slighting:

— Ask no questions and you'll hear no lies.

Like lady, ladylike.

Blazes Boylan's smart tan shoes creaked on the bar floor where he strode. Yes, gold from anear by bronze from afar. Lenehan heard and knew and hailed him:

— See, the conquering hero comes.

Between the car and window, warily walking, went Bloom, unconquered hero. See me he might. The seat he sat on: warm. Black wary hecat walked towards Richie Goulding's legal bag, lifted aloft, saluting.

— *And I from thee . . .*

— I heard you were round, said Blazes Boylan.

He touched to fair Miss Kennedy a rim of his slanted straw. She smiled on him. But sister bronze outsmiled her, preening for him her richer hair, a bosom and a rose.

Boylan bespoke potions.

— What's your cry? Glass of bitter? Glass of bitter, please, and a sloe gin for me. Wire in yet?

Not yet. At four he. All said four.

Cowley's red lugs and bulging apple in the door of the sheriff's office. Avoid. Goulding a chance. What is he doing in the Ormond? Car waiting. Wait.

Hello. Where off to? Something to eat? I too was just. In here. What, Ormond? Best value in Dublin. Is that so? Dining room. Sit tight there. See, not be seen. I think I'll join you. Come on.

Richie led on. Bloom followed bag. Dinner fit for a prince.

Miss Douce reached high to take a flagon, stretching her satin arm, her bust, that all but burst, so high.

— O! O! jerked Lenehan, gasping at each stretch. O!

But easily she seized her prey and led it low in triumph.

— Why don't you grow? asked Blazes Boylan.

Shebronze, dealing from her jar thick syrupy liquor for his lips, looked as it flowed (flower in his coat: who gave him?) and syrupped with her voice:

— Fine goods in small parcels.

That is to say she. Neatly she poured slow syrupy sloe.

— Here's fortune, Blazes said.

He pitched a broad coin down. Coin rang.

— Hold on, said Lenehan, till I . . .

— Fortune, he wished, lifting his bubbled ale.

— *Sceptre* will win in a canter, he said.

— I plunged a bit, said Boylan, winking and drinking. Not on my own, you know. Fancy of a friend of mine.

Lenehan still drank and grinned at his tilted ale and at Miss Douce's lips that all but hummed, not shut, the ocean song her lips had trilled. Idolores. The eastern seas.

Clock whirred. Miss Kennedy passed their way (flower, wonder who gave), bearing away tea tray. Clock clacked.

Miss Douce took Boylan's coin, struck boldly the cash register. It clanged. Clock clacked. Fair one of Egypt, she teased and sorted in the till and hummed and handed coins in change. Look to the west. A clack. For me.

— What time is that? asked Blazes Boylan. Four?

O'clock.

Lenehan, small eyes ahunger on her humming, bust ahumming, tugged Blazes Boylan's elbowsleeve.

— Let's hear the time, he said.

The bag of Goulding, Collis, Ward led Bloom by ryebloom-flowered tables. Aimless he chose with agitated aim, bald Pat attending, a table near the door. Be near. At four. Has he forgotten? Perhaps a trick. Not come: whet appetite. I couldn't do. Wait, wait. Pat, waiter, waited.

Sparkling bronze azureeyed Blazure's sky-blue bow and eyes.

— Go on, pressed Lenehan. There's no one. He never heard.

— . . . *to Flora's lips did hie.*

High, a high note pealed in the treble, clear.

Bronzedouce, communing with her rose that sank and rose, sought Blazes Boylan's flower and eyes.

— Please, please.

He pleaded over returning phrases of avowal.

— *I could not leave thee* . . .

— Afterwits, Miss Douce promised coyly.

— No, now, urged Lenehan. *Sonnez la cloche!* O do! There's no one.

She looked. Quick. Miss Kenn out of earshot. Sudden bent. Two kindling faces watched her bend.

Quavering, the chords strayed from the air, found it again, lost chord, and lost and found it, faltering.

— Go on! Do! *Sonnez!*

Bending, she nipped a peak of skirt above her knee. Delayed. Taunted them still, bending, suspending, with wilful eyes.

— *Sonnez!*

Smack. She set free sudden in rebound her nipped elastic garter smackwarm against her smackable, a woman's, warm-hosed thigh.

— *La cloche!* cried gleeful Lenehan. Trained by owner. No sawdust there.

She smilesmirked supercilious (wept! aren't men?), but, lightward gliding, mild she smiled on Boylan.

— You're the essence of vulgarity, she in gliding said.

Boylan, eyed, eyed. Tossed to fat lips his chalice, drank off his tiny chalice, sucking the last fat violet syrupy drops. His spellbound eyes went after her gliding head as it went down the bar by mirrors, gilded arch for ginger ale, hock and claret glasses shimmering, a spiky shell, where it concerted, mirrored, bronze with sunnier bronze.

Yes, bronze from anearby.

— ... *sweetheart, goodbye!*

— I'm off, said Boylan with impatience.

He slid his chalice brisk away, grasped his change.

— Wait a shake, begged Lenehan, drinking quickly. I wanted to tell you. Tom Rochford ...

— Come on to blazes, said Blazes Boylan, going.

Lenehan gulped to go.

— Got the horn or what? he said. Wait. I'm coming.

He followed the hasty creaking shoes but stood by nimbly by the threshold, saluting forms, a bulky with a slender.

— How do you do, Mr Dollard?

— Eh? How do? How do? Ben Dollard's vague bass answered, turning an instant from Father Cowley's woe. He won't give you any trouble, Bob. Alf Bergan will speak to the long fellow. We'll put a barley straw in that Judas Iscariot's ear this time.

Sighing, Mr Dedalus came through the saloon, a finger soothing an eyelid.

— Hoho, we will, Ben Dollard yodled jollily. Come on, Simon, give us a ditty. We heard the piano.

Bald Pat, bothered waiter, waited for drink orders. Power for Richie.

And Bloom? Let me see. Not make him walk twice. His corns. Four now. How warm this black is. Course nerves a bit. Refracts (is it?) heat. Let me see. Cider. Yes, bottle of cider.

— What's that? Mr Dedalus said. I was only vamping, man.

— Come on, come on, Ben Dollard called. Begone, dull care. Come, Bob.

He ambled Dollard, bulky slops, before them (hold that fellow with the: hold him now) into the saloon. He plumped him Dollard on the stool. His gouty paws plumped chords. Plumped, stopped abrupt.

Bald Pat in the doorway met tealess gold returning. Bothered, he wanted Power and cider. Bronze by the window watched, bronze from afar.

Jingle a tinkle jaunted.

Bloom heard a jing, a little sound. He's off. Light sob of breath Bloom sighed on the silent blue-hued flowers. Jingling. He's gone. Jingle. Hear.

— *Love and War*, Ben, Mr Dedalus said. God be with old times.

Miss Douce's brave eyes, unregarded, turned from the crossblind, smitten by sunlight. Gone. Pensive (who knows?), smitten (the smiting light), she lowered the dropblind with a sliding cord. She drew down pensive (why did he go so quick when I?) about her bronze, over the bar where bald stood by sister gold, inexquisite contrast, contrast inexquisite nonexquisite, slow cool dim sea-green sliding depth of shadow, *eau de Nil.*

— Poor old Goodwin was the pianist that night, Father Cowley reminded them. There was a slight difference of opinion between himself and the Collard grand.

There was.

— A symposium all his own, Mr Dedalus said. The devil wouldn't stop him. He was a crotchety old fellow in the primary stage of drink.

— God, do you remember? Ben bulky Dollard said, turning from the punished keyboard. And, by Japers, I had no wedding garment.

They laughed all three. He had no wed. All trio laughed. No wedding garment.

— Our friend Bloom turned in handy that night, Mr Dedalus said. Where's my pipe, by the way?

He wandered back to the bar to the lost chord pipe. Bald Pat carried two diners' drinks, Richie and Poldy. And Father Cowley laughed again.

— I saved the situation, Ben, I think.

— You did, averred Ben Dollard. I remember those tight trousers too. That was a brilliant idea, Bob.

Father Cowley blushed to his brilliant purply lobes. He saved the situa. Tight trou. Brilliant ide.

— I knew he was on the rocks, he said. The wife was playing the piano in the Coffee Palace on Saturdays for a very trifling consideration and who was it gave me the wheeze she was doing the other business? Do you remember? We had to search all Holles Street to find them till the chap in Keogh's gave us the number. Remember?

Ben remembered, his broad visage wondering.

— By God, she had some luxurious opera cloaks and things there.

Mr Dedalus wandered back, pipe in hand.

— Merrion Square style. Balldresses, by God, and court dresses. He wouldn't take any money either. What? Any God's quantity of cocked hats and boleros and trunk hose. What?

— Ay, ay, Mr Dedalus nodded. Mrs Marion Bloom has left off clothes of all descriptions.

Jingle jaunted down the quays. Blazes sprawled on bounding tyres.

Liver and bacon. Steak and kidney pie. Right, sir. Right, Pat.

Mrs Marion. Met him pike hoses. Smell of burn. Of Paul de Kock. Nice name he.

— What's this her name was? A buxom lassy. Marion . . .

— Tweedy.

— Yes. Is she alive?

— And kicking.

— She was a daughter of . . .

— Daughter of the regiment.

— Yes, begad. I remember the old drum major.

Mr Dedalus struck, whizzed, lit, puffed savoury puff after

— Irish? I don't know, faith. Is she, Simon?

puff after puff, a puff, strong, savoury, crackling.

— Buccinator muscle is . . . What? . . . bit rusty . . . O, she is . . . My Irish Molly, O.

He puffed a pungent plumy blast.

— From the Rock of Gibraltar . . . all the way.

They pined in depth of ocean shadow, gold by the beerpull, bronze by maraschino, thoughtful all two, Mina Kennedy, 4 Lismore Terrace, Drumcondra, with Idolores, a queen, Dolores, silent.

Pat served, uncovered dishes. Leopold cut liver slices. As said before he ate with relish the inner organs, nutty gizzards, fried cod's roe, while

Richie Goulding, Collis, Ward ate steak and kidney, steak then kidney, bite by bite of pie he ate Bloom ate they ate.

Bloom with Goulding, married in silence, ate. Dinners fit for princes.

By Bachelor's Walk jogjaunty jingled Blazes Boylan, bachelor, in sun, in heat, mare's glossy rump atrot, with flick of whip, on bounding tyres: sprawled, warmseated, Boylan impatience, ardentbold. Horn. Have you the? Horn. Have you the? Haw haw horn.

Over their voices Dollard bassooned attack, booming over bombarding chords:

— *When love absorbs my ardent soul* ...

Roll of Bensoulbenjamin rolled to the quivery loveshivery roofpanes.

— War! War! cried Father Cowley. You're the warrior.

— So I am, Ben Warrior laughed. I was thinking of your landlord. Love or money.

He stopped. He wagged huge beard, huge face, over his blunder huge.

— Sure, you'd burst the tympanum of her ear, man, Mr Dedalus said through smoke aroma, with an organ like yours.

In bearded abundant laughter Dollard shook upon the keyboard. He would.

— Not to mention another membrane, Father Cowley added. Halftime, Ben. *Amoroso ma non troppo.* Let me there.

Miss Kennedy served two gentlemen with tankards of cool stout. She passed a remark. It was indeed, first gentleman said, beautiful weather. They drank cool stout. Did she know where the lord lieutenant was going? And heard steelhoofs ringhoof ring. No, she couldn't say. But it would be in the paper. O, she needn't trouble. No trouble. She waved about her outspread *Independent*, searching, the lord lieutenant, her pinnacles of hair slowmoving, lord lieuten. Too much trouble, first gentleman said. O, not in the least. Way he looked that. Lord lieutenant. Gold by bronze heard iron steel.

— ... *my ardent soul,*
    I care not foror the morrow.

In liver gravy Bloom mashed mashed potatoes. *Love and War* someone is. Ben Dollard's famous. Night he ran round to us to borrow a dress suit for that concert. Trousers tight as a drum on him. Musical porkers. Molly did laugh when he went out. Threw herself back across the bed, screaming, kicking. With all his belongings on show. O saints above, I'm drenched! O, the women in the front row! O, I never laughed so many! Well, of course, that's what gives him the base barreltone. For instance eunuchs. Wonder who's playing. Nice touch. Must be Cowley. Musical. Knows whatever note you play. Bad breath he has, poor chap. Stopped.

Miss Douce, engaging, Lydia Douce, bowed to suave solicitor, George Lidwell, gentleman, entering. Good afternoon. She gave her moist, a lady's, hand to his firm clasp. Afternoon. Yes, she was back. To the old dingdong again.

— Your friends are inside, Mr Lidwell.

George Lidwell, suave, solicited, held a lydiahand.

Jingle.

Bloom ate liv as said before. Clean here at least. That chap in the Burton, gummy with gristle. No one here: Goulding and I. Clean tables, flowers, mitres of napkins. Pat to and fro, bald Pat. Nothing to do. Best value in Dub.

Piano again. Cowley it is. Way he sits in to it, like one together, mutual understanding. Tiresome shapers scraping fiddles, eye on the bow end, sawing the cello, remind you of toothache. Her high long snore. Night we were in the box. Trombone under blowing like a grampus, between the acts, other brass chap unscrewing, emptying spittle. Conductor's legs too, bagstrousers, jiggedy jiggedy. Do right to hide them.

Jiggedy jingle jaunty jaunty.

Only the harp. Lovely. Gold glowering light. Girl touched it. Poop of a lovely. Gravy's rather good, fit for a. Golden ship. Erin. The harp that once or twice. Cool hands. Ben Howth, the rhododendrons. We are their harps. I. He. Old. Young.

— Ah, I couldn't, man, Mr Dedalus said, shy, listless.

Strongly.

— Go on, blast you! Ben Dollard growled. Get it out in bits.

— *M'appari*, Simon, Father Cowley said.

Down stage he strode some paces, grave, tall in affliction, his long arms outheld. Hoarsely the apple of his throat hoarsed softly. Softly he sang to a dusty seascape there: *A Last Farewell*. A headland, a ship, a sail upon the billows. Farewell. A lovely girl, her veil awave upon the wind upon the headland, wind around her.

Cowley sang:

— *M'appari tutt'amor:*
  Il mio sguardo l'incontr…

She waved, unhearing Cowley, her veil to one departing, dear one, to wind, love, speeding sail, return.

— Go on, Simon.

– Ah, sure, my dancing days are done, Ben ... Well ...

Mr Dedalus laid his pipe to rest beside the tuning fork and, sitting, touched the obedient keys.

– No, Simon, Father Cowley turned. Play it in the original. One flat.

The keys, obedient, rose higher, told, faltered, confessed, confused.

Up stage strode Father Cowley.

– Here, Simon, I'll accompany you, he said. Get up.

By Graham Lemon's pineapple rock, by Elvery's elephant, jingle jogged.

Steak, kidney, liver, mashed. At meat fit for princes sat princes Bloom and Goulding. Princes at meat they raised and drank, Power and cider.

Most beautiful tenor air ever written, Richie said: *Sonnambula.* He heard Joe Maas sing that one night. Ah, what M'Guckin! Yes. In his way. Choirboy style. Maas was the boy. Massboy. A lyrical tenor, if you like. Never forget it. Never.

Tenderly Bloom over liverless bacon saw the tightened features strain. Backache he. Bright's bright eye. Next item on the programme. Paying the piper. Pills, pounded bread, worth a guinea a box. Stave it off awhile. Sings too: *Down among the dead men.* Appropriate. Kidney pie. Sweets to the. Not making much hand of it. Best value in. Characteristic of him. Power. Particular about his drink. Flaw in the glass, fresh Vartry water. Fecking matches from counters to save. Then squander a sovereign in dribs and drabs. And when he's wanted not a farthing. Screwed refusing to pay his fare. Curious types.

Never would Richie forget that night. As long as he lived: never. In the gods of the old Royal with little Peake. And when the first note.

Speech paused on Richie's lips.

Coming out with a whopper now. Rhapsodies about damn all. Believes his own lies. Does really. Wonderful liar. But want a good memory.

– Which air is that? asked Leopold Bloom.

– *All is lost now.*

Richie cocked his lips apout. A low incipient note sweet banshee murmured: all. A thrush. A throstle. His breath, birdsweet, good teeth he's proud of, fluted with plaintive woe. Is lost. Rich sound. Two notes in one there. Blackbird I heard in the hawthorn valley. Taking my motives he twined and turned them. All most too new call is lost in all. Echo. How sweet the answer. How is that done? All lost now. Mournful he whistled. Fall, surrender, lost.

Bloom bent leopold ear, turning a fringe of doyley down under the vase. Order. Yes, I remember. Lovely air. In sleep she went to him.

Innocence in the moon. Brave, don't know their danger. Still hold her back. Call name. Touch water. Jingle jaunty. Too late. She longed to go. That's why. Woman. As easy stop the sea. Yes: all is lost.

— A beautiful air, said Bloom lost Leopold. I know it well.

Never in all his life had Richie Goulding.

He knows it well too. Or he feels. Still harping on his daughter. Wise child that knows her father, Dedalus said. Me?

Bloom askance over liverless saw. Face of the all is lost. Rollicking Richie once. Jokes old stale now. Wagging his ear. Napkin ring in his eye. Now begging letters he sends his son with. Cross-eyed Walter sir I did sir. Wouldn't trouble only I was expecting some money. Apologise.

Piano again. Sounds better than last time I heard. Tuned probably. Stopped again.

Dollard and Cowley still urged the lingering singer out with it.

— With it, Simon.

— It, Simon.

— Ladies and gentlemen, I am most deeply obliged by your kind solicitations.

— It, Simon.

— I have no money but if you will lend me your attention I shall endeavour to sing to you of a heart bowed down.

By the sandwich bell in screening shadow Lydia her bronze and rose, a lady's grace, gave and withheld: as in cool glaucous *eau de Nil* Mina to tankards two her pinnacles of gold.

The harping chords of prelude closed. A chord, long drawn, expectant, drew a voice away.

— *When first I saw that form endearing,*

Richie turned.

— Si Dedalus' voice, he said.

Brain-tipped, cheek touched with flame, they listened, feeling that flow endearing flow over skin limbs human heart soul spine. Bloom signed to Pat, bald Pat is a waiter hard of hearing, to set ajar the door of the bar. The door of the bar. So. That will do. Pat, waiter, waited, waiting to hear, for he was hard of hear by the door.

— *Sorrow from me seemed to depart.*

Through the hush of air a voice sang to them, low, not rain, not leaves in murmur, like no voice of strings or reeds or what do you call them dulcimers, touching their still ears with words, still hearts of their each his remembered lives. Good, good to hear: sorrow from them each seemed to from both depart when first they heard. When first they saw, lost Richie, Poldy, mercy of beauty, heard from a person wouldn't expect it in the least, her first merciful lovesoft oftloved word.

Love that is singing: love's old sweet song. Bloom unwound slowly the elastic band of his packet. Love's old sweet *sonnez la* gold. Bloom wound a skein round four forkfingers, stretched it, relaxed, and wound it round his troubled double, fourfold, in octave, gyved them fast.

– *Full of hope and all delighted* ...

Tenors get women by the score. Increase their flow. Throw flower at his feet. When will we meet? My head it simply. Jingle all delighted. He can't sing for tall hats. Your head it simply swurls. Perfumed for him. What perfume does your wife? I want to know. Jing. Stop. Knock. Last look at mirror always before she answers the door. The hall. There? How do you? I do well. There? What? Or? Phial of cachous, kissing comfits, in her satchel. Yes? Hands felt for the opulent.

Alas! The voice rose, sighing, changed: loud, full, shining, proud.

– *But, alas, 'twas idle dreaming* ...

Glorious tone he has still. Cork air softer, also their brogue. Silly man! Could have made oceans of money. Singing wrong words. Wore out his wife: now sings. But hard to tell. Only the two themselves. If he doesn't break down. Keep a trot for the avenue. His hands and feet sing too. Drink. Nerves overstrung. Must be abstemious to sing. Jenny Lind soup: stock, sago, raw eggs, half pint of cream. For creamy dreamy.

Tenderness it welled: slow, swelling. Full it throbbed. That's the chat. Ha, give! Take! Throb, a throb, a pulsing proud erect.

Words? Music? No: it's what's behind.

Bloom looped, unlooped, noded, disnoded.

Bloom. Flood of warm jamjam lick-it-up secretness flowed to flow in music out, in desire, dark to lick flow, invading. Tipping her tepping her tapping her topping her. Tup. Pores to dilate dilating. Tup. The joy the feel the warm the. Tup. To pour o'er sluices pouring gushes. Flood, gush, flow, joygush, tupthrob. Now! Language of love.

– ... *ray of hope* ...

Beaming. Lydia for Lidwell squeak scarcely hear so ladylike the muse unsqueaked a ray of hopk.

Martha it is. Coincidence. Just going to write. Lionel's song. Lovely name you have. Can't write. Accept my little pres. Play on her heartstrings, pursestrings too. She's a. I called you naughty boy. Still, the name: Martha. How strange! Today.

The voice of Lionel returned, weaker but unwearied. It sang again to Richie Poldy Lydia Lidwell also sang to Pat open mouth ear waiting to wait. How first he saw that form endearing, how sorrow seemed to part, how look, form, word charmed him Gould Lidwell, won Pat Bloom's heart.

Wish I could see his face though. Explain better. Why the barber in Drago's always looked my face when I spoke his face in the glass. Still, hear it better here than in the bar though farther.

— *Each graceful look* . . .

First night when first I saw her at Mat Dillon's in Terenure. Yellow, black lace she wore. Musical chairs. We two the last. Fate. After her. Fate. Round and round slow. Quick round. We two. All looked. Halt. Down she sat. All ousted looked. Lips laughing. Yellow knees.

— *Charmed my eye* . . .

Singing. *Waiting* she sang. I turned her music. Full voice of perfumes of what perfume does your lilac trees. Bosom I saw, both full, throat warbling. First I saw. She thanked me. Why did she me? Fate. Spanishy eyes. Under a pear tree alone patio this hour in old Madrid one side in shadow Dolores shedolores. At me. Luring. Ah, alluring.

— *Martha! Ah, Martha!*

Quitting all languor Lionel cried in grief, in cry of passion dominant to love to return with deepening yet with rising chords of harmony. In cry of lionel loneliness that she should know, must martha feel. For only her he waited. Where? Here there try there here all try where. Somewhere.

— *Co-ome, thou lost one!*
  Co-ome, thou dear one!

Alone. One love. One hope. One comfort me. Martha, chestnote, return!

— *Come!*

It soared, a bird, it held its flight, a swift pure cry, soar silver orb it leaped serene, speeding, sustained, to come, don't spin it out too long long breath he breath long life, soaring high, high resplendent, aflame, crowned, high in the effulgence symbolistic, high, of the ethereal bosom, high, of the high vast irradiation, everywhere all soaring all around about the all, the endlessnessnessness . . .

— *To me!*

Siopold!

Consumed.

Come. Well sung. All clapped. She ought to. Come. To me, to him, to her, you too, me, us.

— Bravo! Clapclap. Good man, Simon. Clappyclapclap. Encore! Clapclip-clap clap. Sound as a bell. Bravo, Simon! Clapclopclap. Encore, enclap, said, cried, clapped all, Ben Dollard, Lydia Douce, George Lidwell, Pat, Mina Kennedy, two gentlemen with two tankards, Cowley, first gent with tank and bronze Miss Douce and gold Miss Mina.

Blazes Boylan's smart tan shoes creaked on the bar floor, said before. Jingle by monuments of Sir John Gray, Horatio one-handled Nelson, Reverend Father Theobald Mathew, jaunted as said before just now. Atrot, in heat, heatseated. *Cloche. Sonnez la. Cloche. Sonnez la.* Slower the mare went up the hill by the Rotunda, Rutland Square. Too slow for Boylan, blazes Boylan, impatience Boylan, jogged the mare.

An afterclang of Cowley's chords closed, died on the air made richer.

And Richie Goulding drank his Power and Leopold Bloom his cider drank, Lidwell his Guinness, second gentleman said they would partake of two more tankards if she did not mind. Miss Kennedy smirked, disserving, coral lips, at first, at second. She did not mind.

— Seven days in jail, Ben Dollard said, on bread and water. Then you'd sing, Simon, like a garden thrush.

Lionel Simon, singer, laughed. Father Bob Cowley played. Mina Kennedy served. Second gentleman paid. Tom Kernan strutted in. Lydia, admired, admired. But Bloom sang dumb.

Admiring.

Richie, admiring, descanted on that man's glorious voice. He remembered one night long ago. Never forget that night. Si sang *'Twas rank and fame*: in Ned Lambert's 'twas. Good God he never heard in all his life a note like that he never did *then false one we had better part* so clear so God he never heard *since love lives not* a clinking voice ask Lambert he can tell you too.

Goulding, a flush struggling in his pale, told Mr Bloom, face of the night, Si in Ned Lambert's, Dedalus house, sang *'Twas rank and fame.*

He, Mr Bloom, listened while he, Richie Goulding, told him, Mr Bloom, of the night he, Richie, heard him, Si Dedalus, sing *'Twas rank and fame* in his, Ned Lambert's, house.

Brothers-in-law. Relations. We never speak as we pass by. Rift in the lute I think. Treats him with scorn. See. He admires him all the more. The night Si sang. The human voice, two tiny silky cords. Wonderful, more than all the others.

That voice was a lamentation. Calmer now. It's in the silence after that you feel you hear. Vibrations. Now silent air.

Bloom ungyved his crisscrossed hands and with slack fingers plucked the slender catgut thong. It buzzed. He drew and plucked. It twanged. While Goulding talked of Barraclough's voice production. While Tom Kernan, harking back in a kind of retrospective arrangement, talked to listening Father Cowley who played a voluntary, who nodded as he played. While big Ben Dollard talked with Simon Dedalus lighting, who nodded as he smoked, who smoked.

Thou lost one. All songs on that theme. Yet more Bloom stretched his string. Cruel it seems. Let people get fond of each other: lure them on. Then tear asunder. Death. Explos. Knock on the head. Outtohelloutofthat. Human life. Dignam. Ugh, that rat's tail wriggling! Five bob I gave. *Corpus paradisum.* Corncrake croaker: belly like a poisoned pup. Gone. They sing. Forgotten. I too. And one day she with. Leave her: get tired. Suffer then. Snivel. Big Spanishy eyes goggling at nothing. Her wavyavyeavyheavyeav-yevyevyhair un comb:'d.

Yet too much happy bores. He stretched more, more. Are you not happy in your? Twang. It snapped.

Jingle into Dorset Street jinglejingled.

Miss Douce withdrew her satiny arm, reproachful, pleased.

— Don't make half so free, said she, till we are better acquainted.

George Lidwell told her really and truly: but she did not believe.

First gentleman told Mina that was so. She asked him was that so. And second tankard told her so. That that was so.

Miss Douce, Lydia, did not believe: Miss Kennedy, Mina, did not believe: George Lidwell, no: Miss Dou did not: the first, the first: gent with the tank: believe, no, no: did not, Miss Kenn: Lidlydiawell: the tank.

Better write it here. Quills in the post office chewed and twisted.

Bald Pat at a sign drew nigh. A pen and ink. He went. A pad. He went. A pad to blot. He heard, deaf Pat.

— Yes, Mr Bloom said, teasing the curling catgut line. It certainly is. Few lines will do. My present. All that Italian florid music is. Who is this wrote? Know the name you know better. Take out sheet notepaper, envelope: unconcerned. It's so characteristic.

— Grandest number in the whole opera, Goulding said.

— It is, Bloom said.

Numbers it is. All music when you come to think. Two multiplied by two divided by half. Two is twice one. Vibrations. Chords those are. One plus two plus six is seven. Do anything you like with figures, juggling. Always find out this equal to that. Symmetry under a cemetery wall. He doesn't see my mourning. Callous: all for his own gut. Musemathematics. And you think you're listening to the ethereal. But suppose you said it like: Martha, seven times nine minus x is thirty-five thousand. Fall quite flat. It's on account of the sounds it is.

Instance he's playing now. Improvising. Might be what you like till you hear the words. Want to listen sharp. Hard. Begin all right: then hear chords a bit off: feel lost a bit. In and out of sacks, over barrels, through wire fences, obstacle race. Time makes the tune. Question of mood you're in. Still, always nice to hear. Except scales up and down, girls learning. Two together, next-door neighbours. Ought to invent dummy pianos for that. Milly no taste. Queer because we both I mean. *Blumenlied* I bought for her. The name. Playing it slow, a girl, night I came home, the girl. Door of the stables near Cecilia Street.

Bald deaf Pat brought quite flat pad ink pen. Pat set down with ink pen quite flat pad. Pat took plate dish knife fork up. Pat went.

It was the only language, Mr Dedalus said to Ben. He heard them as a boy in Ringabella, Crosshaven, Ringabella, singing their barcaroles. Queenstown Harbour full of Italian ships. Walking, you know, Ben, in the moonlight with those earthquake hats. Blending their voices. God, such music, Ben. Heard as a boy. Cross Ringabella haven mooncarole.

Sour pipe removed he held a shield of hand beside his lips that cooed a moonlight nightcall, clear from anear, a call from afar, replying.

Down the edge of his *Freeman* baton ranged Bloom's your other eye, scanning for where did I see that. Callan, Coleman, Dignam, Patrick A. Heigho! Heigho! Fawcett. Aha! Just the ad I was looking . . .

Hope he's not looking, cute as a rat. He held unfurled his *Freeman*. Can't see now. Remember write Greek ees. Bloom dipped, Bloo mur: dear sir. Dear Henry wrote: dear Mady. Got your lett and flow. Hell did I put? Some pock or oth. It is utterl imposs. Underline *imposs*. To write today.

Bore this. Bored Bloom tambourined gently with I am just reflecting fingers on flat pad Pat brought.

On. Know what I mean. No, change that ee. Accept my poor little pres enclos. Ask her no answ. Hold on. Five Dig. Two about here. Penny the gulls. Elijah is com. Seven Davy Byrne's. Is eight about. Say half a crown. My poor little pres: p.o. two and six. Write me a long. Do you despise? Jingle, have you the? So excited. Why do you call me naught? You naughty too? O, Mairy lost the pin of her. Bye for today. Yes, yes, will tell you. Want to. To keep it up. Call me that other. Other world she wrote.

My patience are exhaust. To keep it up. You must believe. Believe. The tank. It. Is. True.

Folly am I writing? Husbands don't, that's marriage does, their wives. Because I'm away from. Suppose. But how? She must. Keep young. If she found out. Card in my high-grade ha. No, not tell all. Useless pain. If they don't see. Woman. Sauce for the gander.

A hackney car, number three hundred and twenty-four, driver James Barton of number one Harmony Avenue, Donnybrook, on which sat a fare, a young gentleman, stylishly dressed in an indigo-blue serge suit made by George Robert Mesias, tailor and cutter, of number five Eden Quay, and wearing a straw hat, very dressy, bought of John Plasto of number one Great Brunswick Street, hatter. Eh? This is the jingle that joggled and jingled.

By Dlugacz's pork shop bright with tubes of Agudath Netaim forcemeat trotted a gallant-buttocked mare.

— Answering an ad? keen Richie's eyes asked Bloom.

— Yes, Mr Bloom said. Town traveller. Nothing doing, I expect.

Bloom mur: best references. But Henry wrote: it will excite me. You know how. In haste. Henry. Greek ee. Better add postscript. What is he playing now? Improvising? Intermezzo. P.S. The rum tum tum. How will you pun? You punish me? Crooked skirt swinging, whack by. Tell me I want to. Know. O. Course if I didn't I wouldn't ask. La la la ree. Trails off there sad in minor. Why minor sad? Sign: H. They like sad tail at end. P.P.S. La la la ree. I feel so sad today. La ree. So lonely. Dee.

He blotted quick on pad of Pat. Envel. Address. Just copy out of paper. Murmured: Messrs Callan, Coleman and Co., Limited. Henry wrote:

> Miss Martha Clifford
> c/o P.O.
> Dolphin's Barn Lane
> City

Blot over the other so he can't read. Right. Idea prize titbit. Something detective read off blotting pad. Payment at the rate of guinea per col. Matcham often thinks. The laughing witch. Poor Mrs Purefoy. U.P: up.

Too poetical that about the sad. Music did that. Music hath charms, Shakespeare said. Quotations every day in the year. To be or not to be. Wisdom while you wait.

In Gerard's rosery of Fetter Lane he walks, greyed auburn. One life is all. One body. Do. But do.

Done anyhow. Postal order, stamp. Post office lower down. Walk now. Enough. Barney Kiernan's I promised to meet them. Dislike that job. House of mourning. Walk. Pat! Doesn't hear. Deaf beetle he is.

Car near there now. Talk. Talk. Pat! Doesn't. Settling those napkins. Lot of ground he must cover in the day. Paint face behind on him then he'd be two. Wish they'd sing more. Keep my mind off.

Bald Pat who is bothered mitred the napkins. Pat is a waiter hard of his hearing. Pat is a waiter who waits while you wait. Hee hee hee hee. He waits while you wait. Hee hee. A waiter is he. Hee hee hee hee. He waits while you wait. While you wait if you wait he will wait while you wait. Hee hee hee hee. Hoh. Wait while you wait.

Miss Douce, requested, served the same again. Douce now. Douce Lydia. Bronze and rose. She had a gorgeous, simply gorgeous, time. And look at the lovely shell she brought.

To the end of the bar to him she bore lightly the spiked and winding seahorn that he, George Lidwell, solicitor, might hear.

– Listen! she bade him.

Under Tom Kernan's gin-hot words the accompanist wove music slow. Authentic fact. How Walter Bapty lost his voice. Well, sir, the husband took him by the throat. *Scoundrel*, said he. *You'll sing no more love songs.* He did, Sir Tom. Bob Cowley wove. Tenors get wom. Cowley lay back.

Ah, now he heard, she holding it to his ear. Hear! He heard. Wonderful. She held it to her own. And through the sifted light pale gold in contrast glided. To hear.

Tap.

Bloom through the bar door saw a shell held at their ears. He heard more faintly that they heard, each for herself alone, then each for other, hearing, the plash of waves, loudly, a silent roar.

Bronze by a weary gold, anear, afar, they listened.

Her ear too is a shell, the peeping lobe there. Been to the seaside. Lovely seaside girls. Skin tanned raw. Should have put on cold cream first make it brown. Buttered toast. O, and that lotion mustn't forget. Fever near her mouth. Your head it simply. Hair braided over: shell with seaweed. Why do they hide their ears with seaweed hair? And Turks the mouth, why? Her eyes over the sheet, a yashmak. Find the way in. A cave. No admittance except on business.

The sea they think they hear. Singing. A roar. The blood it is. Souse in the ear sometimes. Well, it's a sea. Corpuscle islands.

Wonderful really. So distinct. Again. George Lidwell held its murmur, hearing: then laid it by, gently.

– What are the wild waves saying? he asked her, smiled.

Charming, seasmiling and unanswering, Lydia on Lidwell smiled.

Tap.

By Larry O'Rourke's, by Larry, bold Larry O', Boylan swayed and Boylan turned.

From the forsaken shell Miss Mina glided to her tankards waiting. No, she was not so lonely, archly Miss Douce's head let Mr Lidwell know. Walks in the moonlight by the sea. No, not alone. With whom? She nobly answered: with a gentleman friend.

Bob Cowley's twinkling fingers in the treble played again. The landlord has the prior. A little time. Long John. Big Ben. Lightly he played a light bright tinkling measure for tripping ladies, arch and smiling, and for their gallants, gentlemen friends. One: one, one, one, one, one: two, one, three, four.

Sea, wind, leaves, thunder, water, cows lowing, the cattle market, cocks, hens don't crow, snakes hissss. There's music everywhere. Ruttledge's door: ee creaking. No, that's noise. Minuet of *Don Giovanni* he's playing now. Court dresses of all descriptions in castle chambers dancing. Misery. Peasants outside. Green starving faces eating dock leaves. Nice that is. Look: look, look, look, look, look: you look at us.

That's joyful I can feel. Never have written it. Why? My joy is other joy. But both are joys. Yes, joy it must be. Mere fact of music shows you are. Often thought she was in the dumps till she began to lilt. Then know.

M'Coy valise. My wife and your wife. Squealing cat. Like tearing silk. Tongue when she talks like the clapper of a bell. They can't manage men's intervals. Gap in their voices too. Fill me. I'm warm, dark, open. Molly in *Quis est homo*: Mercadante. My ear against the wall to hear. Want a woman who can deliver the goods.

Jigjog jogged, stopped. Dandy tan shoe of dandy Boylan socks sky-blue clocks came light to earth.

O, look we are so! Chamber music. Could make a kind of pun on that. It is a kind of music I often thought when she. Acoustics that is. Tinkling. Empty vessels make most noise. Because the acoustics, the resonance changes according as the weight of the water is equal to the law of falling water. Like those rhapsodies of Liszt's: Hungarian, gipsy-eyed. Pearls.

Drops. Rain. Diddle iddle addle addle oodle oodle. Hissss. Now. Maybe now. Before.

One rapped on a door, one tapped with a knock, did he knock, Paul de Kock, with a loud proud knocker, with a cock carracarracarra cock. Cockcock.

Tap.

– *Qui sdegno*, Ben, said Father Cowley.

– No, Ben, Tom Kernan interfered. *The Croppy Boy*. Our native Doric.

– Ay, do, Ben, Mr Dedalus said. Good men and true.

– Do, do, they begged in one.

I'll go. Here, Pat, return. Come. He came, he came, he did not stay. To me. How much?

– What key? Six sharps?

– F sharp major, Ben Dollard said.

Bob Cowley's outstretched talons gripped the black deepsounding chords.

Must go, prince Bloom told Richie prince. No, Richie said. Yes, must. Got money somewhere. He's on for a razzle backache spree. Much? He seehears lipspeech. One and nine. Penny for yourself. Here. Give him twopence tip. Deaf, bothered. But perhaps he has wife and family waiting, waiting Patty come home. Hee hee hee hee. Deaf wait while they wait.

But wait. But hear. Chords dark. Lugulugubrious. Low. In a cave of the dark middle earth. Embedded ore. Lump music.

The voice of dark age, of unlove, of earth's fatigue, made grave approach and painful, come from afar, from hoary mountains, called on good men and true. The priest he sought. With him would he speak a word.

Tap.

Ben Dollard's voice. Base barreltone. Doing his level best to sing it. Croak of vast manless moonless womoonless marsh. Other comedown. Big ship chandler's business he had once. Remember: rosiny ropes, ships' lanterns. Failed to the tune of ten thousand pounds. Now in the Iveagh Home. Cubicle number so and so. Number one Bass did that for him.

The priest's at home. A false priest's servant bade him welcome. Step in. The holy father. Curlycues of chords.

Ruin them. Wreck their lives. Then build cubicles to end their days in. Hushaby. Lullaby. Die, dog. Little dog, die.

The voice of warning, solemn warning, told them the youth had entered a lonely hall, told them how solemn fell his footstep there, told them the gloomy chamber, the vested priest sitting to shrive.

Decent soul. Bit addled now. Thinks he'll win in *Answers*. Poets' picture puzzle. We hand you crisp five-pound note. Bird sitting hatching in a nest. *Lay of the Last Minstrel* he thought it was. See blank tee what domestic animal? Tee dash ar most courageous mariner. Good voice he has still. No eunuch yet with all his belongings.

Listen. Bloom listened. Richie Goulding listened. And by the door deaf Pat, bald Pat, tipped Pat, listened.

The chords harped slower.

The voice of penance and of grief came slow, embellished, tremulous. Ben's contrite beard confessed: *in nomine Domini*, in God's name. He knelt. He beat his hand upon his breast, confessing: *mea culpa*.

Latin again. That holds them like birdlime. Priest with the communion corpus for those women. Chap in the mortuary, coffin or coffey, *corpus-nomine*. Wonder where that rat is by now. Scrape.

Tap.

They listened: tankards and Miss Kennedy, George Lidwell eyelid well expressive, full-busted satin, Kernan, Si.

The sighing voice of sorrow sang. His sins. Since Easter he had cursed three times. You bitch's bast. And once at mass time he had gone to play. And once by the churchyard he had passed and for his mother's rest he had not prayed. A boy. A croppy boy.

Deaf Pat held wider ajar the door.

Bronze, listening by the beerpull, gazed far away. Soulfully. Doesn't half know I'm. Molly great dab at seeing anyone looking.

Bronze gazed far sideways. Mirror there. Is that best side of her face? They always know. Knock at the door. Last tip to titivate.

Cockcarracarra.

What do they think when they hear music? Music hath charms. Owls and birds. Way to catch rattlesnakes. Night Michael Gunn gave us the box. Tuning up. Shah of Persia liked that best. Remind him of home sweet home. Wiped his nose in curtain too. Custom his country perhaps. That's music too. Not as bad as it sounds. Tootling. Brasses braying asses through uptrunks. Double basses helpless, gashes in their sides. Woodwinds mooing cows. Semigrand open crocodile music hath jaws. Woodwind like Goodwin's name.

She looked fine. Her crocus dress she wore low cut, belongings on show. Clove her breath was always in theatre when she bent to ask a question. Told her what Spinoza says in that book of poor papa's. Hypnotised, listening. Eyes like that. She bent. Chap in dress circle staring down into her with his opera glass for all he was worth. Beauty of music you must hear twice. Nature woman half a look. God made the country, man the tune. Met him pike hoses. Philosophy. O rocks!

All gone. All fallen. At the siege of Ross his father, at Gorey all his brothers fell. To Wexford, we are the boys of Wexford, he would. Last of his name and race.

I too, last of my race. Milly, young student. Well, my fault perhaps. No son. Rudy. Too late now. Or if not? If not? If still?

He bore no hate.

Hate. Love. Those are names. Rudy. Soon I am old.

Big Ben his voice unfolded. Great voice, Richie Goulding said, a flush struggling in his pale, to Bloom, soon old but when was young.

Ireland comes now. My country above the king. She listens. Who fears to speak of nineteen four? Time to be shoving. Looked enough.

– *Bless me, father*, Dollard the croppy cried. *Bless me and let me go.*

Tap.

Bloom looked, unblessed to go. Got up to kill: on eighteen bob a week. Fellows shell out the dibs. Moonlit walks by the sad sea waves. Want to keep your weather eye open. Those girls, those lovely. Chorus girl's romance. Letters read out for breach of promise. From Chickabiddy's owny Mumpsypum. Laughter in court. Henry. I never signed it. The lovely name you.

Low sank the music, air and words. Then hastened. The false priest rustling soldier from his cassock. A yeoman captain. They know it all by heart. The thrill they itch for. Yeoman cap.

Tap. Tap.

Thrilled, she listened, bending in sympathy to hear.

Blank face. Virgin should say: or fingered only. Write something on it: page. If not, what becomes of them? Decline, despair. Keeps them young. Even admire themselves. See. Play on her lip and blow, body of white woman, a flute alive. Blow gentle. Loud. Three holes all women. Goddess I didn't see. They want it: not too much polite. That's why he gets them. Gold in your pocket, brass in your face. Say something. Make her hear. With look to look: songs without words. Molly that hurdy-gurdy boy. She knew he meant the monkey was sick. Or because so like the Spanish. Understand animals too that way. Solomon did. Gift of nature.

Ventriloquise. My lips closed. Think in my stom. What?

Will? You? I. Want. You. To.

With hoarse rude fury the yeoman cursed, swelling in apoplectic bitch's bastard. A good thought, boy, to come. One hour's your time to live, your last.

Tap. Tap.

Thrill now. Pity they feel. To wipe away a tear for martyrs that want to, dying to, die. For all things dying, for all things born. Poor Mrs Purefoy. Hope she's over. Because their wombs.

A liquid of womb of woman's eyeball gazed under a fence of lashes, calmly, hearing. See real beauty of the eye when she not speaks. On yonder river. At each slow satiny heaving bosom's wave (her heaving embon) red rose rose slowly, sank red rose. Heartbeats: her breath: breath that is life. And all the tiny tiny fernfoils trembled of maidenhair.

But look. The bright stars fade. O rose! Castile. The morn.

Ha. Lidwell. For him then not for. Infatuated. I like that? See her from here though. Popped corks, splashes of beerfroth, stacks of empties.

On the smooth jutting beerpull laid Lydia hand, lightly, plumply, leave it to my hands. All lost in pity for croppy. Fro, to: to, fro: over the polished knob (she knows his eyes, my eyes, her eyes) her thumb and finger passed in pity: passed, reposed and, gently touching, then slid so smoothly, slowly down, a cool firm white enamel baton protruding through their sliding ring.

With a cock with a carra.

Tap. Tap. Tap.

I hold this house. Amen. He gnashed in fury. Traitors swing.

The chords consented. Very sad thing. But had to be.

Get out before the end. Thanks, that was heavenly. Where's my hat? Pass by her. Can leave that *Freeman*. Letter I have. Suppose she were the? No. Walk, walk, walk. Like Cashel Boylo Connoro Coylo Tisdall Maurice Tisntdall Farrell. Waaaaaaalk.

Well, I must be. Are you off? Yrfmstbyes. Blmstup. O'er rye-high blue. Bloom stood up. Ow. Soap feeling rather sticky behind. Must have sweated: music. That lotion, remember. Well, so long. High grade. Card inside, yes.

By deaf Pat in the doorway, straining ear, Bloom passed.

At Geneva Barracks that young man died. At Passage was his body laid. Dolor! O, he dolores! The voice of the mournful chanter called to dolorous prayer.

By rose, by satiny bosom, by the fondling hand, by slops, by empties, by popped corks, greeting in going, past eyes and maidenhair, bronze and faint gold in deep-sea shadow, went Bloom, soft Bloom, I feel so lonely Bloom.

Tap. Tap. Tap.

Pray for him, prayed the bass of Dollard. You who hear in peace. Breathe a prayer, drop a tear, good men, good people. He was the croppy boy.

Scaring eavesdropping boots croppy bootsboy Bloom in the Ormond hallway heard growls and roars of bravo, fat backslapping, their boots all treading, boots not the boots the boy. General chorus off for a swill to wash it down. Glad I avoided.

— Come on, Ben, Simon Dedalus said. By God, you're as good as ever you were.

— Better, said Tomgin Kernan. Most trenchant rendition of that ballad, upon my soul and honour it is.

— Lablache, said Father Cowley.

Ben Dollard bulkily cachucha'd towards the bar, mightily praise-fed and all big roseate, on heavy-footed feet, his gouty fingers nakkering castanets in the air.

Big Benaben Dollard. Big Benben. Big Benben.

Rrr.

And deepmoved all, Simon trumping compassion from foghorn nose, all laughing, they brought him forth, Ben Dollard, in right good cheer.

— You're looking rubicund, George Lidwell said.

Miss Douce composed her rose to wait.

— Ben machree, said Mr Dedalus, clapping Ben's fat back's shoulder-blade. Fit as a fiddle only he has a lot of adipose tissue concealed about his person.

Rrrrrrrsss.

— Fat of death, Simon, Ben Dollard growled.

Richie rift in the lute alone sat: Goulding, Collis, Ward. Uncertainly he waited. Unpaid Pat too.

Tap. Tap. Tap. Tap.

Miss Mina Kennedy brought near her lips to ear of tankard one.

— Mr Dollard, they murmured low.

— Dollard, murmured tankard.

Tank one believed: Miss Kenn when she: that doll he was: she doll: the tank.

He murmured that he knew the name. The name was familiar to him, that is to say. That was to say he had heard the name of. Dollard, was it? Dollard, yes.

Yes, her lips said more loudly, Mr Dollard. He sang that song lovely, murmured Mina. And *The Last Rose of Summer* was a lovely song. Mina loved that song. Tankard loved the song that Mina.

'Tis the last rose of summer dollard left bloom felt wind wound round inside.

Gassy thing that cider: binding too. Wait. Post office up near Reuben J.'s one and eightpence too. Get shut of it. Dodge round by Greek Street. Wish I hadn't promised to meet. Freer in air. Music. Gets on your nerves. Beerpull. Her hand that rocks the cradle rules the. Ben Howth. That rules the world.

Far. Far. Far. Far.

Tap. Tap. Tap. Tap.

Up the quay went Lionelleopold, naughty Henry with letter for Mady, with sweets of sin with frillies for Raoul with met him pike hoses went Poldy on.

Tap blind walked tapping by the tap the curbstone tapping, tap by tap.

Cowley, he stuns himself with it: kind of drunkenness. Better give way only halfway, the way of a man with a maid. Instance enthusiasts. All ears. Not lose a demisemiquaver. Eyes shut. Head nodding in time. Dotty. You daren't budge. Thinking strictly prohibited. Always talking shop. Fiddlefaddle about notes.

All a kind of attempt to talk. Unpleasant when it stops because you never know exac. Organ in Gardiner Street. Old Glynn fifty quid a year. Queer up there in the cockloft alone with stops and locks and keys. Seated all day at the organ. Maunder on for hours, talking to himself or the other fellow, blowing the bellows. Growl, angry, then shriek, cursing (want to have wadding or something in his no don't she cried), then all of a soft sudden wee little wee little pipy wind.

Pwee! A wee little wind piped. Eeee. In Bloom's little wee.

— Was he? Mr Dedalus said, returning with fetched pipe. I was with him this morning at poor little Paddy Dignam's . . .

— Ay, the Lord have mercy on him.

— By the by, there's a tuning fork in there on the . . .

Tap. Tap. Tap. Tap.

— The wife has a fine voice. Or had. What? Lidwell asked.

— O, that must be the tuner, Lydia said to Simonlionel first I saw, forgot it when he was here.

Blind he was she told George Lidwell second I saw. And played so exquisitely, treat to hear. Exquisite contrast: bronzelid, minagold.

— Shout! Ben Dollard shouted, pouring. Sing out!

— 'Ildo! cried Father Cowley.

Rrrrrr.

I feel I want . . .

Tap. Tap. Tap. Tap. Tap.

— Very, Mr Dedalus said, staring hard at a headless sardine.

Under the sandwich bell lay on a bier of bread one lost, one lonely, last sardine of summer. Bloom alone.

— Very, he stared. The lower register, for choice.

Tap. Tap. Tap. Tap. Tap. Tap. Tap. Tap.

Bloom went by Barry's. Wish I could. Wait. That Wonderworker if I had. Twenty-four solicitors in that one house. Litigation. Love one another. Piles of parchment. Messrs Pick and Pocket have power of attorney. Goulding, Collis, Ward.

But for example the chap that wallops the big drum. His vocation. Mickey Rooney's band. Wonder how it first struck him. Sitting at home after pig's cheek and cabbage, nursing it in the armchair. Rehearsing his band part. Pom. Pompedy. Jolly for the wife. Asses' skins. Welt them through life, then wallop after death. Pom. Wallop. Seems to be what you call yashmak or I mean kismet. Fate.

Tap. Tap. A stripling, blind, with a tapping cane came taptaptapping by Daly's window where a mermaid, hair all streaming (but he couldn't see), blew whiffs of a mermaid (blind couldn't), smoke mermaids, coolest whiff of all.

Instruments. A blade of grass, shell of her hands, then blow. Even comb and tissue paper you can knock a tune out of. Molly in her shift in Lombard Street West, hair down. Girl still she was then. Time. I suppose each kind of trade made its own, don't you see? Hunter with a horn. Haw. Have you the? *Cloche. Sonnez la!* Shepherd his pipe. Pwee little wee. Policeman a whistle. Locks and keys? Sweep! Four o'clock's all's well! Sleep! All is lost now. Drum? Pompedy. Wait, I know. Town crier, bumbailiff. Long John. Waken the dead. Pom. Dignam. Poor little *nomine-domine*. Pom. It is music. I mean of course it's all pom pom pom very much what they call *da capo*. Still, you can hear. As we march, we march along, march along. Pom.

I must really. Fff. Now if I did that at a banquet. Just a question of custom. Shah of Persia. Breathe a prayer, drop a tear. All the same he must have been a bit of a natural not to see it was a yeoman cap. Muffled up. Wonder who was that chap at the grave in the brown macin. O, the whore of the lane!

A frowsy whore with black straw sailor hat askew came glazily in the day along the quay towards Mr Bloom. When first he saw that form endearing. Yes, it is. I feel so lonely. Wet night in the lane. Horn. Who had the? Heehaw. Shesaw. Off her beat here. What is she? Hope she. Psst! Any chance of your wash? Knew Molly. Had me decked. Stout lady does be with you in the brown costume. Put you off your stroke, that. Appointment we made knowing we'd never, well hardly ever. Too dear too near to home sweet home. Sees me, does she? Looks a fright in the day. Face like dip. Damn her! O well, she has to live like the rest. Look in here.

In Lionel Marks's antique saleshop window haughty Henry Lionel Leopold dear Henry Flower earnestly Mr Leopold Bloom envisaged battered candlesticks, a melodeon oozing maggoty blowbags. Bargain: six bob. Might learn to play. Cheap. Let her pass. Course everything is dear if you don't want it. That's what good salesman is. Make you buy what he wants to sell. Chap sold me the Swedish razor he shaved me with. Wanted to charge me for the edge he gave it. She's passing now. Six bob.

Must be the cider or perhaps the burgund.

Near bronze from anear near gold from afar they chinked their clinking glasses all, bright-eyed and gallant, before bronze Lydia's tempting last rose of summer, rose of Castile. First Lid, De, Cow, Ker, Doll a fifth. Lidwell, Si Dedalus, Bob Cowley, Kernan and Big Ben Dollard.

Tap. A youth entered a lonely Ormond hall.

Bloom viewed a gallant pictured hero in Lionel Marks's window. Robert Emmet's last words. Seven last words. Of Meyerbeer that is.

— True men like you men.

— Ay, ay, Ben.

— Will lift your glass with us.

They lifted.

Tschink. Tschunk.

Tip. An unseeing stripling stood in the door. He saw not bronze. He saw not gold. Nor Ben nor Bob nor Tom nor Si nor George nor tanks nor Richie nor Pat. Hee hee hee hee. He did not see.

Seabloom, greaseabloom, viewed last words. Softly. *When my country takes her place among.*

Prrprr.

Must be the bur.

Fff. Oo. Rrpr.

Nations of the earth. No one behind. She's passed. *Then and not till then.*
Tram. Kran, kran, kran. Good oppor. Coming. Krandlkrankran. I'm sure
it's the burgund. Yes. One, two. *Let my epitaph be.* Kraaaaaa. *Written. I
have.*

Pprrpffrrppffff.

Done.

I was just passing the time of day with old Troy of the D.M.P. at the corner of Arbour Hill there and be damned but a bloody sweep came along and he near drove his gear into my eye. I turned around to let him have the weight of my tongue when who should I see dodging along Stoneybatter only Joe Hynes.

— 'Lo, Joe, says I. How are you blowing? Did you see that bloody chimney sweep near shove my eye out with his brush?

— Soot's luck, says Joe. Who's the old ballocks you were talking to?

— Old Troy, says I, was in the force. I'm on two minds not to give that fellow in charge for obstructing the thoroughfare with his brooms and ladders.

— What are you doing round those parts? says Joe.

— Devil a much, says I. There's a bloody big foxy thief beyond by the Garrison Church at the corner of Chicken Lane, old Troy was just giving me a wrinkle about him, lifted any God's quantity of tea and sugar to pay three bob a week, said he had a farm in the county Down, off a hop-of-my-thumb by the name of Moses Herzog over there near Heytesbury Street.

— Circumcised? says Joe.

— Ay, says I. A bit off the top. An old plumber named Geraghty. I'm hanging on to his taw now for the past fortnight and I can't get a penny out of him.

— That the lay you're on now? says Joe.

— Ay, says I. How are the mighty fallen! Collector of bad and doubtful debts. But that's the most notorious bloody robber you'd meet in a day's walk and the face on him all pockmarks would hold a shower of rain. *Tell him*, says he, *I dare him*, says he, *and I doubledare him to send you round here again or if he does*, says he, *I'll have him summonsed up before the court, so I will, for trading without a licence.* And he after stuffing himself till he's fit to burst! Jesus, I had to laugh at the little Jewy getting his shirt out. *He drink me my teas. He eat me my sugars. Because he no pay me my moneys?*

For nonperishable goods bought of Moses Herzog, of 13 Saint Kevin's

Parade in the city of Dublin, Wood Quay ward, merchant, hereinafter called the vendor, and sold and delivered to Michael E. Geraghty, Esquire, of 29 Arbour Hill in the city of Dublin, Arran Quay ward, gentleman, hereinafter called the purchaser, *videlicet* five pounds avoirdupois of first choice tea at three shillings and no pence per pound avoirdupois and three stone avoirdupois of sugar, crushed crystal, at threepence per pound avoirdupois, the said purchaser debtor to the said vendor of one pound five shillings and sixpence sterling for value received which amount shall be paid by said purchaser to said vendor in weekly instalments every seven calendar days of three shillings and no pence sterling: and the said nonperishable goods shall not be pawned or pledged or sold or otherwise alienated by the said purchaser but shall be and remain and be held to be the sole and exclusive property of the said vendor to be disposed of at his good will and pleasure until the said amount shall have been duly paid by the said purchaser to the said vendor in the manner herein set forth as this day hereby agreed between the said vendor, his heirs, successors, trustees and assigns of the one part and the said purchaser, his heirs, successors, trustees and assigns of the other part.

— Are you a strict t.t.? says Joe.

— Not taking anything between drinks, says I.

— What about paying our respects to our friend? says Joe.

— Who? says I. Sure, he's out in John of God's off his head, poor man.

— Drinking his own stuff? says Joe.

— Ay, says I. Whiskey and water on the brain.

— Come around to Barney Kiernan's, says Joe. I want to see the Citizen.

— Barney mavourneen's be it, says I. Anything strange or wonderful, Joe?

— Not a word, says Joe. I was up at that meeting in the City Arms.

— What was that, Joe? says I.

— Cattle traders, says Joe, about the foot-and-mouth disease. I want to give the Citizen the hard word about it.

So we went around by the Linen Hall Barracks and the back of the courthouse talking of one thing or another. Decent fellow Joe when he has it but sure like that he never has it. Jesus, I couldn't get over that bloody foxy Geraghty, the daylight robber. *For trading without a licence*, says he.

In Inisfail the fair there lies a land, the land of holy Michan. There rises a watchtower beheld of men afar. There sleep the mighty dead as in life they slept, warriors and princes of high renown. A pleasant land it is in sooth of murmuring waters: fishful streams where sport the gurnard, the plaice, the roach, the halibut, the gibbed haddock, the grilse, the dab, the brill, the flounder, the pollock, the mixed coarse fish generally and other denizens of the aqueous kingdom too numerous to be enumerated. In the mild breezes of the west and of the east the lofty trees wave in different directions their first-class foliage: the wafty sycamore, the Lebanonian cedar, the exalted plane tree, the eugenic eucalyptus and other ornaments of the arboreal world with which that region is thoroughly well supplied. Lovely maidens sit in close proximity to the roots of the lovely trees singing the most lovely songs while they play with all kinds of lovely objects as for example golden ingots, silvery fishes, crans of herrings, drafts of eels, codlings, creels of fingerlings, purple seagems and playful insects. And heroes voyage from afar to woo them: from Eblana to Slievemargy, the peerless princes of unfettered Munster and of Connacht the just and of smooth sleek Leinster and of Cruachan's land and of Armagh the splendid and of the noble district of Boyle, princes, the sons of kings.

And there rises a shining palace whose crystal glittering roof is seen by mariners who traverse the extensive sea in barks built expressly for that purpose: and thither come all herds and fatlings and first fruits of that land, for O'Connell Fitzsimon takes toll of them, a chieftain descended from chieftains. Thither the extremely large wains bring foison of the fields: flaskets of cauliflowers and floats of spinach and pineapple chunks and Rangoon beans and strikes of tomatoes and drums of figs and drills of Swedes and spherical potatoes and tallies of iridescent kale, York and Savoy, and trays of onions, pearls of the earth, and punnets of mushrooms and custard marrows and fat vetches and bere and rape and red green yellow brown russet sweet big bitter ripe pomellated apples and chips of strawberries and sieves of gooseberries, pulpy and pelurious, and strawberries fit for princes and raspberries from their canes.

I dare him, says he, *and I doubledare him.* Come out here, Geraghty, you notorious bloody hill and dale robber!

And by that way wend the herds innumerable of bellwethers and flushed ewes and shearling rams and lambs and stubble geese and medium steers and roaring mares and polled calves and longwools and store sheep and Cuffe's prime springers and culls and sowpigs and baconhogs and the various different varieties of highly distinguished swine and Angus heifers and polly bullocks of immaculate pedigree together with prime premiated milch cows and beeves, and there is ever

281

heard a trampling, cackling, roaring, lowing, bleating, bellowing, rumbling, grunting, champing and chewing of sheep and pigs and heavy-hooved kine from pasturelands of Lusk and Rush and Carrickmines and from the streamy vales of Thomond, from M'Gillicuddy's Reeks the inaccessible and lordly Shannon the unfathomable and from the gentle declivities of the place of the race of Kiar, their udders distended with superabundance of milk, and butts of butter and rennets of cheese and farmer's firkins and targets of lamb and crannocks of corn and oblong eggs in great hundreds, various in size, the agate with the dun.

So we turned into Barney Kiernan's and there, sure enough, was the Citizen up in the corner having a great confab with himself and that bloody mangy mongrel, Garryowen, and he waiting for what the sky would drop in the way of drink.

— There he is, says I, in his glory hole, with his cruiskeen lawn and his load of papers, working for the cause.

The bloody mongrel let a grouse out of him would give you the creeps. Be a corporal work of mercy if someone would take the life of that bloody dog. I'm told for a fact he ate a good part of the breeches off a constabulary man in Santry that came round one time with a blue paper about a licence.

— Stand and deliver, says he.

— That's all right, Citizen, says Joe. Friends here.

— Pass, friends, says he.

Then he rubs his hand in his eye and says he:

— What's your opinion of the times?

Doing the rapparee and Rory of the Hill. But, begob, Joe was equal to the occasion.

— I think the markets are on a rise, says he, sliding his hand down his fork.

So begob the Citizen claps his paw on his knee and he says:

— Foreign wars is the cause of it.

And says Joe, sticking his thumb in his pocket:

— It's the Russians wish to tyrannise.

— Arrah, give over your bloody codding, Joe, says I. I've a thirst on me I wouldn't sell for half a crown.

— Give it a name, Citizen, says Joe.

— Wine of the country, says he.

— What's yours? says Joe.

— Ditto MacAnaspey, says I.

— Three pints, Terry, says Joe. And how's the old heart, Citizen? says he.

— Never better, *a chara*, says he. What, Garry? Are we going to win? Eh?

And with that he took the bloody old towser by the scruff of the neck and, by Jesus, he near throttled him.

The figure seated on a large boulder at the foot of a round tower was that of a broadshouldered deepchested stronglimbed frankeyed redhaired freelyfreckled shaggybearded widemouthed largenosed longheaded deepvoiced barekneed brawnyhanded hairylegged ruddyfaced sinewy-armed hero. From shoulder to shoulder he measured several ells and his rocklike mountainous knees were covered, as was likewise the rest of his body wherever visible, with a strong growth of tawny prickly hair in hue and toughness similar to the mountain gorse (*Ulex europeus*). The wide-winged nostrils, from which bristles of the same tawny hue projected, were of such capaciousness that within their cavernous obscurity the field lark might easily have lodged her nest. The eyes in which a tear and a smile strove ever for the mastery were of the dimensions of a good-sized cauliflower. A powerful current of warm breath issued at regular intervals from the profound cavity of his mouth while in rhythmic resonance the loud strong hale reverberations of his formidable heart thundered rum-blingly, causing the ground, the summit of the lofty tower and the still loftier walls of the cave to vibrate and tremble.

He wore a long unsleeved garment of recently flayed oxhide reaching to the knees in a loose kilt and this was bound about his middle by a girdle of plaited straw and rushes. Beneath this he wore trews of deerskin roughly stitched with gut. His nether extremities were encased in high Balbriggan buskins dyed in lichen purple, the feet being shod with brogues of salted cowhide laced with the windpipe of the same beast. From his girdle hung a row of sea stones which jangled at every movement of his portentous frame and on these were graven with rude yet striking art the tribal images of many Irish heroes and heroines of antiquity: Cuchulain, Conn of the Hundred Battles, Niall of the Nine Hostages, Brian of Kincora, the *Árd Rí* Malachi, Art MacMurrough, Shane O'Neill, Father John Murphy, Owen Roe, Patrick Sarsfield, Red Hugh O'Donnell, Red Jim MacDermott, Soggarth Eoghan O'Growney, Michael Dwyer, Francy Higgins, Henry Joy M'Cracken, Goliath, Horace Wheatley, Thomas Conneff, Peg Woffington, the Village Blacksmith, Captain Moon-light, Captain Boycott, Dante Alighieri, Christopher Columbus, S. Fursa,

S. Brendan, Marshal MacMahon, Charlemagne, Theobald Wolfe Tone, the Mother of the Maccabees, the Last of the Mohicans, the Rose of Castile, the Man for Galway, the Man that Broke the Bank at Monte Carlo, the Man in the Gap, the Woman Who Didn't, Benjamin Franklin, Napoleon Bonaparte, John L. Sullivan, Cleopatra, Savourneen Deelish, Julius Caesar, Paracelsus, Sir Thomas Lipton, William Tell, Michelangelo Hayes, Mohammed, the Bride of Lammermoor, Peter the Hermit, Peter the Packer, Dark Rosaleen, Patrick W. Shakespeare, Brian Confucius, Murtagh Gutenberg, Patricio Velasquez, Captain Nemo, Tristan and Isolde, the first Prince of Wales, Thomas Cook and Son, the Bold Soldier Boy, Arrah na Pogue, Dick Turpin, Ludwig Beethoven, the Colleen Bawn, Waddler Healy, Angus the Culdee, Dolly Mount, Sidney Parade, Ben Howth, Valentine Greatrakes, Adam and Eve, Arthur Wellesley, Boss Croker, Herodotus, Jack the Giantkiller, Gautama Buddha, Lady Godiva, the Lily of Killarney, Balor of the Evil Eye, the Queen of Sheba, Acky Nagle, Joe Nagle, Alessandro Volta, Jeremiah O'Donovan Rossa and Don Philip O'Sullivan Beare. A couched spear of acuminated granite rested by him while at his feet reposed a savage animal of the canine tribe whose stertorous gasps announced that he was sunk in uneasy slumber, a supposition confirmed by hoarse growls and spasmodic movements which his master repressed from time to time by tranquilising blows of a mighty cudgel rudely fashioned out of paleolithic stone.

So anyhow Terry brought the three pints Joe was standing and begob the sight nearly left my eyes when I saw him land out a quid. O, as true as I'm telling you. A good-looking sovereign.

— And there's more where that came from, says he.

— Were you robbing the poorbox, Joe? says I.

— Sweat of my brow, says Joe. 'Twas the prudent member gave me the wheeze.

— I saw him before I met you, says I, sloping around by Pill Lane and Greek Street with his cod's eye counting up all the guts of the fish.

Who comes through Michan's land, bedight in sable armour? O'Bloom, the son of Rory: it is he. Impervious to fear is Rory's son: he of the prudent soul.

— For the old woman of Prince's Street, says the Citizen, the subsidised organ. The pledge-bound party on the floor of the House. And look at this blasted rag, says he. Look at this, says he. *The Irish Independent*, if you please, founded by Parnell to be the workingman's friend. Listen to the births and deaths in the *Irish all for Ireland Independent*, and I'll thank you, and the marriages.

And he starts reading them out:

— Gordon, Barnfield Crescent, Exeter; Redmayne of Iffley, Saint Anne's on Sea, the wife of William T. Redmayne, of a son. How's that, eh? Wright and Flint, Vincent and Gillett to Rotha Marion daughter of Rosa and the late George Alfred Gillett, 179 Clapham Road, Stockwell, Haywood and Ridsdale at Saint Jude's, Kensington, by the Very Reverend Dr Forrest, dean of Worcester. Eh? Deaths. Bristow, at Whitehorse Lane, London: Cann, Stoke Newington, of gastritis and heart disease: Cockburn, at the Moat House, Chepstow . . .

— I know that fellow, says Joe, from bitter experience.

— Cockburn. Dimsey, wife of David Dimsey, late of the Admiralty: Miller, Tottenham, aged eighty-five: Welsh, June 12, at 35 Canning Street, Liverpool, Isabella Helen. How's that for a national press, eh, my brown son! How's that for Martin Murphy, the Bantry jobber!

— Ah, well, says Joe, handing round the booze. Thanks be to God they had the start of us. Drink that, Citizen.

— I will, says he, honourable person.

— Health, Joe, says I. And all down the form.

Ah! Ow! Don't be talking! I was blue mouldy for the want of that pint. Declare to God I could hear it hit the pit of my stomach with a click.

And lo, as they quaffed their cup of joy, a godlike messenger came swiftly in, radiant as the eye of heaven, a comely youth, and behind him there passed an elder of noble gait and countenance bearing the sacred scrolls of law and with him his lady wife, a dame of peerless lineage, fairest of her race.

Little Alf Bergan popped in round the door and hid behind Barney's snug, squeezed up with the laughing. And who was sitting up there in the corner that I hadn't seen, snoring drunk, blind to the world, only Bob Doran. I didn't know what was up and Alf kept making signs out of the door. And begob what was it only that bloody old pantaloon Denis Breen in his bath slippers with two bloody big books tucked under his oxter and the wife hotfoot after him, unfortunate wretched woman, trotting like a poodle. I thought Alf would split.

— Look at him, says he. Breen. He's traipsing all round Dublin with a postcard someone sent him with U.P: up on it to take a li . . .

And he doubled up.

— Take a what? says I.

— Libel action, says he, for ten thousand pounds.

— O hell! says I.

The bloody mongrel began to growl that'd put the fear of God in you seeing something was up but the Citizen gave him a kick in the ribs.

— *Bi i do thost*, says he.

— Who? says Joe.

— Breen, says Alf. He was in John Henry Menton's and then he went round to Collis and Ward's and then Tom Rochford met him and sent him round to the subsheriff's for a lark. O God, I've a pain laughing. U.P: up. The long fellow gave him an eye as good as a process and now the bloody old lunatic is gone round to Green Street to look for a G-man.

— When is Long John going to hang that fellow in Mountjoy? says Joe.

— Bergan, says Bob Doran, waking up. Is that Alf Bergan?

— Yes, says Alf. Hanging? Wait till I show you. Here, Terry, give us a pony. That bloody old fool! Ten thousand pounds. You should have seen Long John's eye. U.P...

And he started laughing.

— Who are you laughing at? says Bob Doran. Is that Bergan?

— Hurry up, Terry boy, says Alf.

Terence O'Ryan heard him and straightway brought him a crystal cup full of the foamy ebon ale which the noble twin brothers Bung Iveagh and Bung Ardilaun brew ever in their divine ale-vats, cunning as the sons of deathless Leda. For they garner the succulent berries of the hop, and mass and sift and bruise and brew them, and they mix therewith sour juices and bring the must to the sacred fire and cease not night or day from their toil, those cunning brothers, lords of the vat.

Then did you, chivalrous Terence, hand forth, as to the manner born, that nectarous beverage and you offered the crystal cup to him that thirsted, the soul of chivalry, in beauty akin to the immortals.

But he, the young chief of the O'Bergan's, could ill brook to be outdone in generous deeds but gave therefor with gracious gesture a testoon of costliest bronze. Thereon embossed in excellent smithwork was seen the image of a queen of regal port, scion of the House of Brunswick, Victoria her name, Her Most Excellent Majesty, by grace of God of the United Kingdom of Great Britain and Ireland and of the British dominions beyond the sea queen, defender of the faith, empress of India, even she, who bore rule, a victress over many peoples, the well beloved, for they knew and loved her from the rising of the sun to the going down thereof, the pale, the dark, the ruddy and the ethiop.

— What's that bloody freemason doing, says the Citizen, prowling up and down outside?

— What's that? says Joe.

— Here you are, says Alf, chucking out the rhino. Talking about hanging, I'll show you something you never saw. Hangmen's letters. Look at here.

So he took a bundle of wisps of letters and envelopes out of his pocket.

— Are you codding? says I.

— Honest injun, says Alf. Read them.

So Joe took up the letters.

— Who were you laughing at? says Bob Doran.

So I saw there was going to be a bit of a dust-up, Bob's a queer chap when the porter's in him, so says I just to make talk:

— How's Willy Murray those times, Alf?

— I don't know, says Alf. I saw him just now in Capel Street with Paddy Dignam. Only I was running after that . . .

— You what? says Joe, throwing down the letters. With who?

— With Dignam, says Alf.

— Is it Paddy? says Joe.

— Yes, says Alf. Why?

— Don't you know he's dead? says Joe.

— Paddy Dignam dead! says Alf.

— Ay, says Joe.

— Sure I'm after seeing him not five minutes ago, says Alf, as plain as a pikestaff.

— Who's dead? says Bob Doran.

— You saw his ghost then, says Joe, God between us and harm.

— What? says Alf. Good Christ, only five . . . What? . . . And Willy Murray with him, the two of them there near what-do-you-call-him's . . . What? Dignam dead?

— What about Dignam? says Bob Doran. Who's talking about . . . ?

— Dead! says Alf. He's no more dead than you are.

— Maybe so, says Joe. They took the liberty of burying him this morning anyhow.

— Paddy? says Alf.

— Ay, says Joe. He paid the debt of nature, God be merciful to him.

– Good Christ! says Alf.

Begob he was what you might call flabbergasted.

In the darkness spirit hands were felt to flutter and when prayer by tantras had been directed to the proper quarter a faint but increasing luminosity of ruby light became gradually visible, the apparition of the etheric double being particularly lifelike owing to the discharge of jivic rays from the crown of the head and face. Communication was effected through the pituitary body and also by means of the orange-fiery and scarlet rays emanating respectively from the sacral region and solar plexus. Questioned by his earthname as to his whereabouts in the heavenworld, he stated that he was now on the path of prālāyā or return but was still submitted to trial at the hands of certain bloodthirsty entities on the lower astral levels. In reply to a question as to his first sensations in the great divide beyond he stated that previously he had seen as in a glass darkly but that those who had passed over had summit possibilities of atmic development opened up to them. Interrogated as to whether life there resembled our experience in the flesh, he stated that he had heard from more favoured beings now in the spirit that their abodes were equipped with every modern home comfort such as tālāfānā, ālāvātār, hātākāldā and wātāklāsāt and that the highest adepts were steeped in waves of volupcy of the very purest nature. He requested a quart of buttermilk and this was brought and evidently afforded relief. Asked if he had any message for the living, he exhorted all who were still at the wrong side of Māyā to acknowledge the true path for it was reported in devanic circles that Mars and Jupiter were out for mischief on the eastern angle where the Ram has power. It was then queried whether there were any special desires on the part of the defunct and the reply was: *We greet you, friends of earth, who are still in the body. Mind C.K. doesn't pile it on.* It was ascertained that the reference was to Mr Cornelius Kelleher, manager of Messrs H.J. O'Neill's popular funeral establishment, a personal friend of the defunct who had been responsible for the carrying out of the interment arrangements. Before departing he requested that it should be told to his dear son Patsy that the other boot which he had been looking for was at present under the commode in the return room and that the pair should be sent to Cullen's to be soled only as the heels were still good. He stated that this had greatly perturbed his peace of mind in the other region and earnestly requested that his desire should be made known. Assurances were given that the matter would be attended to and it was intimated that this had given satisfaction.

He is gone from mortal haunts: O'Dignam, sun of our morning. Fleet was his foot on the bracken: Patrick of the beamy brow. Wail, Banba, with your wind: and wail, O Ocean, with your whirlwind.

– There he is again, says the Citizen, staring out.

– Who? says I.

– Bloom, says he. He's on point duty up and down there for the last ten minutes.

And, begob, I saw his physog do a peep in and then slidder off again.

Little Alf was knocked bawways. Faith, he was.

– Good Christ! says he. I could have sworn it was him.

And says Bob Doran, with the hat on the back of his poll, lowest blackguard in Dublin when he's under the influence:

– Who said Christ is good?

– I beg your parsnips, says Alf.

– Is that a good Christ, says Bob Doran, to take away poor little Willy Dignam?

– Ah, well, says Alf, trying to pass it off. He's over all his troubles.

But Bob Doran shouts out of him:

– He's a bloody ruffian, I say, to take away poor little Willy Dignam.

Terry came down and tipped him the wink to keep quiet, that they didn't want that kind of talk in a respectable licensed premises. And Bob Doran starts doing the weeps about Paddy Dignam, true as you're there.

– The finest man, says he, snivelling, the finest, purest character.

The tear is bloody near your eye. Talking through his bloody hat. Fitter for him to go home to the little sleepwalking bitch he married, Mooney, the bumbailiff's daughter, mother kept a kip in Hardwicke Street, that used to be stravaging about the landings, Bantam Lyons told me that was stopping there, at two in the morning without a stitch on her, exposing her person, open to all comers, fair field and no favour.

– The noblest, the truest, says he. And he's gone, poor little Willy, poor little Paddy Dignam.

And mournful and with a heavy heart he bewept the extinction of that beam of heaven.

Old Garryowen started growling again at Bloom that was skeezing round the door.

– Come in, come on, says the Citizen. He won't eat you.

So Bloom slopes in with his cod's eye on the dog and he asks Terry was Martin Cunningham there.

— O Christ M'Keown, says Joe, reading one of the letters. Listen to this, will you?

And he starts reading out one:

> 7 Hunter Street,
> Liverpool.
>
> To the High Sheriff of Dublin,
> Dublin.
>
> Honoured sir i beg to offer my services in the abovementioned painful case i hanged Joe Gann in Bootle jail on the 12 of Febuary 1900 and i hanged...

— Show us, Joe, says I.

> ... private Arthur Chace for fowl murder of Jessie Tilsit in Pentonville prison and i was assistant when...

— Jesus, says I.

> ... Billington executed the awful murderer Toad Smith...

The Citizen made a grab at the letter.

— Hold hard, says Joe:

> ... i have a special nack of putting the noose once in he can't get out hoping to be favoured i remain, honoured sir, my terms is five ginnees.
>
> H. Rumbold,
> Master Barber.

— And a barbarous bloody barbarian he is too, says the Citizen.

— And the dirty scrawl of the wretch, says Joe. Here, says he, take them to hell out of my sight, Alf. Hello, Bloom, says he, what will you have?

So they started arguing about the point, Bloom saying he wouldn't and he couldn't and excuse him no offence and all to that and then he said well he'd just take a cigar. Gob, he's a prudent member and no mistake.

— Give us one of your prime stinkers, Terry, says Joe.

And Alf was telling us there was one chap sent in a mourning card with a black border round it.

— They're all barbers, says he, from the black country that would hang their own fathers for five quid down and travelling expenses.

And he was telling us there's two fellows waiting below to pull his heels down when he gets the drop and choke him properly and then they chop up the rope after and sell the bits for a few bob a skull.

In the dark land they bide: the vengeful knights of the razor. Their deadly coil they grasp: yea, and therein they lead to Erebus whatsoever wight hath done a deed of blood for I will in nowise suffer it even so saith the Lord.

So they started talking about capital punishment and of course Bloom comes out with the why and the wherefore and all the codology of the business and the old dog smelling him all the time, I'm told those Jewies does have a sort of a queer odour coming off them for dogs, about I don't know what, all deterrent effect and so forth and so on.

— There's one thing it hasn't a deterrent effect on, says Alf.

— What's that? says Joe.

— The poor bugger's tool that's being hanged, says Alf.

— That so? says Joe.

— God's truth, says Alf. I heard that from the head warder that was in Kilmainham when they hanged Joe Brady, the Invincible. He told me when they cut him down after the drop it was standing up in their faces like a poker.

— Ruling passion strong in death, says Joe, as someone said.

— That can be explained by science, says Bloom. It's only a natural phenomenon, don't you see, because on account of the ...

And then he starts with his jawbreakers about phenomenon and science and this phenomenon and the other phenomenon.

The distinguished scientist Herr Professor Luitpold Blumenduft tendered medical evidence to the effect that the instantaneous fracture of the cervical vertebrae and consequent scission of the spinal cord would, according to the best approved tradition of medical science, be calculated to inevitably produce in the human subject a violent ganglionic stimulus of the nerve centres of the genital apparatus, thereby causing the elastic pores of the *corpora cavernosa* to rapidly dilate in such a way as to instantaneously facilitate the flow of blood to that part of the human anatomy known as the penis or male organ, resulting in the phenomenon which has been denominated by the faculty a morbid upwards and outwards philoprogenitive erection *in articulo mortis per diminutionem capitis*.

So of course the Citizen was only waiting for the wink of the word and he starts gassing out of him about the Invincibles and the old guard and the men of sixty-seven and who fears to speak of ninety-eight and Joe with him about all the fellows that were hanged, drawn and transported for the cause by drumhead court-martial and a new Ireland and a new this, that and the other. Talking about new Ireland, he ought to go and get a new dog so he ought. Mangy ravenous brute sniffing and sneezing all round the place and scratching his scabs and round he goes to Bob Doran that was standing Alf a half one sucking up for what he could get. So of course Bob Doran starts doing the bloody fool with his:

— Give us the paw! Give the paw, doggy! Good old doggy! Give the paw here! Give us the paw!

Arrah, bloody end to the paw he'd paw and Alf trying to keep him from tumbling off the bloody stool atop of the bloody old dog and he talking all kinds of drivel about training by kindness and thoroughbred dog and intelligent dog: give you the bloody pip. Then he starts scraping a few bits of old biscuit out of the bottom of a Jacobs tin he told Terry to bring. Gob, he golloped it down like old boots and his tongue hanging out of him a yard long for more. Near ate the tin and all, hungry bloody mongrel.

And the Citizen and Bloom having an argument about the point, the brothers Sheares and Wolfe Tone beyond on Arbour Hill and Robert Emmet and die for your country, the Tommy Moore touch about Sara Curran and she's far from the land. And Bloom, of course, with his knock-me-down cigar putting on swank with his lardy face. Phenomenon! The fat heap he married is a nice old phenomenon with a back on her like a ball alley. Time they were stopping up in the City Arms, Pisser Burke told me, there was an old one there with a cracked loodheramaun of a nephew and Bloom trying to get on the soft side of her doing the mollycoddle playing bezique to come in for a bit of the wampum in her will and not eating meat of a Friday, because the old one was always thumping her craw, and taking the lout out for a walk. And one time he led him the rounds of Dublin and, by the holy farmer, he never cried crack till he brought him home as drunk as a boiled owl and he said he did it to teach him the evils of alcohol. And, by herrings, if the three women didn't near roast him it's a queer story, the old one, Bloom's wife and Mrs O'Dowd that kept the hotel. Jesus, I had to laugh at Pisser Burke taking them off chewing the fat. And Bloom with his *but don't you see?* and *but on the other hand.* And sure, more be token, the lout I'm told was in Power's after, the blender's, round in Cope Street, going home footless in a cab five times in the week after drinking his way through all the samples in the bloody establishment. Phenomenon!

— The memory of the dead, says the Citizen, taking up his pintglass and glaring at Bloom.

— Ay, ay, says Joe.

— You don't grasp my point, says Bloom. What I mean is . . .

— *Sinn féin!* says the Citizen. *Sinn féin amháin!* The friends we love are by our side and the foes we hate before us.

The last farewell was affecting in the extreme. From the belfries far and near the funereal death-bell tolled unceasingly, while all around the gloomy precincts rolled the ominous warning of a hundred muffled drums punctuated by the hollow booming of pieces of ordnance. The deafening claps of thunder and the dazzling flashes of lightning which lit up the ghastly scene testified that the artillery of heaven had lent its supernatural pomp to the already gruesome spectacle. A torrential rain poured down from the floodgates of the angry heavens upon the bared heads of the assembled multitude which numbered at the lowest computation five hundred thousand persons. A posse of Dublin Metropolitan Police superintended by the chief commissioner in person maintained order in the vast throng for whom the York Street Brass and Reed Band whiled away the intervening time by admirably rendering on their black-draped instruments the matchless melody endeared to us from the cradle by Speranza's plaintive muse. Special quick excursion trains and upholstered charabancs had been provided for the comfort of our country cousins of whom there were large contingents. Considerable amusement was caused by the favourite Dublin streetsingers L-n-h-n and M-ll-g-n who sang *The Night before Larry was Stretched* in their usual mirth-provoking fashion. Our two inimitable drolls did a roaring trade with their broadsheets among lovers of the comedy element and nobody who has a corner in his heart for real Irish fun without vulgarity will grudge them their hard-earned pennies. The children of the Male and Female Foundling Hospital who thronged the windows overlooking the scene were delighted with this unexpected addition to the day's entertainment and a word of praise is due to the Little Sisters of the Poor for their excellent idea of affording the poor fatherless and motherless children a genuinely instructive treat. The viceregal house party which included many well-known ladies was chaperoned by Their Excellencies to the most favourable position on the grandstand, while the picturesque foreign delegation known as the Friends of the Emerald Isle was accommodated on a tribune directly opposite. The delegation, present in full force, consisted of Commendatore Bacibaci Beninobenone (the semiparalysed doyen of the party who had to be assisted to his seat by the aid of a powerful steam crane), Monsieur Pierrepaul Petitépatant, the Grandjoker Vladinmire Pokethankertscheff, the Archjoker Leopold Rudolph von Schwanzenbad-Hodenthaler, Countess Marha Virága Kisászony Putrápesthi, Hiram Y.

Bomboost, Count Athanatos Karamelopulos, Ali Baba Backsheesh Rahat Lokum Effendi, Señor Hidalgo Caballero Don Pecadillo y Palabras y Paternoster de la Malora de la Malaria, Hokopoko Harakiri, Hi Hung Chang, Olaf Kobberkeddelsen, Mynheer Trik van Trumps, Pan Poleaxe Paddyrisky, Goosepond Přhklštř Kratchinabritchisitch, Borus Hupinkoff, Herr Hurhausdirektorpräsident Hans Chuechli-Steuerli and National-gymnasiummuseumsanatoriumandsuspensoriumsordinaryprivatdocent-generalhistoryspecialprofessordoctor Kriegfried Überallgemein. All the delegates without exception expressed themselves in the strongest poss-ible heterogeneous terms concerning the nameless barbarity which they had been called upon to witness. An animated altercation (in which all took part) ensued among the F.O.T.E.I. as to whether the eighth or the ninth of March was the correct date of the birth of Ireland's patron saint. In the course of the argument cannonballs, scimitars, boomerangs, blun-derbusses, stinkpots, meatchoppers, umbrellas, catapults, knuckledusters, sandbags and lumps of pig iron were resorted to and blows were freely exchanged. The baby policeman, Constable MacFadden, summoned by special courier from Booterstown, quickly restored order and with light-ning promptitude proposed the seventeenth of the month as a solution equally honourable for both contending parties. The ready-witted nine-footer's suggestion at once appealed to all and was unanimously accepted. Constable MacFadden was heartily congratulated by all the F.O.T.E.I., several of whom were bleeding profusely. Commendatore Beninobenone having been extricated from underneath the presidential armchair, it was explained by his legal adviser Avvocato Pagamimi that the various articles secreted in his thirty-two pockets had been abstracted by him during the affray from the pockets of his junior colleagues in the hope of bringing them to their senses. The objects (which included several hundred ladies' and gentlemen's gold and silver watches) were promptly restored to their rightful owners and general harmony reigned supreme.

Quietly, unassumingly, Rumbold stepped on to the scaffold in faultless morning dress and wearing his favourite flower, the *Gladiolus cruentus*. He announced his presence by that gentle Rumboldian cough which so many have tried (unsuccessfully) to imitate – short, painstaking, yet withal so characteristic of the man. The arrival of the world-renowned headsman was greeted by a roar of acclamation from the huge concourse, the viceregal ladies waving their handkerchiefs in their excitement while the even more excitable foreign delegates cheered vociferously in a medley of cries, *hoch, banzai, eljen, zivio, chinchin, polla kronia, hip hip, vive, Allah,* amid which the ringing *evviva* of the delegate of the land of song (a high double F recalling those piercingly lovely notes with which the eunuch Catalani beglamoured our great-great-grandmothers) was easily distinguishable. It was exactly seventeen o'clock. The signal for prayer was then promptly given by megaphone and in an instant all heads were bared, the commendatore's patriarchal sombrero, which has been in the possession of his family since the revolution of Rienzi, being removed by his medical adviser in attendance, Dr Pippi. The learned prelate who administered the last comforts of holy religion to the hero martyr when about to pay the death penalty knelt in a most Christian spirit in a pool of rainwater, his cassock above his hoary head, and offered up to the throne of grace fervent prayers of supplication. Hard by the block stood the grim figure of the executioner, his visage being concealed in a ten-gallon pot with two circular perforated apertures through which his eyes glowered furiously. As he awaited the fatal signal he tested the edge of his horrible weapon by honing it upon his brawny forearm and decapitated in rapid succession a flock of sheep which had been provided by the admirers of his fell but necessary office. On a handsome mahogany table near him were neatly arranged the quartering knife, the various finely tempered disembowelling appliances (specially supplied by the world-famous firm of cutlers, Messrs John Round and Sons, Sheffield), a terracotta saucepan for the reception of the duodenum, colon, blind intestine and appendix etc. when successfully extracted and two commodious milkjugs destined to receive the most precious blood of the most precious victim. The house steward of the Amalgamated Cats' and Dogs' Home was in attendance to convey these vessels when replenished to that beneficent institution. Quite an excellent repast consisting of rashers and eggs, fried steak and onions done to a nicety, delicious hot breakfast rolls and invigorating tea had been considerately provided by the authorities for the consumption of the central figure of the tragedy who was in capital spirits when prepared for death and evinced the keenest interest in the proceedings from beginning to end. But he, with an abnegation rare in these our times, rose nobly to the occasion and expressed the dying wish (immediately acceded to) that the meal should be divided in aliquot parts among the members of the Sick and Indigent Roomkeepers' Society as a token of his regard and esteem. The *nec* and *non plus ultra* of emotion were reached when the blushing bride-elect burst her way through the serried ranks of the bystanders and flung herself upon the muscular bosom of him who was about to be launched into eternity for her sake. The hero folded her willowy form in a loving embrace, murmuring fondly *Sheila, my own.* Encouraged by this use of her Christian name she kissed passionately all the various suitable areas of his person which the decencies of prison garb permitted her ardour to reach. She swore to him as they mingled the salt streams of their tears that she would ever cherish his memory, that she would never forget her hero boy who went to his death with a song on his lips as if he were but going to a hurling match in Clonturk Park. She brought back to his recollection the happy days of blissful childhood together on the banks of Anna Liffey when they had indulged in the innocent pastimes of the young and, oblivious of the dreadful present, they both laughed heartily, all the spectators, including the venerable pastor, joining in the general merriment. That monster audience simply rocked with delight. But anon they were overcome with grief and clasped their hands for the last time. A fresh torrent of tears burst from their lachrymal ducts and the vast concourse of people, touched to the inmost core, broke into heartrending sobs, not the least affected being the aged prebendary himself. Big strong men, officers of the peace and genial giants of the Royal Irish Constabulary, were making frank use of their handkerchiefs, and it is safe to say that there was not a dry eye in that record assemblage. A most romantic incident occurred when a handsome young Oxford graduate, noted for his chivalry towards the fair sex, stepped forward and, presenting his visiting card, bankbook and genealogical tree, solicited the hand of the hapless young lady, requesting her to name the day, and was accepted on the spot. Every lady in the audience was presented with a tasteful souvenir of the occasion in the shape of a skull-and-crossbones brooch, a timely and generous act which evoked a fresh outburst of emotion: and when the gallant young Oxonian (the bearer, by the way, of one of the most time-honoured names in Albion's history) placed on the finger of his blushing fiancée an expensive engagement ring with emeralds set in the form of a four-leaved shamrock the excitement knew no bounds. Nay, even the stern provost marshal, Lieutenant Colonel Tomkin-Maxwell ffrenchmullan Tomlinson, who presided on the sad occasion, he who had blown a considerable number of sepoys from the cannon mouth without flinching, could not now restrain his natural emotion. With his mailed gauntlet he brushed away a furtive tear and was overheard by those privileged burghers who happened to be in his immediate entourage to murmur to himself in a faltering undertone:

— God blimey if she ain't a clinker, that there bleeding tart. Blimey it makes me kind of bleeding cry, straight it does, when I sees her, cause I thinks of my old mashtub what's waiting for me down Limehouse way.

So then the Citizen begins talking about the Irish language and the Corporation meeting and all to that and the shoneens that can't speak their own language and Joe chipping in because he stuck someone for a quid and Bloom putting in his old goo with his twopenny stump that he cadged off of Joe and talking about the Gaelic League and the antitreating league and drink, the curse of Ireland. Antitreating is about the size of it. Gob, he'd let you pour all manner of drink down his throat till the Lord would call him before you'd ever see the froth of his pint. And one night I went in with a fellow into one of their musical evenings, song and dance about *she could get up on a truss of hay she could my Maureen Lay* and there was a fellow with a Ballyhooly blue-ribbon badge spiffing out of him in Irish and a lot of colleen bawns going about with temperance beverages and selling medals and oranges and lemonade and a few old dry buns, gob, flahoolagh entertainment, don't be talking. Ireland sober is Ireland free. And then an old fellow starts blowing into his bagpipes and all the gougers shuffling their feet to the tune the old cow died of. And one or two sky pilots having an eye around that there was no goings on with the females, hitting below the belt.

So howandever, as I was saying, the old dog seeing the tin was empty starts mousing around by Joe and me. I'd train him by kindness, so I would, if he was my dog. Give him a rousing fine kick now and again where it wouldn't blind him.

— Afraid he'll bite you? says the Citizen, jeering.

— No, says I. But he might take my leg for a lamppost.

So he calls the old dog over.

— What's on you, Garry? says he.

Then he starts hauling and mauling and talking to him in Irish and the old towser growling, letting on to answer, like a duet in the opera. Such growling you never heard as they let off between them. Someone that has nothing better to do ought to write a letter *pro bono publico* to the papers about the muzzling order for a dog the like of that. Growling and grousing and his eye all bloodshot from the drouth is in it and the hydrophobia dropping out of his jaws.

All those who are interested in the spread of human culture among the lower animals (and their name is legion) should make a point of not missing the really marvellous exhibition of cynanthropy given by the famous old Irish red setter wolfdog formerly known by the sobriquet of

Garryowen and recently rechristened by his large circle of friends and acquaintances Owen Garry. The exhibition, which is the result of years of training by kindness and a carefully thought-out dietary system, comprises, among other achievements, the recitation of verse. Our greatest living phonetic expert (wild horses shall not drag it from us!) has left no stone unturned in his efforts to delucidate and compare the verse recited and has found it bears a *striking* resemblance (the italics are ours) to the ranns of ancient Celtic bards. We are not speaking so much of those delightful love songs with which the writer who conceals his identity under the graceful pseudonym of The Little Sweet Branch has familiarised the book-loving world but rather (as a contributor D.O.C. points out in an interesting communication published by an evening contemporary) of the harsher and more personal note which is found in the satirical effusions of the famous Raftery and of Donal MacConsidine, to say nothing of a more modern lyrist at present very much in the public eye. We subjoin a specimen which has been rendered into English by an eminent scholar whose name for the moment we are not at liberty to disclose, though we believe that our readers will find the topical allusion rather more than an indication. The metrical system of the canine original, which recalls the intricate alliterative and isosyllabic rules of the Welsh englyn, is infinitely more complicated, but we believe our readers will agree that the spirit has been well caught. Perhaps it should be added that the effect is greatly increased if Owen's verse be spoken somewhat slowly and indistinctly in a tone suggestive of suppressed rancour.

> *The curse of my curses*
> *Seven days every day*
> *And seven dry Thursdays*
> *On you, Barney Kiernan,*
> *Has no sup of water*
> *To cool my courage,*
> *And my guts red roaring*
> *After Lowrey's lights.*

So he told Terry to bring some water for the dog and, gob, you could hear him lapping it up a mile off. And Joe asked him would he have another.

— I will, says he, *a chara*, to show there's no ill feeling.

Gob, he's not as green as he's cabbage-looking. Arsing around from one pub to another, leaving it to your own honour, with old Giltrap's dog and getting fed up by the ratepayers and corporators. Entertainment for man and beast. And says Joe:

– Could you make a hole in another pint?

– Could a swim duck? says I.

– Same again, Terry, says Joe. Are you sure you won't have anything in the way of liquid refreshment? says he.

– Thank you, no, says Bloom. As a matter of fact I just wanted to meet Martin Cunningham, don't you see, about this insurance of poor Dignam's. Martin asked me to go to the house. You see, he, Dignam I mean, didn't serve any notice of the assignment on the company at the time and nominally under the Act the mortgagee can't recover on the policy.

– Holy Wars, says Joe, laughing, that's a good one if old Shylock is landed. So the wife comes out top dog, what?

– Well, that's a point, says Bloom, for the wife's admirers.

– Whose admirers? says Joe.

– The wife's advisers, I mean, says Bloom.

Then he starts all confused mucking it up about the mortgagor under the Act like the lord chancellor giving it out on the bench and for the benefit of the wife and that a trust is created but on the other hand that Dignam owed Bridgeman the money and if now the wife or the widow contested the mortgagee's right till he near had the head of me addled with his mortgagor under the Act. He was bloody safe he wasn't run in himself under the Act that time as a rogue and vagabond only he had a friend in court. Selling bazaar tickets or what do you call it Royal Hungarian Privileged Lottery. True as you're there. O, commend me to an Israelite! Royal and Privileged Hungarian robbery.

So Bob Doran comes lurching around asking Bloom to tell Mrs Dignam he was sorry for her trouble and he was very sorry about the funeral and to tell her that he said and everyone who knew him said that there was never a truer, a finer than poor little Willy that's dead, to tell her. Choking with bloody foolery. And shaking Bloom's hand doing the tragic to tell her that. Shake hands, brother. You're a rogue and I'm another.

– Let me, said he, so far presume upon our acquaintance which, however slight it may appear if judged by the standard of mere time, is founded, as I hope and believe, on a sentiment of mutual esteem as to request of you this favour. But should I have overstepped the limits of reserve let the sincerity of my feelings be the excuse for my boldness.

– No, rejoined the other. I appreciate to the full the motives which actuate your conduct and I shall discharge the office you entrust to me consoled by the reflection that, though the errand be one of sorrow, this proof of your confidence sweetens in some measure the bitterness of the cup.

– Then suffer me to take your hand, said he. The goodness of your heart, I feel sure, will dictate to you better than my inadequate words the expressions which are most suitable to convey an emotion whose poignancy, were I to give vent to my feelings, would deprive me even of speech.

And off with him and out trying to walk straight. Boozed at five o'clock. Night he was near being lagged only Paddy Leonard knew the bobby, 14A. Blind to the world in a shebeen up in Bride Street after closing time fornicating with two shawls and a bully on guard and drinking porter out of teacups. And calling himself a Frenchy for the shawls, Joseph Manuo, and talking against the Catholic religion, and he serving mass in Adam and Eve's when he was young with his eyes shut, *who wrote the New Testament and the Old Testament*, and hugging and smugging. And the two shawls killed with the laughing, picking his pockets, the bloody fool, and he spilling the porter all over the bed and the two shawls screeching laughing at one another. *How is your testament? Have you got an old testament?* Only Paddy was passing there, I tell you what. Then see him of a Sunday with his little concubine of a wife and she wagging her tail up the aisle of the chapel with her patent boots on her, no less, and her violets, nice as pie, doing the little lady. Jack Mooney's sister. And the old prostitute of a mother procuring rooms to street couples. Gob, Jack made him toe the line. Told him if he didn't patch up the pot, Jesus, he'd kick the shite out of him.

So Terry brought the three pints.

– Here, says Joe, doing the honours. Here, Citizen.

– *Slán leat*, says he.

– Fortune, Joe, says I. Good health, Citizen.

Gob, he had his mouth halfway down the tumbler already. Want a small fortune to keep him in drinks.

– Who is the long fellow running for the mayoralty, Alf? says Joe.

– Friend of yours, says Alf.

– Nannan? says Joe. The mimber?

– I won't mention any names, says Alf.

– I thought so, says Joe. I saw him up at that meeting now with William Field M.P., the cattle traders.

– Hairy Iopas, says the Citizen, that exploded volcano, the darling of all countries and the idol of his own.

So Joe starts telling the Citizen about the foot-and-mouth disease and the cattle traders and taking action in the matter and the Citizen sending them all to the rightabout and Bloom coming out with his sheep-dip for the scab and a hoose drench for coughing calves and the guaranteed remedy for timber tongue. Because he was up one time in a knacker's yard. Walking about with his book and pencil, here's my head and my heels are coming, till Joe Cuffe gave him the order of the boot for giving lip to a grazier. Mister Knowall. Teach your grandmother how to milk ducks. Pisser Burke was telling me in the hotel the wife used to be in rivers of tears sometimes with Mrs O'Dowd crying her eyes out with her eight inches of fat all over her. Couldn't loosen her farting strings but old cod's eye was waltzing around her showing her how to do it. What's your programme today? Ay. Humane methods. Because the poor animals suffer and experts say and the best known remedy that doesn't cause pain to the animal and on the sore spot administer gently. Gob, he'd have a soft hand under a hen.

Ga ga gara. Klook klook klook. Black Liz is our hen. She lays eggs for us. When she lays her egg she is so glad. Gara. Klook klook klook. Then comes good uncle Leo. He puts his hand under Black Liz and takes her fresh egg. Ga ga ga ga gara. Klook klook klook.

– Anyhow, says Joe, Field and Nannetti are going over tonight to London to ask about it on the floor of the House of Commons.

– Are you sure, says Bloom, the councillor is going? I wanted to see him, as it happens.

– Well, he's going off by the mailboat, says Joe, tonight.

– That's too bad, says Bloom. I wanted particularly. Perhaps only Mr Field is going. I couldn't phone. No. You're sure?

– Nannan's going too, says Joe. The League told him to ask a question tomorrow about the commissioner of police forbidding Irish games in the park. What do you think of that, Citizen? The *Sluagh na hÉireann*.

Mr Cowe Conacre (*Multifarnham. Nat.*) – Arising out of the question of my honourable friend, the member for Shillelagh, may I ask the right honourable gentleman whether the government has issued orders that these animals shall be slaughtered though no medical evidence is forthcoming as to their pathological condition?

Mr Allfours (*Tamoshant. Con.*) – Honourable members are already in possession of the evidence produced before a committee of the whole

House. I feel I cannot usefully add anything to that. The answer to the honourable member's question is in the affirmative.

Mr Orelli O'Reilly (*Montenotte. Nat.*) – Have similar orders been issued for the slaughter of human animals who dare to play Irish games in the Phoenix Park?

Mr Allfours – The answer is in the negative.

Mr Cowe Conacre – Has the right honourable gentleman's famous Mitchelstown telegram inspired the policy of the gentlemen on the Treasury bench?

(*O! O!*)

Mr Allfours – I must have notice of that question.

Mr Staylewit (*Buncombe. Ind.*) – Don't hesitate to shoot.

(*Ironical opposition cheers.*)

The speaker – Order! Order!

(*The House rises. Cheers.*)

– There's the man, says Joe, that made the Gaelic sports revival. There he is sitting there. The man that got away James Stephens. The champion of all Ireland at putting the sixteen-pound shot. What was your best throw, Citizen?

– *Ná bac leis*, says the Citizen, letting on to be modest. There was a time I was as good as the next fellow anyhow.

– Put it there, Citizen, says Joe. You were, and a bloody sight better.

– Is that really a fact? says Alf.

– Yes, says Bloom. That's well known. Did you not know that?

So off they started about Irish sports and shoneen games the like of lawn tennis and about hurley and putting the stone and racy of the soil and building up a nation once again and all to that. And of course Bloom had to have his say too about if a fellow had a rower's heart violent exercise was bad. I declare to my antimacassar if you took up a straw from the bloody floor and if you said to Bloom, *Look at that, Bloom. Do you see that straw? That's a straw*, declare to my aunt he'd talk about it for an hour so he would and talk steady.

A most interesting discussion took place in the ancient hall of *Brian O'Ciarnaint's* in *Sráid na Breataine Bheag* under the auspices of *Sluagh na hÉireann* on the revival of ancient Gaelic sports and the importance of physical culture, as understood in ancient Greece and ancient Rome and ancient Ireland, for the development of the race. The venerable president of the noble order was in the chair and the attendance was of large dimensions. After an instructive discourse by the chairman, a magnificent oration eloquently and forcibly expressed, a most interesting and instructive discussion of the usual high standard of excellence ensued as to the desirability of the revivability of the ancient games and sports of our ancient Pan-Celtic forefathers. The well-known and highly respected worker in the cause of our old tongue, Mr Joseph M'Carthy Hynes, made an eloquent appeal for the resuscitation of the ancient Gaelic sports and pastimes, practised morning and evening by Finn MacCool, as calculated to revive the best traditions of manly strength and prowess handed down to us from ancient ages. L. Bloom who met with a mixed reception of applause and hisses having espoused the negative, the vocalist chairman brought the discussion to a close, in response to repeated requests and hearty plaudits from all parts of a bumper house, by a remarkably noteworthy rendering of the immortal Thomas Osborne Davis's evergreen verses (happily too familiar to need recalling here) *A Nation Once Again* in the execution of which the veteran patriot champion may be said without fear of contradiction to have fairly excelled himself. The Irish Caruso-Garibaldi was in superlative form and his stentorian notes were heard to the greatest advantage in the time-honoured anthem sung as only our Citizen can sing it. His superb high-class vocalism, which by its superquality greatly enhanced his already international reputation, was vociferously applauded by the large audience among which were to be noticed many prominent members of the clergy as well as representatives of the press and the bar and the other learned professions. The proceedings then terminated.

Amongst the clergy present were the Very Rev. William Delany S.J., Ll.D., the Rt. Rev. Monsignor Gerald Molloy D.D., the Rev. P.J. Kavanagh C.S.Sp., the Rev. T. Waters C.C., the Rev. John M. Ivers P.P., the Rev. P.J. Cleary O.S.F., the Very Rev. L.J. Hickey O.P., the Very Rev. Friar Nicholas O.S.F.C., the Very Rev. B. Gorman O.D.C., the Rev. T. Maher S.J., the Very Rev. James Murphy S.J., the Rev. John Lavery V.F., the Rev. William Doherty D.D., the Rev. Peter Fagan O.M., the Rev. T. Brangan O.S.A., the Rev. J. Flavin C.C., the Rev. M.A. Hackett P.P., the Rev. W. Hurley C.C., the Rt. Rev. Monsignor M. M'Manus V.G., the Rev. B.R. Slattery O.M.I., the Very Rev. M.D. Scally P.P., the Rev. T.F. Purcell O.P., the Very Rev. Timothy Canon Gorman P.P. and the Rev. J. Flanagan C.C. The laity included P. Fay, T. Quirke etc., etc.

— Talking about violent exercise, says Alf, were you at that Keogh-Bennett match?

— No, says Joe.

— I heard so-and-so made a cool hundred quid over it, says Alf.

— Who? Blazes? says Joe.

And says Bloom:

— What I meant about tennis, for example, is the agility and training the eye.

— Ay, Blazes, says Alf. He let out that Myler was on the beer to run up the odds and he swatting all the time.

— We know him, says the Citizen. The traitor's son. We know what put English gold in his pocket.

— True for you, says Joe.

And Bloom cuts in again about lawn tennis and the circulation of the blood, asking Alf:

— Now, don't you think, Bergan?

— Myler dusted the floor with him, says Alf. Heenan and Sayers was only a bloody fool to it. Handed him the father and mother of a beating. See the little kipper not up to his navel and the big fellow swiping. God, he gave him one last puck in the wind, Queensberry rules and all, made him puke what he never ate.

It was a historic and a hefty battle when Myler and Percy were scheduled to don the gloves for the purse of fifty sovereigns. Handicapped as he was by lack of poundage, Dublin's pet lamb made up for it by superlative skill in ringcraft. The final bout of fireworks was a gruelling for both champions. The welterweight sergeant major had tapped some lively claret in the previous mix-up during which Keogh had been receiver general of rights and lefts, the artilleryman putting in some neat work on the pet's nose, and Myler came on looking groggy. The soldier got to business, leading off with a powerful left jab to which the Irish gladiator retaliated by shooting out a stiff one flush to the point of Bennett's jaw. The redcoat ducked but the Dubliner lifted him with a left hook, the body punch being a fine one. The men came to handigrips. Myler quickly became busy and got his man under, the bout ending with the bulkier man on the ropes, Myler punishing him. The Englishman, whose right eye was nearly closed, took his corner where he was liberally drenched with water and when the bell went came on gamey and brimful of pluck, confident of knocking out the fistic Eblanite in jigtime. It was a fight to a finish and the best man for it. The two fought like tigers and excitement ran fever high. The referee twice cautioned Pucking Percy for holding but the pet was tricky and his footwork a treat to watch. After a brisk exchange of courtesies during which a smart uppercut of the military man brought blood freely from his opponent's mouth, the lamb suddenly waded in all over his man and landed a terrific left to Battling Bennett's stomach, flooring him flat. It was a knockout clean and clever. Amid tense expectation the Portobello bruiser was being counted out when Bennett's second Ole Pfotts Wettstein threw in the towel and the Santry boy was declared victor to the frenzied cheers of the public who broke through the ringropes and fairly mobbed him with delight.

— He knows which side his bread is buttered, says Alf. I hear he's running a concert tour now up in the north.

— He is, says Joe. Isn't he?

— Who? says Bloom. Ah, yes. That's quite true. Yes, a kind of summer tour, you see. Just a holiday.

— Mrs B. is the bright particular star, isn't she? says Joe.

— My wife? says Bloom. She's singing, yes. I think it will be a success too. He's an excellent man to organise. Excellent.

Hoho begob says I to myself, says I. That explains the milk in the coconut and absence of hair on the animal's chest. Blazes doing the tootle on the flute. Concert tour. Dirty Dan the dodger's son off Islandbridge that sold the same horses twice over to the government to fight the Boers. Old Whatwhat. I called about the poor and water rate, Mr Boylan. You what? The water rate, Mr Boylan. You whatwhat? That's the bucko that'll organise her, take my tip. 'Twixt me and you, Caddareesh.

Pride of Calpe's rocky mount, the raven-haired daughter of Tweedy: there grew she to peerless beauty where loquat and almond scent the air. The gardens of Alameda knew her step: the garths of olives knew and bowed. The chaste spouse of Leopold is she: Marion of the bountiful bosoms.

And lo, there entered one of the clan of the O'Molloys, a comely hero of white face yet withal somewhat ruddy, his majesty's counsel learned in the law, and with him the prince and heir of the noble line of Lambert.

— Hello, Ned.

— Hello, Alf.

— Hello, Jack.

— Hello, Joe.

— God save you, says the Citizen.

— Save you kindly, says J.J. What'll it be, Ned?

— Half one, says Ned.

So J.J. ordered the drinks.

— Were you round at the court? says Joe.

— Yes, says J.J. He'll square that, Ned, says he.

— Hope so, says Ned.

Now what were those two at? J.J. getting him off the grand jury list and the other give him a leg over the stile. With his name in Stubbs's. Playing cards, hobnobbing with flash toffs with a swank glass in their eye and drinking fizz and he half smothered in writs and garnishee orders. Pawning his gold watch in Cummins's of Francis Street where no one would know him in the private office when I was there with Pisser releasing his boots out of the pop. What's your name, sir? Dunne, says he. Ay, and done, says I. Gob, he'll come home by weeping cross one of those days, I'm thinking.

— Did you see that bloody lunatic Breen round there? says Alf. U.P: up.

— Yes, says J.J. Looking for a private detective.

— Ay, says Ned. And he wanted right go wrong to address the court only Corny Kelleher got round him telling him to get the handwriting examined first.

— Ten thousand pounds, says Alf, laughing. God, I'd give anything to hear him before a judge and jury.

— Was it you did it, Alf? says Joe. The truth, the whole truth and nothing but the truth, so help you Jimmy Johnson.

— Me? says Alf. Don't cast your nasturtiums on my character.

— Whatever statement you make, says Joe, will be taken down in evidence against you.

— Of course an action would lie, says J.J. It implies that he is not *compos mentis*. U.P: up.

— *Compos* your eye! says Alf, laughing. Do you know that he's balmy? Look at his head. Do you know that some mornings he has to get his hat on with a shoehorn?

— Yes, says J.J., but the truth of a libel is no defence to an indictment for publishing it in the eyes of the law.

— Ha ha, Alf, says Joe.

— Still, says Bloom, on account of the poor woman, I mean his wife.

— Pity about her, says the Citizen. Or any other woman marries a half-and-half.

— How half-and-half? says Bloom. Do you mean he ...

— Half-and-half I mean, says the Citizen. A fellow that's neither fish nor flesh.

— Nor good red herring, says Joe.

306

— That's what I mean, says the Citizen. A pithogue, if you know what that is.

Begob I saw there was trouble coming. And Bloom explaining he meant on account of it being cruel for the wife having to go round after the old stuttering fool. Cruelty to animals so it is to let that bloody poverty-stricken Breen out on grass with his beard out tripping him, bringing down the rain. And she with her nose cock-a-hoop after she married him because a cousin of his old fellow's was pew-opener to the pope. Picture of him on the wall with his Smashall Sweeney's moustaches. The signior Brini from Summerhill, the eyetallyano, papal zouave to the Holy Father, has left the quay and gone to Moss Street. And who was he, tell us? A nobody, two pair back and passage at seven shillings a week, and he covered with all kinds of breastplates bidding defiance to the world.

— And moreover, says J.J., a postcard is publication. It was held to be sufficient evidence of malice in the test case Sadgrove vs. Hole. In my opinion an action might lie.

Six and eightpence, please. Who wants your opinion? Let us drink our pints in peace. Gob, we won't be let even do that much itself.

— Well, good health, Jack, says Ned.

— Good health, Ned, says J.J.

— There he is again, says Joe.

— Where? says Alf.

And begob there he was passing the door with his books under his oxter and the wife beside him and Corny Kelleher with his walleye looking in as they went past, talking to him like a father, trying to sell him a secondhand coffin.

— How did that Canada Swindle case go off? says Joe.

— Remanded, says J.J.

One of the bottlenosed fraternity it was went by the name of James Wought alias Saphiro alias Spark and Spiro put an ad in the papers saying he'd give a passage to Canada for twenty bob. What? Do you see any green in the white of my eye? Course it was a bloody barney. What? Swindled them all, skivvies and bodachs from the county Meath, ay, and his own kidney too. J.J. was telling us there was an ancient Hebrew, Zaretsky or something, weeping in the witness-box with his hat on him, swearing by the holy Moses he was stuck for two quid.

— Who tried the case? says Joe.

— Recorder, says Ned.

— Poor old Sir Frederick, says Alf, you can cod him up to the two eyes.

— Heart as big as a lion, says Ned. Tell him a tale of woe about arrears of rent and a sick wife and a squad of kids and, faith, he'll dissolve in tears on the bench.

— Ay, says Alf. Reuben J. was bloody lucky he didn't clap him in the dock the other day for suing poor little Gumley that's minding stones for the Corporation there near Butt Bridge.

And he starts taking off the old recorder letting on to cry:

— A most scandalous thing! This poor hardworking man! How many children? Ten, did you say?

— Yes, your worship. And my wife has the typhoid.

— And the wife with typhoid fever! Scandalous! Leave the court immediately, sir. No, sir, I'll make no order for payment. How dare you, sir, come up before me and ask me to make an order! A poor hardworking industrious man! I dismiss the case.

And whereas on the sixteenth day of the month of the ox-eyed goddess and in the third week after the feastday of the Holy and Undivided Trinity, the daughter of the skies, the virgin moon, being then in her first quarter, it came to pass that those learned judges repaired them to the halls of law. There Master Courtenay, sitting in his own chamber, gave his rede and Master Justice Andrews, sitting without a jury in the probate court, weighed well and pondered the claim of the first chargeant upon the property in the matter of the will propounded and final testamentary disposition in re the real and personal estate of the late lamented Jacob Halliday, vintner, deceased, versus Livingstone, an infant, of unsound mind, and another. And to the solemn court of Green Street there came Sir Frederick the Falconer. And he sat him there about the hour of five o'clock to administer the law of the brehons at the commission for all that and those parts to be holden in and for the county of the city of Dublin. And there sat with him the High Sanhedrin of the twelve tribes of Iar, for every tribe one man, of the tribe of Patrick and of the tribe of Hugh and of the tribe of Owen and of the tribe of Conn and of the tribe of Oscar and of the tribe of Fergus and of the tribe of Finn and of the tribe of Dermot and of the tribe of Cormac and of the tribe of Kevin and of the tribe of Caoilte and of the tribe of Ossian, there being in all twelve good men and true. And he conjured them by Him who died on rood that they should well and truly try and true deliverance make in the issue joined between their sovereign lord the king and the prisoner at the bar and true verdict give according to the evidence, so help them God and kiss the book. And they rose in their seats, those twelve of Iar, and they swore by the name of Him who is from everlasting that they would do His rightwiseness. And straightway the minions of the law led forth from their donjon keep one whom the sleuthhounds of justice had apprehended in consequence of information received. And they shackled him hand and foot and would take of him ne bail ne mainprise but preferred a charge against him for he was a malefactor.

— Those are nice things, says the Citizen, coming over here to Ireland filling the country with bugs.

So Bloom lets on he heard nothing and he starts talking with Joe, telling him he needn't trouble about that little matter till the first but if he would just say a word to Mr Crawford. And so Joe swore high and holy by this and by that he'd do the devil and all.

— Because, you see, says Bloom, for an advertisement you must have repetition. That's the whole secret.

— Rely on me, says Joe.

— Swindling the peasants, says the Citizen, and the poor of Ireland. We want no more strangers in our house.

— O, I'm sure that will be all right, Hynes, says Bloom. It's just that Keyes, you see …

— Consider that done, says Joe.

— Very kind of you, says Bloom.

— The strangers, says the Citizen. Our own fault. We let them come in. We brought them in. The adulteress and her paramour brought the Saxon robbers here.

— Decree nisi, says J.J.

And Bloom letting on to be awfully deeply interested in nothing, a spider's web in the corner behind the barrel, and the Citizen scowling after him and the old dog at his feet looking up to know who to bite and when.

— A dishonoured wife, says the Citizen, that's what's the cause of all our misfortunes.

— And here she is, says Alf, that was giggling over the *Police Gazette* on the counter with Terry, in all her warpaint.

— Give us a squint at her, says I.

And what was it only one of the smutty Yankee pictures Terry borrows off of Corny Kelleher. Secrets for enlarging your private parts. Misconduct of society belle. Norman W. Tupper, wealthy Chicago contractor, finds pretty but faithless wife in lap of Officer Taylor. Belle in her bloomers misconducting herself and her fancy man feeling for her tickles and Norman W. Tupper bouncing in with his peashooter just in time to be late after she doing the trick of the loop with Officer Taylor.

— O jakers, Jenny, says Joe, how short your shirt is!

— There's hair, Joe, says I. Get a queer old tail-end of corned beef off of that one, what?

So anyhow in came John Wyse Nolan and Lenehan with him with a face on him as long as a late breakfast.

— Well, says the Citizen, what's the latest from the scene of action? What did those tinkers in the City Hall at their caucus meeting decide about the Irish language?

O'Nolan, clad in shining armour, low bending made obeisance to the puissant and high and mighty chief of all Erin and did him to wit of that which had befallen, how that the grave elders of the most obedient city, second of the realm, had met them in the Tholsel and there, after due prayers to the gods who dwell in ether supernal, had taken solemn counsel whereby they might, if so be it might be, bring once more into honour among mortal men the winged speech of the sea-divided Gael.

— It's on the march, says the Citizen. To hell with the bloody brutal Sassenachs and their *patois*.

So J.J. puts in a word, doing the toff about one story was good till you heard another and blinking facts and the Nelson policy, putting your blind eye to the telescope, and drawing up a bill of attainder to impeach a nation and Bloom trying to back him up moderation and botheration and their colonies and their civilisation.

— Their syphilisation, you mean, says the Citizen. To hell with them! The curse of a good-for-nothing God light sideways on the bloody thick-lugged sons of whores' gets! No music and no art and no literature worthy of the name. Any civilisation they have they stole from us. Tongue-tied sons of bastards' ghosts.

— The European family, says J.J....

— They're not European, says the Citizen. I was in Europe with Kevin Egan of Paris. You wouldn't see a trace of them or their language anywhere in Europe except in a *cabinet d'aisance*.

And says John Wyse:

— Full many a flower is born to blush unseen.

And says Lenehan that knows a bit of the lingo:

— *Conspuez les Anglais! Perfide Albion!*

He said and then lifted he in his rude great brawny strengthy hands the medher of dark strong foamy ale and, uttering his tribal slogan *Lámh Dhearg Abú*, he drank to the undoing of his foes, a race of mighty valorous heroes, rulers of the waves, who sit on thrones of alabaster silent as the deathless gods.

— What's up with you, says I to Lenehan. You look like a fellow that had lost a bob and found a tanner.

— Gold Cup, says he.

— Who won, Mr Lenehan? says Terry.

— *Throwaway*, says he, at twenty to one. A rank outsider. And the rest nowhere.

— And Bass's mare? says Terry.

— Still running, says he. We're all in a cart. Boylan plunged two quid on my tip *Sceptre* for himself and a lady friend.

— I had half a crown myself, says Terry, on *Zinfandel* that Mr Flynn gave me. Lord Howard de Walden's.

— Twenty to one, says Lenehan. Such is life in an outhouse. *Throwaway*, says he. Takes the biscuit. Frailty, thy name is *Sceptre*. And talking about bunions ...

So he went over to the biscuit tin Bob Doran left to see if there was anything he could lift on the nod and the old cur after him backing his luck with his mangy snout up. Old Mother Hubbard went to the cupboard.

— Not there, my child, says he.

— Keep your pecker up, says Joe. She'd have won the money only for the other dog.

And J.J. and the Citizen arguing about law and history with Bloom sticking in an odd word.

— Some people, says Bloom, can see the mote in others' eyes but they can't see the beam in their own.

— *Ráiméis*, says the Citizen. There's no one as blind as the fellow that won't see, if you know what that means. Where are our missing twenty millions of Irish should be here today instead of four, our lost tribes? And our potteries and textiles, the finest in the whole world! And our wool that was sold in Rome in the time of Juvenal and our flax and our damask from the looms of Antrim and our Limerick lace and our tanneries and our white flint glass down there by Ballybough and our Huguenot poplin that we have since Jacquard de Lyon and our woven silk and our Foxford tweeds and ivory raised point from the Carmelite convent in New Ross, nothing like it in the whole wide world! Where are the Greek merchants that came through the pillars of Hercules, the Gibraltar now grabbed by the foe of mankind, with gold and Tyrian purple to sell in Wexford at the fair of Carmen? Read Tacitus and Ptolemy, even Giraldus Cambrensis. Wine, peltries, Connemara marble, silver from Tipperary, second to none, our far-famed horses even today, the Irish hobbies, with King Philip of Spain offering to pay customs duties for the right to fish in our waters. What do the yellowjohns of Anglia owe us for our ruined trade and our ruined hearths? And the beds of the Barrow and Shannon they won't deepen with millions of acres of marsh and bog to make us all die of consumption?

– As treeless as Portugal we'll be soon, says John Wyse, or Heligoland with its one tree if something is not done to reafforest the land. Larches, firs, all the trees of the conifer family are going fast. I was reading a report of Lord Castletown's ...

– Save them, says the Citizen. The giant ash of Galway and the chieftain elm of Kildare with a forty-foot bole and an acre of foliage. Save the trees of Ireland for the future men of Ireland on the fair hills of Eire, O.

– Europe has its eyes on you, says Lenehan.

The fashionable international world attended *en masse* this afternoon at the wedding of the chevalier Jean Wyse de Neaulan, grand high chief ranger of the Irish National Foresters, with Miss Fir Conifer of Pine Valley. Lady Sylvester Elmshade, Mrs Barbara Lovebirch, Mrs Poll Ash, Mrs Holly Hazeleyes, Miss Daphne Bays, Miss Dorothy Canebrake, Mrs Clyde Twelvetrees, Mrs Rowan Greene, Mrs Helen Vinegadding, Miss Virginia Creeper, Miss Gladys Beech, Miss Olive Garth, Miss Blanche Maple, Mrs Maud Mahogany, Miss Myra Myrtle, Miss Priscilla Elderflower, Miss Bee Honeysuckle, Miss Grace Poplar, Miss O Mimosa San, Miss Rachel Cedarfrond, the Misses Lilian and Viola Lilac, Miss Timidity Aspenall, Mrs Kitty Dewey-Mosse, Miss May Hawthorne, Mrs Gloriana Palme, Mrs Liana Forrest, Mrs Arabella Blackwood and Mrs Norma Holyoake of Oakholme Regis graced the ceremony by their presence. The bride, who was given away by her father, the M'Conifer of the Glands, looked exquisitely charming in a creation carried out in green mercerised silk, moulded on an underslip of gloaming grey, sashed with a yoke of broad emerald and finished with a triple flounce of darker-hued fringe, the scheme being relieved by bretelles and hip insertions of acorn bronze. The maids of honour, Miss Larch Conifer and Miss Spruce Conifer, sisters of the bride, wore very becoming costumes in the same tone, a dainty motif of plume rose being worked into the pleats in a pinstripe and repeated capriciously in the jade-green toques in the form of heron feathers of pale-tinted coral. Senhor Enrique Flor presided at the organ with his well-known ability and, in addition to the prescribed numbers of the nuptial mass, played a new and striking arrangement of *Woodman, Spare that Tree* at the conclusion of the service. On leaving the Church of Saint Fiacre *in Horto* after the papal blessing the happy pair were subjected to a playful crossfire of hazelnuts, beech-mast, bay leaves, catkins of willow, ivytod, holly berries, mistletoe sprigs and quicken shoots. Mr and Mrs Wyse Conifer Neaulan will spend a quiet honeymoon in the Black Forest.

— And our eyes are on Europe, says the Citizen. We had our trade with Spain and France and with the Flemings before those mongrels were pupped, Spanish ale in Galway, the wine bark on the wine-dark waterway.

— And will again, says Joe.

— And with the help of the holy mother of God we will again, says the Citizen, clapping his thigh. Our harbours that are empty will be full again, Queenstown, Kinsale, Galway, Blacksod Bay, Ventry in the kingdom of Kerry and Killybegs, the third largest harbour in the wide world with a fleet of masts of the Galway Lynches and the Cavan O'Reillys and the O'Kennedys of Dublin when the earl of Desmond could make a treaty with the emperor Charles the Fifth himself. And will again, says he, when the first Irish battleship is seen breasting the waves with our own flag to the fore, none of your Henry Tudor's harps, no, the oldest flag afloat, the flag of the province of Desmond and Thomond, three crowns on a blue field, the three sons of Milesius.

And he took the last swig out of the pint. Moya. All wind and piss like a tanyard cat. Cows in Connacht have long horns. As much as his bloody life is worth to go down and address his tall talk to the assembled multitude in Shanagolden where he daren't show his nose with the Molly Maguires looking for him to let daylight through him for grabbing the holding of an evicted tenant.

— Hear! Hear! to that, says John Wyse. What will you have?

— An imperial yeomanry, says Lenehan, to celebrate the occasion.

— Half one, Terry, says John Wyse, and a hands up. Terry! Are you asleep?

— Yes, sir, says Terry. Small whiskey and bottle of Allsopp. Right, sir.

Hanging over the bloody paper with Alf looking for spicy bits instead of attending to the general public. Picture of a butting match, trying to crack their bloody skulls, one chap going for the other with his head down like a bull at a gate. And another one: *Black Beast Burned in Omaha,*

Ga. A lot of Deadwood Dicks in slouch hats and they firing at a sambo strung up in a tree with his tongue out and a bonfire under him. Gob, they ought to drown him in the sea after and electrocute and crucify him to make sure of their job.

— But what about the fighting navy, says Ned, that keeps our foes at bay?

— I'll tell you what about it, says the Citizen. Hell upon earth it is. Read the revelations that's going on in the papers about flogging on the training ships at Portsmouth. A fellow writes that calls himself *Disgusted One.*

So he starts telling us about corporal punishment and about the crew of tars and officers and rear admirals drawn up in cocked hats and the parson with his Protestant Bible to witness punishment and a young lad brought out, howling for his ma, and they tie him down on the butt-end of a gun.

— A rump and dozen, says the Citizen, was what that old ruffian Sir John Beresford called it, but the modern God's Englishman calls it caning on the breech.

And says John Wyse:

— 'Tis a custom more honoured in the breach than in the observance.

Then he was telling us the master-at-arms comes along with a long cane and he draws out and he flogs the bloody backside off of the poor lad till he yells meila murder.

— That's your glorious British navy, says the Citizen, that bosses the earth. The fellows that never will be slaves, with the only hereditary chamber on the face of God's earth and their land in the hands of a dozen gamehogs and cottonball barons. That's the great empire they boast about of drudges and whipped serfs.

— On which the sun never rises, says Joe.

— And the tragedy of it is, says the Citizen, they believe it. The unfortunate yahoos believe it.

They believe in rod, the scourger almighty, creator of hell upon earth, and in Jacky Tar, the son of a gun, who was conceived of unholy boast, born of the fighting navy, suffered under rump and dozen, was scarified, flayed and curried, yelled like bloody hell, the third day he arose again from the bed, steered into haven and sitteth on his beam end till further orders whence he shall come to drudge for a living and be paid.

— But, says Bloom, isn't discipline the same everywhere? I mean wouldn't it be the same here if you put force against force?

Didn't I tell you? As true as I'm drinking this porter if he was at his last gasp he'd try to downface you that dying was living.

— We'll put force against force, says the Citizen. We have our greater Ireland beyond the sea. They were driven out of house and home in the black '47. Their mud cabins and their shielings by the roadside were laid low by the battering ram and the *Times* rubbed its hands and told the white-livered Saxons there would soon be as few Irish in Ireland as redskins in America. Even the Grand Turk sent us his piastres. But the Sassenach tried to starve the nation at home while the land was full of crops that the British hyenas bought and sold in Rio de Janeiro. Ay, they drove out the peasants in hordes. Twenty thousand of them died in the coffin ships. But those that came to the land of the free remember the land of bondage. And they will come again and with a vengeance, no cravens, the sons of Granuaile, the champions of Kathleen ni Houlihan.

— Perfectly true, says Bloom. But my point was ...

— We are a long time waiting for that day, Citizen, says Ned. Since the poor old woman told us that the French were on the sea and landed at Killala.

— Ay, says John Wyse. We fought for the royal Stuarts that reneged us against the Williamites and they betrayed us. Remember Limerick and the broken treatystone. We gave our best blood to France and Spain, the wild geese. Fontenoy, eh? And Sarsfield and O'Donnell, duke of Tetuan in Spain, and Ulysses Browne of Camus that was field marshal to Maria Theresa. But what did we ever get for it?

— The French! says the Citizen. Set of dancing masters! Do you know what it is? They were never worth a roasted fart to Ireland. Aren't they trying to make an *entente cordiale* now at Tay Pay's dinner party with perfidious Albion? Firebrands of Europe and they always were.

— *Conspuez les Français*, says Lenehan, nobbling his beer.

— And as for the Prooshians and the Hanoverians, says Joe, haven't we had enough of those sausage-eating bastards on the throne from George the Elector down to the German lad and the flatulent old bitch that's dead?

Jesus, I had to laugh at the way he came out with that about the old one with the winkers on her, blind drunk in her royal palace every night of God, old Vic, with her jorum of mountain dew and her coachman carting her up body and bones to roll into bed and she pulling him by the whiskers and singing him old bits of songs about *Ehren on the Rhine* and *Come where the booze is cheaper*.

— Well, says J.J. We have Edward the Peacemaker now.

— Tell that to a fool, says the Citizen. There's a bloody sight more pox than pax about that boyo. Edward Guelph-Wettin!

— And what do you think, says Joe, of the holy boys, the priests and bishops of Ireland, doing up his room in Maynooth in His Satanic Majesty's racing colours and sticking up pictures of all the horses his jockeys rode. The earl of Dublin, no less.

— They ought to have stuck up all the women he rode himself, says little Alf.

And says J.J.:

— Considerations of space influenced their lordships' decision.

— Will you try another, Citizen? says Joe.

— Yes, sir, says he. I will.

— You? says Joe.

— Beholden to you, Joe, says I. May your shadow never grow less.

— Repeat that dose, says Joe.

Bloom was talking and talking with John Wyse and he quite excited with his dunduckety mud-coloured mug on him and his old plum-eyes rolling about.

— Persecution, says he, all the history of the world is full of it. Perpetuating national hatred among nations.

— But do you know what a nation means? says John Wyse.

— Yes, says Bloom.

— What is it? says John Wyse.

— A nation? says Bloom. A nation is the same people living in the same place.

— By God, then, says Ned, laughing, if that's so I'm a nation for I'm living in the same place for the past five years.

So of course everyone had the laugh at Bloom and says he, trying to muck out of it:

— Or also living in different places.

— That covers my case, says Joe.

— What is your nation if I may ask? says the Citizen.

— Ireland, says Bloom. I was born here. Ireland.

The Citizen said nothing, only cleared the spit out of his gullet and, gob, he spat a Red Bank oyster out of him right in the corner.

— After you with the push, Joe, says he, taking out his handkerchief to swab himself dry.

— Here you are, Citizen, says Joe. Take that in your right hand and repeat after me the following words.

The much-treasured and intricately embroidered ancient Irish face-cloth attributed to Solomon of Droma and Manus Tomaltach Óg Mac-Donogh, authors of the Book of Ballymote, was then carefully produced and called forth prolonged admiration. No need to dwell on the legendary beauty of the cornerpieces, the acme of art, wherein one can distinctly discern each of the four evangelists in turn presenting to each of the Four Masters his evangelical symbol, a bogoak sceptre, a North American puma (a far nobler king of beasts than the British article, be it said in passing), a Kerry calf and a golden eagle from Carrantuohill. The scenes depicted on the emunctory field, showing our ancient duns and raths and cromlechs and grianauns and seats of learning and maledictive stones, are as wonderfully beautiful and the pigments as delicate as when the Sligo illuminators gave free rein to their artistic fantasy long long ago in the time of the Barmecides. Glendalough, the lovely lakes of Killarney, the ruins of Clonmacnois, Cong Abbey, Glen Inagh and the Twelve Pins, Ireland's Eye, the Green Hills of Tallaght, Croagh Patrick, the brewery of Messrs Arthur Guinness, Son and Company Limited, Lough Neagh's banks, the vale of Ovoca, Isolde's Tower, the Malpas obelisk, Sir Patrick Dun's Hospital, Cape Clear, the glen of Aherlow, Lynch's Castle, the Scotch House, Rathdown Union Workhouse at Loughlinstown, Tullamore jail, Castleconnel rapids, Kilballymacshonakill, the cross at Monasterboice, Jury's Hotel, S. Patrick's Purgatory, the Salmon Leap, Maynooth College refectory, Curley's Hole, the three birthplaces of the first duke of Wellington, the Rock of Cashel, the Bog of Allen, the Henry Street warehouse, Fingal's Cave – all these moving scenes are still there for us today rendered more beautiful still by the waters of sorrow which have passed over them and by the rich incrustations of time.

— Show us over the drink, says I. Which is which?

— That's mine, says Joe, as the devil said to the dead policeman.

— And I belong to a race too, says Bloom, that is hated and persecuted. Also now. This very moment. This very instant.

Gob, he near burnt his fingers with the butt of his old cigar.

— Robbed, says he. Plundered. Insulted. Persecuted. Taking what belongs to us by right. At this very moment, says he, putting up his fist, sold by auction in Morocco like slaves or cattle.

— Are you talking about the new Jerusalem? says the Citizen.

— I'm talking about injustice, says Bloom.

— Right, says John Wyse. Stand up to it then with force like men.

That's an almanac picture for you. Mark for a softnosed bullet. Old lardyface standing up to the business end of a gun. Gob, he'd adorn a sweeping brush, so he would, if he only had a nurse's apron on him. And then he collapses all of a sudden, twisting around all the opposite, as limp as a wet rag.

— But it's no use, says he. Force, hatred, history, all that. That's not life for men and women, insult and hatred. And everybody knows that it's the very opposite of that that is really life.

— What? says Alf.

— Love, says Bloom. I mean the opposite of hatred. I must go now, says he to John Wyse. Just round to the court a moment to see if Martin is there. If he comes just say I'll be back in a second. Just a moment.

Who's hindering you? And off he pops like greased lightning.

— A new apostle to the gentiles, says the Citizen. Universal love.

— Well, says John Wyse. Isn't that what we're told? Love your neighbour.

— That chap? says the Citizen. Beggar my neighbour is his motto. Love, moya! He's a nice pattern of a Romeo and Juliet.

Love loves to love love. Nurse loves the new chemist. Constable 14A loves Mary Kelly. Gerty MacDowell loves the boy that has the bicycle. M.B. loves a fair gentleman. Li Chi Han lovey up kissy Cha Pu Chow. Jumbo the elephant loves Alice the elephant. Old Mr Verschoyle with the ear trumpet loves old Mrs Verschoyle with the turned-in eye. The man in the brown macintosh loves a lady who is dead. His Majesty the King loves Her Majesty the Queen. Mrs Norman W. Tupper loves Officer Taylor. You love a certain person. And this person loves that other person because everybody loves somebody but God loves everybody.

— Well, Joe, says I, your very good health and song. More power, Citizen.

— Hurrah, there, says Joe.

— The blessing of God and Mary and Patrick on you, says the Citizen.

And he ups with his pint to wet his whistle.

— We know those canters, says he, preaching and picking your pocket. What about sanctimonious Cromwell and his ironsides that put the women and children of Drogheda to the sword with the Bible text *God is love* pasted round the mouth of his cannon? The Bible! Did you read that skit in the *United Irishman* today about that Zulu chief that's visiting England?

— What's that? says Joe.

So the Citizen takes up one of his paraphernalia papers and he starts reading out:

— A delegation of the chief cotton magnates of Manchester was presented yesterday to His Majesty the Alake of Abeokuta by Gold Stick in Waiting, Lord Walkup of Walkup on Eggs, to tender to His Majesty the heartfelt thanks of British traders for the facilities afforded them in his dominions. The delegation partook of luncheon at the conclusion of which the dusky potentate, in the course of a happy speech freely translated by the British chaplain, the Reverend Ananias Praisegod Barebones, tendered his best thanks to Massa Walkup and emphasised the cordial relations existing between Abeokuta and the British Empire, stating that he treasured as one of his dearest possessions an illuminated Bible, the volume of the word of God and the secret of England's greatness, graciously presented to him by the white chief woman, the great squaw Victoria, with a personal dedication from the august hand of the Royal Donor. The Alake then drank a loving cup of first-shot usquebaugh to the toast *Black and White* from the skull of his immediate predecessor in the dynasty, Kakachakachak, surnamed Forty Warts, after which he visited the chief factory of Cottonopolis and signed his mark in the visitors' book, subsequently executing a charming old Abeokutic wardance, in the course of which he swallowed several knives and forks amid hilarious applause from the girl hands.

— Widow woman, says Ned. I wouldn't doubt her. Wonder did he put that Bible to the same use as I would.

— Same only more so, says Lenehan. And thereafter in that fruitful land the broadleafed mango flourished exceedingly.

— Is that by Griffith? says John Wyse.

— No, says the Citizen. It's not signed Shanganagh. It's only initialled: P.

— And a very good initial too, says Joe.

— That's how it's worked, says the Citizen. Trade follows the flag.

— Well, says J.J., if they're any worse than those Belgians in the Congo Free State they must be bad. Did you read that report by a man what's this his name is?

— Casement, says the Citizen. He's an Irishman.

— Yes, that's the man, says J.J. Raping the women and girls and flogging the natives on the belly to squeeze all the red rubber they can out of them.

— I know where he's gone, says Lenehan, cracking his fingers.

— Who? says I.

— Bloom, says he. The courthouse is a blind. He had a few bob on *Throwaway* and he's gone to gather in the shekels.

— Is it that white-eyed kaffir? says the Citizen, that never backed a horse in anger in his life?

— That's where he's gone, says Lenehan. I met Bantam Lyons going to back that horse only I put him off it and he told me Bloom gave him the tip. Bet you what you like he has a hundred shillings to five on. He's the only man in Dublin has it. A dark horse.

— He's a bloody dark horse himself, says Joe.

— Mind, Joe, says I. Show us the entrance out.

— There you are, says Terry.

Goodbye Ireland, I'm going to Gort. So I just went round the back of the yard to pump ship and begob (hundred shillings to five) while I was letting off my (*Throwaway* twenty to) letting off my load gob says I to myself I knew he was uneasy in his (two pints off of Joe and one in Slattery's off) in his mind to get off the mark to (hundred shillings is five quid) and when they were in the (dark horse) Pisser Burke was telling me card party and letting on the child was sick (gob, must have done about a gallon) flabbyarse of a wife speaking down the tube *she's better* or *she's* (ow!) all a plan so he could vamoose with the pool if he won or (Jesus, full up I was) trading without a licence (ow!) Ireland my nation says he (hoik! phthook!) never be up to those bloody (there's the last of it) Jerusalem (ah!) cuckoos.

So anyhow when I got back they were at it dingdong, John Wyse saying it was Bloom gave the ideas for Sinn Féin to Griffith to put in his paper, all kinds of jerrymandering and packed juries and swindling the taxes off of the government and appointing consuls all over the world to walk about selling Irish industries. Robbing Peter to pay Paul. Gob, that puts the bloody kibosh on it if old sloppy eyes is mucking up the show. Give us a bloody chance. God save Ireland from the likes of that bloody mouse-about. Mr Bloom with his argol bargol. And his old fellow before him perpetrating frauds, old Methuselah Bloom, the robbing bagman, that poisoned himself with the prussic acid after he swamping the country with his baubles and his penny diamonds. Loans by post on easy terms. Any amount of money advanced on note of hand. Distance no object. No security. Gob, he's like Lanty MacHale's goat that'd go a piece of the road with everyone.

— Well, it's a fact, says John Wyse. And there's the man now that'll tell you all about it, Martin Cunningham.

Sure enough the castle car drove up with Martin on it and Jack Power with him and a fellow named Crofter or Crofton, pensioner out of the collector general's, an Orangeman Blackburne does have on the registration and he drawing his pay, or Crawford, gallivanting around the country at the king's expense.

Our travellers reached the rustic hostelry and alighted from their palfreys.

— Ho, varlet! cried he, who by his mien seemed the leader of the party. Saucy knave! To us!

So saying he knocked loudly with his swordhilt upon the open lattice.

Mine host came forth at the summons, girding him with his tabard.

— Give you good den, my masters, said he with an obsequious bow.

— Bestir thyself, sirrah! cried he who had knocked. Look to our steeds. And for ourselves give us of your best for i'faith we need it.

— Lackaday, good masters, said the host, my poor house has but a bare larder. I know not what to offer your lordships.

— How now, fellow? cried the second of the party, a man of pleasant countenance. So servest thou the king's messengers, Master Taptun?

An instantaneous change overspread the landlord's visage.

— Cry you mercy, gentlemen, he said humbly. An you be the king's messengers (God shield His Majesty!) you shall not want for aught. The king's friends (God bless His Majesty!) shall not go afasting in my house I warrant me.

— Then about! cried the traveller who had not spoken, a lusty trencherman by his aspect. Hast aught to give us?

Mine host bowed again as he made answer:

— What say you, good masters, to a squab pigeon pasty, some collops of venison, a saddle of veal, widgeon with crisp hog's bacon, a boar's head with pistachios, a bason of jolly custard, a medlar tansy and a flagon of old Rhenish?

— Gadzooks! cried the last speaker. That likes me well. Pistachios!

— Aha! cried he of the pleasant countenance. A poor house and a bare larder, quotha! 'Tis a merry rogue.

So in comes Martin asking where was Bloom.

— *Where is he?* says Lenehan. Defrauding widows and orphans.

— Isn't that a fact, says John Wyse, what I was telling the Citizen about Bloom and the Sinn Féin?

— That's so, says Martin. Or so they allege.

— Who made those allegations? says Alf.

— I, says Joe. I'm the alligator.

— And after all, says John Wyse, why can't a Jew love his country like the next fellow?

— Why not? says J.J., when he's quite sure which country it is.

— Is he a Jew or a gentile or a Holy Roman or a swaddler or what the hell is he? says Ned. Or who is he? No offence, Crofton.

— Who is Junius? says J.J.

— We don't want him, says Crofter the Orangeman or Presbyterian.

— He's a perverted Jew, says Martin, from a place in Hungary and it was he drew up all the plans according to the Hungarian system. We know that in the Castle.

— Isn't he a cousin of Bloom the dentist? says Jack Power.

— Not at all, says Martin. Only namesakes. His name was Virag, the father's name that poisoned himself. He changed it by deed poll, the father did.

— That's the new Messiah for Ireland! says the Citizen. Island of saints and sages!

— Well, they're still waiting for their redeemer, says Martin. For that matter so are we.

— Yes, says J.J., and every male that's born they think it may be their Messiah. And every Jew is in a tall state of excitement, I believe, till he knows if he's a father or a mother.

— Expecting every moment will be his next, says Lenehan.

— O, by God, says Ned, you should have seen Bloom before that son of his that died was born. I met him one day in the South City Market buying a tin of Neave's food six weeks before the wife was delivered.

— *En ventre sa mère*, says J.J.

— Do you call that a man? says the Citizen.

— I wonder did he ever put it out of sight, says Joe.

— Well, there were two children born anyhow, says Jack Power.

— And who does he suspect? says the Citizen.

Gob, there's many a true word spoken in jest. One of those mixed middlings he is. Lying up in the hotel, Pisser was telling me, once a month with headache like a totty with her courses. Do you know what I'm telling you? It'd be an act of God to take a hold of a fellow the like of that and throw him in the bloody sea. Justifiable homicide, so it would. Then sloping off with his five quid without putting up a pint of stuff like a man. Give us your blessing. Not as much as would blind your eye.

— Charity to the neighbour, says Martin. But where is he? We can't wait.

— A wolf in sheep's clothing, says the Citizen. That's what he is. Virag from Hungary! Ahasuerus I call him. Cursed by God.

— Have you time for a brief libation, Martin? says Ned.

— Only one, says Martin. We must be quick. J.J. and S.

— You, Jack? Crofton? Three half ones, Terry.

— Saint Patrick would want to land again at Ballykinlar and convert us, says the Citizen, after allowing things like that to contaminate our shores.

— Well, says Martin, rapping for his glass. God bless all here is my prayer.

— Amen, says the Citizen.

— And I'm sure He will, says Joe.

And at the sound of the sacring bell, headed by a crucifer with acolytes, thurifers, boatbearers, readers, ostiarii, deacons and subdeacons, the blessed company drew nigh of mitred abbots and priors and guardians and monks and friars: the monks of Benedict of Spoleto, Carthusians and Camaldolesi, Cistercians and Olivetans, Oratorians and Vallombrosans and the friars of Augustine, Brigittines, Premonstratensians, Servi, Trinitarians and the children of Peter Nolasco: and therewith from Carmel Mount the children of Elijah Prophet led by Albert Bishop and by Teresa of Avila, calced and other: and friars, brown and grey, sons of poor Francis, Capuchins, Cordeliers, Minimes and Observants and the daughters of Clare: and the sons of Dominic, the Friars Preachers, and the sons of Vincent: and the monks of S. Wolstan: and Ignatius his children: and the confraternity of the Christian Brothers led by the Reverend Brother Edmund Ignatius Rice. And after came all saints and martyrs, virgins and confessors: S. Cyr and S. Isidore Arator and S. James the Less and S. Phocas of Sinope and S. Julian Hospitator and S. Felix de Cantalice and S. Simon Stylites and S. Stephen Protomartyr and S. John of God and S. Ferreol and S. Leugarde and S. Theodotus and S. Vulmar and S. Richard and S. Vincent de Paul and S. Martin of Todi and S. Martin of Tours and S. Alfred and S. Joseph and S. Denis and S. Cornelius and S. Leopold and S. Bernard and S. Terence and S. Edward and S. Owen Caniculus and S. Anonymous and S. Eponymous and S. Pseudonymous and S. Homonymous and S. Paronymous and S. Synonymous and S. Laurence O'Toole and S. James of Dingle and Compostella and S. Columcille and S. Columba and S. Celestine and S. Colman and S. Kevin and S. Brendan and S. Frigidian and S. Senan and S. Fachtna and S. Columbanus and S. Gall and S. Fursey and S. Fintan and S. Fiacre and S. John Nepomuc and S. Thomas Aquinas and S. Ives of Brittany and S. Michan and S. Herman-Joseph and the three patrons of holy youth, S. Aloysius Gonzaga and S. Stanislaus Kostka and S. John Berchmans, and the saints Gervasius, Servasius and Bonifacius and S. Bride and S. Kieran and S. Canice of Kilkenny and S. Jarlath of Tuam and S. Finbarr and S. Pappin of Ballymun and Brother Aloysius Pacificus and Brother Louis Bellicosus and the saints Rose of Lima and of Viterbo and S. Martha of Bethany and S. Mary of Egypt and S. Lucy and S. Brigid and S. Attracta and S. Dympna and S. Ita and S. Marion Calpensis and the Blessed Sister Teresa of the Child Jesus and S. Barbara and S. Scholastica and S. Ursula with eleven thousand virgins. And all came with nimbi and aureoles and gloriae, bearing palms and harps and swords and olive crowns, in robes whereon were woven the blessed symbols of their efficacies, inkhorns, arrows, loaves, cruses, fetters, axes, trees, bridges, babes in a bathtub, shells, wallets, shears, keys, dragons, lilies, buckshot, beards, hogs, lamps, bellows, beehives, soupladles, stars, snakes, anvils, boxes of Vaseline, bells, crutches, forceps, stags' horns, watertight boots, hawks, millstones, eyes on a dish, wax candles, aspergills and unicorns. And as they wended their way by Nelson's Pillar, Henry Street, Mary Street, Capel Street and Little Britain Street chanting the Introit *in Epiphania Domini* which beginneth *Surge, illuminare* and thereafter most sweetly the gradual *Omnes* which saith *de Saba venient* they did divers wonders such as casting out devils, raising the dead to life, multiplying fishes, healing the halt and the blind, discovering various articles which had been mislaid, interpreting and fulfilling the scriptures, blessing and prophesying. And last, beneath a canopy of cloth of gold came the Reverend Father O'Flynn attended by Malachi and Patrick. And when the good fathers had reached the appointed place, the house of Bernard Kiernan and Company Limited, 8, 9 and 10 Little Britain Street, wholesale grocers, wine and brandy shippers, licensed for the sale of beer, wine and spirits for consumption on the premises, the celebrant blessed the house and censed the mullioned windows and the groynes and the vaults and the arrises and the capitals and the pediments and the cornices and the engrailed arches and the spires and the cupolas and sprinkled the lintels thereof with blessed water and prayed that God might bless that house as He had blessed the house of Abraham and Isaac and Jacob and make the angels of His light to inhabit therein. And entering he blessed the viands and the beverages and the company of all the blessed answered his prayers.

— *Adjutorium nostrum in nomine Domini.*

— *Qui fecit coelum et terram.*

— *Dominus vobiscum.*

— *Et cum spiritu tuo.*

And he laid his hands upon that he blessed and gave thanks and he prayed and they all with him prayed:

— *Deus, cujus verbo sanctificantur omnia, benedictionem tuam effunde super creaturas istas: et praesta ut quisquis eis secundum legem et voluntatem Tuam cum gratiarum actione usus fuerit per invocationem sanctissimi nominis Tui corporis sanitatem et animae tutelam Te auctore percipiat per Christum Dominum nostrum.*

— And so say all of us, says Jack.

— Thousand a year, Lambert, says Crofton or Crawford, taking up his John Jameson.

— Right, says Ned. And butter for fish.

I was just looking around to see who the happy thought would strike when be damned but in he comes again letting on to be in a hell of a hurry.

— I was just round at the courthouse, says he, looking for you. I hope I'm not...

— No, says Martin, we're ready.

Courthouse my eye. And your pockets hanging down with gold and silver. Mean bloody scut. Stand us a drink itself. Devil a sweet fear! There's a Jew for you! All for number one. Cute as a shithouse rat. Hundred to five.

— Don't tell anyone, says the Citizen.

— Beg your pardon, says he.

— Come on, boys, says Martin, seeing it was looking blue. Come along now.

— Don't tell anyone, says the Citizen, letting a bawl out of him. It's a secret.

And the bloody dog woke up and let a growl.

— Bye bye all, says Martin.

And he got them out as quick as he could, Jack Power and Crofton or whatever you call him and him in the middle of them letting on to be all at sea and up with them on the bloody jaunting car.

– Off with you, says Martin to the jarvey.

The milk-white dolphin tossed his mane and, rising in the golden poop, the helmsman spread the bellying sail upon the wind and stood off forward with all sail set, the spinnaker to larboard. A many comely nymphs drew nigh to starboard and to larboard and, clinging to the sides of the noble bark, they linked their shining forms as doth the cunning wheelwright when he fashions about the heart of his wheel the equidistant rays whereof each one is sister to another and he binds them all with an outer ring and giveth speed to the feet of men whenas they ride to a hosting or contend for the smile of ladies fair. Even so did they come and set them, those willing nymphs, the undying sisters. And they laughed, sporting in a circle of their foam: and the bark clave the waves.

But begob I was just lowering the heel of the pint when I saw the Citizen getting up to waddle to the door, puffing and blowing with the dropsy, and he cursing the curse of Cromwell on him, bell, book and candle in Irish, spitting and spatting out of him and Joe and little Alf round him like leprechauns trying to peacify him.

– Let me alone, says he.

And begob he got as far as the door and they holding him and he bawls out of him:

– Three cheers for Israel!

Arrah, sit down on the parliamentary side of your arse for Christ's sake and don't be making a public exhibition of yourself. Jesus, there's always some bloody clown or other kicking up a bloody murder about bloody nothing. Gob, it'd turn the porter sour in your guts, so it would.

And all the ragamuffins and sluts of the nation round the door and Martin telling the jarvey to drive ahead and the Citizen bawling and Alf and Joe at him to whisht and he on his high horse about the Jews and the loafers calling for a speech and Jack Power trying to get him to sit down on the car and hold his bloody jaw and a loafer with a patch over his eye starts singing *If the Man in the Moon was a Jew, Jew, Jew* and a slut shouts out of her:

– Eh, mister! Your fly is open, mister!

And says he:

– Mendelssohn was a Jew and Karl Marx and Mercadante and Spinoza. And the Saviour was a Jew and his father was a Jew. Your God.

– He had no father, says Martin. That'll do now. Drive ahead.

– Whose God? says the Citizen.

326

— Well, his uncle was a Jew, says he. Your God was a Jew. Christ was a Jew like me.

Gob, the Citizen made a plunge back into the shop.

— By Jesus, says he, I'll brain that bloody Jewman for using the holy name. By Jesus, I'll crucify him so I will. Give us that biscuit box here.

— Stop! Stop! says Joe.

A large and appreciative gathering of friends and acquaintances from the metropolis and greater Dublin assembled in their thousands to bid farewell to Nagyságos uram Lipóti Virag, late of Messrs Alexander Thom's, printers to His Majesty, on the occasion of his departure for the distant clime of Százharminczbrojúgulyás-Dugulás (Meadow of Murmuring Waters). The ceremony which went off with great éclat was characterised by the most affecting cordiality. An illuminated scroll of ancient Irish vellum, the work of Irish artists, was presented to the distinguished phenomenologist on behalf of a large section of the community and was accompanied by the gift of a silver casket tastefully executed in the style of ancient Celtic ornament, a work which reflects every credit on the makers, Messrs Jacob *agus* Jacob. The departing guest was the recipient of a hearty ovation, many of those who were present being visibly moved when the select orchestra of Irish pipes struck up the well-known strains of *Come Back to Erin,* followed immediately by *Rákóczy's March.* Tar barrels and bonfires were lighted along the coastline of the four seas on the summits of the Hill of Howth, Three Rock Mountain, Sugarloaf, Bray Head, the mountains of Mourne, the Galtees, the Ox and Donegal and Sperrin peaks, the Nagles and the Boggeraghs, the Connemara hills, the reeks of M'Gillicuddy, Slieve Aughty, Slieve Bernagh and Slieve Bloom. Amid cheers that rent the welkin, responded to by answering cheers from a big muster of henchmen on the distant Cambrian and Caledonian hills, the mastodontic pleasure ship slowly moved away saluted by a final floral tribute from the representatives of the fair sex who were present in large numbers while as it proceeded down the river escorted by a flotilla of barges the flags of the Ballast Office and Custom House were dipped in salute as were also those of the electrical power station at the Pigeonhouse and the Poolbeg Light. *Visszontlátásra, kedvés barátom! Visszontlátásra!* Gone but not forgotten!

Gob, the devil wouldn't stop him till he got hold of the bloody tin anyhow and out with him and little Alf hanging on to his elbow and he shouting like a stuck pig, as good as any bloody play in the Queen's Royal Theatre:

– Where is he till I murder him?

And Ned and J.J. paralysed with the laughing.

– Bloody wars, says I, I'll be in for the last gospel.

But as luck would have it the jarvey got the nag's head round the other way and off with him.

– Hold on, Citizen, says Joe. Stop!

Begob he drew his hand and made a swipe and let fly. Mercy of God the sun was in his eyes or he'd have left him for dead. Gob, he near sent it into the county Longford. The bloody nag took fright and the old mongrel after the car like bloody hell and all the populace shouting and laughing and the old tin box clattering along the street.

The catastrophe was terrific and instantaneous in its effect. The observatory of Dunsink registered in all eleven shocks, all of the fifth grade of Mercalli's scale, and there is no record extant of a similar seismic disturbance in our island since the earthquake of 1534, the year of the rebellion of Silken Thomas. The epicentre appears to have been that part of the metropolis which constitutes the Inns Quay ward and parish of Saint Michan covering a surface of forty-one acres, two roods and one square pole or perch. All the lordly residences in the vicinity of the palace of justice were demolished and that noble edifice itself, in which at the time of the catastrophe important legal debates were in progress, is literally a mass of ruins beneath which it is to be feared all the occupants have been buried alive. From the reports of eyewitnesses it transpires that the seismic waves were accompanied by a violent atmospheric perturbation of cyclonic character. An article of headgear since ascertained to belong to the much-respected clerk of the crown and peace Mr George Fottrell and a silk umbrella with gold handle with the engraved initials, crest, coat of arms and house number of the erudite and worshipful chairman of quarter sessions Sir Frederick Falkiner, recorder of Dublin, have been discovered by search parties in remote parts of the island: respectively, the former on the third basaltic ridge of the Giant's Causeway, the latter embedded to the extent of one foot three inches in the sandy beach of Holeopen Bay near the Old Head of Kinsale. Other eyewitnesses depose that they observed an incandescent object of enormous proportions hurtling through the atmosphere at a terrifying velocity in a trajectory directed southwest by west. Messages of condolence and sympathy are being hourly received from all parts of the different continents and the sovereign pontiff has been graciously pleased to decree that a special *missa pro defunctis* shall be celebrated simultaneously by the ordinaries of each and every cathedral church of all the episcopal dioceses subject to the spiritual authority of the Holy See in suffrage of the souls of those faithful departed who have been so unexpectedly called away from our midst. The work of salvage, removal of debris, human remains etc. has been entrusted to Messrs Michael Meade and Son, 159 Great Brunswick Street, and Messrs T. and C. Martin, 77, 78, 79 and 80 North Wall, assisted by the men and officers of the Duke of Cornwall's Light Infantry under the general supervision of H.R.H. Rear Admiral the Right Honourable Sir Hercules Hannibal Habeas Corpus Anderson K.G., K.P., K.T., P.C., K.C.B., M.P., J.P., M.B., D.S.O., S.O.D., M.F.H., M.R.I.A., B.L., Mus. Doc., P.L.G., F.T.C.D., F.R.U.I., F.R.C.P.I., F.R.C.S.I.

You never saw the like of it in all your born puff. Gob, if he got that lottery ticket on the side of his poll he'd remember the Gold Cup, he would so, but begob the Citizen would have been lagged for assault and battery and Joe for aiding and abetting. The jarvey saved his life by furious driving as sure as God made Moses. What? O Jesus, he did. And he let a volley of oaths after him.

— Did I kill him, says he, or what?

And he shouting to the bloody dog:

— After him, Garry! After him, boy!

And the last we saw was the bloody car rounding the corner and old sheepsface on it gesticulating and the bloody mongrel after it with his lugs back for all he was bloody well worth to tear him limb from limb. Hundred to five! Jesus, he took the value of it out of him, I promise you.

When, lo, there came about them all a great brightness and they beheld the chariot wherein He stood ascend to heaven. And they beheld Him in the chariot, clothed upon in the glory of the brightness, having raiment as of the sun, fair as the moon and terrible that for awe they durst not look upon Him. And there came a voice out of heaven, calling: *Elijah! Elijah!* And He answered with a main cry: *Abba! Adonai!* And they beheld Him, even Him, ben Bloom Elijah, amid clouds of angels ascend to the glory of the brightness at an angle of forty-five degrees over Donohoe's in Little Green Street like a shot off a shovel.

The summer evening had begun to fold the world in its mysterious embrace. Far away in the west the sun was setting and the last glow of all too fleeting day lingered lovingly on sea and strand, on the proud promontory of dear old Howth guarding as ever the waters of the bay, on the weed-grown rocks along Sandymount shore and, last but not least, on the quiet church whence there streamed forth at times upon the stillness the voice of prayer to her who is in her pure radiance a beacon ever to the storm-tossed heart of man, Mary, star of the sea.

The three girl friends were seated on the rocks enjoying the evening scene and the air which was fresh but not too chilly. Many a time and oft were they wont to come there to that favourite nook to have a cosy chat beside the sparkling waves and discuss matters feminine – Cissy Caffrey and Gerty MacDowell and Edy Boardman with the baby in the pushcar and Tommy and Jacky Caffrey, two little curlyheaded boys dressed in sailor suits with caps to match and the name *H.M.S. Belleisle* printed on both. For Tommy and Jacky Caffrey were twins, scarce four years old, and very noisy and spoiled twins sometimes, but for all that darling little fellows with bright merry faces and endearing ways about them. They were dabbling in the sand with their spades and buckets, building castles as children do, or playing with their big coloured ball, as happy as the day was long. And Edy Boardman was rocking the chubby baby to and fro in the pushcar while that young gentleman fairly chuckled with delight. He was but eleven months and nine days old and, though still a tiny toddler, was just beginning to lisp his first babyish words. Cissy Caffrey bent over to him to tease his fat little plucks and the dainty dimple in his chin.

– Now, baby, Cissy Caffrey said. Say out big, big. *I want a drink of water.*

And baby prattled after her:

– A jink a jink a jawbo.

Cissy Caffrey cuddled the wee chap for she was awfully fond of children, so patient with little sufferers, and Tommy Caffrey could never be got to take his castor oil unless it was Cissy Caffrey that held his nose and promised him the scatty heel of the loaf of brown bread with golden

330

syrup on. What a persuasive power that girl had! But to be sure baby Boardman was as good as gold, a perfect little dote in his new fancy bib. None of your spoilt beauties, Flora MacFlimsy sort, was Cissy Caffrey. A truer-hearted lass never drew the breath of life, always with a laugh in her gipsylike eyes and a frolicsome word on her cherry-ripe red lips, a girl lovable in the extreme. And Edy Boardman laughed too at the quaint language of little brother.

But just then there was a slight altercation between Master Tommy and Master Jacky. Boys will be boys and our two twins were no exception to this golden rule. The apple of discord was a certain castle of sand which Master Jacky had built and Master Tommy would have it right go wrong that it was to be architecturally improved by a front door like the Martello tower had. But if Master Tommy was headstrong Master Jacky was self-willed too and, true to the maxim that every little Irishman's house is his castle, he fell upon his hated rival and to such purpose that the would-be assailant came to grief and (alas to relate!) the coveted castle too. Needless to say, the cries of discomfited Master Tommy drew the attention of the girl friends.

— Come here, Tommy, his sister called imperatively. At once! And you, Jacky, for shame, to throw poor Tommy in the dirty sand. Wait till I catch you for that.

His eyes misty with unshed tears, Master Tommy came at her call for their big sister's word was law with the twins. And in a sad plight he was too after his misadventure. His little man-o'-war top and unmentionables were full of sand but Cissy was a past mistress in the art of smoothing over life's tiny troubles and very quickly not one speck of sand was to be seen on his smart little suit. Still, the blue eyes were glistening with hot tears that would well up so she kissed away the hurtness and shook her hand at Master Jacky the culprit and said if she was near him she wouldn't be far from him, her eyes dancing in admonition.

— Nasty bold Jacky! she cried.

She put an arm round the little mariner and coaxed winningly:

— What's your name? Butter and cream?

— Tell us who is your sweetheart, spoke Edy Boardman. Is Cissy your sweetheart?

— Nao, tearful Tommy said.

— Is Edy Boardman your sweetheart? Cissy queried.

— Nao, Tommy said.

— I know, Edy Boardman said none too amiably with an arch glance from her shortsighted eyes. I know who is Tommy's sweetheart. Gerty is Tommy's sweetheart.

— Nao, Tommy said on the verge of tears.

Cissy's quick motherwit guessed what was amiss and she whispered to Edy Boardman to take him there behind the pushcar where the gentleman couldn't see and to mind he didn't wet his new tan shoes.

But who was Gerty?

Gerty MacDowell, who was seated near her companions, lost in thought, gazing far away into the distance, was in very truth as fair a specimen of winsome Irish girlhood as one could wish to see. She was pronounced beautiful by all who knew her though, as folks often said, she was more a Giltrap than a MacDowell. Her figure was slight and graceful, inclining even to fragility, but those iron jelloids she had been taking of late had done her a world of good, much better than the Widow Welch's female pills, and she was much better of those discharges she used to get and that tired feeling. The waxen pallor of her face was almost spiritual in its ivorylike purity though her rosebud mouth was a genuine Cupid's bow, Greekly perfect. Her hands were of finely veined alabaster with tapering fingers and as white as lemon juice and queen of ointments could make them, though it was not true that she used to wear kid gloves in bed or take a milk footbath either. Bertha Supple told that once to Edy Boardman, a deliberate lie, when she was black out at daggers drawn with Gerty (the girl chums had of course their little tiffs from time to time like the rest of mortals) and she told her not to let on whatever she did that it was her that told her or she'd never speak to her again. No. Honour where honour is due. There was an innate refinement, a languid queenly hauteur about Gerty which was unmistakably evidenced in her delicate hands and high-arched instep. Had kind fate but willed her to be born a gentlewoman of high degree in her own right and had she only received the benefit of a good education Gerty MacDowell might easily have held her own beside any lady in the land and have seen herself exquisitely gowned with jewels on her brow and patrician suitors at her feet vying with one another to pay their devoirs to her. Mayhap it was this, the love that might have been, that lent to her softly featured face at whiles a look tense with suppressed meaning and that imparted a strange yearning tenderness to the beautiful eyes, a charm few could resist. Why have women such eyes of witchery? Gerty's were of the bluest Irish blue, set off by lustrous lashes and dark expressive brows. Time was when those brows were not so silkily seductive. It was Madame Vera Verity, directress of the Woman Beautiful page of the *Princess's Novelettes*, who had first advised her to try eyebrow liner which gave that haunting expression to the eyes, so becoming in leaders of fashion, and she had never regretted it. Then there was blushing scientifically cured and how to be tall increase your height and you have a beautiful face but your nose? That would suit Mrs Dignam because she had a button one. But Gerty's crowning glory was her wealth of wonderful hair. It was dark brown with a natural wave in it. She had cut it that very morning on account of the new moon and it nestled about her pretty head in a profusion of luxuriant clusters. And pared her nails too, Thursday for wealth. And just now at Edy's words as a telltale flush, delicate as the faintest rose bloom, crept into her cheeks she looked so lovely in her sweet girlish shyness that of a surety God's fair land of Ireland did not hold her equal.

For an instant she was silent with rather sad downcast eyes. She was about to retort but something checked the words on her tongue. Inclination prompted her to speak out: dignity told her to be silent. The pretty lips pouted awhile but then she glanced up with a faint smile and broke out into a joyous little laugh which had in it all the freshness of a young May morning. She knew right well, no one better, what made squinty Edy say that because of him cooling in his attentions when it was simply a lovers' quarrel. As per usual somebody's nose was out of joint about the boy that had the bicycle off the Londonbridge Road always riding up and down in front of her window. Only now his father kept him in in the evenings studying hard to get an exhibition in the intermediate that was on and he was going to go to Trinity College to study for a doctor when he left the High School like his brother W.E. Wylie who was racing in the bicycle races in Trinity College university. Little recked he perhaps for what she felt, that dull aching void in her heart sometimes, piercing to the core. Yet he was young and perchance he might learn to love her in time. They were Protestants in his family and of course Gerty knew who came first and after Him the Blessed Virgin and then Saint Joseph. But he was undeniably handsome with an exquisite nose and he was what he looked, every inch a gentleman, the shape of his head too at the back without his cap on that she would know anywhere, something off the common, and the way he turned the bicycle at the lamp with his hands off the bars and also the nice perfume of those good cigarettes he smoked and besides they were both of a size too, he and she, and that was why Edy Boardman thought she was so frightfully clever because he didn't go and ride up and down in front of her bit of a garden.

Gerty was dressed simply but with the instinctive taste of a votary of Dame Fashion for she felt that there was just a might that he might be out. A neat blouse of electric blue, self-tinted by dolly dyes (because it was expected in the *Lady's Pictorial* that electric blue would be worn), with a smart vee opening down to the division and kerchief pocket (in which she always kept a piece of cotton wool scented with her favourite perfume because the handkerchief spoiled the sit) and a navy three-quarter skirt cut to the stride showed off her slim graceful figure to perfection. She wore a coquettish little love of a hat of wide-leaved nigger straw contrast-trimmed with an underbrim of egg-blue chenille and at the side a butterfly bow of silk to tone. All Tuesday week afternoon she was hunting to match that chenille but at last she found what she wanted at Clery's summer sales, the very it, slightly shop-soiled but you would never notice, seven fingers two and a penny. She did it up all by herself and what joy was hers when she tried it on then, smiling at the lovely reflection which the mirror gave back to her! And when she put it on the waterjug to keep the shape she knew that that would take the shine out of some people she knew. Her shoes were the newest thing in footwear (Edy Boardman prided herself that she was very *petite* but she never had a foot like Gerty MacDowell, a five, and never would, ash, oak or elm) with patent toecaps and just one smart buckle over her high-arched instep. Her well-turned ankle displayed its perfect proportions beneath her skirt and just the proper amount and no more of her shapely limbs encased in finespun hose with high-spliced heels and wide garter tops. As for undies they were Gerty's chief care, and who that knows the fluttering hopes and fears of sweet seventeen (though Gerty would never see seventeen again) can find it in his heart to blame her? She had four dinky sets with awfully pretty stitchery, three garments and nighties extra, and each set slotted with different-coloured ribbons, rose pink, pale blue, mauve and pea-green, and she aired them herself and blued them when they came home from the wash and ironed them and she had a brickbat too to keep the iron on because she wouldn't trust those washerwomen as far as she'd see them, scorching the things. She was wearing the blue for luck, hoping against hope, her own colour and the lucky colour too for a bride to have a bit of blue somewhere on her, because the green she wore that day week brought grief because his father brought him in to study for the intermediate exhibition and because she thought perhaps he might be out because when she was dressing that morning she nearly slipped up the old pair on her inside out and that was for luck and lovers' meetings if you put those things on inside out or if they got untied that he was thinking about you so long as it wasn't of a Friday.

And yet – and yet! That strained look on her face! A gnawing sorrow is there all the time. Her very soul is in her eyes and she would give worlds to be in the privacy of her own familiar chamber where, giving way to tears, she could have a good cry and relieve her pent-up feelings, though not too much because she knew how to cry nicely before the mirror. You are lovely, Gerty, it said. The paly light of evening falls upon a face infinitely sad and wistful. Gerty MacDowell yearns in vain. Yes, she had known from the very first that her daydream, a marriage has been arranged and the wedding bells are ringing for Mrs Reggy Wylie T.C.D. (because the one who married the elder brother would be Mrs Wylie) and in the fashionable intelligence Mrs Gertrude Wylie was wearing a sumptuous confection of grey trimmed with expensive blue fox, was not to be. He was too young to understand. He would not believe in love, a woman's birthright. The night of the party long ago in Stoer's (he was still in short trousers) when they were alone and he stole an arm round her waist she went white to the very lips. He called her little one in a strangely husky voice and snatched a half kiss (the first!) but it was only the end of her nose and then he hastened from the room with a remark about refreshments. Impetuous fellow! Strength of character had never been Reggy Wylie's strong point and he who would woo and win Gerty MacDowell must be a man among men. But waiting, always waiting to be asked and it was leap year too and would soon be over. No prince charming is her beau ideal to lay a rare and wondrous love at her feet but rather a manly man with a strong quiet face who had not found his ideal, perhaps his hair slightly flecked with grey, and who would understand, take her in his sheltering arms, strain her to him in all the strength of his deep passionate nature and comfort her with a long long kiss. It would be like heaven. For such a one she yearns this balmy summer eve. With all the heart of her she longs to be his, his only, his affianced bride for riches for poor, in sickness in health, till death us two part, from this to this day forward.

And while Edy Boardman was with little Tommy behind the pushcar she was just thinking would the day ever come when she could call herself his little wife-to-be. Then they could talk about her till they went blue in the face, Bertha Supple too, and Edy, the little spitfire, because she would be twenty-two in November. She would care for him with creature comforts too for Gerty was womanly wise and knew that a mere man liked that feeling of hominess. Her griddlecakes done to a golden-brown hue and Queen Anne's pudding of delightful creaminess had won golden opinions from all because she had a lucky hand they said also for lighting a fire, dredge in the fine self-raising flour and always stir in the same direction, then cream the milk and sugar and whisk well the white of eggs, though she didn't like the eating part when there were any people that made her shy and often she wondered why you couldn't eat something poetical like violets or roses, and they would have a beautifully appointed drawing room with pictures and engravings and the photograph of grandpapa Giltrap's lovely dog Garryowen that almost talked it was so human and chintz covers for the chairs and that silver toastrack in Clery's summer jumble sales like they have in rich houses. He would be tall with broad shoulders (she had always admired tall men for a husband) and glistening white teeth under his carefully trimmed sweeping moustache and they would go on the Continent for their honeymoon (three wonderful weeks!) and then, when they settled down in a nice snug and cosy little homely house, every morning they would both have brekky, simple but perfectly served, for their own two selves, and before he went out to business he would give his dear little wifey a good hearty hug and gaze for a moment deep down into her eyes.

Edy Boardman asked Tommy Caffrey was he done and he said yes, so then she buttoned up his little knickerbockers for him and told him to run off and play with Jacky and to be good now and not to fight. But Tommy said he wanted the ball and Edy told him no, that baby was playing with the ball and if he took it there'd be wigs on the green, but Tommy said it was his ball and he wanted his ball and he pranced on the ground, if you please. The temper of him! O, he was a man already was little Tommy Caffrey since he was out of pinnies. Edy told him no, no, and to be off now with him and she told Cissy Caffrey not to give in to him.

— You're not my sister, naughty Tommy said. It's my ball.

But Cissy Caffrey told baby Boardman to look up, look up high at her finger, and she snatched the ball quickly and threw it along the sand and Tommy ran after it in full career, having won the day.

— Anything for a quiet life, laughed Ciss.

And she tickled tiny tot's two cheeks to make him forget and played here's the lord mayor, here's his two horses, here's his gingerbread carriage and here he walks in, chinchopper, chinchopper, chinchopper chin. But Edy got as cross as two sticks about him getting his own way like that from everyone always petting him.

— I'd like to give him something, she said, so I would, where I won't say.

— On the bee-o-tee-tom, laughed Cissy merrily.

Gerty MacDowell bent down her head and crimsoned at the idea of Cissy saying an unladylike thing like that out loud she'd be ashamed of her life to say, flushing a deep rosy red, and Edy Boardman said she was sure the gentleman opposite heard what she said. But not a pin cared Ciss.

— Let him! she said with a pert toss of her head and a piquant tilt of her nose. Give it to him too on the same place as quick as I'd look at him.

Madcap Ciss with her golliwog curls! You had to laugh at her sometimes. For instance when she asked you would you have some more Chinese tea and jaspberry ram and when she drew the jugs too and the men's faces on her nails with red ink make you split your sides or when she wanted to go where you know she said she wanted to run and pay a visit to the Miss White. That was just like Cissycums. O, and will you ever forget the evening she dressed up in her father's suit and hat and the burnt-cork moustache and walked down Tritonville Road smoking a cigarette. There was none to come up to her for fun. But she was sincerity itself, one of the bravest and truest hearts heaven ever made, a sterling good friend, not one of your two-faced things, too sweet to be wholesome.

And then there came out upon the air the sound of voices and the pealing anthem of the organ from the old ivyclad church and Gerty's heart was touched. It was the men's temperance retreat conducted by the missioner, the Reverend John Hughes S.J., rosary, sermon and benediction of the Most Blessed Sacrament. They were there gathered together without distinction of social class (and a most edifying spectacle it was to see) in that simple fane beside the waves after the storms of this weary world, kneeling before the feet of the Immaculate, reciting the litany of Our Lady of Loreto, beseeching her to intercede for them, the old familiar words, holy Mary, holy virgin of virgins. How sad to poor Gerty's ears! Had her father only avoided the clutches of the demon drink by taking the pledge or those powders the drink habit cured in *Pearson's Weekly* she might now be rolling in her carriage, second to none. Over and over had she told herself that as she mused by the dying embers in a brown study without the lamp because she hated two lights or oftentimes gazing out

337

of the window dreamily by the hour at the rain falling on the rusty bucket, thinking. But that vile decoction which has ruined so many hearths and homes had cast its shadow over her childhood days. Nay, she had even witnessed in the home circle deeds of violence caused by intemperance and had seen her own father, a prey to the fumes of intoxication, forget himself completely for if there was one thing of all things that Gerty knew it was that the man who lifts his hand to a woman save in the way of kindness deserves to be branded as the lowest of the low.

And still the voices sang in supplication to the Virgin most powerful, Virgin most merciful. And Gerty, rapt in thought, scarce saw or heard her companions or the twins at their boyish gambols or the gentleman off Sandymount Green that Cissy Caffrey called the man that was so like himself passing along the strand taking a short walk. You never saw him any way screwed but still and for all that she would not like him for a father because he was too old or something or on account of his face (it was a palpable case of Doctor Fell) or his carbuncly nose with the pimples on it and his sandy moustache a bit white under his nose. Poor father! With all his faults she loved him still when he sang *Tell me, Mary, how to woo thee* or *My love and cottage near Rochelle* and they had stewed cockles and lettuce with Lazenby's salad dressing for supper and when he sang *The moon hath raised* with Mr Dignam that died suddenly and was buried, God have mercy on him, from a stroke. Her mother's birthday that was and Charley was home on his holidays and Tom and Mr Dignam and Mrs and Patsy and Freddy Dignam and they were to have had a group taken. No one would have thought the end was so near. Now he was laid to rest. And her mother said to him to let that be a warning to him for the rest of his days and he couldn't even go to the funeral on account of the gout and she had to go into town to bring him the letters and samples from his office about Catesby's cork lino, artistic, standard designs, fit for a palace, gives tiptop wear and always bright and cheery in the home.

A sterling good daughter was Gerty, just like a second mother in the house, a ministering angel too with a little heart worth its weight in gold. And when her mother had those raging splitting headaches who was it rubbed the menthol cone on her forehead but Gerty, though she didn't like her mother taking pinches of snuff because it wasn't ladylike and that was the only single thing they ever had words about, taking snuff. Everyone thought the world of her for her gentle ways. It was Gerty who turned off the gas at the main every night and it was Gerty who tacked up on the wall of that place where she never forgot every fortnight the chlorate of lime Mr Tunney the grocer's Christmas almanac picture of *Halcyon Days* where a young gentleman in the costume they used to wear then with a three-cornered hat was offering a bunch of flowers to his ladylove with old-time chivalry through her lattice window. You could see there was a story behind it. The colours were done something lovely. She was robed in a soft clinging white in a studied attitude and the gentleman was in chocolate and he looked a thorough aristocrat. She often looked at them dreamily when she went there for a certain purpose and felt her own arms that were white and soft just like hers with the sleeves back and thought about those times because she had found out in Walker's pronouncing dictionary that belonged to grandpapa Giltrap about the halcyon days what they meant.

The twins were now playing in the most approved brotherly fashion till at last Master Jacky who was really as bold as brass, there was no getting behind that, deliberately kicked the ball as hard as ever he could down towards the seaweedy rocks. Needless to say poor Tommy was not slow to voice his dismay but luckily the gentleman in black who was sitting there by himself came gallantly to the rescue and intercepted the ball. Our two champions claimed their plaything with lusty cries and to avoid trouble Cissy Caffrey called to the gentleman to throw it to her please. The gentleman aimed the ball once or twice and then threw it up the strand towards Cissy Caffrey but it rolled down the slope and stopped right under Gerty's skirt near the little pool by the rock. The twins clamoured again for it and Cissy told her to kick it away and let them fight for it so Gerty drew back her foot but she wished their stupid ball hadn't come rolling down to her and she gave a kick but she missed and Edy and Cissy laughed.

— If you fail try again, Edy Boardman said.

Gerty smiled assent and bit her lip. A delicate pink crept into her pretty cheeks but she was determined to let them see, so she just lifted her skirt a little but just enough and took good aim and gave the ball a jolly good kick and it went ever so far and the two twins after it down towards the shingle. Pure jealousy of course it was, nothing else, trying to draw attention on account of the gentleman opposite looking. She felt the warm flush, a danger signal always with Gerty MacDowell, surging and flaming into her cheeks. Till then they had only exchanged glances of the most casual kind but now under the brim of her new hat she ventured a look at him and the face that met her gaze there in the twilight, wan and strangely drawn, seemed to her the saddest she had ever seen.

Through the open window of the church the fragrant incense was wafted and with it the fragrant names of her who was conceived without stain of original sin. Spiritual vessel, pray for us, honourable vessel, pray for us, vessel of singular devotion, pray for us, mystical rose. And careworn hearts were there and toilers for their daily bread and many who had erred and wandered, their eyes wet with contrition, but for all that bright with hope for the reverend father Father Hughes had told them what the great Saint Bernard had said in his famous prayer of Mary the most pious Virgin's intercessory power, that it was not recorded in any age that those who implored her powerful protection were ever abandoned by her.

The twins were now playing again right merrily, for the troubles of childhood are but as fleeting summer showers. Cissy Caffrey played with baby Boardman till he crowed with glee, clapping baby hands in the air. *Peep* she cried behind the hood of the pushcar and Edy asked where was Cissy gone and then Cissy popped up her head and cried *ah!* and, my word, didn't the little chap enjoy that! And then she told him to say papa:

— Say papa, baby. Say pa pa pa pa pa pa pa.

And baby did his level best to say it for he was very intelligent for eleven months everyone said and big for his age and the picture of health, a perfect little bunch of love, and he would certainly turn out to be something great, they said.

— Haja ja ja haja.

Cissy wiped his little mouth with the dribbling bib and wanted him to sit up properly and say pa pa pa. But when she undid the strap she cried out, holy Saint Denis, that he was possing wet and to double the half blanket the other way under him. Of course His Infant Majesty was most obstreperous at such toilet formalities and he let everyone know it:

— Habaa baaaahabaaa baaaa.

And two great big lovely big tears coursed down his cheeks. It was all no use soothering him with no, no no, baby, no, and telling him about the geegee and where was the puffpuff but Ciss, always ready-witted, gave him in his mouth the teat of the sucking bottle and the young heathen was quickly appeased.

Gerty wished to goodness they would take their squalling baby home out of that and not get on her nerves, no hour to be out, and the little brats of twins. She gazed out towards the distant sea. It was like the paintings that man used to do on the pavement with all the coloured chalks and such a pity too leaving them there to be all blotted out, the evening and the clouds coming out and the Bailey light on Howth, and to hear the music like that and the perfume of those incense they burned in the church like a kind of waft. And while she gazed her heart went pitapat. Yes, it was her he was looking at and there was meaning in his look. His eyes burned into her as though they would search her through and through, read her very soul. Wonderful eyes they were, superbly expressive, but could you trust them? People were so queer. She could see at once by his dark eyes and his pale intellectual face that he was a foreigner, the image of the photo she had of Martin Harvey, the matinée idol, only for the moustache which she preferred because she wasn't stagestruck like Winny Rippingham that wanted they two to always dress the same on account of a play but she could not see whether he had an aquiline nose or a slightly *retroussé* from where he was sitting. He was in deep mourning, she could see that, and the story of a haunting sorrow was written on his face. She would have given worlds to know what it was. He was looking up so intently, so still, and he saw her kick the ball and perhaps he could see the bright steel buckles of her shoes if she swung them like that thoughtfully with the toes down. She was glad that something told her to put on the transparent stockings thinking Reggy Wylie might be out but that was far away. Here was that of which she had so often dreamed. It was he who mattered and there was joy on her face because she wanted him because she felt instinctively that he was like no one else. The very heart of the girl-woman went out to him, her dream husband, because she knew on the instant it was him. If he had suffered, more sinned against than sinning, or even, even, if he had been himself a sinner, a wicked man, she cared not. Even if he was a Protestant or Methodist she could convert him easily if he truly loved her. There were wounds that wanted healing with heartbalm. Those dark eyes had suffered. She was a womanly woman, not like other flighty girls, unfeminine, he had known, those cyclists showing off what they hadn't got, and she just yearned to know all, to forgive all, if she could make him fall in love with her, make him forget the memory of the past. Then mayhap he would embrace her gently like a real man, crushing her soft body to him, and love her, his ownest girlie, for herself alone.

Refuge of sinners. Comfortress of the afflicted. *Ora pro nobis*. Well has it been said that whosoever prays to her with faith and constancy can never be lost or cast away: and fitly is she too a haven of refuge for the afflicted because of the seven dolours which transpierced her own heart. Gerty could picture the whole scene in the church, the stained glass windows lighted up, the candles, the flowers and the blue banners of the Blessed Virgin's sodality, and Father Conroy was helping Canon O'Hanlon at the altar, carrying things in and out with his eyes cast down. He looked almost a saint and his confession box was so quiet and clean and dark and his hands were just like white wax and if ever she became a Dominican nun in their white habit perhaps he might come to the convent for the novena of Saint Dominic. He told her that time when she told him about that in confession, crimsoning up to the very roots of her hair for fear he could see, that she was not to be troubled because that was only the voice of nature and we were all subject to nature's laws, he said, in this life and that that was no sin because that came from the nature of woman instituted by God, he said, and that Our Blessed Lady herself said to the archangel Gabriel be it done unto me according to Thy word. He was so kind and holy and often and often she thought and thought could she work a ruched teacosy with embroidered floral design for him as a present or a clock but they had a clock she noticed on the mantelpiece white and gold with a canarybird that came out of a little house to tell the time the day she went there about the flowers for the forty hours' adoration because it was hard to know what sort of a present to give or perhaps an album of illuminated views of Dublin or someplace.

The exasperating little brats of twins began to quarrel again and Jacky threw the ball out towards the sea and they both ran after it. Little monkeys, common as ditchwater. Someone ought to take them and give them a good hiding for themselves to keep them in their places, the both of them. And Cissy and Edy shouted after them to come back because they were afraid the tide might come in on them and be drowned:

– Jacky! Tommy!

Not they! What a great notion they had! So Cissy said it was the very last time she'd ever bring them out. She jumped up and called them and then she ran down the slope past him, tossing her hair behind her which had a good enough colour if there had been more of it but with all the thingamerry she was always rubbing into it she couldn't get it to grow long because it wasn't natural so she could just go and throw her hat at it. She ran with long gandery strides it was a wonder she didn't rip up her skirt at the side that was too tight on her because there was a lot of the tomboy about Cissy Caffrey and she was a forward piece whenever she thought she had a good opportunity to show off and just because she was a good runner she ran like that so that he could see all the end of her petticoat running and her skinny shanks up as far as possible. It would have served her just right if she had tripped up over something accidentally on purpose with her high crooked French heels on her to make her look tall and got a fine tumble. *Tableau!* That would have been a very charming exposé for a gentleman like that to witness.

Queen of angels, queen of patriarchs, queen of prophets, of all saints, they prayed, queen of the most holy rosary, and then Father Conroy handed the thurible to Canon O'Hanlon and he put in the incense and censed the Blessed Sacrament and Cissy Caffrey caught the two twins and she was itching to give them a ringing good clip on the ear but she didn't because she thought he might be watching but she never made a bigger mistake in all her life because Gerty could see without looking that he never took his eyes off of her and then Canon O'Hanlon handed the thurible back to Father Conroy and knelt down looking up at the Blessed Sacrament and the choir began to sing the *Tantum ergo* and she just swung her foot in and out in time as the music rose and fell to the *tantumer gosa cramen tum*. Three and eleven she paid for those stockings in Sparrow's of George's Street on the Tuesday, no, the Monday before Easter and there wasn't a brack on them and that was what he was looking at, transparent, and not at her insignificant ones that had neither shape nor form (the cheek of her!) because he had eyes in his head to see the difference for himself.

Cissy came up along the strand with the two twins and their ball with her hat anyhow on her to one side after her run and she did look a streel lugging the two kids along with the flimsy blouse she bought only a fortnight before like a rag on her back and a bit of her petticoat hanging like a caricature. Gerty just took off her hat for a moment to settle her hair and a prettier, a daintier head of nutbrown tresses was never seen on a girl's shoulders – a radiant little vision, in sooth, almost maddening in its sweetness. You would have to travel many a long mile before you found a head of hair the like of that. She could almost see the swift answering flash of admiration in his eyes that set her tingling in every nerve. She put on her hat so that she could see from underneath the brim and swung her buckled shoe faster for her breath caught as she read the expression in his eyes. He was eyeing her as a snake eyes its prey. Her woman's instinct told her that she had raised the devil in him and at the thought a burning scarlet swept from throat to brow till the lovely colour of her face became a glorious rose.

Edy Boardman was noticing it too because she was squinting at Gerty, half smiling, with her specs, like an old maid, pretending to nurse the baby. Irritable little gnat she was and always would be and that was why no one could get on with her, poking her nose into what was no concern of hers. And she said to Gerty:

— A penny for your thoughts.

— What? replied Gerty with a smile reinforced by the whitest of teeth. I was only wondering was it late.

Because she wished to goodness they'd take the snotty-nosed twins and the babby home to the mischief out of that so that was why she just gave a gentle hint about it being late. And when Cissy came up Edy asked her the time and Miss Cissy, as glib as you like, said it was half past kissing time, time to kiss again. But Edy wanted to know because they were told to be in early.

— Wait, said Cissy, I'll ask my uncle Peter over there what's the time by his conundrum.

So over she went and when he saw her coming she could see him take his hand out of his pocket, getting nervous, and begin to play with his watchchain, looking up at the church. Passionate nature though he was, Gerty could see that he had enormous control over himself. One moment he had been there, fascinated by a loveliness that made him gaze, the passion seething in his veins, and the next moment it was the quiet grave-faced gentleman, self-control expressed in every line of his distinguished-looking figure.

Cissy said to excuse her would he mind please telling her what was the right time and Gerty could see him taking out his watch, listening to it and looking up and clearing his throat, and he said he was very sorry his watch was stopped but he thought it must be after eight because the sun was set. His voice had a cultured ring in it and though he spoke in measured accents there was a suspicion of a quiver in the mellow tones. Cissy said thanks and came back with her tongue out and said uncle said his waterworks were out of order.

Then they sang the second verse of the *Tantum ergo* and Canon O'Hanlon got up again and censed the Blessed Sacrament and knelt down and told Father Conroy that one of the candles was just going to set fire to the flowers and Father Conroy got up and settled it all right and she could see the gentleman winding his watch and listening to the works and she swung her leg more in and out in time. It was getting darker but he could see and he was looking all the time that he was winding the watch or whatever he was doing to it and then he put it back and put his hands back into his pockets. She felt a kind of a sensation rushing all over her and she knew by the feel of her scalp and that irritation against her stays that that thing must be coming on because the last time too was when she clipped her hair on account of the moon. His dark eyes fixed themselves on her again, drinking in her every contour, literally worshipping at her shrine. If ever there was undisguised admiration in a man's passionate gaze it was there plain to be seen on that man's face. It is for you, Gertrude MacDowell, and you know it.

Edy began to get ready to go and it was high time for her and Gerty noticed that that little hint she gave had had the desired effect because it was a long way along the strand to where there was the place to push up the pushcar and Cissy took off the twins' caps and tidied their hair, to make herself attractive of course, and Canon O'Hanlon stood up with his cope poking up at his neck and Father Conroy handed him the card to read off and he read out *Panem de coelo praestitisti eis* and Edy and Cissy were talking about the time all the time and asking her but Gerty could pay them back in their own coin and she just answered with scathing politeness when Edy asked her was she heartbroken about her best boy throwing her over. Gerty winced sharply. A brief cold blaze shone from her eyes that spoke volumes of scorn immeasurable. It hurt, O yes, it cut deep because Edy had her own quiet way of saying things like that that she knew would wound like the confounded little cat she was. Gerty's lips parted swiftly to frame the word but she fought back the sob that rose to her throat, so slim, so flawless, so beautifully moulded it seemed one an artist might have dreamed of. She had loved him better than he knew. Lighthearted deceiver and fickle like all his sex he would never understand what he had meant to her and for an instant there was in the blue eyes a quick stinging of tears. Their eyes were probing her mercilessly but with a brave effort she sparkled back in sympathy as she glanced at her new conquest for them to see.

– O, responded Gerty, quick as lightning, laughing, and the proud head flashed up. I can throw my cap at who I like because it's leap year.

Her words rang out crystal clear, more musical than the cooing of the ringdove, but they cut the silence icily. There was that in her young voice that told that she was not a one to be lightly trifled with. As for Mr Reggy with his swank and his bit of money she could just chuck him aside as if he was so much filth and never again would she cast as much as a second thought on him and tear his silly postcard into a dozen pieces. And if ever after he dared to presume she could give him one look of measured scorn that would make him shrivel up on the spot. Miss puny little Edy's countenance fell to no slight extent and Gerty could see by her looking as black as thunder that she was simply in a towering rage though she hid it, the little kinnatt, because that shaft had struck home for her petty jealousy and they both knew that she was something aloof, apart, in another sphere, that she was not of them and never would be and there was somebody else too that knew it and saw it so they could put that in their pipe and smoke it.

Edy straightened up baby Boardman to get ready to go and Cissy tucked in the ball and the spades and buckets and it was high time too because the sandman was on his way for Master Boardman junior and Cissy told him too that Billy Winks was coming and that baby was to go deedaws and baby looked just too ducky, laughing up out of his gleeful eyes, and Cissy poked him like that out of fun in his wee fat tummy and baby, without as much as by your leave, sent up his compliments to all and sundry on to his brand-new dribbling bib.

– O my! Puddeny pie! protested Ciss. He has his bib destroyed.

The slight contretemps claimed her attention but in two twos she set that little matter to rights.

Gerty stifled a smothered exclamation and gave a nervous cough and Edy asked what and she was just going to tell her to catch it while it was flying but she was ever ladylike in her deportment so she simply passed it off with consummate tact by saying that that was the benediction because just then the bell rang out from the steeple over the quiet seashore because Canon O'Hanlon was up on the altar with the veil that Father Conroy put round his shoulders giving the benediction with the Blessed Sacrament in his hands.

How moving the scene there in the gathering twilight, the last glimpse of Erin, the touching chimes of those evening bells and at the same time a bat flew forth from the ivied belfry through the dusk, hither, thither, with a tiny lost cry. And she could see far away the lights of the lighthouses so picturesque she would have loved to do with a box of paints because it was easier than to make a man and soon the lamplighter would be going his rounds past the Presbyterian churchgrounds and along by shady Tritonville Avenue where the couples walked and lighting the lamp near her window where Reggy Wylie used to turn his freewheel like she read in that book *The Lamplighter* by Miss Cummins, author of *Mabel Vaughan* and other tales. For Gerty had her dreams that no one knew of. She loved to read poetry and when she got a keepsake from Bertha Supple of that lovely confession album with the coral-pink cover to write her thoughts in she laid it in the drawer of her toilet table which, though it did not err on the side of luxury, was scrupulously neat and clean. It was there she kept her girlish treasure trove, the tortoiseshell combs, her Child of Mary badge, the white-rose scent, the eyebrow liner, her alabaster pouncet box and the ribbons to change when her things came home from the wash, and there were some beautiful thoughts written in it in violet ink that she bought in Hely's of Dame Street for she felt that she too could write poetry if she could only express herself like that poem that appealed to her so deeply that she had copied out of the newspaper she found one evening round the potherbs, *Art thou real, my ideal?* it was called, by Louis J. Walsh, Magherafelt, and after there was something about *Twilight, wilt thou ever?* and ofttimes the beauty of poetry, so sad in its transient loveliness, had misted her eyes with silent tears for she felt that the years were slipping by for her, one by one, and but for that one shortcoming she knew she need fear no competition and that was an accident coming down Dalkey Hill and she always tried to conceal it. But it must end, she felt. If she saw that magic lure in his eyes there would be no holding back for her. Love laughs at locksmiths. She would make the great sacrifice. Her every effort would be to share his thoughts. Dearer than the whole world would she be to him and gild his days with happiness. There was the all-important question and she was dying to know was he a married man or a widower who had lost his wife or some tragedy like the nobleman with the foreign name from the land of song in the novel that had to have her put into a madhouse when she went mad, cruel only to be kind. But even if – what then? Would it make a very great difference? From everything in the least indelicate her fine-bred nature instinctively recoiled. She loathed that sort of person, the fallen women off the accommodation walk beside the Dodder that went with the soldiers and coarse men with no respect for a girl's honour, degrading the sex and being taken up to the police station. No, no: not that. They would be just good friends like a big brother and sister without all that other in spite of the conventions of Society with a big ess. She would be even with Mr Stuckup Wylie whose people didn't want him to marry beneath them. Perhaps it was an old flame he was in mourning for from the days beyond recall. She thought she understood. She would be full of sympathy, try to understand him because men were so different. The old love was waiting, waiting with little white hands stretched out, with blue appealing eyes. Heart of mine! She would follow her dream of love, the dictates of her heart that told her he was her all in all, the only man in all the world for her, for love was the master guide. Nothing else mattered. Come what might she would be wild, untrammelled, free.

Canon O'Hanlon put the Blessed Sacrament back into the tabernacle and genuflected and the choir sang *Laudate Dominum omnes gentes* and then he locked the tabernacle door because the benediction was over and Father Conroy handed him his hat to put on and crosscat Edy asked wasn't she coming but Jacky Caffrey called out:

– O, look, Cissy!

And they all looked was it sheet lightning but Tommy saw it too over the trees beside the church, blue and then green and purple.

– It's fireworks, Cissy Caffrey said.

And they all ran down the strand to see over the houses and the church, helterskelter, Edy with the pushcar with baby Boardman in it and Cissy holding Tommy and Jacky by the hand so they wouldn't fall running.

– Come on, Gerty, Cissy called. It's the bazaar fireworks.

But Gerty was adamant. She had no intention now of being at their beck and call. If they could run like rossies she could sit, so she said she could see from where she was. The eyes that were fastened upon her set her pulses tingling. She looked at him a moment, meeting his glance, and a light broke in upon her. White-hot passion was in that face, passion silent as the grave, and it had made her his. At last they were left alone without the others to pry and pass remarks and she knew he could be trusted to the death, steadfast, a sterling man, a man of inflexible honour to his fingertips. His hands and face were working and a tremor went over her. She leaned back far to look up where the fireworks were and she caught her knee in her hands so as not to fall back looking up and there was no one to see only him and her when she revealed all her graceful beautifully shaped legs like that, supply soft and delicately rounded, and she seemed to hear the panting of his heart, his hoarse breathing, because she knew about the passion of men like that, hot-blooded, because Bertha Supple told her once in dead secret and made her swear she'd never about the gentleman lodger that was staying with them out of the Congested Districts Board that had pictures cut out of papers of those skirtdancers and highkickers and she said he used to do something not very nice that you could imagine sometimes in the bed. But this was altogether different from a thing like that because there was all the difference because she could almost feel him draw her face to his and the first quick hot touch of his handsome lips. Besides there was absolution so long as you didn't do the other thing before being married and there ought to be women priests that would understand without your telling out and Cissy Caffrey too sometimes had that dreamy kind of dreamy look in her eyes so that she too, my dear, and Winny Rippingham so mad about actors' photographs and besides it was on account of that other thing coming on the way it did.

And Jacky Caffrey shouted to look, there was another, and she leaned back and the garters were blue to match on account of the contrast with the transparent and they all saw it and they all shouted to look, look, there it was, and she leaned back ever so far to see the fireworks and something queer was flying about through the air, a soft thing, to and fro, dark. And she saw a long Roman candle going up over the trees, up, up, and, in the tense hush, they were all breathless with excitement as it went higher and higher and she had to lean back more and more to look up after it, high, high, almost out of sight, and her face was suffused with a divine, an entrancing blush from straining back and he could see her other things too, nainsook knickers, the fabric that caresses the skin, better than those other pettiwidth, the green, four and eleven, on account of being white, and she let him and she saw that he saw and then it went so high it went out of sight a moment and she was trembling in every limb from being bent so far back and he had a full view high up above her knee where no one ever not even on the swing or wading and she wasn't ashamed and he wasn't either to look in that immodest way like that because he couldn't resist the sight of the wondrous revealment half offered like those skirtdancers behaving so immodest before gentlemen looking and he kept on looking, looking. She would fain have cried to him chokingly, held out her snowy slender arms to him to come, to feel his lips laid on her white brow, the cry of a young girl's love, a little strangled cry, wrung from her, that cry that has rung through the ages. O! And then a rocket sprang and bang shot blind blank and O! then the Roman candle burst and it was like a sigh of O! and everyone cried O! O! in raptures and it gushed out of it a stream of rain gold hair threads and they shed and ah! they were all greeny dewy stars falling with golden rain, O so lovely, O, soft, sweet, soft!

Then all melted away dewily in the grey air: all was silent. Ah! She glanced at him as she bent forward quickly, a pathetic little glance of piteous protest, of shy reproach, under which he coloured like a girl. He

349

was leaning back against the rock behind. Leopold Bloom (for it is he) stands silent, with bowed head before those young guileless eyes. What a brute he had been! At it again? A fair unsullied soul had called to him and, wretch that he was, how had he answered? An utter cad he had been! He of all men! But there was an infinite store of mercy in those eyes, for him too a word of pardon even though he had erred and sinned and wandered. Should a girl tell? No, a thousand times no. That was their secret, only theirs, alone in the hiding twilight and there was none to know or tell save the little bat that flew so softly through the evening to and fro and little bats don't tell.

Cissy Caffrey whistled, imitating the boys in the football field to show what a great person she was, and then she cried:

– Gerty! Gerty! We're going. Come on. We can see better from farther up.

Gerty had an idea, one of love's little ruses. She slipped a hand into her kerchief pocket and took out the wadding and waved in gay reply of course without letting him and then slipped it back. Wonder if he's too far to. She rose. Was it goodbye? No. She had to go: but they would meet again, there, and she would dream of that till then, till they met tomorrow, of her dream of yestereve. She drew herself up to her full height. Their souls met in a last lingering glance and the eyes, full of a strange shining, that had reached her heart hung enraptured on her sweet flowerlike face. She half smiled at him wanly, a sweet forgiving smile, a smile that verged on tears – and then they parted.

Slowly, without looking back, she went down the uneven strand to Cissy, to Edy, to Jacky and Tommy Caffrey, to little baby Boardman. It was darker now and there were stones and bits of wood on the strand and slippy seaweed. She walked with a certain quiet dignity characteristic of her but with care and very slowly because – because Gerty MacDowell was . . .

Tight boots? No. She's lame! O!

Mr Bloom watched her as she limped away. Poor girl! That's why she's left on the shelf and the others did a sprint. Thought something was wrong by the cut of her jib. Might have a moustache, superfluous hair. Jilted beauty. A defect is ten times worse in a woman. But makes them polite. Glad I didn't know it when she was on show. Hot little devil all the same. I wouldn't mind. Curiosity. Like a nun or a negress or a girl with glasses. That squinty one is delicate. Near her monthlies I expect. Makes them feel ticklish. I have such a bad headache today. Where did I put the letter? Yes, all right. All kinds of crazy longings. Licking pennies. Girl in Tranquilla Convent that nun told me liked to smell rock oil. Virgins go mad in the end I suppose. Sister? How many women in Dublin have it today? Martha, she. Something in the air. That's the moon. But then why don't all women menstruate at the same time, with the same moon I mean? Depends on the time they were born I suppose. Or all start scratch then get out of step. Sometimes Molly and Milly together. Anyhow I got the best of that. Damned glad I didn't do it in the bath this morning over her silly I will punish you letter. Made up for that tramdriver this morning. That gouger M'Coy stopping me to say nothing. And his wife, engagement in the country, valise, voice like a pickaxe. Thankful for small mercies. Cheap too. Yours for the asking. Because they want it themselves. Their natural craving. Shoals of them every evening pouring out of offices. Reserve better. Don't want it they throw it at you. Catch 'em alive, O. Pity they can't see themselves. A dream of well-filled hose. Where was that? Ah, yes. Mutoscope pictures in Capel Street: for men only. Peeping Tom. Willy's hat and what the girls did with it. Do they snapshot those girls or is it all a fake? Lingerie does it. Felt for the curves inside her deshabille. Excites them also when they're dressed up. I'm all clean come and dirty me. And they like dressing one another for the sacrifice. Milly delighted with Molly's new blouse. At first. Put them all on to take them all off. Molly. Why I bought her the violet garters. Us too: the tie he wore, his lovely socks and turned-up trousers. He wore a pair of gaiters the night that first we met. His lovely shirt was shining beneath his what? of jet. Say a woman loses a charm with every pin she takes out. Pinned together. O, Mairy lost the pin of her. Dressed up to the nines for somebody. Fashion part of their charm. Just changes when you're on the track of the secret. Except the east: Mary, Martha: now as then. No reasonable offer refused. She wasn't in a hurry either. Always off to a fellow when they are. They never forget an appointment. Out on spec probably. They believe in chance because like themselves. And the others inclined to give her an odd dig. Girl friends at school, arms round each other's necks or with ten fingers locked, kissing and whispering secrets about nothing in the convent garden. Nuns with whitewashed faces, cool coifs and their rosaries, going up and down, vindictive too for what they can't get. Barbed wire. Be sure now and write to me. And I'll write to you. Now won't you? Molly and Josie Powell. Till Mr Right comes along, then meet once in a blue moon. *Tableau!* O, look who it is for the love of God! How are you at all? What have you been doing with yourself? Kiss and delighted to, kiss, to see you. Picking holes in each other's appearance. You're looking splendid. Sister souls. Showing their teeth at one another. How many have you left? Wouldn't lend each other a pinch of salt.

Ah!

Devils they are when that's coming on them. Dark devilish appearance. Molly often told me feel things a ton weight. Scratch the sole of my foot. O, that way! O, that's exquisite! Feel it myself too. Good to rest once in a way. Wonder if it's bad to go with them then. Safe in one way. Turns milk, makes fiddlestrings snap. Something about withering plants in a garden I read. Besides they say if the flower withers she wears she's a flirt. All are. Daresay she felt I. When you feel like that you often meet what you feel. Liked me or what? Dress they look at. Always know a fellow courting: collar and cuffs. Well, cocks and lions do the same and stags. Same time might prefer a tie undone or something. Trousers? Suppose I when I was? No. Gently does it. Dislike rough and tumble. Kiss in the dark and never tell. Saw something in me. Wonder what. Sooner have me as I am than some poet chap with bear's-grease plastery hair, lovelock over his dexter optic. To aid gentleman in literary. Ought to attend to my appearance my age. Didn't let her see me in profile. Still, you never know. Pretty girls and ugly men marrying. Beauty and the beast. Besides I can't be so if Molly. Took off her hat to show her hair. Wide brim. Bought to hide her face, meeting someone might know her, bend down or carry a bunch of flowers to smell. Hair strong in rut. Ten bob I got for Molly's combings when we were on the rocks in Holles Street. Why not? Suppose he gave her money. Why not? All a prejudice. She's worth ten shillings, fifteen, more, a pound. What? I think so. All that for nothing. Bold hand: Mrs Marion. Did I forget to write address on that letter like the postcard I sent to Flynn? And the day I went to Drimmie's without a necktie. Wrangle with Molly it was put me off. No, I remember. Richie Goulding: he's another. Weight on his mind. Funny my watch stopped at half past four. Dust. Shark liver oil they use to clean. Could do it myself. Save. Was that just when he, she?

O, he did. Into her. She did. Done.

Ah!

Mr Bloom with careful hand recomposed his wet shirt. O Lord, that little limping devil. Begins to feel cold and clammy. Aftereffect not pleasant. Still, you have to get rid of it someway. They don't care. Complimented perhaps. Go home to nicey bread and milky and say night prayers with the kiddies. Well, aren't they? See her as she is spoil all. Must have the stage setting, the rouge, costume, position, music. The name too.

Amours of actresses. Nell Gwyn, Mrs Bracegirdle, Maud Branscombe. Curtain up. Moonlight silver effulgence. Maiden discovered with pensive bosom. Little sweetheart, come and kiss me. Still, I feel. The strength it gives a man. That's the secret of it. Good job I let off then behind the wall coming out of Dignam's. Cider that was. Otherwise I couldn't have. Makes you want to sing after. *Lacaus esant taratara.* Suppose I spoke to her. What about? Bad plan however if you don't know how to end the conversation. Ask them a question they ask you another. Good idea if you're stuck. Gain time. But then you're in a cart. Wonderful of course if you say: good evening: and you see she's on for it: good evening. O, but the dark evening in the Appian Way I nearly spoke to Mrs Clinch thinking she was. Whew! Girl in Meath Street that night. All the dirty things I made her say. All wrong of course. My arks she called it. It's so hard to find one who. Aho! If you don't answer when they solicit must be horrible for them till they harden. And kissed my hand when I gave her the extra two shillings. Parrots. Press the button and the bird will squeak. Wish she hadn't called me sir. O, her mouth in the dark! And you a married man with a single girl! That's what they enjoy. Taking a man from another woman. Or even hear of it. Different with me. Glad to get away from other chap's wife. Eating off his cold plate. Chap in the Burton today spitting back gum-chewed gristle. French letter still in my pocketbook. Cause of half the trouble. But might happen sometime, I don't think. Come in, all is prepared. I dreamt. What? Worst is beginning. How they change the venue when it's not what they like. Ask you do you like mushrooms because she once knew a gentleman who. Or ask you what someone was going to say when he changed his mind and stopped. Yet if I went the whole hog, say: I want to: something like that. Because I did. She too. Offend her, then make it up. Pretend to want something awfully, then cry off for her sake. Flatters them. She must have been thinking of someone else all the time. What harm? Must have since she came to the use of reason, he, he and he. First kiss does the trick. The propitious moment. Something inside them goes pop. Mushy like, tell by their eye, on the sly. First thoughts are best. Remember that till their dying day. Molly, Lieutenant Mulvey that kissed her under the Moorish Wall beside the gardens. Fifteen she told me. But her breasts were developed. Fell asleep then. After Glencree dinner that was when we drove home over the Featherbed mountain. Gnashing her teeth in sleep. Lord mayor had his eye on her too. Val Dillon. Apoplectic.

There she is with them down there for the fireworks. My fireworks. Up like a rocket, down like a stick. And the children, twins they must be, waiting for something to happen. Want to be grown-ups. Dressing in mother's clothes. Time enough understand all the ways of the world. And the dark one with the mop head and the nigger mouth. I knew she could whistle. Mouth made for that. Like Molly. Why that high-class whore in Jammet's wore her veil only to her nose. Would you mind, please, telling me the right time? I'll tell you the right time up a dark lane. Say prunes and prisms forty times every morning, cure for fat lips. Caressing the little boy too. Onlookers see most of the game. Of course they understand birds, animals, babies. In their line.

Didn't look back when she was going down the strand. Wouldn't give that satisfaction. Those girls, those girls, those lovely seaside girls. Fine eyes she had, clear. It's the white of the eye brings that out not so much the pupil. Did she know what I? Course. Like a cat sitting beyond a dog's jump. Woman. Never meet one like that Wilkins in the High School drawing a picture of Venus with all his belongings on show. Call that innocence? Poor idiot! His wife has her work cut out for her. Never see them sit on a bench marked *Wet Paint*. Eyes all over them. Look under the bed for what's not there. Longing to get the fright of their lives. Sharp as needles they are. When I said to Molly the man at the corner of Cuffe Street was good-looking, thought she might like, twigged at once he had a false arm. Had too. Where do they get that? Typist going up Roger Greene's stairs two at a time to show her understandings. Handed down from father to, mother to daughter I mean. Bred in the bone. Milly for example drying her handkerchief on the mirror to save the ironing. Best place for an ad to catch a woman's eye, on a mirror. And when I sent her for Molly's Paisley shawl to Prescott's, by the way that ad I must, carrying home the change in her stocking. Clever little minx! I never told her. Neat way she carries parcels too. Attract men, small thing like that. Holding up her hand, shaking it, to let the blood flow back when it was red. Who did you learn that from? Nobody. Something the nurse taught me. O, don't they know! Three years old she was in front of Molly's dressing table just before we left Lombard Street West: *Me have a nice pace*. Mullingar. Who knows? Way of the world. Young student. Straight on her pins anyway, not like the other. Still, she was game. Lord, I am wet! Devil you are. Swell of her calf. Transparent stockings, stretched to breaking point. Not like that frump today. AE. Rumpled stockings. Or the one in Grafton Street. White. Wow! Beef to the heel.

A monkey-puzzle rocket burst, spluttering in darting crackles. Zrads and zrads, zrads, zrads. And Cissy and Tommy and Jacky ran out to see and Edy after with the pushcar and then Gerty beyond the curve of the rocks. Will she? Watch! Watch! See! Looked round. She smelt an onion. Darling, I saw your. I saw all.

Lord!

Did me good all the same. Off colour after Kiernan's, Dignam's. For this relief much thanks. In *Hamlet* that is. Lord! It was all things combined. Excitement. When she leaned back felt an ache at the butt of my tongue. Your head it simply swurls. He's right. Might have made a worse fool of myself however. Instead of talking about nothing. Then I will tell you all. Still, it was a kind of language between us. It couldn't be? No. Gerty they called her. Might be false name however like my name and the address Dolphin's Barn a blind.

Her maiden name was Jemima Brown
And she lived with her mother in Irishtown.

Place made me think of that, I suppose. All tarred with the same brush. Wiping pens in their stockings. But the ball rolled down to her as if it understood. Every bullet has its billet. Course I never could throw anything straight at school. Crooked as a ram's horn. Sad however because it lasts only a few years till they settle down to potwalloping and papa's pants will soon fit Willy and fuller's earth for the baby when they hold him out to do ah ah. No soft job. Saves them. Keeps them out of harm's way. Nature. Washing child, washing corpse. Dignam. Children's hands always round them. Coconut skulls, monkeys, not even closed at first, sour milk in their swaddles and tainted curds. Oughtn't to have given that child an empty teat to suck. Fill it up with wind. Mrs Beaufoy, Purefoy. Must call to the hospital. Wonder is Nurse Callan there still. She used to look over some nights when Molly was in the Coffee Palace. That young Doctor O'Hare I noticed her brushing his coat. And Mrs Breen and Mrs Dignam once like that too, marriageable. Worst of all at night Mrs Duggan told me in the City Arms. Husband rolling in drunk, stink of pub off him like a polecat. Have that in your nose in the dark, whiff of stale booze. Then ask in the morning: was I drunk last night? Bad policy however to fault the husband. Chickens come home to roost. They stick by one another like glue. Maybe the woman's fault also. That's where Molly can knock spots off them. It's the blood of the south. Moorish. Also the form, the figure. Hands felt for the opulent. Just compare for instance those others. Wife locked up at home, skeleton in the cupboard. Allow me to introduce my. Then they trot you out some kind of a nondescript, wouldn't know what to call her. Always see a fellow's weak point in his wife. Still, there's destiny in it, falling in love. Have their own secrets between them. Chaps that would go to the dogs if some woman didn't take them in hand. Then little chits of girls, height of a shilling in coppers, with little hubbies. As God made them He matched them. Sometimes children turn out well enough. Twice nought makes one. Or old rich chap of seventy and blushing bride. Marry in May and repent in December. This wet is very unpleasant. Stuck. Well, the foreskin is not back. Better detach.

Ow!

Other hand a six-footer with a wifey up to his watch pocket. Long and the short of it. Big he and little she. Very strange about my watch. Wristwatches are always going wrong. Wonder is there any magnetic influence between the person because that was about the time he. Yes, I suppose, at once. Cat's away the mice will play. I remember looking in Pill Lane. Back of everything magnetism. Earth for instance pulling this and being pulled. That causes movement. And time? Well, that's the time the movement takes. Then if one thing stopped the whole gazebo would stop bit by bit. Because it's all arranged that way down to the smallest: no mistakes. Magnetic needle tells you what's going on in the sun, the stars. Little piece of steel iron. When you hold out the fork. Come. Come. Tip. Woman and man that is. Fork and steel. Molly, he. Also that now is magnetism. Dress up and look and suggest and let you see and see more and defy you if you're a man to see that and, like a sneeze coming, legs, look, look, and if you have any guts in you. Tip. Have to let fly.

Wonder how is she feeling in that region. Shame all put on before third person. More put out about a hole in her stocking. Molly, her underjaw stuck out, head back, about the farmer in the riding boots and spurs at the Horse Show. And when the painters were in Lombard Street West. Fine voice that fellow had. How Giuglini began. Smell that I did, like flowers. It was too. Violets. Came from the turpentine probably in the paint. Make their own use of everything. Same time doing it scraped her slipper on the floor so they wouldn't hear. But lots of them can't kick the beam, I think. Keep that thing up for hours. Kind of a general all round over me and half down my back.

Wait. Hm. Hm. Yes. That's her perfume. Why she waved her hand. I leave you this to think of me when I'm far away on the pillow. What is it? Heliotrope? No. Hyacinth? Hm. Roses, I think. She'd like scent of that kind. Sweet and cheap: soon sour. Why Molly likes opopanax. Suits her. With a little jessamine mixed. Her high notes and her low notes. At the dance night she met him. Dance of the Hours. Heat brought it out. She was wearing her black dress and it had the perfume of the time before. Good conductor, is it? Or bad? Light too. Suppose there's some connection. For instance if you go into a cellar where it's dark. Mysterious thing too. Why did I smell it only now? Took its time in coming. Like herself, slow but sure. Suppose it's ever so many millions of tiny grains blown across. Yes, it is. Because those Spice Islands, Cingalese this morning, smell them leagues off. Tell you what it is. It's like a fine fine veil or web they have all over the skin, fine like what do you call it gossamer, and they're always spinning it out of them, fine as anything, like rainbow colours without knowing it. Clings to everything she takes off. Vamp of her stockings. Warm shoes. Stays. Drawers. Little kick taking them off. Bye bye till next time. Then why do they use any other? To balance. Cover up their own. Also the cat likes to sniff in her shift on the bed. Know her smell in a thousand. Bathwater too. Reminds me of strawberries and cream. Wonder where it is really. There or the armpits or under the neck? Because you get it out of all holes and corners. Hyacinth perfume made of oil of ether or something. Muskrats. Bag under their tails. One grain pour off odour for years. Dogs at each other behind. Good evening. Evening. How do you sniff? Hm. Hm. Very well, thank you. Animals go by that. Yes now, look at it that way. We're the same. Some women for instance warn you off when they have their period. Come near. Then get a hogo you could hang your hat on. Like what? Potted herrings gone stale or. Boof! Please keep off the grass.

Perhaps they get a mansmell off us. What though? Cigary gloves Long John had on his desk the other day. Breath? What you eat and drink gives that. No. Mansmell I mean. Must be connected with that because priests that are supposed to be are different. Women buzz round it like flies round treacle. Railed off the altar get on to it at any cost. The tree of forbidden priest. O father, will you? Let me be the first to. That diffuses itself all through the body, permeates. Source of life. And it's extremely curious the smell. Celery sauce. Let me.

Mr Bloom inserted his nose. Hm. Into the. Hm. Opening of his waistcoat. Almonds or. No. Lemons it is. Ah no, that's the soap.

O, by the by, that lotion. I knew there was something on my mind. Never went back and the soap not paid. Dislike carrying bottles like that hag this morning. Hynes might have paid me that three shillings. I could mention Meagher's just to remind him. Still, if he works that paragraph. Two and nine. Bad opinion of me he'll have. Call tomorrow. How much do I owe you? Three and nine? Two and nine, sir. Ah. Might stop him giving credit another time. Lose your customers that way. Pubs do. Fellows run up a bill on the slate and then slink around the back streets into somewhere else.

Here's this nobleman passed before. Blown in from the bay. Just went as far as turn back. Always at home at dinnertime. Looks mangled out: had a good tuck-in. Enjoying nature now. Grace after meals. After supper walk a mile. Sure he has a small bank balance somewhere, government sit. Walk after him now make him awkward like those newsboys me today. Still, you learn something. See ourselves as others see us. So long as women don't mock what matter? That's the way to find out. Ask yourself who is he now. *The Mystery Man on the Beach*, prize titbit story by Mr Leopold Bloom. Payment at the rate of one guinea per column. And that fellow today at the graveside in the brown macintosh. Corns on his kismet however. Healthy perhaps absorb all the. Whistle brings rain they say. Must be some somewhere. Salt in the Ormond damp. The body feels the atmosphere. Old Betty's joints are on the rack. Mother Shipton's prophecy that is about ships around they fly in the twinkling. No. Signs of rain it is. The royal reader. And distant hills seem coming nigh.

Howth. Bailey light. Two, four, six, eight, nine. See. Has to change or they might think it a house. Wreckers. Grace Darling. People afraid of the dark. Also glowworms, cyclists: lighting-up time. Jewels, diamonds flash better. Light is a kind of reassuring. Not going to hurt you. Better now of course than long ago. Country roads. Run you through the small guts for nothing. Still, two types there are you bob up against. Scowl or smile. Pardon! Not at all. Best time to spray plants too, in the shade after the sun. Some light still. Red rays are longest. Roygbiv, Vance taught us, red, orange, yellow, green, blue, indigo, violet. A star I see. Venus? Can't tell yet. Two. When three it's night. Were those nightclouds there all the time? Looks like a phantom ship. No. Wait. Trees are they? An optical illusion. Mirage. Land of the setting sun this. Home Rule sun setting in the southeast. My native land, good night.

Dew falling. Bad for you, dear, to sit on that stone. Brings on white fluxions. Never have little baby then 'less he was big strong fight his way up through. Might get piles myself. Sticks too like a summer cold, sore on the mouth. Cut with grass or paper worst. Friction of the position. Like to be that rock she sat on. O sweet little, you don't know how nice you looked. I begin to like them at that age. Green apples. Grab at all on offer. Suppose it's the only time we cross legs, seated. Also the library today: those girl graduates. Happy chairs under them. But it's the evening influence. They feel all that. Open like flowers, know their hours, sunflowers, Jerusalem artichokes, in ballrooms, chandeliers, avenues under the lamps. Nightstock in Mat Dillon's garden where I kissed her shoulder. Wish I had a full-length oil painting of her then. June that was too I wooed. The year returns. History repeats itself. Ye crags and peaks, I'm with you once again. Life, love, voyage round your own little world. And now? Sad about her lame of course but must be on your guard not to feel too much pity. They take advantage.

All quiet on Howth now. The distant hills seem. Where we. The rhododendrons. I am a fool perhaps. He gets the plums and I the plumstones. Where I come in. All that old hill has seen. Names change: that's all. Lovers: yum yum.

Tired I feel now. Will I get up? O, wait. Drained all the manhood out of me, little wretch. She kissed me. My youth. Never again. Only once it comes. Or hers. Take the train there tomorrow. No. Returning not the same. Like kids your second visit to a house. The new I want. Nothing new under the sun. Care of P.O. Dolphin's Barn. Are you not happy in your? Naughty darling. At Dolphin's Barn, charades in Luke Doyle's house. Mat Dillon and his bevy of daughters: Tiny, Atty, Floey, Mamy, Louy, Hetty. Molly too. Eighty-seven that was. Year before we. And the old major, partial to his drop of spirits. Curious she an only child, I an only child. So it returns. Think you're escaping and run into yourself. Longest way round is the shortest way home. And just when he and she. Circus horse walking in a ring. Rip Van Winkle we played. Rip: tear in Henny Doyle's overcoat. Van: breadvan delivering. Winkle: cockles and periwinkles. Then I did Rip Van Winkle coming back. She leaned on the sideboard watching. Moorish eyes. Twenty years asleep in Sleepy Hollow. All changed. Forgotten. The young are old. His gun rusty from the dew.

Ba. What is that flying about? Swallow? Bat probably. Thinks I'm a tree, so blind. Have birds no smell? Metempsychosis. They believed you could be changed into a tree from grief. Weeping willow. Ba. There he goes. Funny little beggar. Wonder where he lives. Belfry up there very likely. Hanging by his heels in the odour of sanctity. Bell scared him out, I suppose. Mass seems to be over. Could hear them all at it. Pray for us. And pray for us. And pray for us. Good idea the repetition. Same thing with ads. Buy from us. And buy from us. Yes, there's the light in the priest's house. Their frugal meal. Remember about the mistake in the valuation when I was in Thom's. Twenty-eight it is. Two houses they have. Gabriel Conroy's brother is curate. Ba. Again. Wonder why they come out at night like mice. They're a mixed breed. Birds are like hopping mice. What frightens them, light or noise? Better sit still. All instinct. Like the bird in drouth got water out of the end of a jar by throwing in pebbles. Like a little man in a cloak he is with tiny hands. Are they birds or what? Weeny bones. Almost see them glimmering, kind of a bluey white. Colours depend on the light you see. Stare at the sun for example like the eagle then look at a shoe see a blotch blob yellowish. Wants to stamp his trademark on everything. Instance, that cat this morning on the staircase colour of brown turf. Say you never see them with three colours. Not true. That half-tabby white tortoiseshell in the City Arms with the letter em on her forehead. Body fifty different colours. Howth a while ago amethyst. Glass flashing. That's how that wise man what's his name with the burning glass. Then the heather goes on fire. It can't be tourists' matches. What? Perhaps the sticks dry rub together in the wind and light. Or broken bottles in the furze act as a burning glass in the sun. Archimedes. I have it! My memory's not so bad.

Ba. Who knows what they're always flying for. Insects? That bee last week got into the room playing with his shadow on the ceiling. Might be the one bit me, come back to see. Birds too. Never find out. Or what they say. Like our small talk. And says she and says he. Nerve they have to fly over the ocean and back. Lots must be killed in storms, telegraph wires. Dreadful life sailors have too. Big brutes of oceangoing steamers floundering along in the dark, lowing out like sea cows: *Faugh a ballagh!* Out of that, bloody curse to you! Others in vessels, bit of a handkerchief sail, pitched about like snuff at a wake when the stormy winds do blow. Married too. Sometimes away for years at the ends of the earth somewhere. No ends really because it's round. Wife in every port they say. She has a good job if she minds it till Johnny comes marching home again. If ever he does. Smelling the tail end of ports. How can they like the sea? Yet they do. The anchor's weighed. Off he sails with a scapular or a medal on him for luck. Well? And the tephillin, no, what's this they call it, poor papa's father had on his door to touch. That brought us out of the land of Egypt and into the house of bondage. Something in all those superstitions because when you go out never know what dangers. Hanging on to a plank or astride of a beam for grim life, lifebelt round him, gulping salt water, and that's the last of his nibs till the sharks catch hold of him. Do fish ever get seasick?

Then you have a beautiful calm without a cloud, smooth sea, placid, crew and cargo in smithereens, Davy Jones's locker. Moon looking down so peaceful. Not my fault, old cockalorum.

A last long candle wandered up the sky from Mirus Bazaar in search of funds for Mercer's Hospital and broke, drooping, and shed a cluster of violet but one white stars. They floated, fell: they faded. The shepherd's hour: the hour of folding: hour of tryst. From house to house, giving his ever-welcome double knock, went the nine o'clock postman, the glowworm's lamp at his belt gleaming here and there through the laurel hedges. And among the five young trees a hoisted linstock lit the lamp at Leahy's Terrace. By screens of lighted windows, by equal gardens, a shrill voice went crying, wailing: *Evening Telegraph, stop-press edition! Result of the Gold Cup race!* and from the door of Dignam's house a boy ran out and called. Twittering, the bat flew here, flew there. Far out over the sands the coming surf crept, grey. Howth settled for slumber, tired of long days, of yumyum rhododendrons (he was old), and felt gladly the night breeze ruffle his fell of ferns. He lay, but opened a red eye unsleeping, deep and slowly breathing, slumberous but awake. And far on Kish Bank the anchored lightship twinkled, winked at Mr Bloom.

Life those chaps out there must have, stuck in the same spot. Irish Lights Board. Penance for their sins. Coastguards too. Rocket and breeches buoy and lifeboat. Day we went out for the pleasure cruise in the *Erin's King*, throwing them the sack of old papers. Bears in the zoo. Filthy trip. Drunkards out to shake up their livers. Puking overboard to feed the herrings. Nausea. And the women, fear of God in their faces. Milly, no sign of funk. Her blue scarf loose, laughing. Don't know what death is at that age. And then their stomachs clean. But being lost they fear. When we hid behind the tree at Crumlin. I didn't want to. Mamma! Mamma! Babes in the wood. Frightening them with masks too. Throwing them up in the air to catch them. I'll murder you. Is it only half fun? Or children playing battle. Whole earnest. How can people aim guns at each other? Sometimes they go off. Poor kids. Only troubles wildfire and nettlerash. Calomel purge I got her for that. After getting better, asleep with Molly. Very same teeth she has. What do they love? Another themselves? But the morning she chased her with the umbrella. Perhaps so as not to hurt. I felt her pulse. Ticking. Little hand it was: now big. Dearest Papli. All that the hand says when you touch. Loved to count my waistcoat buttons. Her first stays I remember. Made me laugh to see. Little paps to begin with. Left one is more sensitive, I think. Mine too. Nearer the heart. Padding themselves out if fat is in fashion. Her growing pains at night, calling, wakening me. Frightened she was when her nature came on her first. Poor child! Strange moment for the mother too. Brings back her girlhood. Gibraltar. Looking from Buena Vista. O'Hara's Tower. The seabirds screaming. Old Barbary ape that gobbled all his family. Sundown, gunfire for the men to cross the lines. Looking out over the sea she told me. Evening like this, but clear, no clouds. I always thought I'd marry a lord or a rich gentleman with a private yacht. *Buenas noches, señorita. El hombre ama la muchacha hermosa.* Why me? Because you were so foreign from the others.

Better not stick here all night like a limpet. This weather makes you dull. Must be getting on for nine by the light. Go home? Too late for *Leah, Lily of Killarney.* No. Might be still up. Call to the hospital to see. Hope she's over. Long day I've had. Martha, the bath, funeral, house of Keyes, museum with those goddesses, Dedalus' song. Then that bawler in Barney Kiernan's. Got my own back there. Drunken ranters. What I said about his God made him wince. Mistake to hit back. Or? No. Ought to go home and laugh at themselves. Always want to be swilling in company. Afraid to be alone like a child of two. Suppose he hit me. Look at it other way round. Not so bad then. Perhaps not to hurt he meant. Three cheers for Israel. Three cheers for the sister-in-law he hawked about, three fangs in her mouth. Same style of beauty. Particularly nice old party for a cup of tea. The sister of the wife of the wild man of Borneo has just come to town. Imagine that in the early morning at close range. Everyone to his taste, as Morris said when he kissed the cow. But Dignam's put the boots on it. Houses of mourning so depressing because you never know. Anyhow she wants the money. Must call to the Scottish Widows as I promised. Strange name. Takes it for granted we're going to pop off first. That widow on Monday was it outside Cramer's that looked at me. Buried the poor husband but progressing favourably on the premium. Her widow's mite. Well? What do you expect her to do? Must wheedle her way along. Widower I hate to see. Looks so forlorn. Poor man, O'Connor, wife and five children poisoned by mussels here. The sewage. Hopeless. Some good matronly woman in a porkpie hat to mother him. Take him in tow, platter face and a large apron. Ladies' grey flannelette bloomers, three shillings a pair, astonishing bargain. Plain and loved, loved for ever, they say. Ugly:

no woman thinks she is. Love, lie and be handsome for tomorrow we die. See him sometimes walking about trying to find out who played the trick. U.P: up. Fate that is. He, not me. Also a shop, often noticed. Curse seems to dog it. I was born for this too. Dreamt last night? Wait. Something confused. She had red slippers on. Turkish. Wore the breeches. Suppose she does. Would I like her in pyjamas? Damned hard to answer. Nannetti's gone. Mailboat. Near Holyhead by now. Must nail that ad of Keyes's. Work Hynes and Crawford. Petticoats for Molly. She has something to put in them. What's that? Might be money.

Mr Bloom stooped and turned over a piece of paper on the sand. He brought it near his eyes and peered. Letter? No. Can't read. Better go. Better. I'm too tired to move. Page of an old copybook. All those holes and pebbles. Who could count them? Never know what you find. Bottle with story of a treasure in it thrown from a wreck. Parcels post. Children always want to throw things in the sea. Trust? Bread cast on the waters. What's this? Bit of stick.

O! Exhausted that female has me. Not so young now. Will she come here tomorrow? Wait for her somewhere for ever. Must come back. Murderers do. Will I?

Mr Bloom with his stick gently vexed the thick sand at his foot. Write a message for her. Might remain. What?

I.

Some flatfoot tramp on it in the morning. Useless. Washed away. Tide comes here. Saw a pool near her foot. Bend, see my face there, dark mirror, breathe on it it stirs. All these rocks with lines and scars and letters. O, those transparent! Besides, they don't know. What is the meaning of that other world. I called you naughty boy because I do not like.

AM. A.

No room. Let it go.

Mr Bloom effaced the letters with his slow boot. Hopeless thing sand. Nothing grows in it. All fades. No fear of big vessels coming up here. Except Guinness's barges. Round the Kish in eighty days. Done half by design.

He flung his wooden pen away. The stick fell in silted sand, stuck. Now, if you were trying to do that for a week on end you couldn't. Chance. We'll never meet again. But it was lovely. Goodbye, dear. Thanks. Made me feel so young.

Short snooze now if I had. Must be near nine. Liverpool boat long gone. Not even the smoke. And she can do the other. Did too. And Belfast. I won't go. Race there, race back to Ennis. Let him. Just close my eyes a moment. Won't sleep though. Half dream. It never comes the same. Bat again. No harm in him. Just a few.

O sweety all your little girlwhite up I saw dirty bracegirdle made me do love sticky we two naughty Grace Darling she him half past the bed met him pike hoses frillies for Raoul de perfume your wife black hair heave under embon *señorita* young eyes Mulvey plump bubs me breadvan Winkle red slippers she rusty sleep wander years dreams return tail end Agudath swoony lovey showed me her next year in drawers return next in her next her next.

A bat flew. Here. There. Here. Far in the grey a bell chimed. Mr Bloom with open mouth, his left boot sanded sideways, leaned, breathed. Just for a few

Cuckoo.

Cuckoo.

Cuckoo.

The clock on the mantelpiece in the priest's house cooed where Canon O'Hanlon and Father Conroy and the Reverend John Hughes S.J. were taking tea and soda bread and butter and fried mutton chops with catsup and talking about

Cuckoo.

Cuckoo.

Cuckoo.

Because it was a little canarybird that came out of its little house to tell the time that Gerty MacDowell noticed the time that she was there because she was as quick as anything about a thing like that, was Gerty MacDowell, and she noticed at once that that foreign gentleman that was sitting on the rock looking was

Cuckoo.

Cuckoo.

Cuckoo.

Deshil Holles Eamus. Deshil Holles Eamus. Deshil Holles Eamus.

Send us, bright one, light one, Horhorn, quickening and wombfruit.
Send us, bright one, light one, Horhorn, quickening and wombfruit.
Send us, bright one, light one, Horhorn, quickening and wombfruit.

Hoopsa, boyaboy, hoopsa! Hoopsa, boyaboy, hoopsa! Hoopsa, boyaboy, hoopsa!

Universally that person's acumen is esteemed very little perceptive concerning whatsoever matters are being held as most profitably by mortals with sapience endowed to be studied who is ignorant of that which the most in doctrine erudite and certainly by reason of that in them high mind's ornament deserving of veneration constantly maintain when by general consent they affirm that other circumstances being equal by no exterior splendour is the prosperity of a nation more efficaciously asserted than by the measure of how far forward may have progressed the tribute of its solicitude for that proliferent continuance which of evils the original if it be absent when fortunately present constitutes the certain sign of omnipollent nature's incorrupted benefaction. For who is there who anything of some significance has apprehended but is conscious that that exterior splendour may be the surface of a downward-tending and lutulent reality or on the contrary anyone so is there unilluminated as not to perceive that as no nature's boon can contend against the bounty of increase so it behoves every most just citizen to become the exhortator and admonisher of his semblables and to tremble lest what had in the past been by the nation excellently commenced might be in the future not with similar excellence accomplished if an inverecund habit shall have gradually traduced the honourable by ancestors transmitted customs to that thither of profundity that that one was audacious excessively who would have the hardihood to rise affirming that no more odious offence can for anyone be than to oblivious neglect to consign that evangel simultaneously command and promise which on all mortals with prophecy of abundance or with diminution's menace that exalted of reiteratedly procreating function ever irrevocably enjoined?

It is not why therefore we shall wonder if, as the best historians relate, among the Celts, who nothing that was not in its nature admirable admired, the art of medicine shall have been highly honoured. Not to speak of hostels, leperyards, sweating chambers, plaguegraves, their greatest doctors, the O'Shiels, the O'Hickeys, the O'Lees, have sedulously set down the divers methods by which the sick and the relapsed found again health whether the malady had been the trembling withering or loose boyconnell flux. Certainly in every public work which in it anything of gravity contains preparation should be with importance commensurate and therefore a plan was by them adopted (whether by having preconsidered or as the maturation of experience it is difficult in being said which the discrepant opinions of subsequent inquirers are not up to the present congrued to render manifest) whereby maternity was so far from all accident possibility removed that whatever care the patient in that all hardest of woman hour chiefly required and not solely for the copiously opulent but also for her who not being sufficiently moneyed scarcely and often not even scarcely could subsist valiantly and for an inconsiderable emolument was provided.

To her nothing already then and thenceforward was anyway able to be molestful for this chiefly felt all citizens except with proliferent mothers prosperity at all not to can be and as they had received eternity gods mortals generation to befit them her beholding, when the case was so hoving itself, parturient in vehicle thereward carrying desire immense among all one another was impelling on of her to be received in to that domicile. O thing of prudent nation not merely in being seen but also even in being related worthy of being praised that they her by anticipation went seeing mother, that she by them suddenly to be about to be cherished had been begun she felt!

Before born babe bliss had. Within womb won he worship. Whatever in that one case done commodiously done was. A couch by midwives attended with wholesome food reposeful and cleanest swaddles as though forthbringing were now done and by wise foresight set: but to this no less also of what drugs there is need and surgical implements which are pertaining to her case not omitting aspect of all very distracting spectacles in various latitudes by our terrestrial orb offered together with images, divine and human, the cogitation of which by sejunct females is to tumescence conducive or eases issue in the high sunbright well-built fair home of mothers when, ostensibly far gone and reproductive, it is come by her thereto to lie in, her term up.

Some man that wayfaring was stood by house door at night's oncoming. Of Israel's folk was that man that on earth wandering far had fared. Stark ruth of man his errand that him love led to that house.

Of that house A. Horne is lord. Seventy beds keeps he there where teeming mothers are wont that they lie for to thole and bring forth bairns hale so God's angel to Mary quoth. Watchers twey there walk, white sisters in ward sleepless. Smarts they still, sickness soothing: in twelve moons thrice an hundred. Truest bedthanes they twain are, for Horne holding wariest ward.

In ward wary the watcher hearing come that man mild-hearted eft rising with swire ywimpled to him her gate wide undid. Lo, levin leaping lightens in eyeblink Ireland's westward welkin! Full she drad that God the Wreaker all mankind would fordo with water for his evil sins. Christ's rood made she on breastbone and him drew that he would rathe infare under her thatch. That man her will wotting worthful went in Horne's house.

Loth to irk in Horne's hall hat holding the seeker stood. On her stow he ere was living with dear wife and lovesome daughter that then over land and seafloor nine years had long outwandered. Once her in townhithe meeting he to her bow had not doffed. Her to forgive now he craved with good ground of her allowed that that of him swiftseen face, hers, so young then had looked. Light swift her eyes kindled, bloom of blushes his word winning.

As her eyes then ongot his weeds swart therefor sorrow she feared. Glad after she was that ere adread was. Her he asked if O'Hare Doctor tidings sent from far coast and she with grameful sigh him answered that O'Hare Doctor in heaven was. Sad was the man that word to hear that him so heavied in bowels ruthful. All she then told him, ruing death for friend so young, algate sore unwilling God's rightwiseness to withsay. She said that he had a fair sweet death through God His goodness with masspriest to be shriven him, holy housel to eat and sick men's oil to his limbs. The man then right earnest asked the nun of which death the dead man was died and the nun answered him and said that he was died in Mona Island through bellycrab three year agone come Childermas and she prayed to God the Allruthful to have his dear soul in his undeathliness. He heard her sad words, in held hat sad staring. So stood they there both awhile in wanhope sorrowing one with other.

Therefore, everyman, look to that last end that is thy death and the dust that gripeth on every man that is born of woman for as he came naked forth from his mother's womb so naked shall he wend him at the last for to go as he came.

The man that was come into the house then spoke to the nursingwoman and he asked her how it fared with the woman that lay there in childbed. The good nursingwoman answered him and said that that woman was in throes now full three days and that it would be a hard birth unneth to bear but that now in a little it would be. She said thereto that she had seen many births of women but never was none so hard as was that woman's birth. Then she set it forth all to him for because she knew the man that time was had lived nigh that house. The man hearkened to her words for he felt with wonder women's woe in the travail that they have of motherhood and he wondered to look on her face that was a fair face for any man to see but yet was she left after long years a handmaid. Nine twelve bloodflows chiding her childless.

And whiles they spake the door of the castle was opened and there nighed them near a mickle noise as of many that sat there at meat. And there came against the place as they stood a young learning knight yclept Dixon. And the traveller Leopold was couth to him sithen it had happed that they had had ado each with other in the house of our mother of misericord where this learning knight lay by cause the traveller Leopold came there to be healed for he was sore wounded in his breast by a spear wherewith a horrible and dreadful dragon was smitten him for which he did do make a salve of volatile salt and chrism as much as he might suffice. And he said now that he should go into that castle for to make merry with them that were there. And the traveller Leopold said that he should go otherwhither for he was a man of cautels and a subtile. Also the lady was of his avis and repreved the learning knight though she trowed well that the traveller had said thing that was false for his subtility. But the learning knight would not hear say nay nor do her mandement ne have him neither in aught contrarious to his list and he said how it was a marvellous castle. And the traveller Leopold went into the castle for to rest him for a space being sore of limb after many marches environing in divers lands and sometime venery.

And in the castle was set a board that was of the birchwood of Finlandy and it was upheld by four dwarfmen of that country but they durst not move more for enchantment. And on this board were frightful swords and knives that are made in a great cavern by swinking demons out of white flames that they fix in the horns of buffalos and stags that there abound marvellously. And there were vessels that are wrought by magic of Mahound out of seasand and the air by a warlock with his breath that he blares into them like to bubbles. And full fair cheer and rich was on the board that no wight could devise a fuller ne richer. And there was a vat of silver that was moved by craft to open in the which lay strange fishes withouten heads though misbelieving men nie that this be possible thing without they see it. Yet natheless they are so. And these fishes lie in an oily water brought there from Portugal land because of the fatness that therein is which is like to the juices of the olive press. And also it was a marvel to see in that castle how by magic they make a compost out of fecund wheat kidneys out of Chaldee that by aid of certain angry spirits that they do into it swells up wondrously like to a vast mountain. And they teach the serpents there to entwine themselves up on long sticks out of the ground and of the scales of these serpents they brew out a brewage like to mead.

And the learning knight let pour for Childe Leopold a draught of fellowship and a halp thereto the which all they that were there drank every each. And Childe Leopold did up his beaver for to pleasure him and took apertly somewhat in amity for he never drank no manner of mead which he then put by and anon privily he voided it the more part in his neighbour glass and his neighbour wist not of this wile. And he sat down in that castle with them for to rest him there awhile. Thanked be Almighty God.

This meanwhile the good sister stood by the door and begged them at the reverence of Jesu our alther liege Lord to leave their wassailing for there was above one quick with child, a gentle dame, whose time hied fast. Sir Leopold heard in the upfloor cry on high and he wondered what cry that it was, whether of child or woman. I marvel, said he, it be not come or now. Meseems it dureth overlong. And he was ware of and saw a franklin that hight Lenehan on that side the table that was older than any of the tother and for that they both were knights venturous in the one emprise and eke by cause that he was elder he spoke to him fully gently. But, said he, or it be long too she will bring forth by God His bounty and have joy of her childing for she hath waited marvellous long. And the franklin that had drunken said, Expecting each moment to be her next.

Also he took the cup that stood tofore him for him needed never none asking nor desiring of him to drink and, Now drink, said he full delectably, and he quaffed as far as he might to their both's health for he was a passing good man of his lustiness. And Sir Leopold that was the goodliest guest that ever sat in scholars' hall and that was the meekest man and the kindest that ever laid husbandly hand under hen and that was the very gentlest knight of the world, one that ever did minion service to lady gentle, pledged him courtly in the cup. Woman's woe with wonder pondering.

Now let us speak of that fellowship that was there to the intent to be drunken an they might. There was a sort of scholars along either side the board, that is to wit, Dixon yclept junior of Saint Mary Merciable's with other his fellows Lynch and Madden, scholars of medicine, and the franklin that hight Lenehan and one from Alba Longa, one Crotthers, and young Stephen that had mien of a frere that was at head of the board and Costello that men clepen Punch Costello all long of a mastery of him erewhile gested (and of all them, reserved young Stephen, he was the most drunken that demanded still of more mead) and beside the meek Sir Leopold. But on young Malachi they waited for that he promised to have come and such as intended to no goodness said how he had broke his avow. And Sir Leopold sat with them for he bore fast friendship to Sir Simon and to this his son young Stephen and for that his languor becalmed him there after longest wanderings insomuch as they feasted him for that time in the honourablest manner. Ruth rede him, love led on with will to wander, loth to leave.

For they were right witty scholars. And he heard their aresouns each gen other as touching birth and righteousness, young Madden maintaining that put such case it were hard the wife to die (for so it had fallen out a matter of some years agone with a woman of Eblana in Horne's house that now was trespassed out of this world and the self night next before her death all leeches and pothecaries had taken counsel of her case). And they said farther she should live because in the beginning, they said, the woman should bring forth in pain and travail and wherefore they that were of this imagination affirmed how young Madden had said truth for he had conscience to let her die. And not few and of these was young Lynch were in doubt that the world was now right evil governed as it was never other howbeit the mean people believed it otherwise but the law nor his judges did provide no remedy. A redress God grant. This was scant said but all cried with one acclaim, Nay, by our Virgin Mother, the wife should live (sith she was God's creature as well as other) and the babe to die. In colour whereof they waxed hot upon that head what with argument and what for their drinking but the franklin Lenehan was prompt each when to pour them ale so that at the least way mirth might not lack. Then young Madden showed all the whole affair and when they had heard her case how that she was dead and how for holy religion sake by rede of palmer and bedesman and for a vow he had made to Saint Ultan of Ardbraccan her goodman husband would not let her death whereby they were one and all wondrous grieved. To whom young Stephen had these words following, Murmur, sirs, is eke oft among low folk. Both babe and parent now glorify their Maker, the one in limbo gloom, the other in purge fire. But, gramercy, what of those Godpossibled souls that we nightly impossibilise, which is the sin against the Holy Ghost, Very God, Lord and Giver of Life? For, sirs, he said, our mickle of lust is brief. We are means to those small creatures within us and nature, giving that, has other ends than we. Then said Dixon junior to Punch Costello wist he what ends. But he had overmuch drunken and the best word he could have of him was that he would ever dishonest a woman whoso she were, were she wife or maid or leman, if it so fortuned him to be delivered of his spleen of lustihead. Whereat young Stephen presently poured him mead in his cup, saying it was well said if not well done. And Crotthers of Alba Longa sang young Malachi's praise of that beast the unicorn how once in the millennium he cometh by his horn, he all that while, pricked forward with their jibes wherewith they did malice him, witnessing all and several by Saint Foutinus his engines that he was able by grace of his privities to do any manner of thing that lay in man to do. Thereat laughed they all right jocundly only young Stephen and Sir Leopold which never durst laugh too open by reason of a strange humour which he would not bewray and also for that he rued for her that bare whoso she might be or wheresoever. Then spake young Stephen orgulous of Mother Church that would cast him out of her bosom, of law of canons, of Lilith, patron of abortions, of bigness wrought by wind of seeds of brightness or by potency of vampires mouth to mouth or, as Virgilius saith, by the influence of the occident or by the reek of moonflower or an she lie with a woman which her man has but lain with, *effectu secuto*, or peradventure in her bath according to the opinions of Averroës and Moses Maimonides. He said also how at the end of the second month a human soul was infused and how in all our holy mother foldeth ever souls for God's greater glory whereas that earthly mother which was but a dam to bring forth beastly should die by canon for so saith he that holdeth the fisherman's seal, even that blessed Peter on which rock was Holy Church for all ages founded. All they bachelors then asked of Sir Leopold would he in like case so jeopard her person as risk life to save life. A wariness of mind he would answer as fitted all and, laying hand to jaw, he said dissembling, as his wont was, that as it was informed him, who had ever loved the art of physic as might a layman, and agreeing also with his experience of so seldom seen an accident, it was good for that Mother Church belike at one blow had birth and death pence and in such sort deliverly he scaped their question. That is truth, pardy, said Dixon, and, or I err, a pregnant word. Which hearing, young Stephen was a marvellous glad man and he averred that he who stealeth from the poor lendeth to the Lord, for he was ever of a wild manner when he was drunken and that he was now in that taking it appeared eftsoons.

But Sir Leopold was passing grave, maugre his word, by cause he still had pity of the terror-causing shrieking of shrill women in their labour and as he was minded of his good lady Marion that had borne him an only manchild which on his eleventh day on live had died and no man of art could save so dark is destiny. And she was wondrous stricken of heart for that evil hap and for his burial, sore weeping, did him on a fair corselet of lamb's wool, the flower of the flock, lest he might perish utterly and lie akeled (for it was then about the midst of the winter): and now Sir Leopold that had of his body no manchild for an heir looked upon him, his friend's son, and was shut up in sorrow for his forepassed happiness and as sad as he was that him failed a son of such gentle courage (for all accompted him of real parts) so grieved he also in no less measure for young Stephen for that he lived riotously with those wastrels and murdered his goods with whores.

About that present time young Stephen filled full all cups that stood empty of their portion so as there remained but little mo, if some of the prudenter had not shrouded their approach from him that still plied it very busily who, praying for the intentions of the sovereign pontiff, gave them for a pledge the vicar of Christ which also, as he judged, was, by all signs and tokens, vicar of Bray. Now drink we, quod he, of this mazer and quaff ye this mead which is not indeed parcel of my body but my soul's bodiment. Leave ye fraction of bread to them that live by bread alone. Be not afeard neither for any want for this will comfort more than the other will dismay. See ye here. And he showed them glistering coins of the tribute and goldsmiths' notes to the worth of two pounds nineteen shillings that he had, he said, for a song which he writ. They all admired to see the foresaid riches in such dearth of money as was herebefore. His words were then these as followeth: Know all men, he said, time's ruins build eternity's mansions. What means this? Desire's wind blasts the thorntree but after it becomes from a bramblebush to be a rose upon the rood of time. Mark me now. In woman's womb word is made flesh but in the spirit of the maker all flesh that passes becomes the word that shall not pass away. This is the postcreation. *Omnis caro ad te veniet.* No question but her name is puissant who aventried the dear corse of our Agenbuyer, Healer and Herd, our mighty mother and mother most venerable, and Bernardus saith aptly that she hath an *omnipotentiam deiparae supplicem,* that is to wit, an almightiness of petition, because she is the second Eve and she won us, saith Augustine too, whereas that other, our grandam, which we are linked up with by successive anastomosis of navelcords, sold us all, seed, breed and generation, for a penny pippin. But here is the matter now. Or she knew him, that second I say, and was but creature of her creature, *vergine madre, figlia di tuo figlio,* or she knew him not and then stands she in the one denial or ignorance with Peter Piscator, who lives in the house that Jack built, and with Joseph the Joiner, patron of the happy demise of all unhappy marriages, *parce que M. Léo Taxil nous a dit que qui l'avait mise dans cette fichue position, c'était le sacré pigeon, ventre de Dieu! Entweder* transubstantiality *oder* consubstantiality but in no case sub-substantiality. And all cried as one man: Out upon it for a very scurvy word. A pregnancy without joy, he said, a birth without pangs, a body without blemish, a belly without bigness. Let the lewd with faith and fervour worship. With will will we withstand, withsay.

Hereupon Punch Costello dinged with his fist upon the board and would sing a bawdy catch *Staboo Stabella* about a wench that was put in pod of a jolly swashbuckler in Almany which he did straightways now attack

The first three months she was not well, Staboo...

when here Nurse Quigley from the door angerly bid them hist, ye should shame you, nor was it not meet as she remembered them, being her mind was to have all orderly against Lord Andrew came for because she was jealous that no gasteful turmoil might shorten the honour of her guard. It was an ancient and a sad matron of a sedate look and a Christian walking, in habit dun beseeming her megrims and wrinkled visage, nor did her hortative want of it effect for incontinently Punch Costello was of them all embraided and they reclaimed the churl with civil rudeness some to countervail the same and shaked him with menace of blandishments others, whiles all chode with him, a murrain seize the dolt, what a devil he would be at, thou chuff, thou puny, thou got in peasestraw, thou losel, thou chitterling, thou spawn of a rebel, thou dykedropt, thou abortion thou, to shut up his drunken drool out of that like a curse of God ape, the good Sir Leopold that had for his cognisance the flower of quiet, margerain gentle, advising also the time's occasion as most sacred and most worthy to be most sacred. In Horne's house rest should reign.

To be short, this passage was scarce by when Master Dixon of Mary in Eccles, goodly grinning, asked young Stephen what was the reason why he had not cided to take friar's vows and he answered him: obedience in the womb, chastity in the tomb but involuntary poverty all his days. Master Lenehan at this made return that he had heard of those nefarious deeds and how, as he heard hereof counted, he had besmirched the lily virtue of a confiding female which was corruption of minors and they all intershowed it too, waxing merry and toasting to his fathership. But he said very entirely it was clean contrary to their suppose for he was the eternal son and ever virgin. Thereat mirth grew in them the more and they rehearsed to him his curious rite of wedlock for the disrobing and deflowering of spouses as the priests use in Madagascar Island, she to be in guise of white and saffron, her groom in white and grain, with burning of nard tapers, on a bridebed while clerks sung kyries and the anthem *Ut novetur sexus omnis corporis mysterium* till she was there unmaided. He gave them then a much admirable hymen minim by those delicate poets Master John Fletcher and Master Francis Beaumont that is in their *Maid's Tragedy* that was writ for a like twining of lovers, *To bed, to bed* was the burden of it, to be played with accompanable concent upon the virginals. An exquisite dulcet epithalame of most mollificative suadency for juveniles amatory whom the odoriferous flambeaus of the paranymphs have escorted to the quadrupedal proscenium of connubial communion. Well met they were, said Master Dixon, joyed, but, harkee, young sir, better were they named Beau Mount and Lecher for, by my troth, of such a mingling much might come. Young Stephen said indeed to his best remembrance they had but the one doxy between them and she of the stews to make shift with in delights amorous for life ran very high in those days and the custom of the country approved with it. Greater love than this, he said, no man hath, that a man lay down his wife for his friend. Go thou and do likewise. Thus, or words to that effect, saith Zarathustra, sometime regius professor of French letters to the university of Oxtail, nor breathed there ever that man to whom mankind was more beholden. Bring a stranger within thy tower it will go hard but thou wilt have the second-best bed. *Orate, fratres, pro memetipso.* And all the people shall say, Amen. Remember, Erin, thy generations and thy days of old, how thou settedst little by me and by my word and broughtedst in a stranger to my gates to commit fornication in my sight and to wax fat and kick like Jeshurun. Therefore hast thou sinned against my light and hast made me, thy lord, to be the slave of servants. Return, return, Clan Milly: forget me not, O Milesian! Why hast thou done this abomination before me, that thou didst spurn me for a merchant of jalaps and didst deny me to the Roman and to the Indian of dark speech with whom thy daughters did lie luxuriously? Look forth now, my people, upon the land of behest, even from Horeb and from Nebo and from Pisgah and from the Horns of Hatten unto a land flowing with milk and money. But thou hast suckled me with a bitter milk: my moon and my sun thou hast quenched for ever. And thou hast left me alone for ever in the dark ways of my bitterness: and with a kiss of ashes hast thou kissed my mouth. This tenebrosity of the interior, he proceeded to say, hath not been illumined by the wit of the Septuagint nor so much as mentioned, for the Orient from on high which brake hell's gates visited a darkness that was foraneous. Assuefaction minorates atrocities (as Tully saith of his darling Stoics) and Hamlet his father showeth the prince no blister of combustion. The adiaphane in the noon of life is an Egypt's plague which in the nights of prenativity and postmortemity is their most proper *ubi* and *quomodo*. And as the ends and ultimates of all things accord in some mean and measure with their inceptions and originals, that same multiplicit concordance which leads forth growth from birth accomplishing by a retrogressive metamorphosis that minishing and ablation towards the final which is agreeable unto nature, so is it with our subsolar being. The aged sisters draw us into life: we wail, batten, sport, clip, clasp, sunder, dwindle, die: over us dead they bend. First, saved from water of old Nile, among bulrushes, a bed of fasciated wattles: at last, the cavity of a mountain, an occulted sepulchre, amid the conclamation of the hillcat and the ossifrage. And as no man knows the ubicity of his tumulus nor to what ineluctable processes we shall thereby be ushered nor whether to Tophet or to Edenville, in the like way is all hidden when we would backward see from what region of remoteness the whatness of our whoness hath fetched his whenceness.

Thereto Punch Costello roared out mainly, *Étienne, chanson,* but he loudly bid them, lo, Wisdom hath built herself a house, this vast majestic longstablished vault, the crystal palace of the Creator, all in apple-pie order, a penny for him who finds the pea.

> *Behold the mansion reared by dedal Jack,*
> *See the malt stored in many a refluent sack,*
> *In the proud cirque of Jackjohn's bivouac.*

A black crack of noise in the street here, alack, bawled back. Loud on left Thor thundered: in anger awful the hammerhurler. Came now the storm that hist his heart. And Master Lynch bade him have a care to flout and witwanton as the god self was angered for his hellprate and paganry. And he that had erst challenged to be so doughty waxed wan as they might all mark and shrank together and his pitch that was before so haught uplift was now of a sudden quite plucked down and his heart shook within the cage of his breast as he tasted the rumour of that storm. Then did some mock and some jeer and Punch Costello fell hard again to his yale which Master Lenehan vowed he would do after and he was indeed but a word and a blow on any the least colour. But the braggart boaster cried that an old Nobodaddy was in his cups it was muchwhat indifferent and he would not lag behind his lead. But this was only to dye his desperation as cowed he crouched in Horne's hall. He drank indeed and all at one draught to pluck up a heart of any grace for it thundered long rumblingly over all the heavens so that Master Madden, being godly certain whiles, knocked him on his ribs upon that crack of doom and Master Bloom, at the braggart's side, spoke to him calming words to slumber his great fear, advertising how it was no other thing but a hubbub noise that he heard, the discharge of fluid from the thunderhead, look you, having taken place and all of the order of a natural phenomenon.

But was young Boasthard's fear vanquished by Calmer's words? No, for he had in his bosom a spike named Bitterness which could not by words be done away. And was he then neither calm like the one nor godly like the other? He was neither as much as he would have liked to be either. But could he not have endeavoured to have found again as in his youth the bottle Holiness that then he lived withal? Indeed no, for Grace was not there to find that bottle. Heard he then in that clap the voice of the god Bringforth or, what Calmer said, a hubbub of Phenomenon? Heard? Why, he could not but hear both of those things unless he had plugged him up the tube Understanding (which he had not done). For through that tube he saw that he was in the land of Phenomenon where he must for a certain one day die as he was like the rest too a passing show. And would he not accept to die like the rest and pass away? By no means would he though he must nor would he make more shows according as men do with wives which Phenomenon has commanded them to do by the book Law. Then wotted he nought of that other land which is called Believe-on-Me that is the land of promise which behoves to the king Delightful and shall be for ever where there is no death and no birth, neither wiving nor mothering, at which all shall come, as many as believe on it? Yes, Pious had told him of that land and Chaste had pointed him to the way but the reason was that in the way he fell in with a certain whore of an eye-pleasing exterior whose name, she said, is Bird-in-the-Hand and she beguiled him wrongways from the true path by her flatteries that she said to him as, Ho, you pretty man, turn aside hither and I will show you a brave place, and she lay at him so flatteringly that she had him in her grot of shame which is named Two-in-the-Bush or, by some learned men also, Carnal Concupiscence.

This was it what all that company that sat there at commons in Manse of Mothers the most lusted after and if they met with this whore Bird-in-the-Hand (which was within all foul plagues, monsters and a wicked devil) they would strain the last but they would make at her and know her. For regarding Believe-on-Me they said it was nought else but notion and they could conceive no thought of it for, first, Two-in-the-Bush whither she ticed them was the very goodliest grot and in it were four pillows on which were four tickets with these words printed on them, Pickaback and Topsyturvy and Shameface and Cheek by Jowl and, second, for that foul plague Allpox and the monsters they cared not for them for Preservative had given them a stout shield of oxengut and, third, that they might take no hurt neither from Offspring that was that wicked devil by virtue of this same shield which was named Killchild. So were they all in their blind fancy, Mr Cavil and Mr Sometimes Godly, Mr Ape Swillale, Mr False Franklin, Mr Dainty Dixon, Young Boasthard and Mr Cautious Calmer. Wherein, O wretched company, were ye all deceived for that was the voice of the god that was in a very grievous rage that he would presently lift his arm up and spill their souls for their abuses and their spillings done by them contrariwise to his word which forth to bring brenningly biddeth.

So Thursday sixteenth June Patk. Dignam laid in clay of an apoplexy and after hard drought, please God, rained, a bargeman coming in by water a fifty mile or thereabout with turf saying the seed won't sprout, fields looked athirst, very sad-coloured and stunk mightily, the quags and tofts too. Hard to breathe and all the young quicks clean consumed without sprinkle this long while back as no man remembered to be without. The rosy buds all gone brown and spread out blobs and on the hills nought but dry flag and faggots that would catch at first fire. All the world saying, for aught they knew, the big wind of last February a year that did havoc the land so pitifully was a small thing beside this barrenness. But by and by, as said, this evening after sundown, the wind sitting in the west, biggish swollen clouds to be seen as the night increased and the weatherwise poring up at them and some sheet lightnings at first and after, past ten of the clock, one great stroke with a long thunder and in a brace of shakes all scamper pellmell within door for the smoking shower, the men making shelter for their straws with a clout or kerchief, womenfolk skipping off with kirtles catched up soon as the pour came. In Ely Place, Baggot Street, Duke's Lawn, thence through Merrion Green up to Holles Street a swash of water running that was before bone dry and not one chair or coach or fiacre seen about but no more crack after that first. Over against the Rt. Hon. Mr Justice Fitzgibbon's door (that is to sit with Mr Healy the lawyer upon the college lands) Mal. Mulligan, a gentleman's gentleman that had but come from Mr Moore's the writer's (that was a papish but is now, folk say, a good Williamite), chanced against Al. Bannon in a cut bob (which are now in with dance cloaks of Kendal green) that was new got to town from Mullingar with the stage where his coz and Mal. M.'s brother will stay a month yet till Saint Swithin and asks what in the earth he does there, he bound home and he to Andrew Horne's being stayed for to crush a cup of wine, so he said, but would tell him of a skittish heifer, big of her age and beef to the heel, and all this while poured with rain and so both together on to Horne's. There Leop. Bloom of Crawford's journal sitting snug with a covey of wags, likely brangling fellows, Dixon jun., scholar of my Lady of Mercy's, Vin. Lynch, a Scots fellow, Will. Madden, T. Lenehan, very sad about a racer he fancied, and Stephen D. Leop. Bloom there for a languor he had before but was now better, he having dreamed tonight a strange fancy of his dame Mrs Moll with red slippers on in a pair of Turkey trunks which is thought by those in ken to be for an omen of change, and Mistress Purefoy there that got in through pleading her belly and now on the stools, poor body, two days past her term, the midwives sore put to it, and can't deliver, she queasy for a bowl of riceslop that is a shrewd drier up of the insides and her breath very heavy more than good and should be a bullyboy from the knocks, they say, but God give her soon issue. 'Tis her ninth chick to live, I hear, and Lady Day bit off her last chick's nails that was then a twelvemonth and with other three all breast-fed that died written out in a fair hand in the king's Bible. Her hub fifty odd and a Methodist but takes the sacrament and is to be seen any fair Sabbath with a pair of his boys off Bullock Harbour dapping on the sound with a heavy-braked reel or in a punt he has trailing for flounder and pollock and catches a fine bag, I hear. In sum an infinite great fall of rain and all refreshed and will much increase the harvest yet those in ken say after wind and water fire shall come for a prognostication of Malachi's almanac (and I hear that Mr Russell has done a prophetical charm of the same gist out of the Hindustanish for his farmer's gazette) to have three things in all, but this a mere fetch without bottom of reason for old crones and bairns yet sometimes they are found in the right guess with their queerities, no telling how.

With this came up Lenehan to the feet of the table to say how the letter was in that night's gazette and he made a show to find it about him (for he swore with an oath that he had been at pains about it) but on Stephen's persuasion he gave over the search and was bidden to sit near by which he did mighty brisk. He was a kind of sport gentleman that went for a merry-andrew or honest pickle and what belonged of women, horseflesh or hot scandal in the town he had it pat. To tell the truth he was mean in fortunes and for the most part hankered about the coffeehouses and low taverns with crimps, ostlers, bookies, Paul's men, runners, flatcaps, waist-coateers, ladies of the bagnio and other rogues of the game or with a chanceable catchpole or a tipstaff, often at nights till broad day, of whom he picked up between his sackpossets much loose gossip. He took his ordinary at a boilingcook's and if he had but gotten into him a mess of broken victuals or a platter of tripes with a bare tester in his purse in any company he could always bring himself off with his tongue with some randy quip he had from a punk or whatnot that every mother's son of them would burst their sides. The other, Costello that is, hearing this talk asked was it poetry or a tale. Faith, no, he says, Frank (that was his name), 'tis all about Kerry cows that are to be butchered along of the plague. But they can go hang, says he with a wink, for me with their bully beef, a pox on it. There's as good fish in this tin as ever came out of it, and very friendly he offered to take of some salty sprats that stood by which he had eyed wishly in the meantime and found the place which was indeed the chief design of his embassy as he was sharp-set. *Mort aux vaches*, says Frank then in the French language that had been indentured to a brandy shipper that has a winelodge in Bordeaux and he spoke French like a gentleman too. From a child this Frank had been a do-nought that his father, a headborough who could ill keep him to school to learn his letters and the use of the globes, matriculated at the university to study the mechanics but he took the bit between his teeth like a raw colt and was more familiar with the justiciary and the parish beadle than with his volumes. One time he would be a playactor, then a sutler or a welsher, then nought would keep him from the bearpit and the cocking main, then he was for the ocean sea or to hoof it on the roads with the Romany folk, kidnapping a squire's heir by favour of moonlight, fecking maids' linen or choking chickens behind a hedge. He had been off as many times as a cat has lives and back again with naked pockets as many more to his father the headborough who shed a pint of tears as often as he saw him. What, says Mr Leopold, with his hands across, that was earnest to know the drift of it, will they slaughter all? I protest I saw them but this day morning going to the Liverpool boat, says he. I can scarce believe 'tis so bad, says he. And he had experience of the like brood beasts and of springers, greasy hoggets and wether wool, having been some years before actuary for Mr Joseph Cuffe, a worthy salesmaster that drove his trade for livestock and meadow auctions hard by Mr Gavin Low's yard in Prussia Street. I question with you there, says he. More like 'tis the hoose or the timber tongue. Mr Stephen, a little moved but very handsomely, told him no such matter and that he had dispatches from the emperor's chief tailtickler thanking him for the hospitality, that was sending over Doctor Rinderpest, the best-quoted cowcatcher in all Muscovy, with a bolus or two of physic to take the bull by the horns. Come, come, says Mr Vincent, plain dealing. He'll find himself soon on the horns of a dilemma if he meddles with a bull that's Irish, says he. Irish by name and irish by nature, says Mr Stephen, as he sent the ale purling about. An Irish bull in an English chinashop. I conceive you, says Mr Dixon, it is that same bull that was sent to our island by Farmer Nicholas, the bravest cattle breeder of them all, with an emerald ring in his nose. True for you, says Mr Vincent cross the table, and a bull's-eye into the bargain, says he, and a plumper and a portlier bull, says he, never shit on shamrock. He had horns galore, a coat of cloth of gold and a sweet smoky breath coming out of his nostrils so that the women of our island, leaving doughballs and rolling pins, followed after him everywhere, hanging his bulliness in daisychains. What for that, says Mr Dixon, but before he came over Farmer Nicholas that was a eunuch had him properly gelded by a college of doctors who were no better off than himself. So be off now, says he, and do all my cousin-german the Lord Harry tells you and take a farmer's blessing, and with that he slapped his posteriors very soundly. But the slap and the blessing stood him friend, says Mr Vincent, for to make up he taught him a trick worth two of the other so that maid, wife, abbess and widow to this day affirm that they would rather any time of the month whisper in his ear in the dark of a cowhouse or get a lick on the nape from his holy tongue than lie with the finest strapping young ravisher in the four fields of all Ireland. Another then put in his word: And they dressed him, says he, in a point shift and petticoat with a tippet and girdle and ruffles on his wrists and clipped his forelock and rubbed him all over with spermaceti oil and built stables for him at every turn of the road with a gold manger in each full of the best hay in the market so that he could doss and dung to his heart's content. By this time the father of the faithful (for so they called him) was grown so heavy that he could scarce walk to pasture. To remedy which our cozening dames and damsels brought him his fodder in their apron laps and as soon as his belly was full he would rear up on his hindquarters to show their ladyships a mystery and roar and bellow out of him in bulls' language and they all after him. Ay, says another, and so pampered was he that he would suffer nought to grow in all the land but green grass for himself (for that was the only colour to his mind) and there was a board put up on a hillock in the middle of the island with a printed notice, saying: By the Lord Harry, green is the grass that grows on the ground. And, says Mr Dixon, if ever he got scent of a cattle raider in Roscommon or the wilds of Connemara or a husbandman in Sligo that was sowing as much as a handful of mustard or a bag of rapeseed, out he'd run amok over half the countryside rooting up with his horns whatever was planted and all by Lord Harry's orders. There was bad blood between them at first, says Mr Vincent, and the Lord Harry called Farmer Nicholas all the Old Nicks in the world and an old whoremaster that kept seven trulls in his house and

I'll meddle in his matters, says he. I'll make that animal smell hell, says he, with the help of that good pizzle my father left me. But one evening, says Mr Dixon, when the Lord Harry was cleaning his royal pelt to go to dinner after winning a boatrace (he had spade oars for himself but the first rule of the course was that the others were to row with pitchforks) he discovered in himself a wonderful likeness to a bull and on picking up a black-thumbed chapbook that he kept in the pantry he found sure enough that he was a left-handed descendant of the famous champion bull of the Romans, *Bos Bovum*, which is good bog Latin for Boss of the Show. After that, says Mr Vincent, the Lord Harry put his head into a cow's drinking trough in the presence of all his courtiers and pulling it out again told them all his new name. Then, with the water running off him, he got into an old smock and skirt that had belonged to his grandmother and bought a grammar of the bulls' language to study but he could never learn a word of it except the first personal pronoun which he copied out big and got off by heart and if ever he went out for a walk he filled his skirt pockets with chalk to write it up on what took his fancy, the side of a rock or a teahouse table or a bale of cotton or a cork float. In short, he and the bull of Ireland were soon as fast friends as an arse and a shirt. They were, says Mr Stephen, and the end was that the men of the island, seeing no help was toward as the ungrate women were all of the one mind, made a wherry raft, loaded themselves and their bundles of chattels on shipboard, set all masts erect, manned the yards, sprang their luff, heaved to, spread three sheets in the wind, put her head between wind and water, weighed anchor, ported her helm, ran up the Jolly Roger, gave three times three, let the bullgine run, pushed off in their bumboat and put to sea to recover the main of America. Which was the occasion, says Mr Vincent, of the composing by a boatswain of that rollicking chanty:

> *Pope Peter's but a piss-a-bed.*
> *A man's a man for a' that.*

Our worthy acquaintance, Mr Malachi Mulligan, now appeared in the doorway as the students were finishing their apologue accompanied with a friend whom he had just rencountered, a young gentleman, his name Alec Bannon, who had late come to town, it being his intention to buy a colour or a cornetcy in the fencibles and list for the wars. Mr Mulligan was civil enough to express some relish of it and all the more as it jumped with a project of his own for the cure of the very evil that had been touched on. Whereat he handed round to the company a set of pasteboard cards which he had had printed that day at Mr Quinnell's bearing a legend printed in fair italics:

Mr Malachi Mulligan,
Fertiliser and Incubator,
Lambay Island.

His project, as he went on to expound, was to withdraw from the round of idle pleasures such as form the chief business of Sir Fopling Popinjay and Sir Milksop Quidnunc in town and to devote himself to the noblest task for which our bodily organism has been framed. Well, let us hear of it, good my friend, said Mr Dixon. I make no doubt it smacks of wenching. Come, be seated both. 'Tis as cheap sitting as standing. Mr Mulligan accepted of the invitation and, expatiating upon his design, told his hearers that he had been led into this thought by a consideration of the causes of sterility, both the inhibitory and the prohibitory, whether the inhibition in its turn were due to conjugal vexations or to a parsimony of the balance as well as whether the prohibition proceeded from defects congenital or from proclivities acquired. It grieved him plaguily, he said, to see the nuptial couch defrauded of its dearest pledges and to reflect upon so many agreeable females with rich jointures, a prey to the vilest bonzes, who hide their flambeau under a bushel in an uncongenial cloister or lose their womanly bloom and pine in the embraces of some unaccountable muskin when they might multiply the inlets of happiness, sacrificing the inestimable jewel of their sex so sadly when a hundred pretty fellows were at hand to caress: this, he assured them, made his heart weep. To curb this inconvenience (which he concluded to be due to a suppression of latent heat), having advised with certain counsellors of worth and inspected into this matter, he had resolved to purchase in fee simple for ever the freehold of Lambay Island from its holder, Lord Talbot de Malahide, a Tory gentleman of note much in favour with our ascendancy party. He proposed to set up there a national fertilising farm to be named Omphalos with an obelisk hewn and erected after the fashion of Egypt and to offer his dutiful yeoman services for the fecundation of any female of what grade of life soever who should there direct to him with the desire of fulfilling the functions of her natural. Money was no object, he said, nor would he take a penny for his pains. The poorest kitchen-wench no less than the opulent lady of fashion, if so be their constructions and their tempers were warm persuaders for their petitions, would find in him their man. For his nutriment he shewed how he would feed himself exclusively upon a diet of savoury tubercles and fish and coneys there, the flesh of these latter prolific rodents being highly recommended for his purpose, both broiled and stewed with a blade of mace and a pod or two of capsicum chillies. After this homily, which he delivered with much warmth of asseveration, Mr Mulligan in a trice put off from his hat a kerchief with which he had shielded it. They both, it seems, had been overtaken by the rain and for all their mending their pace had taken water, as might be observed by Mr Mulligan's smallclothes of a hodden grey which was now somewhat piebald. His project meanwhile was very favourably entertained by his auditors and won hearty eulogies from all though Mr Dixon of Mary's excepted to it, asking with a finicking air did he purpose also to carry coals to Newcastle. Mr Mulligan however made court to the scholarly by an apt quotation from the classics which, as it dwelt upon his memory, seemed to him a sound and tasteful support of his contention, *Talis ac tanta depravatio hujus seculi, O Quirites, ut matresfamiliarum nostrae lascivas cujuslibet semiviri libici titillationes testibus ponderosis atque excelsis erectionibus centurionum Romanorum magnopere anteponent,* while for those of ruder wit he drove home his point by analogies of the animal kingdom more suitable to their stomach, the buck and doe of the forest glade, the farmyard drake and duck.

Valuing himself not a little upon his elegance, being indeed a proper man of person, this talkative now applied himself to his dress with animadversions of some heat upon the sudden whimsy of the atmospherics while the company lavished their encomiums upon the project he had advanced. The young gentleman, his friend, overjoyed as he was at a passage that had late befallen him, could not forbear to tell it his nearest neighbour. Mr Mulligan, now perceiving the table, asked for whom were those loaves and fishes and, seeing the stranger, he made him a civil bow and said, Pray, sir, was you in need of any professional assistance we could give? Who, upon his offer, thanked him very heartily, though preserving his proper distance, and replied that he was come there about a lady, now an inmate of Horne's house, that was in an interesting condition, poor body, from woman's woe (and here he fetched a deep sigh), to know if her happiness had yet taken place. Mr Dixon, to turn the table, took on to ask of Mr Mulligan himself whether his incipient ventripotence, upon which he rallied him, betokened an ovoblastic gestation in process in the prostatic utricle or male womb or was due, as with the noted physician Mr Austin Meldon, to a malady known as wolf in the stomach. For answer Mr Mulligan, in a gale of laughter at his smalls, smote himself bravely below the diaphragm, exclaiming with an admirable droll mimic of Mother Grogan (the most excellent creature of her sex though 'tis pity she's a trollop): There's a belly that never bore a bastard. This was so happy a conceit that it renewed the storm of mirth and threw the whole room into the most violent agitations of delight. The spry rattle had run on in the same vein of mimicry but for some larum in the antechamber.

Here the listener, who was none other than the Scotch student, a little fume of a fellow, blond as tow, congratulated in the liveliest fashion with the young gentleman and, interrupting the narrative at a salient point, having desired his vis-à-vis with a polite beck to have the obligingness to pass him a flagon of cordial waters, at the same time by a questioning poise of the head (a whole century of polite breeding had not achieved so nice a gesture) to which was united an equivalent but contrary balance of the bottle asked the narrator as plainly as was ever done in words if he might treat him with a cup of it. *Mais bien sûr*, noble stranger, said he cheerily, *et mille compliments*. That you may and very opportunely. There wanted nothing but this cup to crown my felicity. But, gracious heaven, was I left with but a crust in my wallet and a cupful of water from the well, my God, I freely would accept of them and find it in my heart to kneel down upon the ground and give thanks to the powers above for the happiness vouchsafed me by the Giver of good things. With these words he approached the goblet to his lips, took a complacent draught of the cordial, slicked his hair and, opening his bosom, popped out a locket that hung from a silk ribbon, that very picture which he had cherished ever since her hand had wrote therein. Gazing upon those features with a world of tenderness, Ah, Monsieur, he said, had you but beheld her as I did with these eyes at that affecting instant with her dainty tucker and her new coquette cap (a gift for her feastday as she told me prettily) in such an artless disorder, of so melting a tenderness, 'pon my conscience, even you, Monsieur, I weigh, had been impelled by generous nature to deliver yourself wholly into the hands of such an enemy or to quit the field for ever. I declare, I was never so touched in all my life. God, I thank thee, as the Author of my days! Thrice happy will he be whom so amiable a creature will bless with her favours. A sigh of affection gave eloquence to these words and, having replaced the locket in his bosom, he wiped his eyes and sighed again. Beneficent Disseminator of blessings to all Thy creatures, how great and universal must be that sweetest of Thy tyrannies which can hold in thrall the free and the bond, the simple swain and the polished coxcomb, the lover in the heyday of reckless passion and the husband of maturer years. But indeed, sir, I wander from the point. How mingled and imperfect are all our sublunary joys! Maledicity! Would to God that foresight had but remembered me to take my cloak along! I could weep to think of it. Then, though it had poured seven showers, we were neither of us a penny the worse. But, beshrew me, he cried, clapping hand to his forehead, tomorrow will be a new day and, thousand thunders, I know of a *marchand de capotes*, Monsieur Poyntz, from whom I can have for a *livre* as snug a cloak of the French fashion as ever kept a lady from wetting. Tut, tut! cried Le Fécondateur, tripping in, my friend Monsieur Moore, that most accomplished traveller (I have just cracked a half bottle *avec lui* in a circle of the best wits of the town), is my authority that in Cape Horn, *ventre biche*, they have a rain that will wet through any, even the stoutest, cloak. A drenching of that violence, he tells me, *sans blague*, has sent more than one luckless fellow in good earnest posthaste to another world. Pooh! A *livre*! cried Monsieur Lynch. The clumsy things are dear at a sou. One umbrella, were it no bigger than a fairy mushroom, is worth ten such stopgaps. No woman of any wit would wear one. My dear Kitty told me today that she would dance in a deluge before ever she would starve in such an ark of salvation for, as she reminded me (blushing piquantly and whispering in my ear though there was none to snap her words but giddy butterflies), Dame Nature, by the divine blessing, has implanted it in our hearts and it has become a household word that *il y a deux choses* for which the innocence of our original garb, in other circumstances a breach of the proprieties, is the fittest, nay, the only garment. The first, said she (and here my pretty philosopher, as I handed her to her tilbury, to fix my attention gently tipped with her tongue the outer chamber of my ear), the first is a bath ... But at this point a bell tinkling in the hall cut short a discourse which had promised so bravely for the enrichment of our store of knowledge.

Amid the general vacant hilarity of the assembly a bell rang and while all were conjecturing what might be the cause Miss Callan entered and, having spoken a few words in a low tone to young Mr Dixon, retired with a profound bow to the company. The presence even for a moment among a party of debauchees of a woman endued with every quality of modesty and not less severe than beautiful refrained the humorous sallies even of the most licentious but her departure was the signal for an outbreak of ribaldry. Strike me silly, Doc, said Costello, a low fellow who was fuddled, I'll be sworn she has rendezvoused you. A monstrous fine bit of cowflesh! What, you dog? Have you a way with them? Gad's bud, immensely so, said Mr Lynch. The bedside manner it is that they use in the Mater Hospice. Demme, does not Doctor O'Gargle chuck the nuns there under the chin? As I look to be saved, I had it from my Kitty who has been wardmaid there any time these seven months. Lawks-a-mercy, Doctor, cried the young blood in the primrose vest, feigning a womanish simper and with immodest squirmings of his body, how you do tease a body! Drat the man! Bless me, I'm all of a wibblywobbly. Why, you're as bad as dear little Father Cantekissem, that you are! May this pot of four half choke me, cried Costello, if she ain't in the family way. I knows a lady what's got a white swelling quick as I claps eyes on her. The young surgeon, however, rose and begged the company to excuse his retreat as the nurse had just then informed him that he was needed in the ward. Merciful providence had been pleased to put a period to the sufferings of the lady who was *enceinte* which she had borne with a laudable fortitude and she had given birth to a bouncing boy. I want patience, said he, with those who, without wit to enliven or learning to instruct, revile an ennobling profession which, saving the reverence due to the Deity, is the greatest power for happiness upon the earth. What? Malign such an one, the amiable Miss Callan, who is the lustre of her own sex and the astonishment of ours? And at an instant the most momentous that can befall a puny child of clay? Perish the thought! I am positive when I say that if need were I could produce a cloud of witnesses to the excellence of her noble exercitations which, so far from being a byword, should be a glorious incentive in the human breast. I cannot away with them. I shudder to think of the future of a race where the seeds of such malice have been sown and where no right reverence is rendered to mother and maid in house of Horne. Having delivered himself of this rebuke he saluted those present on the by and repaired to the door. A murmur of approval arose from all and some were for ejecting the low soaker without more ado, a design which would have been effected nor would he have received more than his bare deserts had he not abridged his transgression by affirming with a horrid imprecation (for he swore a round hand) that he was as good a son of the true fold as ever drew breath. Stap my vitals, said he, them was always the sentiments of honest Frank Costello which

I was bred up most particular to honour thy father and thy mother by poor dear mamma that had the best hand to a rolypoly or a hasty pudding as you ever see what I always looks back on with a loving heart.

To revert to Mr Bloom who, after his first entry, had been conscious of some impudent mocks which he, however, had borne with them as being the fruits of that age upon which it is commonly charged that it knows not pity. The young sparks, it is true, were as full of extravagancies as overgrown children: the words of their tumultuary discussions were difficultly understood and not often nice: their testiness and outrageous *mots* were such that his intellect resiled from: nor were they scrupulously sensible of the proprieties though their fund of strong animal spirits spoke in their behalf. But the word of Mr Costello was an unwelcome language for him for in he nauseated the wretch that seemed to him a crop-eared creature of a misshapen gibbosity born out of wedlock and thrust like a crookback teethed and feet first into the world, which the dint of the surgeon's pliers in his skull lent indeed a colour to, so as to put him in thought of that missing link of creation's chain desiderated by the late ingenious Mr Darwin. It was now for more than the middle span of our allotted years that he had passed through the thousand vicissitudes of existence and, being of a wary ascendancy and self a man of a rare forecast, he had enjoined his heart to repress all motions of a rising choler and, by intercepting them with the readiest precaution, foster within his breast that plenitude of sufferance which base minds jeer at, rash judgers scorn and all find tolerable and but tolerable. To those who create themselves wits at the cost of feminine delicacy (a habit of mind which he never did hold with), to them he would concede neither to bear the name nor to inherit the tradition of a proper breeding: while for such that, having lost all forbearance, can lose no more, there remained the sharp antidote of experience to cause their insolency to beat a precipitate and inglorious retreat. Not but what he could feel with mettlesome youth which, caring nought for the mows of dotards or the gruntlings of the severe, is ever (as the chaste fancy of the Holy Writer expresses it) for eating of the tree forbid it, yet not so far forth as to pretermit humanity upon any condition soever towards a gentlewoman when she was about her lawful occasions. To conclude, while from the sister's words he had reckoned upon a speedy delivery he was, however, it must be owned, not a little alleviated by the intelligence that the issue so auspicated after an ordeal of such duress now testified once more to the mercy as well as to the bounty of the Supreme Being.

Accordingly he broke his mind to his neighbour, saying that, to express his notion of the thing, his opinion (who ought not perchance to express one) was that one must have a cold constitution and a frigid genius not to be rejoiced by this freshest news of the fruition of her confinement since she had been in such pain through no fault of hers. The dressy young blade said it was her husband's fault that put her in that expectation or at least it ought to be unless she were another Ephesian matron. I must acquaint you, said Mr Crotthers, clapping on the table so as to evoke a resonant comment of emphasis, old Glory Allelujurum was round again today, an elderly man with dundrearies, preferring through his nose a request to have word of Wilhelmina, my life, as he calls her. I bade him hold himself in readiness for that the event would burst anon. 'Slife, I'll be round with you, I cannot but extol the virile potency of the old bucko that could still knock another child out of her. All fell to praising of it, each after his own fashion, though the same young blade held with his former view that another than her conjugal had been the man in the gap, a clerk in orders, a linkboy (virtuous) or an itinerant vendor of articles needed in every household. Singular, communed the guest with himself, the wonderfully unequal faculty of metempsychosis possessed by them, that the puerperal dormitory and the dissecting theatre should be the seminaries of such frivolity, that the mere acquisition of academic titles should suffice to transform in a pinch of time these votaries of levity into exemplary practitioners of an art which most men anywise eminent have esteemed the noblest. But, he further added, it is mayhap to relieve the pent-up feelings that in common oppress them, for I have more than once observed that birds of a feather laugh together.

But with what fitness, let it be asked of the noble lord, his patron, has this alien, whom the concession of a gracious prince has admitted to civic rights, constituted himself the lord paramount of our internal polity? Where is now that gratitude which loyalty should have counselled? During the recent war whenever the enemy had a temporary advantage with his granados did this traitor to his kind not seize that moment to discharge his piece against the empire of which he is a tenant at will while he trembled for the security of his four per cents? Has he forgotten this as he forgets all benefits received? Or is it that from being a deluder of others he has become at last his own dupe, as he is, if report belie him not, his own and his only enjoyer? Far be it from candour to violate the bedchamber of a respectable lady, the daughter of a gallant major, or to cast the most distant reflections upon her virtue, but if he challenges attention there (as it was indeed highly his interest not to have done) then be it so. Unhappy woman, she has been too long and too persistently denied her legitimate prerogative to listen to his objurgations with any other feeling than the derision of the desperate. He says this, a censor of morals, a very pelican in his piety, who did not scruple, oblivious of the ties of nature, to attempt illicit intercourse with a female domestic drawn from the lowest strata of society! Nay, had the hussy's scouring brush not been her tutelary angel it had gone with her as hard as with Hagar the Egyptian! In the question of the grazing lands his peevish asperity is notorious and in Mr Cuffe's hearing brought upon him from an indignant rancher a scathing retort couched in terms as straightforward as they were bucolic. It ill becomes him to preach that gospel. Has he not himself nearer home a seedfield that lies fallow for the want of a ploughshare? A habit reprehensible at puberty and an opprobrium in middle life is second nature to him. If he must dispense his balm of Gilead in nostrums and apothegms of dubious taste to restore to health a generation of unfledged profligates let his practice consist better with the doctrines that now engross him. His marital breast is the repository of secrets which decorum is reluctant to adduce. The lewd suggestions of some faded beauty may console him for a consort neglected and debauched but this new exponent of morals and healer of ills is at his best an exotic tree which, when rooted in its native orient, throve and flourished and was abundant in balm but, transplanted to a clime more temperate, its roots have lost their quondam vigour while the stuff that comes away from it is stagnant, acid and inoperative.

The news was imparted with a circumspection recalling the ceremonial usage of the Sublime Porte by the second female infirmarian to the junior medical officer in residence, who in his turn announced to the delegation that an heir had been born. When he had betaken himself to the women's apartment to assist at the prescribed ceremony of the afterbirth in the presence of the secretary of state for domestic affairs and the members of the privy council, the delegates, silent in unanimous exhaustion and approbation, chafing under the length and solemnity of their vigil and hoping that the joyful occurrence would palliate a licence which the simultaneous absence of abigail and officer rendered the easier, broke out at once into a strife of tongues. In vain the voice of Mr Canvasser Bloom was heard endeavouring to urge, to mollify, to restrain. The moment was too propitious for the display of that discursiveness which seemed the only bond of union among tempers so divergent. Every phase of the situation was successively eviscerated: the prenatal repugnance of uterine brothers, the Caesarean section, posthumity with respect to the father and, that rarer form, with respect to the mother, the fratricidal case known as the Childs Murder and rendered memorable by the impassioned plea of Mr Advocate Bushe which secured the acquittal of the wrongfully accused, the rights of primogeniture and king's bounty touching twins and triplets, miscarriages and infanticides, simulated and dissimulated, acardiac *foetus in foetu*, aprosopia due to a congestion, the agnathia of certain chinless Chinamen (cited by Mr Candidate Mulligan) in consequence of a defective reunion of the maxillary knobs along the medial line so that (as he said) one ear could hear what the other spoke, the benefits of anaesthesia or twilight sleep, the prolongation of labour pains in advanced gravidancy by reason of pressure on the vein, the premature relentment of the amniotic fluid (as exemplified in the actual case) with consequent peril of sepsis to the matrix, artificial insemination by means of syringes, involution of the womb consequent upon the menopause, the problem of the perpetuation of the species in the case of females impregnated by delinquent rape, that distressing manner of delivery called by the Brandenburghers *Sturzgeburt*, the recorded instances of multiseminal, twikindled and monstrous births conceived during the catamenic period or of consanguineous parents – in a word, all the cases of human nativity which Aristotle has classified in his *Masterpiece* with chromolithographic illustrations. The gravest problems of obstetrics and forensic medicine were examined with as much animation as the most popular beliefs on the state of pregnancy such as the forbidding to a gravid woman to step over a country stile lest, by her movement, the navelcord should strangle her creature and the injunction upon her in the event of a yearning, ardently and ineffectually entertained, to place her hand against that part of her person which long usage has consecrated as the seat of castigation. The abnormalities of harelip, breastmole, supernumerary digits, negro's inkle, strawberry mark and port-wine stain were alleged by one as a prima facie and natural hypothetical explanation of swineheaded (the case of Madam Grissel Steevens was not forgotten) or doghaired infants occasionally born. The hypothesis of a plasmic memory, advanced by the Caledonian envoy and worthy of the metaphysical traditions of the land he stood for, envisaged in such cases an arrest of embryonic development at some stage antecedent to the human. An outlandish delegate of a somewhat bestial cast of countenance sustained against both these views with such heat as almost carried conviction the theory of copulation between women and the males of brutes, his authority being his own avouchment in support of fables such as that of the Minotaur which the genius of the elegant Latin poet has handed down to us in the pages of his *Metamorphoses*. The impression made by his words on an assembly so mobile was immediate but short-lived. It was effaced as easily as it had been evoked by an allocution from Mr Candidate Mulligan in that vein of pleasantry which none better than he knew how to affect, postulating as the supremest object of desire a nice clean old man. Contemporaneously, a heated argument having arisen between Mr Delegate Madden and Mr Candidate Lynch regarding the juridical and theological dilemma created in the event of one Siamese twin predeceasing the other, the difficulty by mutual consent was referred to Mr Canvasser Bloom for instant submittal to Mr Coadjutor Deacon Dedalus. Hitherto silent, whether the better to show by preternatural gravity that curial dignity of the garb with which he was invested or in obedience to an inward voice, he delivered briefly and, as some thought, perfunctorily the ecclesiastical ordinance forbidding man to put asunder what God has joined.

But Malachias' tale began to freeze them with horror. He conjured up the scene before them. The secret panel beside the chimney slid back and in the recess appeared – Haines! Which of us did not feel his flesh creep! He had a portfolio full of Celtic literature in one hand, in the other a phial marked *Poison*. Surprise, horror, loathing were depicted on all faces while he eyed them with a ghostly grin. I anticipated some such reception, he began with an eldritch laugh, for which, it seems, history is to blame. Yes, it is true. I am the murderer of Samuel Childs. And how I am punished! The inferno has no terrors for me. This is the appearance is on me. Tare and ages, what way would I be resting at all, he muttered thickly, and I tramping Dublin this while back with my share of songs and himself after me the like of a soulth or a bullawurrus? My hell, and Ireland's, is in this life. It is what I tried, to obliterate my crime. Distractions, rook shooting, the Erse language (he recited some), laudanum (he raised the phial to his lips), camping out. In vain! His spectre stalks me. Dope is my only hope ... Ah! Destruction! The black panther! With a cry he suddenly vanished and the panel slid back. An instant later his head appeared in the door opposite and said: Meet me at Westland Row Station at ten past eleven.

He was gone! Tears gushed from the eyes of the dissipated host. The seer raised his hand to heaven, murmuring: The vendetta of Mananaan! The sage repeated several times that *lex talionis*, The sentimentalist is he who would enjoy without incurring the immense debtorship for a thing done. Malachias, overcome by emotion, ceased. The mystery was unveiled. Haines was the third brother. His real name was Childs. The black panther was himself the ghost of his own father. He drank drugs to obliterate. For this relief much thanks. The lonely house by the graveyard is uninhabited. No soul will live there. The spider pitches her web in the solitude. The nocturnal rat peers from his hole. A curse is on it. It is haunted. Murderer's ground.

What is the age of the soul of man? As she hath the virtue of the chameleon to change her hue at every new approach, to be gay with the merry and mournful with the downcast, so too is her age changeable as her mood. No longer is Leopold, as he sits there, ruminating, chewing the cud of reminiscence, that staid agent of publicity and holder of a modest substance in the funds. A score of years are blown away. He is young Leopold. There, as in a retrospective arrangement, a mirror within a mirror (hey, presto!), he beholdeth himself. That young figure of then is seen, precociously manly, walking on a nipping morning from the old house in Clanbrassil Street to the High School, his booksatchel on him bandolierwise and in it a goodly hunk of wheaten loaf, a mother's thought. Or it is the same figure, a year or so gone over, in his first hard hat (ah, that was a day!), already on the road, a full-fledged traveller for the family firm, equipped with an order book, a scented handkerchief (not for show only), his case of bright trinketware (alas, a thing now of the past!) and a quiverful of compliant smiles for this or that half-won housewife reckoning it out upon her fingertips or for a budding virgin shyly acknowledging (but the heart? tell me!) his studied baisemains? The scent, the smile, but more than these the dark eyes and oleaginous address brought home at duskfall many a commission to the head of the firm seated with Jacob's pipe after like labours in the paternal ingle (a meal of noodles, you may be sure, is aheating) reading through round horned spectacles some paper from the Europe of a month before. But (hey, presto!) the mirror is breathed on and the young knight-errant recedes, shrivels, dwindles to a tiny speck within the mist. Now he is himself paternal and these about him might be his sons. Who can say? The wise father knows his own child. He thinks of a drizzling night in Hatch Street, hard by the bonded stores there, the first. Together (she is a poor waif, a child of shame, yours

393

and mine and of all for a bare shilling and her luckpenny), together they hear the heavy tread of the watch as two raincaped shadows pass the new Royal University. Bridie! Bridie Kelly! He will never forget the name, ever remember the night, first night, the bridenight. They are entwined in nethermost darkness, the willer with the willed, and in an instant (*fiat!*) light shall flood the world. Did heart leap to heart? Nay, fair reader. In a breath 'twas done. But hold! Back! It must not be! In terror the poor girl flees away through the murk. She is the bride of darkness, a daughter of night. She dare not bear the sunny-golden babe of day. No, Leopold! Name and memory solace thee not. That youthful illusion of thy strength was taken from thee – and in vain. No son of thy loins is by thee. There is none now to be for Leopold what Leopold was for Rudolph.

The voices blend and fuse in clouded silence: silence that is the infinity of space: and swiftly, silently, the soul is wafted over regions of cycles of generations that have lived. A region where grey twilight ever descends, never falls, on wide sage-green pasturefields, shedding her dusk, scattering a perennial dew of stars. She follows her mother with ungainly steps, a mare leading her filly foal. Twilight phantoms are they, yet moulded in prophetic grace of structure, slim shapely haunches, a supple tendonous neck, the meek apprehensive skull. They fade, sad phantoms: all is gone. Agudath is a waste land, a home of screech owls and of the sand-blind upupa. Netaim, the golden, is no more. And on the highway of the clouds they come, muttering thunder of rebellion, the ghosts of beasts. Huuh! Hark! Huuh! Parallax stalks behind and goads them, the lancinating lightnings of whose brow are scorpions. Elk and yak, the bulls of Bashan and of Babylon, mammoth and mastodon, they come trooping to the sunken sea, *Lacus Mortis*. Ominous revengeful zodiacal host! They moan, passing upon the clouds, horned and capricorned, the trumpeted with the tusked, the lion-maned, the giant-antlered, snouter and crawler, rodent, ruminant and pachyderm, all their moving moaning multitude, murderers of the sun.

Onward to the dead sea they tramp to drink, unslaked and with horrible gulpings, the salt somnolent inexhaustible flood. And the equine portent grows again, magnified in the deserted heavens, nay, to heaven's own magnitude, till it looms, vast, over the house of Virgo. And, lo, wonder of metempsychosis, it is she, the everlasting bride, harbinger of the daystar, the bride, ever virgin. It is she, Martha, thou lost one, Millicent, the young, the dear, the radiant. How serene does she now arise, a queen among the Pleiades, in the penultimate antelucan hour, shod in sandals of bright gold, coifed with a veil of what do you call it gossamer. It floats, it flows about her starborn flesh, and loose it streams, emerald, sapphire, mauve and heliotrope, sustained on currents of the cold interstellar wind, winding, coiling, simply swirling, writhing in the skies a mysterious writing till, after a myriad metamorphoses of symbol, it blazes, Alpha, a ruby and triangled sign upon the forehead of Taurus.

Francis was reminding Stephen of years before when they had been at school together in Conmee's time. He asked about Glaucon, Alcibiades, Pisistratus. Where were they now? Neither knew. You have spoken of the past and its phantoms, Stephen said. Why think of them? If I call them into life across the waters of Lethe will not the poor ghosts troop to my call? Who supposes it? I, Bous Stephanoumenos, bullock-befriending bard, am lord and giver of their life. He encircled his gadding hair with a coronal of vine leaves, smiling at Vincent. That answer and those leaves, Vincent said to him, will adorn you more fitly when something more, and greatly more, than a capful of light odes can call your genius father. All who wish you well hope this for you. All desire to see you bring forth the work you meditate, to acclaim you Stephanephoros. I heartily wish you may not fail them. O no, Vincent, Lenehan said, laying a hand on the shoulder near him, have no fear. He could not leave his mother an orphan. The young man's face grew dark. All could see how sad it was for him to be reminded of his promise and of his recent loss. He would have withdrawn from the feast had not the noise of voices allayed the smart. Madden had lost five drachmas on *Sceptre* for a whim of the rider's name: Lenehan as much more. He told them of the race. The flag fell and, huuh, off, scamper, the mare ran out freshly with O. Madden up. She was leading the field: all hearts were beating. Even Phyllis could not contain herself. She waved her scarf and cried: Huzzah! *Sceptre* wins! But in the straight on the run home when all were in close order the dark horse *Throwaway* drew level, reached, outstripped her. All was lost now. Phyllis was silent: her eyes were sad anemones. Juno, she cried, I am undone. But her lover consoled her and brought her a bright casket of gold in which lay some oval sugarplums which she partook. A tear fell: one only. A whacking fine whip, said Lenehan, is W. Lane. Four winners yesterday and three today. What rider is like him? Mount him on the camel or the boisterous buffalo, the victory in a hack canter is still his. But let us bear it as was the ancient wont. Mercy on the luckless! Poor *Sceptre*! he said with a light sigh. She is not the filly that she was. Never, by this hand, shall we behold such another. By Gad, sir, a queen of them. Do you remember her, Vincent? I wish you could have seen my queen today, Vincent said, how young she was and radiant (Lalage were scarce fair beside her) in her yellow shoes and frock of muslin, I do not know the right name of it. The chestnuts that shaded us were in bloom: the air drooped with their persuasive odour and with pollen floating by us. In the sunny patches one might easily have cooked on a stone a batch of those buns with Corinth fruit in them that Periplipomenes sells in his booth near the bridge. But she had nought for her teeth but the arm with which I held her and in that she nibbled mischievously when I pressed too close. A week ago she lay ill, four days on the couch, but today she was free, blithe, mocked at peril. She is more taking then. Her posies too! Mad romp that it is, she had pulled her fill as we reclined together. And in your ear, my friend, he said to Francis, you will not think who met us as we left the field. Conmee himself! He was walking by the hedge, reading, I think, a brevier book with, I doubt not, a witty letter in it from Glycera or Chloe to keep the page. The sweet creature turned all colours in her confusion, feigning to reprove a slight disorder in her dress: a slip of underwood clung there, for the very trees adore her. When Conmee had passed she glanced at her lovely echo in the little mirror she carries. But he had been kind. In going by he had blessed us. The gods too are ever kind, Lenehan said. If I had poor luck with Bass's mare perhaps this draught of his may serve me more propensely. He was laying his hand upon a winejar: Malachi saw it and withheld his act, pointing to the stranger and to the scarlet label. Warily, Malachi whispered, preserve a druid silence. His soul is far away. It is as painful perhaps to be awakened from a vision as to be born. Any object, intensely regarded, may be a gate of access to the incorruptible eon of the gods. Do you not think it, Stephen? Theosophos told me so, Stephen answered, whom in a previous existence Egyptian priests initiated into the mysteries of karmic law. The lords of the moon, Theosophos told me, an orange-fiery shipload from planet Alpha of the lunar chain, would not assume the etheric doubles and these were therefore incarnated by the ruby-coloured egos from the second constellation.

However, as a matter of fact though, the preposterous surmise about him being in some description of a doldrums or other or mesmerised, which was entirely due to a misconception of the shallowest character, was not the case at all. The individual whose visual organs were at this juncture commencing to exhibit symptoms of animation was as astute if not astuter than any man living and anybody that conjectured the contrary would have found themselves pretty speedily in the wrong shop. During the past four minutes or thereabouts while the above was going on he had been staring hard at a certain amount of Number One Bass, bottled by Messrs Bass and Co. at Burton-on-Trent, which happened to be situated amongst a lot of others right opposite to where he was and which was certainly calculated to attract anyone's remark on account of its scarlet appearance. He was simply and solely, as it subsequently transpired for reasons best known to himself which put quite an altogether different complexion on the proceedings, after the moment before's observations about boyhood days and the turf recollecting two or three private transactions of his own which the other two were as mutually innocent of as the babe unborn. Eventually, however, both their eyes met and, as soon as it began to dawn on him that the other was endeavouring to help himself to the thing, he involuntarily determined to help him himself and so he accordingly took hold of the neck of the medium-sized glass recipient which contained the fluid sought after and made a capacious hole in it by pouring a lot of it out with, also at the same time, however, a considerable degree of attentiveness in order not to upset any of the beer that was in it about the place.

The debate which ensued was in its scope and progress an epitome of the course of life. Neither place nor council was lacking in dignity. The debaters were the keenest in the land, the theme they were engaged on the loftiest and most vital. The high hall of Horne's house had never beheld an assembly so representative and so varied nor had the old rafters of that establishment ever listened to a language so encyclopaedic. A gallant scene in truth it made. Crotthers was there at the foot of the table in his striking Highland garb, his face glowing from the briny airs of the Mull of Galloway. There too, opposite to him, was Lynch whose countenance bore already the stigmata of early depravity and premature wisdom. Next the Scotchman was the place assigned to Costello, the eccentric, while at his side was seated in stolid repose the squat form of Madden. The chair of the resident, indeed, stood vacant before the hearth but on either flank of it the figure of Bannon in explorer's kit of tweed shorts and salted cowhide brogues contrasted sharply with the primrose elegance and town-bred manners of Malachi Roland St John Mulligan. Lastly, at the head of the board was the young poet who found a refuge from his labours of pedagogy and metaphysical inquisition in the convivial atmosphere of Socratic discussion, while to right and left of him were accommodated the flippant prognosticator, fresh from the hippodrome, and that vigilant wanderer, soiled by the dust of travel and combat and stained by the mire of an indelible dishonour but from whose steadfast and constant heart no lure or peril or threat or degradation could ever efface the image of that voluptuous loveliness which the inspired pencil of Lafayette has limned for ages yet to come.

It had better be stated here and now at the outset that the perverted transcendentalism to which Mr S. Dedalus' (Div. Scep.) contentions would appear to prove him pretty badly addicted runs directly counter to accepted scientific methods. Science, it cannot be too often repeated, deals with tangible phenomena. The man of science like the man in the street has to face hardheaded facts that cannot be blinked and explain them as best he can. There may be, it is true, some questions which science cannot answer – at present – such as the first problem submitted by Mr L. Bloom (Publ. Canv.) regarding the future determination of sex. Must we accept the view of Empedocles of Trinacria that the right ovary (the postmenstrual period, assert others) is responsible for the birth of males, or are the too long neglected spermatozoa or nemasperms the differentiating factors, or is it, as most embryologists incline to opine, such as Culpeper, Spallanzani, Blumenbach, Lusk, Hertwig, Leopold and Valenti, a mixture of both? This would be tantamount to a cooperation (one of nature's favourite devices) between the *nisus formativus* of the nemasperm on the one hand and on the other a happily chosen position, *succubitus felix*, of the passive element. The other problem raised by the same inquirer is scarcely less vital: infant mortality. It is interesting because, as he pertinently remarked, we are all born in the same way but we all die in different ways. Mr M. Mulligan (Hyg. et Eug. Doc.) blames the sanitary conditions in which our grey-lunged citizens contract adenoids, pulmonary complaints etc. by inhaling the bacteria which lurk in dust. These factors, he alleged, and the revolting spectacles offered by our streets, hideous publicity posters, religious ministers of all denominations, mutilated soldiers and sailors, exposed scorbutic cardrivers, the suspended carcasses of dead animals, paranoiac bachelors and unfructified duennas – these, he said, were accountable for any and every falling off in the calibre of the race. Kallipedia, he prophesied, would soon be generally adopted and all the graces of life, genuinely good music, agreeable literature, light philosophy, instructive pictures, plaster-cast reproductions of the classical statues such as Venus and Apollo, artistic coloured photographs of prize babies, all these little attentions would enable ladies who were in a particular condition to pass the intervening months in a most enjoyable manner. Mr J. Crotthers (Disc. Bacc.) attributes some of these demises to abdominal trauma in the case of women workers subjected to heavy labours in the workshop and to marital discipline in the home but by far the vast majority to neglect, private or official, culminating in the exposure of newborn infants, the practice of criminal abortion or the atrocious crime of infanticide. Although the former (we are thinking of neglect) is undoubtedly only too true, the case he cites of nurses forgetting to count the sponges in the peritoneal cavity is too rare to be normative. In fact when one comes to look into it the wonder is that so many pregnancies and deliveries go off so well as they do, all things considered and in spite of our human shortcomings which often balk nature in her intentions. An ingenious suggestion is that thrown out by Mr V. Lynch (Bacc. Arith.) that both natality and mortality as well as all other phenomena of evolution, tidal movements, lunar phases, blood temperatures, diseases in general, everything, in fine, in nature's vast workshop from the extinction of some remote sun to the blossoming of one of the countless flowers which beautify our public parks is subject to a law of numeration as yet unascertained. Still, the plain straightforward question why a child of normally healthy parents and seemingly a healthy child and properly looked after succumbs unaccountably in early childhood (though other children of the same marriage do not) must certainly, in the poet's words, give us pause. Nature, we may rest assured, has her own good and cogent reasons for whatever she does and in all probability such deaths are due to some law of anticipation by which organisms in which morbous germs have taken up their residence (modern science has conclusively shown that only the plasmic substance can be said to be immortal) tend to disappear at an increasingly earlier stage of development, an arrangement which, though productive of pain to some of our feelings (notably the maternal), is nevertheless, some of us think, in the long run beneficial to the race in general in securing thereby the survival of the fittest. Mr S. Dedalus' (Div. Scep.) remark (or should it be called an interruption?) that an omnivorous being which can masticate, deglute, digest and apparently pass through the ordinary channel with pluterperfect imperturbability such multifarious aliments as cancrenous females emaciated by parturition, corpulent professional gentlemen, not to speak of jaundiced politicians and chlorotic nuns, might possibly find gastric relief in an innocent collation of staggering bob reveals as nought else could and in a very unsavoury light the tendency above alluded to. For the enlightenment of those who are not so intimately acquainted with the minutiae of the municipal abattoir as this morbid-minded would-be esthete and embryo philosopher who for all his overweening bumptiousness in things scientific can scarcely distinguish an acid from an alkali prides himself on being, it should perhaps be stated that staggering bob in the vile parlance of our lower-class licensed victuallers signifies the cookable and eatable flesh of a calf newly dropped from its mother. In a recent public controversy with Mr L. Bloom (Publ. Canv.) which took place in the commons' hall of the National Maternity Hospital, 29, 30 and 31 Holles Street, of which, as is well known, Dr A. Horne (Lic. in Midw., F.K.Q.C.P.I.) is the able and popular master, he is reported by eyewitnesses as having stated that once a woman has let the cat into the bag (an esthetic allusion, presumably, to one of the most complicated and marvellous of all nature's processes, the act of sexual congress) she must let it out again or give it life, as he phrased it, to save her own. At the risk of her own, was the telling rejoinder of his interlocutor, none the less effective for the moderate and measured tone in which it was delivered.

Meanwhile the skill and patience of the physician had brought about a happy accouchement. It had been a weary weary while both for patient and doctor. All that surgical skill could do was done and the brave woman had manfully helped. She had. She had fought the good fight and now she was very very happy. Those who have passed on, who have gone before, are happy too as they gaze down and smile upon the touching scene. Reverently look at her as she reclines there (a pretty sight it is to see) with the motherlight in her eyes, that longing hunger for baby fingers, in the first bloom of her new motherhood, breathing a silent prayer of thanksgiving to One above, the Universal Husband. And as her loving eyes behold her babe she wishes only one blessing more, to have her dear Doady there with her to share her joy, to lay in his arms that mite of God's clay, the fruit of their lawful embraces. He is older now (you and I may whisper it) and a trifle stooped in the shoulders, yet in the whirligig of years a grave dignity has come to the conscientious second accountant of the Ulster Bank, College Green branch. O Doady, loved one of old, faithful lifemate now, it may never be again that far off time of the roses! With the old shake of her pretty head she recalls those days. God, how beautiful now across the mist of years! But their children are grouped in her imagination about the bedside, hers and his, Charley, Mary Alice, Frederick Albert (if he had lived), Mamy, Budgy (Victoria Frances), Tom, Violet Constance Louisa, darling little Bobsy (called after our famous hero of the South African war, Lord Bobs of Waterford and Kandahar) and now this last pledge of their union, a Purefoy if ever there was one, with the true Purefoy nose. Young hopeful will be christened Mortimer Edward after the influential third cousin of Mr Purefoy in the Treasury Remembrancer's Office, Dublin Castle. And so time wags on: but Father Cronion has dealt lightly here. No, let no sigh break from that bosom, dear gentle Mina. And Doady, knock the ashes from your pipe, the seasoned briar you still fancy, when the curfew rings for you (may it be the distant day!) and dout the light whereby you read in the Sacred Book, for the oil too has run low, and so with a tranquil heart to bed, to rest. He knows and will call in His own good time. You too have fought the good fight and played loyally your man's part. Sir, to you my hand. Well done, thou good and faithful servant!

There are sins or (let us call them as the world calls them) evil memories which are hidden away by man in the darkest places of the heart but they abide there and wait. He may suffer their memory to grow dim, let them be as though they had not been and all but persuade himself that they were not or at least were otherwise. Yet a chance word will call them forth suddenly and they will rise up to confront him in the most various circumstances, a vision or a dream, or while timbrel and harp soothe his senses or amid the cool silver tranquility of the evening or at the feast at midnight when he is now filled with wine. Not to insult over him will the vision come as over one that lies under her wrath, not for vengeance to cut him off from the living, but shrouded in the piteous vesture of the past, silent, remote, reproachful.

The stranger still regarded on the face before him a slow recession of that false calm there, imposed, as it seemed, by habit or some studied trick, upon words so embittered as to accuse in their speaker an unhealthy sensitiveness, a flair, for the cruder things of life. A scene disengages itself in the observer's memory, evoked, it would seem, by a word of so natural a homeliness as if those days were really present there (as some thought) with their immediate pleasures. A shaven space of lawn one soft May evening, the well-remembered grove of lilacs at Roundtown, purple and white, fragrant slender spectators of the game but with much real interest in the pellets as they run slowly forward over the sward or collide and stop, one by its fellow, with a brief alert shock. And yonder about that grey urn where the water moves at times in thoughtful irrigation you saw another as fragrant sisterhood, Floey, Atty, Tiny and their darker friend with I know not what of arresting in her pose then, Our Lady of the

Cherries, a comely brace of them pendent from an ear, bringing out the foreign warmth of the skin so daintily against the cool ardent fruit. A lad of four or five in linsey-woolsey of ripe damson (blossom time, yes, but there will be cheer in the kindly hearth when ere long the bowls are gathered and hutched) is standing on the urn secured by that circle of girlish fond hands. He frowns a little, just as this young man does now, with a perhaps too conscious enjoyment of the danger but must needs glance at whiles towards where his mother watches from the *piazzetta* giving upon the flowerclose with a faint shadow of remoteness or of reproach (*alles Vergängliche*) in her glad look.

Mark this farther and remember. The end comes suddenly. Enter that antechamber of birth where the studious are assembled and note their faces. Nothing, as it seems, there of rash or violent. Quietude of custody rather, befitting their station in that house, the vigilant watch of shepherds and of angels on that holiest of nights about a crib in Bethlehem of Juda long ago. But as before the lightning the serried stormclouds, heavy with preponderant excess of moisture, in swollen masses turgidly distended, compass earth and sky in one vast slumber, impending above parched field and drowsy oxen and blighted growth of shrub and verdure, till in an instant a flash rives their centres and with the reverberation of the thunder the cloudburst pours its torrent, so and not otherwise in that room of quiet was the transformation, violent and instantaneous, upon the utterance of the Word.

Burke's! outflings my Lord Stephen, giving the cry, and a tag and bobtail of all them after, cockerel, jackanapes, welsher, pilldoctor, punctual Bloom at heels, with a universal grabbing at headgear, ashplants, bilbos, Panama hats and scabbards, Zermatt alpenstocks and whatnot. A dedale of lusty youth, noble every student there. Nurse Callan taken aback in the hallway cannot stay them nor smiling surgeon coming downstairs with news of placentation ended, a full pound if a milligramme. They hark him on. The door! It is open? Ha! They are out tumultuously, off for a minute's race, all bravely legging it, Burke's of Denzille and Holles their ulterior goal. Dixon follows giving them sharp language but raps out an oath, he too, and on. Bloom stays with nurse a thought to send a kind word to happy mother and nurseling up there. Doctor Diet and Doctor Quiet. Looks she too not other now? Ward of watching in Horne's house has told its tale to be read in that washed-out pallor. Then all being gone, a glance of motherwit helping, he whispers close in going: Madam, when comes the storkbird for thee?

The air without is impregnated with raindew moisture, life essence celestial, glistering on Dublin stone there under starshiny *coelum.* God's air, the Allfather's air, scintillant circumambient cessile air. Breathe it deep into thee. By heaven, Theodore Purefoy, thou hast done a doughty deed and no botch! Thou art, I vow, the remarkablest progenitor barring none in this chaffering all-including most farraginous chronicle. Astounding! In her lay a God-framed God-given preformed possibility which thou hast fructified with thy modicum of man's work. Cleave to her! Serve! Toil on, labour like a very bandog and let scholarment and all Malthusiasts go hang. Thou art all their daddies, Theodore. Art drooping under thy load, bemoiled with butcher's bills at home and ingots (not thine!) in the counting house? Head up! For every new-begotten thou shalt gather thy homer of ripe wheat. See, thy fleece is drenched. Dost envy Darby Dullman there with his Joan? A canting jay and a rheum-eyed curdog is all their progeny. Pshaw, I tell thee! He is a mule, a dead gasteropod, without vim or stamina, not worth a cracked kreutzer. Copulation without population! No, say I! Herod's slaughter of the innocents were the truer name. Vegetables, forsooth, and sterile cohabitation! Give her beefsteaks, red, raw, bleeding! She is a hoary pandemonium of ills, enlarged glands, mumps, quinsy, bunions, hay fever, bedsores, ringworm, floating kidney, Derbyshire neck, warts, bilious attacks, gallstones, cold feet, varicose veins. A truce to threnes and trentals and jeremies and all such congenital defunctive music. Twenty years of it, regret them not. With thee it was not as with many that will and would and wait and never – do. Thou sawest thy America, thy life task, and didst charge to cover like the transpontine bison. How saith Zarathustra? *Deine Kuh Trübsal melkest Du. Nun trinkst Du die süsse Milch des Euters.* See! It displodes for thee in abundance. Drink, man, an udderful! Mother's milk, Purefoy, the milk of human kin, milk too of those burgeoning stars overhead, rutilant in thin rainvapour, punch milk, such as those rioters will quaff in their guzzling den, milk of madness, the honey milk of Canaan's land. Thy cow's dug was tough, what? Ay, but her milk is hot and sweet and fattening. No dollop this but thick rich bonnyclabber. To her, old patriarch! Pap! *Per deam Partulam et Pertundam, nunc est bibendum!*

All off for a buster, armstrong, hollering down the street. Bonafides. Where you slep las nigh? Timothy of the battered naggin. Like ole Billyo.

Any brollies or gumboots in the fambly? Where the Henry Nevil's sawbones and ole clo? Sorra one o' me knows. Hurrah there, Dix! Forward to the ribbon counter. Where's Punch? All serene. Jay, look at the drunken minister coming out of the maternity hospal! *Benedicat vos omnipotens Deus, Pater et Filius.* A make, mister. The Denzille Lane boys. Hell, blast ye! Scoot. Righto, Isaacs, shove em out of the bleeding limelight. Yous join uz, dear sir? No hentrusion in life. Lou heap good man. Allee samee dis bunch. *En avant, mes enfants!* Fire away number one on the gun. Burke's! Burke's! Thence they advanced five parasangs. Slattery's Mounted Foot. Where's that bleeding awfur? Parson Steve, apostates' creed! No, no. Mulligan! Abaft there! Shove ahead. Keep a watch on the clock. Chucking-out time. Mullee! What's on you? *Ma mère m'a mariée.* British Beatitudes! *Retamplan Digidi Boum Boum.* Ayes have it. To be printed and bound at the Druiddrum Press by two designing females. Calf covers of pissed-on green. Last word in art shades. Most beautiful book come out of Ireland my time. *Silentium!* Get a spurt on. Tention. Proceed to nearest canteen and there annex liquor stores. March! Tramp, tramp, tramp, the boys are (atitudes!) parching. Beer, beef, business, bibles, bulldogs, battleships, buggery and bishops. Whether on the scaffold high. Beer, beef, trample the bibles. When for Irelandear. Trample the trampellers. Thunderation! Keep the durned millingtary step. We fall. Bishops, boozebox. Halt! Heave to. Rugger. Scrum in. No touch kicking. Wow, my tootsies! You hurt? Most amazingly sorry!

Query. Who's astanding this here do? Proud possessor of damn all. Declare misery. Bet to the ropes. Me nantee saltee. Not a red at me this week gone. Yours? Mead of our fathers for the *Übermensch.* Ditto. Five number ones. You, sir? Ginger cordial. Chase me, the cabby's caudle. Stimulate the caloric. Winding of his ticker. Stopped short never to go again when the old. Absinthe for me, savvy? *Caramba!* Have an eggnog or a prairie oyster. Enemy? Avuncular's got my timepiece. Ten to. Obligated awful. Don't mention it. Got a pectoral trauma, eh, Dix? Pos fact. Got bet be a boomblebee whenever he wus settin sleepin in hes bit garten. Digs up near the Mater. Buckled he is. Know his dona? Yup, sartin I do. Full of a dure. See her in her dishybilly. Peels off a credit. Lovey lovekin. None of your lean kine, not much. Pull down the blind, love. Two Ardilauns. Same here. Look slippery. If you fall don't wait to get up. Five, seven, nine. Fine! Got a prime pair of mince pies, no kid. And her take me to rests and her anker of rum. Must be seen to be believed. Your starving eyes and allbeplastered neck you stole my heart, O gluepot. Sir? Spud again the rheumatiz? All poppycock, you'll scuse me saying. For the hoi polloi. I vear thee beest a gert vool. Well, doc? Back fro Lapland? Your corporosity sagaciating OK? How's the squaws and papooses? Woman-body after going on the straw? Stand and deliver. Password. There's hair. Ours the white death and the ruddy birth. Hi! Spit in your own eye, boss! Mummer's wire. Cribbed out of Meredith. Jesified, orchidised, polycimical Jesuit! Aunty mine's writing Pa Kinch. Baddybad Stephen lead astray goodygood Malachi.

Hurroo! Collar the leather, young un. Roun wi the nappy. Here, Jock braw Hielentman barley bree. Lang may your lum reek and your kailpot boil! My tipple. *Merci.* Here's to us. How's that? Leg before wicket. Don't stain my brand-new sit-in-ems. Give's a shake of pepper, you there. Catch aholt. Caraway seed to carry away. Twig? Shrieks of silence. Every cove to his gentry mort. Venus Pandemos. *Les petites femmes.* Bold bad girl from the town of Mullingar. Tell her I was axing at her. Hauding Sara by the wame. Mine. On the road to Malahide. Me? If she who seduced me had left but the name. What do you want for ninepence? Machree, macruiskeen. Smutty Moll for a mattress jig. And a pull all together. *Ex!*

Waiting, guvnor? Most deciduously. Bet your boots on. Stunned like, seeing as how no shiners is acoming. Underconstumble? He've got the chink. *Ad lib.* Seed near free poun on un a spell ago a said war hisn. Us come right in on your invite, see? Up to you, matey. Out with the oof. Two bar and a wing. You larn that go off of they there Frenchy bilks? Won't wash here for nuts nohow. Lil chile velly solly. Ise de cutest colour coon down our side. Gawds teruth, Chawley. We are nae fou. We're nae tha fou. *Au reservoir, mossoo.* Tanks you.

'Tis, sure. What say? In the speakeasy. Tight. I shee you, shir. Bantam, two days teetee. Bowsing nowt but claretwine. Garn! Have a glint, do. Gum, I'm jiggered. And been to barber he have. Too full for words. With a railway bloke. How come you so? Opera he'd like? Rose of Castile. Rows of cast. Police! Some H_2O for a gent fainted. Look at Bantam's flowers. Gemini, he's going to holler. The colleen bawn. My colleen bawn. O, cheese it! Shut his blurry Dutch oven with a firm hand. Had the winner today till I tipped him a dead cert. The ruffin cly the nab of Stephen Hand as give me the jady coppaleen. He strike a telegram boy paddock wire big bug Bass to the depot. Shove him a joey and grahamise. Mare on form hot order. Guinea to a goosegog. Tell a cram, that. Gospel true. Criminal diversion? I think that yes. Sure thing. Land him in chokeechokee if the harman beck copped the game. Madden back Madden's a maddening back. O lust, our refuge and our strength. Decamping. Must you go? Off to mammy. Stand by. Hide my blushes, someone. All in if he spots me. Come ahome, our Bantam. Horryvar, mong vioo. Dinna forget the cowslips for hersel. Cornfide. Wha gev ye thon colt? Pal to pal. Jannock. Of John Thomas, her spouse. No fake, old man Leo. S'elp me, honest injun. Shiver my timbers if I had. There's a great big holy friar! Vyfor you no me tell? Vel, I ses, if that ain't a sheeny nachez, vel, I vil get misha mishinnah. Through yerd our lord, Amen.

You move a motion? Steve boy, you're going it some. More bluggy drunkables? Will immensely splendiferous stander permit one stooder of most extreme poverty and one largesize grandacious thirst to terminate one expensive inaugurated libation? Give's a breather. Landlord, landlord, have you good wine, Staboo? Hoots, mon, a wee drap to pree. Cut and come again. Right. Boniface! Absinthe the lot. *Nos omnes biberimus viridum toxicum diabolus capiat posterioria nostria.* Closing time, gents. Eh? Rome booze for the Bloom toff. I hear you say onions? Bloo? Cadges ads. Photo's papli, by all that's gorgeous. Play low, pardner. Slide. *Bonsoir la compagnie.* And snares of the poxfiend. Where's the buck and Namby Amby? Skunked. Leg bail. Aweel, ye maun e'en gang yer gates. Checkmate. King to tower. Kind Kristyann, wil yu help yung man hoose frend tuk bungalo kee tu find plais whear tu lay crown of his hed 2 night. Crikey, I'm about sprung. Tarnally doggone my shins if this been't the bestest puttiest longbreak yet. Item, curate, couple of cookies for this child. Cot's plood and prandypalls, none! Not a pite of sheeses? Thrust syphilis down to hell and with him those other licensed spirits. Time, gents! Who wander through the world. Health all! *À la vôtre!*

Golly, whatten tunket's yon guy in the mackintosh? Dusty Rhodes. Peep at his wearables. By mighty! What's he got? Jubilee mutton. Bovril, by James. Wants it real bad. D'ye ken bare socks? Seedy cuss in the Richmond? Rawthere! Thought he had a deposit of lead in his penis. Trumpery insanity. Bartle the Bread we calls him. That, sir, was once a prosperous cit. Man all tattered and torn that married a maiden all forlorn. Slung her hook, she did. Here see lost love. Walking Mackintosh of lonely canyon. Tuck and turn in. Schedule time. Nix for the hornies. Pardon? Seen him today at a runefal? Chum o' yourn passed in his checks? Ludamassy! Pore piccaninnies! Thou'll no be telling me thot, Pold veg! Did ums blubble bigsplash crytears cos frien Padney was took off in black bag? Of all de darkies Massa Pat was verra best. I never see de like sence I was born. *Tiens, tiens,* but it is well sad, that, my faith, yes. O, get, rev on a gradient one in nine. Live-axle drives are souped. Lay you two to one Jenatzy licks him ruddy well hollow. Jappies? High-angle fire, inyah! Sunk by war specials. Be worse for him, says he, nor any Rooshian. Time all. There's eleven of them. Get ye gone. Forward, woozy wobblers! Night. Night. May Allah the Excellent One your soul this night ever tremendously conserve.

Your attention! We're nae tha fou. The Leith police dismisseth us. The least tholice. Ware hawks for the chap puking. Unwell in his abominable regions. Yooka. Night. Mona, my thrue love. Yook. Mona, my own love. Ook.

Hark! Shut your obstropolos. Pflaap! Pflaap! Blaze on. There she goes. Brigade! Bout ship. Mount Street way. Cut up. Pflaap! Tallyho. You not come? Run, skelter, race. Pflaaaap!

Lynch! Hey? Sign on long o' me. Denzille Lane thisaway. Change here for Bawdyhouse. We two, she said, will seek the kips where shady Mary is. Righto, any old time. *Laetabuntur in cubilibus suis.* You coming long? Whisper, who the sooty hell's the johnny in the black duds? Hush! Sinned against the light and even now that day is at hand when he shall come to judge the world by fire. Pflaap! *Ut implerentur scripturae.* Strike up a ballad. Then outspake medical Dick to his comrade medical Davy. Christicle, who's this excrement yellow gospeller on the Merrion Hall? Elijah is coming. Washed in the blood of the Lamb. Come on, you winefizzling ginsizzling boozeguzzling existences! Come on, you doggone bullnecked, beetlebrowed, hogjowled, peanutbrained, weaseleyed four-flushers, false alarms and excess baggage! Come on, you triple extract of infamy! Alexander J. Christ Dowie, that's my name that's yanked to glory most half this planet from 'Frisco Beach to Vladivostok. The Deity ain't no nickel dime bumshow. I put it to you that He's on the square and a corking fine business proposition. He's the grandest thing yet and don't you forget it. Shout salvation in King Jesus. You'll need to rise precious early, you sinner there, if you want to diddle the Almighty God. Pflaaaap! Not half. He's got a coughmixture with a punch in it for you, my friend, in his back pocket. Jest you try it on.

The Mabbot Street entrance of nighttown, before which stretches an uncobbled tramsiding set with skeleton tracks, red and green will-o'-the-wisps and danger signals. Rows of grimy houses with gaping doors. Rare lamps with faint rainbow fans. Round Rabaiotti's halted ice gondola stunted men and women squabble. They grab wafers between which are wedged lumps of coral and copper snow. Sucking, they scatter slowly. Children. The swancomb of the gondola, high-reared, forges on through the murk, white and blue under a lighthouse. Whistles call and answer.

The Calls – Wait, my love, and I'll be with you.
The Answers – Round behind the stable.

A deaf-mute idiot with goggle eyes, his shapeless mouth dribbling, jerks past, shaken in Saint Vitus's dance. A chain of children's hands imprisons him.

The Children – Kithogue! Salute!
The Idiot (*lifts a palsied left arm and gurgles*) – Ghahute!
The Children – Where's the great light?
The Idiot (*gobbling*) – Ghaghahest.

They release him. He jerks on. A pigmy woman swings on a rope slung between two railings, counting. A form sprawled against a dustbin and muffled by its arm and hat snores, groans, grinding growling teeth, and snores again. On a step a gnome totting among a rubbish tip crouches to shoulder a sack of rags and bones. A crone standing by with a smoky oil lamp rams her last bottle in the maw of his sack. He heaves his booty, tugs askew his peaked cap and hobbles off mutely. The crone makes back for her lair, swaying her lamp. A bandy child, asquat on the doorstep with a paper shuttlecock, crawls sidling after her in spurts, clutches her skirt, scrambles up. A drunken navvy grips with both hands the railings of an area, lurching heavily. At a corner two night watch in shoulder capes, their hands upon their staff holsters, loom tall. A plate crashes: a woman screams: a child wails. Oaths of a man roar, mutter, cease. Figures wander, lurk, peer from warrens. In a room lit by a candle stuck in a bottleneck a slut combs out the tatts from the hair of a scrofulous child. Cissy Caffrey's voice, still young, sings shrill from a lane.

Cissy Caffrey
— I gave it to Molly
  Because she was jolly,
  The leg of the duck,
  The leg of the duck.

Private Carr and Private Compton, swaggersticks tight in their oxters, rightabout face and, as they march unsteadily, burst together from their mouths a volleyed fart. Laughter of men from the lane. A hoarse virago retorts.

The Virago – Signs on you, hairy arse. More power the Cavan girl.
Cissy Caffrey – More luck to me. Cavan, Cootehill and Belturbet. (*She sings.*)
  I gave it to Nelly
  To stick in her belly,
  The leg of the duck,
  The leg of the duck.

Private Carr and Private Compton turn and counterretort, their tunics blood-bright in a lampglow, black sockets of caps on their blond cropped polls. Stephen Dedalus and Lynch pass through the crowd close to the redcoats.

Private Compton (*jerks his finger*) – Way for the parson.
Private Carr (*turns and calls*) – What ho, parson!
Cissy Caffrey (*her voice soaring higher*)
  — She has it, she got it,
  Wherever she put it,
  The leg of the duck.

Stephen, flourishing the ashplant in his left hand, chants with joy the Introit for paschal time. Lynch, his jockey cap low on his brow, attends him, a sneer of discontent wrinkling his face.

Stephen – *Vidi aquam egredientem de templo a latere dextro. Alleluia.*

The famished snaggletusks of an elderly bawd protrude from a doorway.

The Bawd (*her voice whispering huskily*) – Sst! Come here till I tell you. Maidenhead inside. Sst!

Stephen (*altius aliquantulum*) – *Et omnes ad quos pervenit aqua ista.*

The Bawd (*spits in their trail her jet of venom*) – Trinity medicals. Fallopian tube. All prick and no pence.

Edy Boardman, sniffling, crouched with Bertha Supple, draws her shawl across her nostrils.

Edy Boardman (*bickering*) – And says the one: I seen you up Faithful Place with your squarepusher, the greaser off the railway, in his come-to-bed hat. Did you, says I. That's not for you to say, says I. You never seen me in the mantrap with a married Highlander, says I. The likes of her! Stag that one is! Stubborn as a mule! And her walking with two fellows the one time, Kilbride the enginedriver and Lance Corporal Oliphant.

Stephen (*triumphaliter*) – *Salvi facti sunt.*

He flourishes his ashplant, shivering the lamp image, shattering light over the world. A liver and white spaniel on the prowl slinks after him, growling. Lynch scares it with a kick.

Lynch – So that?

Stephen (*looks behind*) – So that gesture, not music, not odour, would be a universal language, the gift of tongues, rendering visible not the lay sense but the first entelechy, the structural rhythm.

Lynch – Pornosophical philotheology. Metaphysics in Mecklenburgh Street!

Stephen – We have shrew-ridden Shakespeare and henpecked Socrates. Even the all-wisest Stagyrite was bitted, bridled and mounted by a light-o'-love.

Lynch – Bah!

Stephen – Anyway, who wants two gestures to illustrate a loaf and a jug? This movement illustrates the loaf and jug of bread, or wine I mean, in Omar. Hold my stick.

Lynch – Damn your yellow stick. Where are we going?

Stephen – Lecherous lynx, to *la belle dame sans merci*, Georgina Johnson, *ad deam qui laetificat juventutem meam*.

Stephen thrusts the ashplant on him and slowly holds out his hands, his head going back till both hands are a span from his breast, down turned, in planes intersecting, the fingers about to part, the left being higher.

Lynch – Which is the jug of bread? It skills not. That or the Custom House. Illustrate thou. Here, take your crutch and walk.

They pass. Tommy Caffrey scrambles to a gaslamp and, clasping, climbs in spasms. From the top spur he slides down. Jacky Caffrey clasps to climb. The navvy lurches against the lamp. The twins scuttle off in the dark. The navvy, swaying, presses a forefinger against a wing of his nose and ejects from the farther nostril a long liquid jet of snot. Shouldering the lamp he staggers away through the crowd with his flaring cresset.

Snakes of riverfog creep slowly. From drains, clefts, cesspools, middens, arise on all sides stagnant fumes. A glow leaps in the south beyond the seaward reaches of the river. The navvy, staggering forward, cleaves the crowd and lurches towards the tramsiding. On the farther side under the railway bridge Bloom appears, flushed, panting, cramming bread and chocolate into a side pocket. From Gillen's hairdresser's window a composite portrait shows him gallant Nelson's image. A concave mirror at the side presents to him lovelorn longlost lugubru Booloohoom. Grave Gladstone sees him level, Bloom for Bloom. He passes, struck by the stare of truculent Wellington, but in the convex mirror grin unstruck the bonham eyes and fatchuck cheekchops of Jollypoldy the rixdix doldy.

At Antonio Rabaiotti's door Bloom halts, sweated under the bright arclamp. He disappears. In a moment he reappears and hurries on.

Bloom – Fish and taters. N.g. Ah!

He disappears into Olhausen's, the pork butcher's, under the downcoming rollshutter. A few moments later he emerges from under the shutter, puffing Poldy, blowing Bloohoom. In each hand he holds a parcel, one containing a lukewarm pig's crubeen, the other a cold sheep's trotter sprinkled with whole pepper. He gasps, standing upright. Then, bending to one side, he presses a parcel against his ribs and groans.

Bloom – Stitch in my side. Why did I run?

He takes breath with care and goes forward slowly towards the lamp-set siding. The glow leaps again.

Bloom – What is that? A flasher? Searchlight.

He stands at Cormack's corner, watching.

Bloom – Aurora borealis or a steel foundry? Ah, the brigade, of course. Southside anyhow. Big blaze. Might be his house. Beggar's Bush. We're safe. (*He hums cheerfully.*) London's burning, London's burning! On fire, on fire! (*He catches sight of the navvy lurching through the crowd at the farther side of Talbot Street.*) I'll miss him. Run. Quick. Better cross here.

He darts to cross the road. Urchins shout.

The Urchins – Mind out, mister!

Two cyclists, with lighted paper lanterns aswing, swim by him, grazing him, their bells rattling.

The Bells – Haltyaltyaltyall.
Bloom (*halts erect, stung by a spasm*) – Ow!

He looks round, darts forward suddenly. Through rising fog a dragon sandstrewer, travelling at caution, slews heavily down upon him, its huge red headlight winking, its trolley hissing on the wire. The motorman bangs his footgong.

The Gong – Bang Bang Bla Bak Blud Bugg Bloo.

The brake cracks violently. Bloom, raising a policeman's white-gloved hand, blunders stiff-legged out of the track. The motorman, thrown forward, pugnosed, on the guidewheel, yells as he slides past over chains and keys.

412

The Motorman – Hey, shitbreeches, are you doing the hat trick?

Bloom trickleaps to the curbstone and halts again. He brushes a mudflake from his cheek with a parcelled hand.

Bloom – No thoroughfare. Close shave that but cured the stitch. Must take up Sandow's exercises again. On the hands down. Insure against street accident too. The Providential. (*He feels his trouser pocket.*) Poor mamma's panacea. Heel easily catch in track or bootlace in a cog. Day the wheel of the Black Maria peeled off my shoe at Leonard's Corner. Third time is the charm. Shoe trick. Insolent driver. I ought to report him. Tension makes them nervous. Might be the fellow balked me this morning with that horsey woman. Same style of beauty. Quick of him all the same. The stiff walk. True word spoken in jest. That awful cramp in Lad Lane. Something poisonous I ate. Emblem of luck. Why? Probably lost cattle. Mark of the beast. (*He closes his eyes an instant.*) Bit light in the head. Monthly or effect of the other. Brainfogfag. That tired feeling. Too much for me now. Ow!

A sinister figure leans on plaited legs against O'Beirne's wall, a visage unknown, injected with dark mercury. From under a wide-leaved sombrero the figure regards him with evil eye.

Bloom – *Buenas noches, Señorita Blanca. ¿Qué calle es ésta?*
The Figure (*impassive, raises a signal arm*) – Password. *Sráid Mabbot.*
Bloom – Haha. *Merci.* Esperanto. *Slán leat.* (*He mutters.*) Gaelic League spy, sent by that fire-eater.

He steps forward. A sack-shouldered ragman bars his path. He steps left, ragsackman left.

Bloom – I beg.

He leaps right, sackragman right.

Bloom – I beg.

He swerves, sidles, steps aside, slips past and on.

413

Bloom – Keep to the right, right, right. If there is a signpost planted by the Touring Club at Stepaside, who procured that public boon? I, who lost my way and contributed to the columns of the *Irish Cyclist* the letter headed *In darkest Stepaside*. Keep, keep, keep to the right. Rags and bones at midnight. A fence more likely. First place murderer makes for. Wash off his sins of the world.

Jacky Caffrey, hunted by Tommy Caffrey, runs full tilt against Bloom.

Bloom – O.

Shocked, on weak hams, he halts. Tommy and Jacky vanish there, there. Bloom pats with parcelled hands watchfob, pocketbookpocket, pursepoke, sweets of sin, potato, soap.

Bloom – Beware of pickpockets. Old thieves' dodge. Collide. Then snatch your purse.

The retriever approaches, sniffing, nose to the ground. A sprawled form sneezes. A stooped bearded figure appears, garbed in the long caftan of an elder of Zion and a smoking cap with magenta tassels. Horned spectacles hang down at the wings of the nose. Yellow poison streaks are on the drawn face.

Rudolph – Second half crown waste money today. I told you not go with drunken goy ever. So you catch no money.

Bloom hides the crubeen and trotter behind his back and, crestfallen, feels warm and cold feetmeat.

Bloom – *Ja, ich weiss, papachi.*
Rudolph – What you making down this place? Have you no soul? (*With feeble vulture talons he feels the silent face of Bloom.*) Are you not my son Leopold, the grandson of Leopold? Are you not my dear son Leopold who left the house of his father and left the god of his fathers Abraham and Jacob?
Bloom (*with precaution*) – I suppose so, father. Mosenthal. All that's left of him.

Rudolph (*severely*) – One night they bring you home drunk as dog after spend your good money. What you call them running chaps?

Bloom (*in youth's smart blue Oxford suit with white vestslips, narrow-shouldered, in brown Alpine hat, wearing gent's sterling silver Waterbury keyless watch and double-curb Albert with seal attached, one side of him coated with stiffening mud*) – Harriers, father. Only that once.

Rudolph – Once! Mud head to foot. Cut your hand open. Lockjaw. They make you kaputt, Leopoldleben. You watch them chaps.

Bloom (*weakly*) – They challenged me to a sprint. It was muddy. I slipped.

Rudolph (*with contempt*) – *Goim nachez!* Nice spectacles for your poor mother!

Bloom – Mamma!

Ellen Bloom, in pantomime dame's stringed mobcap, Widow Twankey's crinoline and bustle, blouse with muttonleg sleeves buttoned behind, grey mittens and cameo brooch, her plaited hair in a crispine net, appears over the staircase banisters, a slanted candlestick in her hand, and cries out in shrill alarm.

Ellen Bloom – O blessed Redeemer, what have they done to him! My smelling salts! (*She hauls up a reef of skirt and ransacks the pouch of her striped blay petticoat. A phial, an Agnus Dei, a shrivelled potato and a celluloid doll fall out.*) Sacred Heart of Mary, where were you at all at all?

Bloom, mumbling, his eyes downcast, begins to bestow his parcels in his filled pockets but desists, muttering.

A Voice (*sharply*) – Poldy!

Bloom – Who? (*He ducks and wards off a blow clumsily.*) At your service.

He looks up. Beside a mirage of date palms a handsome woman in Turkish costume stands before him. Opulent curves fill out her scarlet trousers and jacket, slashed with gold. A wide yellow cummerbund girdles her. A white yashmak, violet in the night, covers her face, leaving free only her large dark eyes and raven hair.

Bloom – Molly!

Marion – Molly? Mrs Marion from this out, my dear man, when you speak to me. (*Satirically*) Has poor little hubby cold feet waiting so long?

Bloom (*shifts from foot to foot*) – No, no. Not the least little bit.

He breathes in deep agitation, swallowing gulps of air, questions, hopes, crubeens for her supper, things to tell her, excuses, desires, spellbound. A coin gleams on her forehead. On her feet are jewelled toe-rings. Her anklets are linked by a slender fetterchain. Beside her a camel, hooded with a turreting turban, waits. A silk ladder of innumerable rungs climbs to his bobbing howdah. He ambles near with disgruntled hindquarters. Fiercely she slaps his haunch, her gold-curb wristbangles angriling, scolding him in Moorish.

Marion – Nebrakada! Femininum!

The camel, lifting a foreleg, plucks from a tree a large mango fruit, offers it to his mistress, blinking, in his cloven hoof, then droops his head and, grunting, with uplifted neck, fumbles to kneel. Bloom stoops his back for leapfrog.

Bloom – I can give you ... I mean as your business menagerer ... Mrs Marion ... if you ...

Marion – So you notice some change? (*Her hands pass slowly over her trinketed stomacher, a slow friendly mockery in her eyes.*) O Poldy, Poldy, you are a poor old stick-in-the-mud! Go and see life. See the wide world.

Bloom – I was just going back for that lotion, white wax, orangeflower water. Shop closes early on Thursday. But the first thing in the morning. (*He pats divers pockets.*) This moving kidney. Ah!

He points to the south, then to the east. A cake of new clean lemon soap arises, diffusing light and perfume.

The Soap
– *We're a capital couple are Bloom and I.*
  He brightens the earth, I polish the sky.

The freckled face of Sweny, the druggist, appears in the disk of the soapsun.

Sweny – Three and a penny, please.

Bloom – Yes. For my wife. Mrs Marion. Special recipe.

Marion (*softly*) – Poldy!

Bloom – Yes, ma'am?

Marion – *Ti trema un poco il cuore?*

In disdain she saunters away, humming the duet from *Don Giovanni*, plump as a pampered pouter pigeon.

Bloom – Are you sure about that *Voglio*? I mean the pronunciati...

He follows, followed by the sniffing terrier. The elderly bawd seizes his sleeve, the bristles of her chinmole glittering.

The Bawd – Ten shillings a maidenhead. Fresh thing was never touched. Fifteen. There's no one in it only her old father that's dead drunk.

She points. In the gap of her dark den, furtive, rain-bedraggled, Bridie Kelly stands.

Bridie – Hatch Street. Any good in your mind?

With a squeak she flaps her bat shawl and runs. A burly rough pursues with booted strides. He stumbles on the steps, recovers, plunges into gloom. Weak squeaks of laughter are heard, weaker.

The Bawd (*her wolfeyes shining*) – He's getting his pleasure. You won't get a virgin in the flash houses. Ten shillings. Don't be all night before the polis in plain clothes sees us. Sixty-seven is a bitch.

Leering, Gerty MacDowell limps forward. She draws from behind, ogling, and shows coyly her bloodied clout.

Gerty – With all my worldly goods I thee and thou. (*She murmurs.*) You did that. I hate you.

Bloom – I? When? You're dreaming. I never saw you.

The Bawd – Leave the gentleman alone, you cheat. Writing the

417

gentleman false letters. Streetwalking and soliciting. Better for your mother take the strap to you at the bedpost, hussy like you.

Gerty (*to Bloom*) – When you saw all the secrets of my bottom drawer. (*She paws his sleeve, slobbering.*) Dirty married man! I love you for doing that to me.

She glides away crookedly. Mrs Breen, in man's frieze overcoat with loose bellows pockets, stands in the causeway, her roguish eyes wide open, smiling in all her herbivorous buckteeth.

Mrs Breen – Mr . . .

Bloom (*coughs gravely*) – Madam, when we last had this pleasure by letter dated the sixteenth instant . . .

Mrs Breen – Mr Bloom! You down here in the haunts of sin! I caught you nicely! Scamp!

Bloom (*hurriedly*) – Not so loud my name. Whatever do you think of me? Don't give me away. Walls have ears. How do you do? It's ages since I. You're looking splendid. Absolutely it. Seasonable weather we are having this time of year. Black refracts heat. Shortcut home here. Interesting quarter. Rescue of fallen women. Magdalen Asylum. I am the secretary . . .

Mrs Breen (*holds up a finger*) – Now, don't tell a big fib! I know somebody won't like that. O, just wait till I see Molly! (*Slyly*) Account for yourself this very minute or woe betide you!

Bloom (*looks behind*) – She often said she'd like to visit. Slumming. The exotic, you see. Negro servants too in livery if she had money. Othello. Black brute. Eugene Stratton. Even the bones and cornerman at the Livermore christies. Bohee brothers. Sweep for that matter.

Tom and Sam Bohee, coloured coons, in white duck suits, scarlet socks, upstarched Sambo chokers and large scarlet asters in their buttonholes, leap out. Each has his banjo slung. Their paler, smaller negroid hands jingle the twingtwang wires. Flashing white Kaffir eyes and tusks they rattle through a breakdown in clumsy clogs, twinging, singing, back to back, toe heel, heel toe, with smackfatclacking nigger lips.

Tom and Sam
– There's someone in the house with Dina,
  There's someone in the house, I know,

> *There's someone in the house with Dina,*
> *Playing on the old banjo.*

They whisk black masks from raw babbyfaces: then, chuckling, chortling, strumming, twanging, they diddle diddle cakewalk dance away.

Bloom (*with a sour tenderish smile*) – A little frivol, shall we, if you are so inclined? Would you like me perhaps to embrace you just for a fraction of a second?

Mrs Breen (*screams gaily*) – O, you ruck! You ought to see yourself!

Bloom – For old sake's sake. I only meant a square party, a mixed marriage mingling of our different little conjugals. You know I had a soft corner for you. (*Gloomily*) 'Twas I sent you that valentine of the dear gazelle.

Mrs Breen – Glory Alice, you do look a holy show! Killing simply. (*She puts out her hand inquisitively.*) What are you hiding behind your back? Tell us, there's a dear.

Bloom (*seizes her wrist with his free hand*) – Josie Powell that was, prettiest deb in Dublin. How time flies by! Do you remember, harking back in a retrospective arrangement, Old Christmas night, Georgina Simpson's housewarming, while they were playing the Irving Bishop game, finding the pin blindfold and thought reading? Subject, what is in this snuffbox?

Mrs Breen – You were the lion of the night with your seriocomic recitation and you looked the part. You were always a favourite with the ladies.

Bloom (*squire of dames, in dinner jacket with watered-silk facings, blue masonic badge in his buttonhole, black bow and mother-of-pearl studs, a prismatic champagne glass tilted in his hand*) – Ladies and gentlemen, I give you Ireland, home and beauty.

Mrs Breen – The dear dead days beyond recall. Love's old sweet song.

Bloom (*meaningfully dropping his voice*) – I confess I'm teapot with curiosity to find out whether some person's something is a little teapot at present.

Mrs Breen (*gushingly*) – Tremendously teapot! London's teapot and I'm simply teapot all over me! (*She rubs sides with him.*) After the parlour mystery games and the crackers from the tree we sat on the staircase ottoman. Under the mistletoe. Two is company.

Bloom (*wearing a purple Napoleon hat with an amber half-moon, his* *fingers and thumb passing slowly down to her soft moist meaty palm which she surrenders gently*) – The witching hour of night. I took the splinter out of this hand, carefully, slowly. (*Tenderly, as he slips on her finger a ruby ring*) *Là ci darem la mano.*

Mrs Breen (*in a one-piece evening frock executed in moonlight blue, a tinsel sylph's diadem on her brow, with her dancecard fallen beside her moon-blue satin slipper, curving her palm softly, breathing quickly*) – *Voglio e non* ... You're hot! You're scalding! The left hand nearest the heart.

Bloom – When you made your present choice they said it was beauty and the beast. I can never forgive you for that. (*His clenched fist at his brow*) Think what it means. All you meant to me then. (*Hoarsely*) Woman, it's breaking me!

Denis Breen, whitetallhatted, with Wisdom Hely's sandwich boards, shuffles past them in carpet slippers, his dull beard thrust out, muttering to right and left. Little Alf Bergan, cloaked in the pall of the ace of spades, dogs him to left and right, doubled in laughter.

Alf Bergan (*points jeering at the sandwich boards*) – U.P: up.

Mrs Breen (*to Bloom*) – High jinks below stairs. (*She gives him the glad eye.*) Why didn't you kiss the spot to make it well? You wanted to.

Bloom (*shocked*) – Molly's best friend! Could you?

Mrs Breen (*her pulpy tongue between her lips, offers a pigeon kiss*) – Hnhn. The answer is a lemon. Have you a little present for me there?

Bloom (*offhandedly*) – Kosher. A snack for supper. The home without potted meat is incomplete. I was at *Leah*, Mrs Bandmann-Palmer. Trenchant exponent of Shakespeare. Unfortunately threw away the programme. Rattling good place round there for pigs' feet. Feel.

Richie Goulding, three ladies' hats pinned on his head, appears, weighted to one side by the black legal bag of Collis and Ward on which a skull and crossbones are painted in white limewash. He opens it and shows it full of polonies, kippered herrings, Findon haddies and tight-packed pills.

Richie – Best value in Dub.

Bald Pat, bothered beetle, stands on the curbstone, folding his napkin, waiting to wait. He advances with a tilted dish of spillspilling gravy.

Bald Pat – Steak and kidney. Bottle of lager. Hee hee hee. Wait till I wait.

Richie – Goodgod. Inev erate inall ...

With hanging head he marches doggedly forward. The navvy, lurching by, gores him with his flaming pronghorn.

Richie (*with a cry of pain, his hand to his back*) – Ah! Bright's! Lights!

Bloom (*points to the navvy*) – A spy. Don't attract attention. I hate stupid crowds. I am not on pleasure bent. I am in a grave predicament.

Mrs Breen – Humbugging and deluthering as per usual with your cock and bull story.

Bloom – I want to tell you a little secret about how I came to be here. But you must never tell. Not even Molly. I have a most particular reason.

Mrs Breen (*all agog*) – O, not for worlds.

Bloom – Let's walk on. Shall us?

Mrs Breen – Let's.

The bawd makes an unheeded sign. Bloom walks on with Mrs Breen. The terrier follows, whining piteously, wagging his tail.

The Bawd – Jewman's melt!

Bloom (*in an oatmeal sporting suit, a sprig of woodbine in the lapel, tony buff shirt, shepherd's plaid Saint Andrew's Cross scarftie, white spats, fawn dustcoat on his arm, tawny red brogues, field glasses in bandolier, and a grey billycock hat*) – Do you remember a long long time, years and years ago, just after Milly, Marionette we called her, was weaned, when we all went together to Fairyhouse races, was it?

Mrs Breen (*in smart Saxe tailor-made, white velours hat and spider veil*) – Leopardstown.

Bloom – I mean Leopardstown. And Molly won seven shillings on a three-year-old named *Nevertell* and coming home along by Foxrock in that old five-seater shandrydan of a waggonette, you were in your heyday then, and you had on that new hat of white velours with a surround of molefur that Mrs Hayes advised you to buy because it was marked down to nineteen and eleven, a bit of wire and an old rag of velveteen, and I'll lay you what you like she did it on purpose ...

Mrs Breen – She did, of course, the cat! Don't tell me! Nice adviser!

Bloom – Because it didn't suit you one quarter as well as the other ducky little tammy toque with the bird-of-paradise wing in it that I admired on you and you honestly looked just too fetching in it though it was a pity to kill it, you cruel naughty creature, little mite of a thing with a heart the size of a full stop.

Mrs Breen (*squeezes his arm, simpers*) – Naughty cruel I was!

Bloom (*low, secretly, ever more rapidly*) – And Molly was eating a sandwich of spiced beef out of Mrs Joe Gallaher's lunchbasket. Frankly, though she had her advisers or admirers, I never cared much for her style. She was...

Mrs Breen – Too...

Bloom – Yes. And Molly was laughing because Rogers and Maggot O'Reilly were mimicking a cock as we passed a farmhouse and Marcus Tertius Moses, the tea merchant, drove past us in a gig with his daughter, Dancer Moses was her name, and the poodle in her lap bridled up and you asked me if I ever heard or read or knew or came across...

Mrs Breen (*eagerly*) – Yes, yes, yes, yes, yes, yes, yes.

She fades from his side. Followed by the whining dog he walks on towards hell's gates. In an archway a standing woman, bent forward, her feet apart, pisses cowily. Outside a shuttered pub a bunch of loiterers listen to a tale which their broken-snouted gaffer rasps out with raucous humour. An armless pair of them flop wrestling, growling, in maimed sodden playfight.

The Gaffer (*crouches, his voice twisted in his snout*) – And when Cairns came down from the scaffolding in Beaver Street what was he after doing it into only into the bucket of porter that was there waiting on the shavings for Kirwan's plasterers.

The Loiterers (*guffaw with cleft palates*) – O jays!

Their paint-speckled hats wag. Spattered with size and lime of their lodges, they frisk limblessly about him.

Bloom – Coincidence too. They think it funny. Anything but that. Broad daylight. Trying to walk. Lucky no woman.

The Loiterers – Jays, that's a good one. Glauber salts. O jays, into the men's porter.

Bloom passes. Cheap whores, singly, coupled, shawled, dishevelled, call from lanes, doors, corners.

The Whores
— Are you going far, queer fellow?
— How's your middle leg?
— Got a match on you?
— Eh? Come here till I stiffen it for you.

He plodges through their sump towards the lighted street beyond. From a bulge of window curtains a gramophone rears a battered brazen trunk. In the shadow a shebeenkeeper haggles with the navvy and the two redcoats.

The Navvy (*belching*) — Where's the bloody house?
The Shebeenkeeper — Purdon Street. Shilling a bottle of stout. Respect-able woman.
The Navvy (*gripping the two redcoats, staggers forward with them*) — Come on, you British Army!
Private Carr (*behind his back*) — He ain't half balmy.
Private Compton (*laughs*) — What ho!
Private Carr (*to the navvy*) — Portobello barracks canteen. You ask for Carr. Just Carr.
The Navvy (*shouts*) — We are the boys. Of Wexford.
Private Compton — Say! What price the sergeant major?
Private Carr — Bennett? He's my pal. I love old Bennett.
The Navvy (*shouts*)
— *The galling chain.*
  And free our native land.

He staggers forward, dragging them with him. Bloom stops, at fault. The dog approaches, his tongue outlolling, panting.

Bloom — Wild goose chase this. Disorderly houses. Lord knows where they are gone. Drunks cover distance doublequick. Nice mix-up. Scene at Westland Row. Then jump in first-class with third ticket. Then too far. Train with engine behind. Might have taken me to Malahide or a siding for the night or collision. Second drink does it. Once is a dose. What am I following him for? Still, he's the best of that lot. If I hadn't heard about

Mrs Beaufoy Purefoy I wouldn't have gone and wouldn't have met. Kismet. He'll lose that cash. Relieving office here. Good biz for cheapjacks, organs. What do ye lack? Soon got, soon gone. Might have lost my life too with that mangongwheeltracktrolleyglarejuggernaut only for presence of mind. Can't always save you, though. If I had passed Trulock's window that day two minutes later would have been shot. Absence of body. Still, if bullet only went through my coat get damages for shock, five hundred pounds. What was he? Kildare Street Club toff. God help his gamekeeper.

He gazes ahead, reading on the wall a scrawled chalk legend *Wet Dream* and a phallic design.

Bloom – Odd! Molly drawing on the frosted carriage pane at Kingstown. What's that like?

Gaudy doll-women loll in the lighted doorways, in window embrasures, smoking bird's-eye cigarettes. The odour of the sicksweet weed floats towards him in slow round ovalling wreaths.

The Wreaths – Sweet are the sweets. Sweets of sin.
Bloom – My spine's a bit limp. Go or turn? And this food? Eat it and get all pigsticky. Absurd I am. Waste of money. One and eightpence too much. (*The retriever drives a cold snivelling muzzle against his hand, wagging his tail.*) Strange how they take to me. Even that brute today. Better speak to him first. Like women they like *rencontres*. Stinks like a polecat. *Chacun son goût.* He might be mad. Dog days. Uncertain in his movements. Good fellow! Fido! Good fellow! Garryowen! (*The wolfdog sprawls on his back, wriggling obscenely with begging paws, his long black tongue lolling out.*) Influence of his surroundings. Give and have done with it. Provided nobody. (*Calling encouraging words he shambles back with a furtive poacher's tread, dogged by the setter, into a dark stalestunk corner. He unrolls one parcel and goes to dump the crubeen softly but holds back and feels the trotter.*) Sizeable for threepence. But then I have it in my left hand. Calls for more effort. Why? Smaller from want of use. O, let it slide. Two and six.

With regret he lets the unrolled crubeen and trotter slide. The mastiff mauls the bundle clumsily and gluts himself with growling greed, crunching the bones. Two raincaped watch approach, silent, vigilant. They murmur together.

The Watch – Bloom. Of Bloom. For Bloom. Bloom.

Each lays hand on Bloom's shoulder.

First Watch – Caught in the act. Commit no nuisance.
Bloom (*stammers*) – I am doing good to others.

A covey of gulls, storm petrels, rises hungrily from Liffey slime with Banbury cakes in their beaks.

The Gulls – Kaw kave kankury kake.
Bloom – The friend of man. Trained by kindness.

He points. Bob Doran, toppling from a high barstool, sways over the munching spaniel.

Bob Doran – Towser. Give us the paw. Give the paw.

The bulldog growls, his scruff standing, a gobbet of pig's knuckle between his molars through which rabid scumspittle dribbles. Bob Doran falls silently into an area.

Second Watch – Prevention of cruelty to animals.
Bloom (*enthusiastically*) – A noble work! I scolded that tramdriver on Harold's Cross bridge for ill-using the poor horse with his harness scab. Bad French I got for my pains. Of course it was frosty and the last tram. All tales of circus life are highly demoralising.

Signor Maffei, passion-pale, in liontamer's costume with diamond studs in his shirtfront, steps forward holding a circus paper hoop, a curling carriagewhip and a revolver with which he covers the gorging boarhound.

Signor Maffei (*with a sinister smile*) – Ladies and gentlemen, my educated greyhound. It was I broke in the bucking broncho *Ajax* with my patent spiked saddle for carnivores. Lash under the belly with a knotted thong. Block tackle and a strangling pulley will bring your lion to heel, no matter how fractious, even *Leo ferox* there, the Libyan man-eater. A red-hot crowbar and some liniment rubbing on the burning part produced *Fritz of Amsterdam,* the thinking hyena. (*He glares.*) I possess the Indian sign. The glint of my eye does it with these breastsparklers. (*With a bewitching smile*) I now introduce Mademoiselle Ruby, the pride of the ring.

First Watch – Come. Name and address.

Bloom – I have forgotten for the moment. Ah, yes! (*He takes off his high-grade hat, saluting.*) Dr Bloom, Leopold, dental surgeon. You have heard of von Blum Pasha. Umpteen millions. *Donnerwetter!* Owns half Austria. Egypt. Cousin.

First Watch – Proof.

A card falls from inside the leather headband of Bloom's hat.

Bloom (*in red fez, qadi's dress coat with broad green sash, wearing a false badge of the Legion of Honour, picks up the card hastily and offers it*) – Allow me. My club is the Junior Army and Navy. Solicitors: Messrs John Henry Menton, 27 Bachelor's Walk.

First Watch (*reads*) – Henry Flower. No fixed abode. Unlawfully watching and besetting.

Second Watch – An alibi. You are cautioned.

Bloom (*produces from his heart pocket a crumpled yellow flower*) – This is the flower in question. It was given me by a man. I don't know his name. (*Plausibly*) You know that old joke, rose of Castile. Bloom. The change of name. Virag. (*He murmurs privately and confidentially.*) We are engaged, you see, sergeant. Lady in the case. Love entanglement. (*He shoulders the second watch gently.*) Dash it all. It's a way we gallants have in the navy. Uniform that does it. (*He turns gravely to the first watch.*) Still, of course, you do get your Waterloo sometimes. Drop in some evening and have a glass of old burgundy. (*To the second watch, gaily*) I'll introduce you, inspector. She's game. Do it in the shake of a lamb's tail.

A dark mercurialised face appears, leading a veiled figure.

The Dark Mercury – The Castle is looking for him. He was drummed out of the army.

Martha (*thick-veiled, a crimson halter round her neck, a copy of the* Irish Times *in her hand, in tone of reproach, pointing*) – Henry! Leopold! Lionel, thou lost one! Clear my name.

First Watch (*sternly*) – Come to the station.

Bloom, scared, hats himself, steps back, then, plucking at his heart and lifting his right forearm on the square, gives the sign and dueguard of fellowcraft.

Bloom – No, no, worshipful master, light of love. Mistaken identity. The Lyons mail. Lesurques and Duboscq. You remember the Childs fratricide case. We medical men. By striking him dead with a hatchet. I am wrongfully accused. Better one guilty escape than ninety-nine wrongfully condemned.

Martha (*sobbing behind her veil*) – Breach of promise. My real name is Peggy Griffin. He wrote to me that he was miserable. I'll tell my brother, the Bective rugger fullback, on you, heartless flirt.

Bloom (*behind his hand*) – She's drunk. The woman is inebriated. (*He murmurs vaguely the pass of Ephraim.*) Shitbroleeth.

Second Watch (*tears in his eyes, to Bloom*) – You ought to be thoroughly well ashamed of yourself.

Bloom – Gentlemen of the jury, let me explain. A pure mare's nest. I am a man misunderstood. I am being made a scapegoat of. I am a respectable married man, without a stain on my character. I live in Eccles Street. My wife is the daughter of a most distinguished commander, a gallant upstanding gentleman, what do you call him, Major General Brian Tweedy, one of Britain's fighting men who helped to win our battles. Got his majority for the heroic defence of Rorke's Drift.

First Watch – Regiment.

Bloom (*turns to the gallery*) – The Royal Dublins, boys, the salt of the earth, known the world over. I think I see some old comrades in arms up there among you. The R.D.F. With our own Metropolitan police, guardians of our homes, the pluckiest lads and the finest body of men, as physique, in the service of our sovereign.

A Voice – Turncoat! Up the Boers! Who booed Joe Chamberlain?

Bloom (*his hand on the shoulder of the first watch*) – My old dad too was a J.P. I'm as staunch a Britisher as you are, sir. I fought with the colours for king and country in the absentminded war under General Gough in the Park and was disabled at Spion Kop and Bloemfontein. Was mentioned in dispatches. I did all a white man could. (*With quiet feeling*) Jim Bludso. Hold her nozzle again' the bank.

First Watch – Profession or trade.

Bloom – Well, I follow a literary occupation, author-journalist. In fact we are just bringing out a collection of prize stories of which I am the inventor, something that is an entirely new departure. I am connected with the British and Irish press. If you ring up ...

Myles Crawford strides out jerkily, a quill between his teeth. His scarlet beak blazes within the aureole of his straw hat. He dangles a hank of Spanish onions in one hand and holds with the other hand a telephone receiver nozzle to his ear.

Myles Crawford (*his cock's wattles wagging*) – Hello, seventy-seven eight four. Hello. *Freeman's Urinal* and *Weekly Arsewipe* here. Paralyse Europe. You which? Bluebags? Who writes? Is it Bloom?

Mr Philip Beaufoy, pale-faced, stands in the witness-box, in accurate morning dress, outbreast pocket with peak of handkerchief showing, creased lavender trousers and patent boots. He carries a large portfolio labelled *Matcham's Masterstrokes*.

Beaufoy (*drawls*) – No, you aren't, not by a long shot, if I know it. I don't see it, that's all. No born gentleman, no one with the most rudimentary promptings of a gentleman, would stoop to such particularly loathsome conduct. One of those, my lord. A plagiarist. A soapy sneak masquerading as a littérateur. It's perfectly obvious that with the most inherent baseness he has cribbed some of my best-selling copy, really gorgeous stuff, a perfect gem, the love passages in which are beneath suspicion. The Beaufoy books of love and great possessions, with which your lordship is doubtless familiar, are a household word throughout the kingdom.

Bloom (*murmurs with hangdog meekness*) – That bit about the laughing witch hand in hand I take exception to, if I may ...

Beaufoy (*his lip upcurled, smiles superciliously on the court*) – You funny ass, you! You're too beastly awfully weird for words! I don't think you need overexcessively discommodate yourself in that regard. My literary agent Mr J.B. Pinker is in attendance. I presume, my lord, we shall receive the usual witnesses' fees, shan't we? We are considerably out of pocket over this bally pressman johnny, this jackdaw of Rheims, who has not even been to a university.

Bloom (*indistinctly*) – University of life. Bad art.

Beaufoy (*shouts*) – It's a damnably foul lie, showing the moral rottenness of the man! (*He extends his portfolio.*) We have here damning evidence, the *corpus delicti*, my lord, a specimen of my maturer work disfigured by the hallmark of the beast.

A Voice from the Gallery
   —*Moses, Moses, king of the Jews,*
      Wiped his arse in the Daily News.

Bloom (*bravely*) – Overdrawn.

Beaufoy – You low cad! You ought to be ducked in the horsepond, you rotter! (*To the court*) Why, look at the man's private life! Leading a quadruple existence! Street angel and house devil. Not fit to be mentioned in mixed society! The archconspirator of the age!

Bloom (*to the court*) – And he, a bachelor, how ...

First Watch – The King versus Bloom. Call the woman Driscoll.

The Crier – Mary Driscoll, scullery maid!

Mary Driscoll, a slipshod servant girl, approaches. She has a bucket on the crook of her arm and a scouring brush in her hand.

Second Watch – Another! Are you of the unfortunate class?

Mary Driscoll (*indignantly*) – I'm not a bad one. I bear a respectable character and was four months in my last place. I was in a situation, six pounds a year and my chances with Fridays out, and I had to leave owing to his carryings on.

First Watch – What do you tax him with?

Mary Driscoll – He made a certain suggestion but I thought more of myself as poor as I am.

Bloom (*in house jacket of ripple cloth, flannel trousers, heelless slippers, unshaven, his hair rumpled, softly*) – I treated you white. I gave you mementos, smart emerald garters far above your station. Incautiously I took your part when you were accused of pilfering. There's a medium in all things. Play cricket.

Mary Driscoll (*excitedly*) – As God is looking down on me this night if ever I laid a hand to them oylsters!

First Watch – The offence complained of? Did something happen?

Mary Driscoll – He surprised me in the rear of the premises, your honour, when the missus was out shopping one morning, with a request for a safety pin. He held me and I was discoloured in four places as a result. And he interfered twict with my clothing.

Bloom – She counterassaulted.

Mary Driscoll (*scornfully*) – I had more respect for the scouring brush, so I had. I remonstrated with him, your lord, and he remarked: keep it quiet.

General laughter.

George Fottrell (*clerk of the crown and peace, resonantly*) – Order in court! The accused will now make a bogus statement.

Bloom, pleading not guilty and holding a full-blown water lily, begins a long unintelligible speech. They would hear what counsel had to say in his stirring address to the grand jury. He was down and out but, though branded as a black sheep, if he might say so, he meant to reform, to retrieve the memory of the past in a purely sisterly way and return to nature as a purely domestic animal. A seven-months' child, he had been carefully brought up and nurtured by an aged bedridden parent. There might have been lapses of an erring father but he wanted to turn over a new leaf and now, when at long last in sight of the whipping post, to lead a homely life in the evening of his days, permeated by the affectionate surroundings of the heaving bosom of the family. An acclimatised Britisher, he had seen that summer eve from the footplate of an engine cab of the Loop Line railway company, while the rain refrained from falling, glimpses, as it were, through the windows of loveful households in Dublin city and urban district, of scenes truly rural of happiness of the better land with Dockrell's wallpaper at one and ninepence a dozen, innocent British-born bairns lisping prayers to the Sacred Infant, youthful scholars grappling with their pensums, model young ladies playing on the pianoforte, or anon all with fervour reciting the family rosary round the crackling yule log while in the boreens and green lanes the colleens with their swains strolled what times the strains of the organ-toned melodeon, Britannia metalbound with four acting stops and twelvefold bellows, a sacrifice, greatest bargain ever…

Renewed laughter. He mumbles incoherently. Reporters complain that they cannot hear.

Longhand and Shorthand (*without looking up from their notebooks*) – Loosen his boots.

Professor MacHugh (*from the press table, coughs and calls*) – Cough it up, man. Get it out in bits.

The cross-examination proceeds re Bloom and the bucket. A large bucket. Bloom himself. Bowel trouble. In Beaver Street. Gripe, yes. Quite bad. A plasterer's bucket. By walking stiff-legged. Suffered untold misery. Deadly agony. About noon. Love or burgundy. Yes, some spinach. Crucial moment. He did not look in the bucket. Nobody. Rather a mess. Not completely. A *Tit-Bits* back number.

Uproar and catcalls. Bloom, in a torn frockcoat stained with whitewash, dinged silk hat sideways on his head, a strip of sticking plaster across his nose, talks inaudibly.

J.J. O'Molloy (*in barrister's grey wig and stuff gown, speaking with a voice of pained protest*) – This is no place for indecent levity at the expense of an erring mortal disguised in liquor. We are not in a bear garden nor at an Oxford rag nor is this a travesty of justice. My client is an infant, a poor foreign immigrant who started scratch as a stowaway and is now trying to turn an honest penny. The trumped-up misdemeanour was due to a momentary aberration of heredity, brought on by hallucination, such familiarities as the alleged guilty occurrence being quite permitted in my client's native place, the land of the Pharaoh. Prima facie, I put it to you that there was no attempt at carnally knowing. Intimacy did not occur and the offence complained of by Driscoll, that her virtue was solicited, was not repeated. I would deal in especial with atavism. There have been cases of shipwreck and somnambulism in my client's family. If the accused could speak he could a tale unfold – one of the strangest that have ever been narrated between the covers of a book. He himself, my lord, is a physical wreck from cobbler's weak chest. His submission is that he is of Mongolian extraction and irresponsible for his actions. Not all there, in fact.

Bloom, barefoot, pigeon-breasted, in lascar's vest and trousers, apologetic toes turned in, opens his tiny mole's eyes and looks about him dazedly, passing a slow hand across his forehead. Then he hitches his belt sailor fashion and with a shrug of oriental obeisance salutes the court, pointing one thumb heavenward.

431

Bloom – Him makee velly muchee fine night. (*He begins to lilt simply.*)

   Li li poo lil chile
   Blingee pigfoot evly night
   Payee two shilly . . .

He is howled down.

J.J. O'Molloy (*hotly, to the populace*) – This is a lonehand fight. By Hades, I will not have any client of mine gagged and badgered in this fashion by a pack of curs and laughing hyenas. The Mosaic code has superseded the law of the jungle. I say it and I say it emphatically, without wishing for one moment to defeat the ends of justice, accused was not accessory before the act and prosecutrix has not been tampered with. The young person was treated by defendant as if she were his very own daughter. (*Bloom takes J.J. O'Molloy's hand and raises it to his lips.*) I shall call rebutting evidence to prove up to the hilt that the hidden hand is again at its old game. When in doubt persecute Bloom. My client, an innately bashful man, would be the last man in the world to do anything ungentlemanly which injured modesty could object to or to cast a stone at a girl who took the wrong turning when some dastard, responsible for her condition, had worked his own sweet will on her. He wants to go straight. I regard him as the whitest man I know. He is down on his luck at present owing to the mortgaging of his extensive property at Agudath Netaim in faraway Asia Minor, slides of which will now be shown. (*To Bloom*) I suggest that you will do the handsome thing.

Bloom – A penny in the pound.

The image of the lake of Kinneret with blurred cattle cropping in silver haze is projected on the wall. Moses Dlugacz, ferret-eyed albino, in blue dungarees, stands up in the gallery, holding in each hand an orange citron and a pork kidney.

Dlugacz (*hoarsely*) – Bleibtreustrasse 34, Berlin W.15.

J.J. O'Molloy steps onto a low plinth and holds the lapel of his coat with solemnity. His face lengthens, grows pale and bearded, with the sunken eyes, blotches of phthisis and hectic cheekbones of John F. Taylor. He applies his handkerchief to his mouth and scrutinises the galloping tide of rose-pink blood.

J.J. O'Molloy (*almost voicelessly*) – Excuse me. I am suffering from a severe chill, have recently come from a sickbed. A few well-chosen words. (*He assumes the avian head, foxy moustache and proboscidal eloquence of Seymour Bushe.*) When the angel's book comes to be opened if aught that the pensive bosom has inaugurated of soul-transfigured and of soul-transfiguring deserves to live I say accord the prisoner at the bar the sacred benefit of the doubt.

A paper with something written on it is handed into court.

Bloom (*in court dress*) – Can give best references. Messrs Callan, Coleman. Mr Wisdom Hely J.P. My old chief, Joe Cuffe. Mr V.B. Dillon, ex-lord-mayor of Dublin. I have moved in the charmed circle of the highest ... Queens of Dublin society. (*Carelessly*) I was just chatting this afternoon at the viceregal lodge to my old pals, Sir Robert and Lady Ball, astronomer royal, at the levee. Sir Bob, I said ...

Mrs Yelverton Barry (*in low-corsaged opal balldress and elbow-length ivory gloves, wearing a sable-trimmed brick quilted dolman, a comb of brilliants and a panache of osprey in her hair*) – Arrest him, constable. He wrote me an anonymous letter in prentice backhand when my husband was in the North Riding of Tipperary on the Munster circuit, signed James Lovebirch. He said that he had seen from the gods my peerless globes as I sat in a box of the *Theatre Royal* at a command performance of *La Cigale*. I deeply inflamed him, he said. He made improper overtures to me to misconduct myself at half past four p.m. on the following Thursday, Dunsink time. He offered to send me through the post a work of fiction by Monsieur Paul de Kock entitled *The Girl with the Three Pairs of Stays*.

Mrs Bellingham, in cap and seal coney mantle, wrapped up to the nose, steps out of her brougham and scans through tortoiseshell quizzing glasses which she takes from inside her huge opossum muff.

Mrs Bellingham – Also to me. Yes, I believe it is the same objectionable person. Because he closed my carriage door outside Sir Thornley Stoker's one sleety day during the cold snap of February ninety-three when even the grid of the waste pipe and the ballstop in my bath cistern were frozen. Subsequently he enclosed a bloom of edelweiss culled on the heights, as he said, in my honour. I had it examined by a botanical expert and elicited

433

the information that it was a blossom of the homegrown potato plant purloined from a forcing case of the model farm.

Mrs Yelverton Barry – Shame on him!

A crowd of sluts and ragamuffins surges forward.

The Sluts and Ragamuffins (*screaming*) – Stop thief! Hurrah there, Bluebeard! Three cheers for Ikey Mo!

Second Watch (*produces handcuffs*) – Here are the darbies.

Mrs Bellingham – He addressed me in several handwritings with fulsome compliments as a Venus in furs and alleged profound pity for my frostbound coachman Palmer while in the same breath he expressed himself as envious of his earflaps and fleecy sheepskins and of his fortunate proximity to my person when standing behind my chair wearing my livery and the armorial bearings of the Bellingham escutcheon, garnished *sable* a buck's head couped *or*. He lauded almost extravagantly my nether extremities, my swelling calves in silk hose drawn up to the limit, and eulogised glowingly my other hidden treasures in priceless lace which, he said, he could conjure up. He urged me, stating that he felt it his mission in life to urge me, to defile the marriage bed, to commit adultery at the earliest possible opportunity.

The Honourable Mrs Mervyn Talboys (*in amazon costume, hard hat, cock-spurred jackboots, vermilion waistcoat, fawn musketeer gauntlets with braided drums, long train held up and hunting crop with which she strikes her welt constantly*) – Also me. Because he saw me on the polo ground of the Phoenix Park at the match All Ireland versus The Rest of Ireland. My eyes, I know, shone divinely as I watched Captain Slogger Dennehy of the Inniskillings win the final chukkar on his darling cob *Centaur*. This plebeian Don Juan observed me from behind a hackney car and sent me in double envelopes an obscene photograph, such as are sold after dark on Paris boulevards, insulting to any lady. I have it still. It represents a partially nude señorita, frail and lovely (his wife, as he solemnly assured me, taken by him from nature), practising illicit intercourse with a muscular torero, evidently a blackguard. He urged me to do likewise, to misbehave, to sin with officers of the garrison. He implored me to soil his letter in an unspeakable manner, to chastise him as he richly deserves, to bestride and ride him, to give him a most vicious horsewhipping.

Mrs Bellingham – Me too.

Mrs Yelverton Barry – Me too.

Several highly respectable Dublin ladies hold up improper letters received from Bloom.

The Honourable Mrs Mervyn Talboys (*stamps her jingling spurs in a sudden paroxysm of fury*) – I will, by the God above me. I'll scourge the pigeon-livered cur as long as I can stand over him. I'll flay him alive.

Bloom (*his eyes closing, quails expectantly*) – Here? (*He squirms.*) Again! (*He pants, cringing.*) I love the danger.

The Honourable Mrs Mervyn Talboys – Very much so! I'll make it hot for you. I'll make you dance Jack Latten for that.

Mrs Bellingham – Tan his breech well, the upstart! Write the stars and stripes on it!

Mrs Yelverton Barry – Disgraceful! There's no excuse for him! A married man!

Bloom – All these people. I meant only the spanking idea. A warm tingling glow without effusion. Refined birching to stimulate the circulation.

The Honourable Mrs Mervyn Talboys (*laughs derisively*) – O, did you, my fine fellow? Well, by the living God, you'll get the surprise of your life now, believe me, the most unmerciful hiding a man ever bargained for. You have lashed the dormant tigress in my nature into fury.

Mrs Bellingham (*shakes her muff and quizzing glasses vindictively*) – Make him smart, Hanna dear. Give him ginger. Thrash the mongrel within an inch of his life. The cat-o'-nine-tails. Geld him. Vivisect him.

Bloom (*with hangdog mien, shuddering, shrinking, joins his hands*) – O cold! O shivery! It was your ambrosial beauty. Forget, forgive. Kismet. Let me off this once. (*He offers the other cheek.*)

Mrs Yelverton Barry (*severely*) – Don't do so on any account, Mrs Talboys! He should be soundly trounced!

The Honourable Mrs Mervyn Talboys (*unbuttoning her gauntlet violently*) – I'll do no such thing. Pig dog and always was ever since he was pupped! To dare address me! I'll flog him black and blue in the public streets. I'll dig my spurs in him up to the rowel. He is a well-known cuckold. (*She swishes her hunting crop savagely in the air.*) Take down his trousers without loss of time. Come here, sir! Quick! Ready?

Bloom (*trembling, beginning to obey*) – The weather has been so warm.

Davy Stephens, ringletted, passes with a bevy of barefoot newsboys.

Davy Stephens – *Messenger of the Sacred Heart* and *Evening Telegraph* with Saint Patrick's Day supplement. Containing the new addresses of all the cuckolds in Dublin.

The Very Reverend Canon O'Hanlon in cloth-of-gold cope elevates and exposes a marble timepiece. Before him Father Conroy and the Reverend John Hughes S. J. bend low.

The Timepiece (*unportalling*)
– *Cuckoo.*
Cuckoo.
Cuckoo.

The brass quoits of a bed are heard to jingle.

The Quoits – Jigjag. Jigajiga. Jigjag.

A panel of fog rolls back rapidly, revealing in the jurybox the faces of Martin Cunningham, foreman, silk-hatted, Jack Power, Simon Dedalus, Tom Kernan, Ned Lambert, John Henry Menton, Myles Crawford, Lenehan, Paddy Leonard, Nosey Flynn, M'Coy and the featureless face of a Nameless One.

The Nameless One – Bareback riding. Weight for age. Gob, he organised her.
The Jurors (*all their heads turned to his voice*) – Really?
The Nameless One (*snarls*) – Arse over tip. Hundred shillings to five.
The Jurors (*all their heads bowed in assent*) – Most of us thought as much.
First Watch – He is a marked man. Another girl's plait cut. Wanted: Jack the Ripper. A thousand pounds reward.
Second Watch (*awed, whispers*) – And in black. A Mormon. Anarchist.
The Crier (*loudly*) – Whereas Leopold Bloom of no fixed abode is a well-known dynamitard, forger, bigamist, bawd and cuckold, and a public nuisance to the citizens of Dublin and whereas at this commission of assizes the Most Honourable . . .

His Honour, Sir Frederick Falkiner, recorder of Dublin, in judicial garb of grey stone, rises from the bench, stone-bearded. He bears in his arms an umbrella sceptre. From his forehead arise starkly the Mosaic ram's horns.

The Recorder – I will put an end to this white slave traffic and rid Dublin of this odious pest. Scandalous! (*He dons the black cap.*) Let him be taken, Mr Subsheriff, from the dock where he now stands and detained in custody in Mountjoy Prison during His Majesty's pleasure and there be hanged by the neck until he is dead and therein fail not at your peril or may the Lord have mercy on your soul. Remove him. (*A black skullcap descends upon his head.*)

The subsheriff Long John Fanning appears, smoking a pungent Henry Clay. He scowls and calls with rich rolling utterance.

Long John Fanning – Who'll hang Judas Iscariot?

H. Rumbold, master barber, in a blood-coloured jerkin and tanner's apron, a rope coiled over his shoulder, mounts the block. A life preserver and a nail-studded bludgeon are stuck in his belt. He rubs grimly his grappling hands, knobbed with knuckledusters.

Rumbold (*to the recorder with sinister familiarity*) – Hanging Harry, your Majesty, the Mersey terror. Five guineas a jugular. Neck or nothing.

The bells of George's Church toll slowly, loud dark iron.

The Bells – Heigho! Heigho!
Bloom (*desperately*) – Wait. Stop. Gulls. Good heart. I saw. Innocence. Girl in the monkey house. Zoo. Lewd chimpanzee. (*Breathlessly*) Pelvic basin. Her artless blush unmanned me. (*Overcome with emotion*) I left the precincts. (*He turns to a figure in the crowd, appealing.*) Hynes, may I speak to you? You know me. That three shillings you can keep. If you want a little more . . .
Hynes (*coldly*) – You are a perfect stranger.
Second Watch (*points to the corner*) – The bomb is here.
First Watch – Infernal machine with a time fuse.
Bloom – No, no. Pig's feet. I was at a funeral.
First Watch (*draws his truncheon*) – Liar!

The beagle lifts his snout, showing the grey scorbutic face of Paddy Dignam. He has gnawed all. He exhales a putrid carcass-fed breath. He grows to human size and shape. His dachshund coat becomes a brown mortuary habit. His green eye flashes bloodshot. Half of one ear, all the nose and both thumbs are ghoul-eaten.

Paddy Dignam (*in a hollow voice*) – It is true. It was my funeral. Doctor Finucane pronounced life extinct when I succumbed to the disease from natural causes.

He lifts his mutilated ashen face moonwards and bays lugubriously.

Bloom (*in triumph*) – You hear?
Paddy Dignam – Bloom, I am Paddy Dignam's spirit. List, list. O, list!
Bloom – The voice is the voice of Esau.
Second Watch (*blesses himself*) – How is that possible?
First Watch – It is not in the penny catechism.
Paddy Dignam – By metempsychosis. Spooks.
A Voice – O rocks.
Paddy Dignam (*earnestly*) – Once I was in the employ of Mr J.H. Menton, solicitor, commissioner for oaths and affidavits, of 27 Bachelor's Walk. Now I am defunct, the wall of the heart hypertrophied. Hard lines. The poor wife was awfully cut up. How is she bearing it? Keep her off that bottle of sherry. (*He looks round him.*) A lamp. I must satisfy an animal need. That buttermilk didn't agree with me.

The portly figure of John O'Connell, caretaker, stands forth, holding a bunch of keys tied with crape. Beside him stands Father Coffey, chaplain, toad-bellied, wrynecked, in a surplice and bandanna nightcap, holding sleepily a staff of twisted poppies.

Father Coffey (*yawns, then chants with a hoarse croak*) – Namine. Jacobs. Vobiscuits. Amen.
John O'Connell (*foghorns stormily through his megaphone*) – Dignam, Patrick T., deceased.
Paddy Dignam (*with pricked-up ears, winces*) – Overtones. (*He wriggles forward and places an ear to the ground.*) My master's voice!
John O'Connell – Burial docket letter number U.P. eighty-five thousand. Field seventeen. House of Keys. Plot one hundred and one.

Paddy Dignam listens with visible effort, thinking, his tail stiffpointed, his ears cocked.

Paddy Dignam – Pray for the repose of his soul.

He worms down through a coalhole, his brown habit trailing its tether over rattling pebbles. After him toddles an obese grandfather rat on fungus turtle paws under a grey carapace. Dignam's voice, muffled, is heard baying under ground.

Dignam's Voice – Dignam's dead and gone below.

Tom Rochford, robin-redbreasted, in cap and breeches, jumps from his two-columned machine.

Tom Rochford (*a hand to his breastbone, bows*) – Reuben J. A florin I find him. (*He fixes the manhole with a resolute stare.*) My turn now on. Follow me up to Carlow. (*He executes a daredevil salmon-leap in the air and is engulfed in the coalhole. Two disks on the columns wobble, eyes of nought.*)

All recedes. Bloom plodges forward again through the sump. Kisses chirp amid the rifts of fog. A piano sounds. He stands before a lighted house, listening. The kisses, winging from their bowers, fly about him, twittering, warbling, cooing.

The Kisses (*warbling*) – Leo! (*Twittering*) Icky licky micky sticky for Leo! (*Cooing*) Coo coocoo! Yummyyum! Womwom! (*Warbling*) Big comebig! Pirouette! Leopopold! (*Twittering*) Leeolee! (*Warbling*) O Leo!

They rustle, flutter upon his garments, alight, bright giddy flecks, silvery sequins.

Bloom – A man's touch. Sad music. Church music. Perhaps here.

Zoe Higgins, a young whore in a sapphire slip closed with three bronze buckles, a slim black velvet fillet round her throat, nods, trips down the steps and accosts him.

Zoe – Are you looking for someone? He's inside with his friend.

Bloom – Is this Mrs Mack's?

Zoe – No, eighty-two. Mrs Cohen's. You might go farther and fare worse. Mother Slipperslapper. (*Familiarly*) She's on the job herself tonight with the vet, her tipster, that gives her all the winners and pays for her son in Oxford. Working overtime, but her luck's turned today. (*Suspiciously*) You're not his father, are you?

Bloom – Not I!

Zoe – You both in black. Has little mousey any tickles tonight?

His skin, alert, feels her fingertips approach. A hand slides over his left thigh.

Zoe – How's the nuts?

Bloom – Offside. Curiously they are on the right. Heavier, I suppose. One in a million my tailor, Mesias, says.

Zoe (*in sudden alarm*) – You've a hard chancre.

Bloom – Not likely.

Zoe – I feel it.

Her hand slides into his left trouser pocket and brings out a hard black shrivelled potato. She regards it and Bloom with dumb moist lips.

Bloom – A talisman. Heirloom.

Zoe – For Zoe? For keeps? For being so nice, eh?

She puts the potato greedily into a pocket, then links his arm, cuddling him with supple warmth. He smiles uneasily. Slowly, note by note, oriental music is played. He gazes in the tawny crystal of her eyes, ringed with kohol. His smile softens.

Zoe – You'll know me the next time.

Bloom (*forlornly*) – I never loved a dear gazelle but it was sure to . . .

Gazelles are leaping, feeding, on the mountains. Near are lakes. Round their shores file shadows black of cedar groves. Aroma rises, a strong hairgrowth of resin. It burns, the orient, a sky of sapphire, cleft by the bronze flight of eagles. Under it lies the woman-city, nude, white, still, cool, in luxury. A fountain murmurs among damask roses. Mammoth roses murmur of scarlet winegrapes. A wine of shame, lust, blood, exudes, strangely murmuring.

Zoe (*murmuring singsong with the music, her odalisk lips lusciously smeared with salve of swinefat and rose water*) – Schorach ani wenowach, benoith Hierushaloim.

Bloom (*fascinated*) – I thought you were of good stock by your accent.

Zoe – And you know what thought did?

She bites his ear gently with little gold-stopped teeth, sending on him a cloying breath of stale garlic. The roses draw apart, disclosing a sepulchre of the gold of kings and their mouldering bones.

Bloom (*draws back, mechanically caressing her right bub with a flat awkward hand*) – Are you a Dublin girl?

Zoe (*catches a stray hair deftly and twists it to her coil*) – No bloody fear. I'm English. Have you a swaggerroot?

Bloom (*as before*) – Rarely smoke, dear. Cigar now and then. Childish device. (*Lewdly*) The mouth can be better engaged than with a cylinder of rank weed.

Zoe – Go on. Make a stump speech out of it.

Bloom (*in workman's corduroy overalls, black gansy with red floating tie, and apache cap*) – Mankind is incorrigible. Sir Walter Raleigh brought from the new world that potato and that weed, the one a killer of pestilence by absorption, the other a poisoner of the ear, eye, heart, memory, will, understanding, all. That is to say, he brought the poison a hundred years before another person whose name I forget brought the food. Suicide. Lies. All our habits. Why, look at our public life!

Midnight chimes from distant steeples.

The Chimes – Turn again, Leopold! Lord mayor of Dublin!

Bloom (*in alderman's gown and chain*) – Electors of Arran Quay, Inns Quay, Rotunda, Mountjoy and North Dock, better run a tramline, I say, from the cattle market to the river. That's the music of the future. That's my programme. *Cui bono?* But our buccaneering Vanderdeckens in their phantom ship of finance . . .

An Elector – Three times three for our future chief magistrate!

The aurora borealis of the torchlight procession leaps.

The Torchbearers – Hooray!

Several well-known burgesses, city magnates and freemen of the city shake hands with Bloom and congratulate him. Timothy Harrington, late thrice lord mayor of Dublin, imposing in mayoral scarlet, gold chain and white silk tie, confers with Councillor Lorcan Sherlock, locum tenens. They nod vigorously in agreement.

Late Lord Mayor Harrington (*in scarlet robe, with mace, gold mayoral chain and large white silk scarf*) – That Alderman Sir Leo Bloom's speech be printed at the expense of the ratepayers. That the house in which he was born be ornamented with a commemorative tablet and that the thoroughfare hitherto known as Cow Parlour off Cork Street be henceforth designated Boulevard Bloom.

Councillor Lorcan Sherlock – Carried unanimously.

Bloom (*impassionedly*) – These flying Dutchmen or lying Dutchmen as they recline in their upholstered poop, casting dice, what reck they? Machines is their cry, their chimera, their panacea. Laboursaving apparatuses, supplanters, bugbears, manufactured monsters for mutual murder, hideous hobgoblins produced by a horde of capitalistic lusts upon our prostituted labour. The poor man starves while they are grassing their royal mountain stags or shooting peasants and phartridges in their purblind pomp of pelf and power. But their reign is rover for rever and ever and ev...

Prolonged applause. Venetian masts, maypoles and festal arches spring up. A streamer bearing the legends *Céad Míle Fáilte* and *Mah Ttob Melek Israel* spans the street. All the windows are thronged with sightseers, chiefly ladies. Along the route the regiments of the Royal Dublin Fusiliers, the King's Own Scottish Borderers, the Cameron Highlanders and the Welsh Fusiliers, standing to attention, keep back the crowd. Boys from High School are perched on the lampposts, telegraph poles, window sills, cornices, gutters, chimney pots, railings, rainspouts, whistling and cheering. The pillar of the cloud appears. A fife and drum band is heard in the distance playing the Kol Nidre. The beaters approach with imperial eagles hoisted, trailing banners and waving oriental palms. The chryselephantine papal standard rises high, surrounded by pennons of the civic flag. The van of the procession appears, headed by John Howard Parnell, city marshal, in a chessboard tabard, the Athlone Pursuivant and the Ulster King of Arms. They are followed by the Right Honourable Joseph Hutchinson, lord mayor of Dublin, His Lordship the lord mayor of Cork, Their Worships the mayors of Limerick, Galway, Sligo and Waterford, twenty-eight Irish representative peers, sirdars, grandees and maharajahs bearing the cloth of estate, the Dublin Metropolitan Fire Brigade, the chapter of the saints of finance in their plutocratic order of precedence, the bishop of Down and Connor, His Eminence Michael Cardinal Logue, archbishop of Armagh, primate of all Ireland, His Grace the Most Reverend Dr William Alexander, archbishop of Armagh, primate of all Ireland, the chief rabbi, the Presbyterian moderator, the heads of the Baptist, Anabaptist, Methodist and Moravian chapels, and the honorary secretary of the Society of Friends. After them march the guilds and trades and trainbands with flying colours: coopers, bird fanciers, millwrights, newspaper canvassers, law scriveners, masseurs, vintners, trussmakers, chimney sweeps, lard refiners, tabinet and poplin weavers, farriers, Italian warehousemen, church decorators, bootjack manufacturers, undertakers, silk mercers, lapidaries, salesmasters, corkcutters, assessors of fire losses, dyers and cleaners, export bottlers, fellmongers, ticketwriters, heraldic seal engravers, horse repository hands, bullion brokers, cricket and archery outfitters, riddlemakers, egg and potato factors, hosiers and glovers, plumbing contractors. After them march gentlemen of the bedchamber, Black Rod, Deputy Garter, Gold Stick, the master of horse, the lord great chamberlain, the earl marshal, the high constable carrying the sword of state, Saint Stephen's iron crown, the chalice and bible. Four buglers on foot blow a sennet. Beefeaters reply, winding clarions of welcome. Under an arch of triumph Bloom appears, bareheaded, in a crimson velvet mantle trimmed with ermine, bearing Saint Edward's staff, the orb and sceptre with the dove, the curtana. He is seated on a milk-white horse with long flowing crimson tail, richly caparisoned, with golden headstall. Wild excitement. The ladies from their balconies throw down rose petals. The air is perfumed with essences. The men cheer. Bloom's boys run amid the bystanders with branches of hawthorn and wren bushes.

Bloom's Boys

— *The wren, the wren,*

> *The king of all birds,*
> *Saint Stephen's his day*
> *Was caught in the furze.*

A Blacksmith (*murmurs*) – For the honour of God! And is that Bloom? He scarcely looks thirty-one.

A Pavior and Flagger – That's the famous Bloom now, the world's greatest reformer. Hats off!

All uncover their heads. Women whisper eagerly.

A Millionairess (*richly*) – Isn't he simply wonderful?

A Noblewoman (*nobly*) – All that man has seen!

A Feminist (*masculinely*) – And done!

A Bellhanger – A classic face! He has the forehead of a thinker.

Bloom's weather. A sunburst appears in the northwest.

The Bishop of Down and Connor – I here present your undoubted emperor president and king chairman, the most serene and potent and very puissant ruler of this realm. God save Leopold the First!

All – God save Leopold the First!

Bloom (*in dalmatic and purple mantle, to the bishop of Down and Connor, with dignity*) – Thanks, somewhat eminent sir.

William, Archbishop of Armagh (*in purple stock and shovel hat*) – Will you to your power cause law and justice, in mercy, to be executed in all your judgments in Ireland and territories thereunto belonging?

Bloom (*placing his right hand on his testicles, swears*) – So may the Creator deal with me. All this I promise to do.

Michael, Archbishop of Armagh (*pours a cruse of hairoil over Bloom's head*) – *Gaudium magnum annuntio vobis. Habemus carnificem.* Leopold Patrick Andrew David George, be thou anointed!

Bloom assumes a mantle of cloth of gold and puts on a ruby ring. He ascends and stands on the stone of destiny. The representative peers put on at the same time their twenty-eight crowns. Joybells ring in Christ Church, Saint Patrick's, George's, and gay Malahide. Mirus Bazaar fireworks go up from all sides with symbolical phallopyrotechnic designs. The peers do homage, one by one, approaching and genuflecting.

The Peers – I do become your liege man of life and limb to earthly worship.

Bloom holds up his right hand on which sparkles the Koh-i-noor diamond. His palfrey neighs. Immediate silence. Intercontinental and interplanetary wireless transmitters are set for reception of message.

Bloom – My subjects! We hereby nominate our faithful charger *Copula Felix* hereditary Grand Vizier and announce that we have this day repudiated our former spouse and have bestowed our royal hand upon the princess Selene, the splendour of night.

The former morganatic spouse of Bloom is hastily removed in the Black Maria. The princess Selene, in moon-blue robes, a silver crescent on her head, descends from a Sedan chair, borne by two giants. An outburst of cheering.

John Howard Parnell (*raises the royal standard*) – Illustrious Bloom! Successor to my famous brother!
Bloom (*embraces John Howard Parnell*) – We thank you from our heart, John, for this right royal welcome to green Erin, the promised land of our common ancestors.

The freedom of the city is presented to him embodied in a charter. The keys of Dublin, crossed on a crimson cushion, are given to him. He shows all that he is wearing green socks.

Tom Kernan – You deserve it, your honour.
Bloom – On this day twenty years ago we overcame the hereditary enemy at Ladysmith. Our howitzers and camel swivel guns played on his lines with telling effect. Half a league onward! They charge! All is lost now! Do we yield? No! We drive them headlong! Lo! We charge! Deploying to the left, our light horse swept across the heights of Plevna and, uttering their war cry *Bonafide Sabaoth*, sabred the Saracen gunners to a man.
The Chapel of Freeman Typesetters – Hear! Hear!
John Wyse Nolan – There's the man that got away James Stephens.
A Bluecoat Schoolboy – Bravo!

An Old Resident – You're a credit to your country, sir, that's what you are.

An Applewoman – He's a man like Ireland wants.

Bloom – My beloved subjects, a new era is about to dawn. I, Bloom, tell you verily it is even now at hand. Yea, on the word of a Bloom, ye shall ere long enter into the golden city which is to be, the new Bloomusalem in the Nova Hibernia of the future.

Thirty-two workmen, wearing rosettes, from all the counties of Ireland, under the guidance of Kirwan the builder, construct the new Bloomusalem. It is a colossal edifice with crystal roof, built in the shape of a huge pork kidney, containing forty thousand rooms. In the course of its extension several buildings and monuments are demolished. Government offices are temporarily transferred to railway sheds. Numerous houses are razed to the ground. The inhabitants are lodged in barrels and boxes, all marked in red with the letters L.B. Several paupers fall from a ladder. A part of the walls of Dublin, crowded with loyal sightseers, collapses.

The Sightseers (*dying*) – *Morituri te salutant.* (*They die.*)

A man in a brown macintosh springs up through a trapdoor. He points an elongated finger at Bloom.

The Man in the Macintosh – Don't you believe a word he says. That man is Leopold M'Intosh, the notorious fireraiser. His real name is Higgins.

Bloom – Shoot him! Dog of a Christian! So much for M'Intosh!

A cannonshot. The man in the macintosh disappears. Bloom with his sceptre strikes down poppies. The instantaneous deaths of many powerful enemies, graziers, members of parliament, members of standing committees, are reported. Bloom's bodyguard distribute Maundy money, commemoration medals, loaves and fishes, temperance badges, expensive Henry Clay cigars, free cowbones for soup, rubber preservatives in sealed envelopes tied with gold thread, butterscotch, pineapple rock, billets-doux in the form of cocked hats, ready-made suits, porringers of toad in the hole, bottles of Jeyes' Fluid, purchase stamps, 40 days indulgences, spurious coins, dairy-fed pork sausages, theatre passes, season tickets available for all tramlines, coupons of the Royal and Privileged Hungarian

Lottery, penny-dinner counters, cheap reprints of the World's Twelve Worst Books: *Froggy and Fritz* (politic), *Care of the Baby* (infantilic), *50 Meals for 7/6* (culinic), *Was Jesus a Sun Myth?* (historic), *Expel That Pain* (medic), *Infant's Compendium of the Universe* (cosmic), *Let's All Chortle* (hilaric), *Canvasser's Vade Mecum* (journalic), *Love Letters of Mother Assistant* (erotic), *Who's Who in Space* (astric), *Songs that Reached Our Heart* (melodic), *Pennywise's Way to Wealth* (parsimonic). A general rush and scramble. Women press forward to touch the hem of Bloom's robe. The lady Gwendolen DuBedat bursts through the throng, leaps on his horse and kisses him on both cheeks amid great acclamation. A magnesium flashlight photograph is taken. Babes and sucklings are held up.

The Women – Little father! Little father!
The Babes and Sucklings
– *Clap clap hands till Poldy comes home,*
  Cakes in his pocket for Leo alone.

Bloom, bending down, pokes Baby Boardman gently in the stomach.

Baby Boardman (*hiccups, curdled milk flowing from his mouth*) – Hajajaja.

Bloom (*shaking hands with a blind stripling*) – My more than brother! (*Placing his arms round the shoulders of an old couple*) Dear old friends! (*He plays pussy four-corners with ragged boys and girls.*) Peep! Bopeep! (*He wheels twins in a perambulator.*) Ticktacktwo wouldyousetashoe? (*He performs jugglers' tricks, draws red, orange, yellow, green, blue, indigo and violet silk handkerchiefs from his mouth.*) Roygbiv. 32 feet per second. (*He consoles a widow.*) Absence makes the heart grow younger. (*He dances the Highland fling with grotesque antics.*) Leg it, ye devils! (*He kisses the bedsores of a palsied veteran.*) Honourable wounds! (*He trips up a fat policeman.*) U.P: up. U.P: up. (*He whispers in the ear of a blushing waitress and laughs kindly.*) Ah, naughty, naughty! (*He eats a raw turnip offered him by Maurice Butterly, farmer.*) Fine! Splendid! (*He refuses to accept three shillings offered him by Joseph Hynes, journalist.*) My dear fellow, not at all! (*He gives his coat to a beggar.*) Please accept. (*He takes part in a stomach race with elderly male and female cripples.*) Come on, boys! Wriggle it, girls!

The Citizen (*choked with emotion, brushes aside a tear in his emerald muffler*) – May the good God bless him!

The ram's horns sound for silence. The standard of Zion is hoisted. Bloom uncloaks impressively, revealing obesity, unrolls a paper and reads solemnly.

Bloom – Aleph Beth Gimel Daleth Haggadah Tephillin Kosher Yom Kippur Hanukkah Rosh Hashana B'nai B'rith Bar Mitzvah Matzoth Ashkenazim Meshuggah Tallith.

An official translation is read by Jimmy Henry, assistant town clerk.

Jimmy Henry – The Court of Conscience is now open. His Most Catholic Majesty will now administer open-air justice. Free medical and legal advice, solution of doubles and other problems. All cordially invited. Given at this our loyal city of Dublin in the year 1 of the Paradisiacal Era.

Paddy Leonard – What am I to do about my rates and taxes?

Bloom – Pay them, my friend.

Paddy Leonard – Thank you.

Nosey Flynn – Can I raise a mortgage on my fire insurance?

Bloom (*obdurately*) – Sirs, take notice that by the law of torts you are bound over in your own recognisances for six months in the sum of five pounds.

J.J. O'Molloy – A Daniel did I say? Nay! A Peter O'Brien!

Nosey Flynn – Where do I draw the five pounds?

Pisser Burke – For bladder trouble?

Bloom

– *Acid. nit. hydrochlor. dil.*, 20 minims

   Tinct. nux vom., 5 minims

   Extr. taraxel. liq., 30 minims

   Aq. dest. ter in die.

Chris Callanan – What is the parallax of the subsolar ecliptic of Aldebaran?

Bloom – Pleased to hear from you, Chris. K.11.

Joe Hynes – Why aren't you in uniform?

Bloom – When my progenitor of sainted memory wore the uniform of the Austrian despot in a dank prison where was yours?

Ben Dollard – Pansies?

Bloom – Embellish (beautify) suburban gardens.

Ben Dollard – When twins arrive?

Bloom – Father (pater, dad) starts thinking.

Larry O'Rourke – An eight-day licence for my new premises. You remember me, Sir Leo, when you were in number seven. I'm sending around a dozen of stout for the missus.

Bloom (*coldly*) – You have the advantage of me. Lady Bloom accepts no presents.

Crofton – This is indeed a festivity.

Bloom (*solemnly*) – You call it a festivity. I call it a sacrament.

Alexander Keyes – When will we have our own House of Keys?

Bloom – I stand for the reform of municipal morals and the plain ten commandments. New worlds for old. Union of all, Jew, Moslem and gentile. Three acres and a cow for all children of nature. Saloon motor hearses. Compulsory manual labour for all. All parks open to the public day and night. Electric dishscrubbers. Tuberculosis, lunacy, war and mendicancy must now cease. General amnesty, weekly carnival with masked licence, bonuses for all, Esperanto the universal language with universal brotherhood. No more patriotism of barspongers and dropsical impostors. Free money, free rent, free love and a free lay church in a free lay state.

O'Madden Burke – Free fox in a free henroost.

Davy Byrne (*yawning*) – Iiiiiiiiiaaaaaaach!

Bloom – Mixed races and mixed marriage.

Lenehan – What about mixed bathing?

Bloom explains to those near him his schemes for social regeneration. All agree with him. The keeper of the Kildare Street museum appears, dragging a lorry on which are the shaking statues of several naked goddesses, Venus Kallipyge, Venus Pandemos, Venus Metempsychosis, and plaster figures, also naked, representing the new nine muses, Commerce, Operatic Music, Amor, Publicity, Manufacture, Liberty of Speech, Plural Voting, Gastronomy, Private Hygiene, Seaside Concert Entertainments, Painless Obstetrics and Astronomy for the People.

Father Farley – He is an Episcopalian, an agnostic, an anythingarian seeking to overthrow our holy faith.

Mrs Riordan (*tears up her will*) – I'm disappointed in you! You bad man!

Mother Grogan (*removes her boot to throw it at Bloom*) – You beast! You abominable person!

Nosey Flynn – Give us a tune, Bloom. One of the old sweet songs.

Bloom (*with rollicking humour*)

– *I vowed that I never would leave her,*

  She turned out a cruel deceiver.

  With my tooraloom tooraloom tooraloom tooraloom.

Hoppy Holohan – Good old Bloom! There's nobody like him after all.

Paddy Leonard – Stage Irishman!

Bloom – What railway opera is like a tramline in Gibraltar? The Rows of Casteele.

Laughter.

Lenehan – Plagiarist! Down with Bloom!

The Veiled Sibyl (*enthusiastically*) – I'm a Bloomite and I glory in it. I believe in him in spite of all. I'd give my life for him, the funniest man on earth.

Bloom (*winks at the bystanders*) – I bet she's a bonny lassie.

Theodore Purefoy (*in fishing cap and oilskin jacket*) – He employs a mechanical device to frustrate the sacred ends of nature.

The Veiled Sibyl (*stabs herself*) – My hero god! (*She dies.*)

Many most attractive and enthusiastic women also commit suicide, by stabbing, drowning, drinking prussic acid, aconite, arsenic, opening their veins, refusing food, casting themselves under steamrollers, from the top of Nelson's Pillar, into the great vat of Guinness's brewery, asphyxiating themselves by placing their heads in gas ovens, hanging themselves in stylish garters, leaping from windows of different storeys.

Alexander J. Dowie (*violently*) – Fellow Christians and anti-Bloomites, the man called Bloom is from the roots of hell, a disgrace to Christian men. A fiendish libertine from his earliest years, this stinking goat of Mendes gave precocious signs of infantile debauchery, recalling the cities of the plain, with a dissolute grandam. This vile hypocrite, bronzed with infamy, is the white bull mentioned in the Apocalypse. A worshipper of the Scarlet Woman, intrigue is the very breath of his nostrils. The stake faggots and the cauldron of boiling oil are for him. Caliban!

The Mob – Lynch him! Roast him! He's as bad as Parnell was. Mr Fox!

Mother Grogan throws her boot at Bloom. Several shopkeepers from

Upper and Lower Dorset Street throw objects of little or no commercial value, hambones, condensed-milk tins, unsaleable cabbage, stale bread, sheep's tails, odd pieces of fat.

Bloom (*excitedly*) – This is midsummer madness, some ghastly joke again. By heaven, I am guiltless as the unsunned snow! It was my brother Henry. He is my double. He lives in number 2 Dolphin's Barn. Slander, the viper, has wrongfully accused me. Fellow countrymen, *scéal i mbárr bata cóiste gan capall.* I call on my old friend, Dr Malachi Mulligan, sex specialist, to give medical testimony on my behalf.

Dr Mulligan (*in motor jerkin, green motorgoggles on his brow*) – Dr Bloom is bisexually abnormal. He has recently escaped from Dr Eustace's private asylum for demented gentlemen. Born out of bedlock, hereditary epilepsy is present, the consequence of unbridled lust. Traces of elephantiasis have been discovered among his ascendants. There are marked symptoms of chronic exhibitionism. Ambidexterity is also latent. He is prematurely bald from self-abuse, perversely idealistic in consequence, a reformed rake, and has metal teeth. In consequence of a family complex he has temporarily lost his memory and I believe him to be more sinned against than sinning. I have made a pervaginal examination and, after application of the acid test to 5427 anal, axillary, pectoral and pubic hairs, I declare him to be *virgo intacta.*

Bloom holds his high-grade hat over his genital organs.

Dr Madden – Hypospadias is also marked. In the interest of coming generations I suggest that the parts affected should be preserved in spirits of wine in the national teratological museum.

Dr Crotthers – I have examined the patient's urine. It is albuminoid. Salivation is insufficient, the patellar reflex intermittent.

Dr Punch Costello – The *fetor judaicus* is most perceptible.

Dr Dixon (*reads a bill of health*) – Professor Bloom is a finished example of the new womanly man. His moral nature is simple and lovable. Many have found him a dear man, a dear person. He is a rather quaint fellow on the whole, coy though not feeble-minded in the medical sense. He has written a really beautiful letter, a poem in itself, to the court missionary of the Reformed Priests' Protection Society which clears up everything. He is practically a total abstainer and I can affirm that he sleeps on a straw litter and eats the most Spartan food, cold dried grocer's peas. He wears a hairshirt of pure Irish manufacture winter and summer and scourges himself every Saturday. He was, I understand, at one time a first-class misdemeanant in Glencree Reformatory. Another report states that he was a very posthumous child. I appeal for clemency in the name of the most sacred word our vocal organs have ever been called upon to speak. He is about to have a baby.

General commotion and compassion. Women faint. A wealthy American makes a street collection for Bloom. Gold and silver coins, blank cheques, banknotes, jewels, treasury bonds, maturing bills of exchange, IOU's, wedding rings, watchchains, lockets, necklaces and bracelets are rapidly collected.

Bloom – O, I so want to be a mother.
Mrs Thornton (*in nursetender's gown*) – Embrace me tight, dear. You'll be soon over it. Tight, dear.

Bloom embraces her tightly and bears eight male yellow and white children. They appear on a red-carpeted staircase adorned with expensive plants. All the octuplets are handsome, with valuable metallic faces, well made, respectably dressed and well conducted, speaking five modern languages fluently and interested in various arts and sciences. Each has his name printed in legible letters on his shirtfront: Nasodoro, Goldfinger, Chrysostomos, Maindorée, Silversmile, Silberselber, Vifargent, Panargyros. They are immediately appointed to positions of high public trust in several different countries as managing directors of banks, traffic managers of railways, chairmen of limited liability companies, vice-chairmen of hotel syndicates.

A Voice – Bloom, are you the Messiah ben Joseph or ben David?
Bloom (*darkly*) – You have said it.
Brother Buzz – Then perform a miracle like Father Charles.
Bantam Lyons – Prophesy who will win the Saint Leger.

Bloom walks on a net, covers his left eye with his left ear, passes through several walls, climbs Nelson's Pillar, hangs from the top ledge by his eyelids, eats twelve dozen oysters (shells included), heals several sufferers from king's evil, contracts his face so as to resemble many historical personages, Lord Beaconsfield, Lord Byron, Wat Tyler, Moses of Egypt, Moses Maimonides, Moses Mendelssohn, Henry Irving, Rip Van Winkle, Kossuth, Jean Jacques Rousseau, Baron Leopold Rothschild, Robinson Crusoe, Sherlock Holmes, Pasteur, turns each foot simultaneously in different directions, bids the tide turn back, eclipses the sun by extending his little finger.

Brini, Papal Nuncio (*in papal zouave's uniform, steel cuirasses as breastplate, armplates, thighplates, legplates, large profane moustaches and brown paper mitre*) – *Leopoldi autem generatio.* Moses begat Noah and Noah begat Eunuch and Eunuch begat O'Halloran and O'Halloran begat Guggenheim and Guggenheim begat Agudath and Agudath begat Netaim and Netaim begat Le Hirsch and Le Hirsch begat Jesurum and Jesurum begat MacKay and MacKay begat Ostropolsky and Ostropolsky begat Smerdoz and Smerdoz begat Weiss and Weiss begat Schwarz and Schwarz begat Adrianopoli and Adrianopoli begat Aranjuez and Aranjuez begat Lewy Lawson and Lewy Lawson begat Ichabudonosor and Ichabudonosor begat O'Donnell Magnus and O'Donnell Magnus begat Christbaum and Christbaum begat ben Maimun and ben Maimun begat Dusty Rhodes and Dusty Rhodes begat Benamor and Benamor begat Jones-Smith and Jones-Smith begat Savorgnanovich and Savorgnanovich begat Jasperstone and Jasperstone begat Vingtetunieme and Vingtetunieme begat Szombathely and Szombathely begat Virag and Virag begat Bloom *et vocabitur nomen ejus Emmanuel.*

A Dead Hand (*writes on the wall*) – Bloom is a cod.

Crab (*in bushranger's kit*) – What did you do in the cattlecreep behind Kilbarrack?

A Female Infant (*shakes a rattle*) – And under Ballybough Bridge?

A Holly Bush – And in the Devil's Glen?

Bloom (*blushes furiously all over from frons to nates, three tears falling from his left eye*) – Spare my past.

The Irish Evicted Tenants (*in bodycoats, kneebreeches, with Donnybrook Fair shillelaghs*) – Sjambok him!

Bloom with ass's ears seats himself in the pillory with crossed arms, his feet protruding. He whistles *Don Giovanni, a cenar teco.* Artane orphans, joining hands, caper round him. Girls of the Prison Gate Mission, joining hands, caper round in the opposite direction.

The Artane Orphans
– *You hig, you hog, you dirty dog!*
  You think the ladies love you!
The Prison Gate Girls
– *If you see Kay*
  Tell him he may
  See you in tea
  Tell him from me.

Hornblower (*in ephod and hunting cap, announces*) – And he shall carry the sins of the people to Azazel, the spirit which is in the wilderness, and to Lilith, the nighthag. And they shall stone him and defile him, yea, all from Agudath Netaim and from Mizraim, the land of Ham.

All the people cast soft pantomime stones at Bloom. Many bona fide travellers and ownerless dogs come near him and defile him. Masliansky and Citron approach in gaberdines, wearing long earlocks. They wag their beards at Bloom.

Masliansky and Citron – Belial! Laemlein of Istria, the false Messiah! Abulafia! Recant!

George R. Mesias, Bloom's tailor, appears, a tailor's goose under his arm, presenting a bill.

Mesias – To alteration one pair trousers eleven shillings.
Bloom (*rubs his hands cheerfully*) – Just like old times. Poor Bloom!

Reuben J. Dodd, black-bearded Iscariot, bad shepherd, bearing on his shoulders the drowned corpse of his son, approaches the pillory.

Reuben J. (*whispers hoarsely*) – The squeak is out. A split is gone for the flatties. Nip the first rattler.
The Fire Brigade – Pflaap!

Brother Buzz invests Bloom in a yellow habit with embroidery of painted flames and a high pointed hat. He places a bag of gunpowder round his neck and hands him over to the civil power.

Brother Buzz – Forgive him his trespasses.

Lieutenant Myers of the Dublin Fire Brigade by general request sets fire to Bloom. Lamentations.

The Citizen – Thank heaven!

Bloom (*in a seamless garment marked I.H.S. stands upright amid phoenix flames*) – Weep not for me, O daughters of Erin. (*He exhibits to Dublin reporters traces of burning.*)

The daughters of Erin, in black garments, with large prayerbooks and long lighted candles in their hands, kneel down and pray.

The Daughters of Erin
— *Kidney of Bloom, pray for us.*
Flower of the Bath, pray for us.
Mentor of Menton, pray for us.
Canvasser for the Freeman, pray for us.
Charitable Mason, pray for us.
Wandering Soap, pray for us.
Sweets of Sin, pray for us.
Music without Words, pray for us.
Reprover of the Citizen, pray for us.
Friend of all Frillies, pray for us.
Midwife Most Merciful, pray for us.
Potato Preservative against Plague and Pestilence, pray for us.

A choir of six hundred voices, conducted by Vincent O'Brien, sings the Alleluia Chorus from Handel's *Messiah*, accompanied on the organ by Joseph Glynn. Bloom becomes mute, shrunken, carbonised.

Zoe – Talk away till you're black in the face.

Bloom (*in caubeen with clay pipe stuck in the band, dusty brogues, an emigrant's red handkerchief bundle in his hand, leading a black bog-oak pig by a sugaun, with a smile in his eye*) – Let me be going now, woman of the house, for by all the goats in Connemara I'm after having the father and mother of a bating. (*With a tear in his eye*) All is vanity. Patriotism, sorrow for the dead, music, future of the race. To be or not to be. Life's dream is o'er. End it peacefully. They can live on. (*He gazes far away mournfully.*) I am ruined. A few pastilles of aconite. The blinds drawn. A letter. Then lie back to rest. (*He breathes softly.*) No more. I have lived. Fare. Farewell.

Zoe (*stiffly, her finger in her neckfillet*) – Honest? Till the next time. (*She sneers.*) Suppose you got up the wrong side of the bed or came too quick with your best girl. O, I can read your thoughts!

Bloom (*bitterly*) – Man and woman, love, what is it? A cork and bottle. I'm sick of it. Let everything rip.

Zoe (*in sudden sulks*) – I hate a rotter that's insincere. Give a bleeding whore a chance.

Bloom (*repentantly*) – I am very disagreeable. You are a necessary evil. Where are you from? London?

Zoe (*glibly*) – Hogs-Norton where the pigs plays the organs. I'm Yorkshire born. (*She holds his hand which is feeling for her nipple.*) I say, Tommy Tittlemouse, stop that and begin worse. Have you cash for a short time? Ten shillings?

Bloom (*smiles, nods slowly*) – More, houri, more.

Zoe – And more's mother? (*She pats him offhandedly with velvet paws.*) Are you coming into the music room to see our new pianola? Come and I'll peel off.

Bloom (*feeling his occiput dubiously with the unparalleled embarrassment of a harassed pedlar gauging the symmetry of her peeled pears*) – Somebody would be dreadfully jealous if she knew. The green-eyed monster. (*Earnestly*) You know how difficult it is. I needn't tell you.

Zoe (*flattered*) – What the eye can't see the heart can't grieve for. (*She pats him.*) Come.

Bloom – Laughing witch! The hand that rocks the cradle.

Zoe – Babby!

Bloom (*in baby linen and pelisse, bigheaded, with a caul of dark hair, fixes big eyes on her fluid slip and counts its bronze buckles with a chubby finger, his moist tongue lolling and lisping*) – One two tlee: tlee tloo tlone.

The Buckles – Love me. Love me not. Love me.

Zoe – Silent means consent. (*With little parted talons she captures his hand, her forefinger giving to his palm the passtouch of secret monitor, luring him to doom.*) Hot hands, cold gizzard.

He hesitates amid scents, music, temptations. She leads him towards the steps, drawing him by the odour of her armpits, the vice of her painted eyes, the rustle of her slip in whose sinuous folds lurks the lion reek of all the male brutes that have possessed her.

The Male Brutes (*exhaling sulphur of rut and dung and ramping in their loosebox, faintly roaring, their drugged heads swaying to and fro*) – Good!

Zoe and Bloom reach the doorway where two sister whores are seated. They examine him curiously from under their pencilled brows and smile to his hasty bow. He trips awkwardly.

Zoe (*her lucky hand instantly saving him*) – Hoopsa! Don't fall upstairs.
Bloom – The just man falls seven times. (*He stands aside at the threshold.*) After you is good manners.
Zoe – Ladies first, gentlemen after.

She crosses the threshold. He hesitates. She turns and, holding out her hands, draws him over. He hops. On the antlered rack of the hall hang a man's hat and waterproof. Bloom uncovers himself but, seeing them, frowns, then smiles, preoccupied. A door on the return landing is flung open. A man in purple shirt and grey trousers, brown-socked, passes with an ape's gait, his bald head and goatee beard upheld, hugging a full waterjugjar, his two-tailed black braces dangling at heels. Averting his face quickly, Bloom bends to examine on the hall table the spaniel eyes of a running fox: then, his lifted head sniffing, he follows Zoe into the music room. A shade of mauve tissue paper dims the light of the chandelier. Round and round a moth flies, colliding, escaping. The floor is covered with an oilcloth mosaic of jade and azure and cinnabar rhomboids. Footmarks are stamped over it in all senses, heel to heel, heel to hollow, toe to toe, feet locked, a morris of shuffling feet without body, phantoms, all in a scrimmage higgledypiggledy. The walls are tapestried with a paper of yew fronds and clear glades. In the grate is spread a screen of peacock feathers. Lynch squats cross-legged on the hearthrug of matted hair, his cap back to the front. With a wand he beats time slowly. Kitty Ricketts, a bony pallid whore in navy costume, doeskin gloves rolled back from a coral wristlet, a chain purse in her hand, sits perched on the edge of the table swinging her leg and glancing at herself in the gilt mirror over the mantelpiece. A tag of her corset lace hangs slightly below her jacket. Lynch indicates mockingly the couple at the piano.

Kitty (*coughs behind her hand*) – She's a bit imbecilic. (*She signs with a waggling forefinger.*) Blemblem. (*Lynch lifts up her skirt and white petticoat* *with his wand. She settles them down quickly.*) Respect yourself. (*She hiccups, then bends quickly her sailor hat under which her hair glows, red with henna.*) O, excuse!

Zoe – More limelight, Charley. (*She goes to the chandelier and turns the gas full cock.*)

Kitty (*peers at the gasjet*) – What ails it tonight?

Lynch (*deeply*) – Enter a ghost and hobgoblins.

Zoe – Clap on the back for Zoe.

The wand in Lynch's hand flashes: a brass poker. Stephen stands at the pianola, on which sprawl his hat and ashplant. With two fingers he repeats once more the series of empty fifths. Florry Talbot, a blond feeble goose-white whore in a tatterdemalion gown of mildewed strawberry, lolls spread-eagle in the sofa corner, her limp forearm pendent over the bolster, listening. A heavy stye droops over her sleepy eyelid.

Kitty (*hiccups again with a kick of her horsed foot*) – O, excuse!

Zoe (*promptly*) – Your boy's thinking of you. Tie a knot on your shift.

Kitty Ricketts bends her head. Her boa uncoils, slides, glides over her shoulder, back, arm, chair, to the ground. Lynch lifts the curled caterpillar on his wand. She snakes her neck, nestling. Stephen glances behind at the squatted figure with its cap back to the front.

Stephen – As a matter of fact it is of no importance whether Benedetto Marcello found it or made it. The rite is the poet's rest. It may be an old hymn to Demeter or also illustrate *Coeli enarrant gloriam Domini*. It is susceptible of nodes or modes as far apart as hypophrygian and mixoly-dian and of texts so divergent as priests haihooping round David's that is Circe's or what am I saying Ceres' altar, and David's tip from the stable to his chief bassoonist about the alrightness of his almightiness. *Mais, nom de nom*, that is another pair of trousers. *Jetez la gourme. Faut que jeunesse se passe.* (*He stops, points at Lynch's cap, smiles, laughs.*) Which side is your knowledge bump?

The Cap (*with saturnine spleen*) – Bah! It is because it is. Woman's reason. Jewgreek is Greekjew. Extremes meet. Death is the highest form of life. Bah!

Stephen – You remember fairly accurately all my errors, boasts, mistakes. How long shall I continue to close my eyes to disloyalty? Whetstone!

The Cap – Bah!

Stephen – Here's another for you. (*He frowns.*) The reason is because the fundamental and the dominant are separated by the greatest possible interval which . . .

The Cap – Which? Finish. You can't.

Stephen (*with an effort*) – Interval which. Is the greatest possible ellipse. Consistent with. The ultimate return. The octave. Which.

The Cap – Which?

Outside, the gramophone begins to blare *The Holy City*.

Stephen (*abruptly*) – What went forth to the ends of the world to traverse not itself, God, the sun, Shakespeare, a commercial traveller, having itself traversed in reality itself becomes that self. Wait a moment. Wait a second. Damn that fellow's noise in the street. Self which it itself was ineluctably preconditioned to become. *Ecco!*

Lynch (*with a mocking whinny of laughter grins at Bloom and Zoe Higgins*) – What a learned speech, eh?

Zoe (*briskly*) – God help your head, he knows more than you have forgotten.

With obese stupidity Florry Talbot regards Stephen.

Florry – They say the last day is coming this summer.

Kitty – No!

Zoe (*explodes in laughter*) – Great unjust God!

Florry (*offended*) – Well, it was in the papers about Antichrist. O, my foot's tickling.

Ragged barefoot newsboys, jogging a wagtail kite, patter past, yelling.

The Newsboys – Stop-press edition. Result of the rocking horse races. Sea serpent in the Royal Canal. Safe arrival of Antichrist.

Stephen turns and sees Bloom.

Stephen – A time, times and half a time.

Reuben J. Antichrist, wandering Jew, a clutching hand open on his spine, stumps forward. Across his loins is slung a pilgrim's wallet from which protrude promissory notes and dishonoured bills. Aloft over his shoulder he bears a long boatpole from the hook of which the sodden huddled mass of his only son, saved from Liffey waters, hangs from the slack of its breeches. A hobgoblin in the image of Punch Costello, hipshot, crookbacked, hydrocephalic, prognathic, with receding forehead and Ally Sloper nose, tumbles in somersaults through the gathering darkness.

All – What?

The hobgoblin, his jaws chattering, capers to and fro, goggling his eyes, squeaking, kangaroohopping with outstretched clutching arms, then all at once thrusts his lipless face through the fork of his thighs.

The Hobgoblin – *Il vient! C'est moi! L'homme qui rit! L'homme primigène!* (*He whirls round and round with dervish howls.*) *Sieurs et dames, faites vos jeux!* (*He crouches, juggling. Tiny roulette planets fly from his hands.*) *Les jeux sont faits!* (*The planets rush together, uttering crepitant cracks.*) *Rien n'va plus!* (*The planets, buoyant balloons, sail swollen up and away. He springs off into vacuum.*)
Florry (*sinking into torpor, crossing herself secretly*) – The end of the world!

A female tepid effluvium leaks out from her. Nebulous obscurity occupies space. Through the drifting fog without the gramophone blares over coughs and feet-shuffling.

The Gramophone
– *Jerusalem!*
Open your gates and sing
Hosanna...

A rocket rushes up the sky and bursts. A white star falls from it, proclaiming the consummation of all things and second coming of Elijah. Along an infinite invisible tightrope taut from zenith to nadir the End of the World, a two-headed octopus in gillie's kilts, busby and tartan filibegs, whirls through the murk, head over heels, in the form of the Three Legs of Man.

The End of the World (*with a Scotch accent*) – Wha'll dance the keel row, the keel row, the keel row?

Over the possing drift and choking breathcoughs, Elijah's voice, harsh as a corncrake's, jars on high. Perspiring in a loose lawn surplice with funnel sleeves he is seen, verger-faced, above a rostrum about which the banner of Old Glory is draped. He thumps the parapet.

Elijah – No yapping, if you please, in this booth. Jake Crane, Creole Sue, Dove Campbell, Abe Kirschner, do your coughing with your mouths shut. Say, I am operating all this trunk line. Boys, do it now. God's time is 12.25. Tell mother you'll be there. Rush your order and you play a slick ace. Join on right here. Book through to eternity junction, the nonstop run. Just one word more. Are you a god or a doggone clod? If the second advent came to Coney Island are we ready? Florry Christ, Stephen Christ, Zoe Christ, Bloom Christ, Kitty Christ, Lynch Christ, it's up to you to sense that cosmic force. Have we cold feet about the cosmos? No. Be on the side of the angels. Be a prism. You have that something within, the higher self. You can rub shoulders with a Jesus, a Gautama, an Ingersoll. Are you all in this vibration? I say you are. You once nobble that, congregation, and a buck joyride to heaven becomes a back number. You got me? It's a life-brightener, sure. The hottest stuff ever was. It's the whole pie with jam in. It's just the cutest snappiest line out. It is immense, supersumptuous. It restores. It vibrates. I know and I am some vibrator. Joking apart and getting down to bedrock, A.J. Christ Dowie and the harmonial philosophy, have you got that? OK. Seventy-seven West Sixty-ninth Street. Got me? That's it. You call me up by sunphone any old time. Bumboozers, save your stamps. (*He shouts.*) Now then our glory song. All join heartily in the singing. Encore! (*He sings.*) Jeru ...

The Gramophone (*drowning his voice*) – Whorusalaminyourhighhohhhh ... (*The disk rasps gratingly against the needle.*)

The Three Whores (*covering their ears, squawk*) – Ahhkkk!

Elijah (*in rolled-up shirtsleeves, black in the face, shouts at the top of his voice, his arms uplifted*) – Big Brother up there, Mr President, you hear what I done just been saying to you. Certainly, I sort of believe strong in you, Mr President. I certainly am thinking now Miss Higgins and Miss Ricketts got religion way inside them. Certainly seems to me I don't never see no wusser scared female than the way you been, Miss Florry, just now as I done seed you. Mr President, you come long and help me save our sisters dear. (*He winks at his audience.*) Our Mr President, he twig the whole lot and he ain't saying nothing.

Kitty-Kate – I forgot myself. In a weak moment I erred and did what I did on Constitution Hill. I was confirmed by the bishop and enrolled in the brown scapular. My mother's sister married a Montmorency. It was a working plumber was my ruination when I was pure.

Zoe-Fanny – I let him larrup it into me for the fun of it.

Florry-Teresa – It was in consequence of a port-wine beverage on top of Hennessy's three star. I was guilty with Whelan when he slipped into the bed.

Stephen – In the beginning was the Word, in the end the world without end. Blessed be the eight beatitudes.

The beatitudes, Dixon, Madden, Crotthers, Costello, Lenehan, Bannon, Mulligan and Lynch, in white surgical students' gowns, four abreast, goose-stepping, tramp fast past in noisy marching.

The Beatitudes (*incoherently*) – Beer beef battledog buybull businum barnum buggerum bishop.

Lyster (*in Quaker-grey kneebreeches and broad-brimmed hat, discreetly*) – He is our friend. I need not mention names. Seek thou the light.

He corantos by. Best enters, in hairdresser's attire, shinily laundered, his locks in curlpapers. He leads John Eglinton who wears a mandarin's kimono of Nankeen yellow, lizard-lettered, and a high pagoda hat. Smiling, he lifts the hat and displays a shaven poll from the crown of which bristles a pigtail toupee tied with an orange topknot.

Best – I was just beautifying him, don't you know. A thing of beauty, don't you know, Yeats says, or I mean Keats says.

John Eglinton produces a green-capped dark lantern and flashes it towards a corner.

John Eglinton (*with carping accent*) – Esthetics and cosmetics are for the boudoir. I am out for truth. Plain truth for a plain man. Tanderagee wants the facts and means to get them.

In the cone of the searchlight behind the coalscuttle the bearded figure of Mananaan MacLir, ollav, holy-eyed, broods, chin on knees. He rises slowly. A cold sea wind blows from his druid mouth. About his head writhe eels and elvers. He is encrusted with weeds and shells. His right hand holds a bicycle pump. His left hand grasps a huge crayfish by its two talons.

Mananaan MacLir (*with a voice of waves*) – Aum! Hek! Wal! Ak! Lub! Mor! Ma! White yoghin of the gods. Occult pimander of Hermes Trismegistos. (*With a voice of whistling sea wind*) Punarjanman patsypunjaub! I won't have my leg pulled. It has been said by one: beware the left, the cult of Shakti. (*With a cry of stormbirds*) Shakti, Shiva! Dark-hidden Father! (*He smites with his bicycle pump the crayfish in his left hand. On its cooperative dial glow the twelve signs of the zodiac. He wails with the vehemence of the ocean.*) Aum! Baum! Pyjaum! I am the light of the homestead. I am the dreamery creamery butter.

A skeleton Judas hand strangles the light. The green light wanes to mauve. The gasjet wails whistling.

The Gasjet – Pooah! Pfuiiiiiii!

Zoe runs to the chandelier and, crooking her leg, adjusts the mantle.

Zoe – Who has a fag as I'm here?
Lynch (*tossing a cigarette on to the table*) – Here.
Zoe (*her head perched aside in mock pride*) – Is that the way to hand the *pot* to a lady? (*She stretches up to light the cigarette over the flame, twirling it slowly, showing the brown tufts of her armpits. Lynch with his poker lifts boldly a side of her slip. Bare from her garters up, her flesh appears under the sapphire a nixie's green. She puffs calmly at her cigarette.*) Can you see the beauty spot of my behind?
Lynch – I'm not looking.
Zoe (*makes sheep's eyes*) – No? You wouldn't do a less thing. Would you suck a lemon?

Squinting in mock shame she glances with sidelong meaning at Bloom, then twists round towards him, pulling her slip free of the poker. Blue fluid again flows over her flesh. Bloom stands, smiling desirously, twirling

463

his thumbs. Kitty Ricketts licks her middle finger with her spittle and, gazing in the mirror, smooths both eyebrows.

Lipoti Virag, basilicogrammate, chutes rapidly down through the chimney flue and struts two steps to the left on gawky pink stilts. He is sausaged into several overcoats and wears a brown macintosh under which he holds a roll of parchment. In his left eye flashes the monocle of Cashel Boyle O'Connor Fitzmaurice Tisdall Farrell. On his head is perched an Egyptian pschent. Two quills project over his ears. Heels together, he bows.

Virag – My name is Virag Lipoti, of Szombathely. (*He coughs thoughtfully, drily.*) Promiscuous nakedness is much in evidence hereabouts, eh? Inadvertently her back view revealed the fact that she is not wearing those rather intimate garments of which you are a particular devotee. The injection mark on the thigh I hope you perceived? Good.

Bloom – Granpapachi. But ...

Virag – Number two on the other hand, she of the cherry rouge and coiffeuse white, whose hair owes not a little to our tribal elixir of gopherwood, is in walking costume, and tightly staysed by her sit I should opine. Backbone in front, so to say. Correct me but I always understood that the act so performed by skittish humans with glimpses of lingerie appealed to you in virtue of its exhibitionististicicity. In a word. Hippogriff. Am I right?

Bloom – She is rather lean.

Virag (*not unpleasantly*) – Absolutely! Well observed, and those pannier pockets of the skirt and slightly peg-top effect are devised to suggest bunchiness of hip. A new purchase at some monster sale for which a gull has been mulcted. Meretricious finery to deceive the eye. Observe the attention to details of dustspecks. Never put on you tomorrow what you can wear today. Parallax! (*With a nervous twitch of his head*) Did you hear my brain go snap? Pollysyllabax!

Bloom (*an elbow resting in a hand, a forefinger against his cheek*) – She seems sad.

Virag, his weasel teeth bared yellow, draws down his left eye with a finger and barks hoarsely.

Virag (*cynically*) – Hoax! Beware of the flapper and bogus mournful. Lily of the alley. All possess bachelor's button discovered by Rualdus

Columbus. Tumble her. Columble her. Chameleon. (*More genially*) Well then, permit me to draw your attention to item number three. There is plenty of her visible to the naked eye. Observe the mass of oxygenated vegetable matter on her skull. What ho, she bumps! The ugly duckling of the party, long-casted and deep in keel.

Bloom (*regretfully*) – When you come out without your gun.

Virag – We can do you all brands, mild, medium and strong. Pay your money, take your choice. How happy could you be with either...

Bloom – With...?

Virag (*his tongue upcurling*) – Lyum! Look. Her beam is broad. She is coated with quite a considerable layer of fat. Obviously mammal in weight of bosom, you remark that she has in front well to the fore two protuberances of very respectable dimensions, inclined to fall in the noonday soup-plate, while on her rear lower down are two additional protuberances suggestive of potent rectum and tumescent for palpation which leave nothing to be desired save compactness. Such fleshy parts are the product of careful nurture. When coop-fattened their livers reach an elephantine size. Pellets of new bread with fenugreek and gum benjamin swamped down by potions of green tea endow them during their brief existence with natural pincushions of quite colossal blubber. That suits your book, eh? Fleshhotpots of Egypt to hanker after. Wallow in it. Lycopodium. (*His throat twitches.*) Slapbang! There he goes again.

Bloom – The stye I dislike.

Virag (*arches his eyebrows*) – Contact with a gold ring, they say. *Argumentum ad feminam,* as we said in old Rome and ancient Greece in the consulship of Diplodocus and Ichthyosaurus. For the rest, Eve's sovereign remedy. Not for sale. Hire only. Huguenot. (*He twitches.*) It is a funny sound. (*He coughs encouragingly.*) But possibly it is only a wart. I presume you shall have remembered what I will have taught you on that head? Wheaten meal with honey and nutmeg.

Bloom (*reflecting*) – Wheaten meal with lycopodium and syllabax. This searching ordeal. It has been an unusually fatiguing day, a chapter of accidents. Wait. Bloodwarts, I mean wart's blood spreads warts, you said...

Virag (*severely, his nose hard-humped, his side eye winking*) – Stop twirling your thumbs and have a good old thunk. See, you have forgotten. Exercise your mnemotechnic. *Lacaus esant tara tara.* (*Aside*) He will surely remember.

Bloom – Rosemary also, did I understand you to say, or willpower over parasitic tissues. Then, nay, no, I have an inkling. The touch of a dead hand cures. Mnemo?

Virag (*excitedly*) – I say so. I say so. E'en so. Technic. (*He taps his parchment roll energetically.*) This book tells you how to act, with all descriptive particulars. Consult index for agitated fear of aconite, melancholy of muriatic, priapic pulsatilla. Virag is going to talk about amputation. Our old friend caustic. They must be starved. Snip off with horsehair under the denned neck. But to change the venue to the Bulgar and the Basque, have you made up your mind whether you like or dislike women in male habiliments? (*With a dry snigger*) You intended to devote an entire year to the study of the religious problem and the summer months of 1886 to square the circle and win that million. Pomegranate! From the sublime to the ridiculous is but a step. Pyjamas, let us say? Or stockingette gussetted knickers, closed? Or, put we the case, those complicated combinations, camiknickers? (*He crows derisively.*) Keekeereekee!

Bloom surveys uncertainly the three whores, then gazes at the veiled mauve light, hearing the everflying moth.

Bloom – I wanted then to have now concluded. Nightdress was never. Hence this. But tomorrow is a new day will be. Past was is today. What now is will then morrow as now was be past yester.

Virag (*prompts in a pig's whisper*) – Insects of the day spend their brief existences in reiterated coition, lured by the smell of the inferiorly pulchritudinous female possessing extendified pudendal nerve in dorsal region. Pretty Poll! (*His yellow parrotbeak gabbles nasally.*) They had a proverb in the Carpathians in or about the year five thousand five hundred and fifty of our era. One tablespoonful of honey will attract friend Bruin more than half a dozen barrels of first-choice malt vinegar. Bear's buzz bothers bees. But of this apart. At another time we may resume. We were very pleased, we others. (*He coughs and, bending his brow, rubs his nose thoughtfully with a scooping hand.*) You shall find that these night insects follow the light. An illusion, for remember their complex unadjustable eye. For all these knotty points see the seventeenth book of my *Fundamentals of Sexology* or *The Love Passion* which Doctor L.B. says is the book sensation of the year. Some, to example, there are again whose movements are automatic. Perceive. That is his appropriate sun. Nightbird nightsun nighttown. Chase me, Charley! (*He blows into Bloom's ear.*) Buzz!

Bloom – Bee or bluebottle too other day butting shadow on wall dazed self then me wandered dazed down shirt good job I...

Virag (*his face impassive, laughs in a rich feminine key*) – Splendid! Spanish fly in his fly or mustard plaster on his dibble. (*He gobbles gluttonously with turkey wattles.*) Bubbly jock! Bubbly jock! Where are we? Open sesame! Cometh forth! (*He unrolls his parchment rapidly and reads, his glowworm's nose running backwards over the letters which he claws.*) Stay, good friend. I bring thee thy answer. Red Bank oysters will shortly be upon us. I'm the best o'cook. Those succulent bivalves may help us, and the truffles of Perigord, tubers dislodged through mister omnivorous porker, were unsurpassed in cases of nervous debility or viragitis. Though they stink yet they sting. (*He wags his head with cackling raillery.*) Jocular. With my eyeglass in my ocular. (*He sneezes.*) Amen!

Bloom (*absently*) – Ocularly, woman's bivalve case is worse. Always open sesame. The cloven sex. Why they fear vermin, creeping things. Yet Eve and the serpent contradicts. Not a historical fact. Obvious analogy to my idea. Serpents too are gluttons for woman's milk. Wind their way through miles of omnivorous forest to sucksucculent her breast dry. Like those bubblyjocular Roman matrons one reads of in Elephantuliasis.

His mouth projected in hard wrinkles, eyes stonily forlornly closed, Virag psalms in outlandish monotone.

Virag – That the cows with their those distended udders that they have been the the known...

Bloom – I am going to scream. I beg your pardon. Ah? So. (*He repeats.*) Spontaneously to seek out the saurian's lair in order to entrust their teats to his avid suction. Ant milks aphis. (*Profoundly*) Instinct rules the world. In life. In death.

Head askew, Virag arches his back and hunched wingsholders, peers at the moth out of blear bulged eyes, points a horning claw and cries.

Virag – Who's Ger Ger? Who's dear Gerald? Dear Ger, that you? O, dear, he is Gerald. O, I much fear he shall be most badly burned. Will some pleashe pershon not now impediment so catastrophics mit agitation of first-class tablenumpkin? (*He mews.*) Puss puss puss puss! (*He sighs, draws back and stares sideways down with dropping underjaw.*) Well, well. He doth rest anon. (*He snaps his jaws suddenly on the air.*)

The Moth

— *I'm a tiny tiny thing*
  Ever flying in the spring
  Round and round a ringaring.
  Long ago I was a king,
  Now I do this kind of thing
  On the wing, on the wing!
  Bing!

He rushes against the mauve shade, flapping noisily.

The Moth

— *Pretty pretty pretty pretty pretty pretty petticoats.*

From left upper entrance with two gliding steps Henry Flower comes forward to left front centre. He wears a dark mantle and drooping plumed sombrero. He carries a silver-stringed inlaid dulcimer and a long-stemmed bamboo Jacob's pipe, its clay bowl fashioned as a female head. He wears dark velvet hose and silver-buckled pumps. He has the romantic Saviour's face with flowing locks, thin beard and moustache. His spindlelegs and sparrow feet are those of the tenor Mario, prince of Candia. He settles down his goffered ruffs and moistens his lips with a passage of his amorous tongue.

Henry (*in a low dulcet voice, touching the strings of his guitar*) – There is a flower that bloometh.

Virag truculent, his jowl set, stares at the lamp. Grave Bloom regards Zoe's neck. Henry gallant turns with pendent dewlap to the piano.

Stephen (*to himself*) – Play with your eyes shut. Imitate pa. Filling my belly with husks of swine. Too much of this. I will arise and go to my. Expect this is the. Steve, thou art in a parlous way. Must visit old Deasy or telegraph. Our interview of this morning has left on me a deep impression. Though our ages. Will write fully tomorrow. I'm partially drunk, by the way. (*He touches the keys again.*) Minor chord comes now. Yes. Not much however.

Almidano Artifoni holds out a batonroll of music with vigorous moustachework.

Artifoni – *Ci rifletta. Lei rovina tutto.*

Florry – Sing us something. *Love's old sweet song.*

Stephen – No voice. I am a most finished artist. Lynch, did I show you the letter about the lute?

Florry (*smirking*) – The bird that can sing and won't sing.

The Siamese twins, Philip Drunk and Philip Sober, two Oxford dons with lawnmowers, appear in the window embrasure. Both are masked with Matthew Arnold's face.

Philip Sober – Take a fool's advice. All is not well. Work it out with the butt end of a pencil like a good young idiot. Three pounds twelve you got, two notes, one sovereign, two crowns, two shillings, if youth but knew. Mooney's *en ville*, Mooney's *sur mer*, the Moira, Larchet's, Holles Street Hospital, Burke's. Eh? I am watching you.

Philip Drunk (*impatiently*) – Ah, bosh, man. Go to hell! I paid my way. If I could only find out about octaves. Reduplication of personality. Who was it told me his name? (*His lawnmower begins to purr.*) Aha, yes. *Zoe mou sas agapo*. Have a notion I was here before. When was it? Not Atkinson, his card I have somewhere. Mac somebody. Unmack, I have it. He told me about, hold on, Swinburne was it, no?

Florry – And the song?

Stephen – Spirit is willing but the flesh is weak.

Florry – Are you out of Maynooth? You're like someone I knew once.

Stephen – Out of it now. (*To himself*) Clever.

Philip Drunk and Philip Sober (*their lawnmowers purring with a rigadoon of grasshalms*) – Clever ever. Out of it out of it. By the by, have you the book, the thing, the ashplant? Yes, there it, yes. Cleverever outofitnow. Keep in condition. Do like us.

Zoe – There was a priest down here two nights ago to do his bit of business with his coat buttoned up. You needn't try to hide, I says to him, I know you've a Roman collar.

Virag – Perfectly logical from his standpoint. Fall of man. (*Harshly, his pupils waxing*) To hell with the pope! Nothing new under the sun. I am the Virag who disclosed *The Sex Secrets of Monks and Maidens. Why I Left the Church of Rome.* Read *The Priest, the Woman and the Confessional.* Penrose. Flipperty Jippert. (*He wriggles.*) Woman, undoing with sweet pudor her belt of rush rope, offers her all-moist yoni to man's lingam. Short time after man presents woman with pieces of jungle meat. Woman shows joy and covers herself with featherskins. Man loves her yoni fiercely with big lingam, the stiff one. (*He cries.*) *Coactus volui.* Then giddy woman will run about. Strong man grasps woman's wrist. Woman squeals, bites, spucks. Man, now fierce angry, strikes woman's fat yadgana. (*He chases his tail.*) Piffpaff! Popo! (*He stops, sneezes.*) Pchp! (*He worries his butt.*) Prrrrrht!

Lynch – I hope you gave the good father a penance. Nine Glorias for shooting a bishop.

Zoe (*spouting walrus smoke through her nostrils*) – He couldn't get a connection. Only, you know, sensation. A dry rush.

Bloom – Poor man!

Zoe (*lightly*) – Only for what happened him.

Bloom – How?

A diabolic rictus of black luminosity contracting his visage, Virag cranes his scraggy neck forward. He lifts a mooncalf nozzle and howls.

Virag – *Verfluchte Goim!* He had a father, forty fathers. He never existed. Pig god! He had two left feet. He was Judas Iacchia, a Libyan eunuch, the pope's bastard. (*He leans out on tortured forepaws, elbows bent rigid, his eye agonising in his flat skullneck, and yelps over the mute world.*) A son of a whore. Apocalypse.

Kitty – And Mary Shortall that was in the Lock with the pox she got from Jimmy Pidgeon in the bluecaps had a child off him that couldn't swallow and was smothered with the convulsions in the mattress and we all subscribed for the funeral.

Philip Drunk (*gravely*) – *Qui vous a mise dans cette fichue position, Philippe?*

Philip Sober (*gaily*) – *C'était le sacré pigeon, Philippe.*

Kitty unpins her hat and sets it down calmly, patting her henna hair. And a prettier, a daintier head of winsome curls was never seen on a whore's shoulders. Lynch puts on her hat. She whips it off.

Lynch (*laughs*) – And to such delights has Metchnikoff inoculated anthropoid apes.

Florry (*nods*) – Locomotor ataxy.

Zoe (*gaily*) – O, my dictionary.

Lynch – Three wise virgins.

Virag (*ague-shaken, profuse yellow spawn foaming over his bony epileptic lips*) – She sold love philtres, white wax, orangeflower. Panther, the Roman centurion, polluted her with his genitories. (*He sticks out a flickering phosphorescent scorpion tongue, his hand on his fork.*) Messiah! He burst her tympanum. (*With gibbering baboon's cries he jerks his hips in the cynical spasm.*) Hik! Hek! Hak! Hok! Huk! Kok! Kuk!

Ben Jumbo Dollard, rubicund, musclebound, hairy-nostrilled, huge-bearded, cabbage-eared, shaggy-chested, shock-maned, fat-papped, stands forth, his loins and genitals tightened into a pair of black bathing bagslops. Nakkering castanet bones in his huge padded paws, he yodels jovially in base barreltone.

Ben Dollard – *When love absorbs my ardent soul.*

The virgins, Nurse Callan and Nurse Quigley, burst through the ringkeepers and the ropes and mob him with open arms.

The Virgins (*gushingly*) – Big Ben! Ben machree!
A Voice – Hold that fellow with the bad breeches.
Ben Dollard (*smites his thigh in abundant laughter*) – Hold him now.
Henry (*caressing on his breast a severed female head, murmurs*) – Thine heart, mine love. (*He plucks his lutestrings.*) When first I saw . . .
Virag (*sloughing his skins, his multitudinous plumage moulting*) – Rats! (*He yawns, showing a coal-black throat, and closes his jaws by an upward push of his parchment roll.*) After having said which I took my departure. Farewell. Fare thee well. Dreck!

Henry Flower combs his moustache and beard rapidly with a pocket-comb and gives a cow's lick to his hair. Steered by his rapier, he glides to the door, his wild harp slung behind him. Virag reaches the door in two ungainly stilt-hops, his tail cocked, and deftly claps sideways on the wall a pus-yellow flybill, butting it with his head.

The Flybill – K.11. Post No Bills. Strictly confidential. Dr Hy Franks.
Henry – All is lost now.

Virag unscrews his head in a trice and holds it under his arm.

Virag's Head – Quack!

Exeunt severally.

Stephen (*over his shoulder to Zoe*) – You would have preferred the fighting parson who founded the Protestant error. But beware Antisthenes, the dog sage, and the last end of Arius Heresiarchus. The agony in the closet.

Lynch – All one and the same God to her.

Stephen (*devoutly*) – And sovereign Lord of all things.

Florry (*to Stephen*) – I'm sure you're a spoiled priest. Or a monk.

Lynch – He is. A cardinal's son.

Stephen – Cardinal sin. Monks of the Screw.

His Eminence Simon Stephen Cardinal Dedalus, primate of all Ireland, appears in the doorway, dressed in red soutane, sandals and socks. Seven dwarf simian acolytes, also in red, cardinal sins, uphold his train, peeping under it. He wears a battered silk hat sideways on his head. His thumbs are stuck in his armpits and his palms outspread. Round his neck hangs a rosary of corks ending on his breast in a corkscrew cross. Releasing his thumbs, he invokes grace from on high with large wave gestures and proclaims with bloated pomp.

The Cardinal
– *Conservio lies captured.*
 He lies in the lowest dungeon
 With manacles and chains around his limbs
 Weighing upwards of three tons.

He looks at all for a moment, his right eye closed tight, his left cheek puffed out. Then, unable to repress his merriment, he rocks to and fro, arms akimbo, and sings with broad rollicking humour.

The Cardinal
– *O, the poor little fellow*
 Hihihihihis legs they were yellow
 He was plump, fat and heavy and brisk as a snake
 But some bloody savage

To graize his white cabbage
He murdered Nell Flaherty's duck-loving drake.

A multitude of midges swarms white over his robe. He scratches himself with crossed arms at his ribs, grimacing, and exclaims.

The Cardinal – I'm suffering the agony of the damned. By the hoky fiddle, thanks be to Jesus those funny little chaps are not unanimous. If they were they'd walk me off the face of the bloody globe.

His head aslant, he blesses curtly with fore and middle fingers, imparts the Easter kiss and doubleshuffles off comically, swaying his hat from side to side, shrinking quickly to the size of his trainbearers. The dwarf acolytes, giggling, peeping, nudging, ogling, Easterkissing, zigzag behind him. His voice is heard mellow from afar, merciful, male, melodious.

The Cardinal
– Shall carry my heart to thee,
Shall carry my heart to thee,
And the breath of the balmy night
Shall carry my heart to thee!

The trick doorhandle turns.

The Doorhandle – Theeee!
Zoe – The devil is in that door.

A male form passes down the creaking staircase and is heard taking the waterproof and hat from the rack. Bloom starts forward involuntarily and, half closing the door as he passes, takes the chocolate from his pocket and offers it nervously to Zoe.

Zoe (*sniffs his hair briskly*) – Hmmm! Thank your mother for the rabbits. I'm very fond of what I like.
Bloom (*hearing a male voice in talk with the whores on the doorstep, pricks his ears*) – If it were he? After? Or because not? Or the double event?
Zoe (*tears open the silver foil*) – Fingers was made before forks. (*She breaks off and nibbles a piece, gives a piece to Kitty Ricketts and then turns*

kittenishly to Lynch.) No objection to French lozenges? (*He nods. She taunts him.*) Have it now or wait till you get it? (*He opens his mouth, his head cocked. She whirls the prize in left circle. His head follows. She whirls it back in right circle. He eyes her.*) Catch!

She tosses a piece. With an adroit snap he catches it and bites it through with a crack.

Kitty (*chewing*) – The engineer I was with at the bazaar does have lovely ones. Full of the best liqueurs. And the viceroy was there with his lady. The gas we had on the Toft's hobbyhorses. I'm giddy still.

Bloom, in Svengali's fur overcoat, with folded arms and Napoleonic forelock, frowns in ventriloquial exorcism with piercing eagle glance towards the door. Then, rigid, with left foot advanced, he makes a swift pass with impelling fingers and gives the sign of past master, drawing his right arm downwards from his left shoulder.

Bloom – Go, go, go, I conjure you, whoever you are!

A male cough and tread are heard passing through the mist outside. Bloom's features relax. He places a hand in his waistcoat opening, posing calmly. Zoe offers him chocolate.

Bloom (*solemnly*) – Thanks.
Zoe – Do as you're bid. Here!

A firm heel-clacking tread is heard on the stairs.

Bloom (*takes the chocolate*) – Aphrodisiac? Tansy and pennyroyal. But I bought it. Vanilla calms or? Mnemo. Confused light confuses memory. Red influences lupus. Colours affect women's characters, any they have. This black makes me sad. Eat and be merry for tomorrow. (*He eats.*) Influence taste too, mauve. But it is so long since I. Seems new. Aphro. That priest. Must come. Better late than never. Try truffles at Andrews.

The door opens. Bella Cohen, a massive whoremistress, enters. She is dressed in a three-quarter ivory gown, fringed round the hem with tasselled selvedge, and cools herself, flirting a black horn fan like Minnie Hauck in *Carmen*. On her left hand are wedding and keeper rings. Her eyes are deeply carboned. She has a sprouting moustache. Her olive face is heavy, slightly sweated and full-nosed with orange-tainted nostrils. She has large pendent beryl eardrops.

Bella – My word! I'm all of a mucksweat.

She glances round her at the couples. Then her eyes rest on Bloom with hard insistence. Her large fan winnows wind towards her heated face, neck and embonpoint. Her falcon eyes glitter.

The Fan (*flirting quickly, then slowly*) – Married, I see.
Bloom – Yes. Partly. I have mislaid ...
The Fan (*half opening, then closing*) – And the missus is master. Petticoat government.
Bloom (*looks down with a sheepish grin*) – That is so.
The Fan (*folding together, rests against her left eardrop*) – Have you forgotten me?
Bloom – Nes. Yo.
The Fan (*folded akimbo against her waist*) – Is me her was you dreamed before? Was then she him you us since knew? Am all them and the same now me?

Bella approaches, gently tapping with the fan.

Bloom (*wincing*) – Powerful being. In my eyes read that slumber which women love.
The Fan (*tapping*) – We have met. You are mine. It is fate.
Bloom (*cowed*) – Exuberant female. Enormously I desiderate your domination. I am exhausted, abandoned, no more young. I stand, so to speak, with an unposted letter bearing the extra regulation fee before the too late box of the General Post Office of human life. The door and window open at a right angle cause a draught of thirty-two feet per second according to the law of falling bodies. I have felt this instant a twinge of sciatica in my left gluteal muscle. It runs in our family. Poor dear papa, a widower, was a regular barometer from it. He believed in animal heat. A skin of tabby lined his winter waistcoat. Near the end,

remembering King David and the Shunammite, he shared his bed with Athos, faithful after death. A dog's spittle, as you probably ... (*He winces.*) Ah!

Richie Goulding (*bag-weighted, passes the door*) – Mocking is catch. Best value in Dub. Fit for a prince's. Liver and kidney.

The Fan (*tapping*) – All things end. Be mine. Now.

Bloom (*undecided*) – All now? I should not have parted with my talisman. Rain, exposure at dewfall on the sea rocks, a peccadillo at my time of life. Every phenomenon has a natural cause.

The Fan (*points downwards slowly*) – You may.

Bloom (*looks downwards and perceives her unfastened bootlace*) – We are observed.

The Fan (*points downwards quickly*) – You must.

Bloom (*with desire, with reluctance*) – I can make a true black knot. Learned when I served my time and worked the mail order line for Kellett's. Experienced hand. Every knot says a lot. Let me. In courtesy. I knelt once before today. Ah!

Bella raises her gown slightly and, steadying her pose, lifts to the edge of a chair a plump buskined hoof and a full pastern, silk-socked. Bloom, stiff-legged, ageing, bends over her hoof and with gentle fingers draws out and in her laces.

Bloom (*murmurs lovingly*) – To be a shoefitter in Manfield's was my love's young dream, the darling joys of sweet buttonhooking, to lace up crisscrossed to knee-length the dressy kid footwear, satin-lined, so incredibly impossibly small, of Clyde Road ladies. Even their wax model Raymonde I visited daily to admire her cobweb hose and stick-of-rhubarb toe, as worn in Paris.

The Hoof – Smell my hot goathide. Feel my royal weight.

Bloom (*crosslacing*) – Too tight?

The Hoof – If you bungle, Handy Andy, I'll kick your football for you.

Bloom – Not to lace the wrong eyelet as I did the night of the bazaar dance. Bad luck. Hook in wrong tache of her ... person you mentioned. That night she met ... Now!

He knots the lace. Bella places her foot on the floor. Bloom raises his head. Her heavy face, her eyes, strike him in midbrow. His eyes grow dull, darker and pouched, his nose thickens.

Bloom (*mumbles*) – Awaiting your further orders, we remain, gentlemen...

Bello (*with a hard basilisk stare, in a baritone voice*) – Hound of dishonour!

Bloom (*infatuated*) – Empress!

Bello (*his heavy cheekchops sagging*) – Adorer of the adulterous rump!

Bloom (*plaintively*) – Hugeness!

Bello – Dung devourer!

Bloom (*with sinews semiflexed*) – Magmagnificence!

Bello – Down! (*He taps her on the shoulder with his fan.*) Incline feet forward! Slide left foot one pace back! You will fall. You are falling. On the hands down!

Bloom (*her eyes upturned in the sign of admiration, closing, yaps*) – Truffles!

With a piercing epileptic cry she sinks on all fours, grunting, snuffling, rooting at his feet: then lies, shamming dead, with eyes shut tight, trembling eyelids, bowed upon the ground in the attitude of most excellent master.

Bello, with bobbed hair, purple gills, fat moustache rings round his shaven mouth, in mountaineer's puttees, green silver-buttoned coat, sport skirt and alpine hat with moorcock's feather, his hands stuck deep in his breeches pockets, places his heel on her neck and grinds it in.

Bello – Footstool! Feel my entire weight. Bow, bondslave, before the throne of your despot's glorious heels, so glistening in their proud erectness.

Bloom (*enthralled, bleats*) – I promise never to disobey.

Bello (*laughs loudly*) – Holy smoke! You little know what's in store for you. I'm the Tartar to settle your little lot and break you in! I'll bet Kentucky cocktails all round I shame it out of you, old son. Cheek me, I dare you. If you do, tremble in anticipation of heel discipline to be inflicted in gym costume.

Bloom creeps under the sofa and peers out through the fringe.

Zoe (*widening her slip to screen her*) – She's not here.

Bloom (*closing her eyes*) – She's not here.

Florry (*hiding her with her gown*) – She didn't mean it, Mr Bello. She'll be good, sir.

Kitty – Don't be too hard on her, Mr Bello. Sure you won't, ma'amsir.

Bello (*coaxingly*) – Come, ducky dear, I want a word with you, darling. Just to administer correction. Just a little heart-to-heart talk, sweety. (*Bloom puts out her timid head.*) There's a good girly now. (*Bello grabs her hair violently and drags her forward.*) I only want to correct you for your own good on a soft safe spot. How's that tender behind? O, ever so gently, pet. Begin to get ready.

Bloom (*fainting*) – Don't tear my . . .

Bello (*savagely*) – The nose ring, the pliers, the bastinado, the hanging hook, the knout, I'll make you kiss while the flutes play like the Nubian slave of old. You're in for it this time! I'll make you remember me for the balance of your natural life. (*His forehead veins swollen, his face congested*) I shall sit on your ottoman saddleback every morning after my thumping good breakfast of Matterson's fat ham rashers and a bottle of Guinness's porter. (*He belches.*) And suck my thumping good Stock Exchange cigar while I read the *Licensed Victualler's Gazette.* Very possibly I shall have you slaughtered and skewered in my stables and enjoy a slice of you with crisp crackling from the baking tin, basted and baked like sucking pig with rice and lemon or currant sauce. It will hurt you. (*He twists her arm. Bloom squeals, turning turtle.*)

Bloom – Don't be cruel, nurse! Don't!

Bello (*twisting*) – Another!

Bloom (*screams*) – O, it's hell itself! Every nerve in my body aches like mad!

Bello (*shouts*) – Good, by the rumping jumping general! That's the best bit of news I heard these six weeks. Here, don't keep me waiting, damn you!

He slaps her face.

Bloom (*whimpers*) – You're after hitting me. I'll tell . . .

Bello – Hold him down, girls, till I squat on him.

Zoe – Yes. Walk on him! I will.

Florry – I will. Don't be greedy.

Kitty – No, me. Lend him to me.

The brothel cook, Mrs Keogh, wrinkled, grey-bearded, in a greasy bib, men's grey and green socks and brogues, flour-smeared, a rolling pin stuck with raw pastry in her bare red arm and hand, appears at the door.

Mrs Keogh (*ferociously*) – Can I help?

They hold and pinion Bloom. Bello squats, with a grunt, on Bloom's upturned face, puffing cigarsmoke, nursing a fat leg.

Bello – I see Keating Clay is elected vice-chairman of the Richmond Asylum and, by the by, Guinness's preference shares are at sixteen three-quarters. Curse me for a fool that I didn't buy that lot Craig and Gardner told me about. Just my infernal luck, curse it. And that Goddamned outsider *Throwaway* at twenty to one. (*He quenches his cigar angrily on Bloom's ear.*) Where's that Goddamned cursed ashtray?

Bloom (*goaded, buttocksmothered*) – O! O! Monsters! Cruel one!

Bello – Ask for that every ten minutes. Beg. Pray for it as you never prayed before. (*He thrusts out a figged fist and foul cigar.*) Here, kiss that. Both. Kiss. (*He throws a leg astride and, pressing with horseman's knees, calls in a hard voice.*) Gee up! A cockhorse to Banbury Cross. I'll ride him for the Eclipse Stakes. (*He bends sideways and squeezes his mount's testicles roughly, shouting.*) Ho! Off we pop! I'll nurse you in proper fashion. (*He horserides cockhorse, leaping in the, in the saddle.*) The lady goes a pace a pace and the coachman goes a trot a trot and the gentleman goes a gallop a gallop a gallop a gallop.

Florry (*pulls at Bello*) – Let me on him now. You had enough. I asked before you.

Zoe (*pulling at Florry*) – Me. Me. Are you not finished with him yet, suckeress?

Bloom (*stifling*) – Can't.

Bello – Well, I'm not. Wait. (*He holds in his breath.*) Curse it. Here. This bung's about burst. (*He uncorks himself behind: then, contorting his features, farts stoutly.*) Take that! (*He recorks himself.*) Yes, by Jingo, sixteen three-quarters.

Bloom (*a sweat breaking out over him*) – Not man. (*He sniffs.*) Woman.

Bello (*stands up*) – No more blow hot and cold. What you longed for has come to pass. Henceforth you are unmanned and mine in earnest, a thing under the yoke. Now for your punishment frock. You will shed your male garments, you understand, Ruby Cohen? And don the shot silk luxuriously rustling over head and shoulders. And quickly too!

Bloom (*shrinks*) – Silk, mistress said! O crinkly! Scrapy! Must I tiptouch it with my nails?

Bello (*points to his whores*) – As they are now, so will you be: wigged, singed, perfume-sprayed, rice-powdered, with smooth-shaven armpits. Tape measurements will be taken next your skin. You will be laced with cruel force into vicelike corsets of soft dove coutille with whalebone busk to the diamond-trimmed pelvis, the absolute outside edge, while your figure, plumper than when at large, will be restrained in net-tight frocks, pretty two-ounce petticoats and fringes and things stamped, of course, with my houseflag, creations of lovely lingerie for Alice and nice scent for Alice. Alice will feel the pullpull. Martha and Mary will be a little chilly at first in such delicate thighcasing, but the frilly flimsiness of lace round your bare knees will remind you ...

Bloom (*charming soubrette with dauby cheeks, mustard hair, large male hands and nose, and leering mouth*) – I tried her things on only twice, a small prank, in Holles Street. When we were hard up I washed them to save the laundry bill. My own shirts I turned. It was the purest thrift.

Bello (*jeers*) – Little jobs that make mother pleased, eh? And showed off coquettishly in your domino at the mirror behind close-drawn blinds your unskirted thighs and he-goat's udders in various poses of surrender, eh? Ho ho! I have to laugh! That secondhand black opera-top shift and short trunk-leg naughties all split up the stitches at her last rape that Mrs Miriam Dandrade sold you from the Shelbourne Hotel, eh?

Bloom – Miriam. Black. Demimondaine.

Bello (*guffaws*) – Christ Almighty, it's too tickling, this! You were a nice-looking Miriam when you clipped off your back-gate hairs and lay swooning in the thing across the bed as Mrs Dandrade about to be violated by Lieutenant Smythe-Smythe, Mr Philip Augustus Blockwell M.P., Signor Laci Daremo the robust tenor, blue-eyed Bert the liftboy, Henri Fleury of Gordon Bennett fame, Sheridan the quadroon, Croesus, the varsity wetbob eight from old Trinity, Ponto her splendid Newfoundland, and Bobs, dowager duchess of Manorhamilton. (*He guffaws again.*) Christ, wouldn't it make a Siamese cat laugh!

Bloom (*her hands and features working*) – It was Gerald converted me to be a true corsetlover when I was female impersonator in the High School play *Vice Versa*. It was dear Gerald. He got that kink, fascinated by sister's stays. Now dearest Gerald uses pinky greasepaint and gilds his eyelids. Cult of the beautiful.

Bello (*with wicked glee*) – Beautiful! Give us a breather! When you took your seat with womanish care, lifting your billowy flounces, on the smooth-worn throne.

Bloom – Science. To compare the various joys we each enjoy. (*Earnestly*) And really it's better the position ... because often I used to wet ...

Bello (*sternly*) – No insubordination! The sawdust is there in the corner for you. I gave you strict instructions, didn't I? Do it standing, sir! I'll teach you to behave like a jinkleman! If I catch a trace on your swaddles. Aha! By the ass of the Dorans, you'll find I'm a martinet. The sins of your past are rising against you. Many. Hundreds.

The Sins of the Past (*in a medley of voices*) – He went through a form of clandestine marriage with at least one woman in the shadow of the Black Church. Unspeakable messages he telephoned mentally to Miss Dunne at an address in D'Olier Street while he presented himself indecently to the instrument in the call box. By word and deed he frankly encouraged a nocturnal strumpet to deposit fecal and other matter in an unsanitary outhouse attached to empty premises. In five public conveniences he wrote pencilled messages offering his nuptial partner to all strong-membered males. And by the offensively smelling vitriol works did he not pass night after night by courting couples to see if and what and how much he could see? Did he not lie in bed, the gross boar, gloating over a nauseous fragment of well-used toilet paper presented to him by a nasty harlot, stimulated by gingerbread and a postal order?

Bello (*whistles loudly*) – Say, what was the most revolting piece of obscenity in all your career of crime? Go the whole hog. Puke it out! Be candid for once.

Mute inhuman faces throng forward, leering, vanishing, gibbering: Booloohoom, Poldy Kock, Bootlaces a penny, Cassidy's hag, blind stripling, Larry rhinoceros, the girl, the woman, the whore, the other, the ...

Bloom – Don't ask me! Our mutual faith. Pleasants Street. I only thought the half of the ... I swear on my sacred oath ...

Bello (*peremptorily*) – Answer. Repugnant wretch! I insist on knowing. Tell me something to amuse me, smut or a bloody good ghost story or a bit of poetry, quick, quick, quick! Where? How? What time? With how many? I give you just three seconds. One! Two! Thr...

Bloom (*docile, gurgles*) – I rererepugnosed in rerererepugnant ...

Bello (*imperiously*) – O, get out, you skunk! Hold your tongue! Speak when you're spoken to.

Bloom (*bows*) – Master! Mistress! Mantamer!

He lifts his arms. His bangle bracelets fall.

Bello (*satirically*) – By day you will souse and bat our smelling underclothes, also when we ladies are unwell, and swab out our latrines with dress pinned up and a dishclout tied to your tail. Won't that be nice? (*He places a ruby ring on her finger.*) And there now! With this ring I thee own. Say, *thank you, mistress*.

Bloom – Thank you, mistress.

Bello – You will make the beds, get my tub ready, empty the pisspots in the different rooms, including old Mrs Keogh's the cook's, a sandy one. Ay, and rinse the seven of them well, mind, or lap it up like champagne. Drink me piping hot. Hop! You will dance attendance or I'll lecture you on your misdeeds, Miss Ruby, and spank your bare bot right well, miss, with the hairbrush. You'll be taught the error of your ways. At night your well-creamed braceletted hands will wear fortythree-button gloves new-powdered with talc and having delicately scented fingertips. For such favours knights of old laid down their lives. (*He chuckles.*) My boys will be no end charmed to see you so ladylike, the colonel above all, when they come here the night before the wedding to fondle my new attraction in gilded heels. First, I'll have a go at you myself. A man I know on the turf named Charles Alberta Marsh (I was in bed with him just now and another gentleman out of the Hanaper and Petty Bag office) is on the lookout for a maid of all work at a short knock. Swell the bust. Smile. Droop shoulders. What offers? (*He points.*) For that lot. Trained by owner to fetch and carry, basket in mouth. (*He bares his arm and plunges it elbow-deep in Bloom's vulva.*) There's fine depth for you! What, boys? That give you a hard-on? (*He shoves his arm in a bidder's face.*) Here, wet the deck and wipe it round!

A Bidder – A florin!

Dillon's lacquey rings his handbell.

The Lacquey – Barang!

A Voice – One and eightpence too much.

Charles Alberta Marsh – Must be virgin. Good breath. Clean.

Bello (*gives a rap with his gavel*) – Two bar. Rock-bottom figure and cheap at the price. Fourteen hands high. Touch and examine shis points.

Handle hrim. This downy skin, these soft muscles, this tender flesh. If I had only my gold piercer. And quite easy to milk. Three new-laid gallons a day. A pure stockgetter, due to lay within the hour. His sire's milk record was a thousand gallons of whole milk in forty weeks. Whoa, my jewel! Beg up! Whoa! (*He brands his initial C on Bloom's croup.*) So! Warranted Cohen! What advance on two bob, gentlemen?

A Dark-visaged Man (*in disguised accent*) – Hoondert punt sterlink.

Voices (*subdued*) – For the caliph. Haroun al-Raschid.

Bello (*gaily*) – Right. Let them all come. The scanty, daringly short skirt, riding up at the knee to show a peep of white pantalette, is a potent weapon, and transparent stockings, emerald-gartered, with the long straight seam trailing up beyond the knee, appeal to the better instincts of the blasé man about town. Learn the smooth mincing walk on four-inch Louis XV heels, the Grecian bend with provoking croup, the thighs fluescent, knees modestly kissing. Bring all your powers of fascination to bear on them. Pander to their Gomorrean vices.

Bloom (*bends his blushing face into his armpit and simpers with fore-finger in mouth*) – O, I know what you're hinting at now!

Bello – What else are you good for, an impotent thing like you? (*He stoops and, peering, pokes with his fan rudely under the fat suet folds of Bloom's haunches.*) Up! Up! Manx cat! What have we here? Where's your curly teapot gone to or who docked it on you, cockyolly? Sing, birdy, sing. It's as limp as a boy of six's doing his pooly behind a cart. Buy a bucket or sell your pump. (*Loudly*) Can you do a man's job?

Bloom – Eccles Street ...

Bello (*sarcastically*) – I wouldn't hurt your feelings for the world but there's a man of brawn in possession there. The tables are turned, my gay young fellow! He is something like a full-grown outdoor man. Well for you, you muff, if you had that weapon with knobs and lumps and warts all over it. He shot his bolt, I can tell you! Foot to foot, knee to knee, belly to belly, bubs to breast! He's no eunuch. A shock of red hair he has sticking out of him behind like a furze bush! Wait for nine months, my lad! Holy ginger, it's kicking and coughing up and down in her guts already! That makes you wild, don't it? Touches the spot? (*He spits in contempt.*) Spittoon!

Bloom – I was indecently treated, I ... Inform the police. Hundred pounds. Unmentionable. I ...

Bello – Would if you could, lame duck. A downpour we want, not your drizzle.

Bloom – To drive me mad! Moll! I forgot! Forgive! Moll ... We ... Still ...

Bello (*ruthlessly*) – No, Leopold Bloom. All is changed by woman's will since you slept horizontal in Sleepy Hollow your night of twenty years. Return and see.

Old Sleepy Hollow calls over the wold.

Sleepy Hollow – Rip Van Wink! Rip Van Winkle!

Bloom, in tattered moccasins, with a rusty fowling piece, tiptoeing, fingertipping, his haggard bony bearded face peering through the diamond panes, cries out.

Bloom – I see her! It's she! The first night at Mat Dillon's! But that dress, the green! And her hair is dyed gold and he ...

Bello (*laughs mockingly*) – That's your daughter, you owl, with a Mullingar student.

Milly Bloom, fair-haired, green-vested, slim-sandalled, her blue scarf in the sea wind simply swirling, breaks from the arms of her lover and calls, her young eyes wonder-wide.

Milly – My! It's Papli! But, O Papli, how old you've grown!

Bello – Changed, eh? Our whatnot, our writing table where we never wrote, aunt Hegarty's armchair, our classic reprints of old masters. A man and his men friends are living there in clover. The *Cuckoo's Rest*! Why not? How many women had you, say? Following them up dark streets, flatfoot, exciting them by your smothered grunts. What, you male prostitute? Blameless dames with parcels of groceries. Turn about. Sauce for the goose, my gander, O.

Bloom – They ... I ...

Bello (*cuttingly*) – Their heelmarks will stamp the Brusselette carpet you bought at Wren's auction. In their horseplay with Moll, the romp to find the buck flea in her breeches, they will deface the little statue you carried home in the rain for art for art's sake. They will violate the secrets of your bottom drawer. Pages will be torn from your handbook of astronomy to make them pipespills. And they will spit in your ten-shilling brass fender from Hampton Leedom's.

Bloom – Ten and six. The act of low scoundrels. Let me go. I will return. I will prove ...

A Voice – Swear!

Bloom clenches his fists and crawls forward, a bowie knife between his teeth.

Bello – As a paying guest or a kept man? Too late. You have made your second-best bed and others must lie in it. Your epitaph is written. You are down and out and don't you forget it, old bean.

Bloom – Justice! All Ireland versus one! Has nobody ... ? (*He bites his thumb.*)

Bello – Die and be damned to you if you have any sense of decency or grace about you. I can give you a rare old wine that'll send you skipping to hell and back. Sign a will and leave us any coin you have! If you have none see you damn well get it, steal it, rob it! We'll bury you in our shrubbery jakes where you'll be dead and dirty with old Cuck Cohen, my stepnephew I married, the bloody old gouty procurator and sodomite with a crick in his neck, and my other ten or eleven husbands, whatever the buggers' names were, suffocated in the one cesspool. (*He explodes in a loud phlegmy laugh.*) We'll manure you, Mr Flower! (*He pipes scoffingly.*) Bye bye, Poldy! Bye bye, Papli!

Bloom (*clasps his head*) – My willpower! Memory! I have sinned! I have suff ... (*He weeps tearlessly.*)

Bello (*sneers*) – Crybabby! Crocodile tears!

Bloom, broken, closely veiled for the sacrifice, sobs, his face to the earth. The passing bell is heard. Dark-shawled figures of the circumcised, in sackcloth and ashes, stand by the Wailing Wall: I.M. Shmulowitz, Joseph Goldwater, Moses Herzog, Harris Rosenberg, N. Moisel, I. Citron, Minnie Watchman, J. Masliansky, the Reverend A.L. Abramovitz, *chazan*. With swaying arms they wail in pneuma over the recreant Bloom.

The Circumcised (*in dark guttural chant as they cast Dead Sea fruit upon him, no flowers*) – Shema Israel Adonai Elohenu Adonai Echad.

Voices (*sighing*) – So he's gone. Ah, yes. Yes, indeed. Bloom? Never heard of him. No? Queer kind of chap. There's the widow. That so? Ah, yes.

From the suttee pyre the flame of gum camphire ascends. The pall of incense smoke screens and disperses. Out of her oak frame a nymph with hair unbound, lightly clad in tea-brown art colours, descends from her grotto and, passing under interlacing yews, stands over Bloom.

The Yews (*their leaves whispering*) – Sister. Our sister. Ssh!
The Nymph (*softly*) – Mortal! (*Kindly*) Nay, dost not weepest!

Bloom crawls jellily forward under the boughs, streaked by sunlight.

Bloom (*with dignity*) – This position. I felt it was expected of me. Force of habit.
The Nymph – Mortal! You found me in evil company, highkickers, costermongers, picnicmakers, pugilists, popular generals, immoral panto boys in fleshtights and the nifty shimmy dancers, La Aurora and Karini, musical act, the hit of the century. I was hidden in cheap pink paper that smelt of rock oil. I was surrounded by the stale smut of clubmen, stories to disturb callow youth, ads for transparencies, trued-up dice and bust-pads, proprietary articles and why wear a truss with testimonial from ruptured gentleman. Useful hints to the married.
Bloom (*lifts a turtle head towards her lap*) – We have met before. On another star.
The Nymph (*sadly*) – Rubber goods. Neverrip brand as supplied to the aristocracy. Corsets for men. I cure fits or money refunded. Unsolicited testimonials for Professor Waldmann's wonderful chest exuber. My bust developed four inches in three weeks, reports Mrs Gus Rublin with photo.
Bloom – You mean *Photo Bits*?
The Nymph – I do. You bore me away, framed me in oak and tinsel, set me above your marriage couch. Unseen, one summer eve, you kissed me in four places. And with loving pencil you shaded my eyes, my bosom and my shame.
Bloom (*humbly kisses her long hair*) – Your classic curves, beautiful immortal. I was glad to look on you, to praise you, a thing of beauty, almost to pray.
The Nymph – During dark nights I heard your praise.
Bloom (*quickly*) – Yes, yes. You mean that I ... Sleep reveals the worst side of everyone, children perhaps excepted. I know I fell out of bed or rather was pushed. Steel wine is said to cure snoring. For the rest there is that English invention, pamphlet of which I received some days ago,

incorrectly addressed. It claims to afford a noiseless, inoffensive vent. (*He sighs.*) 'Twas ever thus. Frailty, thy name is marriage.

The Nymph (*her fingers in her ears*) – And words. They are not in my dictionary.

Bloom – You understood them?

The Yews – Ssh!

The Nymph (*covers her face with her hands*) – What have I not seen in that chamber? What must my eyes look down on?

Bloom (*apologetically*) – I know. Soiled personal linen, wrong side up with care. The quoits are loose. From Gibraltar by long sea long ago.

The Nymph (*bends her head*) – Worse, worse!

Bloom (*reflects precautiously*) – That antiquated commode. It wasn't her weight. She scaled just eleven stone nine. She put on nine pounds after weaning. It was a crack and want of glue. Eh? And that absurd orange-keyed utensil which has only one handle.

The sound of a waterfall is heard in bright cascade.

The Waterfall
– *Poulaphouca Poulaphouca*
  Poulaphouca Poulaphouca.

The Yews (*mingling their boughs*) – Listen. Whisper. She is right, our sister. We grew by Poulaphouca waterfall. We gave shade on languorous summer days.

In the background, John Wyse Nolan, in Irish National Foresters' uniform, doffs his plumed hat.

John Wyse Nolan – Prosper! Give shade on languorous days, trees of Ireland!

The Yews (*murmuring*) – Who came to Poulaphouca with the High School excursion? Who left his nut-questing classmates to seek our shade?

Bloom (*scared*) – High School of Poula? Mnemo? Not in full possession of faculties. Concussion. Run over by tram.

The Echo – Sham!

Bloom (*pigeon-breasted, bottle-shouldered, padded, in nondescript juvenile grey and black striped suit, too small for him, white tennis shoes, bordered stockings with turnover tops, and a red school cap with badge*) – I was in my teens, a growing boy. A little then sufficed, a jolting car, the mingling odours of the ladies' cloakroom and lavatory, the throng penned tight on the old Royal stairs, for they love crushes, instinct of the herd, and the dark sexsmelling theatre unbridles vice. Even a price list of their hosiery. And then the heat. There were sunspots that summer. End of school. And tipsycake. Halcyon days.

Halcyon Days, High School boys in blue and white football jerseys and shorts, Master Donald Turnbull, Master Abraham Chatterton, Master Owen Goldberg, Master Jack Meredith, Master Percy Apjohn, stand in a clearing of the trees and shout to Master Leopold Bloom.

The Halcyon Days – Mackerel! Live us again. Hurray! (*They cheer.*)

Bloom (*hobbledehoy, warm-gloved, mammamufflered, starred with spent snowballs, struggles to rise*) – Again! I feel sixteen! What a lark! Let's ring all the bells in Montague Street. (*He cheers feebly.*) Hurray for the High School!

The Echo – Fool!

The Yews (*rustling*) – She is right, our sister. Whisper. (*Whispered kisses are heard in all the wood. Faces of hamadryads peep out from the boles and among the leaves and break, blossoming, into bloom.*) Who profaned our silent shade?

The Nymph (*coyly, through parting fingers*) – There? In the open air?

The Yews (*sweeping downward*) – Sister, yes. And on our virgin sward.

The Waterfall
– *Poulaphouca Poulaphouca*
  Phoucaphouca Phoucaphouca.

The Nymph (*with wide fingers*) – O, infamy!

Bloom – I was precocious. Youth. The fauna. I sacrificed to the god of the forest. The flowers that bloom in the spring. It was pairing time. Capillary attraction is a natural phenomenon. Lotty Clarke, flaxen-haired, I saw at her night toilette through ill-closed curtains with poor papa's opera glasses. The wanton ate grass wildly. She rolled downhill at Rialto Bridge to tempt me with her flow of animal spirits. She climbed their crooked tree and I ... A saint couldn't resist it. The demon possessed me. Besides, who saw?

Staggering Bob, a white-polled calf, thrusts through the foliage a ruminating head with humid nostrils. Large teardrops rolling from his prominent eyes, he snivels.

Staggering Bob – Me. Me see.
Bloom – Simply satisfying a need. I ... (*With pathos*) No girl would when I went girling. Too ugly. They wouldn't play ...

High on Ben Howth through rhododendrons a nannygoat passes, plump-uddered, butty-tailed, dropping currants.

The Nannygoat (*bleats*) – Megeggaggegg! Nannannanny!
Bloom (*hatless, flushed, covered with burrs of thistledown and gorse-spine*) – Regularly engaged. Circumstances alter cases. (*He gazes intently downwards on the water.*) Thirty-two head over heels per second. Press nightmare. Giddy Elijah. Fall from cliff. Sad end of government printer's clerk.

Through silversilent summer air the dummy of Bloom, rolled in a mummy, rolls rotatingly from the Lion's Head cliff into the purple waiting waters.

The Dummymummy – Bbbbblllllblblblblobschb!

Far out in the bay between Bailey and Kish lights the *Erin's King* sails, sending a broadening plume of coalsmoke from her funnel towards the land.
Councillor Nannetti, alone on deck, in dark alpaca, yellow-kite-faced, his hand in his waistcoat opening, declaims.

Councillor Nannetti – When my country takes her place among the nations of the earth, then, and not till then, let my epitaph be written. I have ...
Bloom – Done. Prff!
The Nymph (*loftily*) – We immortals, as you saw today, have not such a place and no hair there either. We are stone cold and pure. We eat electric light. (*She arches her body in lascivious crispation, placing her forefinger in her mouth.*) Spoke to me. Heard from behind. How then could you ... ?
Bloom (*pawing the heather abjectly*) – O, I have been a perfect pig.

Enemas too I have administered. One third of a pint of quassia, to which add a tablespoonful of rock salt. Up the fundament. With Hamilton Long's syringe, the ladies' friend.

The Nymph – In my presence. The powder puff. (*She blushes and makes a knee.*) And the rest!

Bloom (*dejected*) – Yes. *Peccavi!* I have paid homage on that living altar where the back changes name. (*With sudden fervour*) For why should the dainty scented jewelled hand, the hand that rules ... ?

Figures wind serpenting in slow woodland pattern around the tree-stems, cooeeing.

The Voice of Kitty (*in the thicket*) – Show us one of them cushions.

The Voice of Florry – Here.

A grouse wings clumsily through the underwood.

The Voice of Lynch (*in the thicket*) – Whew! Piping hot!

The Voice of Zoe (*in the thicket*) – Came from a hot place.

The Voice of Virag (*a birdchief, blue-streaked and feathered in war panoply, with his assegai, striding through a crackling canebrake over beechmast and acorns*) – Hot! Hot! 'Ware Sitting Bull!

Bloom – It overpowers me. The warm impress of her warm form. Even to sit where a woman has sat, especially with divaricated thighs, as though to grant the last favours, most especially with previously well-uplifted white sateen coatpans. So womanly full. It fills me full.

The Waterfall

– *Phillaphulla Poulaphouca*
  Poulaphouca Poulaphouca.

The Yews – Ssh! Sister, speak!

The Nymph (*eyeless, in nun's white habit, coif and huge-winged wimple, softly, with remote eyes*) – Tranquilla Convent. Sister Agatha. Mount Carmel. The apparitions of Knock and Lourdes. No more desire. (*She reclines her head, sighing.*) Only the ethereal. Where dreamy creamy gull waves o'er the waters dull.

Bloom half rises. His back trousers button snaps.

The Button – Bip!

Two sluts of the Coombe dance rainily by, shawled, yelling flatly.

The Sluts
— *O, Leopold lost the pin of his drawers.*
He didn't know what to do,
To keep it up,
To keep it up.

Bloom (*coldly*) — You have broken the spell. The last straw. If there were only ethereal where would you all be, postulants and novices? Shy but willing, like an ass pissing.

The Yews (*their silver foil of leaves precipitating, their skinny arms ageing and swaying*) — Deciduously!

The Nymph (*her features hardening, gropes in the folds of her habit*) — Sacrilege! To attempt my virtue! (*A large moist stain appears on her robe.*) Sully my innocence! You are not fit to touch the garment of a pure woman. (*She clutches again in her robe.*) Wait, Satan, you'll sing no more love songs. Amen. Amen. Amen. Amen. (*She draws a poniard and, clad in the sheath mail of an elected knight of nine, strikes at his loins.*) Nekum!

Bloom (*starts up, seizes her hand*) — Hoy! Nebrakada! Cat o' nine lives! Fair play, madam. No pruning knife. The fox and the grapes, is it? What do you lack, with your barbed wire? Crucifix not thick enough? (*He clutches her veil.*) A holy abbot you want, or Brophy the lame gardener, or the spoutless statue of the watercarrier, or good Mother Alphonsus, eh, Reynard?

With a cry the nymph flees from him, unveiled, her plaster cast cracking, a cloud of stench escaping from the cracks.

The Nymph — Poli … !
Bloom (*calls after her*) — As if you didn't get it on the double yourselves. No jerks and multiple mucosities all over you. I tried it. Your strength our weakness. What's our stud fee? What will you pay on the nail? You fee men dancers on the Riviera, I read. (*The fleeing nymph raises a keen.*) Eh? I have sixteen years of black slave labour behind me. And would a jury give me five shillings alimony tomorrow, eh? Fool someone else, not me. (*He sniffs.*) Rut. Onions. Stale. Sulphur. Grease.

The figure of Bella Cohen stands before him.

Bella – You'll know me the next time.

Bloom (*composed, regards her*) – Passé. Mutton dressed as lamb. Long in the tooth and superfluous hair. A raw onion the last thing at night would benefit your complexion. And take some double-chin drill. Your eyes are as vapid as the glass eyes of your stuffed fox. They have the dimensions of your other features, that's all. I'm not a triple-screw propeller.

Bella (*contemptuously*) – You're not game, in fact. (*Her sowcunt barks.*) Fbhracht!

Bloom (*contemptuously*) – Clean your nailless middle finger first, your bully's cold spunk is dripping from your cockscomb. Take a handful of hay and wipe yourself.

Bella – I know you, canvasser! Dead cod!

Bloom – I saw him, kipkeeper! Pox and gleet vendor!

Bella (*turns to the piano*) – Which of you was playing the Dead March from *Saul*?

Zoe – Me. Mind your cornflowers. (*She darts to the piano and bangs chords on it with crossed arms.*) The cat's ramble through the slag. (*She glances back.*) Eh? Who's making love to my sweeties? (*She darts back to the table.*) What's yours is mine and what's mine is my own.

Kitty, disconcerted, coats her teeth with the silver paper. Bloom approaches Zoe.

Bloom (*gently*) – Give me back that potato, will you?

Zoe – Forfeits, a fine thing and a superfine thing.

Bloom (*with feeling*) – It is nothing, but, still, a relic of poor mamma.

Zoe
  – *Give a thing and take it back*
  God'll ask you where is that
  You'll say you don't know
  God'll send you down below.

Bloom – There is a memory attached to it. I should like to have it.

Stephen – To have or not to have, that is the question.

Zoe – Here. (*She hauls up a reef of her slip, revealing her bare thigh, and unrolls the potato from the top of her stocking.*) Those that hides knows where to find.

Bella (*frowns*) – Here. This isn't a musical peepshow. And don't you smash that piano. Who's paying here?

She goes to the pianola. Stephen fumbles in his pocket and, taking out a banknote by its corner, hands it to her.

Stephen (*with exaggerated politeness*) – This silken purse I made out of the sow's ear of the public. Madam, excuse me. If you allow me. (*He indicates vaguely Lynch and Bloom.*) We are all in the same sweepstake, Kinch and Lynch. *Dans ce bordel où tenons nostre état.*

Lynch (*calls from the hearth*) – Dedalus! Give her your blessing for me.

Stephen (*hands Bella a coin*) – Gold. She has it.

Bella (*looks at the money, then at Stephen, then at Zoe, Florry and Kitty*) – Do you want three girls? It's ten shillings here.

Stephen (*delightedly*) – A hundred thousand apologies. (*He fumbles again and takes out and hands her two crowns.*) Permit, *brevi manu*, my sight is somewhat troubled.

Bella goes to the table to count the money while Stephen talks to himself in monosyllables. Zoe bends over the table. Kitty leans over Zoe's neck. Lynch gets up, rights his cap and, clasping Kitty's waist, adds his head to the group.

Florry (*strives heavily to rise*) – Ow! My foot's asleep. (*She limps over to the table. Bloom approaches.*)

Bella, Zoe, Kitty, Lynch, Bloom (*chattering and squabbling*) – The gentleman ... ten shillings ... paying for the three ... allow me a moment ... this gentleman pays separate ... who's touching it? ... ow ... mind who you're pinching ... are you staying the night or a short time? ... who did? ... you're a liar, excuse me ... the gentleman paid down like a gentleman ... drink ... it's long after eleven.

Stephen (*at the pianola, making a gesture of abhorrence*) – No bottles! What, eleven? A riddle!

Zoe (*lifting up her pettigown and folding a half sovereign into the top of her stocking*) – Hard earned on the flat of my back.

Lynch (*lifting Kitty from the table*) – Come!

Kitty – Wait. (*She clutches the two crowns.*)

Florry – And me?

Lynch – Hoopla!

He lifts her, carries her and bumps her down on the sofa.

Stephen

      — *The fox crew, the cocks flew,*
       The bells in heaven
       Were striking eleven.
       'Tis time for her poor soul
       To get out of heaven.

Bloom (*quietly lays a half sovereign on the table between Bella and Florry*) — So. Allow me. (*He takes up the pound note.*) Three times ten. We're square.

Bella (*admiringly*) — You're such a slyboots, old cocky. I could kiss you.

Zoe (*points*) — Him? Deep as a draw well.

Lynch bends Kitty back over the sofa and kisses her. Bloom goes with the pound note to Stephen.

Bloom — This is yours.

Stephen — How is that? *Le distrait*, or absentminded beggar. (*He fumbles again in his pocket and draws out a handful of coins. An object falls.*) That fell.

Bloom (*stooping, picks up and hands him a box of matches*) — This.

Stephen — Lucifer. Thanks.

Bloom (*quietly*) — You had better hand over that cash to me to take care of. Why pay more?

Stephen (*hands him all his coins*) — Be just before you are generous.

Bloom — I will, but is it wise? (*He counts.*) One, seven, eleven, and five. Six. Eleven. I don't answer for what you may have lost.

Stephen — Why striking eleven? Proparoxyton. Moment before the next, Lessing says. Thirsty fox. (*He laughs loudly.*) Burying his grandmother. Probably he killed her.

Bloom — That is one pound six and eleven. One pound seven, say.

Stephen — Doesn't matter a rambling damn.

Bloom — No, but ...

Stephen (*comes to the table*) — Cigarette, please. (*Lynch tosses a cigarette from the sofa to the table.*) And so Georgina Johnson is dead and married. (*A cigarette appears on the table. Stephen looks at it.*) Wonder. Parlour magic. Married. Hm. (*He strikes a match and proceeds to light the cigarette with enigmatic melancholy.*)

Lynch (*watching him*) – You would have a better chance of lighting it if you held the match nearer.

Stephen (*brings the match near his eye*) – Lynx eye. Must get glasses. Broke them yesterday. Sixteen years ago. Distance. The eye sees all flat. (*He draws the match away. It goes out.*) Brain thinks. Near: far. Ineluctable modality of the visible. (*He frowns mysteriously.*) Hm. Sphinx. The beast that has two backs at midnight. Married.

Zoe – It was a commercial traveller married her and took her away with him.

Florry (*nods*) – Mr Lambe from London.

Stephen – Lambe of London, who takest away the sins of our world.

Lynch (*embracing Kitty on the sofa, chants deeply*) – *Dona nobis pacem.*

The cigarette slips from Stephen's fingers. Bloom picks it up and throws it into the grate.

Bloom – Don't smoke. You ought to eat. Cursed dog I met. (*To Zoe*) You have nothing?

Zoe – Is he hungry?

Stephen extends his hand to her, smiling, and chants to the air of the blood oath in *The Twilight of the Gods.*

Stephen
– *Hangende Hunger,*
  Fragende Frau,
  Macht uns alle kaputt.

Zoe (*tragically*) – Hamlet, I am thy father's gimlet! (*She takes his hand.*) Blue eyes, beauty. I'll read your hand. (*She points to his forehead.*) No wit, no wrinkles. (*She counts.*) Two, three, Mars, that's courage. (*Stephen shakes his head.*) No kid.

Lynch – Sheet-lightning courage. The youth who could not shiver and shake. (*To Zoe*) Who taught you palmistry?

Zoe (*turns*) – Ask my ballocks that I haven't got. (*To Stephen*) I see it in your face. The eye, like that. (*She frowns with lowered head.*)

Lynch (*laughing, slaps Kitty behind twice*) – Like that. Pandybat.

Twice, loudly, a pandybat cracks. The coffin of the pianola flies open. The bald little round jack-in-the-box head of Father Dolan springs up.

Father Dolan – Any boy want flogging? Broke his glasses? Lazy idle little schemer. See it in your eye.

Mild, benign, rectorial, reproving, the head of Don John Conmee rises from the pianola coffin.

Don John Conmee – Now, Father Dolan! Now. I'm sure that Stephen is a very good little boy!

Zoe (*examining Stephen's palm*) – Woman's hand.

Stephen (*murmurs*) – Continue. Lie. Hold me. Caress. I never could read His handwriting except His criminal thumbprint on the haddock.

Zoe – What day were you born?

Stephen – Thursday. Today.

Zoe – Thursday's child has far to go. (*She traces lines on his hand.*) Line of fate. Influential friends.

Florry (*pointing*) – Imagination.

Zoe – Mount of the moon. You'll meet with a … (*She peers at his hand abruptly.*) I won't tell you what's not good for you. Or do you want to know?

Bloom (*detaches her fingers and offers his palm*) – More harm than good. Here. Read mine.

Bella – Show. (*She turns up Bloom's hand.*) I thought so. Knobby knuckles, for the women.

Zoe – (*peering at Bloom's palm*) – Gridiron. Travels beyond the sea and marry money.

Bloom – Wrong.

Zoe (*quickly*) – O, I see. Short little finger. Henpecked husband. That wrong?

Black Liz, a huge rooster hatching in a chalked circle, rises, stretches her wings and clucks.

Black Liz – Gara. Klook klook klook. (*She sidles from her new-laid egg and waddles off.*)

Bloom (*points to his hand*) – That weal there is an accident. Fell and cut it twenty-two years ago. I was sixteen.

Zoe – I see, says the blind man. Tell us news.

Stephen – See? Moves to one great goal. I am twenty-two. Sixteen years ago he was twenty-two too. Sixteen years ago I twenty-two tumbled.

Twenty-two years ago he sixteen fell off his hobbyhorse. (*He winces.*) Hurt my hand somewhere. Must see a dentist. Money?

Zoe (*peers, twisting Bloom's hand*) – Hold on. Wait. (*She laughs in a frank odd fashion.*) Ha ha ha ha ha! Wait. (*Peering again, she laughs with head flung back.*) Ha ha ha ha ha! (*She whispers to Florry. They giggle. Bloom releases his hand and writes idly on the table in backhand, pencilling slow curves.*)

Florry – What?

A hackney car, number three hundred and twenty-four, with a gallant-buttocked mare, driven by James Barton, Harmony Avenue, Donnybrook, trots past. Blazes Boylan and Lenehan sprawl swaying on the sideseats. The Ormond boots crouches behind on the axle. Sadly over the crossblind Lydia Douce and Mina Kennedy gaze.

The Boots (*jogging, mocks them with thumb and wriggling wormfingers*) – Haw haw, have you the horn?

Bronze by gold they whisper.

Zoe (*to Florry*) – Whisper. (*She whispers again.*)

Over the well of the car Blazes Boylan leans, his boater straw set sideways, a red flower in his mouth. Lenehan, in yachtsman's cap and white shoes, officiously detaches a long hair from Blazes Boylan's coat shoulder.

Lenehan – Ho! What do I here behold? Were you brushing the cobwebs off a few quims?

Boylan (*sated, smiles*) – Plucking a turkey.

Lenehan – A good night's work.

Boylan (*holding up four thick blunt-ungulated fingers, winks*) – Blazes Kate! Up to sample or your money back. (*He holds out a forefinger.*) Smell that.

Lenehan (*smells gleefully*) – Ah! Lobster and mayonnaise. Ah!

Zoe and Florry (*laugh together*) – Ha ha ha ha.

Boylan (*jumps surely from the car and calls loudly for all to hear*) – Hello, Bloom! Mrs Bloom dressed yet?

Bloom (*in flunkey's prune plush coat and kneebreeches, buff stockings and powdered wig*) – I'm afraid not, sir. The last articles ...

Boylan (*tosses him sixpence*) – Here, to buy yourself a gin and splash. (*He hangs his hat smartly on a peg of Bloom's antlered head.*) Show me in. I have a little private business with your wife, you understand?

Bloom – Thank you, sir. Yes, sir. Madam Tweedy is in her bath, sir.

Marion – He ought to feel himself highly honoured. (*She plops splashing out of the water.*) Raoul darling, come and dry me. I'm in my pelt. Only my new hat and a carriage sponge.

Boylan (*a merry twinkle in his eye*) – Topping!

Bella – What? What is it?

Zoe whispers to her.

Marion – Let him look, the pithogue! Pimp! And scourge himself! I'll write to a powerful prostitute, or Bartholomona the bearded woman, to raise weals out on him an inch thick and make him bring me back a signed and stamped receipt.

Boylan (*clasps himself*) – Here, I can't hold this little lot much longer. (*He strides off on stiff cavalry legs.*)

Bella (*laughing*) – Ho ho ho ho.

Boylan (*to Bloom, over his shoulder*) – You can apply your eye to the keyhole and play with yourself while I just go through her a few times.

Bloom – Thank you, sir. I will, sir. May I bring two men chums to witness the deed and take a snapshot? (*He holds out an ointment jar.*) Vaseline, sir? Orangeflower ... ? Lukewarm water ... ?

Kitty (*from the sofa*) – Tell us, Florry. Tell us. What ...

Florry whispers to her. Whispering lovewords murmur, liplapping loudly, poppysmic plopslop.

Mina Kennedy (*her eyes upturned*) – O, it must be like the scent of geraniums and lovely peaches! O, he simply idolises every bit of her! Stuck together! Covered with kisses!

Lydia Douce (*her mouth opening*) – Yumyum. O, he's carrying her round the room doing it! Ride a cockhorse. You could hear them in Paris and New York. Like mouthfuls of strawberries and cream.

Kitty (*laughing*) – Hee hee hee.

Boylan's Voice (*sweetly, hoarsely, in the pit of his stomach*) – Ah! Godblazegrukbrukarchkhrasht!

Marion's Voice (*hoarsely, sweetly, rising to her throat*) – O! Weeshwashtkissinapooisthnapoohuck!

Bloom (*his eyes wildly dilated, clasps himself*) – Show! Hide! Show! Plough her! More! Shoot!

Bella, Zoe, Florry, Kitty – Ho ho! Ha ha! Hee hee!

Lynch (*points*) – The mirror up to nature. (*He laughs.*) Hu hu hu hu hu!

Stephen and Bloom gaze in the mirror. The face of William Shakespeare, beardless, appears there, rigid in facial paralysis, crowned by the reflection of the reindeer-antlered hatrack in the hall.

Shakespeare (*in dignified ventriloquy*) – 'Tis the loud laugh bespeaks the vacant mind. (*To Bloom*) Thou thoughtest as how thou wastest invisible. Gaze. (*He crows with a black capon's laugh.*) Iagogo! How my Oldfellow chokit his Thursdaymornun. Iagogogo!

Bloom (*smiles yellowly at the three whores*) – When will I hear the joke?

Zoe – Before you're twice married and once a widower.

Bloom – Lapses are condoned. Even the great Napoleon, when measurements were taken next the skin after his death . . .

Mrs Dignam, widow woman, her snub nose and cheeks flushed with deathtalk, tears and Tunney's tawny sherry, hurries by in her weeds, her bonnet awry, rouging and powdering her cheeks, lips and nose, a pen chevying her brood of cygnets. Beneath her skirt appear her late husband's everyday trousers and turned-up boots, large eights. She holds a Scottish Widows' insurance policy and a large marquee umbrella under which her brood run with her: Patsy hopping on one shod foot, his collar loose, a hank of pork steaks dangling, Freddy whimpering, Susy with a crying cod's mouth, Alice struggling with the baby. She cuffs them on, her streamers flaunting aloft.

Freddy – Ah, ma, you're dragging me along!

Susy – Mamma, the beeftea is fizzing over!

Shakespeare (*with paralytic rage*) – Weda seca whokilla farst.

The face of Martin Cunningham, bearded, refeatures Shakespeare's beardless face. The marquee umbrella sways drunkenly, the children run aside. Under the umbrella appears Mrs Cunningham in Merry Widow hat and kimono gown. She glides sidling and bowing, twirling Japanesely the umbrella.

Mrs Cunningham (*sings*) – *And they call me the jewel of Asia!*
Martin Cunningham (*gazes on her, impassive*) – Immense! Most bloody awful demirep!
Stephen – *Et exaltabuntur cornua justi.* Queens lay with prize bulls. Remember Pasiphaë for whose lust my grand old grossfather made the first confession box. Forget not Madam Grissel Steevens, nor the suine scions of the house of Lambert. And Noah was drunk with wine. And his ark was open.
Bella – None of that here. Come to the wrong shop.
Lynch – Let him alone. He's back from Paris.
Zoe (*runs to Stephen and links him*) – O, go on! Give us some parleyvoo.

Stephen claps hat on head and leaps over to the fireplace where he stands with shrugged shoulders, finny hands outspread, a painted smile on his face.

Lynch (*pommelling on the sofa*) – Rmm Rmm Rmm Rrrrrrmmmm.
Stephen (*gabbles with marionette jerks*) – Thousand places of entertainment to expense your evenings with lovely ladies saling gloves and other things perhaps hers breast beerchops perfect fashionable house very eccentric where lots cocottes beautiful dressed much about princesses like are dancing cancan and winking there parisian clowneries extra foolish for bachelors foreigns the same if talking a poor english how much smart they are on things love and sensations voluptuous. Misters very selects for is pleasure must to visit heaven and hell show with mortuary candles and they tears silver which occur every night. Perfectly shocking terrific of religion's things mockery seen in universal world. All chic womans which arrive full of modesty then disrobe and squeal loud to see vampire man debauch nun very fresh young with *dessous troublants.* (*He clacks his tongue loudly.*) Ho, là là! Ce pif qu'il a!
Lynch – *Vive le vampire!*
The Whores – Bravo! Parleyvoo!
Stephen (*with head back, laughs loudly, clapping himself, grimacing*) – Great success of laughing. Angels much prostitutes like and holy apostles

big damn ruffians. Demimondaines nicely handsome sparkling of diamonds very amiable costumed. Or do you are fond better what belongs they moderns pleasure turpitude of old mans? (*He points about him with grotesque gestures which Lynch and the whores reply to.*) Caoutchouc statue woman reversible or life-size tompeeptom of virgins nudities very lesbic the kiss five ten times. Enter, gentleman, to see in mirror every positions trapezes all that machine there besides also if desire act awfully bestial butcher's boy pollutes in warm veal liver or omelette on the belly, *pièce de Shakespeare.*

Bella (*clapping her belly, sinks back on the sofa with a shout of laughter*) – An omelette on the … Ho ho ho ho! … omelette on the …

Stephen (*mincingly*) – I love you, sir darling. Speak you englishman tongue for *double entente cordiale.* O yes, *mon loup.* How much cost? Waterloo. Watercloset. (*He ceases suddenly and holds up a forefinger.*)

Bella (*laughing*) – Omelette …

The Whores (*laughing*) – Encore! Encore!

Stephen – Mark me. I dreamt of a watermelon.

Zoe – Go abroad and love a foreign lady.

Lynch – Across the world for a wife.

Florry – Dreams goes by contraries.

Stephen (*extending his arms*) – It was here. Street of harlots. In Serpentine Avenue Beelzebub showed me her, a fubsy widow. Where's the red carpet spread?

Bloom (*approaching Stephen*) – Look …

Stephen – No, I flew. My foes beneath me. And ever shall be. World without end. (*He cries.*) *Pater!* Free!

Bloom – I say, look …

Stephen – Break my spirit, will he? *O merde alors!* (*He cries, his vulture talons sharpened.*) *Holà!* Hillyho!

Simon Dedalus' voice hilloes in answer, somewhat sleepy but ready.

Simon – That's all right. (*He swoops uncertainly through the air, wheeling, uttering cries of heartening, on strong ponderous buzzard wings.*) Ho, boy! Are you going to win? Hoop! Pschatt! Stable with those half-castes. Wouldn't let them within the bawl of an ass. Head up! Keep our flag flying! An eagle *gules* volant in a field *argent* displayed. Ulster King of Arms! Hai hoop! (*He makes the beagle's call, giving tongue.*) Bulbul! Burblblburblbl! Hai, boy!

The fronds and spaces of the wallpaper file rapidly cross country. A stout fox, drawn from covert, brush pointed, having buried his grandmother, runs swift for the open, bright-eyed, seeking badger earth under the leaves. The pack of staghounds follows, noses to the ground, sniffing their quarry, beagle-baying, burblbrbling to be blooded. Ward Union huntsmen and huntswomen ride with them, hot for a kill. From Six Mile Point, Flathouse, Nine Mile Stone, follow the footpeople with knotty sticks, hayforks, salmon gaffs and lassoes, flockmasters with stockwhips, bearbaiters with tom-toms, toreadors with bull swords, grey negroes waving torches. The crowd bawls of dicers, crown and anchor players, thimbleriggers, broadsmen. Crows and touts, hoarse bookies in high wizard hats, clamour deafeningly.

The Crowd
— Card of the races. Racing card!
Ten to one the field!
Tommy on the clay here! Tommy on the clay!
Ten to one bar one! Ten to one bar one!
Try your luck on Spinning Jenny!
Ten to one bar one!
Sell the monkey, boys! Sell the monkey!
I'll give ten to one!
Ten to one bar one!

A dark horse, riderless, bolts like a phantom past the winning post, his mane moonfoaming, his eyeballs stars. The field follows, a bunch of bucking mounts. Skeleton horses: *Sceptre, Maximum the Second, Zinfandel,* the duke of Westminster's *Shotover, Repulse,* the duke of Beaufort's *Ceylon, Prix de Paris.* Dwarfs ride them, rusty-armoured, leaping, leaping in their, in their saddles. Last, in a drizzle of rain, on a broken-winded isabelle nag *Cock of the North,* the favourite, honey cap, green jacket, orange sleeves, Garrett Deasy sits, gripping the reins, a hockeystick at the ready. His nag, stumbling on spavined white-gaitered feet, jogs along the rocky road.

The Orange Lodges (*jeering*) – Get down and push, mister. Last lap! You'll be home the night!

Garrett Deasy, bolt upright, his nail-scraped face plastered with postage stamps, brandishes his hockeystick, his blue eyes flashing in the prism of the chandelier as his mount lopes by at schooling gallop.

Garrett Deasy – *Per vias rectas!*

A yoke of buckets leopards all over him and his rearing nag a torrent of mutton broth with dancing coins of carrots, barley, onions, turnips, potatoes.

The Green Lodges – Soft day, Sir John! Soft day, your honour!

Private Carr, Private Compton and Cissy Caffrey pass beneath the windows, singing in discord.

Stephen – Hark! Our friend, noise in the street.
Zoe (*holds up her hand*) – Stop!
Private Carr, Private Compton and Cissy Caffrey
– Yet I've a sort of a
   Yorkshire relish for …
Zoe – That's me. (*She claps her hands.*) Dance! Dance! (*She runs to the pianola.*) Who has twopence?
Bloom – Who'll … ?
Lynch – (*handing her coins*) – Here.
Stephen (*cracking his fingers impatiently*) – Quick! Quick! Where's my augur's rod?

He runs to the piano and takes his ashplant, beating his foot in tripudium.

Zoe (*turns the drumhandle*) – There.

She drops two pennies in the slot. Gold, pink and violet lights start forth. The drum turns, purring in low hesitation waltz. Professor Goodwin, in a bowknotted periwig, in court dress, wearing a stained Inverness cape, bent in two from incredible age, totters across the room, his hands fluttering. He sits tinily on the piano stool and lifts and beats handless sticks of arms on the keyboard, nodding with damsel's grace, his bowknot bobbing.

Zoe (*twirls round herself, heeltapping*) – Dance. Anybody here for there? Who'll dance? Clear the table.

The pianola, with changing lights, plays in waltz time the prelude of *My Girl's a Yorkshire Girl*. Stephen throws his ashplant on the table and seizes Zoe round the waist. Florry and Bella push the table towards the fireplace. Stephen, arming Zoe with exaggerated grace, begins to waltz her round the room. Bloom stands aside. Her sleeve, falling from gracing arms, reveals a white fleshflower of vaccination. Between the curtains Professor Maginni inserts a leg on the toepoint of which spins a silk hat. With a deft kick he sends it spinning to his crown and, jaunty-hatted, skates in. He wears a slate frockcoat with claret silk lapels, a gorget of cream tulle, a green low-cut waistcoat, stock collar with white kerchief tie, tight lavender trousers, patent pumps and canary gloves. In his buttonhole is an immense blue dahlia. He twirls in reversed directions a clouded cane, then wedges it tight in his oxter. He places a hand lightly on his breastbone, bows and fondles his flower and buttons.

Maginni – The poetry of motion, art of calisthenics. No connection with Madam Leggett Byrne's or Levenston's. Fancy dress balls arranged. Deportment. The Katti Lanner step. So. Watch me! My terpsichorean abilities. (*He minuets forward three paces on tripping bee's feet.*) *Tout le monde en avant! Révérence! Tout le monde en place!*

The prelude ceases. Professor Goodwin, beating vague arms, shrivels, sinks, his live cape falling about the stool. The air, in firmer waltz time, sounds. Stephen and Zoe circle freely. The lights change, glow, fade: gold, rose, violet.

The Pianola
 – *Two young fellows were talking about their girls, girls, girls,*
   Sweethearts they'd left behind...

From a corner the morning hours run out, gold-haired, slim-sandalled, in girlish blue, wasp-waisted, with innocent hands. Nimbly they dance, twirling their skipping ropes. The hours of noon follow in amber gold. Laughing, linked, high haircombs flashing, they catch the sun in mocking mirrors, lifting their arms.

Maginni (*clipclaps glovesilent hands*) – *Carré! Avant deux!* Breathe evenly! *Balancé!*

The morning and noon hours waltz in their places, turning, advancing to each other, shaping their curves, bowing vis-à-vis. Cavaliers behind them arch and suspend their arms, with hands descending to, touching, rising from their shoulders.

Hours – You may touch my.
Cavaliers – May I touch your?
Hours – O, but lightly!
Cavaliers – O, so lightly!
The Pianola
– *My little shy little lass has a waist.*

Zoe and Stephen turn boldly with looser swing. The twilight hours advance from long landshadows, dispersed, lagging, languid-eyed, their cheeks delicate with *cipria* and false faint bloom. They are in grey gauze with darker batsleeves that flutter in the landbreeze.

Maginni – *Avant huit! Traversé! Salut! Cours de mains! Croisé!*

The night hours, one by one, steal to the last place. Morning, noon and twilight hours retreat before them. They are masked, with daggered hair and bracelets of dull bells. Weary, they curchycurchy under veils.

The Bracelets – Heigho! Heigho!
Zoe (*twirling, her hand to her brow*) – O!
Maginni – *Les tiroirs! Chaîne de dames! La corbeille! Dos à dos!*

Arabesquing wearily, they weave a pattern on the floor, weaving, unweaving, curtseying, twirling, simply swirling.

Zoe – I'm giddy!

She frees herself, droops on a chair. Stephen seizes Florry and turns with her.

Maginni – *Boulangère! Les ronds! Les ponts! Chevaux de bois! Escargots!*

Twining, receding, with interchanging hands the night hours link each each with arching arms in a mosaic of movements. Stephen and Florry turn cumbrously.

Maginni – *Dansez avec vos dames! Changez de dames! Donnez le petit bouquet à votre dame! Remerciez!*
The Pianola
– *Best, best of all,*
  Baraabum!
Kitty (*jumps up*) – O, they played that on the hobbyhorses at the Mirus Bazaar!

She runs to Stephen. He leaves Florry brusquely and seizes Kitty. A screaming bittern's harsh high whistle shrieks. Groangrousegurgling, Toft's cumbersome whirligig turns slowly the room right roundabout the room.

The Pianola
– *My girl's a Yorkshire girl.*
Zoe – Yorkshire through and through. Come on, all!

She seizes Florry and waltzes her.

Stephen – *Pas seul!*

He wheels Kitty into Lynch's arms, snatches up his ashplant from the table and takes the floor. All wheel whirl waltz twirl Bloombella Kittylynch Florryzoe jujuby women. Stephen with hat ashplant frogsplits in middle highkicks with skykicking mouth shut hand clasp part under thigh. With clang tinkle boomhammer tallyho hornblower blue green yellow flashes Toft's cumbersome turns with hobbyhorse riders from gilded snakes dangled bowels fandango leaping spurn soil foot and fall again.

The Pianola
– *Though she's a factory lass*
  And wears no fancy clothes.

Closeclutched swift swifter with glareblareflare scudding they scootlootshoot lumbering by. Baraabum!

Tutti – Encore! Bis! Bravo! Encore!
Simon – Think of your mother's people!
Stephen – Dance of death.

Bang fresh barang bang of lacquey's bell, horse, nag, steer, piglings, Conmee on Christass, lame crutch and leg sailor in cockboat armfolded ropepulling hitching stamp hornpipe through and through. Baraabum! On nags hogs bellhorses Gadarene swine Corny in coffin steel shark stone onehandled Nelson two trickies Frauenzimmer plumstained from pram falling bawling. Gum he's a champion. Fuseblue peer from barrel Rev. Evensong Love on hackney jaunt Blazes blind coddoubled bicyclers Dilly with snowcake no fancy clothes. Then in last switchback lumbering up and down bump mashtub sort of viceroy and reine relish for tublumber bumpshire rose. Baraabum!

The couples fall aside. Stephen whirls giddily. Room whirls back. Eyes closed, he totters. Red rails fly spacewards. Stars all around suns turn roundabout. Bright midges dance on walls. He stops dead.

Stephen – Ho!

Stephen's mother, emaciated, rises stark through the floor, in leper grey, with a wreath of faded orange blossoms and a torn bridal veil, her face worn and noseless, green with gravemould. Her hair is scant and lank. She fixes her blue-circled hollow eyesockets on Stephen and opens her toothless mouth, uttering a silent word. A choir of virgins and confessors sing voicelessly.

The Choir
– *Liliata rutilantium te confessorum . . .*
  Jubilantium te virginum . . .

From the top of a tower Buck Mulligan, in parti-coloured jester's dress of puce and yellow, and clown's cap with curling bell, stands gaping at her, a smoking buttered split scone in his hand.

Buck Mulligan – She's beastly dead. The pity of it! Mulligan meets the afflicted mother. (*He upturns his eyes.*) Mercurial Malachi!
The Mother (*with the subtle smile of death's madness*) – I was once the beautiful May Goulding. I am dead.

Stephen (*horror-struck*) – Lemur, who are you? No. What bogeyman's trick is this?

Buck Mulligan (*shakes his curling capbell*) – The mockery of it! Kinch dogsbody killed her bitchbody. She kicked the bucket. (*Tears of molten butter fall from his eyes onto the scone.*) Our great sweet mother! *Epi oinopa ponton.*

The Mother (*comes nearer Stephen, breathing upon him softly her breath of wetted ashes*) – All must go through it, Stephen. More women than men in the world. You too. Time will come.

Stephen (*choking with fright, remorse and horror*) – They say I killed you, mother. He offended your memory. Cancer did it, not I. Destiny.

The Mother (*a green rill of bile trickling from a side of her mouth*) – You sang that song to me. *Love's bitter mystery.*

Stephen (*eagerly*) – Tell me the word, mother, if you know now. The word known to all men.

The Mother – Who saved you the night you jumped into the train at Dalkey with Paddy Lee? Who had pity for you when you were sad among the strangers? Prayer is all powerful. Prayer for the suffering souls in the Ursuline manual and forty days indulgence. Repent, Stephen.

Stephen – The ghoul! Hyena!

The Mother – I pray for you in my other world. Get Dilly to make you that boiled rice every night after your brainwork. Years and years I loved you, O my son, my firstborn, when you lay in my womb.

Zoe (*fanning herself with the gratefan*) – I'm melting!

Florry (*points to Stephen*) – Look! He's white.

Bloom (*goes to the window to open it more*) – Giddy.

The Mother (*with smouldering eyes*) – Repent! O, the fire of hell!

Stephen (*panting*) – His noncorrosive sublimate! The corpsechewer! Raw head and bloody bones.

The Mother (*her face drawing nearer and nearer, sending out an ashen breath*) – Beware! (*She raises her blackened withered right arm slowly with outstretched finger towards Stephen's breast.*) Beware God's hand!

A green crab with malignant red eyes sticks deep its grinning claws in Stephen's heart.

Stephen (*strangled with rage*) – Shite! (*His features grow drawn and grey and old.*)

Bloom (*at the window*) – What?

Stephen – *Ah non, par exemple!* The intellectual imagination! With me all or not at all. *Non serviam!*

Florry – Give him some cold water. Wait. (*She rushes out.*)

The Mother (*wrings her hands slowly, moaning desperately*) – O Sacred Heart of Jesus, have mercy on him! Save him from hell, O Divine Sacred Heart!

Stephen – No! No! No! Break my spirit, all of you, if you can! I'll bring you all to heel!

The Mother (*in the agony of her death rattle*) – Have mercy on Stephen, Lord, for my sake! Inexpressible was my anguish when expiring with love, grief and agony on Mount Calvary.

Stephen – Nothung!

He lifts his ashplant high with both hands and smashes the chandelier. Time's livid final flame leaps and, in the following darkness, ruin of all space, shattered glass and toppling masonry.

The Gasjet – Pwfungg!

Bloom – Stop!

Lynch (*rushes forward and seizes Stephen's hand*) – Here! Hold on! Don't run amok!

Bella – Police!

Stephen, abandoning his ashplant, his head and arms thrown back stark, beats the ground and flies from the room past the whores at the door.

Bella (*screams*) – After him!

The two whores rush to the hall door. Lynch and Kitty and Zoe stampede from the room. They talk excitedly. Bloom follows, returns.

The Whores (*jammed in the doorway, pointing*) – Down there.

Zoe (*pointing*) – There. There's something up.

Bella – Who pays for the lamp? (*She seizes Bloom's coattail.*) Here, you were with him. The lamp's broken.

Bloom (*rushes to the hall, rushes back*) – What lamp, woman?

A Whore – He tore his coat.

Bella (*her eyes hard with anger and cupidity, points*) – Who's to pay for that? Ten shillings. You're a witness.

Bloom (*snatches up Stephen's ashplant*) – Me? Ten shillings? Haven't you lifted enough off him? Didn't he ... ?

Bella (*loudly*) – Here, none of your tall talk. This isn't a brothel. A ten-shilling house.

Bloom, his head under the lamp, pulls the chain. Puling, the gasjet lights up a crushed mauve purple shade. He raises the ashplant.

Bloom – Only the chimney's broken. Here is all he ...

Bella (*shrinks back and screams*) – Jesus! Don't!

Bloom (*warding off a blow*) – To show you how he hit the paper. There's not sixpenceworth of damage done. Ten shillings!

Florry (*with a glass of water, enters*) – Where is he?

Bella – Do you want me to call the police?

Bloom – O, I know. Bulldog on the premises. But he a Trinity student. Patrons of your establishment. Gentlemen that pay the rent. (*He makes a masonic sign.*) Know what I mean? Nephew of the vice-chancellor. You don't want a scandal.

Bella (*angrily*) – Trinity! Coming down here ragging after the boat race and paying nothing. Are you the commander here? Where is he? I'll charge him! Disgrace him, I will! (*She shouts.*) Zoe! Zoe!

Bloom (*urgently*) – And if it were your own son in Oxford? (*Warningly*) I know.

Bella (*almost speechless*) – Who are you? Incog?

Zoe (*in the doorway*) – There's a row on.

Bloom – What? Where? (*He throws a shilling on the table and starts.*) That's for the chimney. Where? I need mountain air.

He hurries out through the hall. The whores point. Florry follows, spilling water from her tilted tumbler. On the doorstep all the whores clustered talk volubly, pointing to the right where the fog has cleared off. From the left arrives a jingling hackney car. It slows to in front of the house. Bloom at the hall door perceives Corny Kelleher who is about to dismount from the car with two silent lechers. He averts his face. Bella from within the hall urges on her whores. They blow ickylickysticky yumyum kisses. Corny Kelleher replies with a ghastly lewd smile. The silent lechers turn to pay the jarvey. Zoe and Kitty still point right. Bloom, parting them swiftly, draws his caliph's hood and poncho and hurries down the steps with sideways face. Incog, Haroun al-Raschid, he flits behind the silent lechers and hastens on by the railings with fleet step of a pard, strewing the drag behind him, torn envelopes drenched in aniseed. The ashplant marks his stride. A pack of bloodhounds, led by Hornblower of Trinity in tallyho cap and an old pair of grey trousers and brandishing a dogwhip, follows from afar, picking up the scent, nearer, baying, panting, at fault, breaking away, throwing their tongues, biting his heels, leaping at his tail. He walks, runs, zigzags, gallops, lugs laid back. He is pelted with gravel, cabbage stumps, biscuit boxes, eggs, potatoes, dead codfish, woman's slipperslappers. After him, fresh-found, the hue and cry zigzag gallops in hot pursuit of follow my leader: 65C, 66C, night watch, John Henry Menton, Wisdom Hely, V.B. Dillon, Councillor Nannetti, Alexander Keyes, Larry O'Rourke, Joe Cuffe, Mrs O'Dowd, Pisser Burke, the Nameless One, Mrs Riordan, the Citizen, Garryowen, Whodoyoucallhim, Strangeface, Fellowthatslike, Sawhimbefore, Chapwithawen, Chris Callanan, Sir Charles Cameron, Benjamin Dollard, Lenehan, Bartell d'Arcy, Joe Hynes, Red Murray, editor Brayden, T.M. Healy, Mr Justice Fitzgibbon, John Howard Parnell, the Reverend Tinned Salmon, Professor Joly, Mrs Breen, Denis Breen, Theodore Purefoy, Mina Purefoy, the Westland Row postmistress, C.P. M'Coy, friend of Lyons, Hoppy Holohan, maninthestreet, othermaninthestreet, Footballboots, pugnosed driver, rich Protestant lady, Davy Byrne, Mrs Ellen M'Guinness, Mrs Joe Gallaher, George Lidwell, Jimmy Henry on corns, Superintendent Laracy, Father Cowley, Crofton out of the collector general's, Dan Dawson, dental surgeon Bloom with tweezers, Mrs Bob Doran, Mrs Kennefick, Mrs Wyse Nolan, John Wyse Nolan, handsomemarriedwomanrubbedagainstwidebehindinClonskeaghtram, the bookseller of *Sweets of Sin*, Miss Dubedatandshedidbedad, Mesdames Gerald and Stanislaus Moran of Roebuck, the managing clerk of Drimmie's, Wetherup, Colonel Hayes, Masliansky, Citron, Penrose, Aaron Figatner, Moses Herzog, Michael E. Geraghty, Inspector Troy, Mrs Galbraith, the constable off Eccles Street corner, old Doctor Brady with stethoscope, the mystery man on the beach, a retriever, Mrs Miriam Dandrade and all her lovers.

The Hue and Cry (*helterskelterpelterwelter*) – He's Bloom! Stop Bloom! Stopabloom! Stopperrobber! Hi! Hi! Stophim on the corner!

At the corner of Beaver Street beneath the scaffolding Bloom panting stops on the fringe of the noisy quarrelling knot, a lot not knowing a jot what hi! hi! row and wrangle round the whowhat brawlaltogether.

Stephen (*with elaborate gestures, breathing deeply and slowly*) – You are my guests. Uninvited. By virtue of the fifth of George and seventh of Edward. History to blame. Fabled by mothers of memory.

Private Carr (*to Cissy Caffrey*) – Was he insulting you?

Stephen – Addressed her in vocative feminine. Probably neuter. Ungenitive.

Voices – No, he didn't. The girl's telling lies. He was in Mrs Cohen's. What's up? Soldier and civilian.

Cissy Caffrey – I was in company with the soldiers and they left me to do, you know, and the young man run up behind me. But I'm faithful to the man that's treating me though I'm only a shilling whore.

Voices – Shesfaithfultheman.

Stephen (*catches sight of Lynch's and Kitty's heads*) – Hail, Sisyphus. (*He points to himself and the others.*) Poetic. Uropoetic.

Cissy Caffrey – Yes, to go with him. And me with a soldier friend.

Private Compton – He doesn't half want a thick ear, the blighter. Biff him one, Harry.

Private Carr (*to Cissy*) – Was he insulting you while me and him was having a piss?

Lord Tennyson (*gentleman poet, in Union Jack blazer and cricket flannels, bareheaded, flowing-bearded*) – Theirs not to reason why.

Private Compton – Biff him, Harry.

Stephen (*to Private Compton*) – I don't know your name but you are quite right. Doctor Swift says one man in armour will beat ten men in their shirts. Shirt is synecdoche. Part for the whole.

Cissy Caffrey (*to the crowd*) – No, I was with the privates.

Stephen (*amiably*) – Why not? The bold soldier boy. In my opinion every lady, for example . . .

Private Carr (*his cap awry, advances to Stephen*) – Say, how would it be, governor, if I was to bash in your jaw?

Stephen (*looks up to the sky*) – How? Very unpleasant. Noble art of self-pretence. Personally, I detest action. (*He waves his hand.*) Hand hurts me slightly. *Enfin, ce sont vos oignons.* (*To Cissy Caffrey*) Some trouble is on here. What is it precisely?

Dolly Gray (*from her balcony, waving her handkerchief, giving the sign* *of the heroine of Jericho*) – Rahab. Cook's son, goodbye. Safe home to Dolly. Dream of the girl you left behind and she will dream of you.

The soldiers turn their swimming eyes.

Bloom (*elbowing through the crowd, plucks Stephen's sleeve vigorously*) – Come now, professor, that carman is waiting.

Stephen (*turns*) – Eh? (*He disengages himself.*) Why should I not speak to him or to any human being who walks upright upon this oblate orange? (*He points his finger.*) I'm not afraid of what I can talk to if I see his eye. Retaining the perpendicular. (*He staggers a pace back.*)

Bloom (*propping him*) – Retain your own.

Stephen (*laughs emptily*) – My centre of gravity is displaced. I have forgotten the trick. Let us sit down somewhere and discuss. Struggle for life is the law of existence, but human philirenists, notably the tsar and the king of England, have invented arbitration. (*He taps his brow.*) But in here it is I must kill the priest and the king.

Biddy the Clap – Did you hear what the professor said? He's a professor out of the college.

Cunty Kate – I did. I heard that.

Biddy the Clap – He expresses himself with such marked refinement of phraseology.

Cunty Kate – Indeed, yes. And at the same time with such apposite trenchancy.

Private Carr (*pulls himself free and comes forward*) – What's that you're saying about my king?

Edward the Seventh appears in an archway. He wears a white jersey on which an image of the Sacred Heart is stitched with the insignia of Garter and Thistle, Golden Fleece, Elephant of Denmark, Skinner's and Probyn's Horse, Lincoln's Inn bencher and Ancient and Honourable Artillery Company of Massachusetts. He sucks a red jujube. He is robed as a grand elect perfect and sublime mason, with trowel and apron marked *Made in Germany*. In his left hand he holds a plasterer's bucket on which is printed *Défense d'uriner*. A roar of welcome greets him.

Edward the Seventh (*slowly, solemnly, but indistinctly*) – Peace, perfect peace. For identification, bucket in my hand. Cheerio, boys. (*He turns to* *his subjects*.) We have come here to witness a clean straight fight and we heartily wish both men the best of good luck. Mahak makar a bak. (*He shakes hands with Private Carr, Private Compton, Stephen, Bloom and Lynch*.)

General applause. Edward the Seventh lifts his bucket graciously in acknowledgment.

Private Carr (*to Stephen*) – Say it again.
Stephen (*nervous, friendly, pulls himself up*) – I understand your point of view, though I have no king myself for the moment. This is the age of patent medicines. A discussion is difficult down here. But this is the point. You die for your country, suppose. (*He places his arm on Private Carr's sleeve*.) Not that I wish it for you. But I say: Let my country die for me. Up to the present it has done so. I didn't want it to die. Damn death. Long live life!

Edward the Seventh, in the garb and with the halo of Joking Jesus, a white jujube in his phosphorescent face, levitates over heaps of slain.

Edward the Seventh
— *My methods are new and are causing surprise.*
    To make the blind see I throw dust in their eyes.
Stephen – Kings and unicorns! (*He falls back a pace*.) Come somewhere and we'll ... What was that girl saying?
Private Compton – Eh, Harry, give him a kick in the knackers. Stick one into Jerry.
Bloom (*to the privates, softly*) – He doesn't know what he's saying. Taken a little more than is good for him. Absinthe. Green-eyed monster. I know him. He's a gentleman, a poet. It's all right.
Stephen (*nods, smiling and laughing*) – Gentleman, patriot, scholar and judge of impostors.
Private Carr – I don't give a bugger who he is.
Private Compton – We don't give a bugger who he is.
Stephen – I seem to annoy them. Green rag to a bull.

Kevin Egan of Paris, in black Spanish tasselled shirt and peep-o'-day-boy's hat, signs to Stephen.

Kevin Egan – H'lo! *Bonjour!* The *vieille ogresse* with the *dents jaunes.*

Patrice Egan peeps from behind, his rabbitface nibbling a quince leaf.

Patrice – *Socialiste!*

Don Emile Patrizio Franz Rupert Pope Hennessy (*in medieval haub-erk, two wild geese volant on his helm, with noble indignation points a mailed hand against the privates*) – Werf those eykes to footboden, big grand porcos of johnyellows todos covered of gravy!

Bloom (*to Stephen*) – Come home. You'll get into trouble.

Stephen (*swaying*) – I don't avoid it. He provokes my intelligence.

Biddy the Clap – One immediately observes that he is of patrician lineage.

The Virago – Green above the red, says he. Wolfe Tone.

The Bawd – The red's as good as the green. And better. Up the soldiers! Up King Edward!

A Rough (*laughs*) – Ay! Hands up to De Wet.

The Citizen, with a huge emerald muffler and shillelagh, calls.

The Citizen
— *May the God above*
 Send down a dove
 With teeth as sharp as razors
 To slit the throats
 Of the English dogs
 That hanged our Irish leaders.

The Croppy Boy, the ropenoose round his neck, gripes in his issuing bowels with both hands.

The Croppy Boy
— *I bear no hate to a living thing,*
 But I love my country beyond the king.

Rumbold, Demon Barber (*accompanied by two black-masked assistants, advances with Gladstone bag which he opens*) – Ladies and gents, cleaver purchased by Mrs Pearcey to slay Hogg. Knife with which Voisin dismem-bered the wife of a compatriot and hid remains in a sheet in the cellar, the unfortunate female's throat being cut from ear to ear. Phial containing arsenic retrieved from the body of Miss Barrow which sent Seddon to the gallows.

He jerks the rope. The assistants leap at the victim's legs and drag him downward, grunting. The croppy boy's tongue protrudes violently.

The Croppy Boy
– *Horhot ho hray hor hother's hest.*

He gives up the ghost. A violent erection of the hanged sends gouts of sperm spouting through his deathclothes onto the cobblestones. Mrs Bellingham, Mrs Yelverton Barry and the Honourable Mrs Mervyn Talboys rush forward with their handkerchiefs to sop it up.

Rumbold – I'm near it myself. (*He undoes the noose.*) Rope which hanged the awful rebel. Ten shillings a time. As supplied to Her Royal Highness. (*He plunges his head into the gaping belly of the hanged and draws out his head again clotted with coiled and smoking entrails.*) My painful duty has now been done. God save the king!

Edward the Seventh dances slowly, solemnly, rattling his bucket, and sings with soft contentment.

Edward the Seventh
– *On Coronation Day, on Coronation Day,*
  O, won't we have a merry time,
  Drinking whisky, beer and wine!
Private Carr – Here. What are you saying about my king?
Stephen (*throws up his hands*) – O, this is too monotonous! Nothing. He wants my money and my life, though want must be his master, for some brutish empire of his. Money I haven't. (*He searches his pockets vaguely.*) Gave it to someone.
Private Carr – Who wants your bleeding money?
Stephen (*tries to move off*) – Will someone tell me where I am least likely to meet these necessary evils? *Ça se voit aussi à Paris.* Not that I . . . But, by Saint Patrick . . . !

The women's heads coalesce. Old Gummy Granny appears, in sugarloaf

516

hat, seated on a toadstool, the deathflower of the potato blight on her breast.

Stephen – Aha! I know you, gammer! Hamlet, revenge! The old sow that eats her farrow!

Old Gummy Granny (*rocking to and fro*) – Ireland's sweetheart, the king of Spain's daughter, alanna. Strangers in my house, bad manners to them! (*She keens with banshee woe.*) Ochone! Ochone! Silk of the kine! (*She wails.*) You met with poor old Ireland and how does she stand?

Stephen – How do I stand you? The hat trick! Where's the third person of the Blessed Trinity? Soggarth Aroon? The Reverend Carrion Crow.

Cissy Caffrey (*shrill*) – Stop them from fighting!

A Rough – Our men retreated.

Private Carr (*tugging at his belt*) – I'll wring the neck of any fucker says a word against my fucking king.

Bloom (*terrified*) – He said nothing. Not a word. A pure misunderstanding.

Private Compton – Go it, Harry. Do him one in the eye. He's a pro-Boer.

Stephen – Did I? When?

Bloom (*to the redcoats*) – We fought for you in South Africa, Irish missile troops. Isn't that history? Royal Dublin Fusiliers. Honoured by our monarch.

The Navvy (*staggering past*) – O, yes! O God, yes! O, make the kwawr a krowawr! O! Bo!

Casqued halberdiers in armour thrust forward a pentice of gutted spearpoints. Major Tweedy, moustached like Turko the Terrible, in bearskin cap with hackle plume and accoutrements, with epaulettes, gilt chevrons and sabretaches, his breast bright with medals, toes the line. He gives the pilgrim warrior's sign of the Knights Templars.

Major Tweedy (*growls gruffly*) – Rorke's Drift! Up, guards, and at them! *Maher shalal hashbaz.*

The Citizen – *Erin go bragh!*

Major Tweedy and the Citizen exhibit to each other medals, decorations, trophies of war, wounds. Both salute with fierce hostility.

Private Carr – I'll do him in.

Private Compton (*moves the crowd back*) – Fair play, here. Make a bleeding butcher's shop of the bugger.

Massed bands blare *Garryowen* and *God Save the King*.

Cissy Caffrey – They're going to fight. For me!

Cunty Kate – The brave and the fair.

Biddy the Clap – Methinks yon sable knight will joust it with the best.

Cunty Kate (*blushing deeply*) – Nay, madam. The gules doublet and merry Saint George for me!

Stephen

– *The harlot's cry from street to street*
  Shall weave old Ireland's winding sheet.

Private Carr (*loosening his belt, shouts*) – I'll wring the neck of any fucking bastard says a word against my bleeding fucking king.

Bloom (*shakes Cissy Caffrey's shoulders*) – Speak, you! Are you struck dumb? You are the link between nations and generations. Speak, woman, sacred life-giver!

Cissy Caffrey (*alarmed, seizes Private Carr's sleeve*) – Amn't I with you? Amn't I your girl? Cissy's your girl. (*She cries.*) Police!

Stephen (*ecstatically, to Cissy Caffrey*)

– *White thy fambles, red thy gan*
  And thy quarrons dainty is.

Voices – Police!

Distant Voices – Dublin's burning! Dublin's burning! On fire, on fire!

Brimstone fires spring up. Dense clouds roll past. Heavy Gatling guns boom. Pandemonium. Troops deploy. Gallop of hoofs. Artillery. Hoarse commands. Bells clang. Backers shout. Drunkards bawl. Whores screech. Foghorns hoot. Cries of valour. Shrieks of dying. Pikes clash on cuirasses. Thieves rob the slain. Birds of prey, winging from the sea, rising from marshlands, swooping from eyries, hover screaming: gannets, cormorants, vultures, goshawks, climbing woodcocks, peregrines, merlins, black-grouse, sea eagles, gulls, albatrosses, barnacle geese. The midnight sun is darkened. The earth trembles. The dead of Dublin from Prospect and Mount Jerome, in white sheepskin overcoats and black goatfell cloaks, arise and appear to many. A chasm opens with a noiseless yawn. Tom Rochford, winner, in athlete's singlet and breeches, arrives at the head of the national hurdle handicap and leaps into the void. He is followed by a race of runners and leapers. In wild attitudes they spring from the brink. Their bodies plunge. Factory lasses with fancy clothes toss red-hot Yorkshire baraabombs. Society ladies lift their skirts above their heads to protect themselves. Laughing witches in red cutty sarks ride through the air on broomsticks. Quakerlyster plasters blisters. It rains dragons' teeth. Armed heroes spring up from furrows. They exchange in amity the pass of Knights of the Red Cross and fight duels with cavalry sabres: Wolfe Tone against Henry Grattan, Smith O'Brien against Daniel O'Connell, Michael Davitt against Isaac Butt, Justin McCarthy against Parnell, Arthur Griffith against John Redmond, John O'Leary against Lear O'Johnny, Lord Edward Fitzgerald against Lord Gerald Fitzedward, the O'Donoghue of the Glens against the Glens of the O'Donoghue. On an eminence, the centre of the earth, rises the field altar of Saint Barbara. Black candles rise from its gospel and epistle horns. From the high barbicans of the tower two shafts of light fall on the smoke-palled altarstone. On the altarstone Mrs Mina Purefoy, goddess of unreason, lies naked, fettered, a chalice resting on her swollen belly. Father Malachi O'Flynn, in a lace petticoat and reversed chasuble, his two left feet back to the front, celebrates camp mass. The Reverend Mr Hugh C. Haines Love M.A., in a plain cassock and mortarboard, his head and collar back to the front, holds over the celebrant's head an open umbrella.

Father Malachi O'Flynn – *Introibo ad altare diaboli.*
The Reverend Mr Haines Love – To the devil which hath made glad my young days.
Father Malachi O'Flynn (*takes from the chalice and elevates a blood-dripping host*) – *Corpus meum.*
The Reverend Mr Haines Love (*raises high behind the celebrant's petticoat, revealing his grey bare hairy buttocks between which a carrot is stuck*) – My body.
The Voice of all the Damned – Htengier Tnetopinmo Dog Drol eht rof, Aiulella!

From on high the voice of Adonai calls.

Adonai – Dooooooooooog!
The Voice of all the Blessed – Alleluia, for the Lord God Omnipotent reigneth!

From on high the voice of Adonai calls.

Adonai – Goooooooooood!

In strident discord, peasants and townsmen of Orange and Green factions sing *Kick the Pope* and *Daily, Daily Sing to Mary.*

Private Carr (*with ferocious articulation*) – I'll do him in, so help me fucking Christ! I'll wring the bastard fucker's bleeding blasted fucking windpipe!

The retriever, nosing on the fringe of the crowd, barks noisily.

Bloom (*runs to Lynch*) – Can't you get him away?
Lynch – He likes dialectic, the universal language. Kitty! (*To Bloom*) Get him away, you. He won't listen to me.

He drags Kitty away.

Stephen (*points*) – Exit Judas. *Et laqueo se suspendit.*
Bloom (*runs to Stephen*) – Come along with me now before worse happens. Here's your stick.
Stephen – Stick, no. Reason. This feast of pure reason.
Old Gummy Granny (*thrusts a dagger towards Stephen's hand*) Remove him, acushla. At 8.35 a.m. you will be in heaven and Ireland will be free. (*She prays.*) O good God, take him!
Cissy Caffrey (*pulling Private Carr*) – Come on, you're boozed. He insulted me but I forgive him. (*Shouting in his ear*) I forgive him for insulting me.
Bloom (*over Stephen's shoulder*) – Yes, go. You see he's incapable.
Private Carr (*breaks loose*) – I'll insult him.

He rushes towards Stephen, fist outstretched, and strikes him in the face. Stephen totters, collapses, falls, stunned. He lies prone, his face to the sky, his hat rolling to the wall. Bloom follows and picks it up.

Major Tweedy (*loudly*) – Carbine in bucket! Cease fire! Salute!
The Retriever (*barking furiously*) – Ute ute ute ute ute ute ute ute.
The Crowd – Let him up! Don't strike him when he's down! Air! Who?

The soldier hit him. He's a professor. Is he hurted? Don't manhandle him! He's fainted!

A Hag – What call had the redcoat to strike the gentleman and he under the influence? Let them go and fight the Boers!

The Bawd – Listen to who's talking! Hasn't the soldier a right to go with his girl? He gave him the coward's blow.

They grab at each other's hair, claw at each other and spit.

The Retriever (*barking*) – Wow wow wow.

Bloom shoves them back.

Bloom (*loudly*) – Get back, stand back!

Private Compton (*tugging his comrade*) – Here. Bugger off, Harry. Here's the cops!

Two raincaped watch, tall, stand in the group.

First Watch – What's wrong here?

Private Compton – We were with this lady. And he insulted us. And assaulted my chum. (*The retriever barks.*) Who owns the bleeding tyke?

Cissy Caffrey (*with expectation*) – Is he bleeding?

A Man (*rising from his knees*) – No. Gone off. He'll come to all right.

Bloom (*glances sharply at the man*) – Leave him to me. I can easily . . .

Second Watch – Who are you? Do you know him?

Private Carr (*lurches towards the watch*) – He insulted my lady friend.

Bloom (*angrily*) – You hit him without provocation. I'm a witness. Constable, take his regimental number.

Second Watch – I don't want your instructions in the discharge of my duty.

Private Compton (*pulling his comrade*) – Here. Bugger off, Harry. Or Bennett'll shove you in the lockup.

Private Carr (*staggering as he is pulled away*) – God fuck old Bennett. He's a white-arsed bugger. I don't give a shit for him.

First Watch (*takes out his notebook*) – What's his name?

Bloom (*peering over the crowd*) – I just see a car there. If you give me a hand a second, sergeant . . .

First Watch – Name and address.

Corny Kelleher, weepers round his hat, a death wreath in his hand, appears among the bystanders.

Bloom (*quickly*) – O, the very man! (*He whispers.*) Simon Dedalus's son. A bit sprung. Get those policemen to move those loafers back.
Second Watch – Night, Mr Kelleher.
Corny Kelleher (*to the watch, with drawling eye*) – That's all right. I know him. Won a bit on the races. Gold Cup. *Throwaway.* (*He laughs.*) Twenty to one. Do you follow me?
First Watch (*turns to the crowd*) – Here, what are you all gaping at? Move on out of that.

The crowd disperses slowly, muttering, down the lane.

Corny Kelleher – Leave it to me, sergeant. That'll be all right. (*He laughs, shaking his head.*) We were often as bad ourselves, ay, or worse. What, eh, what?
First Watch (*laughs*) – I suppose so.
Corny Kelleher (*nudges the second watch*) – Come and wipe your name off the slate. (*He lilts, wagging his head.*) With my tooraloom tooraloom tooraloom tooraloom. What, eh, do you follow me?
Second Watch (*genially*) – Ah, sure, we were too.
Corny Kelleher (*winking*) – Boys will be boys. I've a car round there.
Second Watch – All right, Mr Kelleher. Good night.
Corny Kelleher – I'll see to that.
Bloom (*shakes hands with both of the watch in turn*) – Thank you very much, gentlemen. Thank you. (*He mumbles confidentially.*) We don't want any scandal, you understand. Father is a well-known highly respected citizen. Just a little wild oats, you understand.
First Watch – O, I understand, sir.
Second Watch – That's all right, sir.
First Watch – It was only in case of corporal injuries I'd have had to report it at the station.
Bloom (*nods rapidly*) – Naturally. Quite right. Only your bounden duty.
Second Watch – It's our duty.
Corny Kelleher – Good night, men.
The Watch (*saluting together*) – Night, gentlemen.

They move off with slow heavy tread.

Bloom (*blows*) – Providential you came on the scene. You have a car…?

Corny Kelleher (*laughs, pointing his thumb over his right shoulder to the car brought up against the scaffolding*) – Two commercials that were standing fizz in Jammet's. Like princes, faith. One of them lost two quid on the race. Drowning his grief. And were on for a go with the jolly girls. So I landed them up on Behan's car and down to nighttown.

Bloom – I was just going home by Gardiner Street when I happened to…

Corny Kelleher (*laughs*) – Sure they wanted me to join in with the mots. No, by God, says I. Not for old stagers like myself and yourself. (*He laughs again and leers with lacklustre eye.*) Thanks be to God we have it in the house, what, eh, do you follow me? Hah hah hah!

Bloom (*tries to laugh*) – He he he! Yes. Matter of fact I was just visiting an old friend of mine there, Virag, you don't know him, poor fellow, he's laid up for the past week, and we had a liqueur together and I was just making my way home…

The horse neighs.

The Horse – Hohohohohohoh! Hohohohome!

Corny Kelleher – Sure it was Behan our jarvey there that told me after we left the two commercials in Mrs Cohen's and I told him to pull up. And got off to see. (*He laughs.*) Sober hearsedrivers a speciality. Will I give him a lift home? Where does he hang out? Somewhere in Cabra, what?

Bloom – No, in Sandycove, I believe, from what he let drop.

Stephen, prone, breathes to the stars. Corny Kelleher, asquint, drawls at the horse. Bloom, in gloom, looms down.

Corny Kelleher (*scratches his nape*) – Sandycove! (*He bends down and calls to Stephen.*) Eh! (*He calls again.*) Eh! He's covered with shavings anyhow. Take care they didn't lift anything off him.

Bloom – No, no, no. I have his money and his hat here and stick.

Corny Kelleher – Ah well, he'll get over it. No bones broken. Well, I'll shove along. (*He laughs.*) I've a rendezvous in the morning. Burying the dead. Safe home!

The Horse (*neighs*) – Hohohohohome.
Bloom – Good night. I'll just wait and take him along in a few . . .

Corny Kelleher returns to the outside car and mounts it. The horseharness jingles.

Corny Kelleher (*from the car, standing*) – Night.
Bloom – Night.

The jarvey chucks the reins and raises his whip encouragingly. The car and horse back slowly, awkwardly, and turn. Corny Kelleher on the sideseat sways his head to and fro in sign of mirth at Bloom's plight. The jarvey joins in the mute pantomimic merriment, nodding from the farther seat. Bloom shakes his head in mute mirthful reply. With thumb and palm Corny Kelleher reassures that the two bobbies will allow the sleep to continue, for what else is to be done. With a slow nod Bloom conveys his gratitude, as that is exactly what Stephen needs. The car jingles tooraloom round the corner of the tooraloom lane. Corny Kelleher again reassuralooms with his hand. Bloom with his hand assuralooms Corny Kelleher that he is reassuraloomtay. The tinkling hoofs and jingling harness grow fainter with their tooralooloo looloo lay. Bloom, holding in his hand Stephen's hat, festooned with shavings, and ashplant, stands irresolute. Then he bends to him and shakes him by the shoulder.

Bloom – Eh! Ho! (*There is no answer. He bends again.*) Mr Dedalus! (*There is no answer.*) The name if you call. Somnambulist. (*He bends again and, hesitating, brings his mouth near the face of the prostrate form.*) Stephen! (*There is no answer. He calls again.*) Stephen!
Stephen (*frowns*) – Who? Black panther. Vampire.

He sighs and stretches himself, then murmurs thickly with prolonged vowels.

Stephen
– *Who . . . drive . . . Fergus now*
  And pierce . . . wood's woven shade . . .

He turns on his left side, sighing, doubling himself together.

Bloom – Poetry. Well educated. Pity. (*He bends again and undoes the buttons of Stephen's waistcoat.*) To breathe. (*He brushes the wood shavings from Stephen's clothes with light hand and fingers.*) One pound seven. Not hurt anyhow. (*He listens.*) What?

Stephen (*murmurs*)
– ... *shadows ... the woods*
  ... *white breast ... dim sea.*

He stretches out his arms, sighs again, and curls his body. Bloom, holding the hat and ashplant, stands erect. A dog barks in the distance. Bloom tightens and loosens his grip on the ashplant. He looks down on Stephen's face and form.

Bloom (*communes with the night*) – Face reminds me of his poor mother. In the shady wood. The deep white breast. Ferguson, I think I caught. A girl. Some girl. Best thing could happen him. (*He murmurs.*) ... swear that I will always hail, ever conceal, never reveal, any part or parts, art or arts ... (*He murmurs.*) ... in the rough sands of the sea ... a cabletow's length from the shore ... where the tide ebbs ... and flows ...

Silent, thoughtful, alert, he stands on guard, his fingers at his lips in the attitude of secret master. Against the dark wall a figure appears slowly, a fairy boy of eleven, a changeling, kidnapped, dressed in an Eton suit, with glass shoes and a little bronze helmet, holding a book in his hand. He reads from right to left inaudibly, smiling, kissing the page.

Bloom (*wonderstruck, calls inaudibly*) – Rudy!

Rudy gazes, unseeing, into Bloom's eyes and goes on reading, kissing, smiling. He has a delicate mauve face. On his suit he has diamond and ruby buttons. In his free left hand he holds a slim ivory cane with a violet bowknot. A white lambkin peeps out of his waistcoat pocket.

Part III

PREPARATORY to anything else Mr Bloom brushed off the greater bulk of the shavings and handed Stephen the hat and ashplant and bucked him up generally in orthodox Samaritan fashion, which he very badly needed. His (Stephen's) mind was not exactly what you would call wandering but a bit unsteady and on his expressed desire for some beverage to drink Mr Bloom, in view of the hour it was and there being no pump of Vartry water available for their ablutions, let alone drinking purposes, hit upon an expedient by suggesting, off the reel, the propriety of the cabman's shelter, as it was called, hardly a stone's throw away near Butt Bridge where they might hit upon some drinkables in the shape of a milk and soda or a mineral. But how to get there was the rub. For the nonce he was rather nonplussed but inasmuch as the duty plainly devolved upon him to take some measures on the subject he pondered suitable ways and means during which Stephen repeatedly yawned. So far as he could see he was rather pale in the face so that it occurred to him as highly advisable to get a conveyance of some description which would answer in their then condition, both of them being e.d.ed, particularly Stephen, always assuming that there was such a thing to be found. Accordingly, after a few such preliminaries as brushing, in spite of his having forgotten to take up his rather soapsudsy handkerchief after it had done yeoman service in the shaving line, they both walked together along Beaver Street or, more properly, Lane as far as the farrier's and the distinctly fetid atmosphere of the livery stables at the corner of Montgomery Street where they made tracks to the left, from thence debouching into Amiens Street round by the corner of Dan Bergin's. But, as he confidently anticipated, there was not a sign of a Jehu plying for hire anywhere to be seen except a four-wheeler, probably engaged by some fellows inside on the spree, outside the North Star Hotel and there was no symptom of its budging a quarter of an inch when Mr Bloom, who was anything but a professional whistler, endeavoured to hail it by emitting a kind of a whistle, holding his arms arched over his head, twice.

This was a quandary but, bringing common sense to bear on it, evidently there was nothing for it but put a good face on the matter and foot it, which they accordingly did. So, bevelling around by Mullett's and the Signal House, which they shortly reached, they proceeded perforce in the direction of Amiens Street railway terminus, Mr Bloom being handicapped by the circumstance that one of the back buttons of his trousers had, to vary the time-honoured adage, gone the way of all buttons, though, entering thoroughly into the spirit of the thing, he heroically made light of the mischance. So as neither of them were particularly pressed for time, as it happened, and the temperature refreshing since it cleared up after the recent visitation of Jupiter Pluvius, they dandered along past by where the empty vehicle was waiting without a fare or a jarvey. As it so happened a Dublin United Tramways Company's sand-strewer happening to be returning the elder man recounted to his companion apropos of the incident his own truly miraculous escape of some little while back. They passed the main entrance of the Great Northern railway station, the starting point for Belfast, where of course all traffic was suspended at that late hour, and, passing the back door of the morgue (a not very enticing locality, not to say gruesome to a degree, more especially at night), ultimately gained the Dock Tavern and in due course turned into Store Street, famous for its C Division police station. Between this point and the high, at present unlit, warehouses of Beresford Place Stephen thought to think of Ibsen, associated in his mind somehow with Baird's the stonecutter's in Talbot Place, first turning on the right, while the other who was acting as his *fidus Achates* inhaled with internal satisfaction the smell of James Rourke's City Bakery, situated quite close to where they were, the very palatable odour indeed of our daily bread, of all commodities of the public the primary and most indispensable. Bread, the staff of life, earn your bread. *O, tell me where is fancy bread? At Rourke's the baker's, it is said.*

En route, to his taciturn and, not to put too fine a point on it, not yet perfectly sober companion, Mr Bloom, who at all events was in complete possession of his faculties, never more so, in fact disgustingly sober, spoke a word of caution re the dangers of nighttown, women of ill fame and swell mobsmen, which, barely permissible once in a while, though not as a habitual practice, was of the nature of a regular deathtrap for young fellows of his age, particularly if they had acquired drinking habits, under the influence of liquor unless you knew a little jiujitsu for every contingency as even a fellow on the broad of his back could administer a nasty kick if you didn't look out. Highly providential was the appearance on the scene of Corny Kelleher when Stephen was blissfully unconscious. But for that man in the gap turning up at the eleventh hour the finis might have been that he might have been a candidate for the accident ward or, failing that, the Bridewell and an appearance in the court next day before Mr Tobias or, he being the solicitor rather, old Wall he meant to say or Mahony, which simply spelt ruin for a chap when it got bruited about. The reason he mentioned the fact was that a lot of those policemen, whom he cordially disliked, were admittedly unscrupulous in the service of the Crown and, as Mr Bloom put it, recalling a case or two in the A Division in Clanbrassil Street, prepared to swear a hole through a ten-gallon pot. Never on the spot when wanted, but in quiet parts of the city, Pembroke Road for example, the guardians of the law were well in evidence, the obvious reason being they were paid to protect the upper classes. Another thing he commented on was equipping soldiers with firearms or sidearms of any description, liable to go off at any time, which was tantamount to inciting them against civilians should by any chance they fall out over anything. You frittered away your time, he very sensibly maintained, and health and also character. Besides which, the squander-mania of the thing, fast women of the demimonde ran away with a lot of £ *s.d.* into the bargain and the greatest danger of all was who you got drunk with though, touching the much vexed question of stimulants, he relished a glass of choice old wine in season as both nourishing and bloodmaking and possessing aperient virtues (notably a good burgundy which he was a staunch believer in) still never beyond a certain point where he invariably drew the line as it simply led to trouble all round to say nothing of your being at the tender mercy of others practically. Most of all he commented adversely on the desertion of Stephen by all his pub-hunting confrères but one, a most glaring piece of ratting on the part of his brother medicos under all the circs.

– And that one was Judas, Stephen said, who up to then had said nothing whatsoever of any kind.

Discussing these and kindred topics they made a beeline across the back of the Custom House and passed under the Loop Line Bridge where a brazier of coke burning in front of a sentrybox, or something like one, attracted their rather lagging footsteps. Stephen of his own accord stopped for no special reason to look at the heap of barren cobblestones and by the light emanating from the brazier he could just make out the darker figure of the Corporation watchman inside the gloom of the sentrybox. He began to remember that this had happened or had been mentioned as having happened before but it cost him no small effort before he remembered that he recognised in the sentry a quondam friend of his father's, Gumley. To avoid a meeting he drew nearer to the pillars of the railway bridge.

— Someone saluted you, Mr Bloom said.

A figure of middle height on the prowl, evidently, under the arches saluted again, calling:

— Night!

Stephen of course started rather dizzily and stopped to return the compliment. Mr Bloom, actuated by motives of inherent delicacy inasmuch as he always believed in minding his own business, moved off, but nevertheless remained on the *qui vive* with just a shade of anxiety though not funkyish in the least. Although unusual in the Dublin area, he knew that it was not by any means unknown for desperadoes who had next to nothing to live on to be abroad waylaying and generally terrorising peaceable pedestrians by placing a pistol at their head in some secluded spot outside the city proper, famished loiterers of the Thames Embankment category they might be hanging about there or simply marauders ready to decamp with whatever boodle they could in one fell swoop at a moment's notice, your money or your life, leaving you there to point a moral, gagged and garrotted.

Stephen, that is when the accosting figure came to close quarters, though he was not in an oversober state himself, recognised Corley's breath redolent of rotten cornjuice. Lord John Corley some called him and his genealogy came about in this wise. He was the eldest son of Inspector Corley of the G Division, lately deceased, who had married a certain Katherine Brophy, the daughter of a Louth farmer. His grandfather, Patrick Michael Corley of New Ross, had married the widow of a publican there whose maiden name had been Katherine (also) Talbot. Rumour had it, though not proved, that she descended from the house of the Lords Talbot de Malahide, in whose mansion, really an unquestionably fine residence of its kind and well worth seeing, her mother or aunt or some relative, a woman, as the tale went, of extreme beauty, had enjoyed the distinction of being in service in the washkitchen. This, therefore, was the reason why the still comparatively young though dissolute man who now addressed Stephen was spoken of by some with facetious proclivities as Lord John Corley.

Taking Stephen on one side he had the customary doleful ditty to tell. Not as much as a farthing to purchase a night's lodgings. His friends had all deserted him. Furthermore, he had a row with Lenehan and called him to Stephen a mean bloody swab with a sprinkling of a number of other uncalled-for expressions. He was out of a job and implored of Stephen to tell him where on God's earth he could get something, anything at all, to do. No, it was the daughter of the mother in the washkitchen that was foster sister to the heir of the house or else they were connected through the mother in some way, both occurrences happening at the same time if the whole thing wasn't a complete fabrication from start to finish. Anyhow, he was all in.

— I wouldn't ask you, only, pursued he, on my solemn oath and God knows I'm on the rocks.

— There'll be a job tomorrow or the next day, Stephen told him, in a boys' school at Dalkey for a gentleman usher. Mr Garrett Deasy. Try it. You may mention my name.

— Ah, God, Corley replied, sure I couldn't teach in a school, man. I was never one of your bright ones, he added with a half laugh. I got stuck twice in the junior at the Christian Brothers.

— I have no place to sleep myself, Stephen informed him.

Corley, at the first go-off, was inclined to suspect it was something to do with Stephen being fired out of his digs for bringing in a bloody tart off the street. There was a dosshouse in Marlborough Street, Mrs Maloney's, but it was only a tanner touch and full of undesirables but M'Conachie told him you got a decent enough do in the Brazen Head over in Bridge Street (which was distantly suggestive to the person addressed of Friar Bacon) for a bob. He was starving too though he hadn't said a word about it.

Though this sort of thing went on every other night or very near it, still Stephen's feelings got the better of him in a sense though he knew that Corley's brand-new rigmarole, on a par with the others, was hardly deserving of much credence. However, *haud ignarus malorum miseris succurrere disco* et cetera, as the Latin poet remarks, especially as luck would have it he got paid his screw after every middle of the month on the sixteenth which was the date of the month as a matter of fact though a good bit of the wherewithal was demolished. But the cream of the joke was nothing would get it out of Corley's head that he was living in affluence and hadn't a thing to do but hand out the needful whereas ... He put his hand in a pocket anyhow, not with the idea of finding any food there but thinking he might lend him anything up to a bob or so in lieu so that he might endeavour at all events to get sufficient to eat, but the result was in the negative for, to his chagrin, he found his cash missing. A few broken biscuits were all the result of his investigation. He tried his hardest to recollect for the moment whether he had lost, as well he might have, or left, because in that contingency it was not a pleasant lookout, very much the reverse in fact. He was altogether too fagged out to institute a thorough search though he tried to recollect. About biscuits he dimly remembered. Who now exactly gave them, he wondered, or where was … or did he buy …? However, in another pocket he came across what he surmised in the dark were pennies, erroneously, however, as it turned out.

– Those are half crowns, man, Corley corrected him.

And so in point of fact they turned out to be. Stephen anyhow lent him one of them.

– Thanks, Corley answered, you're a gentleman. I'll pay you back some time. Who's that with you? I saw him a few times in the Bleeding Horse in Camden Street with Boylan the billsticker. You might put in a good word for us to get me taken on there. I'd carry a sandwich board only the girl in the office told me they're full up for the next three weeks, man. God, you've to book ahead, man, you'd think it was for the Carl Rosa. I don't give a shite anyway so long as I get a job, even as a crossing sweeper.

Subsequently, being not quite so down in the mouth after the two and six he got, he informed Stephen about a fellow by the name of Bags Comisky, that he said Stephen knew well, out of Fullam's, the ship chandler's, bookkeeper there, that used to be often round in Nagle's back with O'Mara and a little chap with a stutter the name of Tighe. Anyhow, he was lagged the night before last and fined ten bob for a drunk and disorderly and refusing to go with the constable.

Mr Bloom in the meanwhile kept dodging about in the vicinity of the cobblestones near the brazier of coke in front of the Corporation watchman's sentrybox, who, evidently a glutton for work, it struck him, was having a quiet forty winks for all intents and purposes on his own private account while Dublin slept. He threw an odd eye at the same time now and then at Stephen's anything but immaculately attired interlocutor as if he had seen that nobleman somewhere or other though where he was not in a position to truthfully state nor had he the remotest idea when. Being a levelheaded individual who could give points to not a few in point of shrewd observation, he also remarked on his very dilapidated hat and slouchy wearing apparel, generally testifying to a chronic impecuniosity. Palpably he was one of his hangers-on, but for the matter of that it was merely a question of one preying on his next-door neighbour all round. In every deep, so to put it, a deeper depth. And for the matter of that if the man in the street chanced to be in the dock himself penal servitude, with or without the option of a fine, would be a very *rara avis* altogether. In any case he had a consummate amount of cool assurance intercepting people at that hour of the night or morning. Pretty thick that was certainly.

The pair parted company and Stephen rejoined Mr Bloom who, with his practised eye, was not without perceiving that he had succumbed to the blandiloquence of the other parasite. Alluding to the encounter he said, laughingly, Stephen, that is:

— He's down on his luck. He asked me to ask you to ask somebody named Boylan, a billsticker, to give him a job as a sandwich man.

At this intelligence, in which he seemingly evinced little interest, Mr Bloom gazed abstractedly for the space of half a second or so in the direction of a bucket dredger, rejoicing in the far-famed name of Eblana, moored alongside Custom House Quay and quite possibly out of repair, whereupon he observed evasively:

— Everybody gets their own ration of luck, they say. Now you mention it, his face was familiar to me. But leaving that for the moment, how much did you part with, he queried, if I am not too inquisitive?

— Half a crown, Stephen responded. I daresay he needs it to sleep somewhere.

— Needs! Mr Bloom ejaculated, professing not the least surprise at the intelligence. I can quite credit the assertion and I guarantee he invariably does. Everyone according to his needs and everyone according to his deeds. But, talking about things in general, where, added he with a smile, will you sleep yourself? Walking to Sandycove is out of the question and, even supposing you did, you won't get in after what occurred at Westland Row station. Simply fag out there for nothing. I don't mean to presume to dictate to you in the slightest degree but why did you leave your father's house?

— To seek misfortune, was Stephen's answer.

— I met your respected father on a recent occasion, Mr Bloom diplomatically returned. Today, in fact, or, to be strictly accurate, on yesterday. Where does he live at present? I gathered in the course of conversation that he had moved.

— I believe he is in Dublin somewhere, Stephen answered unconcernedly. Why?

— A gifted man, Mr Bloom said of Mr Dedalus senior, in more respects than one and a born *raconteur* if ever there was one. He takes great pride, quite legitimate, out of you. You could go back, perhaps, he hazarded, still thinking of the very unpleasant scene at Westland Row terminus when it was perfectly evident that the other two, Mulligan, that is, and that English tourist friend of his, who eventually euchred their third companion, were patently trying, as if the whole bally station belonged to them, to give Stephen the slip in the confusion, which they did.

There was no response forthcoming to the suggestion however, such as it was, Stephen's mind's eye being too busily engaged in repicturing his family hearth the last time he saw it, with his sister Dilly sitting by the ingle, her hair hanging down, waiting for some weak Trinidad shell cocoa that was in the soot-coated kettle to be done so that she and he could drink it with the oatmeal water for milk after the Friday herrings they had eaten at two a penny, with an egg apiece for Maggy, Boody and Katey, the cat meanwhile under the mangle devouring a mess of eggshells and charred fish heads and bones on a square of brown paper, in accordance with the third precept of the Church to fast and abstain on the days commanded, it being quarter tense or, if not, ember days or something like that.

— No, Mr Bloom repeated again, I wouldn't personally repose much trust in that boon companion of yours who contributes the humorous element, Dr Mulligan, as a guide, philosopher and friend, if I were in your shoes. He knows which side his bread is buttered on though in all probability he never realised what it is to be without regular meals. Of course you didn't notice as much as I did, but it wouldn't occasion me the least surprise to learn that a pinch of tobacco or some narcotic was put in your drink for some ulterior object.

He understood, however, from all he heard, that Dr Mulligan was a versatile all-round man, by no means confined to medicine only, who was rapidly coming to the fore in his line and, if the report was verified, bade fair to enjoy a flourishing practice in the not too distant future as a tony medical practitioner drawing a handsome fee for his services in addition to which professional status his rescue of that man from certain drowning by artificial respiration and what they call first aid at Skerries, or Malahide was it, was, he was bound to admit, an exceedingly plucky deed which he could not too highly praise, so that frankly he was utterly at a loss to fathom what earthly reason could be at the back of it except he put it down to sheer cussedness or jealousy, pure and simple.

– Except it simply amounts to one thing and he is what they call picking your brains, he ventured to throw out.

The guarded glance of half solicitude half curiosity augmented by friendliness which he gave at Stephen's at present morose expression of features did not throw a flood of light, none at all in fact, on the problem as to whether he had let himself be badly bamboozled, to judge by two or three low-spirited remarks he let drop, or, the other way about, saw through the affair and, for some reason or other best known to himself, allowed matters to more or less ... Grinding poverty did have that effect and he more than conjectured that, high educational abilities though he possessed, he experienced no little difficulty in making both ends meet.

Adjacent to the men's public urinal they perceived an ice-cream car round which a group of presumably Italians in heated altercation were getting rid of voluble expressions in their vivacious language in a particularly animated way, there being some little differences between the parties.

– *Puttana Madonna, che ci dia i quattrini! Ho ragione? Culo rotto!*
– *Intendiamoci. Mezzo sovrano più ...*
– *Dice lui, però!*
– *Mezzo.*
– *Farabutto! Mortacci sui!*
– *Ma ascolta! Cinque la testa più ...*

Mr Bloom and Stephen entered the cabman's shelter, an unpretentious wooden structure, where, prior to then, the former had rarely if ever been before, he having previously whispered to the latter a few hints anent the keeper of it, said to be the once famous Skin-the-Goat, Fitzharris, the Invincible, though he wouldn't vouch for the actual facts which quite possibly there was not one vestige of truth in. A few moments later saw our two noctambules safely seated in a discreet corner only to be greeted by stares from the decidedly miscellaneous collection of waifs and strays and other nondescript specimens of the genus *Homo* already there engaged in eating and drinking diversified by conversation for whom they seemingly formed an object of marked curiosity.

– Now, touching a cup of coffee, Mr Bloom ventured to plausibly suggest to break the ice, it occurs to me you ought to sample something in the shape of solid food, say a roll of some description.

Accordingly his first act was with characteristic sangfroid to order these commodities quietly. The hoi polloi of jarvies or stevedores, or whatever they were, after a cursory examination turned their eyes, apparently dissatisfied, away, though one red-bearded bibulous individual, a portion of whose hair was greyish, a sailor probably, still stared for some appreciable time before transferring his rapt attention to the floor.

Mr Bloom, availing himself of the right of free speech, he having just a bowing acquaintance with the language in dispute, though, to be sure, rather in a quandary over *voglio*, remarked to his protégé in an audible tone of voice apropos of the battle royal in the street which was still raging fast and furious:

— A beautiful language. I mean for singing purposes. Why do you not write your poetry in that language? *Bella Poetria!* It is so melodious and full. *Belladonna. Voglio.*

Stephen, who was trying his dead best to yawn, if he could, suffering from lassitude generally, replied:

— To fill the ear of a cow elephant. They were haggling over money.

— Is that so? Mr Bloom asked. Of course, he subjoined pensively at the inward reflection of there being more languages to start with than were absolutely necessary, it may be only the southern glamour that surrounds it.

The keeper of the shelter in the middle of this tête-à-tête put a boiling swimming cup of a choice concoction labelled coffee on the table and a rather antediluvian specimen of a bun, or so it seemed, after which he beat a retreat to his counter, Mr Bloom determining to have a good square look at him later on so as not to appear to … for which reason he encouraged Stephen to proceed with his eyes while he did the honours by surreptitiously pushing the cup of what was temporarily supposed to be called coffee gradually nearer him.

— Sounds are impostures, Stephen said after a pause of some little time. Like names. Cicero, Podmore. Napoleon, Mr Goodbody. Jesus, Mr Doyle. Shakespeares were as common as Murphies. What's in a name?

— Yes, to be sure, Mr Bloom unaffectedly concurred. Of course. Our name was changed too, he added, pushing the so-called roll across.

The red-bearded sailor, who had his weather eye on the newcomers, boarded Stephen, whom he had singled out for attention in particular, squarely by asking:

— And what might your name be?

Just in the nick of time Mr Bloom touched his companion's boot but Stephen, apparently disregarding the warm pressure from an unexpected quarter, answered:

— Dedalus.

The sailor stared at him heavily from a pair of drowsy baggy eyes, rather bunged up from excessive use of booze, preferably good old Hollands and water.

— You know Simon Dedalus? he asked at length.

— I've heard of him, Stephen said.

Mr Bloom was all at sea for a moment, seeing the others evidently eavesdropping too.

— He's Irish, the seaman bold affirmed, staring still in much the same way and nodding. All Irish.

— All too Irish, Stephen rejoined.

As for Mr Bloom he could neither make head or tail of the whole business and he was just asking himself what possible connection when the sailor of his own accord turned to the other occupants of the shelter with the remark:

— I seen him shoot two eggs off two bottles at fifty yards over his shoulder. The left-hand dead shot.

Though he was slightly hampered by an occasional stammer and his gestures being also clumsy as it was, still he did his best to explain.

— Bottles out there, say. Fifty yards measured. Eggs on the bottles. Cocks his gun over his shoulder. Aims.

He turned his body half round, shut up his right eye completely, then he screwed his features up someway sideways and glared out into the night with an unprepossessing cast of countenance.

— Pom! he then shouted once.

The entire audience waited, anticipating an additional detonation, there being still a further egg.

— Pom! he shouted twice.

Egg two evidently demolished, he nodded and winked, adding bloodthirstily:

— *Buffalo Bill shoots to kill,*
  Never missed nor he never will.

A silence ensued till Mr Bloom for agreeableness' sake just felt like asking him whether it was for a marksmanship competition like the Bisley.

— Beg pardon, the sailor said.

— Long ago? Mr Bloom pursued without flinching a hairsbreadth.

— Why, the sailor replied, relaxing to a certain extent under the magic influence of diamond cut diamond, it might be a matter of ten years. He toured the wide world with Hengler's Royal Circus. I seen him do that in Stockholm.

— Curious coincidence, Mr Bloom confided to Stephen unobtrusively.

— Murphy's my name, the sailor continued. D. B. Murphy of Carrigaloe. Know where that is?

— Queenstown Harbour, Stephen replied.

— That's right, the sailor said. Fort Camden and Fort Carlisle. That's where I hails from. I belongs there. My little woman's down there. She's waiting for me, I know. *For England, home and beauty.* She's my own true wife I haven't seen for seven years now, sailing about.

Mr Bloom could easily picture his advent on this scene, the homecoming to the mariner's roadside shieling after having diddled Davy Jones, a rainy night with a blind moon. Across the world for a wife. Quite a number of stories there were on that particular Alice Ben Bolt topic, Enoch Arden and Rip Van Winkle and does anybody hereabouts remember Caoch O'Leary, a favourite and most trying declamation piece, by the way, of poor John Casey and a bit of perfect poetry in its own small way. Never about the runaway wife coming back, however much devoted to the absentee. The face at the window! Judge of his astonishment when he finally did breast the tape and the awful truth dawned upon him anent his better half, wrecked in his affections. You little expected me but I've come to stay and make a fresh start. There she sits, a grass widow, at the selfsame fireside. Believes me dead. Rocked in the cradle of the deep. And there sits uncle Chubb or Tomkin, as the case might be, the publican of the Crown and Anchor, in shirtsleeves, eating rump steak and onions. No chair for father. Broo! The wind! Her brand-new arrival is on her knee, *post mortem* child. With a high ro! and a randy ro! and my galloping tearing tandy O! Bow to the inevitable. Grin and bear it. I remain with much love your brokenhearted husband, D. B. Murphy.

The sailor, who scarcely seemed to be a Dublin resident, turned to one of the jarvies with the request:

— You don't happen to have such a thing as a spare chaw about you, do you?

The jarvey addressed as it happened had not, but the keeper took a die of plug from his good jacket hanging on a nail and the desired object was passed from hand to hand.

— Thank you, the sailor said.

He deposited the quid in his gob and, chewing and with some slow stammers, proceeded:

— We come up this morning eleven o'clock. The three-master *Rosevean* from Bridgwater with bricks. I shipped to get over. Paid off this afternoon. There's my discharge. See? D.B. Murphy A.B.S.

In confirmation of which statement he extricated from an inside pocket and handed to his neighbour a not very clean-looking folded document.

— You must have seen a fair share of the world, the keeper remarked, leaning on the counter.

— Why, the sailor answered upon reflection upon it, I've circumnavigated a bit since I first joined on. I was in the Red Sea. I was in China and North America and South America. We was chased by pirates one voyage. I seen icebergs plenty, growlers. I was in Stockholm and the Black Sea, the Dardanelles under Captain Dalton, the best bloody man that ever scuttled a ship. I seen Russia. *Gospodi pomilyou.* That's how the Russians prays.

— You seen queer sights, don't be talking, put in a jarvey.

— Why, the sailor said, shifting his partially chewed plug, I seen queer things too, ups and downs. I seen a crocodile bite the fluke of an anchor same as I chew that quid.

He took out of his mouth the pulpy quid and, lodging it between his teeth, bit ferociously:

— Khaan! Like that. And I seen man-eaters in Peru that eats corpses and the livers of horses. Look here. Here they are. A friend of mine sent me.

He fumbled out a picture postcard from his inside pocket, which seemed to be in its way a species of repository, and pushed it along the table. The printed matter on it stated: *Choza de Indios. Beni, Bolivia.*

All focussed their attention on the scene exhibited, a group of savage women in striped loincloths, squatted, blinking, suckling, frowning, sleeping, amid a swarm of infants (there must have been quite a score of them) outside some primitive shanties of osier.

— Chews coca all day long, the communicative tarpaulin added. Stomachs like bread graters. Cuts off their diddies when they can't bear no more children. See them sitting there stark ballock-naked eating a dead horse's liver raw.

His postcard proved a centre of attraction for Messrs the greenhorns for several minutes if not more.

— Know how to keep them off? he inquired generally.

Nobody volunteering a statement, he winked, saying:

— Glass. That boggles 'em. Glass.

Mr Bloom, without evincing surprise, unostentatiously turned over the card to peruse the partially obliterated address and postmark. It ran as follows: *Tarjeta Postal. Señor A. Boudin, Galería Becche, Santiago, Chile*. There was no message evidently, as he took particular notice.

Though not an implicit believer in the lurid story narrated (or the eggsniping transaction for that matter despite William Tell and the Lazarillo-Don Cesar de Bazan incident depicted in *Maritana* on which occasion the former's ball passed through the latter's hat) having detected a discrepancy between his name (assuming he was the person he represented himself to be and not sailing under false colours after having boxed the compass on the strict q.t. somewhere) and the fictitious addressee of the missive which made him nourish some suspicions of our friend's *bona fides*, nevertheless it reminded him in a way of a long-cherished plan he meant to one day realise some Wednesday or Saturday of travelling to London via long sea. Not to say that he had ever travelled extensively to any great extent but he was at heart a born adventurer though by a trick of fate he had consistently remained a landlubber except you call going to Holyhead which was his longest. Martin Cunningham frequently said he would work a pass through Egan but some deuced hitch or other eternally cropped up with the net result that the scheme fell through. But even suppose it did come to planking down the needful and breaking Boyd's heart it was not so dear, purse permitting, a few guineas at the outside, considering the fare to Mullingar where he figured on going was five and six there and back. The trip would benefit health on account of the bracing ozone and be in every way thoroughly pleasurable, especially for a chap whose liver was out of order, seeing the different places along the route, Plymouth, Falmouth, Southampton and so on, culminating in an instructive tour to renew acquaintance with the sights of the great metropolis, the spectacle of our modern Babylon, where doubtless he would see the greatest improvement, Tower, Abbey, wealth of Park Lane. Another thing just struck him as a by no means bad notion was he might have a gaze around on the spot to see about trying to make arrangements about a concert tour of summer music embracing the most prominent pleasure resorts, Margate with mixed bathing and first-rate hydros and spas, Eastbourne, Scarborough, Margate and so on, beautiful Bournemouth, the Channel Islands, and similar bijou spots, which might prove highly remunerative. Not, of course, with a hole and corner scratch company or local ladies on the job, witness Mrs C.P. M'Coy type – lend me your valise and I'll post you the pawnticket. No, something top notch, an all-star Irish cast, the Tweedy-Flower Grand Opera Company, with his own legal consort as leading lady, as a sort of counterblast to the Elster-Grimes and Moody-Manners, perfectly simple matter, and he was quite sanguine of success, providing puffs in the local papers could be managed by some fellow with a bit of bounce who could pull the indispensable wires and thus combine business with pleasure. But who? That was the rub.

Also, without being actually positive, it struck him a great field was to be opened up in the line of opening up new routes to keep pace with the times apropos of the Fishguard-Rosslare route which, it was mooted, was once more on the *tapis* in the circumlocution departments with the usual quantity of red tape and dillydallying of effete fogeydom and dunderheads generally. A great opportunity there certainly was there for push and enterprise to meet the travelling needs of the public at large, the average man, i.e. Brown, Robinson and Co.

It was a subject of regret and absurd as well on the face of it and no small shame to our vaunted society that the man in the street, when the system really needed toning up, for a matter of a couple of paltry pounds was debarred from seeing more of the world they lived in instead of being always and ever cooped up since my old stick-in-the-mud took me for a wife. After all, hang it, they had their eleven and more humdrum months of it and merited a radical change of venue after the grind of city life, in the summertime for choice when Dame Nature is at her spectacular best, constituting nothing short of a new lease of life. There were equally excellent opportunities for vacationists in the home island, delightful sylvan spots for rejuvenation, offering a plethora of attractions as well as a bracing tonic for the system, in and around Dublin and its picturesque environs even, Poulaphouca to which there was a steam tram, but also farther away from the madding crowd in Wicklow, rightly termed the garden of Ireland, an ideal neighbourhood for elderly wheelmen, so long as it didn't come down, and in the wilds of Donegal where, if report spoke true, the *coup d'œil* was exceedingly grand, though the last-named locality was not easily getatable so that the influx of visitors was not as yet all that it might be considering the signal benefits to be derived from it, while Howth with its historic associations and otherwise, Silken Thomas, Grace O'Malley, George IV, rhododendrons several hundred feet above sea level, was a favourite haunt with all sorts and conditions of men, especially in the spring when young men's fancy, though it had its own toll of deaths by falling off the cliffs by design or accidentally, usually, by the way, on their left leg, it being only about three quarters of an hour's run from the Pillar. Because of course up-to-date tourist travelling was as yet merely in its infancy, so to speak, and the accommodation left much to be desired. Interesting to fathom, it seemed to him, from a motive of curiosity pure and simple, was whether it was the traffic that created the route or vice versa or the two sides in fact. He turned back the other side of the card, picture, and passed it along to Stephen.

– I seen a Chinese one time, related the doughty narrator, that had little pills like putty, and he put them in the water and they opened, and every pill was something different. One was a ship, another was a house, another was a flower. Cooks rats in your soup, he appetisingly added, them Chinese does.

Possibly perceiving an expression of dubiosity on their faces, the globetrotter went on, adhering to his adventures:

– And I seen a man killed in Trieste by an Italian chap. Knife in his back. Knife like that.

Whilst speaking he produced a dangerous-looking claspknife, quite in keeping with his character, and held it in the striking position.

– In a knocking shop it was, 'count of a try-on between two smugglers. Fellow hid behind a door, come up behind him. Like that. *Prepare to meet your God*, says he. Chuk! It went into his back up to the butt.

His heavy glance, drowsily roaming about, kind of defied their further questions even should they by any chance want to.

– That's a good bit of steel, repeated he, examining his formidable stiletto.

After which harrowing denouement sufficient to appal the stoutest he snapped the blade to and stowed the weapon in question away as before in his chamber of horrors, otherwise pocket.

– They're great for the cold steel, somebody who was evidently quite in the dark said for the benefit of them all. That was why they thought the Park murders of the Invincibles was done by foreigners on account of them using knives.

At this remark, passed obviously in the spirit of *where ignorance is bliss*, Mr Bloom and Stephen, each in his own particular way, both instinctively exchanged meaning glances, in a religious silence of the strictly *entre nous* variety however, towards where Skin-the-Goat, alias the keeper, not turning a hair, was drawing spurts of liquid from his boiler affair. His inscrutable face, which was really a work of art, a perfect study in itself, beggaring description, conveyed the impression that he didn't understand one jot of what was going on. Funny, very!

There ensued a somewhat lengthy pause. One man was reading in fits and starts a stained-by-coffee evening journal; another, the card with the natives *choza de*; another, the seaman's discharge. Mr Bloom, so far as he was personally concerned, was just pondering in pensive mood. He vividly recollected when the occurrence alluded to took place as well as yesterday, roughly some score of years previously in the days of the land troubles when it took the civilised world by storm, figuratively speaking, early in the eighties, eighty-one to be correct, when he was just turned fifteen.

— Ay, boss, the sailor broke in. Give us back them papers.

The request being complied with, he clawed them up with a scrape.

— Have you seen the Rock of Gibraltar? Mr Bloom inquired.

The sailor grimaced, chewing, in a way that might be read one way or the other as yes, ay, or no.

— Ah, you've touched there too, Mr Bloom said, Europa Point, thinking he had, in the hope that the rover might possibly by some reminiscences … but he failed to do so, simply letting spirt a jet of spew into the sawdust, and shook his head with a sort of lazy scorn.

— What year would that be about? Mr Bloom interrogated. Can you recall the boats?

Our *soi-disant* sailor munched heavily awhile, hungrily, before answering.

— I'm tired of all them rocks in the sea, he said, and boats and ships. Salt junk all the time.

Tired, seemingly, he ceased. His questioner, perceiving that he was not likely to get a great deal of change out of such a wily old customer, fell to woolgathering on the enormous dimensions of the water about the globe. Suffice it to say that, as a casual glance at the map revealed, it covered fully three fourths of it and he fully realised accordingly what it meant to rule the waves. On more than one occasion – a dozen at the lowest – near the North Bull at Dollymount he had remarked a superannuated old salt, evidently derelict, seated habitually on the wall near the not particularly redolent sea, staring quite obliviously at it and it at him, dreaming of fresh woods and pastures new as someone somewhere sings. And it left him wondering why. Possibly he had tried to find out the secret for himself, floundering up and down the antipodes and all that sort of thing and over and under – well, not exactly under – tempting the fates. And the odds were twenty to nil there was really no secret about it at all. Nevertheless, without going into the minutiae of the business, the eloquent fact remained that the sea was there in all its glory and in the natural course of things somebody or other had to sail on it and fly in the face of providence though it merely went to show how people usually contrived to load that sort of onus on to the other fellow like the hell idea and the lottery and insurance which were run on identically the same lines. So that for that very reason, if no other, Lifeboat Sunday was a highly laudable institution to which the public at large, no matter where living, inland or seaside as the case might be, having it brought home to them like that, should extend its gratitude also to the harbourmasters and coastguard service who had to man the rigging and push off and out amid the elements, whatever the season, when duty called, *Ireland expects that every man* and so on, and sometimes had a terrible time of it in the wintertime, not forgetting the Irish lights, the Kish and others, liable to capsize at any moment, rounding which he once with his daughter had experienced some remarkably choppy, not to say stormy, weather.

– There was a fellow sailed with me in the *Rover*, the old sea dog, himself a rover, proceeded, went ashore and took up a soft job as gentleman's valet at six quid a month. Them are his trousers I've on me and he gave me an oilskin and that jackknife. I'm game for that job, shaving and brushup. I hate roaming about. There's my son now, Danny, run off to sea and his mother got him took in a draper's in Cork where he could be drawing easy money.

– What age is he? queried one hearer who, by the way, seen from the side bore a distant resemblance to Henry Campbell, the town clerk, away from the carking cares of office, unwashed, of course, and in a seedy getup and a strong suspicion of nosepaint about the nasal appendage.

– Why, the sailor answered with a slow puzzled utterance, my son Danny? He'd be about eighteen now, way I figure it.

The Skibbereen father hereupon tore open his grey or unclean anyhow shirt with his two hands and scratched away at his chest on which was to be seen an image tattooed in blue Chinese ink intended to represent an anchor.

– There was lice in that bunk in Bridgwater, he remarked, sure as nuts. I must get a wash tomorrow or next day. It's them black lads I objects to. I hate those buggers. Sucks your blood dry, they does.

Seeing they were all looking at his chest, he accommodatingly dragged his shirt more open so that, on top of the time-honoured symbol of the mariner's hope and rest, they had a full view of the figures 6–16 and a young man's side-face looking frowningly rather.

– Tattoo, the exhibitor explained. That was done when we were lying becalmed off Odessa in the Black Sea under Captain Dalton. Fellow the name of Antonio done that. There he is himself, a Greek.

– Did it hurt much doing it? one asked the sailor.

That worthy, however, was busily engaged in collecting round the ... some way in his ... squeezing or ...

– See here, he said, showing Antonio. There he is cursing the mate. And there he is now, he added, the same fellow, pulling the skin with his fingers, some special knack evidently, and he laughing at a yarn.

And in point of fact the young man named Antonio's livid face did actually look like forced smiling and the curious effect excited the unreserved admiration of everybody, including Skin-the-Goat who this time stretched over.

– Ay, ay, sighed the sailor, looking down on his manly chest. He's gone too. Ate by sharks after. Ay, ay.

He let go of the skin so that the profile resumed the normal expression of before.

– Neat bit of work, one longshoreman said.

– And what's the number for? loafer number two queried.

– Eaten alive? a third asked the sailor.

– Ay, ay, sighed again the latter personage, more cheerily this time, with some sort of a half smile for a brief duration only in the direction of the questioner about the number. Ate. A Greek he was.

And then he added, with rather gallows-bird humour considering his alleged end:

– *As bad as old Antonio,*
  For he left me on my ownio.

The face of a streetwalker, glazed and haggard under a black straw hat, peered askew round the door of the shelter, palpably reconnoitring on her own with the object of bringing more grist to her mill. Mr Bloom, scarcely knowing which way to look, turned away on the moment, flusterfied but outwardly calm, and, picking up from the table the pink sheet of the Abbey Street organ which the jarvey, if such he was, had laid aside, he looked at the pink of the paper, though why pink? His reason for so doing was he recognised on the moment round the door the same face he had caught a fleeting glimpse of that afternoon on Ormond Quay, the partially idiotic female of the lane, namely, who knew the lady in the brown costume does be with you (Mrs B.) and begged the chance of his washing. Also why *washing*, which seemed rather vague than not? *Your* washing?

Still, candour compelled him to admit that he had washed his wife's undergarments, when soiled, in Holles Street, and women would and did too a man's similar garments, initialled with Bewley and Draper's marking ink (hers were, that is), if they really loved him, that is to say, love me, love my dirty shirt. Still, just then, being on tenterhooks, he desired the female's room more than her company so it came as a genuine relief when the keeper made her a rude sign to take herself off. Round the side of the *Evening Telegraph* he just caught a fleeting glimpse of her face round the side of the door with a kind of demented glassy grin, showing that she was not exactly all there, viewing with evident amusement the group of gazers round Skipper Murphy's nautical chest and then there was no more of her.

– The gunboat, the keeper said.

– It beats me, Mr Bloom confided to Stephen, medically I am speaking, how a wretched creature like that from the Lock Hospital, reeking with disease, can be barefaced enough to solicit or how any man in his sober senses if he values his health in the least ... Unfortunate creature! Of course, I suppose some man is ultimately responsible for her condition. Still, no matter what the cause is from...

Stephen had not noticed her and shrugged his shoulders, merely remarking:

– In this country people sell much more than she ever had and do a roaring trade. Fear not them that sell the body but have not power to buy the soul. She is a bad merchant. She buys dear and sells cheap.

The elder man, though not by any manner of means an old maid or a prude, said that it was nothing short of a crying scandal that ought to be put a stop to *instanter* to say that women of that stamp (quite apart from any old-maidish squeamishness on the subject), a necessary evil, were not licensed and medically inspected by the proper authorities, a thing he could truthfully state he, as a paterfamilias, was a stalwart advocate of from the very first start. Whoever embarked on a policy of the sort, he said, and ventilated the matter thoroughly would confer a lasting boon on everybody concerned.

– You, as a good Catholic, he observed, talking of body and soul, believe in the soul. Or do you mean the intelligence, the brainpower as such, as distinct from any outside object, the table, let us say, that cup? I believe in that myself because it has been explained by competent men as the convolutions of the grey matter. Otherwise we would never have such inventions as x-rays, for instance. Do you?

Thus cornered, Stephen had to make a superhuman effort of memory to try and concentrate and remember before he could say:

—They tell me on the best authority it is a simple substance and therefore incorruptible. It would be immortal, I understand, but for the possibility of its annihilation by its First Cause, who, from all I can hear, is quite capable of adding that to the number of His other practical jokes, *corruptio per se* and *corruptio per accidens* both being excluded by court etiquette.

Mr Bloom thoroughly acquiesced in the general gist of this though the mystical finesse involved was a bit out of his sublunary depth. Still, he felt bound to enter a demurrer on the head of *simple*, promptly rejoining:

—Simple? I shouldn't think that is the proper word. Of course, I grant you, to concede a point, you do knock across a simple soul once in a blue moon. But what I am anxious to arrive at is, it is one thing for instance to invent those rays Röntgen did, or the telescope like Edison, though I believe it was before his time, Galileo was the man I mean, and the same applies to the laws, for example, of a far-reaching natural phenomenon such as electricity, but it's a horse of quite another colour to say you believe in the existence of a supernatural God.

—O, that, Stephen expostulated, has been proved conclusively by several of the best-known passages in Holy Writ, apart from circumstantial evidence.

On this knotty point, however, the views of the pair, poles apart as they were, both in schooling and everything else, with the marked difference in their respective ages, clashed.

—Has been? the more experienced of the two objected, sticking to his original point with a smile of unbelief. I'm not so sure about that. That's a matter of every man's opinion and, without dragging in the sectarian side of the business, I beg to differ with you *in toto* there. My belief is, to tell you the candid truth, that those bits were genuine forgeries, all of them, put in by monks most probably, or it's the big question of our national poet over again, who precisely wrote them, like *Hamlet* and Bacon, as, you who know your Shakespeare infinitely better than I, of course I needn't tell you. Can't you drink that coffee, by the way? Let me stir it. And take a piece of that bun. It's like one of our skipper's bricks disguised. Still, no one can give what he hasn't got. Try a bit.

—Couldn't, Stephen contrived to get out, his mental organs for the moment refusing to dictate further.

Faultfinding being a proverbially bad hat, Mr Bloom thought well to stir, or try to, the clotted sugar from the bottom of Stephen's cup, and reflected with something approaching acrimony on the Coffee Palace and its temperance (and lucrative) work. To be sure it was a legitimate object and beyond yea or nay did a world of good, shelters such as the present one they were in run on teetotal lines for vagrants at night, concerts, dramatic evenings and useful lectures (admittance free) by qualified men for the lower orders. On the other hand, he had a distinct and painful recollection they paid his wife, Madam Marion Tweedy, who had been prominently associated with it at one time, a very modest remuneration indeed for her pianoplaying. The idea, he was strongly inclined to believe, was to do good and net a profit, there being no competition to speak of. Sulphate of copper poison, SO_4 or something, in some dried peas he remembered reading of in a cheap eatinghouse somewhere but he couldn't remember when it was or where. Anyhow, inspection, medical inspection, of all eatables seemed to him more than ever necessary which possibly accounted for the vogue of Dr Tibble's Vi-Cocoa on account of the medical analysis involved.

— Have a shot at it now, he ventured to say of the coffee after being stirred.

Thus prevailed on to at any rate taste it, Stephen lifted the heavy mug from the brown puddle it clopped out of when taken up by the handle and took a sip of the offending beverage.

— Still, it's solid food, his good genius urged, I'm a stickler for solid food, his one and only reason being not gormandising in the least but regular meals as the *sine qua non* for any kind of proper work, mental or manual. You ought to eat more solid food. You would feel a different man.

— Liquids I can eat, Stephen said. But oblige me by taking away that knife. I can't look at the point of it. It reminds me of Roman history.

Mr Bloom promptly did as suggested and removed out of sight the incriminated article, a blunt horn-handled ordinary knife with nothing particularly Roman or antique about it to the lay eye, observing that the point was the least conspicuous point about it.

— Our mutual friend's stories are like himself, Mr Bloom, apropos of knives, remarked to his confidant *sotto voce*. Do you think they are genuine? He could spin those yarns for hours on end all night long and lie like old boots. Look at him.

Yet still, though his eyes were thick with sleep and sea air, life was full of a host of things and coincidences of a terrible nature and it was quite within the bounds of possibility that it was not an entire fabrication though at first blush there was not much inherent probability in all the spoof he got off his chest being strictly accurate gospel.

He had been meantime taking stock of the individual in front of him and Sherlockholmesing him up ever since he clapped eyes on him. Though a well-preserved man of no little stamina, if a trifle prone to baldness, there was something spurious in the cut of his jib that suggested a jail delivery and it required no violent stretch of imagination to associate such a weird-looking specimen with the oakum and treadmill fraternity. He might even have done for his man, supposing it was his own case he told, as people often did about others, namely that he killed him himself and had served his four or five good-looking years in durance vile, to say nothing of the Antonio personage (no relation to the dramatic personage of identical name who sprang from the pen of our national poet) who expiated his crimes in the melodramatic manner above described. On the other hand, he might be only bluffing, a pardonable weakness, because meeting unmistakable mugs, Dublin residents, like those jarvies wanting news from abroad, would tempt any ancient mariner who sailed the ocean seas to draw the long bow about the schooner *Hesperus* etcetera. And when all was said and done, the lies a fellow told about himself couldn't probably hold a proverbial candle to the wholesale whoppers other fellows coined about him.

– Mind you, I'm not saying that it's all a pure invention, he resumed. Analogous scenes are occasionally, if not often, met with. Giants, though that is rather a far cry, you see once in a way. Marcella, the midget queen. In those waxworks in Henry Street I myself saw some Aztecs, as they are called, sitting bowlegged. They couldn't straighten their legs if you paid them because the muscles here, you see, he proceeded, indicating on his companion the brief outline of the sinews or whatever you like to call them behind the right knee, were utterly powerless from sitting that way so long cramped up, being adored as gods. There's an example again of simple souls.

However, reverting to friend Sinbad and his horrifying adventures (who reminded him a bit of Ludwig, alias Ledwidge, when he occupied the boards of the Gaiety when Michael Gunn was identified with the management in the *Flying Dutchman*, a stupendous success, and his host of admirers came in large numbers, everyone simply flocking to hear him, though ships of any sort, phantom or the reverse, on the stage usually fell a bit flat as also did trains), there was nothing intrinsically incompatible about it, he conceded. On the contrary, that stab in the back touch was quite in keeping with those Italianos, though candidly he was none the less free to admit those ice-creamers and friers in the fish way, not to mention the chip potato variety and so forth, over in little Italy there, near the Coombe, were sober thrifty hardworking fellows except perhaps a bit too given to pothunting the harmless necessary animal of the feline persuasion of others at night so as to have a good old succulent tuck-in with garlic de rigueur off him or her next day on the quiet and, he added, on the cheap.

— Spaniards, for instance, he continued, passionate temperaments like that, impetuous as Old Nick, are given to taking the law into their own hands and give you your quietus doublequick with those poignards they carry in the abdomen. It comes from the great heat, climate generally. My wife is, so to speak, Spanish, half that is. Point of fact she could actually claim Spanish nationality if she wanted, having been born in (technically) Spain, i.e. Gibraltar. She has the Spanish type. Quite dark, regular brunette, black. I, for one, certainly believe climate accounts for character. That's why I asked you if you wrote your poetry in Italian.

— The temperaments at the door, Stephen interposed with, were very passionate about ten shillings. *Roberto ruba roba sua*.

— Quite so, Mr Bloom dittoed.

— Then, Stephen said, staring and rambling on to himself or some unknown listener somewhere, we have the impetuosity of Dante and the isosceles triangle, Miss Portinari, he fell in love with and Leonardo and San Tommaso Mastino.

— It's in the blood, Mr Bloom acceded at once. All are washed in the blood of the sun. Coincidence, I just happened to be in the Kildare Street Museum today, shortly prior to our meeting, if I can so call it, and I was just looking at those antique statues there. The splendid proportions of hips, bosom. You simply don't knock against those kind of women here. An exception here and there. Handsome, yes, pretty in a way, you find, but what I'm talking about is the female form. Besides, they have so little taste in dress, most of them, which greatly enhances a woman's natural beauty, no matter what you say. Rumpled stockings ... it may be, possibly is, a foible of mine, but still it's a thing I simply hate to see.

Interest, however, was starting to flag somewhat all round and the others got on to talking about accidents at sea, ships lost in a fog, collisions with icebergs, all that sort of thing. Shipahoy, of course, had his own say to say. He had doubled the Cape a few odd times and weathered a monsoon, a kind of wind, in the China seas and through all those perils of the deep there was one thing, he declared, stood to him, or words to that effect, a pious medal he had that saved him.

So then after that they drifted on to the wreck off Daunt's Rock, wreck of that ill-fated Norwegian barque – nobody could think of her name for the moment till the jarvey who had really quite a look of Henry Campbell remembered it, *Palme* – on Booterstown Strand. That was the talk of the town that year (Albert William Quill wrote a fine piece of original verse of distinctive merit on the topic for the *Irish Times*), breakers running over her and crowds and crowds on the shore in commotion, petrified with horror. Then someone said something about the case of the S.S. *Lady Cairns* of Swansea, run into by the *Mona* which was on an opposite tack in rather muggyish weather and lost with all hands on deck. No aid was given. Her master, the *Mona*'s, said he was afraid his collision bulkhead would give way. She had no water, it appears, in her hold.

At this stage an incident happened. It having become necessary for him to unfurl a reef, the sailor vacated his seat.

– Let me cross your bows, mate, he said to his neighbour, who was just gently dropping off into a peaceful doze.

He made tracks heavily, slowly, with a dumpy sort of a gait to the door, stepped heavily down the one step there was out of the shelter and bore due left. While he was in the act of getting his bearings, Mr Bloom, who noticed when he stood up that he had two flasks of presumably ship's rum, one sticking out of each pocket, for the private consumption of his burning interior, saw him produce a bottle and uncork or unscrew it and, applying its nozzle to his lips, take a good old delectable swig out of it with a gurgling noise. The irrepressible Bloom, who also had a shrewd suspicion that the old stager went out on a manoeuvre after the counter-attraction in the shape of a female who, however, had disappeared to all intents and purposes, could, by straining, just perceive him, when duly refreshed by his rum puncheon exploit, gazing up at the piers and girders of the Loop Line, rather out of his depth, as of course it was all radically altered since his last visit and greatly improved. Some person or persons invisible directed him to the male urinal erected by the cleansing committee all over the place for the purpose, but, after a brief space of time during which silence reigned supreme, the sailor, evidently giving it a wide berth, eased himself closer at hand, the noise of his bilgewater some little time subsequently splashing on the ground where it apparently woke a horse of the cabrank. A hoof scooped anyway for new foothold after sleep and harness jingled. Slightly disturbed in his sentrybox by the brazier of live coke, the watcher of the Corporation stones, who, though now broken down and fast breaking up, was none other in stern reality than the Gumley aforesaid, now practically on the parish rates, given the temporary job by Pat Tobin in all human probability from dictates of humanity, knowing him before, shifted about and shuffled in his box before composing his limbs again into the arms of Morpheus, a truly amazing piece of hard lines in its most virulent form on a fellow most respectably connected and familiarised with decent home comforts all his life who came in for a cool £100 a year at one time which of course the double-barreled ass proceeded to make general ducks and drakes of. And there he was at the end of his tether after having often painted the town tolerably pink, without a beggarly stiver. He drank, needless to be told, and it pointed only once more a moral when he might quite easily be in a large way of business if – a big if, however – he had contrived to cure himself of his particular partiality.

All, meantime, were loudly lamenting the falling off in Irish shipping, coastwise and foreign as well, which was all part and parcel of the same thing. A Palgrave Murphy boat was put off the ways at Alexandra Basin, the only launch that year. Right enough the harbours were there only no ships ever called.

There were wrecks and wreckers, the keeper said, who was evidently *au fait*.

What he wanted to ascertain was why that ship ran bang against the only rock in Galway Bay when the Galway Harbour Scheme was mooted by a Mr Worthington or some name like that, eh? Ask her captain, he advised them, how much palm oil the British Government gave him for that day's work. Captain John Lever of the Lever Line.

– Am I right, skipper? he queried of the sailor now returning after his private potation and the rest of his exertions.

That worthy, picking up the scent of the fag end of the song or words, growled in would-be music, but with great vim, some kind of chanty or other in seconds or thirds. Mr Bloom's sharp ears heard him then expectorate the plug probably (which it was), so that he must have lodged it for the time being in his fist while he did the drinking and making water jobs and found it a bit sour after the liquid fire in question. Anyhow, in he rolled after his successful libation-*cum*-potation, introducing an atmosphere of drink into the soirée, boisterously trolling, like a veritable son of a sea cook:

554

> – *The biscuits was as hard as brass,*
>   *And the beef as salt as Lot's wife's arse.*
>   *O Johnny Lever!*
>   *Johnny Lever, O!*

After which effusion the redoubtable specimen duly arrived on the scene and, regaining his seat, he sank rather than sat heavily on the form provided.

Skin-the-Goat, assuming he was he, evidently with an axe to grind, was airing his grievances in a forcible-feeble philippic anent the natural resources of Ireland, or something of that sort, which he described in his lengthy dissertation as the richest country bar none on the face of God's earth, far and away superior to England, with coal in large quantities, six million pounds worth of pork exported every year, ten millions between butter and eggs, and all the riches drained out of it by England levying taxes on the poor people that paid through the nose always, and gobbling up the best meat in the market, and a lot more surplus steam in the same vein. The conversation accordingly became general and all agreed that that was a fact. You could grow any mortal thing in Irish soil, he stated, and there was Colonel Everard down there in Navan growing tobacco. Where would you find anywhere the like of Irish bacon? But a day of reckoning, he stated *crescendo* with no uncertain voice, thoroughly monopolising all the conversation, was in store for mighty England, despite her power of pelf, on account of her crimes. There would be a fall and the greatest fall in history. The Germans and the Japs were going to have their little look-in, he affirmed. The Boers were the beginning of the end. Brummagem England was toppling already and her downfall would be Ireland, her Achilles heel, which he explained to them about the vulnerable point of Achilles, the Greek hero, a point his auditors at once seized as he completely gripped their attention by showing the tendon referred to on his boot. His advice to every Irishman was: stay in the land of your birth and work for Ireland and live for Ireland. Ireland, Parnell said, could not spare a single one of her sons.

Silence all round marked the termination of his finale. The impervious navigator heard these lurid tidings undismayed.

– Take a bit of doing, boss, retaliated that rough diamond, palpably a bit peeved, in response to the foregoing truism.

To which cold douche, referring to downfall and so on, the keeper concurred but nevertheless held to his main view.

– Who's the best troops in the army? the grizzled old veteran irately interrogated. And the best jumpers and racers? And the best admirals and generals we've got? Tell me that.

— The Irish for choice, retorted the cabby like Campbell, facial blemishes apart.

— That's right, the old tarpaulin corroborated. The Irish Catholic peasant. He's the backbone of our empire. You know Jem Mullins?

While allowing him his individual opinions, as every man, the keeper added he cared nothing for any empire, ours or his, and considered no Irishman worthy of his salt that served it. Then they began to have a few irascible words when it waxed hotter, both, needless to say, appealing to the listeners who followed the passage of arms with interest so long as they didn't indulge in recriminations and come to blows.

From inside information extending over a series of years Mr Bloom was rather inclined to poohpooh the suggestion as egregious balderdash for, pending that consummation devoutly to be or not to be wished for, he was fully cognisant of the fact that their neighbours across the channel, unless they were much bigger fools than he took them for, rather concealed their strength than the opposite. It was quite on a par with the quixotic idea in certain quarters that in a hundred million years the coal seam of the sister island would be played out and if, as time went on, that turned out to be how the cat jumped all he could personally say on the matter was that as a host of contingencies, equally relevant to the issue, might occur ere then it was highly advisable in the interim to try to make the most of both countries, even though poles apart. Another little interesting point, the amours of whores and chummies, to put it in common parlance, reminded him Irish soldiers had as often fought for England as against her, more so in fact. And now, why? So the scene between the pair of them, the licensee of the place, rumoured to be or have been Fitzharris, the famous Invincible, and the other, obviously bogus, reminded him forcibly as being on all fours with the confidence trick, supposing, that is, it was prearranged, the looker-on seeing least of the game. And as for the lessee or keeper, who probably wasn't the other person at all, he (Bloom), a student of the human soul if anything, couldn't help feeling, and most properly, it was better to give people like that the go-by unless you were a blithering idiot altogether and refuse to have anything to do with them and their felonsetting as a golden rule in private life, there always being the off chance of a Dannyman informer coming forward and turning Queen's evidence – or King's now – to divulge the names of his accomplices, like Denis or Peter Carey, an idea he utterly repudiated. Quite apart from that, he disliked those careers of wrongdoing and crime on principle. Yet, though such criminal propensities had never been an inmate of his bosom in any shape or form, he certainly did feel, and no denying it (while inwardly remaining what he was), a certain kind of admiration for a man who had actually brandished a knife, cold steel, with the courage of his political convictions (though, personally, he would never be a party to any such thing), off the same bat as those love vendettas of the south – have her or swing for her – when the husband frequently, after some words passed between the two concerning her relations with the other lucky man (he having had the pair watched), inflicted fatal injuries on his adored one as a result of an alternative postnuptial liaison by plunging his knife into her, until it just struck him that Fitz, nicknamed Skin-the-Goat, merely drove the car for the actual perpetrators of the outrage and so was not, if he was reliably informed, actually party to the ambush, which in point of fact was the plea some legal luminary saved his skin on. In any case that was very ancient history by now. And as for our friend, the pseudo Skin-the-etcetera, he had transparently outlived his welcome. He ought to have either died naturally or on the scaffold high. Like actresses, always farewell – positively last performance – then come up smiling again. Generous to a fault, of course, temperamental, no economising or any idea of the sort, always snapping at the bone for the shadow. So similarly he had a very shrewd suspicion that Mr Johnny Lever got rid of some £ *s.d.* in the course of his perambulations round the docks in the congenial atmosphere of the Old Ireland Tavern, come back to Erin and so on. Then as for the other, he had heard not so long before the same identical lingo and he told Stephen how he simply but effectually silenced the offender.

– He took umbrage at something or other, that much injured but on the whole even-tempered person declared, I let slip. He called me a Jew. And in a heated fashion, offensively. So I, without deviating from plain facts in the least, told him his God, I mean Christ, was a Jew too, and all his family, like me, though in reality I'm not. That was one for him. A soft answer turns away wrath. He hadn't a word to say for himself as everyone saw. Am I not right?

He turned a long you are wrong gaze on Stephen of timorous dark pride at the soft impeachment, with a glance also of entreaty for he seemed to glean in a kind of a way that it wasn't all exactly . . .

— *Ex quibus*, Stephen mumbled in a noncommittal accent, their two or four eyes conversing, *Christus*, or Bloom his name is or after all any other, *secundum carnem*.

— Of course, Mr Bloom proceeded to stipulate, you must look at both sides of the question. It is hard to lay down any hard and fast rules as to right and wrong but room for improvement all round there certainly is, though every country, they say, our own distressful included, has the government it deserves. But with a little goodwill all round ... It's all very fine to boast of mutual superiority but what about mutual equality? I resent violence or intolerance in any shape or form. It never reaches anything or stops anything. A revolution must come on the due instalments plan. It's a patent absurdity on the face of it to hate people because they live round the corner and speak another vernacular, in the next house so to speak.

— Memorable Bloody Bridge battle and seven minutes' war, Stephen assented, between Skinner's Alley and Ormond Market.

Yes, Mr Bloom thoroughly agreed, entirely endorsing the remark, that was overwhelmingly right. It was, as yet, a manifest fact. And the whole world was full of that sort of thing.

— You just took the words out of my mouth, he said. A hocuspocus of conflicting evidence that candidly you couldn't remotely ...

All those wretched quarrels, in his humble opinion, stirring up bad blood, from some bump of combativeness or gland of some kind, erroneously supposed to be about a punctilio of honour and a flag, were very largely a question of the money question which was at the back of everything, greed and jealousy, people never knowing when to stop.

— They accuse ... , remarked he audibly.

He turned away from the others, who probably ... and spoke nearer to, so as the others ... in case they ...

— Jews, he softly imparted in an aside in Stephen's ear, are accused of ruining. Not a vestige of truth in it, I can safely say. History, would you be surprised to learn, proves up to the hilt Spain decayed when the Inquisition hounded the Jews out and England prospered when Cromwell, an uncommonly able ruffian, who in other respects has much to answer for, imported them. Why? Because they are imbued with the proper spirit. They are practical and are proved to be so. I don't want to indulge in any ... because you know the standard works on the subject, and then, orthodox as you are ... but in the economic, not touching religion, domain the priest spells poverty. Spain again, you saw in the war, compared with go-ahead America. Turkey. It's in the dogma. Because if they didn't believe they'd go straight to heaven when they die they'd try to live better, at least so I think. That's the juggle on which the p.p.'s raise the wind on false pretences. I'm, he resumed with dramatic force, as good an Irishman as that rude person I told you about at the outset and I want to see everyone, concluded he, all creeds and classes *pro rata* having a comfortable tidy-sized income, in no niggard fashion either, something in the neighbourhood of £300 per annum. That's the vital issue at stake and it's feasible and would be provocative of friendlier intercourse between man and man. At least that's my idea for what it's worth. I call that patriotism. *Ubi patria*, as we learned a smattering of in our classical days in alma mater, *vita bene*. Where you can live well, the sense is, if you work.

Over his untastable apology for a cup of coffee, listening to this synopsis of things in general, Stephen stared at nothing in particular. He could hear, of course, all kinds of words changing colour like those crabs about Ringsend in the morning, burrowing quickly into all colours of different sorts of the same sand where they had a home somewhere beneath or seemed to. Then he looked up and saw the eyes that said or didn't say the words the voice he heard said, *if you work*.

— Count me out, he managed to remark, meaning work.

The eyes were surprised at this observation because as he, the person who owned them pro tem, observed, or rather his voice speaking did, all must work, have to, together.

— I mean, of course, the other hastened to affirm, work in the widest possible sense. Also literary labour, not merely for the kudos of the thing. Writing for the newspapers, which is the readiest channel nowadays. That's work too. Important work. After all, from the little I know of you, after all the money expended on your education, you are entitled to recoup yourself and command your price. You have every bit as much right to live by your pen in pursuit of your philosophy as the peasant has. What? You both belong to Ireland, the brain and the brawn. Each is equally important.

— You suspect, Stephen retorted with a sort of a half laugh, that I may be important because I belong to the *faubourg Saint-Patrice* called Ireland for short.

— I would go a step farther, Mr Bloom insinuated.

— But I suspect, Stephen interrupted, that Ireland must be important because it belongs to me.

— What belongs? queried Mr Bloom, bending, fancying he was perhaps under some misapprehension. Excuse me. Unfortunately I didn't catch the latter portion. What was it you … ?

Stephen, patently cross-tempered, repeated … and shoved aside his mug of coffee, or whatever you like to call it, none too politely, adding:

— We can't change the country. Let us change the subject.

At this pertinent suggestion, Mr Bloom, to change the subject, looked down, but in a quandary, as he couldn't tell exactly what construction to put on *belongs to* which sounded rather a far cry. The rebuke of some kind was clearer than the other part. Needless to say, the fumes of his recent orgy spoke then with some asperity in a curious bitter way foreign to his sober state. Probably the home life, to which Mr Bloom attached the utmost importance, had not been all that was needful, or he hadn't been familiarised with the right sort of people. With a touch of fear for the young man beside him, he furtively scrutinised him with an air of some consternation, remembering he had just come back from Paris, the eyes more especially reminding him forcibly of father and sister. Failing to throw much light on the subject, however, he brought to mind instances of cultured fellows that promised so brilliantly nipped in the bud of premature decay and nobody to blame but themselves. For instance, there was the case of O'Callaghan, for one, the half-crazy faddist, respectably connected though of inadequate means, with his mad vagaries, among whose other gay doings when rotto and making himself a nuisance to everybody all round was he was in the habit of ostentatiously sporting in public a suit of brown paper (a fact). And then the usual denouement. After the fun had gone on fast and furious he got landed into hot water and had to be spirited away quietly by a few friends after a strong hint to a blind horse from John Mallon of Lower Castle Yard so as not to be made amenable under Section II of the Criminal Law Amendment Act, certain names of those subpoenaed being handed in but not divulged, for reasons which will occur to anyone with a pick of brains. Briefly, putting two and two together, six sixteen, which he pointedly turned a deaf ear to, Antonio and so forth, jockeys and esthetes and the tattoo which was all the go in the seventies or thereabouts, even in the House of Lords, because early in life the occupant of the throne, then heir apparent, the other members of the upper ten and other high personages simply following in the footsteps of the head of the state, he reflected about the errors of notorieties and crowned heads running counter to morality such as the Cornwall case a number of years before under their veneer in a way scarcely intended by nature, a thing good Mrs Grundy, as the law stands, was terribly down on, though not for the reason they thought they were probably, whatever it was, except women chiefly, who were always fiddling more or less at one another, it being largely a matter of dress and all the rest of it. Ladies who like distinctive underclothing should, and every well-tailored man must, trying to make the gap wider between them by innuendo and give more of a genuine fillip to acts of impropriety between the two, she unbuttoned his and then he untied her, mind the pin, whereas savages in the cannibal islands, say, at ninety degrees in the shade not caring a continental. However, reverting to the original, there were on the other hand others who had forced their way to the top from the lowest rung by the aid of their bootstraps. Sheer force of natural genius, that. With brains, sir.

For which and further reasons he felt it was his interest and duty even to wait on and profit by this unlooked-for occasion, though why he could not exactly tell, being, as it was, already several shillings to the bad, having, in fact, let himself in for it. Still, to cultivate the acquaintance of someone of no uncommon calibre who could provide food for reflection would amply repay any small … Intellectual stimulation as such was, he felt, from time to time a first-rate tonic for the mind. Added to which was the coincidence of meeting, discussion, dance, row, old salt of the here today and gone tomorrow type, night loafers, the whole galaxy of events, all went to make up a miniature cameo of the world we live in, if taken down in writing, especially as the lives of the submerged tenth, viz. coalminers, divers, scavengers etc., were very much under the microscope lately. To improve the shining hour he wondered whether he might meet with anything approaching the same luck as Mr Philip Beaufoy suppose he were to pen something out of the common groove (as he fully intended doing) at the rate of one guinea per column, *My Experiences*, let us say, *in a Cabman's Shelter*.

The pink edition, extra sporting, of the *Telegraph*, tell a graphic lie, lay, as luck would have it, beside his elbow and as he was just puzzling again, far from satisfied, over a country belonging to him and the preceding rebus – the vessel came from Bridgwater and the postcard was addressed to A. Boudin, find the captain's age – his eyes went aimlessly over the respective captions which came under his special province, the all-embracing give us this day our daily press. First he got a bit of a start but it turned out to be only something about somebody named H. du Boyes, agent for typewriters or something like that. Great Battle, Tokio. Love-making in Irish, £200 damages. Gordon Bennett. Emigration Swindle.

Letter from His Grace William ✠. Ascot Meeting, the Gold Cup. Victory of outsider *Throwaway* recalls Derby of '92 when Captain Marshall's dark horse *Sir Hugo* captured the blue riband at long odds. New York Disaster, thousand lives lost. Foot-and-mouth. Funeral of the late Mr Patrick Dignam.

So to change the subject he read about Dignam R.I.P. which, he reflected, was anything but a gay send-off. Or a change of address anyway.

– *This morning* (Hynes put it in, of course) *the remains of the late Mr Patrick Dignam were removed from his residence, No 9 Newbridge Avenue, Sandymount, for interment in Glasnevin. The deceased gentleman was a most popular and genial personality in city life and his demise, after a brief illness, came as a great shock to citizens of all classes by whom he is deeply regretted. The obsequies, at which many friends of the deceased were present, were carried out by* (certainly Hynes wrote it with a nudge from Corny) *Messrs H.J. O'Neill & Son, 164 North Strand Road. The mourners included: Patk. Dignam (son), Bernard Corrigan (brother-in-law), John Henry Menton, solr., Martin Cunningham, John Power .)eatondph 1/8 ador dorador doura- dora* (must be where he called Monks the dayfather about Keyes's ad) *Thomas Kernan, Simon Dedalus, Stephen Dedalus B.A., Edward J. Lambert, Cornelius T. Kelleher, Joseph M'C. Hynes, L. Boom, C.P. M'Coy, – M'Intosh, and several others.*

Nettled not a little by *L. Boom* (as it incorrectly stated) and the line of bitched type, but tickled to death simultaneously by C.P. M'Coy and Stephen Dedalus B.A., who were conspicuous, needless to say, by their total absence (to say nothing of M'Intosh), L. Boom pointed it out to his companion B.A. engaged in stifling another yawn, half nervousness, not forgetting the usual crop of nonsensical howlers of misprints.

– Is that first epistle to the Hebrews, he asked as soon as his bottom jaw would let him, in? Text: open thy mouth and put thy foot in it.

– It is, really, Mr Bloom said (though first he fancied he alluded to the archbishop till he added about foot-and-mouth with which there could be no possible connection), overjoyed to set his mind at rest and a bit flabbergasted at Myles Crawford's after all managing the thing. There.

While the other was reading it on page two Boom (to give him for the nonce his new misnomer) whiled away a few odd leisure moments in fits and starts with the account of the third event at Ascot on page three, his side. Value 1000 sovs., with 3000 sovs. in specie added. For entire colts and fillies. Mr F. Alexander's b.h. *Throwaway*, by *Rightaway-Theale*, 5 yrs, 9 st 4 lb (W. Lane) 1. Lord Howard de Walden's *Zinfandel* (M. Cannon) 2.

Mr W. Bass's *Sceptre* 3. Betting. – 5 to 4 on *Zinfandel*. 20 to 1 *Throwaway* (off). *Throwaway* and *Zinfandel* stood close order. It was anybody's race, then the rank outsider drew to the fore, got long lead, beating Lord Howard de Walden's chestnut colt and Mr W. Bass's bay filly *Sceptre* on a 2½-mile course. Winner trained by Braime. So that Lenehan's version of the business was all pure buncombe. Secured the verdict cleverly by a length. 1000 sovs. with 3000 in specie. Also ran: J. de Bremond's (French horse Bantam Lyons was anxiously inquiring after not in yet but expected any minute) *Maximum II.* Different ways of bringing off a coup. Love-making damages. Though that half-baked Lyons ran off at a tangent in his impetuosity to get left. Of course, gambling eminently lent itself to that sort of thing, though, as the event turned out, the poor fool hadn't much reason to congratulate himself on his pick, the forlorn hope. Guesswork it reduced itself to eventually.

– There was every indication they would arrive at that, he, Bloom, said.

– Who? the other, whose hand by the way was hurt, said.

– One morning you would open the paper, the cabman affirmed, and read, *Return of Parnell.* He bet them what they liked. A Dublin fusilier was in that shelter one night and said he saw him in South Africa. Pride it was killed him. He ought to have done away with himself or lain low for a time after Committee Room No 15 until he was his old self again with no one to point a finger at him. Then they would all to a man have gone down on their marrowbones to him to come back when he had recovered his senses. Dead he wasn't. Simply absconded somewhere. The coffin they brought over was full of stones. He changed his name to DeWet, the Boer general. He made a mistake to fight the priests. And so forth and so on.

All the same Bloom (properly so dubbed) was rather surprised at their memories for in nine cases out of ten it was a case of tarbarrels, and not singly but in their thousands, and then complete oblivion because it was twenty-odd years. Highly unlikely, of course, there was even a shadow of truth in the stones and, even supposing, he thought a return highly inadvisable, all things considered. Something evidently riled them in his death. Either he petered out too tamely of acute pneumonia just when his various different political arrangements were nearing completion or it transpired he owed his death to his having neglected to change his boots and clothes after a wetting when a cold resulted and failing to consult a specialist he being confined to his room till he eventually died of it amid widespread regret before a fortnight was at an end, or quite possibly they were distressed to find the job was taken out of their hands. Of course, nobody being acquainted with his movements even before, there was absolutely no clue as to his whereabouts which were decidedly of the *Alice, where art thou?* order even prior to his starting to go under several aliases such as Fox and Stewart, so the remark which emanated from friend cabby might be within the bounds of possibility. Naturally, then, it would prey on his mind as a born leader of men, which undoubtedly he was, and a commanding figure, a six-footer or at any rate five feet ten or eleven in his stockinged feet, whereas Messrs so-and-so, who, though they weren't even a patch on the former man, ruled the roost after, their redeeming features were very few and far between. It certainly pointed a moral, the idol with feet of clay, and then seventy-two of his trusty henchmen rounding on him with mutual mudslinging. And the identical same with murderers. You had to come back – that haunting sense kind of drew you – to show the understudy in the title role how to. He saw him once on the auspicious occasion when they broke up the type in the *Insuppressible*, or was it *United Ireland*, a privilege he keenly appreciated, and in point of fact handed him his silk hat when it was knocked off and he said *Thank you*, excited as he undoubtedly was under his frigid exterior, notwithstanding the little misadventure mentioned between the cup and the lip – what's bred in the bone. Still, as regards return, you were a lucky dog if they didn't set the terrier at you directly you got back. Then a lot of shillyshally usually followed, Tom for and Dick and Harry against. And then, number one, you came up against the man in possession and had to produce your credentials, like the claimant in the Tichborne case, Roger Charles Tichborne, *Bella* was the boat's name to the best of his recollection he, the heir, went down in, as the evidence went to show, and there was a tattoo mark too in Indian ink, Lord Bellew was it? A more prudent course, as Bloom said to the not overeffusive person beside him, in fact like the distinguished personage under discussion, would have been to sound the lie of the land first, as he might very easily have picked up the details from some pal on board ship and then, when got up to tally with the description given, introduce himself with *Excuse me, my name is so-and-so* or some such commonplace remark.

– That bitch, that English whore, did for him, the shebeen proprietor commented. She put the first nail in his coffin.

– Fine lump of a woman all the same, the *soi-disant* town clerk Henry Campbell remarked, and plenty of her. She loosened many a man's thighs. I seen her picture in a barber's. Her husband was a captain or an officer.

– Ay, Skin-the-Goat amusingly added, he was, and a cottonball one.

This gratuitous contribution of a humorous character occasioned a fair amount of laughter among his entourage. As regards Bloom, he, without the faintest suspicion of a smile, merely gazed in the direction of the door and reflected upon the historic story which had aroused extraordinary interest at the time when the facts, to make matters worse, were made public with the usual affectionate letters that passed between them, full of sweet nothings. First it was strictly platonic till nature intervened and an attachment sprang up between them, till bit by bit matters came to a climax and the matter became the talk of the town till the staggering blow came as a welcome intelligence to not a few evil-disposed, however, who were resolved upon encompassing his downfall, though the thing was public property all along though not to anything like the sensational extent that it subsequently blossomed into. Since their names were coupled, though, since he was her declared favourite, where was the particular necessity to proclaim it to the rank and file from the housetops, the fact, namely, that he had shared her bedroom, which came out in the witness-box on oath, when a thrill went through the packed court literally electrifying everybody, in the shape of witnesses swearing to having witnessed him on such and such a particular date in the act of scrambling out of an upstairs apartment with the assistance of a ladder in night apparel, having gained admittance in the same fashion, a fact that the weeklies, addicted to the lubric a little, simply coined shoals of money out of. Whereas the simple fact of the case was it was simply a case of the husband not being up to the scratch with nothing in common between them beyond the name and then a real man arriving on the scene, strong to the verge of weakness, falling a victim to her siren charms and forgetting home ties, the usual sequel, to bask in the loved one's smiles. The eternal question of the life connubial, needless to say, cropped up. Can real love, supposing there happens to be another chap in the case, exist between married folk? Poser. Though it was no concern of theirs absolutely if he regarded her with affection, carried away by a wave of folly. A magnificent specimen of manhood he was truly, augmented obviously by gifts of a high order, as compared with the other military supernumerary, that is, who was just the usual everyday *farewell, my gallant captain* kind of an individual in the light dragoons, the 18th Hussars to be accurate, and inflammable doubtless (the fallen leader, that is, not the other) in his own peculiar way which she of course, woman, quickly perceived as highly likely to carve his way to fame, which he almost bid fair to do till the priests and ministers of the gospel as a whole, his erstwhile staunch adherents, and his beloved evicted tenants, for whom he had done yeoman service in the rural parts of the country by taking up the cudgels on their behalf in a way that exceeded their most sanguine expectations, very effectually cooked his matrimonial goose, thereby heaping coals of fire on his head much in the same way as the fabled ass's kick. Looking back now in a retrospective kind of arrangement, all seemed a kind of dream. And then coming back was the worst thing you ever did because it went without saying you would feel out of place as things always moved with the times. Why, as he reflected, Irishtown Strand, a locality he had not been in for quite a number of years, looked different somehow since, as it happened, he went to reside on the north side. North or south, however, it was just the well-known case of hot passion, pure and simple, upsetting the applecart with a vengeance and just bore out the very thing he was saying, as she also was Spanish or half so, types that wouldn't do things by halves, passionate abandon of the south, casting every shred of decency to the winds.

–Just bears out what I was saying, he, with glowing bosom, said to Stephen, about blood and the sun. And, if I don't greatly mistake, she was Spanish too.

–The king of Spain's daughter, Stephen answered, adding something or other rather muddled about farewell and adieu to you Spanish onions and the first land called the Deadman and from Ramhead to Scilly was so and so many . . .

–Was she? Bloom ejaculated, surprised, though not astonished by any means. I never heard that rumour before. Possible, especially there, it was, as she lived there. So, Spain.

Carefully avoiding a book in his pocket, *Sweets of*, which reminded him by the by of that Capel Street library book out of date, he took out his pocketbook and, turning over the various contents it contained rapidly, finally he . . .

–Do you consider, by the by, he said, thoughtfully selecting a faded photo which he laid on the table, that a Spanish type?

Stephen, obviously addressed, looked down on the photo showing a large-sized lady, with her fleshy charms on evidence in an open fashion, as she was in the full bloom of womanhood, in evening dress cut ostentatiously low for the occasion to give a liberal display of bosom, with more than vision of breasts, her full lips parted, and some perfect teeth, standing near, ostensibly with gravity, a piano, on the rest of which was

In old Madrid, a ballad, pretty in its way, which was then all the vogue. Her (the lady's) eyes, dark, large, looked at Stephen, about to smile about something to be admired, Lafayette of Westmoreland Street, Dublin's premier photographic artist, being responsible for the esthetic execution.

— Mrs Bloom, my wife, the prima donna Madam Marion Tweedy, Bloom indicated. Taken a few years since. In or about '96. Very like her then.

Beside the young man, he also looked at the photo of the lady now his legal wife who, he intimated, was the accomplished daughter of Major Brian Tweedy and displayed at an early age remarkable proficiency as a singer having even made her bow to the public when her years numbered barely sweet sixteen. As for the face, it was a speaking likeness in expression, but it did not do justice to her figure, which came in for a lot of notice usually and which did not come out to the best advantage in that getup. She could without difficulty, he said, have posed for the ensemble, not to dwell on certain opulent curves of the … He dwelt, being a bit of an artist in his spare time, on the female form in general developmentally because, as it so happened, no later than that afternoon he had seen those Grecian statues, perfectly developed as works of art, in the National Museum. Marble could give the original, shoulders, back, all the symmetry, all the rest, whereas no photo could, because it simply wasn't art, in a word.

The spirit moving him, he would much have liked to follow Jack Tar's good example and leave the likeness there for a very few minutes to speak for itself on the plea he … so that the other could drink in the beauty for himself, her stage presence being, frankly, a treat in itself which the camera could not at all do justice to. But it was scarcely professional etiquette so … though it was a warm pleasant sort of a night now yet wonderfully cool for the season considering, for sunshine after storm … and he did feel a kind of need there and then to follow suit like a kind of inward voice and satisfy a possible need by moving a motion. Nevertheless he sat tight, just viewing the slightly soiled photo creased by opulent curves, none the worse for wear however, and looked away thoughtfully with the intention of not further increasing the other's possible embarrassment while gauging her symmetry of heaving embonpoint. In fact, the slight soiling was only an added charm, like the case of linen slightly soiled, good as new, much better in fact, with the starch out. Suppose she was gone when he … ? *I looked for the lamp which she told me* came into his mind but merely as a passing fancy of his because he then recollected the morning littered bed et cetera and the book about Ruby with met him pike hoses (*sic*) in it which must have fell down sufficiently appropriately beside the domestic chamberpot with apologies to Lindley Murray.

The vicinity of the young man he certainly relished, educated, *distingué*, and impulsive into the bargain, far and away the pick of the bunch, though you wouldn't think he had it in him … yet you would. Besides, he said the picture was handsome which, say what you like, it was, though at the moment she was distinctly stouter. And why not? An awful lot of make-believe went on about that sort of thing involving a lifelong slur with the usual splash page of gutterpress about the same old matrimonial tangle alleging misconduct with professional golfer or the newest stage favourite instead of being honest and aboveboard about the whole business. How they were fated to meet and an attachment sprang up between the two so that their names were coupled in the public eye was told in court with letters containing the habitual mushy and compromising expressions, leaving no loophole, to show that they openly cohabited two or three times a week at some well-known seaside hotel and relations, when the thing ran its normal course, became in due course intimate. Then the decree nisi and the King's Proctor tries to show cause why and, he failing to quash it, nisi was made absolute. But as for that, the two misdemeanants, wrapped up as they largely were in one another, could safely afford to ignore it as they very largely did till the matter was put in the hands of a solicitor who filed a petition for the party wronged in due course. He, Bloom, enjoyed the distinction of being close to Erin's uncrowned king in the flesh when the thing occurred on the historic fracas when the fallen leader's – who notoriously stuck to his guns to the last drop even when clothed in the mantle of adultery – (leader's) trusty henchmen to the number of ten or a dozen or possibly even more than that penetrated into the printing works of the *Insuppressible* or, no, it was *United Ireland* (a by no means, by the by, appropriate appellative) and broke up the typecases with hammers or something like that all on account of some scurrilous effusions from the facile pens of the O'Brienite scribes at the usual mudslinging occupation reflecting on the erstwhile tribune's private morals. Though palpably a radically altered man he was still a commanding figure, though carelessly garbed as usual, with that look of settled purpose which went a long way with the shillyshallyers till they discovered to their vast discomfiture that their idol had feet of clay, after placing him upon a pedestal, which she, however, was the first to perceive. As those were particularly hot times, in the general hullaballoo

Bloom sustained a minor injury from a nasty prod of some chap's elbow in the crowd that of course congregated lodging some place about the pit of the stomach, fortunately not of a grave character. His hat (Parnell's), a silk one, was inadvertently knocked off and, as a matter of strict history, Bloom was the man who picked it up in the crush after witnessing the occurrence, meaning to return it to him (and return it to him he did with the utmost celerity), who, panting and hatless and whose thoughts were miles away from his hat at the time ... all the same, being a gentleman born with a stake in the country (he, as a matter of fact, having gone into it more for the kudos of the thing than anything else), what's bred in the bone, instilled into him in infancy at his mother's knee in the shape of knowing what good form was, came out at once because he turned round to the donor and thanked him with perfect aplomb, saying *Thank you, sir*, though in a very different tone of voice from the ornament of the legal profession whose headgear Bloom also set to rights earlier in the course of the day, history repeating itself with a difference, after the burial of a mutual friend when they had left him alone in his glory after the grim task of having committed his remains to the grave.

On the other hand, what incensed him more inwardly was the blatant jokes of the cabmen and so on, who passed it all off as a jest, laughing immoderately, pretending to understand everything, the why and the wherefore, and in reality not knowing their own minds, it being a case for the two parties themselves unless it ensued that the legitimate husband happened to be a party to it owing to some anonymous letter from the usual boy Jones who happened to come across them at the crucial moment in a loving position locked in one another's arms, drawing attention to their illicit proceedings and leading up to a domestic rumpus and the erring fair one begging forgiveness of her lord and master upon her knees and promising to sever the connection and not receive his visits any more if only the aggrieved husband would overlook the matter and let bygones be bygones, with tears in her eyes, though possibly with her tongue in her fair cheek at the same time, as quite possibly there were several others. He personally, being of a sceptical bias, believed, and didn't make the smallest bones about saying so either, that man, or men in the plural, were always hanging around on the waiting list about a lady, even supposing she was the best wife in the world and they got on fairly well together for the sake of argument, when, neglecting her duties, she chose to be tired of wedded life and was on for a little flutter in polite debauchery, to press their attentions on her with improper intent, the upshot being that her affections centred on another, the cause of many liaisons between still attractive married women getting on for fair and forty and younger men, no doubt, as several famous cases of feminine infatuation proved up to the hilt.

It was a thousand pities a young fellow blessed with an allowance of brains, as his neighbour obviously was, should waste his valuable time with profligate women who might present him with a nice dose to last him his lifetime. In the nature of single blessedness he would one day take unto himself a wife when Miss Right came on the scene, but in the interim ladies' society was a *conditio sine qua non* though he had the gravest possible doubts, not that he wanted in the smallest to pump Stephen about Miss Ferguson (who was very possibly the particular lodestar who brought him down to Irishtown so early in the morning), as to whether he would find much satisfaction basking in the boy and girl courtship idea and the company of smirking misses without a penny to their names bi- or tri-weekly with the orthodox preliminary canter of compliment-paying and walking out leading up to fond lovers' ways and flowers and chocs. To think of him house and homeless, rooked by some landlady worse than any stepmother, was really too bad at his age. The queer things he suddenly popped out with, rather like his father, attracted the elder man. But something substantial he certainly ought to eat, even were it only an eggflip made on unadulterated maternal nutriment or, failing that, the homely Humpty Dumpty boiled.

– At what o'clock did you dine? he questioned of the slim form and tired though unwrinkled face.

– Some time yesterday, Stephen said.

– Yesterday! exclaimed Bloom, till he remembered it was already tomorrow, Friday. Ah, you mean it's after twelve!

– The day before yesterday, Stephen said, improving on himself.

Literally astounded at this piece of intelligence, Bloom reflected. Though they didn't see eye to eye in everything, a certain analogy there somehow was, as if both their minds (though one was several years the other's senior) were travelling, so to speak, in the one train of thought. At his age when dabbling in politics, roughly some score of years previously when he had been a quasi-aspirant to parliamentary honours in the Buckshot Forster days, he too, he recollected in retrospect (which was a source of keen satisfaction in itself), had had a sneaking regard for those same ultra ideas. For instance, when the evicted tenants question, then at its first inception, bulked largely in people's mind, though, it goes without saying, not contributing a copper to the cause or pinning his faith absolutely to its dictums, some of which wouldn't exactly hold water, he at the outset, in principle at all events, was in thorough sympathy with peasant possession as voicing the trend of modern opinion, a partiality, however, which, realising his mistake, he was subsequently partially cured of, and even was twitted with going a step further than Michael Davitt in the striking views he at one time inculcated as a back-to-the-lander, which was one reason he strongly resented the innuendo put upon him in so barefaced a fashion by our friend at the gathering of the clans in Barney Kiernan's so that he, though often considerably misunderstood and the least pugnacious of mortals, be it repeated, departed from his customary habit to give him (metaphorically) one in the gizzard, though so far as politics themselves were concerned he was only too conscious of the casualties invariably resulting from propaganda and displays of mutual animosity and the misery and suffering it entailed as a foregone conclusion on fine young fellows chiefly, destruction of the fittest, in a word.

Anyhow, upon weighing up the pros and cons, getting on for one as it was, it was high time to be retiring for the night. The crux was it was a bit risky to bring him home as eventualities might possibly ensue (somebody having a temper of her own sometimes) and spoil the hash altogether as on the night he misguidedly brought home a dog (breed unknown) with a lame paw (not that the cases were either identical or the reverse, though he had hurt his hand too) to Ontario Terrace, as he very distinctly remembered, having been there, so to speak. On the other hand it was altogether far and away too late for the Sandymount or Sandycove suggestion so that he was in some perplexity as to which of the two alternatives ... Everything pointed to the fact that it behoved him to avail himself to the full of the opportunity, all things considered. His initial impression was that he was a bit standoffish and not overeffusive but it grew on him someway. For one thing he mightn't what you call jump at the idea, if approached, and what mostly worried him was he didn't know how to lead up to it or word it exactly, supposing he did entertain the proposal, as it would afford him very great personal pleasure if he would allow him to help to put coin in his way or some wardrobe, if found suitable. At all events, he wound up by concluding, eschewing for the nonce hidebound precedent, a cup of Epps's cocoa and, for the matter of that, a shakedown for the night plus the use of a rug or two and overcoat doubled into a pillow ... At least he would be in safe hands and as warm as a toast on a trivet. He failed to perceive any very vast amount of harm in that, always with the proviso no rumpus of any sort was kicked up. A move had to be made because that merry old soul, the grass widower in question who appeared to be glued to the spot, didn't appear in any particular hurry to wend his way home to his dearly beloved Queenstown and it was highly likely some sponger's bawdyhouse of retired beauties off Sheriff Street Lower where age was no bar would be the best clue to that equivocal character's whereabouts for a few days to come, alternately racking their feelings (the mermaids') with six-chamber revolver anecdotes verging on the tropical calculated to freeze the marrow of anybody's bones and mauling their large-sized charms betweenwhiles with rough-and-tumble gusto to the accompaniment of large potations of potheen and the usual blarney about himself for as to who in reality he was: let x equal my right name and address, as Mr Algebra remarks *passim*. At the same time he inwardly chuckled over his gentle repartee to the blood-and-ouns champion about his God being a Jew. People could put up with being bitten by a wolf but what properly riled them was a bite from a sheep. The most vulnerable point too of tender Achilles. Your God was a. Phew! ... Because mostly they appeared to imagine he came from Carrick-on-Shannon or somewhereabouts in the county Sligo.

—I propose, our hero eventually suggested after mature reflection, as it's rather stuffy here, you just come home with me and talk things over. My diggings are quite close in the vicinity. You can't drink that stuff. Do you like cocoa? Wait, I'll just pay this lot.

The best plan clearly being to clear out, the remainder being plain sailing, he beckoned, while prudently pocketing the photo, to the keeper of the shanty, who didn't seem to...

—Yes, that's the best, he assured Stephen, to whom for the matter of that the Brazen Head or him or anywhere else was all more or less...

All kinds of Utopian plans were flashing through his (Bloom's) busy brain, education (the genuine article), literature, journalism, prize titbits, up-to-date billing, concert tours in English watering resorts packed with hydros and seaside theatres, turning money away, duets in Italian with the accent perfectly true to nature, and a quantity of other things, no necessity of course to tell the world and his wife from the housetops about it. An opening was all was wanted and a slice of luck. Because he more than suspected he had his father's voice to bank his hopes on, which it was quite on the cards he had, so it would be just as well, by the way no harm, to trail the conversation in the direction of that particular red herring just to . . .

The cabby read out of the paper he had got hold of that the former viceroy, Earl Cadogan, had presided at the Cabdrivers' Association dinner in London somewhere. Silence with a yawn or two accompanied this thrilling announcement. Then the old specimen in the corner who appeared to have some spark of vitality left read out that Sir Anthony MacDonnell had left Euston for the Chief Secretary's Lodge or words to that effect. To which absorbing piece of intelligence echo answered, why.

– Give us a squint at that literature, grandfather, the ancient mariner put in, manifesting some natural impatience.

– And welcome, answered the elderly party thus addressed.

The sailor lugged out from a case he had a pair of greenish goggles which he very slowly hooked over his nose and both ears.

– Are you bad in the eyes? the sympathetic personage like the town clerk queried.

– Why, answered the seafarer with the tartan beard, who seemingly was a bit of a literary cove in his own small way, staring out of sea-green portholes as you might well describe them as, I uses goggles reading. Sand in the Red Sea done that. One time I could read a book in the dark, manner of speaking. *The Arabian Nights Entertainment* was my favourite and *Red as a Rose is She.*

Hereupon he pawed the journal open and pored upon Lord only knows what, found drowned or the exploits of King Willow, Iremonger having made a hundred and something second wicket not out for Notts. During which time (completely regardless of Ire) the keeper was intensely occupied loosening an apparently new or secondhand boot, which manifestly pinched him, as he muttered against whoever it was sold it, and all of them, those sufficiently awake enough to be picked out by their facial expressions that is to say, were either simply looking on glumly or passing a trivial remark.

To cut a long story short Bloom, grasping the situation, was the first to rise from his seat so as not to outstay their welcome, having first and foremost, being as good as his word that he would foot the bill for the occasion, taken the wise precaution to unobtrusively motion to mine host as a parting shot a scarcely perceptible sign when the others were not looking to the effect that the amount due was forthcoming, making a grand total of fourpence (the amount he deposited unobtrusively in four coppers, literally the last of the Mohicans), he having previously spotted on the printed price list for all who ran to read opposite to him in unmistakable figures, coffee 2d, confectionery do., and honestly well worth twice the money once in a way, as Wetherup used to remark.

— Come, he counselled to close the séance.

Seeing that the ruse worked and the coast was clear, they left the shelter or shanty together and the elite society of oilskin and company whom nothing short of an earthquake would move out of their *dolce far niente*. Stephen, who confessed to still feeling poorly and fagged out, paused at the ... for a moment ... the door to ...

— One thing I never understood, he said, to be original on the spur of the moment. Why they put tables upside down at night, I mean chairs upside down, on the tables in cafés.

To which impromptu the neverfailing Bloom replied without a moment's hesitation, saying straight off:

— To sweep the floor in the morning.

So saying he skipped around nimbly, considering, frankly at the same time apologetic, to get on his companion's right, a habit of his, by the by, his right side being, in classical idiom, his tender Achilles. The night air was certainly now a treat to breathe though Stephen was a bit weak on his pins.

— It will (the air) do you good, Bloom said, meaning also the walk, in a moment. The only thing is to walk, then you'll feel a different man. Come. It's not far. Lean on me.

Accordingly he passed his left arm in Stephen's right and led him on accordingly.

— Yes, Stephen said uncertainly, because he thought he felt a strange kind of flesh of a different man approach him, sinewless and wobbly and all that.

Anyhow, they passed the sentrybox with stones, brazier etc. where the municipal supernumerary, ex-Gumley, was still to all intents and purposes wrapped in the arms of Murphy, as the adage has it, dreaming of fresh fields and pastures new. And apropos of coffin of stones, the analogy was not at all bad as it was in fact a stoning to death on the part of seventy-two out of eighty-odd constituencies that ratted at the time of the split and chiefly the belauded peasant class, probably the selfsame evicted tenants he had put in their holdings.

So they passed on to chatting about music, a form of art for which Bloom, as a pure amateur, possessed the greatest love, as they made tracks arm in arm across Beresford Place. Wagnerian music, though confessedly grand in its way, was a bit too heavy for Bloom and hard to follow at the first go-off, but the music of Mercadante's *Huguenots*, Meyerbeer's *Seven Last Words on the Cross* and Mozart's *Twelfth Mass* he simply revelled in, the Gloria in that being to his mind the acme of first-class music as such, literally knocking everything else into a cocked hat. He infinitely preferred the sacred music of the Catholic Church to anything the opposite shop could offer in that line such as those Moody and Sankey hymns or *Bid me to live and I will live thy protestant to be.* He also yielded to none in his admiration of Rossini's *Stabat Mater*, a work simply abounding in immortal numbers in which his wife, Madam Marion Tweedy, made a hit, a veritable sensation, he might safely say, greatly adding to her other laurels and putting the others totally in the shade, in the Jesuit Fathers' church in Upper Gardiner Street, the sacred edifice being thronged to the doors to hear her with virtuosos, or virtuosi rather. There was the unanimous opinion that there was none to come up to her and, suffice it to say in a place of worship for music of a sacred character, there was a generally voiced desire for an encore. On the whole, though favouring preferably light opera of the *Don Giovanni* description, and *Martha*, a gem in its line, he had a *penchant*, though with only a surface knowledge, for the severe classical school such as Mendelssohn. And talking of that, taking it for granted he knew all about the old favourites, he mentioned *par excellence* Lionel's air in *Martha, M'appari*, which, curiously enough, he had heard, or overheard to be more accurate, on yesterday, a privilege he keenly appreciated, from the lips of Stephen's respected father, sung to perfection, a capital study of the number, in fact, which made all the others take a back seat. Stephen, in reply to a politely put query, said he didn't sing it but launched out into praises of Shakespeare's songs, at least of in or about that period, the lutenist Dowland who lived in Fetter Lane near Gerard the herbalist, who *annos ludendo hausi, Doulandus*, an instrument he was contemplating purchasing from Mr Arnold Dolmetsch, whom Bloom did not quite recall though the name certainly sounded familiar, for sixty-five guineas, and Farnaby and son with their *dux* and *comes* conceits and Byrd (William) who played the virginals, he said, in the Queen's Chapel or anywhere else he found them and one Tomkins who made toys or airs and John Bull.

On the roadway, beyond the swingchains which they were approaching whilst still speaking, a horse, dragging a sweeper, paced on the paven ground, brushing up a long swathe of mire, so that with the noise Bloom was not perfectly certain whether he had caught aright the allusion to sixty-five guineas and John Bull. He inquired if it was John Bull the political celebrity of that ilk, as it struck him, the two identical names, as a striking coincidence.

By the chains, the horse slowly swerved to turn, which perceiving, Bloom, who was keeping a sharp lookout as usual, plucked the other's sleeve gently, jocosely remarking:

— Our lives are in peril tonight. Beware of the steamroller.

They thereupon stopped. Bloom looked at the head of a horse not worth anything like sixty-five guineas suddenly in evidence in the dark, quite near, so that it seemed new, a different grouping of bones and even flesh, because palpably it was a fourwalker, a hipshaker, a black-buttocker, a taildangler, a headhanger, putting his hind foot foremost the while the lord of his creation sat on the perch, busy with his thoughts. But such a good poor brute he was sorry he hadn't a lump of sugar, but, as he wisely reflected, you could scarcely be prepared for every emergency that might crop up. He was just a big foolish nervous noodly kind of a horse, without a second care in the world. But even a dog, he reflected, take that mongrel in Barney Kiernan's, of the same size, would be a holy horror to face. But it was no animal's fault in particular if he was built that way, like the camel, ship of the desert, distilling grapes into potheen in his hump. Nine tenths of them all could be caged or trained, nothing beyond the art of man barring the bees: whale with a harpoon hairpin; alligator, tickle the small of his back and he sees the joke; chalk a circle for a rooster; tiger, my eagle eye. These timely reflections anent the brutes of the field occupied his mind, somewhat distracted from Stephen's words, while the ship of the street was manoeuvring and Stephen went on about the highly interesting old . . .

— What's this I was saying? Ah, yes! My wife, he intimated, plunging *in medias res*, would have the greatest of pleasure in making your acquaintance as she is passionately attached to music of any kind.

He looked sideways in a friendly fashion at the side-face of Stephen, image of his mother, which was not quite the same as the usual blackguard type they unquestionably had an indubitable hankering after as he was perhaps not that way built.

Still, supposing he had his father's gift, as he more than suspected, it opened up new vistas in his mind such as Lady Fingall's Irish Industries' concert on the preceding Monday and aristocracy in general.

Exquisite variations he was now describing on an air *Youth here has an end* by Jan Pieters Sweelinck, a Dutchman of Amsterdam where the frows come from. Even more he liked an old German song of Johannes Jeep about the clear sea and the voices of sirens, sweet murderers of men, which boggled Bloom a bit:

— *Von der Sirenen Listigkeit*
  Tun die Poeten dichten.

These opening bars he sang and translated extempore. Bloom, nodding, said he perfectly understood and begged him to go on by all means, which he did.

A phenomenally beautiful tenor voice like that, the rarest of boons, which Bloom appreciated at the very first note he got out, could easily, if properly handled by some recognised authority on voice production such as Barraclough, and being able to read music into the bargain, command its own price where baritones were ten a penny and procure for its fortunate possessor in the near future an *entrée* into fashionable houses in the best residential quarters of financial magnates in a large way of business and titled people where, with his university degree of B.A. (a huge ad in its way) and gentlemanly bearing to all the more influence the good impression, he would infallibly score a distinct success, being blessed with brains, which also could be utilised for the purpose, and other requisites, if his clothes were properly attended to, so as to the better worm his way into their good graces as he, a youthful tyro in society's sartorial niceties, hardly understood how a little thing like that could militate against you. It was in fact only a matter of months and he could easily foresee him participating in their musical and artistic *conversaziones* during the festivities of the Christmas season, for choice, causing a slight flutter in the dovecotes of the fair sex and being made a lot of by ladies out for sensation, cases of which, as he happened to know, were on record – in fact, without giving the show away, he himself once upon a time, if he cared to, could easily have … Added to which, of course, would be the pecuniary emolument, by no means to be sneezed at, going hand in hand with his tuition fees. Not, he parenthesised, that for the sake of filthy lucre he need necessarily embrace the lyric platform as a walk in life for any lengthy space of time but a step in the required direction it was, beyond yea or nay, and both monetarily and mentally it contained no reflection on his dignity in the smallest and it often turned in uncommonly handy to be handed a cheque at a much needed moment when every little helped. Besides, though taste latterly had deteriorated to a degree, original music like that, different from the conventional rut, would rapidly have a great vogue as it would be a decided novelty for Dublin's musical world after the usual hackneyed run of catchy tenor solos foisted on a confiding public by Ivan St Austell and Hilton St Just and their *genus omne*. Yes, beyond a shadow of a doubt he could, with all the cards in his hand, and he had a capital opening, make a name for himself and win a high place in the city's esteem where he could command a stiff figure and, booking ahead, give a grand concert for the patrons of the King Street house, given a backer-up, if one were forthcoming to kick him upstairs, so to speak – a big if, however – with some impetus of the go-ahead sort to obviate the inevitable procrastination which often tripped up a too much feted prince of good fellows and it need not detract from the other by one iota as, being his own master, he would have heaps of time to practise literature in his spare moments when desirous of so doing without its clashing with his vocal career or containing anything derogatory whatsoever as it was a matter for himself alone. In fact, he had the ball at his feet and that was the very reason why the other, possessed of a remarkably sharp nose for smelling a rat of any sort, hung on to him at all.

The horse was just then...

And later on at a propitious opportunity he purposed (Bloom did), without anyway prying into his private affairs on the *fools step in where angels* principle, advising him to sever his connection with a certain budding practitioner who, he noticed, was prone to disparage, and even, to a slight extent, with some hilarious pretext, when not present, to deprecate him, or whatever you like to call it, which, in Bloom's humble opinion, threw a nasty sidelight on that side of a person's character, no pun intended.

The horse, having reached the end of his tether, so to speak, halted, and, rearing high a proud feathering tail, added his quota by letting fall on the floor, which the brush would soon brush up and polish, three smoking globes of turds. Slowly, three times, one after another, from a full crupper, he mired. And humanely his driver waited till he (or she) had ended, patient in his scythed car.

Side by side Bloom, profiting by the contretemps, with Stephen passed through the gap of the chains, divided by the upright, and, stepping over a strand of mire, went across towards Gardiner Street Lower, Stephen singing more boldly, but not loudly, the end of the ballad:

– *Und alle Schiffe brechen.*

The driver never said a word, good, bad or indifferent but merely watched the two figures, *as he sat on his low-backed car*, both black, one full, one lean, walk towards the railway bridge, *to be married by Father Maher*. As they walked they at times stopped and walked again, continuing their tête-à-tête (which of course he was utterly out of) about sirens, enemies of man's reason, mingled with a number of other topics of the same category, usurpers, historical cases of the kind, while the man in the sweeper car or you might as well call it in the sleeper car who in any case couldn't possibly hear because they were too far simply sat in his seat near the end of Lower Gardiner Street *and looked after their low-backed car*.

What parallel courses did Bloom and Stephen follow returning?

Starting united, both at normal walking pace, from Beresford Place they followed in the order named Lower and Middle Gardiner Streets and Mountjoy Square West: then, at reduced pace, each bearing left, Gardiner's Place by an inadvertence as far as the farther corner of Temple Street North: then, at reduced pace with interruptions of halt, bearing right, Temple Street North as far as Hardwicke Place. Approaching, disparate, at relaxed walking pace they crossed both the circus before George's Church diametrically, the chord in any circle being less than the arc which it subtends.

Of what did the duumvirate deliberate during their itinerary?

Music, literature, Ireland, Dublin, Paris, friendship, woman, prostitution, diet, the influence of gaslight or the light of arc and glowlamps on the growth of adjoining paraheliotropic trees, exposed Corporation emergency dustbuckets, the Roman Catholic Church, ecclesiastical celibacy, the Irish nation, Jesuit education, careers, the study of medicine, the past day, the maleficent influence of the pre-Sabbath, Stephen's collapse.

Did Bloom discover common factors of similarity between their respective like and unlike reactions to experience?

Both were sensitive to artistic impressions, musical in preference to plastic or pictorial. Both preferred a continental to an insular manner of life, a cisatlantic to a transatlantic place of residence. Both indurated by early domestic training and an inherited tenacity of heterodox resistance professed their disbelief in many orthodox religious, national, social and ethical doctrines. Both admitted the alternately stimulating and obtunding influence of heterosexual magnetism.

Were their views on some points divergent?

Stephen dissented openly from Bloom's views on the importance of dietary and civic self-help while Bloom dissented tacitly from Stephen's views on the eternal affirmation of the spirit of man in literature. Bloom assented covertly to Stephen's rectification of the anachronism involved in assigning the date of the conversion of the Irish nation to Christianity from druidism by Patrick, son of Calpurnius son of Potitus son of Odysseus, sent by Pope Celestine I in the year 432 in the reign of Leary to the year 260 or thereabouts in the reign of Cormac MacArt, † A.D. 266 suffocated by imperfect deglutition of aliment at Sletty and interred at Rossnaree. The collapse which Bloom ascribed to gastric inanition and certain chemical compounds of varying degrees of adulteration and alcoholic strength, accelerated by mental exertion and the velocity of rapid circular motion in a relaxing atmosphere, Stephen attributed to the reapparition of a matutinal cloud (perceived by both from two different points of observation, Sandycove and Dublin) at first no bigger than a woman's hand.

Was there one point on which their views were equal and negative?
The influence of gaslight or electric light on the growth of adjoining paraheliotropic trees.

Had Bloom discussed similar subjects during nocturnal perambulations in the past?
In 1884 with Owen Goldberg and Donald Turnbull at night on public thoroughfares between Longwood Avenue and Leonard's Corner, and Leonard's Corner and Synge Street, and Synge Street and Bloomfield Avenue. In 1885 with Percy Apjohn in the evenings reclined against the wall between Gibraltar Villa and Bloomfield House in Crumlin, barony of Uppercross. In 1886 occasionally with casual acquaintances and prospective purchasers on doorsteps, in front parlours, in third-class railway carriages of suburban lines. In 1888 frequently with Major Brian Tweedy and his daughter Miss Marion Tweedy, together and separately, on the lounge in Matthew Dillon's house in Roundtown. Once in 1892 and once in 1893 with Julius (Juda) Masliansky, on both occasions in the parlour of his (Bloom's) house in Lombard Street West.

What reflection concerning the irregular sequence of dates 1884, 1885, 1886, 1888, 1892, 1893, 1904 did Bloom make before their arrival at their destination?
He reflected that the progressive extension of the field of individual development and experience was regressively accompanied by a restriction of the converse domain of interindividual relations.

As in what ways?
From inexistence to existence he came to many and was as one

received: existence with existence he was with any as any with any: from existence to nonexistence gone he would be by all as none perceived.

What action did Bloom make on their arrival at their destination?

At the house steps of the 4th of the equidifferent uneven numbers, number 7 Eccles Street, he inserted his hand mechanically into the back pocket of his trousers to obtain his latchkey.

Was it there?

It was in the corresponding pocket of the trousers which he had worn on the day but one preceding.

Why was he doubly irritated?

Because he had forgotten and because he remembered that he had reminded himself twice not to forget.

What were then the alternatives before the respectively premeditatedly and inadvertently keyless couple?

To enter or not to enter. To knock or not to knock.

Bloom's decision?

A stratagem. Resting his feet on the dwarf wall, he climbed over the area railings, compressed his hat on his head, grasped two points at the lower union of rails and stiles, lowered his body gradually by its length of five feet nine inches and a half to within two feet ten inches of the area pavement and allowed his body to move freely in space by separating himself from the railings and crouching in preparation for the impact of the fall.

Did he fall?

By his body's known weight of eleven stone and four pounds in avoirdupois measure, as certified by the graduated machine for periodical self-weighing in the premises of Francis Froedman, pharmaceutical chemist, of 19 Frederick Street North, on the last Feast of the Ascension, to wit, the twelfth day of May of the bissextile year one thousand nine hundred and four of the Christian Era (Jewish Era five thousand six hundred and sixty-four, Mohammedan Era one thousand three hundred and twenty-two), Golden Number 5, Epact 13, Solar Cycle 9, Dominical Letters CB, Roman Indiction 2, Julian Period 6617, MCMIV.

Did he rise uninjured by concussion?

Regaining new stable equilibrium he rose uninjured though concussed by the impact, raised the latch of the area door by the exertion of force at its freely moving flange, by leverage of the first kind applied at its fulcrum gained retarded access to the kitchen through the subadjacent scullery, ignited a lucifer match by friction, set free inflammable coal gas by turning on the vent cock, lit a high flame which by regulating he reduced to quiescent candescence and lit finally a portable candle.

What discrete succession of images did Stephen meanwhile perceive?

Reclined against the area railings he perceived through the transparent kitchen panes a man regulating a gas flame of 14 CP, a man lighting a candle of 1 CP, a man removing in turn each of his two boots, a man leaving the kitchen holding a candle.

Did the man reappear elsewhere?

After a lapse of four minutes the glimmer of his candle was discernible through the semitransparent semicircular glass fanlight over the hall door. The hall door turned gradually on its hinges. In the open space of the doorway the man reappeared, without his hat, with his candle.

Did Stephen obey his sign?

Yes, entering softly, he helped to close and chain the door and followed softly along the hallway the man's back and listed feet and lighted candle past a lighted crevice of doorway on the left and carefully down a turning staircase of more than five steps into the kitchen of Bloom's house.

What did Bloom do?

He extinguished the candle by a sharp expiration of breath upon its flame, drew two spoon-seat deal chairs to the hearthstone, one for Stephen with its back to the area window, the other for himself when necessary, knelt on one knee, composed in the grate a pyre of crosslaid resin-tipped sticks and various coloured papers and irregular polygons of best Abram coal at twenty-one shillings a ton from the yard of Messrs Flower and M'Donald of 14 D'Olier Street and kindled it at three projecting points of paper with one ignited lucifer match, thereby releasing the potential energy contained in the fuel by allowing its carbon and hydrogen elements to enter into free union with the oxygen of the air.

Of what similar apparitions did Stephen think?

Of others elsewhere in other times who, kneeling on one knee or on two, had kindled fires for him: of Brother Michael in the infirmary of the college of the Society of Jesus at Clongowes Wood, Sallins, in the county of Kildare: of his father Simon Dedalus in an unfurnished room of his first residence in Dublin, number 13 Fitzgibbon Street: of his godmother Miss Kate Morkan in the house of her dying sister Miss Julia Morkan at 15 Usher's Island: of his aunt Sara, wife of Richie (Richard Goulding), in the kitchen of their lodgings at number 62 Clanbrassil Street: of his mother Mary in the kitchen of number 12 North Richmond Street on the morning of the Feast of Saint Francis Xavier 1898: of the dean of studies, Father Butt, in the physics theatre of University College, numbers 84A-87 Stephen's Green South: of his sister Dilly (Delia) in his father's house in Cabra.

What did Stephen see on raising his gaze to the height of a yard from the fire towards the opposite wall?

Under a row of five coiled spring housebells a curvilinear rope stretched between two holdfasts athwart across the recess beside the chimney pier from which hung four small-sized square handkerchiefs folded unattached consecutively in adjacent rectangles and one pair of ladies' grey hose with lisle suspender tops and feet in their habitual position clamped by three erect wooden pegs two at their outer extremities and the third at their point of junction.

What did Bloom see on the range?

On the right (smaller) hob a blue enamelled saucepan: on the left (larger) hob a black iron kettle.

What did Bloom do at the range?

He removed the saucepan to the left hob, raised and carried the iron kettle to the sink in order to tap the current by turning the faucet to let it flow.

Did it flow?

Yes. From Roundwood reservoir in County Wicklow, of a cubic capacity of 2400 million gallons, percolating through a subterranean aqueduct of filter mains of single and double pipage, constructed at an initial plant cost of £5 per linear yard, by way of the Dargle, Rathdown, Glen of the Downs and Callowhill to the 26-acre reservoir at Stillorgan, a distance of 22 statute miles, and thence through a system of relieving tanks by a gradient of 250 feet to the city boundary at Eustace Bridge, Upper Leeson Street, though from prolonged summer drouth and daily supply of 12½ million gallons the water had fallen below the sill of the overflow weir for which reason the borough surveyor and waterworks engineer, Mr Spencer

Harty C.E., on the instructions of the waterworks committee had prohibited the use of municipal water for purposes other than those of consumption (envisaging the possibility of recourse being had to the impotable water of the Grand and Royal Canals as in 1893), particularly as the South Dublin Guardians, notwithstanding their ration of 15 gallons per day per pauper supplied through a 6-inch meter, had been convicted of a wastage of 20,000 gallons per night by a reading of their meter on the affirmation of the law agent of the Corporation, Mr Ignatius Rice, solicitor, thereby acting to the detriment of another section of the public, self-supporting taxpayers, solvent, sound.

What in water did Bloom, waterlover, drawer of water, watercarrier, returning to the range, admire?

Its universality: its democratic equality and constancy to its nature in seeking its own level: its vastness in the ocean of Mercator's projection: its unplumbed profundity in the Marianne Trench of the Pacific, exceeding 6000 fathoms: the restlessness of its waves and surface particles visiting in turn all points of its seaboard: the independence of its units: the variability of states of sea: its hydrostatic quiescence in calm: its hydrokinetic turgidity in neap and spring tides: its subsidence after devastation: its sterility in the circumpolar icecaps, arctic and antarctic: its climatic and commercial significance: its preponderance of 3 to 1 over the dry land of the globe: its indisputable hegemony extending in square leagues over all the region below the subequatorial tropic of Capricorn: the multisecular stability of its primeval basin: its luteofulvous bed: its capacity to dissolve and hold in solution all soluble substances including millions of tons of the most precious metals: its slow erosions of peninsulas and islands: its persistent formation of homothetic islands, peninsulas and downward-tending promontories: its alluvial deposits: its weight and volume and density: its imperturbability in lagoons, atolls and highland tarns: its gradation of colours in the torrid and temperate and frigid zones: its vehicular ramifications in continental lake-contained streams and confluent oceanflowing rivers with their tributaries and transoceanic currents, gulf stream, north and south equatorial courses: its violence in seaquakes, waterspouts, artesian wells, eruptions, torrents, eddies, freshets, spates, groundswells, watersheds, water partings, geysers, cataracts, whirlpools, maelstroms, inundations, deluges, cloudbursts: its vast circumterrestrial ahorizontal curve: its secrecy in springs and in latent humidity, revealed by rhabdomantic and hygrometric instruments, exemplified by the well by the hole in the wall at Ashtown gate and by saturation of air, distillation of dew: the simplicity of its composition, two constituent parts of hydrogen with one constituent part of oxygen: its healing virtues: its buoyancy in the waters of the Dead Sea: its persevering penetrativeness in runnels, gullies, inadequate dams, leaks on shipboard: its properties for cleansing, quenching thirst and fire, nourishing vegetation: its infallibility as paradigm and paragon: its metamorphoses as vapour, mist, cloud, rain, sleet, snow, hail: its strength in rigid hydrants: its variety of forms in loughs and bays and gulfs and bights and guts and lagoons and atolls and archipelagos and sounds and fjords and minches and tidal estuaries and arms of sea: its solidity in glaciers, icebergs, ice floes: its docility in working hydraulic millwheels, turbines, dynamos, electric power stations, bleachworks, tanneries, scutchmills: its utility in canals, rivers if navigable, floating and graving docks: its potentiality derivable from harnessed tides or watercourses falling from level to level: its submarine fauna and flora (anacoustic, photophobe) numerically, if not literally, the premier inhabitants of the globe: its ubiquity as constituting 90% of the human body: the noxiousness of its effluvia in lacustrine marshes, pestilential fens, faded flowerwater, stagnant pools in the waning moon.

Having set the half-filled kettle on the now burning coals, why did he return to the still flowing tap?

To wash his soiled hands with a partially consumed tablet of Barrington's lemon-flavoured soap, to which paper still adhered, bought thirteen hours previously for fourpence and still unpaid for, in fresh cold neverchanging everchanging water and dry them, face and hands, in a long red-bordered holland cloth passed over a wooden revolving roller.

What reason did Stephen give for declining Bloom's offer?

That he was hydrophobe, hating partial contact by immersion or total by submersion in cold water (his last bath having taken place in the month of October of the preceding year), disliking the aqueous substances of glass and crystal, distrusting aquacities of thought and language.

What impeded Bloom from giving Stephen counsels of hygiene and prophylactic to which should be added suggestions concerning a preliminary wetting of the head and contraction of the muscles with rapid splashing of the face and neck and thoracic and epigastric region in case of sea or river bathing, the parts of the human anatomy most sensitive to cold being the nape, stomach and thenar or sole of foot?

The incompatibility of aquacity with the erratic originality of genius.

What additional didactic counsels did he similarly repress?

Dietary: concerning the respective percentage of protein and caloric energy in bacon, salt ling and butter, the absence of the former in the last named and the abundance of the latter in the first named.

Which seemed to the host to be the predominant qualities of his guest?

Confidence in himself, an equal and opposite power of abandonment and recuperation.

What concomitant phenomenon took place in the vessel of liquid by the agency of fire?

The phenomenon of ebullition. Fanned by a constant updraught of ventilation between the kitchen and the chimney flue, ignition was communicated from the faggots of precombustible fuel to polyhedral masses of bituminous coal, containing in compressed mineral form the foliated fossilised decidua of primeval forests which had in turn derived their vegetative existence from the sun, primal source of heat (radiant, transmitted through omnipresent luminiferous diathermanous ether). Heat (convected, a mode of motion developed by such combustion) was constantly and increasingly conveyed from the source of calorification to the liquid contained in the vessel, being radiated through the uneven unpolished dark surface of the metal iron, in part reflected, in part absorbed, in part transmitted, gradually raising the temperature of the water from normal to boiling point, a rise in temperature expressible as the result of an expenditure of 162 thermal units needed to raise 1 pound of water from 50° to 212° Fahrenheit.

What announced the accomplishment of this rise in temperature?

A double falciform ejection of water vapour from under the kettlelid at both sides simultaneously.

For what personal purpose could Bloom have applied the water so boiled?

To shave himself.

What advantages attended shaving by night?

A softer beard: a softer brush if intentionally allowed to remain from shave to shave in its agglutinated lather: a softer skin if unexpectedly encountering female acquaintances in remote places at incustomary hours: quiet reflections upon the course of the day: a cleaner sensation when awaking after a fresher sleep: since matutinal noises, premonitions and perturbations, a clattered milkcan, a postman's double knock, a paper read, reread while lathering, relathering the same spot, a shock, a shot, with thought of aught he sought though fraught with nought, might cause a faster rate of shaving and a nick on which incision plaster with precision cut and humected and applied adhered: which was to be done.

Why did absence of light disturb him less than presence of noise?

Because of the surety of the sense of touch in his firm full masculine feminine passive active hand.

What quality did it (his hand) possess but with what counteracting influence?

The operative surgical quality but that he was reluctant to shed human blood even when the end justified the means, preferring, in their natural order, heliotherapy, psychophysicotherapeutics, osteopathic surgery.

What lay under exposure on the lower, middle and upper shelves of the kitchen dresser, opened by Bloom?

On the lower shelf five vertical breakfast plates, six horizontal breakfast saucers on which rested inverted breakfast cups, a moustache cup, uninverted, and saucer of Crown Derby, four white gold-rimmed eggcups, an open shammy purse displaying coins, mostly copper, and a phial of aromatic (violet) comfits. On the middle shelf a chipped eggcup containing pepper, a drum of table salt, four conglomerated black olives in oleaginous paper, an empty pot of Plumtree's potted meat, an oval wicker basket bedded with fibre and containing one Jersey pear, a half-empty bottle of William Gilbey and Co.'s white invalid port, half disrobed of its swathe of coral-pink tissue paper, a packet of Epps's soluble cocoa, five ounces of Anne Lynch's choice tea at 2/- per lb in a crinkled lead-paper bag, a cylindrical canister containing the best crystallised lump sugar, two onions, one, the larger, Spanish, entire, the other, smaller, Irish, bisected with augmented surface and more redolent, a jar of Irish Model Dairy cream, a brown crockery jug containing a noggin and a quarter of soured adulterated milk, converted by heat into water, acidulous serum and semisolidified curds, which, added to the quantity subtracted for Mrs

Bloom's and Mrs Fleming's breakfasts, made one imperial pint, the total quantity originally delivered, two cloves, a halfpenny and a small dish containing a slice of fresh rib steak. On the upper shelf a battery of jamjars (empty) of various sizes and provenances.

What attracted his attention lying on the apron of the dresser?
Four polygonal fragments of two lacerated scarlet betting tickets, numbered 8 87, 8 86.

What reminiscences temporarily corrugated his brow?
Reminiscences of coincidences, truth stranger than fiction, preindicative of the result of the Gold Cup flat handicap, the official and definitive result of which he had read in the *Evening Telegraph*, late pink edition, in the cabman's shelter at Butt Bridge.

Where had previous intimations of the result, effected or projected, been received by him?
In Bernard Kiernan's licensed premises, 8, 9 and 10 Little Britain Street: in David Byrne's licensed premises, 21 Duke Street: in O'Connell Street Lower outside Graham Lemon's when a dark man had placed in his hand a throwaway (subsequently thrown away) advertising Elijah, restorer of the church in Zion: in Lincoln Place outside the premises of F.W. Sweny and Co. Limited, dispensing chemists, when, when Frederick M. (Bantam) Lyons had rapidly and successively requested, perused and restituted the copy of the current issue of the *Freeman's Journal and National Press* which he had been about to throw away (subsequently thrown away), he had proceeded towards the oriental edifice of the Turkish and Warm Baths, 11 Leinster Street, with the light of inspiration shining in his countenance and bearing in his arms the secret of the race, graven in the language of prediction.

What qualifying considerations allayed his perturbations?
The difficulties of interpretation, since the significance of any event followed its occurrence as variably as the acoustic report followed the electrical discharge, and of counterestimating against an actual loss by failure to interpret the total sum of possible losses proceeding originally from a successful interpretation.

His mood?
He had not risked, he did not expect, he had not been disappointed, he was satisfied.

What satisfied him?

To have sustained no positive loss. To have brought a positive gain to others. Light to the gentiles.

How did Bloom prepare a collation for a gentile?

He poured into two teacups two level spoonfuls, four in all, of Epps's soluble cocoa and proceeded according to the directions for use printed on the label, to each adding after sufficient time for infusion the prescribed ingredients for diffusion in the manner and in the quantity prescribed.

What supererogatory marks of special hospitality did the host show his guest?

Relinquishing his symposiarchal right to the moustache cup of imitation Crown Derby presented to him by his only daughter, Millicent (Milly), he substituted a cup identical with that of his guest and served extraordinarily to his guest and, in reduced measure, to himself the viscous cream ordinarily reserved for the breakfast of his wife Marion (Molly).

Was the guest conscious of and did he acknowledge these marks of hospitality?

His attention was directed to them by his host jocosely and he accepted them seriously as they drank in jocoserious silence Epps's mass-product, the creature cocoa.

Were there marks of hospitality which the host contemplated but suppressed, reserving them for another and for himself on future occasions to complete the act begun?

The reparation of a fissure of the length of 1½ inches in the right side of his guest's jacket. A gift to his guest of one of the four lady's handkerchiefs, if and when ascertained to be in a presentable condition.

Who drank more quickly?

Bloom, having the advantage of ten seconds at the initiation and taking, from the concave surface of a spoon along the handle of which a steady flow of heat was conducted, three sips to his opponent's one, six to two, nine to three.

What cerebration accompanied his frequentative act?

Concluding by inspection but erroneously that his silent companion was engaged in mental composition he reflected on the pleasures derived from literature of instruction rather than of amusement as he himself had applied to the works of William Shakespeare more than once for the solution of difficult problems in imaginary or real life.

Had he found their solution?

In spite of careful and repeated reading of certain classical passages, aided by a glossary, he had derived imperfect conviction from the text, the answers not bearing on all points.

What lines concluded his first piece of original verse, written by him, potential poet, at the age of 11 in 1877 on the occasion of the offering of three prizes of 10/-, 5/- and 2/6 respectively for competition by the *Shamrock*, a weekly newspaper?

> *An ambition to squint*
> *At my verses in print*
> *Makes me hope that for these you'll find room.*
> *If you so condescend*
> *Then please place at the end*
> *The name of yours truly, L. Bloom.*

Did he find four separating forces between his temporary guest and him?

Name, age, race, creed.

What anagrams had he made on his name in youth?

> Leopold Bloom
> Ellpodbomool
> Molldopeloob
> Bollopedoom
> Old Ollebo M.P.

What acrostic upon the abbreviation of his first name had he (kinetic poet) sent to Miss Marion (Molly) Tweedy on the 14 February 1888?

> **P**oets oft have sung in rhyme
> **O**f music sweet their praise divine.
> **L**et them hymn it nine times nine.
> **D**earer far than song or wine,
> **Y**ou are mine. The world is mine.

What had prevented him from completing a topical song (music by R.G. Johnston) on the events of the past, or fixtures for the actual, years, entitled *If Brian Boru could but come back and see old Dublin now,* commissioned by Michael Gunn, lessee of the Gaiety Theatre, 46, 47, 48, 49 South King Street, and to be introduced into the sixth scene, the valley of diamonds, of the second edition (30 January 1893) of the grand annual Christmas pantomime *Sinbad the Sailor* (produced by R. Shelton 26 December 1892, written by Greenleaf Withers, scenery by George A. Jackson and Cecil Hicks, costumes by Mrs and Miss Whelan under the personal supervision of Mrs Michael Gunn, ballets by Jessie Noir, harlequinade by Thomas Otto) and sung by Nellie Bouverie, principal girl?

Firstly, oscillation between events of imperial and of local interest, the anticipated diamond jubilee of Queen Victoria (born 1820, acceded 1837) and the posticipated opening of the new municipal fish market: secondly, apprehension of opposition from extreme circles on the questions of the respective visits of Their Royal Highnesses the duke and duchess of York (real) and of His Majesty King Brian Boru (imaginary): thirdly, a conflict between professional etiquette and professional emulation concerning the recent erections of the Grand Lyric Hall on Burgh Quay and the Theatre Royal in Hawkins Street: fourthly, distraction resultant from compassion for Nellie Bouverie's non-intellectual, non-political, non-topical expression of countenance and concupiscence caused by Nellie Bouverie's revelations of white articles of non-intellectual, non-political, non-topical underclothing while she (Nellie Bouverie) was in the articles: fifthly, the difficulties of the selection of appropriate music and humorous allusions from *Everybody's Book of Jokes* (1000 pages and a laugh in every one): sixthly, the rhymes, homophonous and cacophonous, associated with the names of the new lord mayor Daniel Tallon, the new high sheriff Thomas Pile and the new solicitor general Dunbar Plunket Barton.

What relation existed between their ages?

16 years before in 1888 when Bloom was of Stephen's present age Stephen was 6. 16 years after in 1920 when Stephen would be of Bloom's present age Bloom would be 54. In 1936 when Bloom would be 70 and Stephen 54 their ages initially in the ratio of 16 to 0 would be as 17½ to 13½, the proportion increasing and the disparity diminishing according as arbitrary future years were added, for if the proportion existing in 1883 had continued immutable, conceiving that to be possible, till then, then in 1904 when Stephen was 22 Bloom would be 374 and in 1920 when Stephen would be 38, as Bloom then was, Bloom would be 646 while in 1952 when Stephen would have attained the maximum postdiluvian age of 70 Bloom, being 1190 years alive having been born in the year 762,

would have surpassed by 221 years the maximum antediluvian age, that of Methuselah, 969 years, while if Stephen would continue to live until he would attain that age in the year A.D. 3072 Bloom would have been obliged to have been alive 20,230 years, having been obliged to have been born in the year 17,158 B.C.

What events might nullify these calculations?

The cessation of existence of both or either, the inauguration of a new era or calendar, the annihilation of the world and consequent extermination of the human species, inevitable but unpredictable.

How many previous encounters proved their preexisting acquaintance?

Two. The first in the lilac garden of Matthew Dillon's house, Medina Villa, Kimmage Road, Roundtown, in 1887, in the company of Stephen's mother, Stephen being then of the age of 5 and reluctant to give his hand in salutation. The second in the coffee room of Breslin's Hotel on a rainy Sunday in the January of 1892, in the company of Stephen's father and Stephen's granduncle, Stephen being then 5 years older.

Did Bloom accept the invitation to dinner given then by the son and afterwards seconded by the father?

Very gratefully, with grateful appreciation, with sincere appreciative gratitude, in appreciatively grateful sincerity of regret, he declined.

Did their conversation on the subject of these reminiscences reveal a third connecting link between them?

Mrs Riordan (Dante), a widow of independent means, had resided in the house of Stephen's parents from 1 September 1888 to 29 December 1891 and had also resided during the years 1892, 1893 and 1894 in the City Arms Hotel owned by Elizabeth O'Dowd of 55 Prussia Street where, during parts of the years 1893 and 1894, she had been a constant informant of Bloom who resided also in the same hotel, being at that time a clerk in the employment of Joseph Cuffe of 5 Smithfield for the superintendence of sales in the adjacent Dublin cattle market on the North Circular Road.

Had he performed any special corporal work of mercy for her?

He had sometimes propelled her on warm summer evenings, an infirm widow of independent, if limited, means, in her convalescent Bath chair with slow revolutions of its wheels as far as the corner of the North Circular Road opposite Mr Gavin Low's place of business where she had remained for a certain time scanning through his one-lensed binocular field glasses unrecognisable citizens on tramcars, roadster bicycles equipped with inflated pneumatic tyres, hackney carriages, tandems, private and hired landaus, dogcarts, pony traps and brakes passing from the city to the Phoenix Park and vice versa.

Why could he then support that his vigil with the greater equanimity?

Because in middle youth he had often sat observing through a rondel of bossed glass of a multicoloured pane the spectacle offered with continual changes of the thoroughfare without, pedestrians, quadrupeds, velocipedes, vehicles, passing slowly, quickly, evenly, round and round and round the rim of a round and round precipitous globe.

What distinct different memories had each of her now eight years deceased?

The older, her bezique cards and counters, her Skye terrier, her supposititious wealth, her lapses of responsiveness and incipient catarrhal deafness: the younger, her lamp of colza oil before the statue of the Immaculate Conception, her green and maroon brushes for Charles Stewart Parnell and for Michael Davitt, her tissue papers.

Were there no means still remaining to him to achieve the rejuvenation which these reminiscences divulged to a younger companion rendered the more desirable?

The indoor exercises, formerly intermittently practised, subsequently abandoned, prescribed in Eugen Sandow's *Physical Strength and How to Obtain It* which, designed particularly for commercial men engaged in sedentary occupations, were to be made with mental concentration in front of a mirror so as to bring into play the various families of muscles and produce successively a pleasant rigidity, a more pleasant relaxation and the most pleasant repristination of juvenile agility.

Had any special agility been his in earlier youth?

Though ringweight lifting had been beyond his strength and the full circle gyration beyond his courage, yet as a High School scholar he had excelled in his stable and protracted execution of the half-lever movement on the parallel bars in consequence of his abnormally developed abdominal muscles.

Did either openly allude to their racial difference?
Neither.

What, reduced to their simplest reciprocal form, were Bloom's thoughts about Stephen's thoughts about Bloom and Bloom's thoughts about Stephen's thoughts about Bloom's thoughts about Stephen?

He thought that he thought that he was a Jew whereas he knew that he knew that he knew that he was not.

What, the enclosures of reticence removed, were their respective parentages?

Bloom, only born male transubstantial heir of Rudolf Virag (subsequently Rudolph Bloom) of Szombathely, Vienna, Budapest, Milan, London and Dublin, and of Ellen Higgins, second daughter of Julius Higgins (born Karoly) and Fanny Higgins (born Hegarty). Stephen, eldest surviving male consubstantial heir of Simon Dedalus of Cork and Dublin, and of Mary, daughter of Richard Goulding and Christina Goulding (born Grier).

Had Bloom and Stephen been baptised, and where and by whom, cleric or layman?

Bloom (three times): by the Reverend Mr Gilmer Johnston M.A., alone, in the Protestant church of Saint Nicholas Without, Coombe: by James O'Connor, Philip Gilligan and James Fitzpatrick, together, under a pump in the village of Swords: and by the Reverend Charles Malone C.C. in the church of the Three Patrons, Rathgar. Stephen (once) by the Reverend Charles Malone C.C., alone, in the church of the Three Patrons, Rathgar.

Did they find their educational careers similar?

Substituting Stephen for Bloom, Stoom would have passed successively through a dame's school and the High School. Substituting Bloom for Stephen, Blephen would have passed successively through the preparatory, junior, middle and senior grades of the intermediate and through the matriculation, first arts, second arts and arts degree courses of the Royal University.

Why did Bloom refrain from stating that he had frequented the university of life?

Because of his fluctuating incertitude as to whether this observation had or had not been already made by him to Stephen or by Stephen to him.

What two temperaments did they individually represent?

The scientific. The artistic.

What proofs did Bloom adduce to prove that his tendency was towards applied, rather than towards pure, science?

Certain possible inventions of which he had cogitated when reclining in a state of supine repletion to aid digestion, stimulated by his appreciation of the importance of inventions now common but once revolutionary, for example the aeronautic parachute, the reflecting telescope, the spiral corkscrew, the safety pin, the mineral water siphon, the canal lock with winch and sluice, the suction pump.

Were these inventions principally intended for an improved scheme of kindergarten?

Yes, rendering obsolete popguns, elastic air bladders, games of hazard, catapults. They comprised astronomical kaleidoscopes exhibiting the twelve constellations of the zodiac from Aries to Pisces, miniature mechanical orreries, arithmetical gelatine lozenges, geometrical to correspond with zoological biscuits, globe-map playing balls, historically costumed dolls.

What also stimulated him in his cogitations?

The financial success achieved by Ephraim Marks and Charles A. James, the former by his 1*d* bazaar at 42 George's Street South, the latter at his 6½*d* shop and world's fancy fair and waxwork exhibition at 30 Henry Street, admission 2*d*, children 1*d*: the infinite possibilities hitherto unexploited of the modern art of advertisement if condensed in triliteral monoïdeal symbols, vertically of maximum visibility (divined), horizontally of maximum legibility (deciphered) and of magnetising efficacy to arrest involuntary attention, to interest, to convince, to decide.

Such as?

K. 11. Kino's 11/- Trousers.

House of Keys. Alexander J. Keyes.

Such as not?

Look at this long candle. Calculate when it burns out and you receive gratis 1 pair of our special non-compo boots, guaranteed 1 candlepower. Address: Barclay and Cook, 104 Talbot Street.

Bacilikil (Insect Powder).

Veribest (Boot Blacking).

Uwantit (Combined pocket two-blade penknife with corkscrew, nail file and pipe cleaner).

Such as never?
What is home without Plumtree's Potted Meat?
Incomplete.
With it an abode of bliss.
Manufactured by George Plumtree, 23 Merchants' Quay, Dublin, put up in 4-oz pots, and inserted by Councillor Joseph P. Nannetti M.P., Rotunda Ward, 19 Hardwicke Street, under the obituary notices and anniversaries of deceases. The name of the label is Plumtree. A plum tree in a meatpot, registered trademark. Beware of imitations. Peatmot. Trumplee. Moutpat. Plamtroo.

Which example did he adduce to induce Stephen to deduce that originality, though producing its own reward, does not invariably conduce to success?

His own ideated and rejected project of an illuminated showcart, drawn by a beast of burden, in which two smartly dressed girls were to be seated engaged in writing.

What suggested scene was then constructed by Stephen?

Solitary hotel in mountain pass. Autumn. Twilight. Fire lit. In dark corner young man seated. Young woman enters. Restless. Solitary. She sits. She goes to window. She stands. She sits. Twilight. She thinks. On solitary hotel paper she writes. She thinks. She writes. She sighs. Wheels and hoofs. She hurries out. He comes from his dark corner. He seizes solitary paper. He holds it towards fire. Twilight. He reads. Solitary.

What?

In sloping, upright and backhands: Queen's Hotel, Queen's Hotel, Queen's Hotel, Queen's Ho . . .

What suggested scene was then reconstructed by Bloom?

The Queen's Hotel, Ennis, County Clare, where Rudolph Bloom (Rudolf Virag) died on the evening of the 27 June 1886, at some hour unstated, in consequence of an overdose of monkshood (aconite) self-administered in the form of a neuralgic liniment composed of 2 parts of aconite liniment to 1 of chloroform liniment (purchased by him at 10.20 a.m. on the morning of 27 June 1886 at the medical hall of Francis Dennehy, 17 Church Street, Ennis) after having, though not in consequence of having, purchased at 3.15 p.m. on the afternoon of 27 June 1886 a new boater straw hat, extra smart (after having, though not in consequence of having, purchased at the hour and in the place aforesaid the toxin aforesaid), at the general drapery store of James Cullen, 4 Main Street, Ennis.

Did he attribute this homonymity to information or coincidence or intuition?

Coincidence.

Did he depict the scene verbally for his guest to see?

He preferred himself to see another's face and listen to another's words by which potential narration was realised and kinetic temperament relieved.

Did he see only a second coincidence in the second scene narrated to him, described by the narrator as *A Pisgah Sight of Palestine* or *The Parable of the Plums*?

It, with the preceding scene and with others unnarrated but existent by implication, to which add essays on various subjects or moral apothegms (e.g. *My Favourite Hero* or *Procrastination is the Thief of Time*) composed during school years, seemed to him to contain in itself and in conjunction with the personal equation certain possibilities of financial, social, personal and sexual success, whether specially collected and selected as model pedagogic themes (of cent per cent merit) for the use of preparatory and junior grade students, or contributed in printed form, following the precedent of Philip Beaufoy or Doctor Dick or Heblon's *Studies in Blue*, to a publication of certified circulation and solvency, or employed verbally as intellectual stimulation for sympathetic auditors, tacitly appreciative of successful narrative and confidently augurative of successful achievement, during the increasingly longer nights gradually following the summer solstice on the day but three following, *videlicet* Tuesday, 21 June (Saint Aloysius Gonzaga), sunrise 3.33 a.m., sunset 8.29 p.m.

Which domestic problem as much as, if not more than, any other frequently engaged his mind?

What to do with our wives.

What had been his hypothetical singular solutions?

Parlour games (dominoes, halma, tiddledywinks, spillikins, cup and ball, nap, spoil five, bezique, twenty-five, beggar my neighbour, draughts, chess or backgammon): embroidery, darning or knitting for the Police-Aided Children's Clothing Society: musical duets, mandoline and guitar, piano and flute, guitar and piano: legal scrivenery or envelope addressing: bi-weekly visits to variety entertainments: commercial activity as pleasantly commanding and pleasingly obeyed mistress proprietress in a cool dairy shop or warm cigar divan: the clandestine satisfaction of erotic irritation in masculine brothels, state-inspected and medically controlled: social visits, at regular infrequent prevented intervals and with regular frequent preventive superintendence, to and from female acquaintances of recognised respectability in the vicinity: courses of evening instruction specially designed to render liberal instruction agreeable.

What instances of deficient mental development in his wife inclined him in favour of the last-mentioned (ninth) solution?

In unoccupied moments she had more than once covered a sheet of paper with signs and hieroglyphics which she stated were Greek and Irish and Hebrew characters. She had interrogated constantly at varying intervals as to the correct method of writing the capital initial of the name of a city in Canada, Quebec. She understood little of political complications, internal, or balance of power, external. In calculating the addenda of bills she frequently had recourse to digital aid. After completion of laconic epistolary compositions she abandoned the implement of calligraphy in the encaustic pigment, exposed to the corrosive action of copperas, green vitriol and nutgall. Unusual polysyllables of foreign origin she interpreted phonetically or by false analogy or by both: metempsychosis (met him pike hoses), alias (a mendacious person mentioned in sacred scripture).

What compensated in the false balance of her intelligence for these and such deficiencies of judgment regarding persons, places and things?

The false apparent parallelism of all perpendicular arms of all balances, proved true by construction. The counterbalance of her proficiency of judgment regarding one person, proved true by experiment.

How had he attempted to remedy this state of comparative ignorance?

Variously. By leaving in a conspicuous place a certain book open at a certain page: by assuming in her, when alluding explanatorily, latent knowledge: by open ridicule in her presence of some absent other's ignorant lapse.

With what success had he attempted direct instruction?

She followed not all, a part of the whole, gave attention with interest, comprehended with surprise, with care repeated, with greater difficulty remembered, forgot with ease, with misgiving reremembered, rerepeated with error.

What system had proved more effective?
Indirect suggestion implicating self-interest.

Example?
She disliked umbrella with rain, he liked woman with umbrella, she disliked new hat with rain, he liked woman with new hat, he bought new hat with rain, she carried umbrella with new hat.

Accepting the analogy implied in his guest's parable, which examples of postexilic eminence did he adduce?
Three seekers of the pure truth, Moses of Egypt, Moses Maimonides, author of *Moreh Nebukim* (Guide of the Perplexed), and Moses Mendelssohn, of such eminence that from Moses (of Egypt) to Moses (Mendelssohn) there arose none like Moses (Maimonides).

What statement was made, under correction, by Bloom concerning a fourth seeker of pure truth, by name Aristotle, mentioned, with permission, by Stephen?
That the seeker mentioned had been a pupil of a rabbinical philosopher, name uncertain.

Were other anapocryphal illustrious sons of the law and children of a selected or rejected race mentioned?
Felix Mendelssohn-Bartholdy (composer), Baruch Spinoza (philosopher), Daniel Mendoza (pugilist), Ferdinand Lassalle (reformer, duellist).

What fragments of verse from the ancient Hebrew and ancient Irish languages were cited with modulations of voice and translation of texts by guest to host and by host to guest?
By Stephen: *siúl, siúl, siúl a rún, siúl go socair agus siúl go ciúin* (walk, walk, walk, my dear, walk in safety, walk with care).
By Bloom: *kifeloch harimon rakatejch m'baad l'zamatejch* (thy temple amid thy hair is as a slice of pomegranate).

How was a glyphic comparison of the phonic symbols of both languages made in substantiation of the oral comparison?
By juxtaposition. On the penultimate blank page of a book of inferior literary style, entitled *Sweets of Sin* (produced by Bloom and so manipulated that its front cover came in contact with the surface of the table),

600

with a pencil (supplied by Stephen) Stephen wrote the Irish characters for gee, ah, dee, em, simple and modified, and Bloom in turn wrote the Hebrew characters gimel, aleph, daleth and (in the absence of mem) a substituted qoph, explaining their arithmetical values as ordinal and cardinal numbers, *videlicet* 3, 1, 4 and 100.

Was the knowledge possessed by both of each of these languages, the extinct and the revived, theoretical or practical?
Theoretical, being confined to certain grammatical rules of accidence and syntax and practically excluding vocabulary.

What points of contact existed between these languages and between the peoples who spoke them?
The presence of guttural sounds, diacritic aspirations, epenthetic and servile letters in both languages: their antiquity, both having been taught on the plain of Shinar 242 years after the deluge in the seminary instituted by Fenius Farsaigh, descendant of Noah, progenitor of Israel, and ascendant of Heber and Heremon, progenitors of Ireland: their vast archaeological, genealogical, hagiographical, exegetical, homiletic, toponomastic, historical and religious literatures, comprising the works of rabbis and culdees, Torah, Talmud (Mishnah and Gemara), Masorah, Pentateuch, Book of the Dun Cow, Book of Ballymote, Garland of Howth, Book of Kells: their dispersal, persecution, survival and revival: the isolation of their synagogical and ecclesiastical rites in ghetto (Saint Mary's Abbey) and masshouse (Adam and Eve's Tavern): the proscription of their national costumes in penal laws and Jewish dress acts: the restoration in Chanah David of Zion and the possibility of Irish political autonomy or devolution.

What anthem did Bloom chant partially in anticipation of that multiple, ethnically irreducible consummation?

> *Kolod balejwaw pnimah*
> *Nefesch jehudi homijah.*

Why was the chant arrested at the conclusion of this first distich?
In consequence of defective mnemotechnic.

How did the chanter compensate for this deficiency?
By a periphrastic version of the general text.

In what common study did their mutual reflections merge?
The increasing simplification traceable from the Egyptian epigraphic

hieroglyphs to the Greek and Roman alphabets and the anticipation of modern stenography and telegraphic code in the cuneiform inscriptions (Semitic) and the virgular quinquecostate ogham writing (Celtic).

Did the guest comply with his host's request?
Doubly, by appending his signature in Irish and Roman characters.

What was Stephen's auditive sensation?
He heard in a profound ancient male unfamiliar melody the accumulation of the past.

What was Bloom's visual sensation?
He saw in a quick young male familiar form the predestination of a future.

What were Stephen's and Bloom's quasi-simultaneous volitional quasi-sensations of concealed identities?
Visually, Stephen's: the traditional figure of hypostasis, depicted by Johannes Damascenus, Lentulus Romanus and Epiphanius Monachus as leucodermic, sexipedalian, with wine-dark hair.
Auditively, Bloom's: the traditional accent of the ecstasy of catastrophe.

What future careers had been possible for Bloom in the past and with what exemplars?
In the church, Roman, Anglican or Nonconformist: exemplars, the Very Reverend John Conmee S.J., the Reverend G. Salmon D.D., provost of Trinity College, Dr Alexander J. Dowie. At the bar, English or Irish: exemplars, Seymour Bushe K.C., Rufus Isaacs K.C. On the stage, modern or Shakespearean: exemplars, Charles Wyndham, high comedian, Osmond Tearle († 1901), exponent of Shakespeare.

Did the host encourage his guest to chant in a modulated voice a strange legend on an allied theme?
Reassuringly, their place, where none could hear them talk, being secluded: reassured, the decocted beverages, allowing for subsolid residual sediment of a mechanical mixture, water plus sugar plus cream plus cocoa, having been consumed.

Recite the first (major) part of this chanted legend.

> *Little Harry Hughes and his schoolfellows all*
> *Went out for to play ball.*
> *And the very first ball little Harry Hughes played*

He drove it o'er the Jew's garden wall.
And the very second ball little Harry Hughes played
He broke the Jew's windows all.

How did the son of Rudolph receive this first part?

With unmixed feeling. Smiling, a Jew, he heard with pleasure and saw the unbroken kitchen window.

Recite the second part (minor) of the legend.

> *Then out there came the Jew's daughter*
> *And she all dressed in green.*
> *'Come back, come back, you pretty little boy,*
> *And play your ball again.'*
>
> *'I can't come back and I won't come back*
> *Without my schoolfellows all.*
> *For if my master he did hear*
> *He'd make it a sorry ball.'*
>
> *She took him by the lily-white hand*
> *And led him along the hall*

Until she led him to a room
Where none could hear him call.

She took a penknife out of her pocket
And cut off his little head.
And now he'll play his ball no more
For he lies among the dead.

Then out there came the Jew's daugh - ter And she all dressed in

green. 'Come _ back, come back, you _ pret-ty lit-tle boy, And

play your ball a - gain. _____ And play your ball a - gain.'

How did the father of Millicent receive this second part?

With mixed feelings. Unsmiling, he heard and saw with wonder a Jew's daughter all dressed in green.

Condense Stephen's commentary.

One of all, the least of all, is the victim predestined. Once by inadvertence, twice by design, he challenges his destiny. It comes when he is abandoned and challenges him reluctant and, as an apparition of hope and youth, holds him unresisting. It leads him to a strange habitation, to a secret infidel apartment, and there, implacable, immolates him, consenting.

Why was the host (victim predestined) sad?

He wished that a tale of a deed by him should by him be told but a tale of a deed not by him should by him not be told.

Why was the host (reluctant, unresisting) still?

In accordance with the law of the conservation of energy.

Why was the host (secret infidel) silent?

He weighed the possible evidences for and against ritual murder: the incitation of the hierarchy, the superstition of the populace, the propagation of rumour in continued fraction of veridicity, the envy of opulence, the influence of retaliation, the sporadic reappearance of atavistic delinquency, the mitigating circumstances of fanaticism, hypnotic suggestion and somnambulism.

From which (if any) of these mental or physical disorders was he not totally immune?

From hypnotic suggestion: once, waking, he had not recognised his sleeping apartment: more than once, waking, he had been for an indefinite time incapable of moving or uttering sounds. From somnambulism: once, sleeping, his body had risen, crouched and crawled in the direction of a heatless fire and, having attained its destination, there, curled, unheated, in night attire had lain, sleeping.

Had this latter or any cognate phenomenon declared itself in any member of his family?

Twice, in Holles Street and in Ontario Terrace, his daughter Millicent (Milly) at the ages of 6 and 8 years had uttered in sleep an exclamation of terror and had replied to the interrogations of two figures in night attire with a vacant mute expression.

What other infantile memories had he of her?

15 June 1889. A querulous newborn female infant crying to cause and lessen congestion. A child renamed Padney Socks she shook with shocks her moneybox: counted his three free moneypenny buttons, one, tloo, tlee: a doll, a boy, a sailor, she cast away: blond, born of two dark, she had blond ancestry, remote, a violation, Herr Hauptmann Hainau, Austrian army, proximate, a hallucination, Lieutenant Mulvey, British navy.

What endemic characteristics were present?

Conversely, the nasal and frontal formation was derived in a direct line of lineage which, though interrupted, would continue at distant intervals to more distant intervals to its most distant intervals.

What memories had he of her adolescence?

She relegated her hoop and skipping rope to a recess. On the Duke's Lawn, entreated by an English visitor, she declined to permit him to make and take away her photographic image (objection not stated). On the South Circular Road in the company of Elsa Potter, followed by an individual of sinister aspect, she went halfway down Stamer Street and turned abruptly back (reason of change not stated). On the vigil of the 15th anniversary of her birth she wrote a letter from Mullingar, County

Westmeath, making a brief allusion to a local student (faculty and year not stated).

Did that first division, portending a second division, afflict him?
Less than he had imagined, more than he had hoped.

What second departure was contemporaneously perceived by him similarly, if differently?
A temporary departure of his cat.

Why similarly, why differently?
Similarly, because actuated by a secret purpose: the quest of a new male (Mullingar student) or of a healing herb (valerian). Differently, because of different possible returns to the inhabitants or to the habitation.

In what other respects were their differences similar?
In passivity, in economy, in the instinct of tradition, in unexpectedness.

As?
Inasmuch as, leaning, she sustained her blond hair for him to ribbon it for her (cf. neck-arching cat). Moreover, on the free surface of the lake in Stephen's Green amid inverted reflections of trees her uncommented spit, describing concentric circles of water rings, indicated by the constancy of its permanence the locus of a somnolent prostrate fish (cf. mouse-watching cat). Again, in order to remember the date, combatants, issue and consequences of a famous military engagement she pulled a plait of her hair (cf. ear-washing cat). Furthermore, Silly Milly, she dreamed of having had an unspoken unremembered conversation with a horse whose name had been Joseph to whom (to which) she had offered a tumblerful of lemonade which it (he) had appeared to have accepted (cf. hearth-dreaming cat). Hence, in passivity, in economy, in the instinct of tradition, in unexpectedness, their differences were similar.

In what way had he utilised gifts (1) an owl, 2) a clock), given as matrimonial auguries, to interest and to instruct her?
As object lessons to explain: 1) the nature and habits of oviparous animals, the possibility of aerial flight, certain abnormalities of vision, the secular process of imbalsamation: 2) the principle of the pendulum, exemplified in bob, wheelgear and regulator, the translation in terms of human or social regulation of the various positions of clockwise movable indicators on an unmoving dial, the exactitude of the recurrence per hour

of an instant in each hour when the longer and the shorter indicator were at the same angle of inclination, *videlicet* 5⁵/₁₁ minutes past each hour per hour in arithmetical progression.

In what manners did she reciprocate?

She remembered: on the 27th anniversary of his birth she presented to him a breakfast moustache cup of imitation Crown Derby porcelain ware. She provided: at quarter day or thereabouts if or when purchases had been made by him not for her she showed herself attentive to his necessities, anticipating his desires. She admired: a natural phenomenon having been explained by him to her she expressed the immediate desire to possess without gradual acquisition a fraction of his science, the moiety, the quarter, a thousandth part.

What proposal did Bloom, diambulist, father of Milly, somnambulist, make to Stephen, noctambulist?

To pass in repose the hours intervening between Thursday (proper) and Friday (normal) on an extemporised cubicle in the apartment immediately above the kitchen and immediately adjacent to the sleeping apartment of his host and hostess.

What various advantages would or might have resulted from a prolongation of such an extemporisation?

For the guest: security of domicile and seclusion of study. For the host: rejuvenation of intelligence, vicarious satisfaction. For the hostess: disintegration of obsession, acquisition of correct Italian pronunciation.

Why might these several provisional contingencies between a guest and a hostess not necessarily preclude or be precluded by a permanent eventuality of reconciliatory union between a schoolfellow and a Jew's daughter?

Because the way to daughter led through mother, the way to mother through daughter.

To what inconsequent polysyllabic question of his host did the guest return a monosyllabic negative answer?

If he had known the late Mrs Emily Sinico, accidentally killed at Sydney Parade railway station, 14 November 1903.

What inchoate corollary statement was consequently suppressed by the host?

A statement explanatory of his absence on the occasion of the interment of Mrs Mary Dedalus (born Goulding), 26 June 1903, vigil of the anniversary of the decease of Rudolph Bloom (born Virag).

Was the proposal of asylum accepted?
Promptly, inexplicably, with amicability, gratefully, it was declined.

What exchange of money took place between host and guest?
The former returned to the latter, without interest, a sum of money (£1-7-0), one pound seven shillings sterling, advanced by the latter to the former.

What counterproposals were alternately advanced, accepted, modified, declined, restated in other terms, reaccepted, ratified, reconfirmed?
To inaugurate a prearranged course of Italian instruction, place the residence of the instructed. To inaugurate a course of vocal instruction, place the residence of the instructress. To inaugurate a series of static, semistatic and peripatetic intellectual dialogues, places the residence of both speakers (if both speakers were resident in the same place), the Ship Hotel and Tavern, 5 Lower Abbey Street (W. and E. Connery, proprietors), the National Library of Ireland, 9 Kildare Street, the National Maternity Hospital, 29, 30 and 31 Holles Street, a public garden, the vicinity of a place of worship, a conjunction of two or more public thoroughfares, the point of bisection of a right line drawn between their residences (if both speakers were resident in different places).

What rendered problematic for Bloom the realisation of these mutually self-excluding propositions?
The irreparability of the past: once at a performance of Albert Hengler's circus in the Rotunda, Rutland Square, Dublin, an intuitive parti-coloured clown in quest of paternity had penetrated from the ring to a place in the auditorium where Bloom, solitary, was seated and had publicly declared to an exhilarated audience that he (Bloom) was his (the clown's) papa. The imprevidibility of the future: once in the summer of 1898 he (Bloom) had marked a florin (2/-) with three notches on the milled edge and tendered it in payment of an account due to and received by J. and T. Davy, family grocers, 1 Charlemont Mall, Grand Canal, for circulation on the waters of civic finance for possible, circuitous or direct, return.

Was the clown Bloom's son?
No.

Had Bloom's coin returned?

Never.

Why would a recurrent frustration the more depress him?

Because at the critical turning point of human existence he desired to amend many social conditions the product of inequality and avarice and international animosity.

He believed then that human life was infinitely perfectible, eliminating these conditions?

There remained the generic conditions imposed by natural as distinct from human law as integral parts of the human whole: the necessity of destruction to procure alimentary sustenance: the painful character of the ultimate functions of separate existence, the agonies of birth and death: the monotonous menstruation of simian and (particularly) human females extending from the age of puberty to the menopause: inevitable accidents at sea, in mines and factories: certain very painful maladies and their resultant surgical operations: innate lunacy and congenital criminality: decimating epidemics: catastrophic cataclysms which make terror the basis of human mentality: seismic upheavals the epicentres of which are located in densely populated regions: the fact of vital growth, through convulsions of metamorphosis, from infancy through maturity to decay.

Why did he desist from speculation?

Because it was a task for a superior intelligence to substitute other more acceptable phenomena in the place of the less acceptable phenomena to be removed.

Did Stephen participate in his dejection?

He affirmed his significance as a conscious rational animal proceeding syllogistically from the known to the unknown and a conscious rational reagent between a micro and a macrocosm ineluctably constructed upon the incertitude of the void.

Was this affirmation apprehended by Bloom?

Not verbally. Substantially.

What comforted his misapprehension?

That as a competent keyless citizen he had proceeded energetically from the unknown to the known through the incertitude of the void.

In what order of precedence, with what attendant ceremony, was the exodus from the house of bondage to the wilderness of inhabitation effected?

Lighted Candle in Stick
borne by
BLOOM
Diaconal Hat on Ashplant
borne by
STEPHEN

With what intonation *secreto* of what commemorative psalm?
The 113th, *modus peregrinus*: *In exitu Israhel de Aegypto domus Jacob de populo barbaro.*

What did each do at the door of egress?
Bloom set the candlestick on the floor. Stephen put the hat on his head.

For what creature was the door of egress a door of ingress?
For a cat.

What spectacle confronted them when they, first the host, then the guest, emerged from obscurity, silently, doubly dark, by a passage from the rear of the house into the penumbra of the garden?
The heaventree of stars hung with humid night-blue fruit.

With what meditations did Bloom accompany his demonstration to his companion of various constellations?
Meditations of evolution increasingly vaster: of the moon invisible in incipient lunation, approaching perigee: of the infinite lactiginous scintillating uncondensed Milky Way, discernible by daylight by an observer placed at the lower end of a cylindrical vertical shaft 5000 ft deep sunk from the surface towards the centre of the earth: of Sirius (Alpha in Canis Major) 9 light-years (51,000,000,000,000 miles) distant and in volume 3,000,000 times the dimension of our planet: of Arcturus: of the precession of equinoxes: of Orion with belt and sextuple sun Theta and Nebula in which myriads of our solar systems could be contained: of moribund and of nascent new stars such as Nova in 1901: of our system plunging towards the constellation of Hercules: of the parallax or parallactic drift of so-called fixed stars, in reality evermoving wanderers from immeasurably remote eons to infinitely remote futures, in comparison with which the years, threescore and ten, of allotted human life formed a parenthesis of infinitesimal brevity.

Were there obverse meditations of involution increasingly less vast?

Of the eons of geological periods recorded in the stratifications of the earth: of the myriad minute entomological organic existences concealed in cavities of the earth, beneath removable stones, in hives and mounds: of microbes, germs, bacteria, bacilli, spermatozoa: of the incalculable trillions of billions of millions of imperceptible molecules contained by cohesion of molecular affinity in a single pinhead: of the universe of human serum constellated with red and white bodies, themselves universes of void space constellated with other bodies, each, in continuity, its universe of divisible component bodies of which each was again divisible in divisions of redivisible component bodies, dividends and divisors ever diminishing without actual division till, if the progress were carried far enough, nought nowhere was never reached.

Why did he not elaborate these calculations to a more precise result?

Because some years previously in 1886 when occupied with the problem of the quadrature of the circle he had learned of the existence of a number computed to a relative degree of accuracy to be of such magnitude and of so many places, e.g. the 9th power of the 9th power of 9, that, the result having been obtained, 33 closely printed volumes of 1000 pages each of innumerable quires and reams of India paper would have to be requisitioned in order to contain the complete tale of its printed integers of units, tens, hundreds, thousands, tens of thousands, hundreds of thousands, millions, tens of millions, hundreds of millions, billions, the nucleus of the nebula of every digit of every series containing succinctly the potentiality of being raised to the utmost kinetic elaboration of any power of any of its powers.

Did he find the problems of the inhabitability of the planets and their satellites by a race, given in species, and of the possible social and moral redemption of said race by a redeemer, easier of solution?

Of a different order of difficulty. Conscious that the human organism, normally capable of sustaining an atmospheric pressure of 14.6 pounds per square inch, when elevated to a considerable altitude in the terrestrial atmosphere suffered with arithmetical progression of intensity, according as the line of demarcation between troposphere and stratosphere was approximated, from nasal hemorrhage, impeded respiration and vertigo, when proposing this problem for solution he had conjectured as a working hypothesis which could not be proved impossible that a more adaptable and differently anatomically constructed race of beings might subsist otherwise under sufficient and equivalent Martian, Mercurial, Venusian, Jovian, Saturnian, Neptunian or Uranian conditions, though an apogean humanity of beings created in varying forms, with finite differences resulting, similar to the whole and to one another would probably there as here remain inalterably and inalienably attached to vanities, to vanities of vanities and to all that is vanity.

And the problem of possible redemption?
The minor was proved by the major.

Which various features of the constellations were in turn considered?
The various colours significant of various degrees of vitality (white, yellow, crimson, vermilion, cinnabar): their degrees of brilliancy: their magnitudes revealed up to and including the 7th: their positions: the waggoner's star: Walsingham Way: the chariot of David: the annular cinctures of Saturn: the condensation of spiral nebulae into suns: the interdependent gyrations of double suns: the independent asynchronous discoveries of Galileo, Simon Marius, Piazzi, Leverrier, Herschel, Galle: the systematisations attempted by Bode and Kepler of cubes of distances and squares of times of revolution: the almost infinite compressibility of hirsute comets and their vast elliptical egressive and reentrant orbits from perihelion to aphelion: the sidereal origin of meteoric stones: the Libyan floods on Mars about the period of the birth of the younger astroscopist: the annual recurrence of meteoric showers about the period of the Feast of Saint Lawrence (martyr, 10 August): the monthly recurrence known as the new moon with the old moon in her arms: the posited influence of celestial on human bodies: the appearance of a star (1st magnitude) of exceeding brilliancy (a new luminous sun generated by the collision and amalgamation in incandescence of two nonluminous ex-suns) dominating by night and day about the period of the birth of William Shakespeare over Delta in the recumbent neversetting constellation of Cassiopeia and of a star (2nd magnitude) of similar origin but of lesser brilliancy which had appeared in and disappeared from the constellation of the Corona Septentrionalis about the period of the birth of Leopold Bloom and of other stars of (presumably) similar origin which had (effectively or presumably) appeared in and disappeared from the constellation of Andromeda about the period of the birth of Stephen Dedalus and in and from the constellation of Auriga some years after the birth and death of Rudolph Bloom, junior, and in and from other constellations some years before or after the birth or death of other persons: the attendant phenom-

ena of eclipses, solar and lunar, from immersion to emersion, abatement of wind, transit of shadow, taciturnity of winged creatures, emergence of nocturnal or crepuscular animals, persistence of infernal light, obscurity of terrestrial waters, pallor of human beings.

His (Bloom's) logical conclusion, having weighed the matter and allowing for possible error?

That it was not a heaventree, not a heavengrot, not a heavenbeast, not a heavenman. That it was a Utopia, there being no known method from the known to the unknown: an infinity renderable equally finite by the suppositious apposition of one or more bodies equally of the same and of different magnitudes: a mobility of illusory forms immobilised in space, remobilised in air: a past which possibly had ceased to exist as a present before its probable spectators had entered actual present existence.

Was he more convinced of the esthetic value of the spectacle?

Indubitably, in consequence of the reiterated examples of poets in the delirium of the frenzy of attachment or in the abasement of rejection invoking ardent sympathetic constellations or the frigidity of the satellite of their planet.

Did he then accept as an article of belief the theory of astrological influences upon sublunary disasters?

It seemed to him as possible of proof as of confutation, and the nomenclature employed in its selenographical charts as attributable to verifiable intuition as to fallacious analogy: the Lake of Dreams, the Sea of Rains, the Gulf of Dews, the Ocean of Fecundity.

What special affinities appeared to him to exist between the moon and woman?

Her antiquity in preceding and surviving successive tellurian generations: her nocturnal predominance: her satellitic dependence: her luminary reflection: her constancy under all her phases, rising and setting by her appointed times, waxing and waning: the forced invariability of her aspect: her indeterminate response to inaffirmative interrogation: her potency over effluent and refluent waters: her power to enamour, to mortify, to invest with beauty, to render insane, to incite to and aid delinquency: the tranquil inscrutability of her visage: the terribility of her isolated dominant implacable resplendent propinquity: her omens of tempest and of calm: the stimulation of her light, her motion and her presence: the admonition of her craters, her arid seas, her silence: her splendour, when visible: her attraction, when invisible.

What visible luminous sign attracted Bloom's, who attracted Stephen's, gaze?

In the second storey (rear) of his (Bloom's) house the light of a paraffin-oil lamp with oblique shade projected on a screen of roller blind supplied by Frank O'Hara, window blind, curtain pole and revolving shutter manufacturer, 17 Aungier Street.

How did he elucidate the mystery of an invisible attractive person, his wife Marion (Molly) Bloom, denoted by a visible splendid sign, a lamp?

With indirect and direct verbal allusions or affirmations: with subdued affection and admiration: with description: with impediment: with suggestion.

Both then were silent?

Silent, each contemplating the other in both mirrors of the reciprocal flesh of theirhisnothis fellowfaces.

Were they indefinitely inactive?

At Stephen's suggestion, at Bloom's instigation, both, first Stephen, then Bloom, in penumbra urinated, their sides contiguous, their organs of micturition reciprocally rendered invisible by manual circumposition, their gazes, first Bloom's, then Stephen's, elevated to the projected luminous and semiluminous shadow.

Similarly?

The trajectories of their, first sequent, then simultaneous, urinations were dissimilar: Bloom's longer, less irruent, in the incomplete form of the bifurcated penultimate alphabetical letter, who in his ultimate year at High School (1880) had been capable of attaining the point of greatest altitude against the whole concurrent strength of the institution, 210 scholars: Stephen's higher, more sibilant, who in the ultimate hours of the previous day had augmented by diuretic consumption an insistent vesical pressure.

What different problems presented themselves to each concerning the invisible audible collateral organ of the other?

To Bloom: the problems of irritability, tumescence, rigidity, reactivity, dimension, sanitariness, pilosity. To Stephen: the problem of the sacerdotal integrity of Jesus circumcised (1 January, holiday of obligation to hear

614

mass and abstain from unnecessary servile work) and the problem as to whether the divine prepuce, the carnal bridal ring of the Holy Roman Catholic Apostolic Church, conserved in Calcata, were deserving of simple hyperdulia or of the fourth degree of latria accorded to the abscission of such divine excrescences as hair and toenails.

What celestial sign was by both simultaneously observed?

A star precipitated with great apparent velocity across the firmament from Vega in the Lyre above the zenith beyond the star group of the Tress of Berenice towards the zodiacal sign of Leo.

How did the centripetal remainer afford egress to the centrifugal departer?

By inserting the barrel of a ferruginated male key in the hole of an unstable female lock, obtaining a purchase on the bow of the key and turning its wards from right to left, withdrawing a bolt from its staple, pulling inward spasmodically an obsolescent unhinged door and revealing an aperture for free egress and free ingress.

How did they take leave, one of the other, in separation?

Standing perpendicular at the same door and on different sides of its base, the lines of their valedictory arms meeting at any point and forming any angle less than the sum of two right angles.

What sound accompanied the union of their tangent, the disunion of their (respectively) centrifugal and centripetal hands?

The sound of the peal of the hour of the night by the chime of the bells in the church of Saint George.

What echoes of that sound were by both and each heard?

By Stephen:

Liliata rutilantium. Turma circumdet.
Jubilantium te virginum. Chorus excipiat.

By Bloom:

Heigho, heigho,
Heigho, heigho.

Where were the several members of the company which with Bloom that day at the bidding of that peal had travelled from Sandymount in the south to Glasnevin in the north?

Martin Cunningham (in bed), Jack Power (in bed), Simon Dedalus (in bed), Ned Lambert (in bed), Tom Kernan (in bed), Joe Hynes (in bed), John Henry Menton (in bed), Bernard Corrigan (in bed), Patsy Dignam (in bed), Paddy Dignam (in the grave).

Alone, what did Bloom hear?
The double reverberation of retreating feet on the heavenborn earth, the double vibration of a Jew's harp in the resonant lane.

Alone, what did Bloom feel?
The cold of interstellar space, near to absolute zero and hundreds of degrees below the freezing points of Fahrenheit, Centigrade or Réaumur: the incipient intimations of proximate dawn.

Of what did bellchime and handtouch and footstep and lonechill remind him?
Of companions now in various manners in different places defunct: Percy Apjohn (killed in action, Modder River), Philip Gilligan (phthisis, Jervis Street Hospital), Matthew F. Kane (accidental drowning, Dublin Bay), Philip Moisel (pyemia, Heytesbury Street), Michael Hart (phthisis, Mater Misericordiae Hospital), Patrick Dignam (apoplexy, Sandymount).

What prospect of what phenomena inclined him to remain?
The disparition of three final stars, the diffusion of daybreak, the apparition of a new solar disk.

Had he ever been a spectator of those phenomena?
Once in 1887 after a protracted performance of charades in the house of Luke Doyle, Dolphin's Barn, he had awaited with patience the apparition of the diurnal phenomenon, seated on a wall, his gaze turned in the direction of Mizrach, the east.

He remembered the initial paraphenomena?
More active air, a matutinal distant cock, ecclesiastical clocks at various points, avian music, the isolated tread of an early wayfarer, the visible diffusion of the light of an invisible luminous body, the first golden limb of the resurgent sun perceptible low on the horizon.

Did he remain?
With deep inspiration he returned, retraversing the garden, reentering the passage, reclosing the door. With brief suspiration he reassumed the candle, reascended the stairs, reapproached the door of the front room, hall floor, and reentered.

What suddenly arrested his ingress?

The right temporal lobe of the hollow sphere of his cranium came into contact with a solid timber angle where, an infinitesimal but sensible fraction of a second later, a painful sensation was located in consequence of antecedent sensations transmitted and registered.

Describe the alterations effected in the disposition of the articles of furniture.

A sofa upholstered in prune plush had been translocated from opposite the door to the ingleside near the compactly furled Union Jack (an alteration which he had frequently intended to execute): the blue and white checker inlaid majolica-topped table had been placed opposite the door in the place vacated by the prune plush sofa: the walnut sideboard (a projecting angle of which had momentarily arrested his ingress) had been moved from its position beside the door to a more advantageous but more perilous position in front of the door: two chairs had been moved from right and left of the ingleside to the position originally occupied by the blue and white checker inlaid majolica-topped table.

Describe them.

One: a squat stuffed easy chair with stout arms extended and back slanted to the rear which, repelled in recoil, had then upturned an irregular fringe of a rectangular rug and now displayed on its amply upholstered seat a centralised diffusing and diminishing discolouration. The other: a slender splayfoot chair of glossy cane curves, placed directly opposite the former, its frame from top to seat and from seat to base being varnished dark brown, its seat being a bright circle of white plaited rush.

What significances attached to these two chairs?

Significances of similitude, of posture, of symbolism, of circumstantial evidence, of testimonial supermanence.

What occupied the position originally occupied by the sideboard?

A vertical piano (Cadby) with exposed keyboard, its closed coffin supporting a pair of long yellow ladies' gloves and an emerald ashtray containing four consumed matches, a partly consumed cigarette and two discoloured ends of cigarettes, its music rest supporting the music in the key of G natural for voice and piano of *Love's Old Sweet Song* (words by G. Clifton Bingham, composed by J. L. Molloy, sung by Madam Antoinette

Sterling) open at the last page with the final indications ad libitum, forte, pedal, animato, sustained pedal, ritardando, close.

With what sensations did Bloom contemplate in rotation these objects?

With strain, elevating a candlestick: with pain, feeling on his right temple a contused tumescence: with attention, focussing his gaze on a large dull passive and a slender bright active: with solicitation, bending and downturning the upturned rug fringe: with amusement, remembering Dr Malachi Mulligan's scheme of colour containing the gradation of green: with pleasure, repeating the words and antecedent act and perceiving through various channels of internal sensibility the consequent and concomitant tepid pleasant diffusion of gradual discolouration.

His next proceeding?

From an open box on the majolica-topped table he extracted a black diminutive cone, one inch in height, placed it on its circular base on a small tin plate, placed his candlestick on the right corner of the mantelpiece, produced from his waistcoat a folded page of prospectus (illustrated) entitled Agudath Netaim, unfolded the same, examined it superficially, rolled it into a thin cylinder, ignited it in the candle flame, applied it when ignited to the apex of the cone till the latter reached the stage of rutilance, placed the cylinder in the basin of the candlestick disposing its unconsumed part in such a manner as to facilitate total combustion.

What followed this operation?

The truncated conical crater summit of the diminutive volcano emitted a vertical and serpentine fume redolent of aromatic oriental incense.

What homothetic objects, other than the candlestick, stood on the mantelpiece?

A timepiece of striated Connemara marble, stopped at the hour of 4.46 a.m. on the 21 March 1896, matrimonial gift of Matthew Dillon: a dwarf tree of glacial arborescence under a transparent bellshade, matrimonial gift of Luke and Caroline Doyle: an embalmed owl, matrimonial gift of Alderman John Hooper.

What interchanges of looks took place between these three objects and Bloom?

In the mirror of the gilt-bordered pierglass the undecorated back of the dwarf tree regarded the upright back of the embalmed owl. Before the mirror the matrimonial gift of Alderman John Hooper with a clear melancholy wise bright motionless compassionate gaze regarded Bloom, while Bloom with obscure tranquil profound motionless compassionate gaze regarded the matrimonial gift of Luke and Caroline Doyle.

What composite asymmetrical image in the mirror then attracted his attention?

The image of a solitary (ipsorelative) mutable (aliorelative) man.

Why solitary (ipsorelative)?

> *Brothers and sisters had he none,*
> *Yet that man's father was his grandfather's son.*

Why mutable (aliorelative)?

From infancy to maturity he had resembled his maternal procreatrix. From maturity to senility he would increasingly resemble his paternal procreator.

What final visual impression was communicated to him by the mirror?

The optical reflection of several inverted volumes improperly arranged and not in the order of their common letters with scintillating titles on the two bookshelves opposite.

Catalogue these books.

Thom's Dublin Post Office Directory, 1886.

Denis Florence M'Carthy's *Poetical Works* (copper-beech leaf bookmark at
    p.5).

Shakespeare's *Works* (dark crimson morocco, gold-tooled).

The Useful Ready Reckoner (brown cloth).

The Secret History of the Court of Charles II (red cloth, tooled binding).

The Child's Guide (blue cloth).

The Beauties of Killarney (wrappers).

When We Were Boys by William O'Brien M.P. (green cloth, slightly faded,
    envelope bookmark at p.217).

Thoughts from Spinoza (maroon leather).

The Story of the Heavens by Sir Robert Ball (blue cloth).

Ellis's *Three Visits to Madagascar* (brown cloth, title obliterated).

The Stark Munro Letters by A. Conan Doyle (black cloth binding, bearing
    white letter-number ticket), property of the City of Dublin Public
    Library, 106 Capel Street, lent 21 May (Whitsun Eve) 1904, due 4 June
    1904, 13 days overdue.

Voyages in China by "Viator" (re-covered with brown paper, red ink title).

Philosophy of the Talmud (sewn pamphlet).

Lockhart's *Life of Napoleon* (cover wanting, marginal annotations,
 minimising victories, aggrandising defeats of the protagonist).
Soll und Haben by Gustav Freytag (black boards, Gothic characters,
 cigarette coupon bookmark at p.24).
Hozier's *History of the Russo-Turkish War* (brown cloth, 2 volumes, with
 gummed label, Garrison Library, Governor's Parade, Gibraltar, on verso
 of cover).
Laurence Bloomfield in Ireland by William Allingham (second edition,
 green cloth, gilt trefoil design, previous owner's name on recto of flyleaf
 erased).
A Handbook of Astronomy (cover, brown leather, detached, 5 plates,
 antique letterpress long primer, author's footnotes nonpareil, marginal
 clues brevier, captions small pica).
The Hidden Life of Christ (black boards).
In the Track of the Sun (yellow cloth, title page missing, recurrent title
 intestation).
Physical Strength and How to Obtain It by Eugen Sandow (red cloth).
Short but yet Plain Elements of Geometry written in French by F. Ignat.
 Pardies and rendered into Engliſh by John Harris D.D., London,
 printed for R. Knaplock at the Biſhop's Head, MDCCXI, with
 dedicatory epiſtle to his worthy friend Charles Cox, eſquire, Member of
 Parliament for the burgh of Southwark and having ink calligraphed
 statement on the flyleaf certifying that the book was the property of
 Michael Gallagher, dated this 10th day of May 1822 and requeſting the
 perſon who should find it, if the book should be loſt or go aſtray, to
 reſtore it to Michael Gallagher, carpenter, Dufery Gate, Enniſcorthy,
 County Wexford, the fineſt place in the world.

What reflections occupied his mind during the process of reversion of
the inverted volumes?

The necessity of order, a place for everything and everything in its
place: the deficient appreciation of literature possessed by females: the
incongruity of an apple incuneated in a tumbler and of an umbrella
inclined in a close-stool: the insecurity of hiding any secret document
behind, beneath or between the pages of a book.

Which volume was the largest in bulk?
Hozier's *History of the Russo-Turkish War.*

What among other data did the second volume of the work in question
contain?

The name of a decisive battle (forgotten), frequently remembered by a decisive officer, Major Brian Cooper Tweedy (remembered).

Why, firstly and secondly, did he not consult the work in question?

Firstly, in order to exercise mnemotechnic: secondly, because after an interval of amnesia when, seated at the central table, about to consult the work in question, he remembered by mnemotechnic the name of the military engagement, Plevna.

What caused him consolation in his sitting posture?

The candour, nudity, pose, tranquillity, youth, grace, sex, counsel, of a statue erect in the centre of the table, an image of Narcissus purchased by auction from P.A. Wren, 9 Bachelor's Walk.

What caused him irritation in his sitting posture?

Inhibitory pressure of collar (size 17) and waistcoat (5 buttons), two articles of clothing superfluous in the costume of mature males and inelastic to alterations of mass by expansion.

How was the irritation allayed?

He removed his collar, with contained black necktie and collapsible stud, from his neck to a position on the left of the table. He unbuttoned successively in reversed direction waistcoat, trousers, shirt and vest along the medial line of irregular incrispated black hairs extending in triangular convergence from the pelvic basin over the circumference of the abdomen and umbilicular fossicle along the medial line of nodes to the intersection of the sixth pectoral ribs, thence produced both ways at right angles and terminating in circles described about two equidistant points, right and left, on the summits of the mammary prominences. He unbraced successively each of six minus one braced trouser buttons, arranged in pairs, of which one incomplete.

What involuntary actions followed?

He compressed between 2 fingers the flesh circumjacent to a cicatrice in the left infracostal region below the diaphragm resulting from a sting inflicted 3 weeks and 3 days previously (23 May 1904) by a bee. He scratched imprecisely with his right hand, though insensible of prurience, various points and surfaces of his partly exposed, wholly abluted, skin. He inserted his left hand into the left lower pocket of his waistcoat and extracted and replaced a silver coin (1 shilling) placed there (presumably) on the occasion (17 November 1903) of the interment of Mrs Emily Sinico, Sydney Parade.

Compile the budget for 16 June 1904.

Debit	£	s	d	Credit	£	s	d
1 Pork kidney	0	0	3	Cash in hand	0	4	9
1 Copy *Freeman's Journal*	0	0	1	Commission recd. *Freeman's Journal*	1	7	6
1 Bath and gratification	0	1	6	Loan (Stephen Dedalus)	1	6	11
Tram fare	0	0	1		£ 2-	19-	2
1 In Memoriam Patrick Dignam	0	5	0				
2 Banbury cakes	0	0	1				
1 Lunch	0	0	7				
1 Renewal fee for book	0	1	0				
1 Packet notepaper and envelopes	0	0	2				
1 Dinner and gratification	0	2	0				
1 Postal order and stamp	0	2	8				
Tram fare	0	0	1				
Train fare	0	0	1				
1 Cake Fry's plain chocolate	0	0	1				
1 Square soda bread	0	0	4				
1 Pig's foot	0	0	4				
1 Sheep's trotter	0	0	3				
Mrs Cohen	0	11	0				
1 Coffee and bun	0	0	4				
Loan (Stephen Dedalus) refunded	1	7	0				
BALANCE	0	6	3				
	£ 2-	19-	2				

Did the process of divestiture continue?

Sensible of a benignant persistent ache in his footsoles he extended his foot to one side and observed the creases, protuberances and salient points caused by foot pressure in the course of walking repeatedly in several different directions, then, inclined, he disnoded the laceknots, unhooked and loosened the laces, took off each of his two boots for the second time, detached the partially moistened right sock through the fore part of which the nail of his great toe had again effracted, raised his right foot and, having unhooked a purple elastic sock suspender, took off his right sock, placed his unclothed right foot on the margin of the seat of his chair, picked at and gently lacerated the protruding part of the great toenail, raised the part lacerated to his nostrils and inhaled the odour of the quick, then, with satisfaction, threw away the lacerated ungual fragment.

Why with satisfaction?

Because the odour inhaled corresponded to other odours inhaled of other ungual fragments, picked and lacerated by Master Bloom, pupil of Mrs Ellis's juvenile school, patiently each night in the act of brief genuflection and nocturnal prayer and ambitious meditation.

In what ultimate ambition had all concurrent and consecutive ambitions now coalesced?

Not to inherit by right of primogeniture, gavelkind or borough-English or to possess in perpetuity an extensive demesne of a sufficient number of acres, roods and perches, statute land measure (valuation £42), of grazing turbary surrounding a baronial hall with gatelodge and carriage drive nor, on the other hand, a terrace house or semidetached villa, described as *Rus in Urbe* or *Qui Si Sana*, but to purchase by private treaty in fee simple a thatched bungalow-shaped 2-storey dwelling house of southerly aspect, surmounted by vane and lightning conductor connected with the earth, with porch covered by parasitic plants (ivy or Virginia creeper), hall door, olive-green, with smart carriage finish and neat doorbrasses, stucco front with gilt tracery at eaves and gable, rising, if possible, upon a gentle eminence with agreeable prospect from balcony with stone pillar parapet over unoccupied and unoccupiable interjacent pastures and standing in 5 or 6 acres of its own ground at such a distance from the nearest public thoroughfare as to render its houselights visible at night above and through a quickset hornbeam hedge of topiary cutting, situate at a given point not less than 1 statute mile from the periphery of the metropolis within a time limit of not more than 15 minutes from tram or train line (e.g. Dundrum, south, or Sutton, north, both localities equally reported by trial to resemble the terrestrial poles in being favourable climates for phthisical subjects), the premises to be held under fee-farm grant, lease 999 years, the messuage to consist of 1 drawing room with bay window (2 lancets), thermometer affixed, 1 sitting room, 4 bedrooms, 2 servants' rooms, tiled kitchen with close range and scullery, lounge hall fitted with linen wallpresses, fumed oak sectional bookcase containing the *Encyclopaedia Britannica* and *New Century Dictionary*, transverse obsolete medieval and oriental weapons, dinner gong, alabaster lamp, bowl pendant, vulcanite automatic telephone receiver with adjacent directory, hand-tufted Axminster carpet with cream ground and trellis border, loo table with pillar and claw legs, hearth with massive firebrasses and ormolu mantel chronometer clock, guaranteed timekeeper with cathedral chime, barometer with hygrographic chart, comfortable lounge settees and corner fitments upholstered in ruby plush with good springing and sunk centre, three-banner Japanese screen and cuspidors (club style, rich wine-coloured leather, gloss renewable with a minimum of labour by use of linseed oil and vinegar) and pyramidically prismatic central chandelier lustre, bentwood perch with finger-tame parrot (expurgated language), embossed mural paper at 10/- per dozen with transverse swags of carmine floral design and top crown frieze: staircase, three continuous flights at successive right angles, of varnished clear-grained oak, treads and risers, newel, balusters and handrail, with stepped-up panel dado, dressed with camphorated wax: bathroom, hot and cold supply, reclining and shower: watercloset on mezzanine provided with opaque single-pane oblong window, tip-up seat, bracket lamp, brass tie rod and brace, armrests, footstool and artistic oleograph on inner face of door: ditto, plain: servants' apartments with separate sanitary and hygienic necessaries for cook, general and between-maid (salary, rising by biennial unearned increments of £2, with comprehensive fidelity insurance, annual bonus (£1) and retiring allowance (based on the 65 system) after 30 years' service), pantry, buttery, larder, refrigerator, outoffices, coal and wood cellarage with wine bin (still and sparkling vintages) for distinguished guests, if entertained to dinner (evening dress), carbon monoxide gas supply throughout.

What additional attractions might the grounds contain?

As addenda, a tennis and fives court, a shrubbery, a glass summerhouse with tropical palms and equipped in the best botanical manner, a rockery with waterspray, a beehive arranged on humane principles, oval flower-beds in rectangular grassplots set with eccentric ellipses of scarlet and chrome tulips, blue scillas, crocuses, polyanthus, sweet william, sweet pea and lily of the valley (bulbs obtainable from Sir James W. Mackey Limited, wholesale and retail seed and bulb merchants and nurserymen, agents for chemical manures, 23 Sackville Street Upper), an orchard, kitchen garden and vinery protected against illegal trespassers by glass-topped mural enclosures, a lumber shed with padlock for various inventoried implements.

As?

Eeltraps, lobster pots, fishing rods, hatchet, steelyard, grindstone, clod-crusher, swatheturner, carriage sack, telescope ladder, 10-tooth rake, washing clogs, haytedder, tumbling rake, billhook, paintpot, brush, hoe and so on.

What improvements might be subsequently introduced?

A rabbitry and fowlrun, a dovecote, a botanical conservatory, 2 ham-mocks (lady's and gentleman's), a sundial, shaded and sheltered by laburnum or lilac trees, an exotically harmonically accorded Japanese tinkle gatebell affixed to left lateral gatepost, a capacious water butt, a lawnmower with side delivery and grassbox, a lawnsprinkler with hydraulic hose.

What facilities of transit were desirable?

When city bound, frequent connection by train or tram from their respective intermediate station or terminal. When country bound, a velocipede, a chainless freewheel roadster cycle with side basket-car attached, or draught conveyance, a donkey with wicker trap or smart phaeton with good working solidungular cob (roan gelding, 14h.).

What might be the name of this erigible or erected residence?

Bloom Cottage. Saint Leopold's. Flowerville.

Could Bloom of 7 Eccles Street foresee Bloom of Flowerville?

In loose all-wool garments, with Harris tweed cap, price 8/6, and useful garden boots with elastic gussets, with watering can, planting aligned young fir trees, syringing, pruning, staking, sowing hayseed, trundling a weed-laden wheelbarrow without excessive fatigue at sunset amid the scent of new-mown hay, ameliorating the soil, multiplying wisdom, achieving longevity.

What syllabus of intellectual pursuits was simultaneously possible?

Snapshot photography, comparative study of religions, folklore relative to various amatory and superstitious practices, contemplation of the celestial constellations.

What lighter recreations?

Outdoor: garden and fieldwork, cycling on level macadamised causeways, ascents of moderately high hills, natation in secluded fresh water and unmolested river-boating in secure wherry or light coracle with kedge anchor on reaches free from weirs and rapids (period of estivation), vespertinal perambulation or equestrian circumprocession with inspection of sterile landscape and contrastingly agreeable cottagers' fires of smoking peat turves (period of hibernation). Indoor: discussion in tepid security of unsolved historical and criminal problems, lecture of unexpurgated exotic erotic masterpieces, house carpentry with toolbox containing hammer, awl, nails, screws, tintacks, gimlet, tweezers, bullnose plane and turnscrew.

Might he become a gentleman farmer of field produce and livestock?

Not impossibly, with 1 or 2 stripper cows, 1 pike of upland hay and requisite farming implements, e.g. an end-to-end churn, a turnip pulper etc.

What would be his civic functions and social status among the county families and landed gentry?

Arranged successively in ascending powers of hierarchical order, that of gardener, groundsman, cultivator, breeder and, at the zenith of his career, resident magistrate or justice of the peace, with a family crest and coat of arms and appropriate classical motto (*Semper paratus*), duly recorded in the court directory (Bloom, Leopold P., M.P., P.C., K.P., LL.D. *honoris causa*, Bloomville, Dundrum) and mentioned in court and fashionable intelligence (Mr and Mrs Leopold Bloom have left Kingstown for England).

What course of action did he outline for himself in such capacity?

A course that lay between undue clemency and excessive rigour: the dispensation, in a heterogeneous society of arbitrary classes incessantly rearranged in terms of greater and lesser social inequality, of unbiassed homogeneous indisputable justice, tempered with mitigations of the widest possible latitude but exactable to the uttermost farthing with confiscation of estate, real and personal, to the Crown. Loyal to the highest constituted power in the land, actuated by an innate love of rectitude his aims would be the strict maintenance of public order, the repression of many abuses though not of all simultaneously (every measure of reform or retrenchment being a preliminary solution to be contained by fluxion in the final solution), the upholding of the letter of the law (common, statute and law merchant) against all traversers in covin and trespassers acting in contravention of bylaws and regulations, all resuscitators (by trespass and petty larceny of kindlings) of venville rights obsolete by desuetude, all orotund instigators of international persecution, all perpetuators of international animosities, all menial molestors of domestic conviviality, all recalcitrant violators of domestic connubiality.

Prove that he had loved rectitude from his earliest youth.

To Master Percy Apjohn at High School in 1880 he had divulged his disbelief in the tenets of the Irish (Protestant) Church (to which his father Rudolf Virag, later Rudolph Bloom, had been converted from the Israelitic faith and communion in 1865 by the Society for Promoting Christianity among the Jews) subsequently abjured by him in favour of Roman Catholicism at the epoch of and with a view to his matrimony in 1888. To Daniel Magrane and Francis Wade in 1882 during a juvenile friendship (terminated by the premature emigration of the former) he had advocated during nocturnal perambulations the political theory of colonial (e.g. Canadian) expansion and the evolutionary theories of Charles Darwin expounded in *The Descent of Man* and *The Origin of Species*. In 1885 he had publicly expressed his adherence to the collective and national economic programme advocated by James Fintan Lalor, John Fisher Murray, John Mitchel, J.F.X. O'Brien and others, the agrarian policy of Michael Davitt, the constitutional agitation of Charles Stewart Parnell (M.P. for Cork City), the programme of peace, retrenchment and reform of William Ewart Gladstone (M.P. for Midlothian, N.B.) and, in support of his political convictions, had climbed up into a secure position amid the ramifications of a tree on Northumberland Road to see the entrance (2 February 1888) into the capital of a demonstrative torchlight procession of 20,000 torchbearers, divided into 120 trade corporations, bearing 2000 torches in escort of the marquess of Ripon and (honest) John Morley.

How much and how did he propose to pay for this country residence?

As per prospectus of the Industrious Foreign Acclimatised Nationalised Friendly State-Aided Building Society (incorporated 1874), a maximum of £60 per annum, being ⅙ of an assured income derived from gilt-edged securities, representing at 5% simple interest a capital of £1200 (estimate of price at 20 years purchase), of which ⅓ to be paid on acquisition and the balance in the form of annual rent, viz. £800 plus 2½% interest on the same, repayable quarterly in equal instalments until extinction by amortisation of loan advanced for purchase within a period of 20 years, amounting to an annual rental of £64, head rent included, the title deeds to remain in possession of the lender or lenders with a saving clause envisaging forced sale, foreclosure and mutual compensation in the event of protracted failure to pay the terms assigned, otherwise the messuage to become the absolute property of the tenant-occupier upon expiry of the period of years stipulated.

What rapid but insecure means to opulence might facilitate immediate purchase?

A private wireless telegraph which would transmit by dot and dash system the result of a national equine handicap (flat or steeplechase) of 1 or more miles and furlongs won by an outsider at odds of 50 to 1 at Ascot at 3.08 p.m. (Greenwich time), the message being received and available for betting purposes in Dublin at 2.59 p.m. (Dunsink time). The unexpected discovery of an object of great monetary value, precious stone, valuable adhesive or impressed postage stamps (7 schilling, mauve, imperforate, Hamburg, 1866: 4 pence, rose, blue paper, perforate, Great Britain, 1855: 1 franc, stone, official, rouletted, diagonal surcharge, Luxemburg, 1878), antique dynastical ring, unique relic, in unusual repositories or by unusual means: from the air (dropped by an eagle in flight), by fire (amid the carbonised remains of an incendiated edifice), in the sea (amid flotsam, jetsam, lagan and derelict), on earth (in the gizzard of a comestible fowl). A Spanish prisoner's donation of a distant treasure of valuables or specie or bullion lodged with a solvent banking corporation 100 years previously at 5% compound interest of the collective worth of £5,000,000 stg (five million pounds sterling). A contract with an inconsiderate contractee for the delivery of 32 consignments of some given commodity in consideration of cash payment on delivery per delivery at the initial rate of ¼d to be increased constantly in the geometrical progression of 2 (¼d, ½d, 1d, 2d, 4d, 8d, 1s 4d, 2s 8d, to 32 terms). A prepared scheme based on a study of the laws of probability to break the bank at Monte Carlo. A solution of the secular problem of the quadrature of the circle, government premium £1,000,000 sterling.

Was vast wealth acquirable through industrial channels?

The reclamation of dunams of waste arenary soil, proposed in the prospectus of Agudath Netaim, Bleibtreustrasse 34, Berlin W.15, by the cultivation of orange plantations and melon fields and by reafforestation. The utilisation of waste paper, fells of sewer rodents, human excrement possessing chemical properties, in view of the vast production of the first, vast number of the second and immense quantity of the third, every normal human being of average vitality and appetite producing annually, cancelling byproducts of water, a sum total of 80 lb (mixed animal and vegetable diet), to be multiplied by 4,386,035, the total population of Ireland according to the census returns of 1901.

Were there schemes of wider scope?

A scheme to be formulated and submitted for approval to the harbour commissioners for the exploitation of white coal (hydraulic power), obtained by hydroelectric plant at peak of tide at Dublin Bar or at head of water at Poulaphouca or Powerscourt or catchment basins of main streams, for the economic production of 500,000 W.H.P. of electricity. A scheme to enclose the peninsular delta of the North Bull at Dollymount and erect on the space of the foreland, used for golf links and rifle ranges, an asphalted esplanade with casinos, booths, shooting galleries, hotels, boarding houses, reading rooms, establishments for mixed bathing. A scheme for the use of dogvans and goatvans for the delivery of early morning milk. A scheme for the development of Irish tourist traffic in and around Dublin by means of petrol-propelled riverboats plying in the fluvial fairway between Island Bridge and Ringsend, charabancs, narrow gauge local railways, and pleasure steamers for coastwise navigation (10/- per person per day, guide, trilingual, included). A scheme for the repristination of passenger and goods traffic over Irish waterways, when freed from weedbeds. A scheme to connect by tramline the cattle market (North Circular Road and Prussia Street) with the quays (Sheriff Street Lower and East Wall), parallel with the Link Line railway laid (in conjunction with the Great Southern and Western railway line) between the cattle park, Liffey Junction, and terminus of Midland Great Western Railway, 43 to 45 North Wall, in proximity to the terminal stations or Dublin branches of Great Central Railway, Midland Railway of England, City of Dublin

Steam Packet Company, Lancashire and Yorkshire Railway Company, Dublin and Glasgow Steam Packet Company, The Glasgow, Dublin and Londonderry Steam Packet Company (Laird line), British and Irish Steam Packet Company, Dublin and Morecambe Steamers, London and North-Western Railway Company, Dublin Port and Docks Board landing sheds, and transit sheds of Palgrave, Murphy and Company, steamship owners, agents for steamers from Mediterranean, Spain, Portugal, France, Belgium and Holland &c. and for Liverpool Underwriters' Association, the cost of acquired rolling stock for animal transport and of additional mileage operated by the Dublin United Tramways Company Limited to be covered by graziers' fees.

Positing what protasis would the contraction for such several schemes become a natural and necessary apodosis?

Given a guarantee equal to the sum sought, the support, by deed of gift and transfer vouchers during donor's lifetime or by bequest after donor's painless extinction, of eminent financiers (Blum Pasha, Rothschild, Guggenheim, Hirsch, Montefiore, Morgan, Rockefeller) possessing fortunes in 6 figures, amassed during a successful life, and joining capital with opportunity the thing required was done.

What eventuality would render him independent of such wealth?

The independent discovery of a goldseam of inexhaustible ore.

For what reason did he meditate on schemes so difficult of realisation?

It was one of his axioms that similar meditations, or the automatic relation to himself of a narrative concerning himself, or tranquil recollection of the past, when practised habitually before retiring for the night alleviated fatigue and produced as a result sound repose and renovated vitality.

His justifications?

As a physicist he had learned that of the 70 years of complete human life at least 2/7, viz. 20 years, are passed in sleep. As a philosopher he knew that at the termination of any allotted life only an infinitesimal part of any person's desires has been realised. As a physiologist he believed in the artificial placation of malignant agencies chiefly operative during somnolence.

What did he fear?

The committal of homicide or suicide during sleep by an aberration of the light of reason, the incommensurable categorical intelligence situated in the cerebral convolutions.

What were habitually his final meditations?

Of some one sole unique advertisement to cause passers to stop in wonder, a poster novelty, with all extraneous accretions excluded, reduced to its simplest and most efficient terms not exceeding the span of casual vision and congruous with the velocity of modern life.

What did the first drawer unlocked contain?

A Vere Foster's handwriting copybook, property of Milly (Millicent) Bloom, certain pages of which bore diagram drawings, marked *Papli*, which showed a large globular head with 5 hairs erect, 2 eyes in profile, the trunk full front with 3 large buttons, 1 triangular foot: 2 fading photographs of Queen Alexandra of England and of Maud Branscombe, actress and professional beauty: a Yuletide card bearing on it a pictorial representation of a parasitic plant, the legend *Mizpah*, the date Xmas 1892, the name of the senders Mr & Mrs M. Comerford, the versicle *May this Yuletide bring to thee, Joy and peace and welcome glee*: a butt of red partly liquefied sealing wax, obtained from the stores department of Messrs Hely's Ltd, 27, 28, 29 and 30 Dame Street: a box containing the remainder of a gross of gilt "J" pen-nibs, obtained from same department of same firm: an old sandglass which rolled, containing sand which rolled: a sealed prophecy (never unsealed) written by Leopold Bloom in 1886 concerning the consequences of the passing into law of William Ewart Gladstone's Home Rule bill of 1886 (never passed into law): a bazaar ticket, No. 2004, of Saint Kevin's Charity Fair, price 6*d*, 100 prizes: an infantile epistle, dated small em *monday*, reading capital pee *Papli* comma capital aitch *How are you* note of interrogation capital eye *I am very well* full stop new paragraph signature with flourishes capital em *Milly* no stop: a cameo brooch, property of Ellen Bloom (born Higgins), deceased: a cameo scarfpin, property of Rudolph Bloom (born Virag), deceased: 3 typewritten letters, addressee Henry Flower, c/o P.O. Westland Row, addresser Martha Clifford, c/o P.O. Dolphin's Barn: the transliterated name and address of the addresser of the 3 letters in reversed alphabetic boustrophedonic punctated quadrilinear cryptogram (vowels suppressed), N.IGS./WI.UU.OX/W.OKS.MH/MI.Y: a press cutting from an English weekly periodical *Modern Society*, subject corporal chastisement in girls' schools: a pink ribbon which had festooned an Easter egg in the year 1899: two partly uncoiled rubber preservatives with reserve pockets, purchased by post from Box 32, P.O. Charing Cross,

London W.C.: 1 pack of 1 dozen cream-laid envelopes and feint-ruled notepaper, watermarked, now reduced by 3: some assorted Austro-Hungarian coins: 2 coupons of the Royal and Privileged Hungarian Lottery: a low-power magnifying glass: 2 erotic photocards, showing a) buccal coition between nude señorita (rear presentation, superior position) and nude torero (fore presentation, inferior position), b) anal violation by male religious (fully clothed, eyes abject) of female religious (partly clothed, eyes direct), purchased by post from Box 32, P.O. Charing Cross, London W.C.: a press cutting of recipe for renovation of old tan boots: a 1*d* adhesive stamp, lavender, of the reign of Queen Victoria: a chart of the measurements of Leopold Bloom compiled before, during and after 2 months' consecutive use of Sandow-Whiteley's pulley exerciser (men's 15/-, athlete's 20/-), viz. chest 28 in. and 29½ in., biceps 9 in. and 10 in., forearm 8½ in. and 9 in., thigh 16 in. and 20 in., calf 11 in. and 12 in.: 1 prospectus of The Wonderworker, the world's greatest remedy for rectal complaints, direct from Wonderworker, Coventry House, South Place, London E.C., addressed (erroneously) to Mrs L. Bloom, with brief accompanying note commencing (erroneously) *Dear Madam.*

Quote the textual terms in which the prospectus claimed notable advantages for this thaumaturgic remedy.

It heals and soothes while you sleep, in case of trouble in breaking wind, assists nature in the most formidable way, ensuring instant relief in the discharge of gases, keeping parts clean and free natural action, an initial outlay of 7/6 making a new man of you and life worth living. Ladies find Wonderworker especially useful, a pleasant surprise when they note delightful result like a cool drink of fresh spring water on a sultry summer's day. Recommend it to your lady and gentlemen friends, lasts a lifetime. Insert long round end. Wonderworker.

Were there testimonials?

Numerous. From clergyman, British naval officer, well-known author, city man, hospital nurse, lady, mother of five, absentminded beggar.

How did absentminded beggar's concluding testimonial conclude?

What a pity the government did not supply our men with Wonderworkers during the South African campaign! What a relief it would have been!

What object did Bloom add to this collection of objects?

A 4th typewritten letter received by Henry Flower (let H.F. be L.B.) from Martha Clifford (find M.C.).

What pleasant reflection accompanied this action?

The reflection that, apart from the letter in question, his magnetic face, form and address had been favourably received during the course of the preceding day by a wife (Mrs Josephine Breen, born Josie Powell), a nurse (Miss Callan, Christian name unknown), a maid (Gertrude (Gerty), family name unknown).

What possibility suggested itself?

The possibility of exercising virile power of fascination in the not immediate future after an expensive repast in a private apartment in the company of an elegant courtesan, of corporal beauty, moderately mercenary, variously instructed, a lady by origin.

What did the 2nd drawer contain?

Documents: the birth certificate of Leopold Paula Bloom: an endowment assurance policy of £500 in the Scottish Widows' Assurance Society, intestated Millicent (Milly) Bloom, coming into force at 25 years as with profit policy of £430, £462–10–0 and £500 at 60 years or death, 65 years or death and death, respectively, or with profit policy (paid up) of £299–10–0 together with cash payment of £133–10–0, at option: a bank passbook issued by the Ulster Bank, College Green branch, showing statement of a/c for half year ending 31 December 1903, balance in depositor's favour £18–14–6 (eighteen pounds fourteen shillings and sixpence sterling), net personalty: certificate of possession of £900 Canadian 4% (inscribed) government stock (free of stamp duty): dockets of the Catholic Cemeteries' (Glasnevin) Committee relative to a graveplot purchased: a local press cutting concerning change of name by deed poll.

Quote the textual terms of this notice.

I, Rudolph Virag, now resident at No. 52 Clanbrassil Street, Dublin, formerly of Szombathely in the kingdom of Hungary, hereby give notice that I have assumed and intend henceforth upon all occasions and at all times to be known by the name of Rudolph Bloom.

What other objects relative to Rudolph Bloom (born Virag) were in the 2nd drawer?

An indistinct daguerreotype of Rudolph Virag and his father Leopold Virag executed in the year 1852 in the portrait atelier of their (respectively) 1st and 2nd cousin, Stefan Virag of Szekesfehervar, Hungary. An ancient haggadah book in which a pair of horn-rimmed convex spectacles inserted marked the passage of thanksgiving in the ritual prayers for

Pesach (Passover): a photocard of the Queen's Hotel, Ennis, proprietor, Rudolph Bloom: an envelope addressed *To My Dear Son Leopold.*

What fractions of phrases did the lecture of those five whole words evoke?

Tomorrow will be a week that I received ... it is no use Leopold to be ... with your dear mother ... that is not more to stand ... to her ... all for me is out ... be kind to Athos, Leopold ... my dear son ... always ... of me ... *das Herz* ... *Gott* ... *dein* ...

What reminiscences of a human subject suffering from progressive melancholia did these objects evoke in Bloom?

An old man, widower, unkempt of hair, in bed, with head covered, sighing: an infirm dog, Athos: aconite, resorted to by increasing doses of grains and scruples as a palliative of recrudescent neuralgia: the face in death of a septuagenarian, suicide by poison.

Why did Bloom experience a sentiment of remorse?

Because in immature impatience he had treated with disrespect certain beliefs and practices.

As?

The prohibition of the use of fleshmeat and milk at one meal: the hebdomadary symposium of incoordinately abstract, perfervidly concrete, mercantile co-exreligionist ex-compatriots: the circumcision of male infants: the supernatural character of Judaic scripture: the ineffability of the tetragrammaton: the sanctity of the Sabbath.

How did these beliefs and practices now appear to him?

Not more rational than they had then appeared, not less rational than other beliefs and practices now appeared.

What first reminiscence had he of Rudolph Bloom (deceased)?

Rudolph Bloom (deceased) narrated to his son Leopold Bloom (aged 6) a retrospective arrangement of migrations and settlements in and between Dublin, London, Florence, Milan, Vienna, Budapest, Szombathely, with statements of satisfaction (his grandfather having seen Maria Theresa, empress of Austria, queen of Hungary), with commercial advice (having taken care of pence, the pounds having taken care of themselves). Leopold Bloom (aged 6) had accompanied these narrations by constant consulta- tion of a geographical map of Europe (political) and by suggestions for the establishment of affiliated business premises in the various centres mentioned.

Had time equally but differently obliterated the memory of these migrations in narrator and listener?

In narrator by the access of years and in consequence of the use of narcotic toxin: in listener by the access of years and in consequence of the action of distraction upon vicarious experiences.

What idiosyncrasies of the narrator were concomitant products of amnesia?

Occasionally he ate without having previously removed his hat. Occasionally he drank voraciously the juice of gooseberry fool from an inclined plate. Occasionally he removed from his lips the traces of food by means of a lacerated envelope or other accessible fragment of paper.

What two phenomena of senescence were more frequent?

The myopic digital calculation of coins, eructation consequent upon repletion.

What objects offered partial consolation for these reminiscences?

The endowment policy, the bank passbook, the certificate of the possession of scrip.

Reduce Bloom by cross multiplication of reverses of fortune, from which these supports protected him, and by elimination of all positive values to a negligible negative irrational unreal quantity.

Successively, in descending helotic order: poverty, that of the outdoor hawker of imitation jewellery, the dun for the recovery of bad and doubtful debts, the poor rate and deputy cess collector: mendicancy, that of the fraudulent bankrupt with negligible assets paying ¼d in the £, sandwich man, distributor of throwaways, nocturnal vagrant, insinuating sycophant, maimed sailor, blind stripling, superannuated bailiff's man, marfeast, lickplate, spoilsport, pickthank, eccentric public laughingstock seated on bench of public park under discarded perforated umbrella: destitution, the inmate of Old Man's House (Royal Hospital), Kilmainham, the inmate of Simpson's Hospital for reduced but respectable men permanently disabled by gout or want of sight: nadir of misery, the aged impotent disfranchised rate-supported moribund lunatic pauper.

With which attendant indignities?

The unsympathetic indifference of previously amiable females, the contempt of muscular males, the acceptance of fragments of bread, the simulated ignorance of casual acquaintances, the latration of illegitimate unlicensed vagabond dogs, the infantile discharge of decomposed vegetable missiles, worth little or nothing, nothing, or less than nothing.

By what could such a situation be precluded?
By decease (change of state): by departure (change of place).

Which preferably?
The latter, by the line of least resistance.

What considerations rendered departure not entirely undesirable?
Constant cohabitation impeding mutual toleration of personal defects. The habit of independent purchase increasingly cultivated. The necessity to counteract by impermanent sojourn the permanence of arrest.

What considerations rendered departure not irrational?
The parties concerned, uniting, had increased and multiplied, which being done, offspring produced and educed to maturity, the parties, if not disunited, were obliged to reunite for increase and multiplication, which was absurd, to form by reunion the original couple of uniting parties, which was impossible.

What considerations rendered departure desirable?
The attractive character of certain localities in Ireland and abroad, as represented in general geographical maps of polychrome design or in special ordnance survey charts by employment of scale numerals and hachures.

In Ireland?
The cliffs of Moher, the windy wilds of Connemara, Lough Neagh with submerged petrified city, the Giant's Causeway, Fort Camden and Fort Carlisle, the Golden Vale of Tipperary, the islands of Aran, the pastures of royal Meath, Brigid's oak in Kildare, the Queen's Island shipyard in Belfast, the Salmon Leap, the lakes of Killarney.

Abroad?
Ceylon (with spice gardens supplying tea to Thomas Kernan, agent for Pulbrook, Robertson and Co., 2 Mincing Lane, London E.C., and 43 Dame Street, Dublin), Jerusalem, the holy city (with mosque of Omar and gate

of Damascus, goal of aspiration), the straits of Gibraltar (the unique birthplace of Marion Tweedy), the Parthenon (containing statues of nude Grecian divinities), the Wall Street money market (which controlled international finance), the Plaza de Toros at La Linea, Spain (where O'Hara of the Camerons had slain the bull), Niagara (over which no human being had passed with impunity), the land of the Eskimos (eaters of soap), the forbidden country of Tibet (from which no traveller returns), the bay of Naples (to see which was to die), the Dead Sea.

Under what guidance, following what signs?

At sea, septentrional, by night the Pole star, located at the point of intersection of the line from Beta to Alpha in Ursa Major produced and extended externally to Omega and the hypotenuse of the right-angled triangle formed by the line Alpha Omega so produced, the line Alpha Delta of Ursa Major and the line from Delta of Ursa Major to Delta of Cassiopeia. On land, meridional, a bispherical moon, revealed in imperfect varying phases of lunation through the posterior interstice of the imperfectly occluded skirt of a carnose negligent perambulating female, a pillar of the cloud by day.

What public advertisement would divulge the occultation of the departed?

£5 reward, lost, stolen or strayed from his residence 7 Eccles Street, missing gent about 40, answering to the name of Bloom, Leopold (Poldy), height 5 ft. 9½ inches, full build, olive complexion, may have since grown a beard, when last seen was wearing a black suit. Above sum will be paid for information leading to his discovery.

What universal binomial denominations would be his as entity and nonentity?

Assumed by any or known to none. Everyman or Noman.

What tributes his?

Honour and gifts of strangers, the friends of Everyman. A nymph immortal, beauty, the bride of Noman.

Would the departed never nowhere nohow reappear?

Ever he would wander, self-compelled, to the extreme limit of his cometary orbit, beyond the fixed stars and variable suns and telescopic planets, astronomical waifs and strays, to the extreme boundary of space, passing from land to land, among peoples, amid events. Somewhere imperceptibly he would hear and somehow reluctantly, sun-compelled, obey the summons of recall. Whence, disappearing from the constellation of the Northern Crown, he would somehow reappear reborn above Delta in the constellation of Cassiopeia and after incalculable eons of peregrination return, an estranged avenger, a wreaker of justice on malefactors, a dark crusader, a sleeper awakened, with financial resources (by supposition) surpassing those of Rothschild or of the silver king.

What would render such return irrational?

An unsatisfactory equation between an exodus and return in time through reversible space and an exodus and return in space through irreversible time.

What play of forces, inducing inertia, rendered departure undesirable?

The lateness of the hour, rendering procrastinatory: the obscurity of the night, rendering invisible: the uncertainty of thoroughfares, rendering perilous: the necessity for repose, obviating movement: the proximity of an occupied bed, obviating research: the anticipation of warmth (human) tempered with coolness (linen), obviating desire and rendering desirable: the statue of Narcissus, sound without echo, desired desire.

What advantages were possessed by an occupied as distinct from an unoccupied bed?

The removal of nocturnal solitude, the superior quality of human (mature female) to inhuman (hot-water jar) calefaction, the stimulation of matutinal contact, the economy of mangling done on the premises in the case of trousers accurately folded and placed lengthwise between the spring mattress (striped) and the woollen mattress (biscuit section).

What past consecutive causes, before rising preapprehended, of accumulated fatigue did Bloom, before rising, silently recapitulate?

The preparation of breakfast (burnt offering): intestinal congestion and premeditative defecation (holy of holies): the bath (rite of John): the funeral (rite of Samuel): the advertisement of Alexander Keyes (Urim and Thummim): the unsubstantial lunch (rite of Melchizedek): the visit to museum and national library (holy place): the book hunt along Bedford Row, Merchants' Arch, Wellington Quay (Simhath Torah): the music in the Ormond Hotel (Shira ha'Shirim): the altercation with a truculent troglodyte in Bernard Kiernan's premises (holocaust): a blank period of time including a cardrive, a visit to a house of mourning, a leavetaking (wilderness): the eroticism produced by feminine exhibitionism (rite of

Onan): the prolonged delivery of Mrs Mina Purefoy (heave offering): the visit to the disorderly house of Mrs Bella Cohen, 82 Tyrone Street Lower, and subsequent brawl and chance-medley in Beaver Street (Armageddon): nocturnal perambulation to and from the cabman's shelter, Butt Bridge (atonement).

What self-imposed enigma did Bloom, about to rise in order to go, so as to conclude lest he should not conclude, involuntarily apprehend?

The cause of a brief sharp unforeseen heard loud lone crack emitted by the insentient material of a strain-veined timber table.

What self-involved enigma did Bloom, risen, going, gathering multicoloured multiform multitudinous garments, voluntarily apprehending not comprehend?

Who was M'Intosh?

What self-evident enigma pondered with desultory constancy during 30 years did Bloom now, having effected natural obscurity by the extinction of artificial light, silently suddenly comprehend?

Where was Moses when the candle went out?

What imperfections in a perfect day did Bloom, walking, charged with collected articles of recently divested male wearing apparel, silently successively enumerate?

A provisional failure to obtain renewal of an advertisement: to obtain a certain quantity of tea from Thomas Kernan (agent for Pulbrook, Robertson and Co., 43 Dame Street, Dublin, and 2 Mincing Lane, London E.C.): to certify the presence or absence of posterior rectal orifice in the case of Hellenic female divinities: to obtain admission (gratuitous or paid) to the performance of *Leah* by Mrs Bandmann-Palmer at the Gaiety Theatre, 46, 47, 48, 49 South King Street.

What impression of an absent face did Bloom, arrested, silently recall?

The face of her father, the late Major Brian Cooper Tweedy, Royal Dublin Fusiliers, of Gibraltar and Rehoboth, Dolphin's Barn.

What recurrent impressions of the same were possible by hypothesis?

Retreating, at the terminus of the Great Northern Railway, Amiens Street, with constant uniform acceleration, along parallel lines meeting at infinity, if produced: along parallel lines reproduced from infinity, with constant uniform retardation, at the terminus of the Great Northern Railway, Amiens Street, returning.

What miscellaneous effects of female personal wearing apparel were perceived by him?

A pair of new inodorous half-silk black ladies' hose, a pair of new violet garters, a pair of outsize ladies' drawers of India mull, cut on generous lines, redolent of opopanax, jessamine and Muratti's Turkish cigarettes, and containing a long bright steel safety pin, folded curvilinear, a camisole of batiste with thin lace border, an accordion underskirt of blue silk moirette, all these objects being disposed irregularly on the top of a rectangular trunk, quadruple-battened, having capped corners, with multicoloured labels, initialled on its fore side in white lettering B.C.T. (Brian Cooper Tweedy).

What impersonal objects were perceived?

A commode, one leg fractured, totally covered by square cretonne cutting, apple design, on which rested a lady's black straw hat. Orange-keyed ware, bought of Henry Price, china merchant, 16A South City Market, disposed irregularly on the washstand and floor and consisting of basin, soapdish and brushtray (on the washstand, together), pitcher and night article (on the floor, separate).

Bloom's acts?

He deposited the articles of clothing on a chair, removed his remaining articles of clothing, took from beneath the bolster at the head of the bed a folded long white nightshirt, inserted his head and arms into the proper apertures of the nightshirt, removed a pillow from the head to the foot of the bed, prepared the bed linen accordingly and entered the bed.

How?

With circumspection, as invariably when entering an abode (his own or not his own): with solicitude, the snake-spiral springs of the mattress being old, the brass quoits and pendent viper radii loose and tremulous under stress and strain: prudently, as entering a lair or ambush of lust or adders: lightly, the less to disturb: reverently, the bed of conception and of birth, of consummation of marriage and of breach of marriage, of sleep and of death.

What did his limbs, when gradually extended, encounter?

New clean bed linen, additional odours, the presence of a human form, female, hers, the imprint of a human form, male, not his, some crumbs, some flakes of potted meat, recooked, which he removed.

640

If he had smiled why would he have smiled?

To reflect that each one who enters imagines himself to be the first to enter whereas he is always the last term of a preceding series even if the first term of a succeeding one, each imagining himself to be first, last, only and alone, whereas he is neither first nor last nor only nor alone in a series originating in and repeated to infinity.

What preceding series?

Assuming Mulvey to be the first term of his series, Mulvey, Penrose, Bartell d'Arcy, Professor Goodwin, Julius Masliansky, John Henry Menton, Father Bernard Corrigan, a farmer at the Royal Dublin Society's Horse Show, Maggot O'Reilly, Matthew Dillon, Valentine Blake Dillon (lord mayor of Dublin), Christopher Callanan, Lenehan, an Italian organ grinder, an unknown gentleman in the Gaiety Theatre, Benjamin Dollard, Simon Dedalus, Andrew (Pisser) Burke, Joseph Cuffe, Wisdom Hely, Alderman John Hooper, Dr Francis Brady, Father Sebastian of Mount Argus, a bootblack at the General Post Office, Hugh E. (Blazes) Boylan, and so each and so on to no last term.

What were his reflections concerning the last member of this series and late occupant of the bed?

Reflections on his vigour (a bounder), corporal proportion (a billsticker), commercial ability (a bester), impressionability (a boaster).

Why for the observer impressionability in addition to vigour, corporal proportion and commercial ability?

Because he had observed with augmenting frequency in the preceding members of the same series the same concupiscence, inflammably transmitted, first with alarm, then with understanding, then with desire, finally with fatigue, with alternating symptoms of epicene comprehension and apprehension.

With what antagonistic sentiments were his subsequent reflections affected?

Envy, jealousy, abnegation, equanimity.

Envy?

Of a bodily and mental male organism specially adapted for the superincumbent posture of energetic human copulation and energetic piston and cylinder movement necessary for the complete satisfaction of a constant but not acute concupiscence resident in a bodily and mental female organism, passive but not obtuse.

Jealousy?

Because a nature, full and volatile in its free state, was alternately the agent and reagent of attraction. Because attraction between agent(s) and reagent(s) at all instants varied, with inverse proportion of increase and decrease, with incessant circular extension and radial reentrance. Because the controlled contemplation of the fluctuation of attraction produced, if desired, a fluctuation of pleasure.

Abnegation?

In virtue of a) acquaintance initiated in September 1903 in the establishment of George Mesias, merchant tailor and outfitter, 5 Eden Quay, b) hospitality extended and received in kind, reciprocated and reappropriated in person, c) comparative youth subject to impulses of ambition and magnanimity, collegial altruism and amorous egoism, d) extraracial attraction, intraracial inhibition, supraracial prerogative, e) an imminent provincial musical tour, common current expenses, net proceeds divided.

Equanimity?

As as natural as any and every natural act of a nature, expressed or understood, executed in natured nature by natural creatures in accordance with his, her and their natured natures of dissimilar similarity. As not as calamitous as a cataclysmic annihilation of the planet in consequence of a collision with a dark sun. As less reprehensible than theft, highway robbery, cruelty to children and animals, obtaining money under false pretences, forgery, embezzlement, misappropriation of public money, betrayal of public trust, malingering, mayhem, corruption of minors, criminal libel, blackmail, contempt of court, arson, treason, felony, mutiny on the high seas, trespass, burglary, jailbreaking, practice of unnatural vice, desertion from armed forces in the field, perjury, poaching, usury, intelligence with the king's enemies, impersonation, criminal assault, manslaughter, wilful and premeditated murder. As not more abnormal than all other parallel processes of adaptation to altered conditions of existence resulting in a reciprocal equilibrium between the bodily organism and its attendant circumstances, foods, beverages, acquired habits, indulged inclinations, significant disease. As more than inevitable, irreparable.

Why more abnegation than jealousy, less envy than equanimity?

From outrage (matrimony) to outrage (adultery) there arose nought but outrage (copulation), yet the matrimonial violator of the matrimonially violated had not been outraged by the adulterous violator of the adulterously violated.

What retribution, if any?

Assassination, never, as two wrongs did not make one right. Duel by combat, no. Divorce, not now. Exposure by mechanical artifice (automatic bed) or individual testimony (concealed ocular witnesses), not yet. Suit for damages by legal influence or simulation of assault with evidence of injuries sustained (self-inflicted), not impossibly. Hush money by moral influence, possibly. If any, positively, connivance, introduction of emulation (material, a prosperous rival agency of publicity: moral, a successful rival agent of intimacy), depreciation, alienation, humiliation, separation protecting the one separated from the other, protecting the separator from both.

By what reflections did he, a conscious reactor against the void of incertitude, justify to himself his sentiments?

The preordained frangibility of the hymen: the presupposed intangibility of the thing in itself: the incongruity and disproportion between the self-prolonging tension of the thing proposed to be done and the self-abbreviating relaxation of the thing done: the fallaciously inferred debility of the female: the muscularity of the male: the variations of ethical codes: the natural grammatical transition by inversion involving no alteration of sense of an aorist preterite proposition (parsed as masculine subject, monosyllabic onomatopoeic transitive verb, direct feminine object) from the active voice into its correlative aorist preterite proposition (parsed as feminine subject, auxiliary verb and quasi-monosyllabic onomatopoeic past participle, complementary masculine agent) in the passive voice: the continued production of seminators by generation: the continual production of semen by distillation: the futility of triumph or protest or vindication: the inanity of extolled virtue: the lethargy of nescient matter: the apathy of the stars.

In what final satisfaction did these antagonistic sentiments and reflections, reduced to their simplest forms, converge?

Satisfaction at the ubiquity in eastern and western terrestrial hemispheres in all habitable lands and islands explored or unexplored (the land of the midnight sun, the islands of the blessed, the isles of Greece, the land of promise) of adipose anterior and posterior female hemispheres, redolent of milk and honey and of excretory sanguine and seminal warmth, reminiscent of secular families of curves of amplitude, insusceptible of moods of impression or of contrarieties of expression, expressive of mute immutable mature animality.

The visible signs of antesatisfaction?
An approximate erection: a solicitous adversion: a gradual elevation: a tentative revelation: a silent contemplation.

Then?
He kissed the plump mellow yellow smellow melons of her rump, on each plump melonous hemisphere, in their mellow yellow furrow, with obscure prolonged provocative melonsmellonous osculation.

The visible signs of postsatisfaction?
A silent contemplation: a tentative velation: a gradual abasement: a solicitous aversion: a proximate erection.

What followed this silent action?
Somnolent invocation, less somnolent recognition, incipient excitation, catechetical interrogation.

With what modifications did the narrator reply to this interrogation?
Negative: he omitted to mention the clandestine correspondence between Martha Clifford and Henry Flower, the public altercation at, in and in the vicinity of the licensed premises of Bernard Kiernan and Co. Limited, 8, 9 and 10 Little Britain Street, the erotic provocation and response thereto caused by the exhibitionism of Gertrude (Gerty), surname unknown. Positive: he included mention of a performance by Mrs Bandmann-Palmer of *Leah* at the Gaiety Theatre, 46, 47, 48, 49 South King Street, an invitation to supper at Wynn's (Murphy's) Hotel, 35, 36 and 37 Lower Abbey Street, a volume of peccaminous pornographical tendency entitled *Sweets of Sin*, anonymous author a gentleman of fashion, a temporary concussion caused by a falsely calculated movement in the course of a postcenal gymnastic display, the victim (since completely recovered) being Stephen Dedalus, professor and author, eldest surviving son of Simon Dedalus, of no fixed occupation, an aeronautical feat executed by him (narrator) in the presence of a witness, the professor

and author aforesaid, with promptitude of decision and gymnastic flexibility.

Was the narration otherwise unaltered by modifications?
Absolutely.

Which event or person emerged as the salient point of his narration?
Stephen Dedalus, professor and author.

What limitations of activity and inhibitions of conjugal rights were perceived by listener and narrator concerning themselves during the course of this intermittent and increasingly more laconic narration?

By the listener, a limitation of fertility. Inasmuch as marriage had been celebrated 1 calendar month after the 18th anniversary of her birth (8 September 1870), viz. 8 October 1888, and consummated on the same date, with female issue born 15 June 1889, marriage having been anticipatorily consummated on 10 September of the same year, and complete carnal intercourse with ejaculation of semen within the natural female organ having last taken place 5 weeks previous, viz. 27 November 1893, to the birth on 29 December 1893 of second (and only male) issue, deceased 9 January 1894 aged 11 days, there remained a period of 10 years, 6 months and 19 days during which carnal intercourse had been incomplete, without ejaculation of semen within the natural female organ. By the narrator, a limitation of activity, mental and corporal. Inasmuch as complete mental intercourse between himself and the listener had not taken place since the consummation of puberty, indicated by catamenial hemorrhage, of the female issue of narrator and listener, 15 September 1903, there remained a period of 9 months and 1 day during which, in consequence of a preestablished natural comprehension in incomprehension between the consummated females (listener and issue), complete corporal liberty of action had been circumscribed.

How?
By various reiterated feminine interrogations concerning the masculine destination whither, the place where, the time at which, the duration for which, the object with which, in the case of temporary absences, projected or effected.

What moved visibly above the listener's and the narrator's invisible thoughts?

The upcast reflection of a lamp and shade, an inconstant series of concentric circles of varying gradations of light and shadow.

In what directions did listener and narrator lie?

Listener, SE by E: Narrator, NW by W: on the 53rd parallel of latitude, N, and 6th meridian of longitude, W: at an angle of 45° to the terrestrial equator.

In what state of rest or motion?

At rest, relatively to themselves and to each other. In motion, being each and both carried eastward, forward and rearward respectively, by the proper perpetual motion of the earth through everchanging tracks of neverchanging space.

In what posture?

Listener: reclined semilaterally, left, left hand under head, right leg extended in a straight line and resting on left leg, flexed, in the attitude of Gaia-Tellus, fulfilled, recumbent, big with seed. Narrator: reclined laterally, left, with right and left legs flexed, the index finger and thumb of the right hand resting on the bridge of the nose, in the attitude depicted in a snapshot photograph made by Percy Apjohn, the childman weary, the manchild in the womb.

Womb? Weary?

He rests. He has travelled.

With?

Sinbad the Sailor and Tinbad the Tailor and Jinbad the Jailer and Whinbad the Whaler and Ninbad the Nailer and Finbad the Failer and Binbad the Bailer and Pinbad the Pailer and Minbad the Mailer and Hinbad the Hailer and Rinbad the Railer and Dinbad the Kailer and Vinbad the Quailer and Linbad the Yailer and Xinbad the Phthailer.

When?

Going to dark bed there was a square round Sinbad the Sailor roc's auk's egg in the night of the bed of all the auks of the rocs of Darkinbad the Brightdayler.

Where?

●

Yes because he never did a thing like that before as ask to get his breakfast in bed with a couple of eggs since the City Arms Hotel when he used to be pretending to be laid up with a sick voice doing His Highness to make himself interesting for that old faggot Mrs Riordan that he thought he had a great leg of and she never left us a farthing all for masses for herself and her soul greatest miser ever was actually afraid to lay out 4*d* for her methylated spirit telling me all her ailments she had too much old chat in her about politics and earthquakes and the end of the world let us have a bit of fun first God help the world if all the women were her sort down on bathing suits and low necks of course nobody wanted her to wear them I suppose she was pious because no man would look at her twice I hope I'll never be like her a wonder she didn't want us to cover our faces but she was a well-educated woman certainly and her gabby talk about Mr Riordan here and Mr Riordan there I suppose he was glad to get shut of her and her dog smelling my fur and always edging to get up under my petticoats especially then still I like that in him polite to old women like that and waiters and beggars too he's not proud out of nothing but not always if ever he got anything really serious the matter with him it's much better for them to go into a hospital where everything is clean but I suppose I'd have to dring it into him for a month yes and then we'd have a hospital nurse next thing on the carpet have him staying there till they throw him out or a nun maybe like the smutty photo he has she's as much a nun as I'm not yes because they're so weak and puling when they're sick they want a woman to get well if his nose bleeds you'd think it was O tragic and that dying-looking one off the South Circular when he sprained his foot at the choir party at the Sugarloaf mountain the day I wore that dress Miss Stack bringing him flowers the worst old ones she could find at the bottom of the basket anything at all to get into a man's bedroom with her old maid's voice trying to imagine he was dying on account of her *to never see thy face again* though he looked more like a man with his beard a bit grown in the bed father was the same besides I hate bandaging and dosing when he cut his toe with the razor paring his corns afraid he'd get blood poisoning but if it was a

thing I was sick then we'd see what attention only of course the woman
hides it not to give all the trouble they do yes he came somewhere I'm
sure by his appetite anyway love it's not or he'd be off his feed thinking
of her so either it was one of those night women if it was down there he
was really and the hotel story he made up a pack of lies to hide it planning
it Hynes kept me who did I meet ah yes I met do you remember Menton
and who else who let me see that big babbyface I saw him and he not
long married flirting with a young girl at Poole's Myriorama and turned
my back on him when he slinked out looking quite conscious what harm
but he had the impudence to make up to me one time well done to him
mouth almighty and his boiled eyes of all the big stupoes I ever met and
that's called a solicitor only for I hate having a long wrangle in bed or else
if it's not that it's some little bitch or other he got in with somewhere or
picked up on the sly if they only knew him as well as I do yes because the
day before yesterday he was scribbling something a letter when I came
into the front room to show him Dignam's death in the paper as if
something told me and he covered it up with the blotting paper pretending to be thinking about business so very probably that was it to
somebody who thinks she has a softy in him because all men get a bit
like that at his age especially getting on to forty he is now so as to wheedle
any money she can out of him no fool like an old fool and then the usual
kissing my bottom was to hide it not that I care two straws now who he
does it with or knew before that way though I'd like to find out so long as
I don't have the two of them under my nose all the time like that slut that
Mary we had in Ontario Terrace padding out her false bottom to excite
him bad enough to get the smell of those painted women off him once or
twice I had a suspicion by getting him to come near me when I found the
long hair on his coat without that one when I went into the kitchen
pretending he was drinking water one woman is not enough for them it
was all his fault of course ruining servants then proposing that she could
eat at our table on Christmas Day if you please O no thank you not in my
house stealing my potatoes and the oysters 2/6 per dozen going out to
see her aunt if you please common robbery so it was but I was sure he
had something on with that one it takes me to find out a thing like that
he said you have no proof it was her proof O yes her aunt was very fond
of oysters but I told her what I thought of her suggesting me to go out to
be alone with her I wouldn't lower myself to spy on them the garters I
found in her room the Friday she was out that was enough for me a little
bit too much her face swelled up on her with temper when I gave her her

648

week's notice I saw to that better do without them altogether do out the rooms myself quicker only for the damn cooking and throwing out the dirt I gave it to him anyhow either she or me leaves the house I couldn't even touch him if I thought he was with a dirty barefaced liar and sloven like that one denying it up to my face and singing about the place in the WC too because she knew she was too well off yes because he couldn't possibly do without it that long so he must do it somewhere and the last time he came on my bottom when was it the night Boylan gave my hand a great squeeze going along by the Tolka *in my hand there steals another* I just pressed the back of his like that with my thumb to squeeze back singing *The young May moon she's beaming love* because he has an idea about him and me he's not such a fool he said I'm dining out and going to the Gaiety though I'm not going to give him the satisfaction in any case God knows he's a change in a way not to be always and ever wearing the same old hat unless I paid some nice-looking boy to do it since I can't do it myself a young boy would like me I'd confuse him a little alone with him if we were I'd let him see my garters the new ones and make him turn red looking at him seduce him I know what boys feel with that down on their cheek doing that frigging drawing out the thing by the hour question and answer would you do this that and the other with the coalman yes with a bishop yes I would because I told him about some dean or bishop was sitting beside me in the Jews' Temples gardens when I was knitting that woollen thing a stranger to Dublin what place was it and so on about the monuments and he tired me out with statues encouraging him making him worse than he is who is in your mind now tell me who are you thinking of who is it tell me his name who tell me who the German Emperor is it yes imagine I'm him think of him can you feel him trying to make a whore of me what he never will he ought to give it up now at this age of his life simply ruination for any woman and no satisfaction in it pretending to like it till he comes and then finish it off myself anyway and it makes your lips pale anyhow it's done now once and for all with all the talk of the world about it people make it's only the first time after that it's just the ordinary do it and think no more about it why can't you kiss a man without going and marrying him first you sometimes love to wildly when you feel that way so nice all over you you can't help yourself I wish some man or other would take me sometime when he's there and kiss me in his arms there's nothing like a kiss long and hot down to your soul almost paralyses you then I hate that confession when I used to go to Father Corrigan he touched me Father

and what harm if he did where and I said on the canal bank like a fool
but whereabouts on your person my child on the leg behind high up was
it yes rather high up was it where you sit down yes O Lord couldn't he
say bottom right out and have done with it what has that got to do with
it and did you whatever way he put it I forget no Father and I always
think of the real father what did he want to know for when I already
confessed it to God he had a nice fat hand the palm moist always I
wouldn't mind feeling it neither would he I'd say by the bull neck in his
horse collar I wonder did he know me in the box I could see his face he
couldn't see mine of course he'd never turn or let on still his eyes were
red when his father died they're lost for a woman of course must be
terrible when a man cries let alone them I'd like to be embraced by one
in his vestments and the smell of incense off him like the pope besides
there's no danger with a Priest if you're married he's too careful about
himself then give something to HH the pope for a penance I wonder was
he satisfied with me one thing I didn't like his slapping me behind going
away so familiarly in the hall though I laughed I'm not a horse or an ass
am I I suppose he was thinking of his father's I wonder is he awake
thinking of me or dreaming am I in it who gave him that flower he said
he bought he smelt of some kind of drink not whiskey or stout or perhaps
the sweety kind of paste they stick their bills up with some liqueur I'd like
to sip those rich-looking green and yellow expensive drinks those stage-
door Johnnies drink with the opera hats I tasted once with my finger
dipped out of that American that had the squirrel talking stamps with
father he had all he could do to keep himself from falling asleep after the
last time after we took the port and potted meat it had a fine salty taste
yes because I felt lovely and tired myself and fell asleep as sound as a top
the moment I popped straight into bed till that thunder woke me up God
be merciful to us I thought the heavens were coming down about us to
punish us when I blessed myself and said a Hail Mary like those awful
thunderbolts in Gibraltar as if the world was coming to an end and then
they come and tell you there's no God what could you do if it was
running and rushing about nothing only make an act of contrition the
candle I lit that evening in Whitefriars' Street chapel for the month of May
see it brought its luck though he'd scoff if he heard because he never
goes to church mass or meeting he says your soul you have no soul inside
only grey matter because he doesn't know what it is to have one yes
when I lit the lamp because he must have come three or four times with
that tremendous big red brute of a thing he has I thought the vein or

whatever the dickens they call it was going to burst though his nose is not so big after I took off all my things with the blinds down after my hour's dressing and perfuming and combing it like iron or some kind of a thick crowbar standing all the time he must have eaten oysters I think a few dozen he was in great singing voice no I never in all my life felt anyone had one the size of that to make you feel full up he must have eaten a whole sheep after what's the idea making us like that with a big hole in the middle of us or like a Stallion driving it up into you because that's all they want out of you with that determined vicious look in his eye I had to half shut my eyes still he hasn't such a tremendous amount of spunk in him when I made him pull out and do it on me considering how big it is so much the better in case any of it wasn't washed out properly the last time I let him finish it in me nice invention they made for women for him to get all the pleasure but if someone gave them a touch of it themselves they'd know what I went through with Milly nobody would believe cutting her teeth too and Mina Purefoy's husband give us a swing out of your whiskers filling her up with a child or twins once a year as regular as the clock always with a smell of children off her the one they called Budgers or something like a nigger with a shock of hair on it *Jesusjack the child is a black* the last time I was there a squad of them falling over one another and bawling you couldn't hear your ears supposed to be healthy not satisfied till they have us swollen out like elephants or I don't know what supposing I risked having another not off him though still if he was married I'm sure he'd have a fine strong child but I don't know Poldy has more spunk in him yes that'd be awfully jolly I suppose it was meeting Josie Powell and the funeral and thinking about me and Boylan set him off well he can think what he likes now if that'll do him any good I know they were spooning a bit when I came on the scene he was dancing and sitting out with her the night of Georgina Simpson's housewarming and then he wanted to ram it down my neck it was on account of not liking to see her a wallflower that was why we had the stand-up row over politics he began it not me when he said about Our Lord being a carpenter at last he made me cry of course a woman is so sensitive about everything I was fuming with myself after for giving in only for I knew he was gone on me and the first socialist he said He was he annoyed me so much I couldn't put him into a temper still he knows a lot of mixed-up things especially about the body and the insides I often wanted to study up that myself what we have inside us in that *Family Physician* I could always hear his voice talking when the room was crowded and watch him after that I pretended I had a coolness on with her over him because he used to be a bit on the jealous side whenever he asked who are you going to and I said over to Floey and he made me the present of Lord Byron's poems and the three pairs of gloves so that finished that I could quite easily get him to make it up any time I know how I'd even supposing he got in with her again and was going out to see her somewhere I'd know if he refused to eat the onions I know plenty of ways ask him to tuck down the collar of my blouse or touch him with my veil and gloves on going out one kiss then would send them all spinning however all right we'll see then let him go to her she of course would only be too delighted to pretend she's mad in love with him that I wouldn't so much mind I'd just go to her and ask her do you love him and look her square in the eyes she couldn't fool me but he might imagine he was and make a declaration to her with his plabbery kind of a manner like he did to me though I had the devil's own job to get it out of him though I liked him for that it showed he could hold in and wasn't to be got for the asking he was on the pop of asking me too the night in the kitchen I was rolling the potato cake there's something I want to say to you only for I put him off letting on I was in a temper with my hands and arms full of pasty flour in any case I let out too much the night before talking of dreams so I didn't want to let him know more than was good for him she used to be always embracing me Josie whenever he was there meaning him of course glauming me over and when I said I washed up and down as far as possible asking me and did you wash possible the women are always egging on to that putting it on thick when he's there they know by his sly eye blinking a bit putting on the indifferent when they come out with something the kind he is what spoils him I don't wonder in the least because he was very handsome at that time trying to look like Lord Byron I said I liked though he was too beautiful for a man and he was too a little before we got engaged afterwards though she didn't like it so much the day I was in fits of laughing with the giggles I couldn't stop about all my hairpins falling out one after another with the mass of hair I had you're always in great humour she said yes because it grigged her because she knew what it meant because I used to tell her a good bit of what went on between us not all but just enough to make her mouth water but that wasn't my fault she didn't darken the door much after we were married I wonder what she's got like now after living with that dotty husband of hers she had her face beginning to look drawn and run down the last time I saw her she must have been just after a row with him because I saw on the moment she was edging to draw down a conversation about husbands and talk about him to run him down what was it she told me O yes that sometimes he used to go to bed with his muddy boots on when the maggot takes him just imagine having to get into bed with a thing like that that might murder you any moment what a man well it's not the one way everyone goes mad Poldy anyhow whatever he does always wipes his feet on the mat when he comes in wet or shine and always blacks his own boots too and he always takes off his hat when he comes up in the street like then and now he's going about in his slippers to look for £10000 for a postcard U P up O Sweetheart May wouldn't a thing like that simply bore you stiff to extinction actually too stupid even to take his boots off now what could you make of a man like that I'd rather die twenty times over than marry another of their sex of course he'd never find another woman like me to put up with him the way I do know me come sleep with me yes and he knows that too at the bottom of his heart take that Mrs Maybrick that poisoned her husband for what I wonder in love with some other man yes it was found out on her wasn't she the downright villain to go and do a thing like that of course some men can be dreadfully aggravating drive you mad and always the worst word in the world what do they ask us to marry them for if we're so bad as all that comes to yes because they can't get on without us white Arsenic she put in his tea off flypaper wasn't it I wonder why they call it that if I asked him he'd say it's from the Greek leave us as wise as we were before she must have been madly in love with the other fellow to run the chance of being hanged O she didn't care if that was her nature what could she do besides they're not brutes enough to go and hang a woman surely are they

they're all so different Boylan talking about the shape of my foot he noticed at once even before he was introduced when I was in the DBC with Poldy laughing and trying to listen I was waggling my foot we both ordered two teas and plain bread and butter I saw him looking with his two old maids of sisters when I stood up and asked the girl where it was what do I care with it dropping out of me and that black closed breeches he made me buy takes you half an hour to let them down wetting all myself always with some brand-new fad every other week such a long one I did I forgot my suede gloves on the seat behind that I never got after some robber of a woman and he wanted me to put it in the *Irish Times* lost in the ladies' lavatory DBC Dame Street finder return to Mrs Marion Bloom and I saw his eyes on my feet going out through the

turning door he was looking when I looked back and I went there for tea
two days after in the hope but he wasn't now how did that excite him
because I was crossing them when we were in the other room first he
meant the shoes that are too tight to walk in my hand is nice like that if I
only had a ring with the stone for my month a nice aquamarine I'll stick
him for one and a gold bracelet I don't like my foot so much still I made
him spend once with my foot the night after Goodwin's botch-up of a
concert so cold and windy it was well we had that rum in the house to
mull and the fire wasn't black out when he asked to take off my stockings
lying on the hearthrug in Lombard Street West and another time it was
my muddy boots he'd like me to walk in all the horses' dung I could find
but of course he's not natural like the rest of the world that I what did he
say I could give nine points in ten to Katti Lanner and beat her what does
that mean I asked him I forget what he said because the stop-press edition
just passed and the man with the curly hair in the Lucan Dairy that's so
polite I think I saw his face before somewhere I noticed him when I was
tasting the butter so I took my time Bartell d'Arcy too that he used to
make fun of when he commenced kissing me on the choir stairs after I
sang Gounod's Ave Maria *what are we waiting for O my heart kiss me
straight on the brow and part* which is my brown part he was pretty hot
for all his tinny voice too my low notes he was always raving about if you
can believe him I liked the way he used his mouth singing then he said
wasn't it terrible to do that there in a place like that I don't see anything
so terrible about it I'll tell him about that some day not now and surprise
him ay and I'll take him there and show him the very place too we did it
so now there you are like it or lump it he thinks nothing can happen
without him knowing he hadn't an idea about my mother till we were
engaged otherwise he'd never have got me so cheap as he did he was ten
times worse himself anyhow begging me to give him a tiny bit cut off my
drawers that was the evening coming along Kenilworth Square he kissed
me in the eye of my glove and I had to take it off asking me questions is
it permitted to inquire the shape of my bedroom so I let him keep it as if I
forgot it to think of me when I saw him slip it into his pocket of course
he's mad on the subject of drawers that's plain to be seen always skeezing
at those brazen-faced things on the bicycles with their skirts blowing up
to their navels even when Milly and I were out with him at the open-air
fete that one in the cream muslin standing right against the sun so he
could see every atom she had on when he saw me from behind following
in the rain I saw him before he saw me however standing at the corner of

the Harold's Cross Road with a new raincoat on him with the muffler in the Zingari colours to show off his complexion and the brown hat looking slyboots as usual what was he doing there where he'd no business they can go and get whatever they like from anything at all with a skirt on it and we're not to ask any questions but they want to know where were you where are you going I could feel him coming along skulking after me his eyes on my neck he had been keeping away from the house he felt it was getting too warm for him so I half turned and stopped then he pestered me to say yes till I took off my glove slowly watching him he said my openwork sleeves were too cold for the rain anything for an excuse to put his hand anear me drawers drawers the whole blessed time till I promised to give him the pair off my doll to carry about in his waistcoat pocket O Maria Santisima he did look a big fool dreeping in the rain splendid set of teeth he had made me hungry to look at them and beseeched of me to lift the orange petticoat I had on with the sunray pleats that there was nobody he said he'd kneel down in the wet if I didn't so persevering he would too and ruin his new raincoat you never know what freak they'd take alone with you they're so savage for it if anyone was passing so I lifted them a bit and touched his trousers outside the way I used to Gardner after with my ring hand to keep him from doing worse where it was too public I was dying to find out was he circumcised he was shaking like a jelly all over they want to do everything too quick take all the pleasure out of it and father waiting all the time for his dinner he told me to say I left my purse in the butcher's and had to go back for it what a Deceiver then he wrote me that letter with all those words in it how could he have the nerve to face any woman after his company manners making it so awkward after when we met asking me have I offended you with my eyelids down of course he saw I wasn't he had a few brains not like that other fool Henny Doyle he was always breaking or tearing something in the charades I hate an unlucky man and if I knew what it meant of course I had to say no for form's sake I don't understand you I said and wasn't it natural so it is of course it used to be written up with a picture of a woman's on that wall in Gibraltar with that word I couldn't find anywhere only for children seeing it too young then writing every morning a letter sometimes twice a day I liked the way he made love then he knew the way to take a woman when he sent me the eight big poppies because mine was the 8th then I wrote the night he kissed my heart at Dolphin's Barn I couldn't describe it simply it makes you feel like nothing on earth but he never knew how to embrace well like

Gardner I hope he'll come on Monday as he said at the same time four I hate people who come at all hours answer the door you think it's the vegetables then it's somebody and you all undressed or the door of the filthy sloppy kitchen blows open the day old frostyface Goodwin called about the concert in Lombard Street and I just after dinner all flushed and tossed with boiling old stew don't look at me Professor I had to say I'm a fright yes but he was a real old gent in his way it was impossible to be more respectful nobody to say you're out you have to peep out through the blind like the messenger boy today I thought it was a putoff first him sending the port and the peaches first and I was just beginning to yawn with nerves thinking he was trying to make a fool of me when I knew his tattarrattat at the door he must have been a bit late because it was quarter after three when I saw the two Dedalus girls coming from school I never know the time even that watch he gave me never seems to go properly I'd want to get it looked after when I threw the penny to that lame sailor *for England home and beauty* when I was whistling *there is a charming girl I love* and I hadn't even put on my clean shift or powdered myself or a thing then this day week we're to go to Belfast just as well he has to go to Ennis for his father's anniversary the 27th it wouldn't be pleasant if he did suppose our rooms at the hotel were beside each other and any fooling went on in the new bed I couldn't tell him to stop and not bother me with him in the next room or perhaps some Protestant clergyman with a cough knocking on the wall then he'd never believe the next day we didn't do something it's all very well a husband but you can't fool a lover after me telling him we never did anything of course he didn't believe me no it's better he's going where he is besides something always happens with him the time going to the Mallow Concert at Maryborough ordering boiling soup for the two of us then the bell rang out he walks down the platform with the soup splashing about taking spoonfuls of it hadn't he the nerve and the waiter after him making a holy show of us screeching and confusion for the engine to start but he wouldn't pay till he finished it the two gentlemen in the third-class carriage said he was quite right so he was too he's so pigheaded sometimes when he gets a thing into his head a good job he was able to open the carriage door with his knife or they'd have taken us on to Cork I suppose that was done out of revenge on him O I love jaunting in a train or a car with lovely soft cushions I wonder will he take a first-class for me he might want to do it in the train by tipping the guard well O I suppose there'll be the usual idiots of men gaping at us with their eyes as stupid as ever they can possibly be that was an exceptional man that common workman that left us alone in the carriage that day going to Howth I'd like to find out something about him one or two tunnels perhaps then you have to look out of the window all the nicer then coming back suppose I never came back what would they say eloped with him that gets you on on the stage the last concert I sang at where it's over a year ago when was it Saint Teresa's Hall Clarendon Street little chits of missies they have now singing Kathleen Kearney and her like on account of father being in the army and my singing *The absentminded beggar* and wearing a brooch for Lord Roberts when I had the map of it all and Poldy not Irish enough was it him managed it this time I wouldn't put it past him like he got me on to sing in the *Stabat Mater* by going around saying he was putting *Lead kindly light* to music I put him up to that till the Jesuits found out he was a freemason thumping the piano *lead Thou me on* copied from some old opera yes and he was going about with some of them Sinner Fein lately or whatever they call themselves talking his usual trash and nonsense he says that little man he showed me without the neck is very intelligent the coming man Griffith is he well he doesn't look it that's all I can say still it must have been him he knew there was a boycott I hate the mention of their politics after the war that Pretoria and Ladysmith and Bloemfontein where Gardner Lieut Stanley G 8th Bn 2nd East Lancs Rgt of enteric fever he was a lovely fellow in khaki and just the right height over me I'm sure he was brave too he said I was lovely the evening we kissed goodbye at the canal lock my Irish beauty he was pale with excitement about going away or we'd be seen from the road he couldn't stand properly and I so hot as I never felt they could have made their peace in the beginning or old Oom Paul and the rest of the other old Krugers go and fight it out between them instead of dragging on for years killing any fine-looking men there were with their fever if he was even decently shot it wouldn't have been so bad I love to see a regiment pass in review the first time I saw the Spanish cavalry at La Roque it was lovely after looking across the bay from Algeciras all the lights of the Rock like fireflies or those sham battles on the Fifteen Acres the Black Watch with their kilts in time at the march past the 10th Hussars the Prince of Wales' Own or the Lancers *O the Lancers they're grand* or the Dublins that won Tugela his father made his money over selling the horses for the cavalry well he could buy me a nice present up in Belfast after what I gave him they've lovely linen up there or one of those nice kimono things I must buy a mothball like I had before to keep in the drawer with them it would be exciting going round with him shopping buying those things in a new city better leave this ring behind want to keep turning and turning to get it over the knuckle there or they might bell it round the town in their papers or tell the police on me but they'd think we're married O let them all go and smother themselves for the fat lot I care he has plenty of money and he's not a marrying man so somebody better get it out of him if I could find out whether he likes me I looked a bit washy of course when I looked close in the handglass powdering a mirror never gives you the expression besides scrooching down on me like that all the time with his big hipbones he's heavy too with his hairy chest for this heat always having to lie down for them better for him put it into me from behind the way Mrs Masliansky told me her husband made her like the dogs do it and stick out her tongue as far as ever she could and he so quiet and mild with his tingating cither can you ever be up to men the way it takes them lovely stuff in that blue suit he had on and stylish tie and socks with the sky-blue silk things on them he's certainly well off I know by the cut his clothes have and his heavy watch but he was like a perfect devil for a few minutes after he came back with the stop-press tearing up the tickets and swearing blazes because he lost twenty quid he said he lost over that outsider that won and half he put on for me on account of Lenehan's tip cursing him to the lowest pits that sponger he was making free with me after the Glencree dinner coming back that long joult over the Featherbed mountain after the lord Mayor looking at me with his dirty eyes Val Dillon that big heathen I first noticed him at dessert when I was cracking the nuts with my teeth I wished I could have picked every morsel of that chicken out of my fingers it was so tasty and browned and as tender as anything only for I didn't want to eat everything on my plate those forks and fishslicers were hallmarked silver too I wish I had some I could easily have slipped a couple into my muff when I was playing with them then always hanging out of them for money in a restaurant for the bit you put down your throat we have to be thankful for our mangy cup of tea itself as a great compliment to be noticed the way the world is divided in any case if it's going to go on I want at least two other good chemises for one thing and but I don't know what kind of drawers he likes none at all I think didn't he say yes and half the girls in Gibraltar never wore them either naked as God made them that Andalusian singing her manola she didn't make much secret of what she hadn't yes and the second pair of silkette stockings is laddered after one day's wear I could have brought them back to Lewers this morning and kicked up a row and made that one change them only not to upset myself and run the risk of walking into him and ruining the whole thing and one of those kid-fitting corsets I'd want advertised cheap in *The Gentlewoman* with elastic gores on the hips he saved the one I have but that's no good what did they say they give a delightful figure line 11/6 obviating that unsightly broad appearance across the lower back to reduce flesh my belly is a bit too big I'll have to knock off the stout at dinner or am I getting too fond of it the last they sent from O'Rourke's was as flat as a pancake he makes his money easy Larry they call him the old mangy parcel he sent at Christmas a cottage cake and a bottle of hogwash he tried to palm off as claret that he couldn't get anyone to drink God spare his spit for fear he'd die of the drouth or I must do a few breathing exercises I wonder is that antifat any good might overdo it the thin ones are not so much the fashion now garters that much I have the violet pair I wore today that's all he bought me out of the cheque he got on the first O no there was the face lotion I finished the last of yesterday that made my skin like new I told him over and over again get that made up in the same place and don't forget it God only knows whether he did after all I said to him I'll know by the bottle anyway if not I suppose I'll only have to wash in my piss like beef tea or chicken soup with some of that opopanax and violet I thought it was beginning to look coarse or old a bit the skin underneath is much finer where it peeled off there on my finger after the burn it's a pity it isn't all like that and the four paltry handkerchiefs about 6/- in all sure you can't get on in this world without style all going on food and rent when I get it I'll lash it around I tell you in fine style I always want to throw a handful of tea into the pot measuring and mincing if I buy a pair of old brogues itself do you like those new shoes yes how much were they I've no clothes at all the brown costume and the skirt and jacket and the one at the cleaners three what's that for any woman cutting up this old hat and patching up the other the men won't look at you and women try to walk on you because they know you've no man then with all the things getting dearer every day for the four years more I have of life up to thirty-five no I'm what am I at all I'll be thirty-three in September will I what O well look at that Mrs Galbraith she's much older than me I saw her when I was out last week her beauty's on the wane she was a lovely woman magnificent head of hair on her down to her waist tossing it back like that like Kitty O'Shea in Grantham Street first thing I did every morning to look across see her combing it as if she loved it and was full of it pity I only got to know her the day before we left and that Mrs Langtry the

Jersey Lily the Prince of Wales was in love with I suppose he's like the first man going the roads only for the name of a king they're all made the one way only a black man's I'd like to try a beauty up to what was she forty-five there was some funny story about the jealous old husband what was it at all and an oyster knife he went no he made her wear a kind of a tin thing round her and the Prince of Wales yes he had the oyster knife can't be true a thing like that like some of those books he brings me the works of Master François Somebody supposed to be a priest about a child born out of her ear because her bumgut fell out a nice word for any priest to write and her a – e as if any fool wouldn't know what that meant I hate that pretending of all things with that old blackguard's face on him anybody can see it's not true and that *Ruby* and *Fair Tyrants* he brought me that twice I remember when I came to page 50 the part about where she hangs him up out of a hook with a cord flagellate sure there's nothing for a woman in that all invention made up about he drinking the champagne out of her slipper after the ball was over like the infant Jesus in the crib at Inchicore in the Blessed Virgin's arms sure no woman could have a child that big taken out of her and I thought first it came out of her side because how could she go to the chamber when she wanted to and she a rich lady of course she felt honoured H R H he was in Gibraltar the year I was born I bet he found lilies there too where he planted the tree he planted more than that in his time he might have planted me too if he'd come a bit sooner then I wouldn't be here as I am he ought to chuck that *Freeman* with the paltry few shillings he knocks out of it and go into an office or something where he'd get regular pay or a bank where they could put him up on a throne to count the money all the day of course he prefers pottering about the house so you can't stir with him any side what's your programme today I wish he'd even smoke a pipe like father to get the smell of a man or pretending to be mooching about for advertisements when he could have been in Mr Cuffe's still only for what he did then sending me to try and patch it up I could have got him promoted there to be the manager he gave me a great *mirada* once or twice first he was as stiff as the mischief really and truly Mrs Bloom only I felt rotten simply with the old rubbishy dress that I lost the leads out of the tails with no cut in it but they're coming into fashion again I bought it simply to please him I knew it was no good by the finish pity I changed my mind of going to Todd and Burns as I said and not Lee's it was just like the shop itself rummage sale a lot of trash I hate those rich shops get on your nerves Nothing kills me altogether only he thinks he knows a great lot about a woman's dress and cooking mathering everything he can scour off the shelves into it if I went by his advices every blessed hat I put on does that suit me yes take that that's all right the one like a wedding cake standing up miles off my head he said suited me or the dish cover one coming down on my backside on pins and needles about the shopgirl in that place in Grafton Street I had the misfortune to bring him into and she as insolent as ever she could be with her smirk saying I'm afraid we're giving you too much trouble what she's there for but I stared it out of her yes he was awfully stiff and no wonder but he changed the second time he looked Poldy pigheaded as usual like the soup but I could see him looking very hard at my chest when he stood up to open the door for me it was nice of him to show me out in any case I'm extremely sorry Mrs Bloom believe me without making it too marked the first time after him being insulted and me being supposed to be his wife I just half smiled I know my chest was out that way at the door when he said I'm extremely sorry and I'm sure you were

yes I think he made them a bit firmer sucking them like that so long he made me thirsty titties he calls them I had to laugh yes this one anyhow stiff the nipple gets for the least thing I'll get him to keep that up and I'll take those eggs beaten up with marsala fatten them out for him what are all those veins and things curious the way it's made two the same in case of twins they're supposed to represent beauty placed up there like those statues in the museum one of them pretending to hide it with her hand are they so beautiful of course compared with what a man looks like with his two bags full and his other thing hanging down out of him or sticking up at you like a hatrack no wonder they hide it with a cabbage leaf that disgusting Cameron Highlander behind the meat market or that other wretch with the red head behind the tree where the statue of the fish used to be when I was passing pretending he was pissing standing out for me to see it with his baby clothes up to one side the Queen's Own they were a nice lot it's well the Surreys relieved them they're always trying to show it to you every time nearly I passed outside the men's greenhouse near the Harcourt Street station just to try some fellow or other trying to catch my eye as if it was one of the seven wonders of the world O and the stink of those rotten places the night coming home with Poldy after the Comerfords' party oranges and lemonade to make you feel nice and watery I went into one of them it was so biting cold I couldn't keep it in when was that '93 the canal was frozen yes it was a few months after a pity a couple of the Camerons weren't there to see me squatting in the men's place *meadero* I tried to draw a picture of it before I tore it up like a sausage or something I wonder they're not afraid going about of getting a kick or a bang of something there the woman is beauty of course that's admitted when he said I could pose for a picture naked to some rich fellow in Holles Street when he lost the job in Hely's and I was selling the clothes and strumming in the Coffee Palace would I be like that *Bath of the Nymph* with my hair down yes only she's younger or I'm a little like that dirty bitch in that Spanish photo he has nymphs used they go about like that I asked him about her and that word met something with hoses in it and he came out with some jawbreakers about the incarnation he never can explain a thing simply the way a body can understand then he goes and burns the bottom out of the pan all for his Kidney this one not so much there's the mark of his teeth still where he tried to bite the nipple I had to scream out aren't they fearful trying to hurt you I had a great breast of milk with Milly enough for two what was the reason of that he said I could have got a pound a week as a wet nurse all swelled out the morning that delicate-looking student that stopped in number 28 with the Citrons Penrose nearly caught me washing through the window only for I snapped up the towel to my face that was his studenting hurt me they used to weaning her till he got Doctor Brady to give me the belladonna prescription I had to get him to suck them they were so hard he said it was sweeter and thicker than cow's then he wanted to milk me into the tea well he's beyond everything I declare somebody ought to put him in the *Budget* if I only could remember the one half of the things and write a book out of it *The Works of Master Poldy* yes and it's so much smoother the skin much an hour he was at them I'm sure by the clock like some kind of a big infant I had at me they want everything in their mouth all the pleasure those men get out of a woman I can feel his mouth O Lord I must stretch myself I wished he was here or somebody to let myself go with and come again like that I feel all fire inside me or if I could dream it when he made me spend the second time tickling me behind with his finger I was coming for about five minutes with my legs round him I had to hug him after O Lord I wanted to shout out all sorts of things fuck or shit or anything at all only not to look ugly or those lines from the strain who knows the way he'd take it you want to feel your way with a man they're not all like him thank God some of them want you to be so nice about it I noticed the contrast he does it and doesn't talk I gave my eyes that look with my hair a bit loose from the tumbling and my tongue between my lips up to him the savage brute Thursday Friday one Saturday two Sunday three O Lord I can't wait till Monday

frseeeeeeeeefronnnng train somewhere whistling the strength those engines have in them like big giants and the water rolling all over and out of them all sides like the end of *Love's old sweeeetsonnnng* the poor men that have to be out all the night from their wives and families in those roasting engines stifling it was today I'm glad I burned the half of those old *Freeman*s and *Photo Bits* leaving things like that lying about he's getting very careless and threw the rest of them up in the WC I'll get him to cut them tomorrow for me instead of having them there for the next year to get a few pence for them have him asking where's last January's paper and all those old overcoats I bundled out of the hall making the place hotter than it is that rain was lovely and refreshing just after my beauty sleep I thought it was going to get like Gibraltar my goodness the heat there before the levanter came on black as night and the glare of the Rock standing up in it like a big giant compared with their Three Rock mountain they think is so great with the red sentries here and there the poplars and they all white hot and the smell of the rainwater in those tanks watching the sun all the time weltering down on you faded all that lovely frock father's friend Mrs Stanhope sent me from the B Marché Paris what a shame my dearest Doggerina she wrote on it she was very nice what's this her other name was just a pc to tell you I sent the little present have just had a jolly warm bath and feel a *very* clean dog now enjoyed it Wogger she called him Wogger w'd give anything to be back in Gib and hear you sing *Waiting* and *In old Madrid* Concone is the name of those exercises he bought me one of those new some word I couldn't make out shawls amusing things but tear for the least thing still they're lovely I think don't you will always think of the lovely teas we had together scrumptious currant scones and raspberry wafers I adore well now dearest Doggerina be sure and write soon kind she left out regards to your father also Captain Groves with love yrs aff'ly Hester xxxxx she didn't look a bit married just like a girl he was years older than her Wogger he was awfully fond of me when he held down the wire with his foot for me to step over at the bullfight at La Linea when that matador Gomez was given the bull's ear these clothes we have to wear whoever invented them expecting you to walk up Killiney hill then for example at that picnic all staysed up you can't do a blessed thing in them in a crowd run or jump out of the way that's why I was afraid when that other ferocious old Bull began to charge the banderilleros with the sashes and

the two things in their hats and the brutes of men shouting *bravo toro*
sure the women were as bad in their nice white mantillas ripping all the
whole insides out of those poor horses I never heard of such a thing in all
my life yes he used to break his heart at me taking off the dog barking in
Bell Lane poor brute and it sick what became of them ever I suppose
they're dead long ago the two of them it's like all through a mist makes
you feel so old I made the scones of course I had everything all to myself
then a girl Hester we used to compare our hair mine was thicker than
hers she showed me how to settle it at the back when I put it up and
what's this else how to make a knot on a thread with the one hand we
were like cousins what age was I then the night of the storm I slept in her
bed she had her arms round me then we were fighting in the morning
with the pillow what fun he was watching me whenever he got an
opportunity at the band on the Alameda esplanade when I was with
father and Captain Groves I looked up at the church first and then at the
windows then down and our eyes met I felt something go through me
like all needles my eyes were dancing I remember after when I looked at
myself in the glass hardly recognised myself the change he was attractive
to a girl in spite of his being a little bald intelligent-looking disappointed
and gay at the same time he was like Thomas in *The Shadow of Ashlydyat*
I had a splendid skin from the sun and the excitement like a rose I didn't
get a wink of sleep it wouldn't have been nice on account of her but I
could have stopped it in time she gave me *The Moonstone* to read that
was the first I read of Wilkie Collins *East Lynne* I read and *The Shadow of
Ashlydyat* Mrs Henry Wood *Henry Dunbar* by that other woman I lent
him afterwards with Mulvey's photo in it so as he could see I wasn't
without and Lord Lytton *Eugene Aram Molly Bawn* she gave me by Mrs
Hungerford on account of the name I don't like books with a Molly in
them like that one he brought me about the one from Flanders a whore
always shoplifting anything she could cloth and stuff and yards of it O
this blanket is too heavy on me that's better I haven't even one decent
nightdress this thing gets all rolled under me besides him and his fooling
that's better I used to be weltering then in the heat my shift drenched
with the sweat stuck in the cheeks of my bottom on the chair when I
stood up they were so fattish and firm when I got up on the sofa cushions
to see with my clothes up and the bugs tons of them at night and the
mosquito nets I couldn't read a line Lord how long ago it seems centuries
of course they never came back and she didn't put her address right on it
either she may have noticed her Wogger people were always going away

and we never I remember that day with the waves and the boats with their high heads rocking and the smell of ship those Officers' uniforms on shore leave made me seasick he didn't say anything he was very serious I had the high-buttoned boots on and my skirt was blowing she kissed me six or seven times didn't I cry yes I believe I did or near it my lips were taittering when I said goodbye she had a Gorgeous wrap of some special kind of blue colour on her for the voyage made very peculiarly to one side like and it was extremely pretty it got as dull as the devil after they went I was almost planning to run away mad out of it somewhere we're never easy where we are father or aunt or marriage *waiting always waiting to guiiiide him toooo me waiting nor speeeed his flying feet* their damn guns bursting and booming all over the shop especially the Queen's birthday and throwing everything down in all directions if you didn't open the windows when General Ulysses Grant whoever he was or did supposed to be some great fellow landed off the ship and old Sprague the consul that was there from before the Flood dressed up poor man and he in mourning for the son then the same old bugles for reveille in the morning and drums rolling and the unfortunate poor devils of soldiers walking about with mess tins smelling the place more than the old long-bearded Jews in their jellibees and Levites assembly and sound clear and gunfire for the men to cross the Lines and the warden marching with his keys to lock the gates and the bagpipes and only Captain Groves and father talking about Rorke's Drift and Plevna and Sir Garnet Wolseley and Gordon at Khartoum lighting their pipes for them every time they went out drunken old devil with his grog on the window sill catch him leaving any of it picking his nose trying to think of some other dirty story to tell up in a corner but he never forgot himself when I was there sending me out of the room on some blind excuse paying his compliments the Bushmills whiskey talking of course but he'd do the same to the next woman that came along I suppose he died of galloping drink ages ago the days like years not a letter from a living soul except the odd few I posted to myself with bits of paper in them so bored sometimes I could fight with my nails listening to that old Arab with the one eye and his he-ass of an instrument singing his he-ah he-ah a-he-ah all my compriments on your hotchapotch of your he-ass as bad as now with the hands hanging off me looking out of the window if there was a nice fellow even in the opposite house that medical in Holles Street the nurse was after when I put on my gloves and hat at the window to show I was going out not a notion what I meant aren't they thick never understand what you say even you'd want to print it up on a big poster for them not even if you shake hands twice with the left he didn't recognise me either when I half frowned at him outside Westland Row chapel where does their great intelligence come in I'd like to know grey matter they have it all in their tail if you ask me those country gougers up in the City Arms intelligence they had a damn sight less than the bulls and cows they were selling the meat and the coalman's bell that noisy bugger trying to swindle me with the wrong bill he took out of his hat what a pair of paws and pots and pans and kettles to mend any broken bottles for a poor man today and no visitors or post ever except his cheques or some advertisement like that Wonderworker they sent him addressed *Dear Madam* only his letter and the card from Milly this morning see she wrote a letter to him who did I get the last letter from O Mrs Dwenn now what possessed her to write from Canada after so many years to know the recipe I had for *pisto madrileno* Floey Dillon since she wrote to say she was married to a very rich architect if I'm to believe all I hear with a villa and eight rooms her father was an awfully nice man he was near seventy always good-humoured well now Miss Tweedy or Miss Gillespie there's the pyannyer that was a solid silver coffee service he had too on the mahogany sideboard then dying so far away I hate people that have always their poor story to tell everybody has their own troubles that poor Nancy Blake died a month ago of acute pneumonia well I didn't know her so well as all that she was Floey's friend more than mine poor Nancy it's a bother having to answer he always tells me the wrong things and no stops to say like making a speech your sad bereavement symp*h*athy I always make that mistake and ne*w*phew with two doubleyous in I hope he'll write me a longer letter the next time if it's a thing he really likes me O thanks be to the great God I got somebody to give me what I badly wanted to put some heart up into me you've no chances at all in this place like you used long ago I wish somebody would write me a love letter his wasn't much and I told him he could write what he liked yours ever Hugh Boylan *In old Madrid* stuff silly women believe *love is sighing I am dying* still if he wrote it I suppose there'd be some truth in it true or no it fills up your whole day and life always something to think about every moment and see it all round you like a new world I could write the answer in bed to let him imagine me short just a few words not those long crossed letters Atty Dillon used to write to the fellow that was something in the Four Courts that jilted her after out of *The Ladies' Letter Writer* when I told her to say a few simple words he could twist how he liked not acting with precipat precip itancy with equal candour the greatest earthly happiness answer to a gentleman's proposal affirmatively my goodness there's nothing else it's all very fine for them but as for being a woman as soon as you're old they might as well throw you out in the bottom of the ashpit.

Mulvey's was the first when I was in bed that morning and Mrs Rubio brought it in with the coffee she stood there standing when I asked her to hand me a and I pointing at them I couldn't think of the word a hairpin to open it with *ah horquilla* disobliging old thing and it staring her in the face with her switch of false hair on her and vain about her appearance ugly as she was near eighty or a hundred her face a mass of wrinkles with all her religion domineering because she never could get over the Atlantic fleet coming in half the ships of the world and the Union Jack flying with all her carabineros because four drunken English sailors took all the Rock from them and because I didn't run into mass often enough in Santa Maria to please her with her shawl up on her except when there was a marriage on with all her miracles of the saints and her black Blessed Virgin with the silver dress and the sun dancing three times on Easter Sunday morning and when the priest was going by with the bell bringing the vatican to the dying blessing herself for His Majestad an admirer he signed it I near jumped out of my skin I wanted to pick him up when I saw him following me along the Calle Real in the shopwindow then he tipped me just in passing but I never thought he'd write making an appointment I had it inside my petticoat bodice all day reading it up in every hole and corner while father was up at the drill instructing to find out by the handwriting or the language of stamps singing I remember *Shall I wear a white rose* and I wanted to put on the old stupid clock to near the time he was the first man kissed me under the Moorish Wall *My sweetheart when a boy* it never entered my head what kissing meant till he put his tongue in my mouth his mouth was sweetlike young I put my knee up to him a few times to learn the way what did I tell him I was engaged for for fun to the son of a Spanish nobleman named Don Miguel de la Flora and he believed me that I was to be married to him in three years' time there's many a true word spoken in jest *there is a flower that bloometh* a few things I told him true about myself just for him to be imagining the Spanish girls he didn't like I suppose one of them wouldn't have him I got him excited he crushed all the flowers on my bosom he brought me he couldn't count the pesetas and the perragordas till I taught him Cappoquin he came from he said on the Blackwater but it was too short then the day before he left May yes it was May when the infant king of Spain was born I'm always like that in the spring I'd like a new fellow every year up on the tiptop under the Rock Gun near O'Hara's Tower I told him it was struck by lightning and all about the old Barbary apes they sent to Clapham without a tail careering all over the show on each other's back Mrs Rubio said she was a regular old rock scorpion robbing the chickens out of Ince's Farm and throw stones at you if you went anear he was looking at me I had that white blouse on open in the front to encourage him as much as I could without too openly they were just beginning to be plump I said I was tired we lay over the Fig Tree Cave a wild place I suppose it must be the highest rock in existence the galleries and casemates and those frightful rocks and Saint Michael's Cave with the icicles or whatever they call them hanging down and ladders all the mud plotching my boots I'm sure that's the way down the monkeys go under the sea to Africa when they die the ships out far like chips that was the Malta boat passing yes the sea and the sky you could do what you liked lie there for ever he caressed them outside they love doing that it's the roundness there I was leaning over him with my white rice-straw hat to take the newness out of it the left side of my face the best my blouse open for his last day transparent kind of shirt he had I could see his chest pink he wanted to touch mine with his for a moment but I wouldn't let him he was awfully put out first for fear you never know consumption or leave me with a child *embarazada* that old servant Ines told me that one drop even if it got into you at all after I tried with the Banana but I was afraid it might break and get lost up in me somewhere because they once took something down out of a woman that was up there for years covered with lime salts they're all mad to get in there where they come out of you'd think they could never go far enough up and then they're done with you in a way till the next time yes because there's a wonderful feeling there so tender all the time how did we finish it off yes O yes I pulled him off into my handkerchief pretending not to be excited but I opened my legs I wouldn't let him touch me inside my petticoat because I had a skirt opening up the side I tormented the life out of him first tickling him I loved rousing that dog in the hotel rrrsssstt awokwokawok his eyes shut and a bird flying below us he was shy all the same I liked him like that moaning I made him blush a little when I got over him that way when I unbuttoned him and took his out and drew back the skin it had a kind of eye in it they're all Buttons men down the middle on the wrong side of them Molly darling he called me what was his name Jack Joe Harry Mulvey was it yes I think a lieutenant he was rather fair he had a laughing kind of a voice so I went round to the whatyoucallit everything was whatyoucallit moustache had he he said he'd come back Lord it's just like yesterday to me and if I was married he'd do it to me and I promised him yes faithfully I'd let him block me now flying perhaps he's dead or killed or a captain or admiral it's nearly twenty years if I said Fig Tree Cave he would if he came up behind me and put his hands over my eyes to guess who I might recognise him he's young still about forty perhaps he's married some girl on the Blackwater and is quite changed they all do they haven't half the character a woman has she little knows what I did with her beloved husband before he ever dreamt of her in broad daylight too in the sight of the whole world you might say they could have put an article about it in the *Chronicle* I was a bit wild after when I blew out the old bag the biscuits were in from Benadi Bros and exploded it Lord what a bang all the woodcocks and pigeons screaming coming back the same way that we went over Middle Hill round by the old guardhouse and the Jews' burial place pretending to read out the Hebrew on them I wanted to fire his pistol he said he hadn't one he didn't know what to make of me with his peak cap on that he always wore crooked as often as I settled it straight HMS *Calypso* swinging my hat that old Bishop that spoke off the altar his long preach about woman's higher functions about girls now riding the bicycle and wearing peak caps and the new woman bloomers God send him sense and me more money I suppose they're called after him I never thought that would be my name Bloom when I used to write it in print to see how it looked on a visiting card or practising for the butcher and oblige M Bloom you're looking blooming Josie used to say after I married him well it's better than Breen or Briggs does brig or those awful names with bottom in them Mrs Ramsbottom or some other kind of a bottom Mulvey I wouldn't go mad about either or suppose I divorced him Mrs Boylan my mother whoever she was might have given me a nicer name the Lord knows after the lovely one she had Lunita Laredo the fun we had running along Willis's Road to Europa Point twisting in and out all round the other side of Jersey they were shaking and dancing about in my blouse like Milly's little ones now when she runs up the stairs I loved looking down at them I was jumping up at the pepper trees and the white poplars pulling the leaves off and throwing them at him he went to India he was to write the voyages those men have to make to the ends of the world and back it's the least they might get a squeeze or two at a woman while they can going out to be drowned or blown up somewhere I went up Windmill Hill to the Flats that Sunday morning with Captain Rubio's that was dead spyglass like the sentry had he said he'd have one or two from on board I wore that frock from the B Marché Paris and the coral necklace the straits shining I could see over to Morocco almost the bay of Tangier white and the Atlas mountain with snow on it and the straits like a river so clear Harry Molly darling I was thinking of him on the sea all the time after at mass when my petticoat began to slip down at the elevation weeks and weeks I kept the handkerchief under my pillow for the smell of him there was no decent perfume to be got in that Gibraltar only that cheap *peau d'Espagne* that faded and left a stink on you more than anything else I wanted to give him a memento he gave me that clumsy Claddagh ring for luck that I gave Gardner going to South Africa where those Boers killed him with their war and fever but they were well beaten all the same as if it brought its bad luck with it like an opal or pearl still it must have been pure 18-carat gold because it was very heavy but what could you get in a place like that the sand-frog shower from Africa and that derelict ship that came up to the harbour *Marie* the *Marie* whatyoucallit no he hadn't a moustache that was Gardner yes I can see his face clean-shaven frseeeeeeeeeeeeeeeeeeeeefrong that train again weeping tone *once in the dear deaead days beyondre call* close my eyes breath my lips forward kiss sad look eyes open piano *ere o'er the world the mists began* I hate that istsbeg *comes love's sweet soooooooooong* I'll let that out full when I get in front of the footlights again Kathleen Kearney and her lot of squealers Miss This Miss That Miss Theother lot of sparrowfarts skitting around talking about politics they know as much about as my backside anything in the world to make themselves someway interesting Irish homemade beauties soldier's daughter am I ay and whose are you bootmakers' and publicans' I beg your pardon coach I thought you were a wheelbarrow they'd die down dead off their feet if ever they got a chance of walking down the Alameda on an officer's arm like me on the band night my eyes flashing my bust that they haven't passion God help their poor head I knew more about men and life when I was fifteen than they'll all know at fifty they don't know how to sing a song like that Gardner said no man could look at my mouth and teeth smiling like that and not think of it I was afraid he mightn't like my accent first he so English all father left me in spite of his stamps I've my mother's eyes and figure anyhow he always said they're so snotty about themselves some of those cads he wasn't a bit like that he was dead gone on my lips let them get a husband first that's fit to be looked at and a daughter like mine or see if they can excite a swell with money that can pick and choose whoever he wants like Boylan to do it four or five times locked in each other's arms or the voice either I could have been a prima donna only I married him *comes loooove's old* deep down chin back not too much make it double *My lady's bower* is too long for an encore about the moated grange at twilight and vaulted rooms yes I'll sing *Winds that blow from the south* that he gave after the choir-stairs performance I'll change that lace on my black dress to show off my bubs and I'll yes by God I'll get that big fan mended make them burst with envy my hole is itching me always when I think of him I feel I want to I feel some wind in me better go easy not wake him have him at it again slobbering after washing every bit of myself back belly and sides if we had even a bath itself or my own room anyway I wish he'd sleep in some bed by himself with his cold feet on me give us room even to let a fart God or do the least thing better yes hold them like that a bit on my side piano quietly *sweeeee* there's that train far away pianissimo *eeeeeee* one more *tsong*

that was a relief wherever you be let your wind go free who knows if that pork chop I took with my cup of tea after was quite good with the heat I couldn't smell anything off it I'm sure that queer-looking man in the pork butcher's is a great rogue I hope that lamp is not smoking fill my nose up with smuts better than having him leaving the gas on all night I couldn't rest easy in my bed in Gibraltar even getting up to see why am I so damned nervous about that though I like it in the winter it's more company O Lord it was rotten cold too that winter when I was only about ten was I yes I had the big doll with all the funny clothes dressing her up and undressing that icy wind skeeting across from those mountains the something Nevada Sierra Nevada standing at the fire with the little bit of a short shift I had up to heat myself I loved dancing about in it then make a race back into bed I'm sure that fellow opposite used to be there the whole time watching with the lights out in the summer and I in my skin hopping around I used to love myself then stripped at the washstand dabbing and creaming only when it came to the chamber performance I put out the light too so then there were two of us goodbye to my sleep for this night anyhow I hope he's not going to get in with those medicals leading him astray to imagine he's young again coming in at four in the morning it must be if not more still he had the manners not to wake me what do they find to gabber about all night squandering money and getting drunker and drunker couldn't they drink water then he starts giving us his orders for eggs and tea and Findon haddy and hot buttered toast I suppose we'll have him sitting up like the king of the country pumping the wrong end of the spoon up and down in his egg wherever he learned that from and I love to hear him falling up the stairs of a morning with the cups rattling on the tray and then play with the cat she rubs up against you for her own sake I wonder has she fleas she's as bad as a woman always licking and lecking but I hate their claws I wonder do they see anything that we can't staring like that always when she sits at the top of the stairs so long and listening as I wait what a robber too that lovely fresh plaice I bought I think I'll get a bit of fish tomorrow or today is it Friday yes I will with some blancmange with blackcurrant jam like long ago not those two-pound pots of mixed plum and apple from the London and Newcastle Williams and Woods goes twice as far only for the bones I hate those eels cod yes I'll get a nice piece of cod I'm always getting enough for three forgetting anyway I'm sick of that everlasting butcher's meat from Buckley's loin chops and leg beef and rib steak and scrag of mutton and calf's pluck the very name is enough or a picnic suppose we all gave 5/- each or let him pay it and invite some other woman for him who Mrs Fleming and drive out to the Furry Glen or the Strawberry Beds we'd have him examining all the horses' toenails first like he does with the letters no not with Boylan there yes with some cold veal and ham mixed sandwiches there are little houses down at the bottom of the banks there on purpose but it's as hot as blazes he says not a bank holiday anyhow I hate those ruck of Mary Ann coalboxes out for the day Whit Monday is a cursed day too no wonder that bee bit him better the seaside but I'd never again in this life get into a boat with him after him at Bray telling the boatman he knew how to row if anyone asked could he ride the steeplechase for the Gold Cup he'd say yes then it came on to get rough the old thing crookeding about and the weight all down my side telling me pull the right reins now pull the left and the tide all swamping in floods in through the bottom and his oar slipping out of the stirrup it's a mercy we weren't all drowned he can swim of course me no there's no danger whatsoever keep yourself calm in his flannel trousers I'd like to have tattered them down off him before all the people and give him what that one calls flagellate till he was black and blue do him all the good in the world only for that long-nosed chap I don't know who he is with that other beauty Burke out of the City Arms Hotel was there spying around as usual on the slip always where he wasn't wanted if there was a row on you'd vomit a better face there was no love lost between us that's one consolation I wonder what kind is that book he

672

brought me *Sweets of Sin* by A Gentleman of Fashion some other Mr de Kock I suppose the people gave him that nickname going about with his tube from one woman to another I couldn't even change my new white shoes all ruined with the salt water and the hat I had with that feather all blowy and tossed on me how annoying and provoking because the smell of the sea excited me of course the sardines and the bream in Catalan Bay round the back of the Rock they were fine all silver in the fishermen's baskets old Luigi near a hundred they said came from Genoa and the tall old chap with the earrings I don't like a man you have to climb up to to get at I suppose they're all dead and rotten long ago besides I don't like being alone in this big barracks of a place at night I suppose I'll have to put up with it I never brought a bit of salt in even when we moved in the confusion musical academy he was going to make on the first floor drawing room with a brass plate or Bloom's Private Hotel he suggested go and ruin himself altogether the way his father did down in Ennis like all the things he told father he was going to do and me but I saw through him telling me all the lovely places we could go for the honeymoon Venice by moonlight with the gondolas and the lake of Como he had a picture cut out of some paper of and mandolines and lanterns O how nice I said whatever I liked he was going to do immediately if not sooner *will you be my man will you carry my can* he ought to get a leather medal with a putty rim for all the plans he invents then leaving us here all day you'd never know what old beggar at the door for a crust with his long story might be a tramp and put his foot in the way to prevent me shutting it like that picture of that hardened criminal he was called in *Lloyd's Weekly News* twenty years in jail then he comes out and murders an old woman for her money imagine his poor wife or mother or whoever she is such a face you'd run miles away from I couldn't rest easy till I bolted all the doors and windows to make sure but it's worse again being locked up like in a prison or a madhouse they ought to be all shot or the cat-o'-nine-tails a big brute like that that would attack a poor old woman to murder her in her bed I'd cut them off him so I would not that he'd be much use still better than nothing the night I was sure I heard burglars in the kitchen and he went down in his shirt with a candle and a poker as if he was looking for a mouse as white as a sheet frightened out of his wits making as much noise as he possibly could for the burglars' benefit there isn't much to steal indeed the Lord knows still it's the feeling especially now with Milly away such an idea for him to send the girl down there to learn to take photographs on account of his grandfather instead of sending her to Skerry's Academy where she'd have to learn not like me getting all 1s at school only he'd do a thing like that all the same on account of me and Boylan that's why he did it I'm certain the way he plots and plans everything out I couldn't turn round with her in the place lately unless I bolted the door first gave me the fidgets coming in without knocking first when I put the chair against the door just as I was washing myself there below with the glove get on your nerves then doing the loglady all day put her in a glass case with two at a time to look at her if he knew she broke off the hand off that little gimcrack statue with her roughness and carelessness before she left that I got that little Italian boy to mend so that you can't see the join for 2/- wouldn't even teem the potatoes for you of course she's right not to ruin her hands I noticed he was always talking to her lately at the table explaining things in the paper and she pretending to understand sly of course that comes from his side of the house he can't say I pretend things can he I'm too honest as a matter of fact and helping her into her coat but if there was anything wrong with her it's me she'd tell not him I suppose he thinks I'm finished out and laid on the shelf well I'm not no nor anything like it we'll see we'll see now she's well on for flirting too with Tom Devin's two sons imitating me whistling with those romps of Murray girls calling for her can Milly come out please she's in great demand to pick what they can out of her round in Nelson Street riding Harry Devin's bicycle at night it's as well he sent her where she is she was just getting out of bounds wanting to go on the skating rink and smoking their cigarettes through their nose I smelt it off her dress when I was biting off the thread of the button I sewed on to the bottom of her jacket she couldn't hide much from me I tell you only I oughtn't to have stitched it and it on her it brings a parting and the last plum pudding too split in two halves see it comes out no matter what they say her tongue is a bit too long for my taste your blouse is open too low she says to me the pan calling the kettle blackbottom and I had to tell her not to cock her legs up like that on show on the window sill before all the people passing they all look at her like me when I was her age of course any old rag looks well on you then a great touch-me-not too in her own way at *The Only Way* in the Theatre Royal take your foot away out of that I hate people touching me afraid of her life I'd crush her skirt with the pleats a lot of that touching must go on in theatres in the crush in the dark they're always trying to wiggle up to you that fellow in the pit at the Gaiety for Beerbohm Tree in *Trilby* the last time I'll ever go there to be squashed like that for any Trilby or

Barebum every two minutes tipping me there and looking away he's a bit daft I think I saw him after trying to get near two stylish-dressed ladies outside Switzer's window at the same little game I recognised him on the moment the face and everything but he didn't remember me yes and she didn't even want me to kiss her at the Broadstone going away well I hope she'll get someone to dance attendance on her the way I did when she was down with the mumps and her glands swollen where's this and where's that of course she can't feel anything deep yet I never came properly till I was what twenty-two or so it went into the wrong place always only the usual girls' nonsense and giggling that Conny Connolly writing to her in white ink on black paper sealed with sealing wax though she clapped when the curtain came down because he looked so handsome then we had Martin Harvey for breakfast dinner and supper I thought to myself afterwards it must be real love if a man gives up his life for her that way for nothing I suppose there are a few men like that left it's hard to believe in it though unless it really happened to me the majority of them with not a particle of love in their natures to find two people like that nowadays full up of each other that would feel the same way as you do they're usually a bit foolish in the head his father must have been a bit queer to go and poison himself after her still poor old man I suppose he felt lost she's always making love to my things too the few old rags I have wanting to put her hair up at fifteen my powder too only ruin her skin on her she's time enough for that all her life after of course she's restless knowing she's pretty with her lips so red a pity they won't stay that way I was too but there's no use going to the fair with the thing answering me like a fishwoman when I asked her to go for a half a stone of potatoes the day we met Mrs Joe Gallaher at the trotting matches and she pretended not to see us in her trap with Friery the solicitor we weren't grand enough till I gave her two damn fine cracks across the ear for herself take that now for answering me like that and that for your impudence she had me that exasperated of course contradicting I was bad-tempered too because how was it there was a weed in the tea or I didn't sleep the night before cheese I ate was it and I told her over and over again not to leave knives crossed like that because she has nobody to command her as she said herself well if he doesn't correct her faith I will that was the last time she turned on the tear tap I was just like that myself they daren't order me about the place it's his fault of course having the two of us slaving here instead of getting in a woman long ago am I ever going to have a proper servant again of course then she'd see

675

him coming I'd have to let her know or she'd revenge it aren't they a nuisance that old Mrs Fleming you have to be walking round after her putting the things into her hands sneezing and farting into the pots well of course she's old she can't help it a good job I found that rotten old smelly dishcloth that got lost behind the dresser I knew there was something and opened the area window to let out the smell bringing in his friends to entertain them like the night he walked home with a dog if you please that might have been mad especially Simon Dedalus' son his father such a criticiser with his glasses up with his tall hat on him at the cricket match and a great big hole in his sock one thing laughing at the other and his son that got all those prizes for whatever he won them in the intermediate imagine climbing over the railings if anybody saw him that knew us I wonder he didn't tear a big hole in his grand funeral trousers as if the one nature gave wasn't enough for anybody hawking him down into the dirty old kitchen now is he right in his head I ask pity it wasn't washing day my old pair of drawers might have been hanging up too on the line on exhibition for all he'd ever care with the iron mould mark the stupid old bundle burned on them he might think was something else and she never even rendered down the fat I told her and now she's going such as she was on account of her paralysed husband getting worse there's always something wrong with them disease or they have to go under an operation or if it's not that it's drink and he beats her I'll have to hunt around again for someone every day I get up there's some new thing on sweet God sweet God well when I'm stretched out dead in my grave I suppose I'll have some peace I want to get up a minute if I'm let wait O Jesus wait yes that thing has come on me yes now wouldn't that afflict you of course all the poking and rooting and ploughing he had up in me now what am I to do Friday Saturday Sunday wouldn't that pester the soul out of a body unless he likes it some men do God knows there's always something wrong with us five days every three or four weeks usual monthly auction isn't it simply sickening that night it came on me like that the one and only time we were in a box that Michael Gunn gave him to see Mrs Kendal and her husband at the Gaiety something he did about insurance for him in Drimmie's I was fit to be tied though I wouldn't give in with that gentleman of fashion staring down at me with his glasses and him the other side of me talking about Spinoza and his soul that's dead I suppose millions of years ago I smiled the best I could all in a swamp leaning forward as if I was interested having to sit it out then to the last tag I won't forget that *Wife of Scarli* in a hurry supposed to be a fast play about adultery that idiot in the gallery hissing the woman adulteress he shouted I suppose he went and had a woman in the next lane running round all the back ways after to make up for it I wish he had what I had then he'd boo I bet the cat itself is better off than us have we too much blood up in us or what O patience above it's pouring out of me like the sea anyhow he didn't make me pregnant as big as he is I don't want to ruin the clean sheets I just put on I suppose the clean linen I wore brought it on too damn it damn it and they always want to see a stain on the bed to know you're a virgin for them all that's troubling them they're such fools too you could be a widow or divorced forty times over a daub of red ink would do or blackberry juice no that's too purply O Jamesy let me up out of this pooh sweets of sin whoever suggested that business for women what between clothes and cooking and children this damned old bed too jingling like the dickens I suppose they could hear us away over the other side of the Park till I suggested to put the quilt on the floor with the pillow under my bottom I wonder is it nicer in the day I think it is easy I think I'll cut all this hair off me there scalding me I might look like a young girl wouldn't he get the great suck-in the next time he turned up my clothes on me I'd give anything to see his face where's the chamber gone easy I've a holy horror of its breaking under me after that old commode I wonder was I too heavy sitting on his knee I made him sit on the easy chair purposely when I took off only my blouse and skirt first in the other room he was so busy where he oughtn't to be he never felt me I hope my breath was sweet after those kissing comfits easy God I remember one time I could scout it out straight whistling like a man almost easy O Lord how noisy I hope they're bubbles on it for a wad of money from some fellow I'll have to perfume it in the morning don't forget I bet he never saw a better pair of thighs than that look how white they are the smoothest place is right there between this bit here how soft like a peach easy God I wouldn't mind being a man and get up on a lovely woman O Lord what a row you're making like the Jersey Lily easy easy *O how the waters come down at Lahore*

who knows is there anything the matter with my insides or have I something growing in me getting that thing like that every week when was it last I Whit Monday yes it's only about three weeks I ought to go to the doctor only it would be like before I married him when I had that white thing coming from me and Floey made me go to that dry old stick Dr Collins for women's diseases on Pembroke Road your vagina he called it I suppose that's how he got all the gilt mirrors and carpets getting round those rich ones off Stephen's Green running up to him for every little fiddlefaddle her vagina and her Cochin-China they've money of course so they're all right I wouldn't marry him not if he was the last man in the world besides there's something queer about their children always smelling around those filthy bitches all sides asking me if what I did had an offensive odour what did he want me to do but the one thing gold maybe what a question if I smathered it all over his wrinkly old face for him with all my compriments I suppose he'd know then and could you pass it easily pass what I thought he was talking about the Rock of Gibraltar the way he put it that's a very nice invention too by the way only I like letting myself down after in the hole as far as I can squeeze and pull the chain then to flush it nice cool pins and needles still there's something in it I suppose I always used to know by Milly's when she was a child whether she had worms or not still all the same paying him for that how much is that doctor one guinea please and asking me had I frequent omissions where do those old fellows get all the words they have omissions with his shortsighted eyes on me cocked sideways I wouldn't trust him too far to give me chloroform or God knows what else still I liked him when he sat down to write the thing out frowning so severe his nose intelligent like that you be damned you lying strap O anything no matter who except an idiot he was clever enough to spot that of course that was all thinking of him and his mad crazy letters my Precious one everything connected with your glorious Body *everything* underlined that comes from it is a thing of beauty and of joy for ever something he got out of some nonsensical book that he had me always at myself four and five times a day sometimes and I said I hadn't are you sure O yes I said I am quite sure in a way that shut him up I knew what was coming next only natural weakness it was he excited me I don't know how the first night ever we met when I was living in Rehoboth Terrace we stood staring at one another for about ten minutes as if we met somewhere I suppose on account of my being Jewess-looking after my mother he used to amuse me the things he said with the half-sloothering smile on him and all the Doyles said he was going to stand for a member of Parliament O wasn't I the born fool to believe all his blather about Home Rule and the Land League sending me that long strool of a song out of *The Huguenots* to sing in French to be more classy *O beau pays de La Touraine* that I never even sang once explaining and rigmaroling about religion and persecution he won't let you enjoy anything naturally then might he

678

as a great favour the very first opportunity he got a chance in Brighton
Square running into my bedroom pretending the ink got on his hands to
wash it off with the Albion milk and sulphur soap I used to use and the
gelatine still round it O I laughed myself sick at him that day I better not
make an all-night sitting on this affair they ought to make chambers a
natural size so that a woman could sit on it properly he kneels down to
do it I suppose there isn't in all creation another man with the habits he
has look at the way he's sleeping at the foot of the bed how can he
without a hard bolster it's well he doesn't kick or he might knock out all
my teeth breathing with his hand on his nose like that Indian god he
took me to show me one wet Sunday in the museum in Kildare Street all
yellow in a pinafore lying on his side on his hand with his ten toes
sticking out that he said was a bigger religion than the Jews and Our
Lord's both put together all over Asia imitating him as he's always
imitating everybody I suppose he used to sleep at the foot of the bed too
with his big square feet up in his wife's mouth damn this stinking thing
anyway where's this those napkins are ah yes I know I hope the old press
doesn't creak ah I knew it would he's sleeping hard had a good time
somewhere still she must have given him great value for his money of
course he has to pay for it from her O this nuisance of a thing I hope
they'll have something better for us in the other world tying ourselves up
God help us that's all right for tonight now the lumpy old jingly bed
always reminds me of old Cohen I suppose he scratched himself in it
often enough and he thinks father bought it from Lord Napier that I used
to admire when I was a little girl because I told him easy piano O I like
my bed God here we are as bad as ever after sixteen years how many
houses were we in at all Raymond Terrace and Ontario Terrace and
Lombard Street and Holles Street and he goes about whistling every time
we're on the run again his *Huguenots* or *The frogs' march* pretending to
help the men with our four sticks of furniture and then the City Arms
Hotel worse and worse says Warden Daly that charming place on the
landing always somebody inside praying then leaving all their stinks after
them always know who was in there last every time we're just getting on
right something happens or he puts his big foot in it Thom's and Hely's
and Mr Cuffe's and Drimmie's either he's going to be run into prison over
his old lottery tickets that was to be all our salvations or he goes and gives
impudence we'll have him coming home with the sack soon out of the
Freeman too like the rest on account of those Sinner Fein or the freemasons then we'll see if the little man he showed me dribbling along in the

wet all by himself round by Coady's Lane will give him much consolation that he says is so capable and sincerely Irish he is indeed judging by the sincerity of the trousers I saw on him wait there's George's Church bells wait three-quarters the hour one wait two o'clock well that's a nice hour of the night for him to be coming home at to anybody climbing down into the area if anybody saw him I'll knock him off that little habit tomorrow first I'll look at his shirt to see or I'll see if he has that French letter still in his pocketbook I suppose he thinks I don't know deceitful men all their twenty pockets aren't enough for their lies then why should we tell them even if it's the truth they don't believe you then tucked up in bed like those babies in the *Aristocrat's Masterpiece* he brought me another time as if we hadn't enough of that in real life without some old Aristocrat or whatever his name is disgusting you more with those rotten pictures children with two heads and no legs that's the kind of villainy they're always dreaming about with not another thing in their empty heads they ought to get slow poison the half of them then tea and toast for him buttered on both sides and new-laid eggs I suppose I'm nothing any more when I wouldn't let him lick me in Holles Street one night man man tyrant as ever for the one thing he slept on the floor half the night naked the way the Jews used when somebody dies belonged to them and wouldn't eat any breakfast or speak a word wanting to be petted so I thought I stood out enough for one time and let him he does it all wrong too thinking only of his own pleasure his tongue is too flat or I don't know what he forgets that why then I don't I'll make him do it again if he doesn't mind himself and lock him down to sleep in the coal cellar with the blackbeetles I wonder was it her Josie off her head with my castoffs he's such a born liar too no he'd never have the courage with a married woman that's why he wants me and Boylan though as for her Denis as she calls him that forlorn-looking spectacle you couldn't call him a husband yes it's some little bitch he's got in with even when I was with him with Milly at the College races that Hornblower with the child's bonnet on the top of his nob let us into by the back way he was throwing his sheep's eyes at those two doing skirt duty up and down I tried to wink at him first no use of course and that's the way his money goes this is the fruits of Mr Paddy Dignam yes they were all in great style at the grand funeral in the paper Boylan brought in if they saw a real officer's funeral that'd be something reversed arms muffled drums the poor horse walking behind in black L Boom and Tom Kernan that drunken little barrelly man that bit his tongue off falling down the men's WC drunk in some place or other and Martin Cunningham and the two Dedaluses and Fanny M'Coy's husband white head of cabbage skinny thing with a turn in her eye trying to sing my songs she'd want to be born all over again and her old green dress with the low neck as she can't attract them any other way like dabbling on a rainy day I see it all now plainly and they call that friendship killing and then burying one another and they all with their wives and families at home more especially Jack Power keeping that barmaid he does of course his wife is always sick or going to be sick or just getting better of it and he's a good-looking man still though he's getting a bit grey over the ears they're a nice lot all of them well they're not going to get my husband again into their clutches if I can help it making fun of him then behind his back I know well when he goes on with his idiotics because he has sense enough not to squander every penny piece he earns down their gullets and looks after his wife and family good-for-nothings poor Paddy Dignam all the same I'm sorry in a way for him what are his wife and five children going to do unless he was insured comical little teetotum always stuck up in some pub corner and her or her son waiting *Bill Bailey won't you please come home* her widow's weeds won't improve her appearance they're awfully becoming though if you're good-looking what men wasn't he yes he was at the Glencree dinner and Ben Dollard base barreltone the night he borrowed the swallowtail to sing out of in Holles Street squeezed and squashed into them and grinning all over his big Dolly face like a well-whipped child's botty didn't he look a balmy ballocks sure enough that must have been a spectacle on the stage imagine paying 5/- in the preserved seats for that to see him trotting off in his trowlers and Simon Dedalus too he was always turning up half screwed singing the second verse first *The old love is the new* was one of his *so sweetly sang the maiden on the hawthorn bough* he was always on for flirtyfying too when I sang *Maritana* with him at Freddy Mayer's private opera he had a delicious glorious voice *Phoebe dearest goodbye sweetheart sweet*heart he always sang it not like Bartell d'Arcy sweet *tart* goodbye of course he had the gift of the voice so there was no art in it all over you like a warm shower bath *O Maritana wildwood flower* we sang splendidly though it was a bit too high for my register even transposed and he was married at the time to May Goulding but then he'd say or do something to knock the good out of it he's a widower now I wonder what sort is his son he says he's an author and going to be a university professor of Italian and I'm to take lessons what is he driving at now showing him my photo it's not good of me I ought to have got it taken in drapery that never looks out of fashion still I look young in it I wonder he didn't make him a present of it altogether and me too after all why not I saw him driving down to the Kingsbridge station with his father and mother I was in mourning that's eleven years ago now yes he'd be eleven though what was the good in going into mourning for what was neither one thing nor the other the first cry was enough for me I heard the deathwatch too ticking in the wall of course he insisted he'd go into mourning for the cat I suppose he's a man now by this time he was an innocent boy then and a darling little fellow in his Lord Fauntleroy suit and curly hair like a prince on the stage when I saw him at Mat Dillon's he liked me too I remember they all do wait by God yes wait yes hold on he was on the cards this morning when I laid out the deck union with a young stranger neither dark nor fair you met before I thought it meant him but he's no chicken nor a stranger either besides my face was turned the other way what was the seventh card after that the 10 of spades for a journey by land then there was a letter on its way and scandals too the three queens and the 8 of diamonds for a rise in society yes wait it all came out and two red 8s for new garments look at that and didn't I dream something too yes there was something about poetry in it I hope he hasn't long greasy hair hanging into his eyes or standing up like a Red Indian what do they go about like that for only getting themselves and their poetry laughed at I always liked poetry when I was a girl first I thought he was a poet like Lord Byron and not an ounce of it in his composition I thought he was quite different I wonder is he too young he's about wait '88 I was married '88 Milly is fifteen yesterday '89 what age was he then at Dillon's five or six about '88 I suppose he's twenty or more I'm not too old for him if he's twenty-three or twenty-four I hope he's not that stuck-up university student sort no otherwise he wouldn't go sitting down in the old kitchen with him taking Epps's cocoa and talking of course he pretended to understand it all probably he told him he was out of Trinity College he's very young to be a professor I hope he's not a professor like Goodwin was he was a patent professor of John Jameson they all write about some woman in their poetry well I suppose he won't find many like me *where softly sighs of love the light guitar* where poetry is in the air the blue sea and the moon shining so beautifully coming back on the nightboat from Tarifa the lighthouse at Europa Point the guitar that fellow played was so expressive will I ever go back there again all new faces *two glancing eyes a lattice hid* I'll sing that for him they're my eyes if he's anything of a poet *two eyes as darkly bright as love's*

682

own star aren't those beautiful words *as love's young star* it'll be a change
the Lord knows to have an intelligent person to talk to about yourself not
always listening to him and Billy Prescott's ad and Keyes's ad and Tom
the Devil's ad then if anything goes wrong in their business we have to
suffer I'm sure he's very distinguished I'd like to meet a man like that
God not those other ruck besides he's young those fine young men I
could see down in Margate Strand bathing place from the side of the rock
standing up in the sun naked like a God or something and then plunging
into the sea with them why aren't all men like that there'd be some
consolation for a woman like that lovely little statue he bought I could
look at him all day long curly head and his shoulders his finger up for
you to listen there's real beauty and poetry for you I often felt I wanted to
kiss him all over also his lovely young cock there so simple I wouldn't
mind taking him in my mouth if nobody was looking as if it was asking
you to suck it so clean and white he looks with his boyish face I would
too in half a minute even if some of it went down what is it it's only like
gruel or the dew there's no danger besides he'd be so clean compared
with those pigs of men I suppose never dream of washing it from one
year's end to the other the most of them only that's what gives the
women the moustaches I'm sure it'll be grand if I can only get in with a
handsome young poet at my age I'll throw them the first thing in the
morning till I see if the wish card comes out or I'll try pairing the lady
herself and see if he comes out I'll read and study all I can find or learn a
bit off by heart if I knew who he likes so he won't think me stupid if he
thinks all women are the same and I can teach him the other part I'll
make him feel all over him till he half faints under me then he'll write
about me lover and mistress publicly too with our two photographs in all
the papers when he becomes famous O but then what am I going to do
about him though

   no that's no way for him has he no manners nor no refinement nor no
nothing in his nature slapping us behind like that on my bottom because
I didn't call him Hugh the ignoramus that doesn't know poetry from a
cabbage that's what you get for not keeping them in their proper place
pulling off his shoes and trousers there on the chair before me so
barefaced without even asking permission and standing out that vulgar
way in the half of a shirt they wear to be admired like a priest or a butcher
or those old hypocrites in the time of Julius Caesar of course he's right
enough in his way to pass the time as a joke sure you might as well be in
bed with what with a lion God I'm sure he'd have something better to say

for himself an old Lion would O well I suppose it's because they were so plump and tempting in my short petticoat he couldn't resist they excite myself sometimes it's well for men all the amount of pleasure they get off a woman's body we're so round and white for them always I wish I was one myself for a change just to try with that thing they have swelling up on you so hard and at the same time so soft when you touch it *my uncle John has a thing long* I heard those cornerboys saying passing the corner of Marrowbone Lane *my aunt Mary has a thing hairy* because it was dark and they knew a girl was passing it didn't make me blush why should it either it's only nature and he puts his thing long into my aunt Mary's hairy et cetera and turns out to be you put the handle in a sweeping brush men again all over they can pick and choose what they please a married woman or a fast widow or a girl for their different tastes like those houses round behind Irish Street no but we're to be always chained up they're not going to be chaining me up no damn fear once I start I tell you for their stupid husband's jealousy why can't we all remain friends over it instead of quarrelling her husband found it out what they did together well naturally and if he did can he undo it he's *coronado* anyway whatever he does and then he going to the other mad extreme about the wife in *Fair Tyrants* of course the man never even casts a second thought on the husband or wife either it's the woman he wants and he gets her what else were we given all those desires for I'd like to know I can't help it if I'm young still can I it's a wonder I'm not an old shrivelled hag before my time living with him so cold never embracing me except sometimes when he's asleep the wrong end of me not knowing I suppose who he has any man that'd kiss a woman's bottom I'd throw my hat at him after that he'd kiss anything unnatural where we haven't one atom of any kind of expression in us all of us the same two lumps of lard before ever I'd do that to a man pfooh the dirty brutes the mere thought is enough *I kiss the feet of you señorita* there's some sense in that didn't he kiss our hall door yes he did what a madman nobody understands his cracked ideas but me still of course a woman wants to be embraced twenty times a day almost to make her look young no matter by who so long as to be in love or loved by somebody if the fellow you want isn't there sometimes by the Lord God I was thinking would I go around by the quays there some dark evening where nobody'd know me and pick up a sailor off the sea that'd be hot on for it and not care a pin whose I was only do it off up in a gate somewhere or one of those wild-looking gipsies in Rathfarnham had their camp pitched near the Bloomfield laundry to try and steal our things if

they could I only sent mine there a few times for the name model laundry
sending me back over and over some old one's odd stockings that
blackguard-looking fellow with the fine eyes peeling a switch attack me
in the dark and ride me up against the wall without a word or a murderer
anybody what they do themselves the fine gentlemen in their silk hats
that KC lives up somewhere this way coming out of Hardwicke Lane the
night he gave us the fish supper on account of winning over the boxing
match of course it was for me he gave it I knew him by his gaiters and
the walk and when I turned round a minute after just to see there was a
woman after coming out of it too some filthy prostitute then he goes
home to his wife after that only I suppose the half of those sailors are
rotten again with disease O move over your big carcass out of that for the
love of Mike listen to him *the winds that waft my sighs to thee* so well he
may sleep and sigh the great Suggester Don Poldo de la Flora if he knew
how he came out on the cards this morning he'd have something to sigh
for a dark man in some perplexity between two 7s too in prison for Lord
knows what he does that I don't know and I'm to be slooching around
down in the kitchen to get his lordship his breakfast while he's rolled up
like a mummy will I indeed did you ever see me running I'd just like to
see myself at it show them attention and they treat you like dirt I don't
care what anybody says it'd be much better for the world to be governed
by the women in it you wouldn't see women going and killing one
another and slaughtering when do you ever see women rolling around
drunk like they do or gambling every penny they have and losing it on
horses yes because a woman whatever she does she knows where to stop
sure they wouldn't be in the world at all only for us they don't know what
it is to be a woman and a mother how could they where would they all of
them be if they hadn't all a mother to look after them what I never had
that's why I suppose he's running wild now out at night away from his
books and studies and not living at home on account of the usual rowy
house I suppose well it's a poor case that those that have a fine son like
that they're not satisfied and I none was he not able to make one it wasn't
my fault we came together when I was watching the two dogs up in her
behind in the middle of the naked street that disheartened me altogether
I suppose I oughtn't to have buried him in that little woolly jacket I
knitted crying as I was but give it to some poor child but I knew well I'd
never have another our first death too it was we were never the same
since O I'm not going to think myself into the glooms about that any
more I wonder why he wouldn't stay the night I felt all the time it was

somebody strange he brought in instead of roving around the city meeting God knows who nightwalkers and pickpockets his poor mother wouldn't like that if she was alive ruining himself for life perhaps still it's a lovely hour so silent I used to love coming home after dances the air of the night they have friends they can talk to we've none either he wants what he won't get or it's some woman ready to stick her knife in you I hate that in women no wonder they treat us the way they do we are a dreadful lot of bitches I suppose it's all the troubles we have makes us so snappy I'm not like that he could easy have slept in there on the sofa in the other room I suppose he was as shy as a boy he being so young hardly twenty of me in the next room he'd have heard me on the chamber arrah what harm Dedalus I wonder it's like those names in Gibraltar Delapaz Delagracia they had the devil's queer names there Father Vilaplana of Santa Maria that gave me the rosary Rosales y O'Reilly in the Calle las Siete Revueltas and Pisimbo and Mrs Opisso in Governor Street O what a name I'd go and drown myself in the first river if I had a name like her O my and all the bits of streets Paradise Ramp and Bedlam Ramp and Rodger's Ramp and Crutchett's Ramp and the Devil's Gap Steps well small blame to me if I am a harumscarum I know I am a bit I declare to God I don't feel a day older than then I wonder could I get my tongue round any of the Spanish *como esta usted muy bien gracias y usted* see I haven't forgotten it all I thought I had only for the grammar a noun is the name of any person place or thing pity I never tried to read that novel cantankerous Mrs Rubio lent me by Valera with the questions in it all upside down the two ways I always knew we'd go away in the end I can tell him the Spanish and he tell me the Italian then he'll see I'm not so ignorant what a pity he didn't stay I'm sure the poor fellow was dead tired and wanted a good sleep badly I could have brought him in his breakfast in bed with a bit of toast so long as I didn't do it on the knife for bad luck or if the woman was going her rounds with the watercress and something nice and tasty there are a few olives in the kitchen he might like I never could bear the look of them in Abrines I could do the *criada* the room looks all right since I changed it the other way you see something was telling me all the time I'd have to introduce myself not knowing me from Adam very funny wouldn't it I'm his wife or pretend we were in Spain with him half awake without a God's notion where he is *dos huevos estrellados señor* Lord the cracked things come into my head sometimes it'd be great fun supposing he stayed with us why not there's the room upstairs empty and Milly's bed in the back room he could do his writing and studies at the table in there for all the scribbling he does at it and if he wants to read in bed in the morning like me as he's making the breakfast for one he can make it for two I'm sure I'm not going to take in lodgers off the street for him if he takes a gazebo of a house like this I'd love to have a long talk with an intelligent well-educated person I'd have to get a nice pair of red slippers like those Turks with the fez used to sell or yellow and a nice semitransparent morning gown that I badly want or a peach-blossom dressing jacket like the one long ago in Walpole's only 8/6 or 18/6 I'll just give him one more chance I'll get up early in the morning I'm sick of Cohen's old bed in any case I might go over to the markets to see all the vegetables and cabbages and tomatoes and carrots and all kinds of splendid fruits all coming in lovely and fresh who knows who'd be the first man I'd meet they're out looking for it in the morning Mamy Dillon used to say they are and the night too that was her massgoing I'd love a big juicy pear now to melt in your mouth like when I used to be in the longing way then I'll throw him up his eggs and tea in the moustache cup she gave him to make his mouth bigger I suppose he'd like my nice cream too I know what I'll do I'll go about rather gay not too much singing a bit now and then *Mi fa pietà Masetto* then I'll start dressing myself to go out *Presto non son più forte* I'll put on my best shift and drawers let him have a good eyeful out of that to make his micky stand for him I'll let him know if that's what he wanted that his wife is fucked yes and damn well fucked too up to my neck nearly not by him five or six times hand-running there's the mark of his spunk on the clean sheet I wouldn't bother to even iron it out that ought to satisfy him if you don't believe me feel my belly unless I made him stand there and put him into me I've a mind to tell him every scrap and make him do it out in front of me serve him right it's all his own fault if I am an adulteress as the thing in the gallery said O much about it if that's all the harm ever we did in this vale of tears God knows it's not much doesn't everybody only they hide it I suppose that's what a woman is supposed to be there for or He wouldn't have made us the way He did so attractive to men then if he wants to kiss my bottom I'll drag open my drawers and bulge it right out in his face as large as life he can stick his tongue seven miles up my hole as he's there my brown part then I'll tell him I want £1 or perhaps 30/- I'll tell him I want to buy underclothes then if he gives me that well he won't be too bad I don't want to soak it all out of him like other women do I could often have written out a fine cheque for myself and write his name on it for a couple of pounds a few times he forgot to lock it up besides he won't spend it I'll let him do it off on me behind provided he doesn't smear all my good drawers O I suppose that can't be helped I'll do the indifferent one or two questions I'll know by the answers when he's like that he can't keep a thing back I know every turn in him I'll tighten my bottom well and let out a few smutty words smellrump or lick my shit or the first mad thing comes into my head then I'll suggest about yes O wait now sonny my turn is coming I'll be quite gay and friendly over it O but I was forgetting this bloody pest of a thing pfooh you wouldn't know which to laugh or cry we're such a mixture of plum and apple no I'll have to wear the old things so much the better it'll be more pointed he'll never know whether he did it or not there that's good enough for you any old thing at all then I'll wipe him off me just like a business his omission then I'll go out I'll have him eyeing up at the ceiling where is she gone now make him want me that's the only way a quarter after what an unearthly hour I suppose they're just getting up in China now combing out their pigtails for the day we'll soon have the nuns ringing the angelus they've nobody coming in to spoil their sleep except an odd priest or two for his night office or the alarm clock next door at cockshout clattering the brains out of itself let me see if I can doze off one two three four five what kind of flowers are those they invented like the stars the wallpaper in Lombard Street was much nicer the apron he gave me was like that something only I only wore it twice better lower this lamp and try again so as I can get up early I'll go to Lambe's there beside Findlater's and get them to send us some flowers to put about the place in case he brings him home tomorrow today I mean no no Friday's an unlucky day first I want to do the place up someway the dust grows in it I think while I'm asleep then we can have music and cigarettes I can accompany him first I must clean the keys of the piano with milk what'll I wear *shall I wear a white rose* or those fairy cakes in Lipton's I love the smell of a rich big shop at $7\frac{1}{2}d$ a pound or the other ones with the cherries in them and the pinky sugar $11d$ a couple of pounds of those a nice plant for the middle of the table I'd get that cheaper in wait where's this I saw them not long ago I love flowers I'd love to have the whole place swimming in roses God of heaven there's nothing like nature the wild mountains then the sea and the waves rushing then the beautiful country with the fields of oats and wheat and all kinds of things and all the fine cattle going about that would do your heart good to see rivers and lakes and flowers all sorts of shapes and smells and colours springing up even out of the ditches primroses and violets nature it is as for them saying there's no God I wouldn't give a snap of my two fingers for all their learning why don't they go and create something I often asked him atheists or whatever they call themselves go and wash the cobbles off themselves first then they go howling for the priest and they dying and why why because they're afraid of hell on account of their bad conscience ah yes I know them well who was the first person in the universe before there was anybody that made it all who ah that they don't know neither do I so there you are they might as well try to stop the sun from rising tomorrow the sun shines for you he said the day we were lying among the rhododendrons on Howth Head in the grey tweed suit and his straw hat the day I got him to propose to me yes first I gave him the bit of seedcake out of my mouth and it was leap year like now yes sixteen years ago my God after that long kiss I near lost my breath yes he said I was a flower of the mountain yes so we are flowers all a woman's body yes that was one true thing he said in his life and the sun shines for you today yes that was why I liked him because I saw he understood or felt what a woman is and I knew I could always get round him and I gave him all the pleasure I could leading him on till he asked me to say yes and I wouldn't answer first only looked out over the sea and the sky I was thinking of so many things he didn't know of Mulvey and Mr Stanhope and Hester and father and old Captain Groves and the sailors playing All Birds Fly and I Say Stoop and Washing Up Dishes they called it on the pier and the sentry in front of the Governor's house with the thing round his white helmet poor devil half roasted and the Spanish girls laughing in their shawls and their tall combs and the auctions in the morning the Greeks and the Jews and the Arabs and the devil knows who else from all the ends of Europe and Duke Street and the fowl market all clucking outside Larby Sharon's and the poor donkeys slipping half asleep and the vague fellows in the cloaks asleep in the shade on the steps and the big wheels of the carts of the bulls and the old castle thousands of years old yes and those handsome Moors all in white and turbans like kings asking you to sit down in their little bit of a shop and Ronda with the old windows of the posadas *two glancing eyes a lattice hid* for her lover to kiss the iron and the wine shops half open at night and the castanets and the night we missed the boat at Algeciras the watchman going about serene with his lamp and O that awful deepdown torrent O and the sea the sea crimson sometimes like fire and the glorious sunsets and the fig trees in the Alameda Gardens yes and all the queer little streets and the pink and blue and yellow houses and the rose gardens and the jessamine and geraniums and cactuses and Gibraltar as a girl where I was a Flower of the mountain yes when I put the rose in my hair like the Andalusian girls used *or shall I wear a red* yes and how he kissed me under the Moorish Wall and I thought well as well him as another and then I asked him with my eyes to ask again yes and then he asked me would I yes to say yes my mountain flower and first I put my arms around him yes and drew him down to me so he could feel my breasts all perfume yes and his heart was going like mad and yes I said yes I will Yes.

Trieste-Zurich-Paris,
1914–1921.

Appendix

Episode 18, 'Penelope', in its alternative format

Yes because he never did a thing like that before as ask to get his breakfast in bed with a couple of eggs since the City Arms Hotel when he used to be pretending to be laid up with a sick voice doing His Highness to make himself interesting for that old faggot Mrs Riordan that he thought he had a great leg of and she never left us a farthing all for masses for herself and her soul greatest miser ever was actually afraid to lay out 4d for her methylated spirit telling me all her ailments she had too much old chat in her about politics and earthquakes and the end of the world let us have a bit of fun first God help the world if all the women were her sort down on bathing suits and low necks of course nobody wanted her to wear them I suppose she was pious because no man would look at her twice I hope Ill never be like her a wonder she didnt want us to cover our faces but she was a well-educated woman certainly and her gabby talk about Mr Riordan here and Mr Riordan there I suppose he was glad to get shut of her and her dog smelling my fur and always edging to get up under my petticoats especially then still I like that in him polite to old women like that and waiters and beggars too hes not proud out of nothing but not always if ever he got anything really serious the matter with him its much better for them to go into a hospital where everything is clean but I suppose Id have to dring it into him for a month yes and then wed have a hospital nurse next thing on the carpet have him staying there till they throw him out or a nun maybe like the smutty photo he has shes as much a nun as Im not yes because theyre so weak and puling when theyre sick they want a woman to get well if his nose bleeds youd think it was O tragic and that dying-looking one off the South Circular when he sprained his foot at the choir party at the Sugarloaf mountain the day I wore that dress Miss Stack bringing him flowers the worst old ones she could find at the bottom of the basket anything at all to get into a mans bedroom with her old maids voice trying to imagine he was dying on account of her *to never see thy face again* though he looked more like a man with his beard a bit grown in the bed father was the same besides

I hate bandaging and dosing when he cut his toe with the razor paring his corns afraid hed get blood poisoning but if it was a thing I was sick then wed see what attention only of course the woman hides it not to give all the trouble they do yes he came somewhere Im sure by his appetite anyway love its not or hed be off his feed thinking of her so either it was one of those night women if it was down there he was really and the hotel story he made up a pack of lies to hide it planning it Hynes kept me who did I meet ah yes I met do you remember Menton and who else who let me see that big babbyface I saw him and he not long married flirting with a young girl at Pooles Myriorama and turned my back on him when he slinked out looking quite conscious what harm but he had the impudence to make up to me one time well done to him mouth almighty and his boiled eyes of all the big stupoes I ever met and thats called a solicitor only for I hate having a long wrangle in bed or else if its not that its some little bitch or other he got in with somewhere or picked up on the sly if they only knew him as well as I do yes because the day before yesterday he was scribbling something a letter when I came into the front room to show him Dignams death in the paper as if something told me and he covered it up with the blotting paper pretending to be thinking about business so very probably that was it to somebody who thinks she has a softy in him because all men get a bit like that at his age especially getting on to forty he is now so as to wheedle any money she can out of him no fool like an old fool and then the usual kissing my bottom was to hide it not that I care two straws now who he does it with or knew before that way though Id like to find out so long as I dont have the two of them under my nose all the time like that slut that Mary we had in Ontario Terrace padding out her false bottom to excite him bad enough to get the smell of those painted women off him once or twice I had a suspicion by getting him to come near me when I found the long hair on his coat without that one when I went into the kitchen pretending he was drinking water 1 woman is not enough for them it was all his fault of course ruining servants then proposing that she could eat at our table on Christmas Day if you please O no thank you not in my house stealing my potatoes and the oysters 2/6 per doz going out to see her aunt if you please common robbery so it was but I was sure he had something on with that one it takes me to find out a thing like that he said you have no proof it was her proof O yes her aunt was very fond of oysters but I told her what I thought of her suggesting me to go out to be alone with her I wouldnt lower myself to spy on them the garters I found in her room the

Friday she was out that was enough for me a little bit too much her face swelled up on her with temper when I gave her her weeks notice I saw to that better do without them altogether do out the rooms myself quicker only for the damn cooking and throwing out the dirt I gave it to him anyhow either she or me leaves the house I couldnt even touch him if I thought he was with a dirty barefaced liar and sloven like that one denying it up to my face and singing about the place in the WC too because she knew she was too well off yes because he couldnt possibly do without it that long so he must do it somewhere and the last time he came on my bottom when was it the night Boylan gave my hand a great squeeze going along by the Tolka *in my hand there steals another* I just pressed the back of his like that with my thumb to squeeze back singing *The young May moon shes beaming love* because he has an idea about him and me hes not such a fool he said Im dining out and going to the Gaiety though Im not going to give him the satisfaction in any case God knows hes a change in a way not to be always and ever wearing the same old hat unless I paid some nice-looking boy to do it since I cant do it myself a young boy would like me Id confuse him a little alone with him if we were Id let him see my garters the new ones and make him turn red looking at him seduce him I know what boys feel with that down on their cheek doing that frigging drawing out the thing by the hour question and answer would you do this that and the other with the coalman yes with a bishop yes I would because I told him about some dean or bishop was sitting beside me in the Jews Temples gardens when I was knitting that woollen thing a stranger to Dublin what place was it and so on about the monuments and he tired me out with statues encouraging him making him worse than he is who is in your mind now tell me who are you thinking of who is it tell me his name who tell me who the German Emperor is it yes imagine Im him think of him can you feel him trying to make a whore of me what he never will he ought to give it up now at this age of his life simply ruination for any woman and no satisfaction in it pretending to like it till he comes and then finish it off myself anyway and it makes your lips pale anyhow its done now once and for all with all the talk of the world about it people make its only the first time after that its just the ordinary do it and think no more about it why cant you kiss a man without going and marrying him first you sometimes love to wildly when you feel that way so nice all over you you cant help yourself I wish some man or other would take me sometime when hes there and kiss me in his arms theres nothing like a kiss long and hot down to your soul almost paralyses you then I hate that confession when I used to go to Father Corrigan he touched me Father and what harm if he did where and I said on the canal bank like a fool but whereabouts on your person my child on the leg behind high up was it yes rather high up was it where you sit down yes O Lord couldnt he say bottom right out and have done with it what has that got to do with it and did you whatever way he put it I forget no Father and I always think of the real father what did he want to know for when I already confessed it to God he had a nice fat hand the palm moist always I wouldnt mind feeling it neither would he Id say by the bull neck in his horse collar I wonder did he know me in the box I could see his face he couldnt see mine of course hed never turn or let on still his eyes were red when his father died theyre lost for a woman of course must be terrible when a man cries let alone them Id like to be embraced by one in his vestments and the smell of incense off him like the pope besides theres no danger with a Priest if youre married hes too careful about himself then give something to HH the pope for a penance I wonder was he satisfied with me one thing I didnt like his slapping me behind going away so familiarly in the hall though I laughed Im not a horse or an ass am I I suppose he was thinking of his fathers I wonder is he awake thinking of me or dreaming am I in it who gave him that flower he said he bought he smelt of some kind of drink not whiskey or stout or perhaps the sweety kind of paste they stick their bills up with some liqueur Id like to sip those rich-looking green and yellow expensive drinks those stage-door Johnnies drink with the opera hats I tasted once with my finger dipped out of that American that had the squirrel talking stamps with father he had all he could do to keep himself from falling asleep after the last time after we took the port and potted meat it had a fine salty taste yes because I felt lovely and tired myself and fell asleep as sound as a top the moment I popped straight into bed till that thunder woke me up God be merciful to us I thought the heavens were coming down about us to punish us when I blessed myself and said a Hail Mary like those awful thunderbolts in Gibraltar as if the world was coming to an end and then they come and tell you theres no God what could you do if it was running and rushing about nothing only make an act of contrition the candle I lit that evening in Whitefriars Street chapel for the month of May see it brought its luck though hed scoff if he heard because he never goes to church mass or meeting he says your soul you have no soul inside only grey matter because he doesnt know what it is to have one yes when I lit the lamp because he must have come 3 or 4 times with that tremendous big red brute of a thing he has I thought the vein or whatever the dickens they call it was going to burst though his nose is not so big after I took off all my things with the blinds down after my hours dressing and perfuming and combing it like iron or some kind of a thick crowbar standing all the time he must have eaten oysters I think a few dozen he was in great singing voice no I never in all my life felt anyone had one the size of that to make you feel full up he must have eaten a whole sheep after whats the idea making us like that with a big hole in the middle of us or like a Stallion driving it up into you because thats all they want out of you with that determined vicious look in his eye I had to half shut my eyes still he hasnt such a tremendous amount of spunk in him when I made him pull out and do it on me considering how big it is so much the better in case any of it wasnt washed out properly the last time I let him finish it in me nice invention they made for women for him to get all the pleasure but if someone gave them a touch of it themselves theyd know what I went through with Milly nobody would believe cutting her teeth too and Mina Purefoys husband give us a swing out of your whiskers filling her up with a child or twins once a year as regular as the clock always with a smell of children off her the one they called Budgers or something like a nigger with a shock of hair on it *Jesusjack the child is a black* the last time I was there a squad of them falling over one another and bawling you couldnt hear your ears supposed to be healthy not satisfied till they have us swollen out like elephants or I dont know what supposing I risked having another not off him though still if he was married Im sure hed have a fine strong child but I dont know Poldy has more spunk in him yes thatd be awfully jolly I suppose it was meeting Josie Powell and the funeral and thinking about me and Boylan set him off well he can think what he likes now if thatll do him any good I know they were spooning a bit when I came on the scene he was dancing and sitting out with her the night of Georgina Simpsons housewarming and then he wanted to ram it down my neck it was on account of not liking to see her a wallflower that was why we had the stand-up row over politics he began it not me when he said about Our Lord being a carpenter at last he made me cry of course a woman is so sensitive about everything I was fuming with myself after for giving in only for I knew he was gone on me and the first socialist he said He was he annoyed me so much I couldnt put him into a temper still he knows a lot of mixed-up things especially about the body and the insides I often wanted to study up that myself what we have inside us in that *Family Physician* I could always hear his voice talking when the room was crowded and watch him after that I pretended I had a coolness on with her over him because he used to be a bit on the jealous side whenever he asked who are you going to and I said over to Floey and he made me the present of Lord Byrons poems and the three pairs of gloves so that finished that I could quite easily get him to make it up any time I know how Id even supposing he got in with her again and was going out to see her somewhere Id know if he refused to eat the onions I know plenty of ways ask him to tuck down the collar of my blouse or touch him with my veil and gloves on going out 1 kiss then would send them all spinning however all right well see then let him go to her she of course would only be too delighted to pretend shes mad in love with him that I wouldnt so much mind Id just go to her and ask her do you love him and look her square in the eyes she couldnt fool me but he might imagine he was and make a declaration to her with his plabbery kind of a manner like he did to me though I had the devils own job to get it out of him though I liked him for that it showed he could hold in and wasnt to be got for the asking he was on the pop of asking me too the night in the kitchen I was rolling the potato cake theres something I want to say to you only for I put him off letting on I was in a temper with my hands and arms full of pasty flour in any case I let out too much the night before talking of dreams so I didnt want to let him know more than was good for him she used to be always embracing me Josie whenever he was there meaning him of course glauming me over and when I said I washed up and down as far as possible asking me and did you wash possible the women are always egging on to that putting it on thick when hes there they know by his sly eye blinking a bit putting on the indifferent when they come out with something the kind he is what spoils him I dont wonder in the least because he was very handsome at that time trying to look like Lord Byron I said I liked though he was too beautiful for a man and he was too a little before we got engaged afterwards though she didnt like it so much the day I was in fits of laughing with the giggles I couldnt stop about all my hairpins falling out one after another with the mass of hair I had youre always in great humour she said yes because it grigged her because she knew what it meant because I used to tell her a good bit of what went on between us not all but just enough to make her mouth water but that wasnt my fault she didnt darken the door much after we were married I wonder what shes got like now after living with that dotty husband of hers she had her face beginning to look drawn and run down the last time I saw her she must have been just after a row with him because I saw on the moment she was edging to draw down a conversation about husbands and talk about him to run him down what was it she told me O yes that sometimes he used to go to bed with his muddy boots on when the maggot takes him just imagine having to get into bed with a thing like that that might murder you any moment what a man well its not the one way everyone goes mad Poldy anyhow whatever he does always wipes his feet on the mat when he comes in wet or shine and always blacks his own boots too and he always takes off his hat when he comes up in the street like then and now hes going about in his slippers to look for £10000 for a postcard U P up O Sweetheart May wouldnt a thing like that simply bore you stiff to extinction actually too stupid even to take his boots off now what could you make of a man like that Id rather die 20 times over than marry another of their sex of course hed never find another woman like me to put up with him the way I do know me come sleep with me yes and he knows that too at the bottom of his heart take that Mrs Maybrick that poisoned her husband for what I wonder in love with some other man yes it was found out on her wasnt she the downright villain to go and do a thing like that of course some men can be dreadfully aggravating drive you mad and always the worst word in the world what do they ask us to marry them for if were so bad as all that comes to yes because they cant get on without us white Arsenic she put in his tea off flypaper wasnt it I wonder why they call it that if I asked him hed say its from the Greek leave us as wise as we were before she must have been madly in love with the other fellow to run the chance of being hanged O she didnt care if that was her nature what could she do besides theyre not brutes enough to go and hang a woman surely are they

theyre all so different Boylan talking about the shape of my foot he noticed at once even before he was introduced when I was in the DBC with Poldy laughing and trying to listen I was waggling my foot we both ordered 2 teas and plain bread and butter I saw him looking with his two old maids of sisters when I stood up and asked the girl where it was what do I care with it dropping out of me and that black closed breeches he made me buy takes you half an hour to let them down wetting all myself always with some brand-new fad every other week such a long one I did I forgot my suede gloves on the seat behind that I never got after some robber of a woman and he wanted me to put it in the *Irish Times* lost in the ladies lavatory DBC Dame Street finder return to Mrs Marion Bloom and I saw his eyes on my feet going out through the turning door he was looking when I looked back and I went there for tea 2 days after in the hope but he wasnt now how did that excite him because I was crossing them when we were in the other room first he meant the shoes that are too tight to walk in my hand is nice like that if I only had a ring with the stone for my month a nice aquamarine Ill stick him for one and a gold bracelet I dont like my foot so much still I made him spend once with my foot the night after Goodwins botch-up of a concert so cold and windy it was well we had that rum in the house to mull and the fire wasnt black out when he asked to take off my stockings lying on the hearthrug in Lombard Street West and another time it was my muddy boots hed like me to walk in all the horses dung I could find but of course hes not natural like the rest of the world that I what did he say I could give 9 points in 10 to Katti Lanner and beat her what does that mean I asked him I forget what he said because the stop-press edition just passed and the man with the curly hair in the Lucan Dairy thats so polite I think I saw his face before somewhere I noticed him when I was tasting the butter so I took my time Bartell dArcy too that he used to make fun of when he commenced kissing me on the choir stairs after I sang Gounods Ave Maria *what are we waiting for O my heart kiss me straight on the brow and part* which is my brown part he was pretty hot for all his tinny voice too my low notes he was always raving about if you can believe him I liked the way he used his mouth singing then he said wasnt it terrible to do that there in a place like that I dont see anything so terrible about it Ill tell him about that some day not now and surprise him ay and Ill take him there and show him the very place too we did it so now there you are like it or lump it he thinks nothing can happen without him knowing he hadnt an idea about my mother till we were engaged otherwise hed never have got me so cheap as he did he was 10 times worse himself anyhow begging me to give him a tiny bit cut off my drawers that was the evening coming along Kenilworth Square he kissed me in the eye of my glove and I had to take it off asking me questions is it permitted to inquire the shape of my bedroom so I let him keep it as if I forgot it to think of me when I saw him slip it into his pocket of course hes mad on the subject of drawers thats plain to be seen always skeezing at those brazen-faced things on the bicycles with their skirts blowing up to their navels even when Milly and I were out with him at the open-air fete that one in the cream muslin standing right against the sun so he could see every atom she had on when he saw me from behind following in the rain I saw him before he saw me however standing at the corner of the

Harolds Cross Road with a new raincoat on him with the muffler in the Zingari colours to show off his complexion and the brown hat looking slyboots as usual what was he doing there where hed no business they can go and get whatever they like from anything at all with a skirt on it and were not to ask any questions but they want to know where were you where are you going I could feel him coming along skulking after me his eyes on my neck he had been keeping away from the house he felt it was getting too warm for him so I half turned and stopped then he pestered me to say yes till I took off my glove slowly watching him he said my openwork sleeves were too cold for the rain anything for an excuse to put his hand anear me drawers drawers the whole blessed time till I promised to give him the pair off my doll to carry about in his waistcoat pocket O Maria Santisima he did look a big fool dreeping in the rain splendid set of teeth he had made me hungry to look at them and beseeched of me to lift the orange petticoat I had on with the sunray pleats that there was nobody he said hed kneel down in the wet if I didnt so persevering he would too and ruin his new raincoat you never know what freak theyd take alone with you theyre so savage for it if anyone was passing so I lifted them a bit and touched his trousers outside the way I used to Gardner after with my ring hand to keep him from doing worse where it was too public I was dying to find out was he circumcised he was shaking like a jelly all over they want to do everything too quick take all the pleasure out of it and father waiting all the time for his dinner he told me to say I left my purse in the butchers and had to go back for it what a Deceiver then he wrote me that letter with all those words in it how could he have the nerve to face any woman after his company manners making it so awkward after when we met asking me have I offended you with my eyelids down of course he saw I wasnt he had a few brains not like that other fool Henny Doyle he was always breaking or tearing something in the charades I hate an unlucky man and if I knew what it meant of course I had to say no for forms sake I dont understand you I said and wasnt it natural so it is of course it used to be written up with a picture of a womans on that wall in Gibraltar with that word I couldnt find anywhere only for children seeing it too young then writing every morning a letter sometimes twice a day I liked the way he made love then he knew the way to take a woman when he sent me the 8 big poppies because mine was the 8th then I wrote the night he kissed my heart at Dolphins Barn I couldnt describe it simply it makes you feel like nothing on earth but he never knew how to embrace well like Gardner I hope hell come on

Monday as he said at the same time four I hate people who come at all hours answer the door you think its the vegetables then its somebody and you all undressed or the door of the filthy sloppy kitchen blows open the day old frostyface Goodwin called about the concert in Lombard Street and I just after dinner all flushed and tossed with boiling old stew dont look at me Professor I had to say Im a fright yes but he was a real old gent in his way it was impossible to be more respectful nobody to say youre out you have to peep out through the blind like the messenger boy today I thought it was a putoff first him sending the port and the peaches first and I was just beginning to yawn with nerves thinking he was trying to make a fool of me when I knew his tattarrattat at the door he must have been a bit late because it was ¼ after 3 when I saw the 2 Dedalus girls coming from school I never know the time even that watch he gave me never seems to go properly Id want to get it looked after when I threw the penny to that lame sailor *for England home and beauty* when I was whistling *there is a charming girl I love* and I hadnt even put on my clean shift or powdered myself or a thing then this day week were to go to Belfast just as well he has to go to Ennis for his fathers anniversary the 27th it wouldnt be pleasant if he did suppose our rooms at the hotel were beside each other and any fooling went on in the new bed I couldnt tell him to stop and not bother me with him in the next room or perhaps some Protestant clergyman with a cough knocking on the wall then hed never believe the next day we didnt do something its all very well a husband but you cant fool a lover after me telling him we never did anything of course he didnt believe me no its better hes going where he is besides something always happens with him the time going to the Mallow Concert at Maryborough ordering boiling soup for the two of us then the bell rang out he walks down the platform with the soup splashing about taking spoonfuls of it hadnt he the nerve and the waiter after him making a holy show of us screeching and confusion for the engine to start but he wouldnt pay till he finished it the two gentlemen in the 3rd class carriage said he was quite right so he was too hes so pigheaded sometimes when he gets a thing into his head a good job he was able to open the carriage door with his knife or theyd have taken us on to Cork I suppose that was done out of revenge on him O I love jaunting in a train or a car with lovely soft cushions I wonder will he take a 1st class for me he might want to do it in the train by tipping the guard well O I suppose therell be the usual idiots of men gaping at us with their eyes as stupid as ever they can possibly be that was an exceptional man that common workman that left us alone in the carriage that day going to Howth Id like to find out something about him 1 or 2 tunnels perhaps then you have to look out of the window all the nicer then coming back suppose I never came back what would they say eloped with him that gets you on on the stage the last concert I sang at where its over a year ago when was it St Teresas Hall Clarendon St little chits of missies they have now singing Kathleen Kearney and her like on account of father being in the army and my singing *The absentminded beggar* and wearing a brooch for Lord Roberts when I had the map of it all and Poldy not Irish enough was it him managed it this time I wouldnt put it past him like he got me on to sing in the *Stabat Mater* by going around saying he was putting *Lead kindly light* to music I put him up to that till the Jesuits found out he was a freemason thumping the piano *lead Thou me on* copied from some old opera yes and he was going about with some of them Sinner Fein lately or whatever they call themselves talking his usual trash and nonsense he says that little man he showed me without the neck is very intelligent the coming man Griffith is he well he doesnt look it thats all I can say still it must have been him he knew there was a boycott I hate the mention of their politics after the war that Pretoria and Ladysmith and Bloemfontein where Gardner Lieut Stanley G 8th Bn 2nd East Lancs Rgt of enteric fever he was a lovely fellow in khaki and just the right height over me Im sure he was brave too he said I was lovely the evening we kissed goodbye at the canal lock my Irish beauty he was pale with excitement about going away or wed be seen from the road he couldnt stand properly and I so hot as I never felt they could have made their peace in the beginning or old Oom Paul and the rest of the other old Krugers go and fight it out between them instead of dragging on for years killing any fine-looking men there were with their fever if he was even decently shot it wouldnt have been so bad I love to see a regiment pass in review the first time I saw the Spanish cavalry at La Roque it was lovely after looking across the bay from Algeciras all the lights of the Rock like fireflies or those sham battles on the 15 Acres the Black Watch with their kilts in time at the march past the 10th Hussars the Prince of Wales Own or the Lancers *O the Lancers theyre grand* or the Dublins that won Tugela his father made his money over selling the horses for the cavalry well he could buy me a nice present up in Belfast after what I gave him theyve lovely linen up there or one of those nice kimono things I must buy a mothball like I had before to keep in the drawer with them it would be exciting going round with him shopping buying those things in a new city better leave this ring behind want to keep turning and turning to get it over the knuckle there or they might bell it round the town in their papers or tell the police on me but theyd think were married O let them all go and smother themselves for the fat lot I care he has plenty of money and hes not a marrying man so somebody better get it out of him if I could find out whether he likes me I looked a bit washy of course when I looked close in the handglass powdering a mirror never gives you the expression besides scrooching down on me like that all the time with his big hipbones hes heavy too with his hairy chest for this heat always having to lie down for them better for him put it into me from behind the way Mrs Masliansky told me her husband made her like the dogs do it and stick out her tongue as far as ever she could and he so quiet and mild with his tingating cither can you ever be up to men the way it takes them lovely stuff in that blue suit he had on and stylish tie and socks with the sky-blue silk things on them hes certainly well off I know by the cut his clothes have and his heavy watch but he was like a perfect devil for a few minutes after he came back with the stop-press tearing up the tickets and swearing blazes because he lost 20 quid he said he lost over that outsider that won and half he put on for me on account of Lenehans tip cursing him to the lowest pits that sponger he was making free with me after the Glencree dinner coming back that long joult over the Featherbed moun- tain after the lord Mayor looking at me with his dirty eyes Val Dillon that big heathen I first noticed him at dessert when I was cracking the nuts with my teeth I wished I could have picked every morsel of that chicken out of my fingers it was so tasty and browned and as tender as anything only for I didnt want to eat everything on my plate those forks and fishslicers were hallmarked silver too I wish I had some I could easily have slipped a couple into my muff when I was playing with them then always hanging out of them for money in a restaurant for the bit you put down your throat we have to be thankful for our mangy cup of tea itself as a great compliment to be noticed the way the world is divided in any case if its going to go on I want at least two other good chemises for one thing and but I dont know what kind of drawers he likes none at all I think didnt he say yes and half the girls in Gibraltar never wore them either naked as God made them that Andalusian singing her manola she didnt make much secret of what she hadnt yes and the second pair of silkette stockings is laddered after one days wear I could have brought them back to Lewers this morning and kicked up a row and made that one change them only not to upset myself and run the risk of walking into him and ruining the whole thing and one of those kid-fitting corsets Id want advertised cheap in *The Gentlewoman* with elastic gores on the hips he saved the one I have but thats no good what did they say they give a delightful figure line 11/6 obviating that unsightly broad appearance across the lower back to reduce flesh my belly is a bit too big Ill have to knock off the stout at dinner or am I getting too fond of it the last they sent from ORourkes was as flat as a pancake he makes his money easy Larry they call him the old mangy parcel he sent at Xmas a cottage cake and a bottle of hogwash he tried to palm off as claret that he couldnt get anyone to drink God spare his spit for fear hed die of the drouth or I must do a few breathing exercises I wonder is that antifat any good might overdo it the thin ones are not so much the fashion now garters that much I have the violet pair I wore today thats all he bought me out of the cheque he got on the first O no there was the face lotion I finished the last of yesterday that made my skin like new I told him over and over again get that made up in the same place and dont forget it God only knows whether he did after all I said to him Ill know by the bottle anyway if not I suppose Ill only have to wash in my piss like beef tea or chicken soup with some of that opopanax and violet I thought it was beginning to look coarse or old a bit the skin underneath is much finer where it peeled off there on my finger after the burn its a pity it isnt all like that and the four paltry handkerchiefs about 6/- in all sure you cant get on in this world without style all going on food and rent when I get it Ill lash it around I tell you in fine style I always want to throw a handful of tea into the pot measuring and mincing if I buy a pair of old brogues itself do you like those new shoes yes how much were they Ive no clothes at all the brown costume and the skirt and jacket and the one at the cleaners 3 whats that for any woman cutting up this old hat and patching up the other the men wont look at you and women try to walk on you because they know youve no man then with all the things getting dearer every day for the 4 years more I have of life up to 35 no Im what am I at all Ill be 33 in September will I what O well look at that Mrs Galbraith shes much older than me I saw her when I was out last week her beautys on the wane she was a lovely woman magnificent head of hair on her down to her waist tossing it back like that like Kitty OShea in Grantham Street 1st thing I did every morning to look across see her combing it as if she loved it and was full of it pity I only got to know her the day before we left and that Mrs Langtry the Jersey Lily the Prince of Wales was in love with I suppose hes like the first man going the roads only for the name of

a king theyre all made the one way only a black mans Id like to try a
beauty up to what was she 45 there was some funny story about the
jealous old husband what was it at all and an oyster knife he went no he
made her wear a kind of a tin thing round her and the Prince of Wales
yes he had the oyster knife cant be true a thing like that like some of
those books he brings me the works of Master Francois Somebody
supposed to be a priest about a child born out of her ear because her
bumgut fell out a nice word for any priest to write and her a – e as if any
fool wouldnt know what that meant I hate that pretending of all things
with that old blackguards face on him anybody can see its not true and
that *Ruby* and *Fair Tyrants* he brought me that twice I remember when I
came to page 50 the part about where she hangs him up out of a hook
with a cord flagellate sure theres nothing for a woman in that all invention
made up about he drinking the champagne out of her slipper after the
ball was over like the infant Jesus in the crib at Inchicore in the Blessed
Virgins arms sure no woman could have a child that big taken out of her
and I thought first it came out of her side because how could she go to
the chamber when she wanted to and she a rich lady of course she felt
honoured HRH he was in Gibraltar the year I was born I bet he found
lilies there too where he planted the tree he planted more than that in his
time he might have planted me too if hed come a bit sooner then I
wouldnt be here as I am he ought to chuck that *Freeman* with the paltry
few shillings he knocks out of it and go into an office or something where
hed get regular pay or a bank where they could put him up on a throne
to count the money all the day of course he prefers pottering about the
house so you cant stir with him any side whats your programme today I
wish hed even smoke a pipe like father to get the smell of a man or
pretending to be mooching about for advertisements when he could have
been in Mr Cuffes still only for what he did then sending me to try and
patch it up I could have got him promoted there to be the manager he
gave me a great *mirada* once or twice first he was as stiff as the mischief
really and truly Mrs Bloom only I felt rotten simply with the old rubbishy
dress that I lost the leads out of the tails with no cut in it but theyre
coming into fashion again I bought it simply to please him I knew it was
no good by the finish pity I changed my mind of going to Todd and Burns
as I said and not Lees it was just like the shop itself rummage sale a lot of
trash I hate those rich shops get on your nerves Nothing kills me
altogether only he thinks he knows a great lot about a womans dress and
cooking mathering everything he can scour off the shelves into it if I went

by his advices every blessed hat I put on does that suit me yes take that thats all right the one like a wedding cake standing up miles off my head he said suited me or the dish cover one coming down on my backside on pins and needles about the shopgirl in that place in Grafton Street I had the misfortune to bring him into and she as insolent as ever she could be with her smirk saying Im afraid were giving you too much trouble what shes there for but I stared it out of her yes he was awfully stiff and no wonder but he changed the second time he looked Poldy pigheaded as usual like the soup but I could see him looking very hard at my chest when he stood up to open the door for me it was nice of him to show me out in any case Im extremely sorry Mrs Bloom believe me without making it too marked the first time after him being insulted and me being supposed to be his wife I just half smiled I know my chest was out that way at the door when he said Im extremely sorry and Im sure you were

yes I think he made them a bit firmer sucking them like that so long he made me thirsty titties he calls them I had to laugh yes this one anyhow stiff the nipple gets for the least thing Ill get him to keep that up and Ill take those eggs beaten up with marsala fatten them out for him what are all those veins and things curious the way its made 2 the same in case of twins theyre supposed to represent beauty placed up there like those statues in the museum one of them pretending to hide it with her hand are they so beautiful of course compared with what a man looks like with his two bags full and his other thing hanging down out of him or sticking up at you like a hatrack no wonder they hide it with a cabbage leaf that disgusting Cameron Highlander behind the meat market or that other wretch with the red head behind the tree where the statue of the fish used to be when I was passing pretending he was pissing standing out for me to see it with his baby clothes up to one side the Queens Own they were a nice lot its well the Surreys relieved them theyre always trying to show it to you every time nearly I passed outside the mens greenhouse near the Harcourt Street station just to try some fellow or other trying to catch my eye as if it was 1 of the 7 wonders of the world O and the stink of those rotten places the night coming home with Poldy after the Comerfords party oranges and lemonade to make you feel nice and watery I went into 1 of them it was so biting cold I couldnt keep it in when was that 93 the canal was frozen yes it was a few months after a pity a couple of the Camerons werent there to see me squatting in the mens place *meadero* I tried to draw a picture of it before I tore it up like a sausage or something I wonder theyre not afraid going about of getting a kick or a bang of something there the woman is beauty of course thats admitted when he said I could pose for a picture naked to some rich fellow in Holles Street when he lost the job in Helys and I was selling the clothes and strumming in the Coffee Palace would I be like that *Bath of the Nymph* with my hair down yes only shes younger or Im a little like that dirty bitch in that Spanish photo he has nymphs used they go about like that I asked him about her and that word met something with hoses in it and he came out with some jawbreakers about the incarnation he never can explain a thing simply the way a body can understand then he goes and burns the bottom out of the pan all for his Kidney this one not so much theres the mark of his teeth still where he tried to bite the nipple I had to scream out arent they fearful trying to hurt you I had a great breast of milk with Milly enough for two what was the reason of that he said I could have got a pound a week as a wet nurse all swelled out the morning that delicate-looking student that stopped in no 28 with the Citrons Penrose nearly caught me washing through the window only for I snapped up the towel to my face that was his studenting hurt me they used to weaning her till he got Doctor Brady to give me the belladonna prescription I had to get him to suck them they were so hard he said it was sweeter and thicker than cows then he wanted to milk me into the tea well hes beyond everything I declare somebody ought to put him in the *Budget* if I only could remember the 1 half of the things and write a book out of it *The Works of Master Poldy* yes and its so much smoother the skin much an hour he was at them Im sure by the clock like some kind of a big infant I had at me they want everything in their mouth all the pleasure those men get out of a woman I can feel his mouth O Lord I must stretch myself I wished he was here or somebody to let myself go with and come again like that I feel all fire inside me or if I could dream it when he made me spend the 2nd time tickling me behind with his finger I was coming for about 5 minutes with my legs round him I had to hug him after O Lord I wanted to shout out all sorts of things fuck or shit or anything at all only not to look ugly or those lines from the strain who knows the way hed take it you want to feel your way with a man theyre not all like him thank God some of them want you to be so nice about it I noticed the contrast he does it and doesnt talk I gave my eyes that look with my hair a bit loose from the tumbling and my tongue between my lips up to him the savage brute Thursday Friday one Saturday two Sunday three O Lord I cant wait till Monday

frseeeeeeeeefronnnng train somewhere whistling the strength those engines have in them like big giants and the water rolling all over and out of them all sides like the end of *Loves old sweeeetsonnnng* the poor men that have to be out all the night from their wives and families in those roasting engines stifling it was today Im glad I burned the half of those old *Freeman*s and *Photo Bits* leaving things like that lying about hes getting very careless and threw the rest of them up in the WC Ill get him to cut them tomorrow for me instead of having them there for the next year to get a few pence for them have him asking wheres last Januarys paper and all those old overcoats I bundled out of the hall making the place hotter than it is that rain was lovely and refreshing just after my beauty sleep I thought it was going to get like Gibraltar my goodness the heat there before the levanter came on black as night and the glare of the Rock standing up in it like a big giant compared with their 3 Rock mountain they think is so great with the red sentries here and there the poplars and they all white hot and the smell of the rainwater in those tanks watching the sun all the time weltering down on you faded all that lovely frock fathers friend Mrs Stanhope sent me from the B Marche Paris what a shame my dearest Doggerina she wrote on it she was very nice whats this her other name was just a pc to tell you I sent the little present have just had a jolly warm bath and feel a *very* clean dog now enjoyed it Wogger she called him Wogger wd give anything to be back in Gib and hear you sing *Waiting* and *In old Madrid* Concone is the name of those exercises he bought me one of those new some word I couldnt make out shawls amusing things but tear for the least thing still theyre lovely I think dont you will always think of the lovely teas we had together scrumptious currant scones and raspberry wafers I adore well now dearest Doggerina be sure and write soon kind she left out regards to your father also Captain Groves with love yrs affly Hester xxxxx she didnt look a bit married just like a girl he was years older than her Wogger he was awfully fond of me when he held down the wire with his foot for me to step over at the bullfight at La Linea when that matador Gomez was given the bulls ear these clothes we have to wear whoever invented them expecting you to walk up Killiney hill then for example at that picnic all staysed up you cant do a blessed thing in them in a crowd run or jump out of the way thats why I was afraid when that other ferocious old Bull began to charge the banderilleros with the sashes and the 2 things in their hats and the brutes of men shouting *bravo toro* sure the women were as bad in their nice white mantillas ripping all the whole insides out of those poor horses I never heard of such a thing in all my life yes he used to break his heart at me taking off the dog barking in Bell Lane poor brute and it sick what became of them ever I suppose theyre dead long ago the 2 of them its like all through a mist makes you feel so old I made the scones of course I had everything all to myself then a girl Hester we used to compare our hair mine was thicker than hers she showed me how to settle it at the back when I put it up and whats this else how to make a knot on a thread with the one hand we were like cousins what age was I then the night of the storm I slept in her bed she had her arms round me then we were fighting in the morning with the pillow what fun he was watching me whenever he got an opportunity at the band on the Alameda esplanade when I was with father and Captain Groves I looked up at the church first and then at the windows then down and our eyes met I felt something go through me like all needles my eyes were dancing I remember after when I looked at myself in the glass hardly recognised myself the change he was attractive to a girl in spite of his being a little bald intelligent-looking disappointed and gay at the same time he was like Thomas in *The Shadow of Ashlydyat* I had a splendid skin from the sun and the excitement like a rose I didnt get a wink of sleep it wouldnt have been nice on account of her but I could have stopped it in time she gave me *The Moonstone* to read that was the first I read of Wilkie Collins *East Lynne* I read and *The Shadow of Ashlydyat* Mrs Henry Wood *Henry Dunbar* by that other woman I lent him afterwards with Mulveys photo in it so as he could see I wasnt without and Lord Lytton *Eugene Aram Molly Bawn* she gave me by Mrs Hungerford on account of the name I dont like books with a Molly in them like that one he brought me about the one from Flanders a whore always shoplifting anything she could cloth and stuff and yards of it O this blanket is too heavy on me thats better I havent even one decent nightdress this thing gets all rolled under me besides him and his fooling thats better I used to be weltering then in the heat my shift drenched with the sweat stuck in the cheeks of my bottom on the chair when I stood up they were so fattish and firm when I got up on the sofa cushions to see with my clothes up and the bugs tons of them at night and the mosquito nets I couldnt read a line Lord how long ago it seems centuries of course they never came back and she didnt put her address right on it either she may have noticed her Wogger people were always going away and we never I remember that day with the waves and the boats with their high heads rocking and the smell of ship those Officers uniforms on shore leave made me seasick he didnt say anything he was very serious I had the high-buttoned boots on and my skirt was blowing she kissed me six or seven times didnt I cry yes I believe I did or near it my lips were taittering when I said goodbye she had a Gorgeous wrap of some special kind of blue colour on her for the voyage made very peculiarly to one side like and it was extremely pretty it got as dull as the devil after they went I was almost planning to run away mad out of it somewhere were never easy where we are father or aunt or marriage *waiting always waiting to guiiiide him toooo me waiting nor speeeed his flying feet* their damn guns bursting and booming all over the shop especially the Queens birthday and throwing everything down in all directions if you didnt open the windows when General Ulysses Grant whoever he was or did supposed to be some great fellow landed off the ship and old Sprague the consul that was there from before the Flood dressed up poor man and he in mourning for the son then the same old bugles for reveille in the morning and drums rolling and the unfortunate poor devils of soldiers walking about with mess tins smelling the place more than the old long-bearded Jews in their jellibees and Levites assembly and sound clear and gunfire for the men to cross the Lines and the warden marching with his keys to lock the gates and the bagpipes and only Captain Groves and father talking about Rorkes Drift and Plevna and Sir Garnet Wolseley and Gordon at Khartoum lighting their pipes for them every time they went out drunken old devil with his grog on the window sill catch him leaving any of it picking his nose trying to think of some other dirty story to tell up in a corner but he never forgot himself when I was there sending me out of the room on some blind excuse paying his compliments the Bushmills whiskey talking of course but hed do the same to the next woman that came along I suppose he died of galloping drink ages ago the days like years not a letter from a living soul except the odd few I posted to myself with bits of paper in them so bored sometimes I could fight with my nails listening to that old Arab with the one eye and his he-ass of an instrument singing his he-ah he-ah a-he-ah all my compriments on your hotchapotch of your he-ass as bad as now with the hands hanging off me looking out of the window if there was a nice fellow even in the opposite house that medical in Holles Street the nurse was after when I put on my gloves and hat at the window to show I was going out not a notion what I meant arent they thick never understand what you say even youd want to print it up on a big poster for them not even if you shake hands twice with the left he didnt recognise me either when I half frowned at him outside Westland Row chapel where does their great intelligence come in Id like to know grey matter they have it all in their tail if you ask me those country gougers up in the City Arms intelligence they had a damn sight less than the bulls and cows they were selling the meat and the coalmans bell that noisy bugger trying to swindle me with the wrong bill he took out of his hat what a pair of paws and pots and pans and kettles to mend any broken bottles for a poor man today and no visitors or post ever except his cheques or some advertisement like that Wonderworker they sent him addressed *Dear Madam* only his letter and the card from Milly this morning see she wrote a letter to him who did I get the last letter from O Mrs Dwenn now what possessed her to write from Canada after so many years to know the recipe I had for *pisto madrileno* Floey Dillon since she wrote to say she was married to a very rich architect if Im to believe all I hear with a villa and eight rooms her father was an awfully nice man he was near seventy always good-humoured well now Miss Tweedy or Miss Gillespie theres the pyannyer that was a solid silver coffee service he had too on the mahogany sideboard then dying so far away I hate people that have always their poor story to tell everybody has their own troubles that poor Nancy Blake died a month ago of acute pneumonia well I didnt know her so well as all that she was Floeys friend more than mine poor Nancy its a bother having to answer he always tells me the wrong things and no stops to say like making a speech your sad bereavement symphathy I always make that mistake and newphew with 2 doubleyous in I hope hell write me a longer letter the next time if its a thing he really likes me O thanks be to the great God I got somebody to give me what I badly wanted to put some heart up into me youve no chances at all in this place like you used long ago I wish somebody would write me a love letter his wasnt much and I told him he could write what he liked yours ever Hugh Boylan *In old Madrid* stuff silly women believe *love is sighing I am dying* still if he wrote it I suppose thered be some truth in it true or no it fills up your whole day and life always something to think about every moment and see it all round you like a new world I could write the answer in bed to let him imagine me short just a few words not those long crossed letters Atty Dillon used to write to the fellow that was something in the Four Courts that jilted her after out of *The Ladies Letter Writer* when I told her to say a few simple words he could twist how he liked not acting with precipat precip itancy with equal candour the greatest earthly happiness answer to a gentlemans proposal affirmatively my goodness theres nothing else its all very fine for them but as for being a woman as soon as youre old they might as well throw you out in the bottom of the ashpit.

Mulveys was the first when I was in bed that morning and Mrs Rubio brought it in with the coffee she stood there standing when I asked her to hand me a and I pointing at them I couldnt think of the word a hairpin to open it with *ah horquilla* disobliging old thing and it staring her in the face with her switch of false hair on her and vain about her appearance ugly as she was near 80 or a 100 her face a mass of wrinkles with all her religion domineering because she never could get over the Atlantic fleet coming in half the ships of the world and the Union Jack flying with all her carabineros because 4 drunken English sailors took all the Rock from them and because I didnt run into mass often enough in Santa Maria to please her with her shawl up on her except when there was a marriage on with all her miracles of the saints and her black Blessed Virgin with the silver dress and the sun dancing 3 times on Easter Sunday morning and when the priest was going by with the bell bringing the vatican to the dying blessing herself for His Majestad an admirer he signed it I near jumped out of my skin I wanted to pick him up when I saw him following me along the Calle Real in the shopwindow then he tipped me just in passing but I never thought hed write making an appointment I had it inside my petticoat bodice all day reading it up in every hole and corner while father was up at the drill instructing to find out by the handwriting or the language of stamps singing I remember *Shall I wear a white rose* and I wanted to put on the old stupid clock to near the time he was the first man kissed me under the Moorish Wall *My sweetheart when a boy* it never entered my head what kissing meant till he put his tongue in my mouth his mouth was sweetlike young I put my knee up to him a few times to learn the way what did I tell him I was engaged for for fun to the son of a Spanish nobleman named Don Miguel de la Flora and he believed me that I was to be married to him in 3 years time theres many a true word spoken in jest *there is a flower that bloometh* a few things I told him true about myself just for him to be imagining the Spanish girls he didnt like I suppose one of them wouldnt have him I got him excited he crushed all the flowers on my bosom he brought me he couldnt count the pesetas and the perragordas till I taught him Cappoquin he came from he said on the Blackwater but it was too short then the day before he left May yes it was May when the infant king of Spain was born Im always like that in the spring Id like a new fellow every year up on the tiptop under the Rock Gun near OHaras Tower I told him it was struck by lightning and all about the old Barbary apes they sent to Clapham without a tail careering all over the show on each others back Mrs Rubio said she was a regular old rock scorpion robbing the chickens out of Inces Farm and throw stones at you if you went anear he was looking at me I had that white blouse on open in the front to encourage him as much as I could without too openly they were just beginning to be plump I said I was tired we lay over the Fig Tree Cave a wild place I suppose it must be the highest rock in existence the galleries and casemates and those frightful rocks and Saint Michaels Cave with the icicles or whatever they call them hanging down and ladders all the mud plotching my boots Im sure thats the way down the monkeys go under the sea to Africa when they die the ships out far like chips that was the Malta boat passing yes the sea and the sky you could do what you liked lie there for ever he caressed them outside they love doing that its the roundness there I was leaning over him with my white rice-straw hat to take the newness out of it the left side of my face the best my blouse open for his last day transparent kind of shirt he had I could see his chest pink he wanted to touch mine with his for a moment but I wouldnt let him he was awfully put out first for fear you never know consumption or leave me with a child *embarazada* that old servant Ines told me that one drop even if it got into you at all after I tried with the Banana but I was afraid it might break and get lost up in me somewhere because they once took something down out of a woman that was up there for years covered with lime salts theyre all mad to get in there where they come out of youd think they could never go far enough up and then theyre done with you in a way till the next time yes because theres a wonderful feeling there so tender all the time how did we finish it off yes O yes I pulled him off into my handkerchief pretending not to be excited but I opened my legs I wouldnt let him touch me inside my petticoat because I had a skirt opening up the side I tormented the life out of him first tickling him I loved rousing that dog in the hotel rrrsssstt awokwokawok his eyes shut and a bird flying below us he was shy all the same I liked him like that moaning I made him blush a little when I got over him that way when I unbuttoned him and took his out and drew back the skin it had a kind of eye in it theyre all Buttons men down the middle on the wrong side of them Molly darling he called me what was his name Jack Joe Harry Mulvey was it yes I think a lieutenant he was rather fair he had a laughing kind of a voice so I went round to the whatyoucallit everything was whatyoucallit moustache had he he said hed come back Lord its just like yesterday to me and if I was married hed do it to me and I promised him yes faithfully Id let him block me now flying perhaps hes dead or killed or a captain or admiral its nearly 20 years if I said Fig Tree Cave he would if he came up behind me and put his hands over my eyes to guess who I might recognise him hes young still about 40 perhaps hes married some girl on the Blackwater and is quite changed they all do they havent half the character a woman has she little knows what I did with her beloved husband before he ever dreamt of her in broad daylight too in the sight of the whole world you might say they could have put an article about it in the *Chronicle* I was a bit wild after when I blew out the old bag the biscuits were in from Benadi Bros and exploded it Lord what a bang all the woodcocks and pigeons screaming coming back the same way that we went over Middle Hill round by the old guardhouse and the Jews burial place pretending to read out the Hebrew on them I wanted to fire his pistol he said he hadnt one he didnt know what to make of me with his peak cap on that he always wore crooked as often as I settled it straight H M S *Calypso* swinging my hat that old Bishop that spoke off the altar his long preach about womans higher functions about girls now riding the bicycle and wearing peak caps and the new woman bloomers God send him sense and me more money I suppose theyre called after him I never thought that would be my name Bloom when I used to write it in print to see how it looked on a visiting card or practising for the butcher and oblige M Bloom youre looking blooming Josie used to say after I married him well its better than Breen or Briggs does brig or those awful names with bottom in them Mrs Ramsbottom or some other kind of a bottom Mulvey I wouldnt go mad about either or suppose I divorced him Mrs Boylan my mother whoever she was might have given me a nicer name the Lord knows after the lovely one she had Lunita Laredo the fun we had running along Williss Road to Europa Point twisting in and out all round the other side of Jersey they were shaking and dancing about in my blouse like Millys little ones now when she runs up the stairs I loved looking down at them I was jumping up at the pepper trees and the white poplars pulling the leaves off and throwing them at him he went to India he was to write the voyages those men have to make to the ends of the world and back its the least they might get a squeeze or two at a woman while they can going out to be drowned or blown up somewhere I went up Windmill Hill to the Flats that Sunday morning with Captain Rubios that was dead spyglass like the sentry had he said hed have one or two from on board I wore that frock from the B Marche Paris and the coral necklace the straits shining I could see over to Morocco almost the bay of Tangier white and the Atlas mountain with snow on it and the straits like a river so clear

Harry Molly darling I was thinking of him on the sea all the time after at mass when my petticoat began to slip down at the elevation weeks and weeks I kept the handkerchief under my pillow for the smell of him there was no decent perfume to be got in that Gibraltar only that cheap *peau dEspagne* that faded and left a stink on you more than anything else I wanted to give him a memento he gave me that clumsy Claddagh ring for luck that I gave Gardner going to South Africa where those Boers killed him with their war and fever but they were well beaten all the same as if it brought its bad luck with it like an opal or pearl still it must have been pure 18-carat gold because it was very heavy but what could you get in a place like that the sand-frog shower from Africa and that derelict ship that came up to the harbour *Marie* the *Marie* whatyoucallit no he hadnt a moustache that was Gardner yes I can see his face clean-shaven frseeeeeeeeeeeeeeeeeeeeeeefrong that train again weeping tone *once in the dear deaead days beyondre call* close my eyes breath my lips forward kiss sad look eyes open piano *ere oer the world the mists began* I hate that istsbeg *comes loves sweet soooooooooong* Ill let that out full when I get in front of the footlights again Kathleen Kearney and her lot of squealers Miss This Miss That Miss Theother lot of sparrowfarts skitting around talking about politics they know as much about as my backside anything in the world to make themselves someway interesting Irish homemade beauties soldiers daughter am I ay and whose are you bootmakers and publicans I beg your pardon coach I thought you were a wheelbarrow theyd die down dead off their feet if ever they got a chance of walking down the Alameda on an officers arm like me on the band night my eyes flashing my bust that they havent passion God help their poor head I knew more about men and life when I was 15 than theyll all know at 50 they dont know how to sing a song like that Gardner said no man could look at my mouth and teeth smiling like that and not think of it I was afraid he mightnt like my accent first he so English all father left me in spite of his stamps Ive my mothers eyes and figure anyhow he always said theyre so snotty about themselves some of those cads he wasnt a bit like that he was dead gone on my lips let them get a husband first thats fit to be looked at and a daughter like mine or see if they can excite a swell with money that can pick and choose whoever he wants like Boylan to do it 4 or 5 times locked in each others arms or the voice either I could have been a prima donna only I married him *comes looooves old* deep down chin back not too much make it double *My ladys bower* is too long for an encore about the moated grange at twilight and vaulted rooms yes

Ill sing *Winds that blow from the south* that he gave after the choir-stairs performance Ill change that lace on my black dress to show off my bubs and Ill yes by God Ill get that big fan mended make them burst with envy my hole is itching me always when I think of him I feel I want to I feel some wind in me better go easy not wake him have him at it again slobbering after washing every bit of myself back belly and sides if we had even a bath itself or my own room anyway I wish hed sleep in some bed by himself with his cold feet on me give us room even to let a fart God or do the least thing better yes hold them like that a bit on my side piano quietly *sweeeee* theres that train far away pianissimo *eeeeeee* one more *tsong*

that was a relief wherever you be let your wind go free who knows if that pork chop I took with my cup of tea after was quite good with the heat I couldnt smell anything off it Im sure that queer-looking man in the pork butchers is a great rogue I hope that lamp is not smoking fill my nose up with smuts better than having him leaving the gas on all night I couldnt rest easy in my bed in Gibraltar even getting up to see why am I so damned nervous about that though I like it in the winter its more company O Lord it was rotten cold too that winter when I was only about ten was I yes I had the big doll with all the funny clothes dressing her up and undressing that icy wind skeeting across from those mountains the something Nevada Sierra Nevada standing at the fire with the little bit of a short shift I had up to heat myself I loved dancing about in it then make a race back into bed Im sure that fellow opposite used to be there the whole time watching with the lights out in the summer and I in my skin hopping around I used to love myself then stripped at the washstand dabbing and creaming only when it came to the chamber performance I put out the light too so then there were 2 of us goodbye to my sleep for this night anyhow I hope hes not going to get in with those medicals leading him astray to imagine hes young again coming in at 4 in the morning it must be if not more still he had the manners not to wake me what do they find to gabber about all night squandering money and getting drunker and drunker couldnt they drink water then he starts giving us his orders for eggs and tea and Findon haddy and hot buttered toast I suppose well have him sitting up like the king of the country pumping the wrong end of the spoon up and down in his egg wherever he learned that from and I love to hear him falling up the stairs of a morning with the cups rattling on the tray and then play with the cat she rubs up against you for her own sake I wonder has she fleas shes as bad as a woman always licking and lecking but I hate their claws I wonder do they see anything that we cant staring like that always when she sits at the top of the stairs so long and listening as I wait what a robber too that lovely fresh plaice I bought I think Ill get a bit of fish tomorrow or today is it Friday yes I will with some blancmange with blackcurrant jam like long ago not those 2-lb pots of mixed plum and apple from the London and Newcastle Williams and Woods goes twice as far only for the bones I hate those eels cod yes Ill get a nice piece of cod Im always getting enough for 3 forgetting anyway Im sick of that everlasting butchers meat from Buckleys loin chops and leg beef and rib steak and scrag of mutton and calfs pluck the very name is enough or a picnic suppose we all gave 5/- each or let him pay it and invite some other woman for him who Mrs Fleming and drive out to the Furry Glen or the Strawberry Beds wed have him examining all the horses toenails first like he does with the letters no not with Boylan there yes with some cold veal and ham mixed sandwiches there are little houses down at the bottom of the banks there on purpose but its as hot as blazes he says not a bank holiday anyhow I hate those ruck of Mary Ann coalboxes out for the day Whit Monday is a cursed day too no wonder that bee bit him better the seaside but Id never again in this life get into a boat with him after him at Bray telling the boatman he knew how to row if anyone asked could he ride the steeplechase for the Gold Cup hed say yes then it came on to get rough the old thing crookeding about and the weight all down my side telling me pull the right reins now pull the left and the tide all swamping in floods in through the bottom and his oar slipping out of the stirrup its a mercy we werent all drowned he can swim of course me no theres no danger whatsoever keep yourself calm in his flannel trousers Id like to have tattered them down off him before all the people and give him what that one calls flagellate till he was black and blue do him all the good in the world only for that long-nosed chap I dont know who he is with that other beauty Burke out of the City Arms Hotel was there spying around as usual on the slip always where he wasnt wanted if there was a row on youd vomit a better face there was no love lost between us thats 1 consolation I wonder what kind is that book he brought me *Sweets of Sin* by A Gentleman of Fashion some other Mr de Kock I suppose the people gave him that nickname going about with his tube from one woman to another I couldnt even change my new white shoes all ruined with the salt water and the hat I had with that feather all blowy and tossed on me how annoying and provoking because the smell of the sea excited me of course the sardines and the bream in Catalan Bay round the back of the Rock they were fine all silver in the fishermens baskets old Luigi near a hundred they said came from Genoa and the tall old chap with the earrings I dont like a man you have to climb up to to get at I suppose theyre all dead and rotten long ago besides I dont like being alone in this big barracks of a place at night I suppose Ill have to put up with it I never brought a bit of salt in even when we moved in the confusion musical academy he was going to make on the first floor drawing room with a brass plate or Blooms Private Hotel he suggested go and ruin himself altogether the way his father did down in Ennis like all the things he told father he was going to do and me but I saw through him telling me all the lovely places we could go for the honeymoon Venice by moonlight with the gondolas and the lake of Como he had a picture cut out of some paper of and mandolines and lanterns O how nice I said whatever I liked he was going to do immediately if not sooner *will you be my man will you carry my can* he ought to get a leather medal with a putty rim for all the plans he invents then leaving us here all day youd never know what old beggar at the door for a crust with his long story might be a tramp and put his foot in the way to prevent me shutting it like that picture of that hardened criminal he was called in *Lloyds Weekly News* 20 years in jail then he comes out and murders an old woman for her money imagine his poor wife or mother or whoever she is such a face youd run miles away from I couldnt rest easy till I bolted all the doors and windows to make sure but its worse again being locked up like in a prison or a madhouse they ought to be all shot or the cat-o-nine-tails a big brute like that that would attack a poor old woman to murder her in her bed Id cut them off him so I would not that hed be much use still better than nothing the night I was sure I heard burglars in the kitchen and he went down in his shirt with a candle and a poker as if he was looking for a mouse as white as a sheet frightened out of his wits making as much noise as he possibly could for the burglars benefit there isnt much to steal indeed the Lord knows still its the feeling especially now with Milly away such an idea for him to send the girl down there to learn to take photographs on account of his grandfather instead of sending her to Skerrys Academy where shed have to learn not like me getting all 1s at school only hed do a thing like that all the same on account of me and Boylan thats why he did it Im certain the way he plots and plans everything out I couldnt turn round with her in the place lately unless I bolted the door first gave me the fidgets coming in without knocking first when I put the chair against the door just as I was washing myself there below with the glove get on your nerves then doing the loglady all day put her in a glass case with two at a time to look at her if he knew she broke off the hand off that little gimcrack statue with her roughness and carelessness before she left that I got that little Italian boy to mend so that you cant see the join for 2/- wouldnt even teem the potatoes for you of course shes right not to ruin her hands I noticed he was always talking to her lately at the table explaining things in the paper and she pretending to understand sly of course that comes from his side of the house he cant say I pretend things can he Im too honest as a matter of fact and helping her into her coat but if there was anything wrong with her its me shed tell not him I suppose he thinks Im finished out and laid on the shelf well Im not no nor anything like it well see well see now shes well on for flirting too with Tom Devins two sons imitating me whistling with those romps of Murray girls calling for her can Milly come out please shes in great demand to pick what they can out of her round in Nelson Street riding Harry Devins bicycle at night its as well he sent her where she is she was just getting out of bounds wanting to go on the skating rink and smoking their cigarettes through their nose I smelt it off her dress when I was biting off the thread of the button I sewed on to the bottom of her jacket she couldnt hide much from me I tell you only I oughtnt to have stitched it and it on her it brings a parting and the last plum pudding too split in 2 halves see it comes out no matter what they say her tongue is a bit too long for my taste your blouse is open too low she says to me the pan calling the kettle blackbottom and I had to tell her not to cock her legs up like that on show on the window sill before all the people passing they all look at her like me when I was her age of course any old rag looks well on you then a great touch-me-not too in her own way at *The Only Way* in the Theatre Royal take your foot away out of that I hate people touching me afraid of her life Id crush her skirt with the pleats a lot of that touching must go on in theatres in the crush in the dark theyre always trying to wiggle up to you that fellow in the pit at the Gaiety for Beerbohm Tree in *Trilby* the last time Ill ever go there to be squashed like that for any Trilby or Barebum every two minutes tipping me there and looking away hes a bit daft I think I saw him after trying to get near two stylish-dressed ladies outside Switzers window at the same little game I recognised him on the moment the face and everything but he didnt remember me yes and she didnt even want me to kiss her at the Broadstone going away well I hope shell get someone to dance attendance on her the way I did when she was down with the mumps and her glands swollen wheres this and wheres that of course she cant feel anything deep yet I never came properly till I was what 22 or so it went into the wrong place always only the usual girls nonsense and giggling that Conny Connolly writing to her in white ink on black paper sealed with sealing wax though she clapped when the curtain came down because he looked so handsome then we had Martin Harvey for breakfast dinner and supper I thought to myself afterwards it must be real love if a man gives up his life for her that way for nothing I suppose there are a few men like that left its hard to believe in it though unless it really happened to me the majority of them with not a particle of love in their natures to find two people like that nowadays full up of each other that would feel the same way as you do theyre usually a bit foolish in the head his father must have been a bit queer to go and poison himself after her still poor old man I suppose he felt lost shes always making love to my things too the few old rags I have wanting to put her hair up at 15 my powder too only ruin her skin on her shes time enough for that all her life after of course shes restless knowing shes pretty with her lips so red a pity they wont stay that way I was too but theres no use going to the fair with the thing answering me like a fishwoman when I asked her to go for a half a stone of potatoes the day we met Mrs Joe Gallaher at the trotting matches and she pretended not to see us in her trap with Friery the solicitor we werent grand enough till I gave her 2 damn fine cracks across the ear for herself take that now for answering me like that and that for your impudence she had me that exasperated of course contradicting I was bad-tempered too because how was it there was a weed in the tea or I didnt sleep the night before cheese I ate was it and I told her over and over again not to leave knives crossed like that because she has nobody to command her as she said herself well if he doesnt correct her faith I will that was the last time she turned on the tear tap I was just like that myself they darent order me about the place its his fault of course having the two of us slaving here instead of getting in a woman long ago am I ever going to have a proper servant again of course then shed see him coming Id have to let her know or shed revenge it arent they a nuisance that old Mrs Fleming you have to be walking round after her putting the things into her hands sneezing and farting into the pots well of course shes old she cant help it a good job I found that rotten old smelly dishcloth that got lost behind the dresser I knew there was something and opened the area window to let out the smell bringing in his friends to entertain them like the night he walked home with a dog if you please that might have been mad especially Simon Dedalus son his father such a criticiser with his glasses up with his tall hat on him at the cricket match and a great big hole in his sock one thing laughing at the other and his son that got all those prizes for whatever he won them in the intermediate imagine climbing over the railings if anybody saw him that knew us I wonder he didnt tear a big hole in his grand funeral trousers as if the one nature gave wasnt enough for anybody hawking him down into the dirty old kitchen now is he right in his head I ask pity it wasnt washing day my old pair of drawers might have been hanging up too on the line on exhibition for all hed ever care with the iron mould mark the stupid old bundle burned on them he might think was something else and she never even rendered down the fat I told her and now shes going such as she was on account of her paralysed husband getting worse theres always something wrong with them disease or they have to go under an operation or if its not that its drink and he beats her Ill have to hunt around again for someone every day I get up theres some new thing on sweet God sweet God well when Im stretched out dead in my grave I suppose Ill have some peace I want to get up a minute if Im let wait O Jesus wait yes that thing has come on me yes now wouldnt that afflict you of course all the poking and rooting and ploughing he had up in me now what am I to do Friday Saturday Sunday wouldnt that pester the soul out of a body unless he likes it some men do God knows theres always something wrong with us 5 days every 3 or 4 weeks usual monthly auction isnt it simply sickening that night it came on me like that the one and only time we were in a box that Michael Gunn gave him to see Mrs Kendal and her husband at the Gaiety something he did about insurance for him in Drimmies I was fit to be tied though I wouldnt give in with that gentleman of fashion staring down at me with his glasses and him the other side of me talking about Spinoza and his soul thats dead I suppose millions of years ago I smiled the best I could all in a swamp leaning forward as if I was interested having to sit it out then to the last tag I wont forget that *Wife of Scarli* in a hurry supposed to be a fast play about adultery that idiot in the gallery hissing the woman adulteress he shouted I suppose he went and had a woman in the next lane running round all the back ways after to make up for it I wish he had what I had then hed boo I bet the cat itself is better off than us have we too much blood up in us or what O patience above its pouring out of me like the sea anyhow he didnt make me pregnant as big as he is I dont want to ruin the clean sheets I just put on I suppose the clean linen I wore brought it on too damn it damn it and they always want to see a stain on the bed to know youre a virgin for them all thats troubling them theyre such fools too you could be a widow or divorced 40 times over a daub of red ink would do or blackberry juice no thats too purply O Jamesy let me up out of this pooh sweets of sin whoever suggested that business for women what between clothes and cooking and children this damned old bed too jingling like the dickens I suppose they could hear us away over the other side of the Park till I suggested to put the quilt on the floor with the pillow under my bottom I wonder is it nicer in the day I think it is easy I think Ill cut all this hair off me there scalding me I might look like a young girl wouldnt he get the great suck-in the next time he turned up my clothes on me Id give anything to see his face wheres the chamber gone easy Ive a holy horror of its breaking under me after that old commode I wonder was I too heavy sitting on his knee I made him sit on the easy chair purposely when I took off only my blouse and skirt first in the other room he was so busy where he oughtnt to be he never felt me I hope my breath was sweet after those kissing comfits easy God I remember one time I could scout it out straight whistling like a man almost easy O Lord how noisy I hope theyre bubbles on it for a wad of money from some fellow Ill have to perfume it in the morning dont forget I bet he never saw a better pair of thighs than that look how white they are the smoothest place is right there between this bit here how soft like a peach easy God I wouldnt mind being a man and get up on a lovely woman O Lord what a row youre making like the Jersey Lily easy easy *O how the waters come down at Lahore*

who knows is there anything the matter with my insides or have I something growing in me getting that thing like that every week when was it last I Whit Monday yes its only about 3 weeks I ought to go to the doctor only it would be like before I married him when I had that white thing coming from me and Floey made me go to that dry old stick Dr Collins for womens diseases on Pembroke Road your vagina he called it I suppose thats how he got all the gilt mirrors and carpets getting round those rich ones off Stephens Green running up to him for every little fiddlefaddle her vagina and her Cochin-China theyve money of course so theyre all right I wouldnt marry him not if he was the last man in the world besides theres something queer about their children always smell-ing around those filthy bitches all sides asking me if what I did had an offensive odour what did he want me to do but the one thing gold maybe what a question if I smathered it all over his wrinkly old face for him with all my compriments I suppose hed know then and could you pass it easily pass what I thought he was talking about the Rock of Gibraltar the way he put it thats a very nice invention too by the way only I like letting myself down after in the hole as far as I can squeeze and pull the chain then to flush it nice cool pins and needles still theres something in it I suppose I always used to know by Millys when she was a child whether she had worms or not still all the same paying him for that how much is that doctor one guinea please and asking me had I frequent omissions where do those old fellows get all the words they have omissions with his shortsighted eyes on me cocked sideways I wouldnt trust him too far to give me chloroform or God knows what else still I liked him when he sat down to write the thing out frowning so severe his nose intelligent like that you be damned you lying strap O anything no matter who except an idiot he was clever enough to spot that of course that was all thinking of him and his mad crazy letters my Precious one everything connected with your glorious Body *everything* underlined that comes from it is a thing of beauty and of joy for ever something he got out of some nonsensical book that he had me always at myself 4 and 5 times a day sometimes and I said I hadnt are you sure O yes I said I am quite sure in a way that shut him up I knew what was coming next only natural weakness it was he excited me I dont know how the first night ever we met when I was living in Rehoboth Terrace we stood staring at one another for about 10 minutes as if we met somewhere I suppose on account of my being Jewess-looking after my mother he used to amuse me the things he said with the half-sloothering smile on him and all the Doyles said he was going to stand for a member of Parliament O wasnt I the born fool to believe all his blather about Home Rule and the Land League sending me that long strool of a song out of *The Huguenots* to sing in French to be more classy *O beau pays de La Touraine* that I never even sang once explaining and rigmaroling about religion and persecution he wont let you enjoy anything naturally then might he as a great favour the very 1st opportunity he got a chance in Brighton Square running into my bedroom pretending the ink got on his hands to wash it off with the Albion milk and sulphur soap I used to use and the gelatine still round it O I laughed myself sick at him that day I better not make an all-night sitting on this affair they ought to make chambers a natural size so that a woman could sit on it properly he kneels down to do it I suppose there isnt in all creation another man with the habits he has look at the way hes sleeping at the foot of the bed how can he without a hard bolster its

724

well he doesnt kick or he might knock out all my teeth breathing with his hand on his nose like that Indian god he took me to show me one wet Sunday in the museum in Kildare Street all yellow in a pinafore lying on his side on his hand with his ten toes sticking out that he said was a bigger religion than the Jews and Our Lords both put together all over Asia imitating him as hes always imitating everybody I suppose he used to sleep at the foot of the bed too with his big square feet up in his wifes mouth damn this stinking thing anyway wheres this those napkins are ah yes I know I hope the old press doesnt creak ah I knew it would hes sleeping hard had a good time somewhere still she must have given him great value for his money of course he has to pay for it from her O this nuisance of a thing I hope theyll have something better for us in the other world tying ourselves up God help us thats all right for tonight now the lumpy old jingly bed always reminds me of old Cohen I suppose he scratched himself in it often enough and he thinks father bought it from Lord Napier that I used to admire when I was a little girl because I told him easy piano O I like my bed God here we are as bad as ever after 16 years how many houses were we in at all Raymond Terrace and Ontario Terrace and Lombard Street and Holles Street and he goes about whistling every time were on the run again his *Huguenots* or *The frogs march* pretending to help the men with our 4 sticks of furniture and then the City Arms Hotel worse and worse says Warden Daly that charming place on the landing always somebody inside praying then leaving all their stinks after them always know who was in there last every time were just getting on right something happens or he puts his big foot in it Thoms and Helys and Mr Cuffes and Drimmies either hes going to be run into prison over his old lottery tickets that was to be all our salvations or he goes and gives impudence well have him coming home with the sack soon out of the *Freeman* too like the rest on account of those Sinner Fein or the freemasons then well see if the little man he showed me dribbling along in the wet all by himself round by Coadys Lane will give him much consolation that he says is so capable and sincerely Irish he is indeed judging by the sincerity of the trousers I saw on him wait theres Georges Church bells wait 3 quarters the hour 1 wait 2 oclock well thats a nice hour of the night for him to be coming home at to anybody climbing down into the area if anybody saw him Ill knock him off that little habit tomorrow first Ill look at his shirt to see or Ill see if he has that French letter still in his pocketbook I suppose he thinks I dont know deceitful men all their 20 pockets arent enough for their lies then why should we tell them even if its the truth they dont believe you then tucked up in bed like those babies in the *Aristocrats Masterpiece* he brought me another time as if we hadnt enough of that in real life without some old Aristocrat or whatever his name is disgusting you more with those rotten pictures children with two heads and no legs thats the kind of villainy theyre always dreaming about with not another thing in their empty heads they ought to get slow poison the half of them then tea and toast for him buttered on both sides and new-laid eggs I suppose Im nothing any more when I wouldnt let him lick me in Holles Street one night man man tyrant as ever for the one thing he slept on the floor half the night naked the way the Jews used when somebody dies belonged to them and wouldnt eat any breakfast or speak a word wanting to be petted so I thought I stood out enough for one time and let him he does it all wrong too thinking only of his own pleasure his tongue is too flat or I dont know what he forgets that why then I dont Ill make him do it again if he doesnt mind himself and lock him down to sleep in the coal cellar with the blackbeetles I wonder was it her Josie off her head with my castoffs hes such a born liar too no hed never have the courage with a married woman thats why he wants me and Boylan though as for her Denis as she calls him that forlorn-looking spectacle you couldnt call him a husband yes its some little bitch hes got in with even when I was with him with Milly at the College races that Hornblower with the childs bonnet on the top of his nob let us into by the back way he was throwing his sheeps eyes at those two doing skirt duty up and down I tried to wink at him first no use of course and thats the way his money goes this is the fruits of Mr Paddy Dignam yes they were all in great style at the grand funeral in the paper Boylan brought in if they saw a real officers funeral thatd be something reversed arms muffled drums the poor horse walking behind in black L Boom and Tom Kernan that drunken little barrelly man that bit his tongue off falling down the mens WC drunk in some place or other and Martin Cunningham and the two Dedaluses and Fanny MCoys husband white head of cabbage skinny thing with a turn in her eye trying to sing my songs shed want to be born all over again and her old green dress with the low neck as she cant attract them any other way like dabbling on a rainy day I see it all now plainly and they call that friendship killing and then burying one another and they all with their wives and families at home more especially Jack Power keeping that barmaid he does of course his wife is always sick or going to be sick or just getting better of it and hes a good-looking man still though hes getting a bit grey over the ears theyre a nice lot all of them well theyre not going to get my husband again into their clutches if I can help it making fun of him then behind his back I know well when he goes on with his idiotics because he has sense enough not to squander every penny piece he earns down their gullets and looks after his wife and family good-for-nothings poor Paddy Dignam all the same Im sorry in a way for him what are his wife and 5 children going to do unless he was insured comical little teetotum always stuck up in some pub corner and her or her son waiting *Bill Bailey wont you please come home* her widows weeds wont improve her appearance theyre awfully becoming though if youre good-looking what men wasnt he yes he was at the Glencree dinner and Ben Dollard base barreltone the night he borrowed the swallowtail to sing out of in Holles Street squeezed and squashed into them and grinning all over his big Dolly face like a well-whipped childs botty didnt he look a balmy ballocks sure enough that must have been a spectacle on the stage imagine paying 5/- in the preserved seats for that to see him trotting off in his trowlers and Simon Dedalus too he was always turning up half screwed singing the second verse first *The old love is the new* was one of his *so sweetly sang the maiden on the hawthorn bough* he was always on for flirtyfying too when I sang *Maritana* with him at Freddy Mayers private opera he had a delicious glorious voice *Phoebe dearest goodbye sweetheart sweet*heart he always sang it not like Bartell dArcy sweet *tart* goodbye of course he had the gift of the voice so there was no art in it all over you like a warm shower bath *O Maritana wildwood flower* we sang splendidly though it was a bit too high for my register even transposed and he was married at the time to May Goulding but then hed say or do something to knock the good out of it hes a widower now I wonder what sort is his son he says hes an author and going to be a university professor of Italian and Im to take lessons what is he driving at now showing him my photo its not good of me I ought to have got it taken in drapery that never looks out of fashion still I look young in it I wonder he didnt make him a present of it altogether and me too after all why not I saw him driving down to the Kingsbridge station with his father and mother I was in mourning thats 11 years ago now yes hed be 11 though what was the good in going into mourning for what was neither one thing nor the other the first cry was enough for me I heard the deathwatch too ticking in the wall of course he insisted hed go into mourning for the cat I suppose hes a man now by this time he was an innocent boy then and a darling little fellow in his Lord Fauntleroy suit and curly hair like a prince on the stage when I saw him at Mat Dillons he liked me too I remember they all do wait by God yes wait yes hold on he was on the cards this morning when I laid out the deck union with a young stranger neither dark nor fair you met before I thought it meant him but hes no chicken nor a stranger either besides my face was turned the other way what was the 7th card after that the 10 of spades for a journey by land then there was a letter on its way and scandals too the 3 queens and the 8 of diamonds for a rise in society yes wait it all came out and 2 red 8s for new garments look at that and didnt I dream something too yes there was something about poetry in it I hope he hasnt long greasy hair hanging into his eyes or standing up like a Red Indian what do they go about like that for only getting themselves and their poetry laughed at I always liked poetry when I was a girl first I thought he was a poet like Lord Byron and not an ounce of it in his composition I thought he was quite different I wonder is he too young hes about wait 88 I was married 88 Milly is 15 yesterday 89 what age was he then at Dillons 5 or 6 about 88 I suppose hes 20 or more Im not too old for him if hes 23 or 24 I hope hes not that stuck-up university student sort no otherwise he wouldnt go sitting down in the old kitchen with him taking Eppss cocoa and talking of course he pretended to understand it all probably he told him he was out of Trinity College hes very young to be a professor I hope hes not a professor like Goodwin was he was a patent professor of John Jameson they all write about some woman in their poetry well I suppose he wont find many like me *where softly sighs of love the light guitar* where poetry is in the air the blue sea and the moon shining so beautifully coming back on the nightboat from Tarifa the lighthouse at Europa Point the guitar that fellow played was so expressive will I ever go back there again all new faces *two glancing eyes a lattice hid* Ill sing that for him theyre my eyes if hes anything of a poet *two eyes as darkly bright as loves own star* arent those beautiful words *as loves young star* itll be a change the Lord knows to have an intelligent person to talk to about yourself not always listening to him and Billy Prescotts ad and Keyess ad and Tom the Devils ad then if anything goes wrong in their business we have to suffer Im sure hes very distinguished Id like to meet a man like that God not those other ruck besides hes young those fine young men I could see down in Margate Strand bathing place from the side of the rock standing up in the sun naked like a God or something and then plunging into the sea with them why arent all men like that thered be some consolation for a woman like that lovely little statue he bought I could look at him all day long curly head and his shoulders his finger up for you to listen theres real beauty and poetry for you I often felt I wanted to kiss him all over also his lovely young cock there so simple I wouldnt mind taking him in my mouth if nobody was looking as if it was asking you to suck it so clean and white he looks with his boyish face I would too in ½ a minute even if some of it went down what is it its only like gruel or the dew theres no danger besides hed be so clean compared with those pigs of men I suppose never dream of washing it from 1 years end to the other the most of them only thats what gives the women the moustaches Im sure itll be grand if I can only get in with a handsome young poet at my age Ill throw them the 1st thing in the morning till I see if the wish card comes out or Ill try pairing the lady herself and see if he comes out Ill read and study all I can find or learn a bit off by heart if I knew who he likes so he wont think me stupid if he thinks all women are the same and I can teach him the other part Ill make him feel all over him till he half faints under me then hell write about me lover and mistress publicly too with our 2 photographs in all the papers when he becomes famous O but then what am I going to do about him though

    no thats no way for him has he no manners nor no refinement nor no nothing in his nature slapping us behind like that on my bottom because I didnt call him Hugh the ignoramus that doesnt know poetry from a cabbage thats what you get for not keeping them in their proper place pulling off his shoes and trousers there on the chair before me so barefaced without even asking permission and standing out that vulgar way in the half of a shirt they wear to be admired like a priest or a butcher or those old hypocrites in the time of Julius Caesar of course hes right enough in his way to pass the time as a joke sure you might as well be in bed with what with a lion God Im sure hed have something better to say for himself an old Lion would O well I suppose its because they were so plump and tempting in my short petticoat he couldnt resist they excite myself sometimes its well for men all the amount of pleasure they get off a womans body were so round and white for them always I wish I was one myself for a change just to try with that thing they have swelling up on you so hard and at the same time so soft when you touch it *my uncle John has a thing long* I heard those cornerboys saying passing the corner of Marrowbone Lane *my aunt Mary has a thing hairy* because it was dark and they knew a girl was passing it didnt make me blush why should it either its only nature and he puts his thing long into my aunt Marys hairy et cetera and turns out to be you put the handle in a sweeping brush men again all over they can pick and choose what they please a married woman or a fast widow or a girl for their different tastes like those houses round behind Irish Street no but were to be always chained up theyre not going to be chaining me up no damn fear once I start I tell you for their stupid husbands jealousy why cant we all remain friends over it instead of quarrelling her husband found it out what they did together well naturally and if he did can he undo it hes *coronado* anyway whatever he does and then he going to the other mad extreme about the wife in *Fair Tyrants* of course the man never even casts a 2nd thought on the husband or wife either its the woman he wants and he gets her what else were we given all those desires for Id like to know I cant help it if Im young still can I its a wonder Im not an old shrivelled hag before my time living with him so cold never embracing me except sometimes when hes asleep the wrong end of me not knowing I suppose who he has any man thatd kiss a womans bottom Id throw my hat at him after that hed kiss anything unnatural where we havent 1 atom of any kind of expression in us all of us the same 2 lumps of lard before ever Id do that to a man pfooh the dirty brutes the mere thought is enough *I kiss the feet of you senorita* theres some sense in that didnt he kiss our hall door yes he did what a madman nobody understands his cracked ideas but me still of course a woman wants to be embraced 20 times a day almost to make her look young no matter by who so long as to be in love or loved by somebody if the fellow you want isnt there sometimes by the Lord God I was thinking would I go around by the quays there some dark evening where nobodyd know me and pick up a sailor off the sea thatd be hot on for it and not care a pin whose I was only do it off up in a gate somewhere or one of those wild-looking gipsies in Rathfarnham had their camp pitched near the Bloomfield laundry to try and steal our things if they could I only sent mine there a few times for the name model laundry sending me back over and over some old ones odd stockings that blackguard-looking fellow with the fine eyes peeling a switch attack me in the dark and ride me up against the wall without a word or a murderer anybody what they do themselves the fine gentlemen in their silk hats that KC lives up somewhere this way coming out of Hardwicke Lane the night he gave us the fish supper on account of winning over the boxing match of course it was for me he gave it I knew him by his gaiters and the walk and when I turned round a minute after just to see there was a woman after coming out of it too some filthy prostitute then he goes home to his wife after that only I suppose the half of those sailors are rotten again with disease

O move over your big carcass out of that for the love of Mike listen to him *the winds that waft my sighs to thee* so well he may sleep and sigh the great Suggester Don Poldo de la Flora if he knew how he came out on the cards this morning hed have something to sigh for a dark man in some perplexity between 2 7s too in prison for Lord knows what he does that I dont know and Im to be slooching around down in the kitchen to get his lordship his breakfast while hes rolled up like a mummy will I indeed did you ever see me running Id just like to see myself at it show them attention and they treat you like dirt I dont care what anybody says itd be much better for the world to be governed by the women in it you wouldnt see women going and killing one another and slaughtering when do you ever see women rolling around drunk like they do or gambling every penny they have and losing it on horses yes because a woman whatever she does she knows where to stop sure they wouldnt be in the world at all only for us they dont know what it is to be a woman and a mother how could they where would they all of them be if they hadnt all a mother to look after them what I never had thats why I suppose hes running wild now out at night away from his books and studies and not living at home on account of the usual rowy house I suppose well its a poor case that those that have a fine son like that theyre not satisfied and I none was he not able to make one it wasnt my fault we came together when I was watching the two dogs up in her behind in the middle of the naked street that disheartened me altogether I suppose I oughtnt to have buried him in that little woolly jacket I knitted crying as I was but give it to some poor child but I knew well Id never have another our 1st death too it was we were never the same since O Im not going to think myself into the glooms about that any more I wonder why he wouldnt stay the night I felt all the time it was somebody strange he brought in instead of roving around the city meeting God knows who nightwalkers and pickpockets his poor mother wouldnt like that if she was alive ruining himself for life perhaps still its a lovely hour so silent I used to love coming home after dances the air of the night they have friends they can talk to weve none either he wants what he wont get or its some woman ready to stick her knife in you I hate that in women no wonder they treat us the way they do we are a dreadful lot of bitches I suppose its all the troubles we have makes us so snappy Im not like that he could easy have slept in there on the sofa in the other room I suppose he was as shy as a boy he being so young hardly 20 of me in the next room hed have heard me on the chamber arrah what harm Dedalus I wonder its like those names in Gibraltar Delapaz Delagracia they had the devils queer names there Father Vilaplana of Santa Maria that gave me the rosary Rosales y OReilly in the Calle las Siete Revueltas and Pisimbo and Mrs Opisso in Governor Street O what a name Id go and drown myself in the first river if I had a name like her O my and all the bits of streets Paradise Ramp and Bedlam Ramp and Rodgers Ramp and Crutchetts Ramp and the Devils Gap Steps well small blame to me if I am a harumscarum I know I am a bit I declare to God I dont feel a day older than then I wonder could I get my tongue round any of the Spanish *como esta usted muy bien gracias y usted* see I havent forgotten it all I thought I had only for the grammar a noun is the name of any person place or thing pity I never tried to read that novel cantankerous Mrs Rubio lent me by Valera with the questions in it all upside down the two ways I always knew wed go away in the end I can tell him the Spanish and he tell me the Italian then hell see Im not so ignorant what a pity he didnt stay Im sure the poor fellow was dead tired and wanted a good sleep badly I could have brought him in his breakfast in bed with a bit of toast so long as I didnt do it on the knife for bad luck or if the woman was going her rounds with the watercress and something nice and tasty there are a few olives in the kitchen he might like I never could bear the look of them in Abrines I could do the *criada* the room looks all right since I changed it the other way you see something was telling me all the time Id have to introduce myself not knowing me from Adam very funny wouldnt it Im his wife or pretend we were in Spain with him half awake without a Gods notion where he is *dos huevos estrellados senor* Lord the cracked things come into my head sometimes itd be great fun supposing he stayed with us why not theres the room upstairs empty and Millys bed in the back room he could do his writing and studies at the table in there for all the scribbling he does at it and if he wants to read in bed in the morning like me as hes making the breakfast for 1 he can make it for 2 Im sure Im not going to take in lodgers off the street for him if he takes a gazebo of a house like this Id love to have a long talk with an intelligent well-educated person Id have to get a nice pair of red slippers like those Turks with the fez used to sell or yellow and a nice semitransparent morning gown that I badly want or a peach-blossom dressing jacket like the one long ago in Walpoles only 8/6 or 18/6 Ill just give him one more chance Ill get up early in the morning Im sick of Cohens old bed in any case I might go over to the markets to see all the vegetables and cabbages and tomatoes and carrots and all kinds of splendid fruits all coming in lovely and fresh who knows whod be the 1st man Id meet theyre out looking for it in the morning Mamy Dillon used to say they are and the night too that was her massgoing Id love a big juicy pear now to melt in your mouth like when I used to be in the longing way then Ill throw him up his eggs and tea in the moustache cup she gave him to make his mouth bigger I suppose hed like my nice cream too I know what Ill do Ill go about rather gay not too much singing a bit now and then *Mi fa pieta Masetto* then Ill start dressing myself to go out *Presto non son piu forte* Ill put on my best shift and drawers let him have a good eyeful out of that to make his micky stand for him Ill let him know if thats what he wanted that his wife is fucked yes and damn well fucked too up to my neck nearly not by him 5 or 6 times hand-running theres the mark of his spunk on the clean sheet I wouldnt bother to even iron it out that ought to satisfy him if you dont believe me feel my belly unless I made him stand there and put him into me Ive a mind to tell him every scrap and make him do it out in front of me serve him right its all his own fault if I am an adulteress as the thing in the gallery said O much about it if thats all the harm ever we did in this vale of tears God knows its not much doesnt everybody only they hide it I suppose thats what a woman is supposed to be there for or He wouldnt have made us the way He did so attractive to men then if he wants to kiss my bottom Ill drag open my drawers and bulge it right out in his face as large as life he can stick his tongue 7 miles up my hole as hes there my brown part then Ill tell him I want £1 or perhaps 30/- Ill tell him I want to buy underclothes then if he gives me that well he wont be too bad I dont want to soak it all out of him like other women do I could often have written out a fine cheque for myself and write his name on it for a couple of pounds a few times he forgot to lock it up besides he wont spend it Ill let him do it off on me behind provided he doesnt smear all my good drawers O I suppose that cant be helped Ill do the indifferent 1 or 2 questions Ill know by the answers when hes like that he cant keep a thing back I know every turn in him Ill tighten my bottom well and let out a few smutty words smellrump or lick my shit or the first mad thing comes into my head then Ill suggest about yes O wait now sonny my turn is coming Ill be quite gay and friendly over it O but I was forgetting this bloody pest of a thing pfooh you wouldnt know which to laugh or cry were such a mixture of plum and apple no Ill have to wear the old things so much the better itll be more pointed hell never know whether he did it or not there thats good enough for you any old thing at all then Ill wipe him off me just like a business his omission then Ill go out Ill have him eyeing up at the ceiling where is she gone now make him want me thats the only way a quarter after what an unearthly hour I suppose theyre just getting up in China now combing out their pigtails for the day well soon have the nuns ringing the angelus theyve nobody coming in to spoil their sleep except an odd priest or two for his night office or the alarm clock next door at cockshout clattering the brains out of itself let me see if I can doze off 1 2 3 4 5 what kind of flowers are those they invented like the stars the wallpaper in Lombard Street was much nicer the apron he gave me was like that something only I only wore it twice better lower this lamp and try again so as I can get up early Ill go to Lambes there beside Findlaters and get them to send us some flowers to put about the place in case he brings him home tomorrow today I mean no no Fridays an unlucky day first I want to do the place up someway the dust grows in it I think while Im asleep then we can have music and cigarettes I can accompany him first I must clean the keys of the piano with milk whatll I wear *shall I wear a white rose* or those fairy cakes in Liptons I love the smell of a rich big shop at 7½*d* a lb or the other ones with the cherries in them and the pinky sugar 11*d* a couple of lbs of those a nice plant for the middle of the table Id get that cheaper in wait wheres this I saw them not long ago I love flowers Id love to have the whole place swimming in roses God of heaven theres nothing like nature the wild mountains then the sea and the waves rushing then the beautiful country with the fields of oats and wheat and all kinds of things and all the fine cattle going about that would do your heart good to see rivers and lakes and flowers all sorts of shapes and smells and colours springing up even out of the ditches primroses and violets nature it is as for them saying theres no God I wouldnt give a snap of my two fingers for all their learning why dont they go and create something I often asked him atheists or whatever they call themselves go and wash the cobbles off themselves first then they go howling for the priest and they dying and why why because theyre afraid of hell on account of their bad conscience ah yes I know them well who was the first person in the universe before there was anybody that made it all who ah that they dont know neither do I so there you are they might as well try to stop the sun from rising tomorrow the sun shines for you he said the day we were lying among the rhododendrons on Howth Head in the grey tweed suit and his straw hat the day I got him to propose to me yes first I gave him the bit of seedcake out of my mouth and it was leap year like now yes 16 years ago my God after that long kiss I near lost my breath yes he said I was a flower of the mountain yes so we are flowers all a womans body yes that was one true thing he said in his life and the sun shines for you today yes that was why I liked him because I saw he understood or felt what a woman is and I knew I could always get round him and I gave him all the pleasure I could leading him on till he asked me to say yes and I wouldnt answer first only looked out over the sea and the sky I was thinking of so many things he didnt know of Mulvey and Mr Stanhope and Hester and father and old Captain Groves and the sailors playing All Birds Fly and I Say Stoop and Washing Up Dishes they called it on the pier and the sentry in front of the Governors house with the thing round his white helmet poor devil half roasted and the Spanish girls laughing in their shawls and their tall combs and the auctions in the morning the Greeks and the Jews and the Arabs and the devil knows who else from all the ends of Europe and Duke Street and the fowl market all clucking outside Larby Sharons and the poor donkeys slipping half asleep and the vague fellows in the cloaks asleep in the shade on the steps and the big wheels of the carts of the bulls and the old castle thousands of years old yes and those handsome Moors all in white and turbans like kings asking you to sit down in their little bit of a shop and Ronda with the old windows of the posadas *2 glancing eyes a lattice hid* for her lover to kiss the iron and the wine shops half open at night and the castanets and the night we missed the boat at Algeciras the watchman going about serene with his lamp and O that awful deepdown torrent O and the sea the sea crimson sometimes like fire and the glorious sunsets and the fig trees in the Alameda Gardens yes and all the queer little streets and the pink and blue and yellow houses and the rose gardens and the jessamine and geraniums and cactuses and Gibraltar as a girl where I was a Flower of the mountain yes when I put the rose in my hair like the Andalusian girls used *or shall I wear a red* yes and how he kissed me under the Moorish Wall and I thought well as well him as another and then I asked him with my eyes to ask again yes and then he asked me would I yes to say yes my mountain flower and first I put my arms around him yes and drew him down to me so he could feel my breasts all perfume yes and his heart was going like mad and yes I said yes I will Yes.

Trieste-Zurich-Paris,
1914–1921.

A *Ulysses* Chronology

DUBLIN 1902 – The compilation of the *Epiphanies* is begun.

PARIS February to March 1903 – 'Aristotle' notebook on aesthetics is compiled.

DUBLIN Summer 1903 – *Stephen Hero* is begun.

January 1904 – The narrative essay *A Portrait of the Artist* is written.

Early July 1904 – *Dubliners* is begun.

13 July 1904 – Funeral of Mat Kane (model for 'Hades') takes place.

POLA November 1904 – 'Aquinas' notebook on aesthetics is compiled.

TRIESTE June 1905 – Work on *Stephen Hero* (incomplete) is suspended.

ROME 25 September 1906 – A short story, 'Ulysses', is conceived for *Dubliners*.

TRIESTE 20 September 1907 – *Dubliners* is completed.

September 1907 – *Stephen Hero* (suspended since 1905) is abandoned and *A Portrait of the Artist as a Young Man* is begun.

1911 – Joyce throws manuscript of *A Portrait* into the fire; it is rescued.

11 November 1912 – Joyce gives lecture on *Hamlet* at the Università del Popolo.

Autumn 1913 – *Exiles* is begun.

November 1913 – The 'Notes for *Exiles*' are compiled.

1913/1914 – *A Portrait* (Doherty) extension is written but laid aside.

Early 1914 – *A Portrait* manuscript is completed.

15 June 1914 – *Dubliners* is published.

August 1914 – *Giacomo Joyce* manuscript is written.

Spring 1915 – *Exiles* is completed.

Spring/Summer 1915 – Doherty fragment is expanded to form a beginning to a 'sequel' to *A Portrait* to be entitled 'Ulysses'.

16 June 1915 – First episode of the 'sequel' to *A Portrait* (an early version of 'Telemachus') is completed. (Novel is set on 8 October 1904.)

ZURICH   July 1915 – The typescript of *Exiles* is prepared.

October 1916 – First part, part of middle and part of end of the 'sequel' to *A Portrait* are completed. (Novel is set on 8 October 1904.)

November 1916 – Joyce suffers a nervous collapse.

December 1916 – *A Portrait of the Artist as a Young Man* is published in the United States.

January 1917 – Joyce has a first attack of glaucoma.

22 February 1917 – First subvention from Harriet Weaver arrives.

1917 – *Ulysses* is reconceived and divorced from *A Portrait*.

29 May 1917 – The earliest known mention by Joyce of Leopold Bloom.

Summer/Autumn 1917 – The earliest *Ulysses* notebooks, MSS VI.D.7 and VIII.A.8, are compiled. Leopold Bloom is fleshed out. (Novel is set on 16 June 1904.)

COMPOSITION OF *ULYSSES*
DATES OF COMPLETION OF THE FAIR COPIES

PART I. TELEMACHIAD (STEPHEN DEDALUS)

LOCARNO   Late November 1917 – Episode 1: Telemachus

Mid-December 1917 – Episode 2: Nestor

ZURICH   End of January 1918 – Episode 3: Proteus

PART II. ODYSSEY (THE WANDERINGS)

Mid-March 1918 – Episode 4: Calypso

Early April 1918 – Episode 5: Lotus Eaters

Mid-May 1918 – Episode 6: Hades

Mid-August 1918 – Episode 7: Aeolus

Late October 1918 – Episode 8: Lestrygonians

End December 1918 – Episode 9: Scylla and Charybdis

End January 1919 – Episode 10: Wandering Rocks

Mid-May 1919 – Episode 11: Sirens

September 1919 – Episode 12: Cyclops

TRIESTE   Early February 1920 – Episode 13: Nausicaa

Mid-May 1920 – Episode 14: Oxen of the Sun

PARIS   Late December 1920 – Episode 15: Circe

PART III. NOSTOS (THE HOMECOMING)

February 1921 – Episode 16: Eumaeus

Mid-September 1921 – Episode 18: Penelope

Late October 1921 – Episode 17: Ithaca

Acknowledgements

An entire history of scholarship lies behind this edition, and I am indebted to the many individuals who contributed to it. In particular I must thank Hans Walter Gabler, Wolfhard Steppe and Claus Melchior. Their 1984 edition of *Ulysses* radically and for ever changed textual scholarship and in the process educated a generation of Joyceans. Among the more astute commentators on that edition I should mention Charles Peake, David Hayman, Fritz Senn, Clive Hart, Philip Gaskell, Hugh Kenner, Vincent Deane and John Turner. John Kidd, in his inimitable way, contributed not alone by raising public awareness of many of the problems involved in editorial matters but also by drawing attention to many details of presentation. In addition I must acknowledge the contributions of the scholars who founded and solidified *Ulysses* manuscript studies: Jack Dalton, Walton Litz, Norman Silverstein, Philip Herring, Clive Driver, Michael Groden, Myron Schwartzmann and Rodney Owen. A great debt also is owed to the production team that worked with me in preparing this edition: Jonathan Riley, Peter Straus, Tanya Stobbs, Wilf Dickie, Chris Gibson, Michelle Thompson, Nicholas Blake, Nadya Kooznetzoff and (in Dublin) Antony Farrell and Brendan Barrington. Finally, for assistance throughout every stage of the preparation of the Reader's Edition I owe most of all to John O'Hanlon.

For the paperback edition, twenty minor emendations have been made. I am grateful to Vincent Deane, John Kidd, Fritz Senn, Gerry Dukes and John O'Hanlon for pointing these out.